The Disestablishment of Paradise

Also by Phillip Mann from Gollancz,
available at www.sfgateway.com:

The Disestablishment of Paradise

A NOVEL IN FIVE PARTS PLUS DOCUMENTS

Phillip Mann

The right of Phillip Mann to be identified as the author
of this work has been asserted by him in accordance with the
Copyright, Designs and Patents Act 1988.

First published in Great Britain in 2013
by Gollancz
An imprint of the Orion Publishing Group
Orion House, 5 Upper St Martin's Lane,
London WC2H 9EA
An Hachette UK Company
This edition published in Great Britain in 2014
by Gollancz

1 3 5 7 9 10 8 6 4 2

A CIP catalogue record for this book
is available from the British Library.

ISBN 978 0 575 13263 4

Typeset by Input Data Services Ltd, Bridgwater, Somerset

Printed in Great Britain by CPI Group (UK) Ltd, Croydon CR0 4YY

The Orion Publishing Group's policy is to use papers
that are natural, renewable and recyclable products and
made from wood grown in sustainable forests. The logging
and manufacturing processes are expected to conform to
the environmental regulations of the country of origin.

www.phillipmann.co.nz
www.orionbooks.co.uk
www.gollancz.co.uk

For my grandchildren
Jasper, Poppy and Ianto
in the hope that they inherit
a world more peaceful than Paradise.

Be thou, Spirit fierce,
My spirit! be thou me, impetuous one!
Drive my dead thoughts over the universe,
Like wither'd leaves, to quicken a new birth;
And, by the incantation of this verse,
Scatter, as from an unextinguish'd hearth
Ashes and sparks, my words among mankind!
Be through my lips to unawaken'd earth
The trumpet of a prophecy! O Wind,
If Winter comes, can Spring be far behind?

From the final verse of Percy Bysshe Shelley's
'Ode to the West Wind'

This book is dedicated to Sister Hilda,
late of Anchor Hold-over-Europa.

Good friend and teacher
Wise guide and counsellor
Strong as the strung bow of Odysseus chasing demons,
Gentle as the Great Mother you so loved to quote.
In gratitude.

Hera Melhuish

Contents

Part Four **Paradise Menacing**

Part Five **Michelangelo-Reaper**

Documents

Introduction

The book you are now reading reveals the experiences of Dr Hera Melhuish during her last few months on the planet Paradise. Dr Melhuish, let us recall, was the last human being to escape from Paradise. None have returned since and none will ever do so, for that planet is now closed to us. Absolutely. Thus this biography, as much the biography of that world as of the woman, while it does not end in death, has something equally final about it.

It will come as a surprise to some readers that a writer such as myself, better known (if known at all) as a writer of fiction for children, should now turn my hand to a work of non-fiction, a biographical work no less. In explanation let me say that this was not an honour I sought. The invitation to collaborate with Dr Melhuish was completely unforeseen. However, it arrived on my desk during one of the dark periods of my creative life – a time that all writers know well – when I was full of doubt and seeking a new direction. Thus the timing of her letter, as with so much else concerning Paradise, had a certain appropriateness.

At that time my knowledge of Dr Hera Melhuish consisted only of what was available on the public record. She had been director of the Observation, Regeneration and Botanic Expansion (ORBE) project on Paradise at the time of the planet's Disestablishment. Dismissed from this position for alleged misconduct, she nevertheless contrived to return to the planet on a solo mission and was, for a significant time, the only human being there. After a near-fatal accident, Dr Melhuish was joined by her 'research assistant' Mack – of whom more later. Together they discovered, and saved, the last living example of the *Dendron Peripatetica*, hitherto believed extinct. Later Mack died after encountering a rogue Michelangelo-Reaper, and Hera continued her journey alone across this now hostile planet. She was finally rescued

1

just before the shuttle platform over Paradise began its final disintegration.

These are the bare bones of Dr Melhuish's story. However, it was the live transmission of the programme called *The Saving of the Dendron* which most caught the attention of the general public. Many of you will remember this programme, which was in continuous transmission for almost three days and did more to awaken public awareness of the deep issues behind our journeying into space than the thousands of documents issued annually by the Space Council.

For me, this broadcast was a seminal moment in my life. For the first time I witnessed the kind of contact with an alien life form that I had dreamed about since being a child. Not only did the Dendron fulfil the deepest needs of my imagination, but I was one of those many viewers who felt the impact of the creature's psychic presence at the moment of its severance. We were attending a birth, and while the delight of that moment has dimmed over time, its memory lingers in the most private parts of my being. It was a very pure and personal contact, and any doubts I may have had concerning the cultural importance of alien contact were dispelled by what I saw and felt. In those few moments I became vividly aware of the possibilities offered by our venture into space, and at the same time critical of what we had accomplished to date.

Before making a formal acceptance of Dr Melhuish's offer, I reviewed the tri-vid *The Saving of the Dendron*. I also read most of Dr Melhuish's published works, and this almost undid the entire project for I discovered that Hera Melhuish is herself a fine writer. I could not understand why she could not undertake the task herself. For those who do not know her work, *Tales of Io and Me* is a delightful collection of bedtime stories for children. They have as their heroine a certain little girl who, not unlike their author, travels widely, having adventures in strange places. *Of Canals and Caves* is a personal memoir which gives a spirited account of Hera's diving explorations in the deep subterranean lakes on Mars and her discovery there of the luminous burrow worms. In *Beyond Orion*, written shortly after she joined the ORBE project on Paradise, Hera offers her vision of the possibilities for space travel via fractal gates and our responsibilities concerning alien contact. In sum, the scathing prose of her political pamphlet 'Saving Gaia' is matched by the light-hearted humour of her various stories for children. Stirring stuff! I found in these books a breadth of vision which I could share.

At the end of my reading I wrote to Hera. I had three main concerns. Firstly, I freely admitted that my scientific knowledge is superficial. What I do not know, I invent – a practice well suited to fiction but hardly acceptable for a scientific inquiry. Secondly, I felt Dr Melhuish, on the evidence of her own works, was well qualified to handle her own story. And finally, why me? My strengths, such as they are, are in the fanciful, the dark and the mysterious. When I come down to earth I become leaden. I prefer the storm to the rainbow. I have also been criticized because my stories are pagan in background and savage in event. In sum, I could name ten or twenty writers whom I would regard as more qualified than me to tell her biography. But of course it was not really a biography that she wanted; it was an evocation.

Her reply to me was characteristically direct.

To hell with the science. You can leave that to me, not that there will be much science in the story I want to tell. The nearest we will come to physics is pataphysics! If we talk briefly about the 'survival of the fittest', we will talk longer about love and courage, reason and sacrifice.

The first thing to realize is that most of the things that happened on Paradise can not be explained in a rational way – which is not to say they don't have a reason. Paradise was never rational in our way, and the challenge is to understand it in its own terms. That in turn will tell us about the greater reality of the universe.

You wonder why I do not write my own story. The truth is I have tried many times – but am too close to it. When I try to write about those days, I find myself so close to the events that I become like a log of wood in the fire, unable to help myself or stop the burning. There is so much I want to tell. I want to reveal why Paradise was disestablished in the first place – that itself is a dirty story, and I to my shame was no saint. I want to convey the impact Earth had on that solitary world and how it learned to respond in self-defence. I want to tell what it was like to stand inside the living body of a Dendron as its codds beat to survive. I want to tell why I am covered with the dark stains of the weeping

3

Michelangelo, and to tell in detail what happened to Mack, who is the unsung hero of all my adventures.

Let me confess something. At the inquiry after my rescue from Paradise I said that Mack was killed by a Michelangelo-Reaper. That is not strictly true. Mack, who was dearer to me than my own shadow, chose to join with the Reaper, while I, who loved him and Paradise more than myself and would have stayed there willingly as a slave if need be, was, in effect, dismissed both by him and the planet. My consolation has been my memories and my awareness that 'They also serve who only stand and wait.' It was the pain and privacy of that parting which kept me silent for many years. Can you understand that? I think you can for it is women's logic, as old as time. But I knew I would have to speak out one day. Well, now is the time. Now, like the Ancient Mariner, I feel an irresistible urge to tell my tale. And you must help me. You must question me until, like the sea in Yvegeny's poem, I begin to yield up my monsters.

Whatever else it does, the writing must convey the deeper, more imaginative order which underlies all those experiences. I have admired your books, enjoying the strange creatures you create from your imagination, your sense of wonder, as well as your willingness to acknowledge the darkness that can hide in the heart of man. If your style is slightly old-fashioned, as some of your critics maintain, that to me is an advantage, as is your gentle wit. In sum, I feel confident you are the best equipped person to tell this story. And if it is more understood by the children, well so be it.

Receiving this letter, I felt as though a door into a secret garden had opened before me. I did not hesitate. I stepped through.

A few days later I set off to visit Hera. I wanted to arrange how we were to proceed. And, to be frank, I was more than a little curious to know what she would be like in the flesh.

I was, of course, familiar with the tri-vid images of her: short of stature even for a woman, fine features, a stubborn jaw, enviably slim and with her long hair drawn back and pinned so tightly as to give her face an Asian cast. Even soused and gleaming with the sap of the Dendron, as I first saw her in the tri-vid, she nevertheless managed to convey a somewhat neat and prim impression.

Much of all this remains. She has neither put on weight or dwindled, and her voice for the most part retains a deep cultured tone. But the marks of Paradise are on her – her 'love bites' or ' tear-stains', as she calls them. One is on the forehead and one on her right cheek. Her neck and arms are also marked, as is, she informs me, the rest of her body. These marks have become darker with the passing of the years. Sometimes they become sore and angry – at which times strange things must be happening on Paradise, for it is reaching out and afflicting her. If, when this resonance is really severe, she turns her gaze on you, she can, without meaning to, seem to stare coldly through you. It is the imperious look of a hawk or a basilisk. And she will apologize for this when she sees you fidget. At those times, as I eventually came to understand, she is resonating – a very important word if you wish to understand Dr Hera Melhuish – by which she means that she is both here and there, experiencing direct communion with distant Paradise while sitting in your workroom. It took me a long time to accept this, and even now I do not really understand who or what she is communicating with. Lastly, as regards her primness, you will discover if you read on that there is nothing prim about Hera Melhuish – far from it.

However, it is the raw energy of the woman which provides the most abiding memory and for which I was unprepared. It is there at all times, whether making a sketch with quick deft strokes or cackling at some bawdy memory, gesticulating wildly for emphasis or pinning you with her bright eyes. That energy, she informs me, is the wild spirit of the Dendron, which she received into her mind and body and is now lodged there, and which may, as she avers, keep her alive for many years or snuff her out without warning, perhaps by accident through an excess of love. Suffice to say that it is the loving, spirited Dendron rather than the dread Michelangelo which is the true alien in her, and for that we should be glad.

We agreed upon a procedure. Hera would talk and I would record her words and ask questions to draw her out. The talk could ramble, following its own logic. No topic, no matter how intimate, was off limits. And we would keep going until we had reached agreement or impasse. Arguing was also anticipated and proved unavoidable. We would meet as often as necessary.

In this way raw material was generated, which I could then edit

5

and shape as I saw fit. The style of the writing was left up to me. Hera's preference was for me to tell a story and to treat her as I would a character in a novel. This proved remarkably easy.

However, as I discovered more about Paradise and Hera, my view of the narrative changed. Sometimes, when describing events, Hera attained a clarity that I could never have matched in composition. I saw no need to improve upon what nature had supplied. Thus I have frequently used her words as spoken during our interviews. Also, to give a clearer image of Paradise, I have included a short collection of documents selected from writers who had first-hand experience of that planet. These include stories written by young Sasha Malik, who was born on Paradise, as well as passages from the daybooks of the agricultural pioneers Mayday and Marie Newton and some personal speculations by the late Professor Israel Shapiro. These documents, gathered at the end of the book, will I hope add variety and background to the story.

Hera also wished me to avoid specialist scientific vocabulary. 'We are not writing a textbook,' she said on more than one occasion. 'Keep it simple and sweet.' Thus, while I might have relished sounding erudite, you will find that I frequently refer to the creatures of Paradise as plants rather than bio-forms or some such equally neutral term. I do this simply because that is how they were most often seen and spoken about, even by specialists. But this must not blind us to the fact that, while there are distinct parallels with the botanic life of Earth, when we speak of the entities of Paradise we are dealing with life forms which derive from a wholly alien environment.

Initially we met at Hera's small apartment on Anchor Hold-over-Europa. Later, as the project neared completion, we met at my studio on Albertini-over-Terra. During each visit Hera would read and correct what I had written. I was glad to observe that, as we progressed in the project, her corrections became less – a sure sign that either I was becoming more accurate as I grew to know my subject, or that she was forgetting and letting the imaginative world of fiction become the truth.

One difficulty we encountered from the outset was that, as a consequence of her calamitous departure from Paradise, Hera had lost all her notebooks, diaries, memos of meetings, personal records, sketches, photographs and so forth. They are still down there no doubt, on Paradise, preserved in that lacquered state in which Paradise embalms all things of Earth. And so we talked. We talked long and late. We talked until I began to see through her eyes. Sometimes we talked until there were no more words and we just stared out into space or fell asleep where we sat.

I am not the 'Spirit Wild' that Shelley speaks of in his 'Ode to the West Wind', the poem which Hera chose to open her story. But this book is. As Hera stated during one of our meetings, 'I hope the book will help us think about what we are and how we fit into the vast scheme of things. What we need now is not more knowledge, but to understand what we already know.'

I wish to conclude this introduction with two quite different images.

The first is taken from a drawing which Hera made during her first visit to my studio on Albertini. She called the sketch *The Horse and the Woodpecker*, and I have it framed on the wall before me even as I write.

The sketch depicts two women – they could be sisters separated by a decade – sitting together at a wooden table. The room in which they sit is my studio – a bit junk-strewn, very cluttered, with books covering one wall and a transcriber tucked away in an alcove away from the window. There is an empty bottle of wine on the floor and a half-full bottle on the table between the women. Their heads are almost touching as they study a sketch that the older woman is drawing. It is a Dendron in motion, its crest high and its flags waving. And yes, lest there be any confusion, I am the somewhat horsy one in the picture, and Hera the quick woodpecker.

Behind the women, beyond the curved translucent wall, is the busy darkness of space, sparkling with stars and enlivened by the sudden flashes of the Manson screen as it randomizes particles that could threaten our small haven. In the centre hangs the lapis lazuli disc of the Earth – blue and white and wholly beautiful in the full light of the sun.

But they are not looking at the Earth. They are many light years away in their minds, talking about Paradise. I hope you will think of this homely image when the going gets hard and we retreat from the comfortable and human.

My second image is more abstract. It is that of a labyrinth.

A labyrinth is not a maze, it is a journey. You begin by facing your desire, whether it be to find yourself, or Jerusalem, or enlightenment, and you follow a path of knowledge. Once committed you can not leave that path. Sometimes it is direct and your destination is clear before you. At other times it leads you to the side, and this is a time for reflection and the discovery of wider perspectives. Sometimes it seems to lead you directly away from your heart's desire, and that is a dark night of the soul, a time of severe testing when your closest companion is despair. But always the path of the labyrinth turns again. It approaches the point from which you began, but it is a new point, a new departure. And eventually, by being persistent, you find your way to your heart's desire.

That, at day's end, is how I have come to see this work, and how I invite you to understand it.

We begin with an introduction to Paradise.

PART ONE

The Political Tale

1

Concerning Paradise

Paradise was named by the captain of the prospect ship *Scorpion*, the first craft to make its way there from the fractal gate Proxima MINADEC-over-Phobos. The captain's name was Estelle Richter and she was just nineteen years old! We should remember that in the early days of fractal travel only the young could cope with the stress of passing through the fractal threshold. Why? Opinions, as they say, differ, but what is certain is that the young are more fearless, more optimistic, more confident of their sexual power and less weighted down by guilt than their jaded elders, and these qualities were important in the early days of fractal travel – and still are, for they diminish the risk of nightmare.

The *Scorpion* emerged from the temporary fractal gate established above the new world, and its crew found themselves staring out at a shining green and blue planet with twin moons.

Early indications of the planet were very positive. Measurements were made by means of an unmanned probe which touched down on the surface, first at a river delta and then at several other locations including the mountain tops and mid-ocean. But it was obvious to anyone who cared to look that the planet contained life. It was there in the dynamic swirling clouds, in the shining lakes reflecting the sun, in the deep blue wind-ruffled seas and the vivid green of the land.

Can we for a moment imagine the excitement of those young pioneers, as they gathered together to see the results of all the automatic diagnostic tests? Though the new planet was just a little smaller than Mars, its gravity was only slightly less than Earth normal. Good for sport and *Scorpion*-cramped limbs. The air was – yes, astonishingly – breathable, according to analysis. It was perhaps even tonic, being a bit richer in oxygen. And that *was* indeed H_2O in the seas and rivers, not blue acid. And look at the tall trees, which reached up with broad flat leaves. Look at the high waves crashing on the shore and the lime-green meadows where you could follow the footsteps of the wind as it swirled up into the hills . . . Look at the red flowers bobbing like balloons in the valleys! All the colours could have been taken from a child's palette. Strange only were the faint shimmering lines of energy, like the fading pattern of a rainbow, in the misty valleys; that, and the total absence of animals. There were no insects either, or nibbling fish. Flowers without insects? Seas without fish? Why? Why? How? Captain Estelle Richter did not delay but decided to investigate immediately.

As a name, Paradise was a happy choice. Unlike most worlds, this planet was not hostile to the kind of life that we represent. In ways beyond analysis, the air was sweet to breathe, the water pure to the taste, the seas buoyant, and there was a springy dense grass (later called brevet) for a tumble – and perhaps most extraordinary of all, fruits which were found to be edible.

The popular story is that it was Captain Estelle who picked and nibbled the first Paradise plum. The plum tree was growing by the shore close to where they had landed. She stared up into its branches and then in a single act of defiance, in contravention of all contact protocols and common sense, she reached up among the dark spade-shaped leaves and, as she reportedly said later, the fruit seemed to 'leap into' her hand. She bit into its flesh before anyone could stop her. The juice in her mouth startled her and the perfume made her senses reel, and she ate the entire fruit – licking her fingers – including the seeds, which she crunched and swallowed. Was woman ever so 'giddy and bold'? Then, before the eyes of her astonished crew, she confidently removed her survival suit and waded naked into the sea, trailing her fingers behind her in the water, saying – if we are to believe the story – 'Look at me. I'm Aphrodite. And I'm reclaiming Paradise.' A symbolic act if ever there was one. Thus was the planet named, and a physical contact not too far removed from both baptism and the act of lovemaking took place. I suspect that in making her remarks Captain Estelle was remembering a wonderful painting by Botticelli. It is doubtful that the name Paradise had any specific biblical connotations for the young captain, or that in seeking out fruit she was consciously mirroring the actions of our mother Eve.

I am struck by the contrast between these young adventurers and the staunch early astronauts from Earth who left their flags and bootprints and cars on the Moon. What a contrast too between new-found Paradise and the molten or freezing, harsh, dark and sterile worlds the crew visited most frequently. Her companions did not delay but stripped off and followed their leader into the sea. There is an old saying, 'Innocence begets innocence.' If we believe this, then we can be confident that there was no damage done in this first meeting of species. But how interesting it would have been to peer into the mind of Paradise at the moment when Estelle bit the fruit or breasted the sea, for I am sure those contacts were keenly felt in that psychically alive and innocent world.

As Estelle later explained, 'When we came to leave I had one last swim. I have never felt such well-being.' And that evidently was what the crew of the *Scorpion* and most subsequent visitors felt during their first contact. I say *most* because a small but significant number of people have always found Paradise an uncomfortable place to dwell.

I am saddened to report that the log of the *Scorpion*, as well as other early visual recordings of Paradise (including details of its subsequent commercial exploitation) were lost in the catastrophic fire which destroyed the entire Proxima MINADEC-over-Phobos torus. The rumour, widely believed at the time, was that the fire was the result of arson, and though this was never proved it is a fact that the directors of MINADEC (once the Mineral and Natural Resource Development Company) were under investigation for tax evasion and improper use of their prospect licence. The loss of these early records is irredeemable, and one can only lament that, as with Hera's own documentation, the records of Paradise have an awkward habit of vanishing.

Within months of the *Scorpion*'s visit, the planet was being opened up commercially. MINADEC had a fifty-year licence for all its activities.

The miners, prospectors and lumberjacks that MINADEC sent to Paradise, while we know they visited and left their mark on almost every part of that planet, left few written accounts – graffiti apart. Their culture was essentially oral. It thrived at the well head and the pit face, round the campfires and in the mess huts. And, like so much else of value, it died with them. We have some of their songs and drawings and letters – and of course there are the eye-witness accounts written by young Sasha Malik, whose works we will dip into later. Many of the names used by the prospectors and miners became established. Thus the two moons which liven the night sky are called Gin and Tonic. The continents were named after certain distinguishing features. Chain, for instance, when seen from the air, can be seen to be a long thin continent with many promontories and inland lakes. Hammer and neighbouring Anvil require more imaginative interpretations to see the likeness. The continent called Horse has one large headland which does, somewhat, resemble the head of a horse, and Ball is, well, Ball is circular, and that is all that one can say. Some islands are named after composers, some after the names of settlers, some after hometowns on Earth (such as New Syracuse), and some features, like Baby Cry Falls, record important events such as the birth of the first child on Paradise.

Upon expiry of the commercial licence, Paradise was thrown open to agricultural colonists. Among these, one couple, Mayday and Marie Newton, wrote a daybook, in which they set down in homely detail the day-to-day life of the pioneer farmers. These men and women, apart from being visionaries with an urge to build families and create a new world, and who shared a common love of Paradise, were all trained in the basic arts of survival. They could both butcher and nurture. But by the time of their arrival I suspect that Paradise was already turning against invaders.

Despite their best efforts, agriculture on Paradise became harder as the years passed, and no one could explain why. During the first fifty years of colonization, the animals – initially imported in embryo and raised with care – failed to prosper and eventually the last goats and horses died out.

Fresh seed stock was brought in from Earth but this too, after initial success, gradually failed. Fruit would not set and seeds would not germinate, or when they did were sickly. The formation of the Observation, Regeneration and Botanic Expansion project was the result of efforts to bring scientific expertise to bear on this problem.

The failure of ORBE to make any significant difference to the agricultural situation was initially blamed on the lack of suitable equipment. Later it was claimed that its founder, Professor Israel

14

Shapiro, was only interested in his own research and had no real sympathy for the agricultural colonists' dilemma. From my reading, I would say that that is putting the matter mildly. He made it clear on numerous occasions that he found the presence of the 'aggies' on Paradise irksome.

On the death of Shapiro, Dr Hera Melhuish became head of the ORBE project. She held this position for eleven stormy years. But even she, despite many initiatives, could not halt the gradual agricultural decline.

And so we come to the fatal year: the year of Disestablishment.

When we enter her story, Dr Hera Melhuish is feeling well pleased with herself. After months of debate she has managed to defeat proposals which would have opened Paradise to tourism. Moreover the ORBE project research, if not spectacular, is stable and well funded. Her own programme of native out-planting is going well. Her delight in Paradise is as great as that of Marie Newton or the young Estelle Richter, though her aims are vastly different.

And now she is doing what she most enjoys: 'working in the garden' as she called it. It is a fine sunny morning and she is outside, her sleeves rolled up, tending the plants of Paradise.

2

Political Games

Hera was working at the southern tip of Royal Straits, at the dangerous place where the island of Lennon comes closest to the steep cliffs of Horse. It is dangerous because of the rip tide that comes roaring through the narrow strait when the two moons of Paradise are pulling together. This is, of course, also a time of extreme low tide, and that was why Hera and her student assistant were there. They were trying to establish a new submarine seedbed for the spongy green pancake wrack which had once been common in that region but was now, like so much else, in decline.

The work was going well on that fine sunny morning when the peaceful routine was broken by the shrill *bleep-bleep* of a high-priority call demanding attention. The student worker, on shore and unpacking supplies at the time, took the message. It was from Hemi Katene, the administrator at ORBE HQ, and he was asking to speak to Hera urgently.

That lady was some fifty feet out from the shore, down on her knees, leaning over the side of one of the flat-bottomed barges used for marine work. She was reaching out, her arms brown in the clear water, and trying to attach a cable to bolts bedded in a rock just under the surface. The boat bobbed under her, striking her uncomfortably under the arms and splashing water up into her face. Reluctantly Hera was coming to the decision that she would have to don a wetsuit and plunge fully into the water.

'Tell him I'm busy,' she called through clenched teeth and without looking up. Time was short as this particular rock only became accessible at extreme low tide.

'He says it's urgent,' called the student worker, raising the radio phone above her head and waving it.

The loop in the cable passed over the bolt head and Hera began to screw it tight. 'OK, I'm coming,' she called, 'Be there in a mo.' She completed a twist where strands of wire were sticking out sharply – they had already scratched her arm – and snipped off the pointed parts and twisted them under. Satisfied, she loosened the anchor rope and started to pull the barge back to the shore. 'This'd better be good,' she said as she climbed out onto the rocks and accepted the phone. 'You go out there and take over. I've got the first two ends tied but we need to secure the central piece. And watch out for the bloody wire ends.'

The student set off and Hera climbed up to where she could sit on one of the rocks and dry out in the sun. 'Hello there, Hemi. This is Hera. What's the trouble?'

'Yeah, sorry to bother you, but it's pretty important, eh? I've just had a call from Captain Abhuradin. Priority alph—'

'She's not still going on about that tourism proposal is she? I thought we'd scotched that one.'

'No, no. This is something else. No details as yet but, according to Abhuradin, she's just received a message from Space Council head office. Evidently the Economic Subcommittee has just come out of a long session. They've passed a resolution suggesting that three planet colonies be disestablished – and we are one of them.'

'What?'

'Yes. The recommendation is due to be discussed at a full Council meeting in a few weeks and if it is passed then it will be actioned immediately. Part of the new fast-track initiatives.'

'But they can't just—'

'I know, that's what I said. But it is definite. Old Ahab's no happier than you are. She wants to see you as soon as possible. This afternoon if you can get back here. There'll be a shuttle waiting.'

Hera was silent for a moment. She didn't trust snap announcements like this. In her experience, they usually meant that someone had been plotting for quite a while and now was striking fast to minimize resistance. The fact that it was the Economic Subcommittee that had come up with the proposal made matters worse. That committee had become more militant of late, the result of a change of head, a new broom sweeping clean. Some woman (Hera had been told her name but had forgotten it), a hardliner by repute, had taken over. No doubt they had been stewing over the latest production

17

statistics for Paradise. 'When did Abhuradin hear the news?'

'Just a short time ago, she said.'

'She hasn't been sitting on it?'

'Look, I've no idea. But I don't think so. She didn't sound happy, I can tell you that.'

'Does anyone else know?'

'No. Don't think so. Alpha coding, so that's just us. She didn't want to tell me, but I told her you were out in the field and probably wouldn't respond unless you knew what the fuss was.'

'Yeah. Good lad. OK. I'm on my way. Call all the heads of departments in. Tell them to drop whatever they are doing and, if they are within three hours' flying time, to get back to HQ pronto. If not, tell them to stand by for a tri-vid link. Don't tell them what the issue is. I don't want a lot of gabble on the airwaves until we've had a chance to talk. I want a quick meeting before I go up top. And you start gathering statistics. Usual stuff – number of out-plantings, endangered species, economies of scale and so on. And get on to the hospital too; get any info you can on how the anti-toxin programme is working.'

'Will do.'

'I'll give you an ETA as soon as I'm airborne. We've got a battle on our hands, sunshine.'

She broke contact.

The student working out on the barge called across the water to her: 'Bad news?'

'I've got to get back to HQ,' answered Hera. She glanced at her watch. 'I'm going to have to leave you here. You'll have to camp out overnight.'

The student grinned. 'Suits me,' she said. They had planned to camp anyway, so the tents were already up and there was food.

'I reckon you've got two hours' maximum working time before the tide changes. When the tide does turn, get out of it. Don't play silly buggers. All right? Winch the barge up like I showed you and then climb up as high as you can and get round to where the strait narrows. Enjoy the view. When the surge comes it is one of the sights of Paradise. It comes right through here. A twenty-foot wave, breaking all the way. You won't regret it.'

With that Hera ran over to the small cove where they had moored the powerboat. She spread its solar panels and engaged the engine.

'I'll send the cutter back for you tomorrow,' she called, and with a wave was on her way, skimming over the surface of the shallow straits. Low tide was a dangerous time and she stood on a tool-box to look out for the warning sign of waves breaking on water. A strong sea was running against her in the middle of the strait, but once she had bounced through that she rounded the headland where the calypso lilies trailed their long fronds in the water, and was gone.

At the Calypso Station, itself no more than a radio point and a landing pad, she took the survey and survival (SAS) flyer and was in the air in minutes.

The meeting got under way as soon as Hera arrived at ORBE HQ. Those section chiefs who were too far away were already linked by tri-vid, and could be seen in miniature, sitting atop their projection mats with backgrounds of desert or jungle or mountain peak behind them.

All members of the ORBE project were field workers; all were used to living rough and taking care of themselves – and they were not unused to emergencies either. Hair pinned up or shaven-headed, stubble-jawed or bearded, they arrived as they were, in their work clothes, which could be anything from full protection suits if they were working amid dangerous plants like the sugar lilies or the umbrella trees, or in a variety of brightly coloured shirts and shorts if they had been in the fields or greenhouses. Hera was typical, her greying hair held back by a red bandanna and her trousers stained from contact with the dark green pancake wrack.

She outlined the situation quickly, for there was little to say and no new messages had arrived. 'So I wanted to talk to everyone. Get some feedback from you on how we ought to deal with this. We've faced emergencies before, and come out all right, but this is a bit more radical. Obviously, the first thing we need to do is get more info on what the proposal actually is. We don't know what we are fighting until we know exactly what those monkeys on the Economic Subcommittee are suggesting.' There was a murmur of agreement from round the table. 'Right. But we must not just stand back and wait until they respond. We know enough already. We know the kinds of minds we are dealing with. We know that we are not loved by those who cannot see the trees for the timber. And

19

if Ahab is right, we only have a few weeks, and that means that someone is manipulating the timetable behind the scenes. We're on a war footing from now on, lads and lasses. We are going to need all the friends in high places we can get, so get your address books out. And let's not be downhearted – we've fought battles before, and have won, and we do have plenty of friends. So. OK. Any comments?'

For most of the people at the table the news was such a shock that they were having trouble getting their heads round it. They sputtered rather than fired.

'Surely what they are doing is unconstitutional,' said Tania Kowalski, a tough-looking biochemist who had seen action among the dying sequoia of northern California, and who knew all about legal battles.

'I doubt it,' replied Hera. 'These are the ones who write the rules. They're all lawyers and accountants. They'll be working within guidelines. The most we might be able to do is challenge those guidelines. But that takes time.'

'Well, lodge a protest anyway,' said Tania. 'Let them know they're in for a fight. We'll sort out the details later.'

'Point taken. Make a note, Hemi.'

Peter Knight, a young specialist in land reclamation who had only been part of the ORBE team for a few months, raised his hand. 'Can't we get them out here? Just show them what we are doing. Take them round. Show them the Largo Archipelago where the MINADEC chemical dump was. What you've done there is fantastic. Get them to see it. Once they see what we are doing they'll change their minds. We did that on Mirabai when we had a funding crisis and it worked.'

Hera smiled a weary smile. 'They'll have done their homework, Peter. They'll know all about Paradise. To them the situation is cut and dried. They'll have looked at how much the Paradise colony costs in subsidies and maintenance. They'll have weighed those against alternative demands for capital investment – new planets waiting to be opened up – and against the income and advantage derived from the present investment in Paradise. And that's it. As far as they are concerned this planet is in deficit. A generation or two ago this would not have happened.' She looked round the room and those who had spent longest working on Paradise, and knew its history, nodded. 'But now?' Hera looked at Peter Knight. 'Here's an irony for you, Dr Knight. The ORBE project owes its existence to a resolution passed by that same Economic Subcommittee almost thirty years ago.' Peter's surprise showed on his face. 'Yes. Its origin was not to do with ecology – that was the slant that Prof Shapiro gave it. Originally the ORBE project was created to solve the problems that were developing in Paradise's agro-economy. And that is why the Econ Com lawyers always think of us as troubleshooters – green marines, forest fixers, you name it.' Hera gestured to the sky in disgust. 'And you are absolutely right, Peter: they don't know the full story about what we do on Paradise, but that's not for lack of us trying to explain. We've had delegations and fact-finding missions by the bucketload. The last was just eight months ago.'

One of the ORBE workers who had joined by tri-vid, Rita Honeyball, cut into the conversation. 'Hera love, you could solve this problem in one hit. Do we have any good news on the Paradise plum? If we could give them a Paradise plum for breakfast they'd be eating out of our snapsa. They'd be falling over themselves to invest again.'

Hera grinned. 'Keep it clean, Rita.' And then she turned and pointed to a tall spectacled man wearing the traditional white lab coat of a technician. 'Moritz? What news on the plum? Have you got a miracle for us?'

Moritz stood up and spread his hands. He spoke quickly but with a heavy accent. 'Well. Progress we are making, yes. We know the toxins in the fruit yes, but ... they change, they change so fast. Occasionally we have fruit without toxin. But plum next to it has double dose. How is done is a mystery ...'

'So the answer's no, is it, Moritz?' asked Rita.

'Yes. No. It is.' Hera addressed Peter Knight again. 'So there you have it. The problem in a nutshell. Bio-forms mutating faster than we can keep up. We don't know quite what's gone wrong here but we believe that given time we can find out.'

Hemi had been trying to catch Hera's attention for some time. He seized his chance. 'Message came in a few minutes ago. The shuttle's just landing. It'll take off as soon as you are aboard.'

'Wish me luck,' said Hera, looking round the sombre faces, and she picked up her papers from the table. 'I'll report back tonight.'

'Before you go ...' the voice was a rumble and came from Pietr Z, a big man with a spade-shaped grizzled beard and long hair coiled in a knot held in place with a goose quill. No one could ever pronounce his last name to his satisfaction, so he had given up and just used Z. Pietr had been one of the founder members of the ORBE project. He was slowly spoken and could not be rushed.

'Well I've got—' began Hera.

'You've got time to listen to what I have to say. From what you tell us, they may try to disestablish this lovely planet because it is not economic. It may or may not be, we don't know. But if it is disestablished for economic reasons, that may be its saviour.' Hera, who had been tapping the table with her papers anxious to get going, stopped and looked at him, as did all the others round the table. 'Personally I don't give a toss whether there are aggies here or not, as long as they leave the umbrella trees alone.' He paused, tugged on his beard and glanced round with a fierce and angry look, leaving no one in any doubt about what he would do if someone did interfere with his beloved palms. 'But if they do close down the commercial side, they could leave us intact. We could survive. We only cost a few beans, less than the Space Council's booze bill, and perhaps without worrying about quotas we could even get more work done. So listen, young Hera. Don't you go blowing up and getting stirred up and waving your arms like a windmill. You push for us to stay and ditch the rest.'

There were nods of agreement from many members, though those who were involved most closely with the farming projects shook their heads. 'We ought to talk to the farmers before we say anything,' one of them called. 'Have they been contacted yet?'

But his voice was drowned out by Pietr Z, who had now stood up. 'And one more thing. You take that ridiculous headband off and make yourself look pretty. Put a bit of make-up on like that lovely Captain Abracadabra. She knows how to dress for a party. She makes a man feel good just looking at her, eh boys? And you never know, she might just spring a tri-vid link on you and you don't want to speak to the secretary general looking like Sinbad the Pirate. There, I've finished.'

Some of the people looked away to hide their laughter. Hera's lips pursed. And then she too smiled and nodded. The point that Pietr had made about the tri-vid was true. And it was well known that there was no love lost between Hera and Captain Abhuradin, the manager of the platform. 'Thank you, Pietr. I'll bear what you say in mind. Now I'm off to the powder room – for gunpowder.'

And she left.

While she could not, nor had she any desire to, emulate Captain Abhuradin, Hera did keep the shuttle waiting while she showered and yes, she did put some make-up on, as well as her dress uniform, which she had not worn for eight months.

'How do I look?' she asked Hemi. 'Would Pietr approve?'

'To hell with Pietr,' said Hemi. 'I'd take you out on a date any time. I've just had a call from up above, wanting to know where you were. They're getting anxious.'

'And?'

'There was a lot of static on the line, but I told her you were busy but wouldn't be long. Good luck.'

Hemi watched her go. *There was this to be said for Hera*, he thought, sizing her up with the eyes of the young and hungry, *She actually has no idea that she's attractive. Slim, light of step, never has to diet – bit old for me, but hey, if I was fifty . . .*

The waiting shuttle was one of the small six-seaters – fast and economical. Hera lay back, felt the pop in her ears as the pressure doors sealed, and then was pressed back in her couch by the acceleration. When she stepped out onto the shuttle platform a few minutes later, the captain was waiting to greet her, poised and graceful as ever and with her long dark hair pinned up neatly.

'At last,' she said. 'I was beginning to wonder what had happened to you. That young fellow who takes your messages . . .'

'Hemi. He is my administrator.'

'Yes, Hemi. Did he give you all my messages?'

'As far as I know?'

'Did he tell you I've booked a fractal link-thru to Space Central?'

'No, he didn't tell me that.'

'Well I have. It's in about five minutes. That was why I was getting worried. I didn't think it would take you so long. I was dreading you'd turn up dressed in overalls and sandals.'

'If I'd known there was a link-thru planned I would. You should have told me.'

'Yes, I don't know what happened there. I'll check with my secretary. Anyway, as luck has it the times between here and Central are nearly in sync at present. They are bit ahead of us so they will all have had their dinner – which may be to our advantage.' She paused, obviously relieved, and then added. 'Well, you are here now. It's a long time since I've seen you wearing your uniform. It suits you. You should wear it more often. Just a minute, you have your collar twisted.' The captain insisted on straightening the collar and smoothing the shoulders.

Hera twisted away. 'You should have made sure I knew about the fractal link. Damn it. I may need documents . . .'

'It is at their request. They want to tell us what is happening. And you won't need any documents. It is not a hearing. And you'd better check with your young admin boy down there. Frankly, I found him quite unhelpful when I spoke to him.'

The two women moved into the studio where the fractal transmissions took place and took their places opposite one another, facing the black animation mat where the figures they would be speaking to would appear. The technician in charge adjusted the chairs when they had sat down and made sure they were comfortable and within the fractal focus. 'I'm holding signal now,' he informed them. 'Just do a quick voice test.'

'Peter Piper picked a peck of pickled pepper,' said Captain Abhuradin.

'All that is necessary for the powers of evil to triumph is for a few good women to do nothing,' said Hera.

'OK, great. We're holding resonance; just waiting for them to join. In about a minute's time.'

'Who will we be speaking to?' asked Hera, addressing the captain and trying to keep her voice steady and even.

'The secretary general of the Space Council, Tim Isherwood, will be there, definitely. He might have called in one or two others. It won't be a long meeting. I know he's got something coming up later in the evening. You and I can talk afterwards.'

A bell rang softly, and a moment later a light began to shimmer in the space above the tri-vid mat. Both women sat straight and still while the light grew stronger.

'Counting,' came the soft voice of the technician. 'Five, four, three, two . . . . .'

Two signals were meeting, one from the space platform above Paradise, the other from the Space Council in the giant space station

24

called Central, which turned above Luna. Each signal was directly beamed to a fractal point not far from its own orbit – say, two seconds of light time distant. It was here that the signals were bent through another dimension, where they then met and joined in a never-never land. In a place of paradox. A place which only existed because the signals existed, just as they only found one another because the dimension existed. A place where nothing could ever reside, but which could be passed through. As in the quantum world below, so in the depths of interstellar space above.

The shimmering light intensified and grew taller. Briefly it showed the figure of a man with punk-white hair, a clown face and wearing a shocking-green dress, but then the image flickered and reset itself. Hera and Captain Abhuradin found themselves in the offices of the Space Council. Facing them was a man in a long gown of cardinal red and with a face as black as ebony. He was staring straight at them but smiling at some joke that they had not heard.

'I think I saw you before you saw me,' he explained. 'I have been waiting several seconds. You both look very charming, if I may say so. A pleasure to see you. Inez.' He bowed briefly to Captain Abhuradin. 'And you too, Hera. Now we don't have very long so we will get down to business straight away. Obviously you have received the bad news and want more facts. But possibly it may not have come as a complete surprise. Am I right?'

'It was a complete surprise, Secretary Isherwood,' said Hera. 'I can't speak for Captain Abhuradin, but we at the ORBE project would have appreciated prior warning that the future development of Paradise was in question.'

Still smiling, the secretary general turned to Captain Abhuradin. 'And you, Inez?'

'Rumours only, Tim. Just rumours. There are always plenty of them, but no definite word.'

'Well, all colony worlds are under constant review, as you know, and Paradise is no exception. Indeed, its economic prominence in the past has meant that it has been one of the standards by which other worlds were judged. However, be that as it may. Hera, I think I can put your mind at rest and say that the research undertaken by the Economic Subcommittee over the last two years has been very thorough and their decision has not been reached lightly.' He raised his hand, for Hera had been about to speak. 'Nor, may I say without

25

wanting to prejudice any review hearings, is it likely to be over-turned lightly in view of the generally worsening economic climate which confronts us and the increasing demands being placed on our limited res—'

Hera broke in. 'I am grateful for the assurance, Secretary Isherwood, that the committee's work has been thorough, but wonder why, *in being* thorough, they did not feel it necessary to speak to us. We are, after all, on the ground in Paradise and would have been willing to help.'

The secretary general nodded and smiled his affable smile. 'Would you like to speak to the head of the Economic Subcommittee? Dr van Terfel is with me here. Perhaps an explanation will—'

'I would like that very much,' said Hera, her voice beginning to sound grim.

Immediately Tim Isherwood beckoned away to his side and a woman stepped into view, joining him on the tri-vid mat. She was older, perhaps in her late sixties, but nothing in her manner or bear-ing suggested that age had impaired or mellowed her. Everything about her was neat and precise and hard-edged. Her blonde hair, naturally curly and with just a hint of grey, reached her shoulders. On her face were half-glasses with golden rims, and the eyes that peered over them were large and clear and had a cold intensity. She wore a dark blue suit over a pale blue shirt, and the only ostentation was a small silver brooch in the shape of a guillotine.

'Dr Hera Melhuish, I would like you to meet Dr Hilder van Terfel, head of the Economic Subcommittee.' The secretary general with-drew to the back.

Both women smiled tightly at one another. 'We have not had the pleasure of meeting before,' said Dr van Terfel, 'but I have heard a lot about you, Dr Melhuish. Now in what way can I help you?'

'The lack of consultation is a matter of grave concern to all of us. In an event as momentous as a Disestablishment we feel your first step should have been to consult those involved, and we will be seeking an official review of the decision, which, as you must real-ize, prejudices our work at a most critical stage.'

Dr van Terfel nodded as though to confirm that this was the first question she had expected. 'Yes, the issue of consultation was discussed in committee and the feeling was that there had been enough reports and visits over the critical period under review. I am referring to the past ten years up to the present. But please do convey my regrets to your members and accept my own personal apology for any distress caused by our decision. Such things are a shock when first encountered, but we are resilient beings, are we not, otherwise we would not be here. And of course all employees will be redeployed unless of retiring age. There is no question of dismissal. We do not live in the Dark Ages. But there is one other thing that I would like you to convey to your members. Please make them aware that we have to make decisions affecting the future of over a hundred and fifty planets, all of which are competing for limited resources. Everyone feels for their own future and their own planet as much as you feel for Paradise. And I can assure you that the decisions we take are not taken lightly, and are based on rigorous criteria and clear guidelines.'

'I will convey your apology to the members of the ORBE project on Paradise.' said Hera. 'But I am afraid they will feel that your committee's decision was taken in ignorance of the true details of our work, which is dynamic and changes daily since we deal with living things and not balance sheets. In this instance—'

'Forgive me for interrupting, but are you telling me that in the eight months since the last fact-finding mission there have been significant changes in your programme? Some radical new initiatives taken or new major discoveries made? The Paradise plum revitalized perhaps? Or are you continuing with your programme along the lines already well established?'

'The established programme continues, as it must, and with successes in all areas – but in parallel with that new discoveries are made daily.'

'I am sure they are. Indeed it would be a serious matter were there not some ongoing new perceptions given the level of funding you are accorded, but I said *major* discoveries, *significant* changes, *radical new* initiatives. My reference to the Paradise plum was by way of jest. We have rather given up hope on that, I fear. You see, Dr Melhuish, we are not interested in the run-of-the-mill discoveries which are, or should be, part of the daily work of any well run department. We are only interested in developments that are, in the purest sense of the word, significant. If there have been such, we have not heard of them, even though our research department monitors the papers published by your agency. Equally, any new and exciting discovery usually shows up as a request for a special development grant, for, as you know, new discoveries always cost more money than old.' Her lips pursed in a tight smile. 'In the ORBE project we have detected no such applications.'

'You underestimate the value of what you call run-of-the-mill research. That is what great discoveries are based on.'

'So where are the great discoveries?'

'Given time—'

'Ah yes, given time, anything is possible. Given time, we could all achieve enlightenment. But alas we work in the mundane here and now. In this world time is both money and resources. And while you, Dr Melhuish, may have plenty of time, the rest of us, and especially those planets whose natural resources are just on the point of being opened for commercial exploitation and who are hurting for valuable investment, do not.'

'Research does not move at the same timescale as capital investment.'

'Evidently not. And that is precisely our concern.'

The two women glared icily at one another.

Finally Dr van Terfel said, 'You know, Dr Melhuish, I think in a situation such as this – I mean where we are considering the future of a well developed planet – the Economic Subcommittee would have been prepared to be more flexible had you yourself been more flexible regarding the tourism issue. But in view of the Council's resolution in your favour on that matter, the committee discounted the possibility of terminating the agricultural sector since there was nothing of economic significance to take its place. Unless you are hinting at a possible rethink of your position . . .? The simple fact is that Paradise is failing miserably on an economic level, and has been for years, as you are fully aware. And you and your team at the ORBE project, despite massive funding, seem unable to do anything to halt that decline.'

'We are not miracle workers.'

Hera saw Secretary General Isherwood glance at his watch and then say something off camera. Time was running out.

She said, 'There is no question of our making a change in our stance on tourism. However, a point was raised today during the brief time we had to discuss your committee's suggestion –'

'Recommendation.'

'– and that was, if the problem with Paradise is simply a commercial one, then perhaps the commercial arm could be gradually phased out while leaving the research arm intact.'

'You mean close down the agricultural sector and leave you to continue as you are?'

'Well, yes. I wouldn't put it quite like—'

'Without any independent income beyond what you can gain from patents?'

'Yes. After all, the ORBE project is not really very expensive to run. And with the commercial pressure removed we could concentrate all our efforts on the deeper problems. We have many lines of research that are—'

Dr Hilder van Terfel cut across her. 'It costs twenty-three million solas per annum, give or take a few thousand, just to keep human beings down there on Paradise. That is mainly for wages, food supply, transport and equipment. In addition, we would have to factor in the costs of maintaining a fully equipped space platform. Say another twenty-three million, when you add in staffing, depreciation and maintenance. So forty-six million solas per annum. Pure cost. No return. But the promise of a great discovery sometime.' She paused, and laughter could be heard beyond the animation mat. 'I think we would find that a rather hard idea to sell to anyone, like selling sand to Mars. But it is an interesting proposal, and one that we had not considered.' She paused again and then added slowly, 'I trust, in view of your earlier comments on consultation, that this proposal has been discussed with the farming and agricultural sectors on Paradise and that they are in agreement?' She turned slightly away from Hera. 'Captain Abhuradin?'

The captain sat up straight and more or less came to attention in her seat. 'Well, er, no, such a proposal has not been discussed. In fact, this is the first time I have heard of it.'

'Really.' There was a dramatic pause and then Dr van Terfel turned back to Hera and studied her for a moment over her glasses. 'I regret, Dr Melhuish, that until such time as your proposal has been discussed with all parties concerned, it would not be appropriate for it to be discussed in this forum. We can not risk being accused of favouritism or making backroom deals.'

At this point the secretary general intervened smoothly: 'Ladies, I hate to break up a party, but I for one have another meeting to

attend, and I know that Dr van Terfel has contact time scheduled with the two other worlds that have been recommended
for Disestablishment. I propose that we call it a day for the time
being. Your request for an appeal has been noted, Hera, and will
be actioned tomorrow. However, the time frame is short – all part
of our efficiency drive – so the appeal may be heard the day before
the next Council meeting, which is –' he looked away and received
some information from one of the aides in attendance '– which is
. . . in exactly four weeks' time.' He turned immediately to Captain
Abhuradin before Hera could speak. 'Now, Inez, you have not had
much part to play in this debate. How have you and your staff
reacted to the news?'

'Well, there was shock and some dismay, naturally, and we will
be very sad to depart. But I think we all are pretty professional
about these things. We all knew that no planetary posting is permanent. Most are already thinking about the posting they would
like to put in for, and some may seek to take early retirement.'

'To be expected. And I think in cases such as these, where a
change of appointment is the result of a policy change and not a
matter of discipline, the Space Council can afford to be generous.
The same goes for your team, Hera. And now I think we must end.
This has been a most fruitful and frank exchange and I would like
to thank all parties for their participation. Till the next time. Au
revoir.'

The figures of Dr van Terfel and Secretary Isherwood shrank
suddenly to a point of light which then blinked out.

Captain Abhuradin let out a breath. 'Well, that van Terfel woman
is something else, isn't she?'

Hera did not want to speak for the moment. She was in turmoil.
She felt outmanoeuvred, humiliated even. More particularly, she
felt she had been set up by Abhuradin, who, for all Hera knew,
might have had prior information or secret talks with the Space
Council. She looked across at the captain, who was sitting back in
her chair, had undone the top button of her uniform jacket and was
now paying attention to her make-up.

'This was your idea, wasn't it?'

Captain Abhuradin looked across at her in surprise. 'What do
you mean *my* idea? And why are you looking at me like that?
I've told you already that Tim Isherwood asked me to set up the

meeting, which I did. I didn't realize it was going to be so short. And you have nothing to complain about. You got the lion's share of the time. There were a number of things I would have liked to say, but we ran out of time.' She closed the small make-up mirror with a snap.

'As far as I am concerned it was a trap. I was a fool to agree to a conference. In fact I didn't agree to it; it was sprung on me. And I think you were responsible for that.'

The young technician who had set up the tri-vid link and who had now come back into the studio, stood looking at the two women in some embarrassment. 'Er . . . will that be all?'

'Yes, that will be all, thank you,' said Abhuradin crisply. 'Are there any more calls logged or is this studio free?'

'No. No more calls.'

'Good. Close the door when you go. And we don't want to be disturbed. Understood?'

'Yes, ma'am.' He came to attention and saluted.

'Dismissed.'

As soon as the door was closed, Abhuradin rounded on Hera. 'How dare you speak to me like that, and in front of one of my junior technicians! And how dare you accuse me of complicity in some scheme?' Hera began to speak but Abhuradin rode over her. 'No. You've had your say. Now you listen to me for a change. You are going to have to stop this behaviour. Being suspicious of everyone, going round attacking anyone who has a different idea to yourself, behaving as if you are some kind of messiah on a divine mission. Oh yes, I know you've got qualifications as long as your arm, but that doesn't make you right or good. Only clever – clever and finally ridiculous.'

'If all you want to do is insult me, I'm leaving. I have more valuable things to get on with.'

'Yes, I'm sure you do. Well run away then. Start gingering up your forces. Write a report, for all the good it will do you, and then sit back feeling God-almighty virtuous. But what I want you to realize is that it is *your* fault that Paradise is being disestablished.'

'*My* fault?'

'Yes. You heard her, the van Terfel woman. She said if only you'd been a bit flexible. Taken the tourism proposal.'

'That again.'

31

'Yes, that again. We all see the dangers of tourism just as much as you, but no one was ever suggesting that we turn the planet into an expensive sex haven like Gerard's Barn. But something could have been done, something that was appropriate, something that you could have had a say in – and that would have been enough to keep Paradise alive. Well, you blew all the proposals out of the water, and now you see what has happened? The moderates on the Council didn't want to disestablish Paradise, but you left them no arguments. And if we did have enemies on the Council, well, you gave them a loaded gun with which to shoot us. Congratulations, Dr Melhuish.'

'You are talking rubbish. What van Terfel was suggesting was just the thin edge of a wedge, and you know that. Once you let the developers get a toe in the door you never get rid of them. First it would have been adventure holidays – all sweet and innocent – climbing in the Staniforth Mountains. But then something for the old folks, eh? A sanatorium by a quiet lagoon at Largo. Next, recreational diving in the Celeste Deep. And what about something for the kiddies? Within a year we'd see mechanical models of the great Dendron clumping about giving children's rides at Kithaeron. As soon as Paradise returned a profit – and Paradise would have turned a big profit, no question – it would be finished. In fact, Paradise would have ended up subsidizing the whole bloody space programme. Forget about agriculture. Agriculture is nothing. When the big boys move in they play for keeps. And the only way to keep them out is to not let them in in the first place. Now if that is all you have to say . . .'

'You stupid, stupid, stupid woman!' Hera's mouth opened. No one had ever spoken to her like that. 'You know nothing about the real world, do you? That's why people like you are so dangerous. You can't bend. You can't negotiate. You don't care about people, only your blessed plants. Well get back to them, Dr Melhuish, and don't think about the people who are going to leave Paradise, people who love Paradise just as much as you, people who now will have to tear up their lives and start again because of you.'

'I suppose you're one of them.'

'Yes. I am, actually. I plan to take early retirement in a few months and I can think of few places I'd rather live than here. It is the most beautiful place I have ever known.'

'Oh yes? Run a little hotel maybe? A little souvenir shop and café on the side?'

'Take that sneer off your face. I'm getting married at the end of the year and hope to start a family.'

That stopped Hera. 'You?' Hera would have suspected many things of the attractive Inez Abhuradin but the thought of her settling down and pushing a pram! 'You?' She repeated.

'Me what?'

'Getting married.'

'It is not so extraordinary. I'm sure you learned something about human chemistry when you were at university. And yes, I do take a keen interest in the economic well-being of Paradise, because I do not want to see it ruined. In my view this would have been a rather nice place to bring up children. Or do you not think of such things?' Hera did not reply. 'But worst of all, Dr Melhuish, worst of all is to know that you haven't a clue about what is really going on now. Have you?'

'I'm not sure I know what you mean.'

'That meeting just now. What do you think it was about?'

Hera thought for a moment. 'Well. They were trying to make a fool of me, thanks to you. And that van Terfel woman was clearly primed. But overall I think they were trying to calm us down so that we wouldn't make too much of a fuss. Buy us off with promises of redundancy payouts. It is an old trick.'

'Wrong, Dr Melhuish. Zero out of ten, Dr Melhuish.' Abhuradin was speaking more softly now and approached Hera until she was very close. 'They had a number of agendas, one of which was winding you up so that you would make a fuss and demand an appeal.'

'Why?'

'Because they want you out of the way. When the appeal comes, they'll crush you. I don't know how, but they will. They will have something over you, and their planning is probably well advanced already. And then, when you are safely out of the way, they'll close down Paradise, for a while.'

'What do you mean "for a while"? Stop talking in riddles. If you know something that I don't . . .'

'I know no more than you. But I understand how these things are done. You watch. They'll disestablish Paradise all right. But they'll leave the space platform in place. This platform on which we are standing. I stake my career on it.'

'And why would they do that? You heard what that van Terfel woman said about it costing so much money to keep the platform open.'

Captain Abhuradin looked at her in disbelief, and then she spoke very slowly and distinctly. 'After about five years, or ten maybe, depending on sensibilities, someone somewhere will come up with the bright notion that a place is needed for recreation. And then someone from somewhere else will remember and say, "What about that derelict old planet Paradise?" Then they'll talk to someone in high places, who will tell them, "Sorry, there is an environmental restriction order placed on Paradise." Shock! Horror! "But we won't do any harm. In fact we will enhance the environment. Take me to your leader." And within a couple of years they'll be in. And all your nightmares about kiddies' rides and old folks' homes will come true ... but it will be worse. It will be a hundred times worse. It will be more terrible than you can ever imagine because there will be no one here to stop it. Not me. Not you. That is why they need to get rid of you and all your friends at ORBE – and me too, because I am not thought of as a friend. Come back in ten years and then we'll see you weep. Those lovely mountains. Those clear seas. No fish there at the moment, I understand. Is that right?' Hera nodded. 'Well there will be. Specially engineered game fish – freshwater marlin and swordfish. I wouldn't mind betting that Dr van Terfel has already taken out shares in her grandson's name. She knows a bargain when she sees one. And she knows a sucker too.'

'What you are saying is nonsense.' Hera tried to sound confident, but her voice sounded weak even to her own ears. 'Secretary Isherwood signed the environmental decree. It is ironclad. "No tourism on Paradise".'

'Did he? Is it? Well, perhaps you know more about men and politics than I do. But if I look at Secretary Isherwood, with his bright red robe and his smiling face, I see a man who is political to the core. You don't get to his position without being a bit corrupt. Nothing illegal, mind you – too smart for that. You can be corrupt without being illegal you know ... or perhaps you don't. Perhaps you are all saints down there in your greenhouses. But at the end of the day, smiling Timothy Isherwood will come up smelling of roses.

When the time is right and the price is right he will find reasons to sell Paradise to the highest bidder. He will introduce a policy review or some such to overturn the environment order. Don't look so shocked, Hera. Use your brain for a change.' She paused and then added, 'Like a lot of clever people, the only thing you don't ever seem to realize is that the enemy is at least as clever as you are. The difference being that they have vastly more power than you and absolutely no hesitation about using it.'

Captain Abhuradin paused, saddened by the import of her own speech. When she next spoke her tone was more measured.

'Your clever quotation earlier about a few good women doing nothing ... Well in my view there *are* only a few good women and a few good men too – Tim Isherwood is probably one of the better ones – and the good people have to sleep sometimes, and that is when the bad boys do their business. Goodbye, Hera. Go back down and join your own kind. Write your report.'

Hera stood still. Abhuradin's words had shocked her, and, as happened to her when in a state of shock, she had momentarily become a block of wood. The awful reality behind Abhuradin's words was dawning on her. Finally she spoke and her voice was small. 'Will you be coming to the judicial review?'

'Not unless I am ordered to attend. I shall not be putting in an official submission. No point. But in any case ...'

'In any case what?'

'In any case, I do not want to be there and see you humiliated.'

There were no more words. Hera returned to the ORBE station, and when she reached the surface Hemi was waiting for her. He was anxious. 'Hell, Hera, you're never going to forgive me for this. I missed this message for you. It got mixed with some routine stuff. It was from Captain Howavyabin. The secretary general, Timothy Isherwood, has asked her to set up a fractal video link. She wanted to let you know. Sorry.' He looked at her, his face in an exaggerated wince as though about to be hit by a flying brick. 'Was it OK?'

3

A Moment of Madness

Hera did not blow up at Hemi. She simply nodded tightly, and then excused herself and went home. She needed to be alone.

Sitting in her tidy apartment, staring out of the window, Hera could see, above the adjacent buildings, the flapping pennants on the masts of the small flotilla of yachts in the marina. If even half of the things that Abhuradin had mentioned came true, those yachts would soon be counted in their millions. Even so, how she wished she could just climb aboard one, cast off and sail away. But running away was out of the question.

What a fool she had been not to see it all sooner! The plans had been carefully laid by the Space Council. Smarmy bloody Timothy Isherwood and that crone van Terfel! Ugh! Abhuradin had been right all along: she had, from her limited perspective, seen what was happening. And Hera, who prided herself on having a dirty mind when it came to politics, had not seen the danger. God, would she butcher them if she had them in front of her right now? But they were probably smiling over cocktails at this very minute, grinning and clinking glasses.

Hera stood up. She needed to do something, something different, to commit an outrage of some kind. But what? *What?* And a sudden thought came to her.

She found her keys where she had thrown them and went back to ORBE HQ. She did not enter the main office but went to the building next door, close to the small Shapiro Library, and entered the cryogenics lab. All the researchers had their own facilities here, and Hera's containers were in a small side room. She tapped in the access code and opened the fridge door. This was a special fridge where she kept historic samples of fruits and leaves and seeds. She removed a stainless-steel container on the top of which glowed a panel showing that the contents were held at a constant 34.7°F. Methodically she switched off all lights, closed and locked all doors and then carried the container to her shilo. There was a grim determination about her movements.

Back in her kitchen, she set the container down and turned off its refrigeration controls. This released a magnetic lock. Carefully she unscrewed the lid and set it aside. Then she tipped the container into a clean white bowl. Out rolled an object slightly smaller than her fist. It was a Paradise plum, a vintage one, well over a hundred years old, picked in its prime, long before the plums became toxic. As she watched, the plum responded to the warmth of the room. Slowly it changed colour, a bloom came to its skin and its perfume reached her – one of the quintessential smells of Paradise. She touched it and could feel that special tightness that one can detect on the skin of fruit when it is just coming to ripeness and can be bruised so easily.

The plum was a gift to Hera, and a note was tied to its stem on which was written in a wavering hand, *'For my dear H. In memory. Issy'.*[1]

Strange to relate, but Hera, who knew so much about the plants of Paradise, had never tasted a Paradise plum, although Shapiro had on occasion invited her to join him. He had always claimed that the plum brought wisdom and relief from pain. Well, Hera had never followed Shapiro's recommendation, for he was a renowned addict, but now ... now she was in need of something that would dull the ache inside her. Perhaps the bonus would be sweet oblivion. At least it would be one in the eye for the greedy plum-hungry Hilder van Terfel.

Quite conscious that what she held in her hand was worth many thousands of solas, Hera placed the plum on the cutting board, selected a sharp knife and slit it open. The knife cut through the flesh easily and the two halves fell apart, spilling clear seeds that leaked a blue juice with the texture of fine oil. The veined red flesh was firm. Hera scooped out the seeds and set them aside. She was

---

[1] This is the plum referred to by Professor Israel Shapiro in Document 5, the plum he left to Hera in his will.

no Estelle Richter and had no impetuous desire to crunch and swallow. Instead she took the two halves and squeezed them above a glass. The juice ran red, and within that redness were threads of deep blue, which, like oil with water, never mixed with the juice, but rather coiled on its surface.

When the run of juice reduced to a trickle, she set the cut halves aside. Their colour was changing again, darkening.

Hera raised her glass. It was half full. 'Here's to you, old man. May you rest in peace. And to you, Estelle – wherever you found rest for your adventurous spirit. And to you, Hilder van Terfel. May you live to regret the day you chose to disestablish Paradise.'

She put the beaker to her lips and sipped. Then she opened her lips wide and drank.

It was the smell of the plum that smote her first, like sweet incense curling in her mind. Then, as the juice found its way down her throat and to her stomach, she tasted all its colours and it made her legs feel weak so she had to lean back against the counter. She was aware as her eyes gradually lost focus and everything seemed to shine and seethe with light. For a moment she felt every hair on her body stir, and the sound of her breathing was loud. She felt the juice spread along her arms and out to the tips of her fingers; it coursed down the inside of her legs and into her toes. She felt it swirl in her heart and in her womb and it made her sigh.

And then, just as she was raising the beaker to her lips to drink what remained, she felt her stomach contract and heave beyond any control. She twisted round, managing to get her head over the kitchen sink just in time.

She had to grip the taps to keep herself from falling as her body convulsed. It was as though she was being beaten, as though someone was standing behind her and hitting her. But she could not cry out. It was as much as she could do to hang on, to catch breath and hope that her body would survive and purge itself.

How long she stayed like this Hera did not know, but finally she contained nothing more. She drank water and vomited it. But she persisted in drinking and eventually she was able to keep the water down and began to feel better. Gradually her vision cleared. She became aware that her skin was puffy at wrists and ankles, that she was wet with sweat, that she had peed herself, and her hair felt lank and clammy. The final, residual effect, however, was on her sense of smell. Everything smelled foul – especially her own body and the mess in the sink. This last was so strong that all she could do was turn away from it to stumble to the window and gulp the clean air. That was better. Not far away was a Tattersall weed; its blue flowers were open and the sweetness of its perfume reached her. Finally, when she could breathe more normally, she made her way through to the shower cubicle, holding on to the walls all the way. There she stripped as quickly as she could, pulling off her damp clothes and kicking them aside. The shower began to flow and she washed and shampooed and soaped until she was pink.

Hera experienced two more attacks of nausea while she showered, and after the second she felt distinctly better. Something had finally left her and she was able to towel herself dry without shaking.

She found clean clothes, bundled up her old things and sealed them in a plastic bag and threw them into the garbage container.

When she came back into the kitchen, there were the remains of the plum. The seeds had lost their clear lustre and turned to slush. The squeezed halves of the plum had dribbled juice all over the counter and it had dried in sticky veins. The juice in the beaker had thickened and was now unmistakably like congealing blood.

What had she done? The question hit her like a body blow. What had she done? What moment of madness had gripped her? How, how, how could she make amends?

She scooped up the remains of the plum and its seeds. She took them out into her small garden and there, under the light of the moon called Tonic, which had now risen over the horizon, she buried them, offering a prayer to Paradise and asking for forgiveness. There was nothing else she could do. Finally, she cleaned the knife and the cutting board, scrubbing them and putting them in the automatic cleanser just for good measure.

Finally, drained and white, she switched out the lights, went back outside and stood for a while in her garden staring up at Tonic, and then quietly made her way to bed.

Lying there, curled up on her side with her arms crossed and holding herself tight, she wondered what wisdom had come to her. It was, she decided, that she had come perilously close to crossing a boundary of innocence. In trying to taste the plum, she had gone against something deep in her nature, and her body, with a wisdom of its own, had taken over and cleansed her – and she was so glad. She was Hera still.

She should have known better, of course, and for that she could not readily forgive herself. It had been a moment of madness. *What fools we women are sometimes!* And now it had passed. And it had left her whole, in possession of her faculties and, in all the ways that really mattered, undamaged.

She wondered, even as she began to doze, how people had managed to eat those things, and faintly she seemed to hear Shapiro's wheezing laugh. 'It takes practice, Hera . . . and a certain amount of self-disgust at the beast in us.'

And when Hera woke up she was clear-eyed and ready for battle.

4

Political Games – Concluded

The following morning Hera dispatched two formal messages.

The first was to Abhuradin acknowledging that Hemi had indeed received the captain's message but had neglected to inform her. The second was to the Space Council applying for a special review hearing.

To the first message Hera received no answer and she had to wait two days for a reply from the Space Council. Their communication, when it arrived, was a brief acknowledgment from a certain M. Hackabout inviting the senior management team of the ORBE project to present their arguments in writing. Dr Melhuish was assured that if the review panel considered the arguments carried sufficient weight then the Recommendation of Disestablishment served on Paradise would be put on hold and a formal public hearing held. Hera noted with some optimism that the review committee was to be chaired by Ishriba, a senior diplomat who had, in his youth, been a fractal pilot. He had visited Paradise many times and knew the work of the ORBE project well.

Hera prepared her submission carefully. She argued that the absence of consultation by the Economic Subcommittee was an unacceptable breach of protocol. She maintained that the Economic Subcommittee was in error regarding the scientific work of the ORBE project and appended a list of successful projects which, she claimed, would have a bearing not only on the future of Paradise but on the shape of future space exploration. Her strongest argument was saved till last – that space exploration being still in its infancy, the difficulties being encountered on Paradise were to be valued as evidence of the 'dimension of the alien'. Far from disestablishing Paradise and hence closing the ORBE project down, she argued that it should be given a wider mandate than merely to service the agricultural needs of Paradise. It should, she claimed, 'become the main scientific arm of the Space Council dealing with non-terran bio-forms'. Her final paragraph was full of characteristic bravura.

So here is where we now stand. Paradise is a unique world. In all our wanderings in space to date we have not encountered another world like it. We have encountered life, yes, in the warm caves on Mars, on other worlds, but nothing like Paradise. But we will, and stranger worlds too, which will baffle us even more than Paradise does now. Paradise is well named. But let its name not blind us to the fact that it is a vast and largely unknown alien world – it is not a second Earth or an idealized Earth. I sometimes wish it was just called X or Z so that its name did not provoke such high expectations – but yet its name is good, for on Paradise we confront life in an abundant, vigorous, pristine and alien state, and there is so much to learn from it. The parallels with structures we are familiar with from Earth are remarkable, but so are the differences. We have really hardly begun. Let us look upon the agricultural work we have done to date as one big experiment, for that is what it truly is. And any scientist will tell you that you learn as much, if not more, from experiments that fail as from those that succeed. We study. We learn. We adapt. We try again. And we will succeed. But there must be no retreat. The ORBE project was never conceived as a fly-by-night one-issue project, but as a place of contact between the human and the 'other', a place of learning and discovery. It demonstrates our faith in the future and represents the finest traditions of our science. And of course it costs money. But to disestablish Paradise and abort the ORBE project now is akin to stopping Galileo just as he was on his way up the steps of the leaning tower of Pisa, or Newton as he was about to sit down in his orchard, or Archimedes when just about to take a bath, or Einstein because his experiments took place in his mind, in his vision, and lesser minds could not understand them. Let us not make that mistake.

A week after submitting her letter Hera received the following reply from the secretary of the Special Review Committee of the

Space Council.

Dr Hera Melhuish
Director ORBE project
Paradise

The Special Review Committee has considered your submission
re the Disestablishment of Paradise. After due deliberation, the
Committee has concluded that your letter provides insufficient
grounds for the summoning of a full review hearing. No further
action will be taken on this matter. The committee will therefore
recommend that the Disestablishment of Paradise proceed as
proposed.

M. Hackabout
Secretary to the Review Committee

White-faced, Hera pinned the letter up on the board for all to see. It
was greeted with anger, frustration, disbelief and talk of revolution
– the entire ORBE project seethed with such feelings.

Hera contacted the Settlers' Agricultural Association (SAA) to
see what their reaction was, but they were strangely unresponsive,
evasive even. That night stones were thrown through the front
windows of the ORBE HQ.

The very next morning Hera was informed by the legal division
of the Space Council that serious allegations of malpractice had
been lodged against the ORBE project by members of that same
Settlers' Agricultural Association and that the project was to be
audited forthwith. She was ordered to make all files, letters and
fractal transcripts available to the investigative body. She was also
informed that she would be summonsed in due course to answer
any allegations that were found to be substantiated.

Later that very same day agents from the Audit Unit began to
arrive at the shuttle port. All filing cabinets and computers were
immediately seized and sealed and taken to the New Syracuse
Library for evaluation. The library was placed under guard. The
reaction of the ORBE staff was, predictably, one of outrage. Who
had ordered this? Why? On what grounds? But answers were slow
in coming. The only assurances they received were that the cabinets and computers would be returned as soon as their contents

had been viewed and, where relevant, copied. That left many feeling very uneasy.

Soon the entire ORBE HQ was alive with AU agents. They had a mandate signed by Tim Isherwood himself, giving them wide powers. They could investigate anything and everything, from financial records to the suspected use of ORBE equipment for personal activities. They behaved in a manner that seemed calculated to create maximum disruption and irritation.

Work ground to a halt. Tempers flared, resulting in flat disobedience and non-cooperation. Passwords were withheld and someone crashed the entire computer and communications network. It fell to Hera to try and calm the situation – which, as one wit observed, was like asking the fire to cool the pot. But she did broker a deal whereby the computers and filing cabinets were returned in exchange for sworn assurances that no data would be destroyed until vetted. Magically the network repaired itself and work recommenced. But everyone was shaken, not least Hera, who had never experienced the full abrasive impact of bureaucratic ruthlessness.

Special audit teams went out to the various outposts where experimental work was taking place. This led to a clash at the umbrella tree plantation. One of the investigators urinated under a tree and Pietr Z, already fuming from answering questions about how his work helped farmers trying to grow corn, grabbed the man and threw him off the observation platform and into the marsh which surrounded the trees. There he became entangled in the Talking Jenny and almost drowned. By the time he was rescued Pietr Z had run off into the dense thickets surrounding the plantation, thickets in which he knew every path and glade. Pietr Z was never caught or seen again.

Worst of all were the agents who specialized in personal interrogation. These were led by a big heavy-jawed man named Stefan Diamond. He had eyes that stared and were unsmiling, a manner that always suggested that he disbelieved what he had been told, an ability to simply keep asking the same question time after time and a slowness in note taking that was clearly deliberate. His team were all cast from the same mould. They sat in on meetings, and the easy, candid and salacious back and forth of argument that had previously characterized such meetings came to an abrupt end. People started to talk like automatons, knowing that every word was being recorded. Or else they were heavily ironic and used the technical jargon of their discipline to confuse and mock their interlocutors. They referred to them as scatophaga, merdivora, escherichia and Symplocarpi foetidi. It did not make them popular but helped them feel a lot better.

The same agents also began to interview individual members of the ORBE project. They asked about personal research work, about dealings with the agricultural sector, about how ORBE funding was distributed, and whether clear directives regarding their work priorities were received from senior management. All conversations were recorded with warnings that any false information or failure to disclose information could form the grounds for later action – though it was not clear what that action might be.

Morale plummeted among ORBE personnel. Meetings between friends took place in greenhouses, or by the sea where there were no Auriculae aconitae listening.

Hera, of course, came in for very close scrutiny and had the indignity of being suspended while on duty. She was locked out of her office and denied access to her files.

One night Tania Kowalski was woken up by knocking on her door. Hera was in a terrible state, shaking and hardly able to stand. Tania's first thought was that Hera had been raped. She brought her into the small lounge and sat her down and held her in her arms and rocked her and tried to make sense of what had happened. It was rape but not of the sexual kind – of the mind and sensibilities.

That evening Hera had gone to her laboratory and discovered that someone, despite the big warning sign, had disabled the alarm and then turned off the power to the cryogenic units. All the bioform samples dating right back to the early days of Paradise were now slush. The loss was irreplaceable. This could only have been deliberate.

Shocked and distraught, Hera had returned to her shilo to find the front door open, a window smashed and there, hanging on the veranda by a cord, was a Tattersall weed. It had been trimmed so that the blue flower resembled a head, and four of its spiky limbs were like arms and legs. It was draped in some of Hera's underwear. Grotesquely it turned in the light breeze.

Hera, afraid to go into the house, had run all the way to Tania's cabin.

Next morning there was no sign of the hanging Tattersall weed and no one owned up to the damage in the deep-freeze lab.

Hera stayed with Tania after that. And when she moved about New Syracuse she was always accompanied. The theory was that it was members of the Settlers' Agricultural Association who had done these things and there was whispered talk of reprisals, which Hera tried to stop, but she felt the weakening of her authority.

Then, with no warning, the audit ended as quickly as it had begun. The Audit Unit personnel simply packed up and took passage off planet without any explanation.

The ORBE workers were left dazed, insecure and baffled. What had it all been about? Thousands of documents had been copied but none were of what you could call an incriminating nature – embarrassing possibly, comic frequently, scatological often and sometimes brutally frank. Simply the ephemera of busy, clever people.

There were no financial irregularities. ORBE *did* work efficiently. They knew it; everyone knew it – and if some of its members were disrespectful and looked a bit scruffy, that was their choice. There was nothing untidy about their minds.

But relations with the Settlers' Agricultural Association dropped to an all-time low. Fights broke out, and the aggies, who had always had a certain contempt for the scientists, discovered what it meant to tangle with the range-hardened and self-sufficient men and women of the ORBE project, for they could give better than they received when it came to a fight.

The only gleam of hope was that the Space Council had not yet ratified the Economic Subcommittee recommendation. A crucial debate was scheduled to take place just seven days after the audit agents had departed.

On the day of the debate, the times between Central and Paradise were divergent. Using fractal time, dawn on Central was late afternoon on Paradise. As the day wore on, members of ORBE gradually gathered at their HQ. Not far away, in the Settlers' Club, the members of the SAA held their own gathering.

At five thirty in the evening the news came through. Everyone knew that the debate would have been fierce, but the news when it came was delivered in a flat and unemotional manner: 'The Space Council after due deliberation has voted in favour of disestablishing Paradise. Action: immediate.'

It was over.

The news was a body blow. No, it was worse. It was an execution.

Though Hera had tried to prepare herself, when she heard the news it made her physically sick and she had to retire to one of the toilets at the ORBE HQ.

When she came out, some people had already left and had taken bottles down to the beach, there to vent their hurt and rage. Others sat red-eyed. That night Hera admitted herself to the small hospital in New Syracuse. Nervous exhaustion was the diagnosis, but they might just as well have said heartbreak or grief.

And it was there, early in the morning of the next day, that she received an official summons ordering her to attend a disciplinary hearing at the Audit Unit offices on Central. Evidently there were questions she needed to answer. Allegations of misconduct. Irregularities had been found in her stewardship of the ORBE project.

Had the universe turned to clockwork? Hera wondered, each day mindlessly bringing worse tidings. The hearing, which would be open to the public, was scheduled to take place in two days. Wearily Hera contacted Tania Kowalski, who agreed to accompany her to Central.

On the day of departure Captain Abhuradin was waiting for Hera at the shuttle platform. This was not the captain that Hera was used to. Her face looked scrubbed and severe. Her hair was held back and her face lacked make-up. She was wearing fatigues with a black armband. The space platform was already noise with new people arriving to conduct the Disestablishment.

'They did it,' said Hera flatly.

'They always meant to,' answered Abhuradin. 'Here, I have a letter for you.' She saw a sudden look of fear cross Hera's face. 'Don't worry. It's not official; it's from me. Something I've been meaning to say since . . . since the last time we met.' She pressed the letter into Hera's hands. After a slight hesitation, she leaned forward and gave Hera a light kiss on the cheek. 'Good luck.'

Hera endured a terrible passage through the fractal. Where, she

47

wondered, and from what black depth of her psyche, did such nightmares come?

The only shred of comfort for her was Abhuradin's letter.

Dear Hera,

I said some terrible things to you after that meeting with Isherwood, and I am very sorry. I was very angry, but I rarely lose my temper like that. It has quite unsettled me. It tells me that my decision to quit the service at the end of the year is the right decision for me, though I have offered to stay on and perform the 'last rites' now that the Space Council has voted to proceed with the Disestablishment.

This is a terrible day. Like you, I take no joy in anything at present. I am not sure what is going on, but I hope the bad things I predicted do not come to pass.

I was rude to you, and for that I am deeply sorry, but I was also trying to tell you the truth as I see it.

Captain Inez Abhuradin
Alpha Platform-over-Paradise

The letter came as a complete surprise to Hera. She found it difficult to accept that it was from a woman who until today she had regarded as an enemy. How little she had known her. And how right the elegant Captain Abhuradin had been!

Hera was still wobbly on her feet when she and Tania reached Central. It was half past seven in the evening, local time.

An official from the Audit Unit, a strong-looking young man with cropped hair, was there to meet them. 'Hi,' he said. 'I'm Kris. I'm your minder. I was one of the team down on Paradise. Nice place. Sorry to hear what's happened. But that's progress, eh?'

Once through the security doors, reporters were waiting. They pushed their instruments in front of Hera's face and shouted questions. It was as much as Tania and Kris, assisted by one of the security guards, could do to shield Hera and get her into the safety of the lift leading up to the Space Council offices.

'I wasn't expecting that,' said Hera when the sliding doors had hissed shut. 'How did they know I was coming?'

The young man shrugged. 'This place leaks like a sieve when

they want it to. Don't worry. We've booked an apartment for you in the secure wing. You won't be troubled there.'

'The secure wing?' asked Tania. 'Isn't that just for people on trial?'

'And VIPs,' said the young man smoothly.

A soft ringing tone announced that the lift had reached the apartment level. From there Kris conducted them to a pleasant suite of rooms on the outer ring of the torus, from which they had a view of the cratered face of the moon turning slowly beneath them. 'The hearing will take place at ten tomorrow, but I will come to collect you at nine. Breakfast will be delivered at seven thirty. You can make your selection by call-up. Have a pleasant evening.'

The door closed, and Tania, who had a streetwise and suspicious turn to her mind, counted to ten and then tried it. The door opened.

Kris, halfway down the corridor, turned and smiled.

At exactly nine a.m. the next morning Kris tapped on the door. The two women were ready.

Kris conducted them to the main office of the Audit Unit, where Stefan Diamond – unsmiling as ever – handed her some forms. With him was a man Hera had not expected to see, a friend, Senator Jack Stephenson.

Jack Stephenson, formerly an Olympic swimming champion, was now an influential member of the Space Council, chairing several committees. He was also a loyal supporter of the ORBE project, and it was largely due to his influence that the tourism proposals had been so roundly defeated.

'I came as soon as I heard they'd brought you over to Central,' he said. 'I've no idea what this is all about.' He gestured around, including Stefan Diamond in the movement. 'I imagine you have more pressing concerns than this, Hera.' Then, in sudden irritation, he turned and addressed Stefan Diamond. 'Get the women a coffee or something, man. And then, please, I would like to speak to them for a few minutes in private.'

Stefan Diamond shrugged and gestured to Kris, who took their orders and then departed. 'I would remind you that the hearing begins in thirty-five minutes' time,' said Diamond, 'so you have about fifteen minutes.' And he left.

Tania picked up the papers Diamond had left on the table. 'If it is

49

all the same to you, I think I'll take a stroll outside and have a squiz at these. Then I can brief you,' she said. 'You talk in private.'

Jack Stephenson took a small electronic monitor from his pocket and placed it on the table between them. Immediately it began to flash and emit a polytonal signal, indicating that recording devices were operating. 'And you can turn them off too,' said Stephenson loudly. 'And if I find out that any part of our conversation has been listened to, you'll be answerable to the Disciplinary Committee, which I chair.' Seconds later the monitor became silent and its light faded.

Stephenson looked at Hera for a few moments. 'Been tough, eh?' She nodded. 'I understand they got you out of hospital.'

'It was my own choice,' said Hera.

'Well if I'd known, I'd have told you not to come. You could have told them to stuff it. Hell, there's plenty of time for this kind of circus later. Not that it is relevant now anyway.' He paused and sighed deeply. 'I am so sorry,' he said quietly. 'So, very, very sorry. I thought we had the numbers. Just. It was a hell of a debate. There was blood on the floor of the chamber. I've never been through a session like it. It has absolutely split the Council in half. But they got us with a couple of abstentions, Apolinari and de Loutherberg – God knows who pressured them – and poor Elvira Estaing couldn't be there. She was on her way but suffered a heart attack in Suva. She is still in intensive care.' Hera put her hand to her mouth but said nothing. In her mind she was aware of another tick of the clockwork. 'We really missed Elvira's voice at the debate. I think she would have won over the abstentions. And of course smiling Secretary Tim cast his vote with the Lady Hilder party and that was it: fifty-seven to fifty-five.'

'Can't we appeal?' It was said without enthusiasm.

'I've already done so. But I don't have any hopes. It was all so sudden and now positions are entrenched. In any case, the people on the Review Committee, all except old Ishriba, voted for Disestablishment. Times are changing. We are into a new phase of some sort. There is a lot of ignorance out there selling itself as pragmatism, and God knows where it will end. For the first time, Hera, I am really afraid for the future.'

'Well, you did what you could,' said Hera. 'And thank you for that.'

'The bad news is, and I am afraid I am getting cynical in my old age, that I think one of the reasons they have brought you here so quickly is to get you off planet. By the time you get back to Paradise the first demolition teams will already be on the ground. That's how quickly things are happening. They probably thought you might stage a protest.'

Hera made a sound, a quiet sound such as a cat makes when it is dying, a small involuntary keening which could almost have been a sound of love. Then she said, very softly, 'Who is doing this, Jack? Who?'

Stephenson shrugged and shook his head. 'I have no idea. There may be one person or several people ... One day maybe we will find out, but I am not sure that names matter now. You know, Hera, as days pass I seem to meet more and more people who don't seem to like the light of day. People who are not comfortable with ideas like beauty or love or self-sacrifice, and for whom the only truth is what they can hold in their hand, the power they can wield, the advantage they can take. These people don't have to talk to one another; they know one another by their smell. And what I fear most now is that these people, whoever they are, will come to control what is happening in space. And if they do, we as a race will make the same mistake as we always have. We will try to control by force what we could perfectly well live with by reason alone.'

Hera had never seen Jack Stephenson so despondent.

'Well, look at me,' he said, rallying. 'And I came here to offer you support.'

'And you are, Jack.'

There was a tap at the door and Kris brought in the coffee. 'Just to let you know there are seven minutes until we have to go down to the hearing. I'll be taking you down.' He withdrew without waiting for a reply.

Hera and Jack Stephenson were silent.

Inside Hera it was as though all her emotions were colours and they were spinning round in her head. She did not know what she thought or what she felt any more. And then, apropos of nothing, she said, 'There were people I knew on the fractal transit, people I've known for years. Some of them looked away when they saw me.' She paused. 'Isn't that sad? I've had people be rude before, but they didn't seem to want to know me. Why?' She was silent for a

51

moment. 'And there were photographers waiting too. I felt like a criminal. None of us understand what is happening. One day we are told we are going to be disestablished. Then we are told we are going to be audited, and the next thing we know all these strange men arrive and start bossing us about as though they owned the place. I've never seen guns on Paradise before, except in the museum. Why guns . . .?'

'How did your people take it?'

'Not well. But it got to me.'

Stephenson nodded. 'Well, the audit people were on a fishing expedition. As far as I can make out, a group of SAA members made a formal complaint direct to Tim Isherwood saying that funds were being misappropriated by ORBE and that they were not getting the level of support they were entitled to.'

'What? Who were they?'

'William and Proctor Newton and young Elizabeth Pears.'

'I might have known! And Isherwood took them seriously. The Newtons are as mad as March hares. Proctor Newton hears voices, and no one can understand what William is talking about most of the time. As for Lizzie Pears . . . well, she's just a mixed-up girl. Why didn't Isherwood check with us first?'

'Because he didn't want to. He handed the matter over to the Economic Subcommittee and Lady Hilder handed it straight over to the Audit Unit, saying – and I quote – since there was "such controversy about the future of Paradise at present, please investigate the ORBE project thoroughly and report back as soon as possible".'

'How do you know this?'

'Leaked memo. The powers of darkness are not the only ones with their angels, Hera.'

'And *have* they found anything?'

'No idea. They will have found the normal amount of dirt that lies in the crannies of any decent, well run, honest organization. We used to call it oil of discretion. But is your conscience clear?'

'Completely. There was nothing to find. Tania Kowalski reckons it was a jack-up. She thinks they might have tried to plant something. She's full of conspiracy theories.'

'She might be right.'

'But the Newton twins and Lizzie Pears. I mean to say . . . I know they're odd, but not wicked. The aggies can be a pain – suspicious, always wanting more, never satisfied – but now they are hurt as much as the rest of us. I suppose they want someone to blame, and have chosen me. Misplaced anger. They can't blame God, so they blame us.'

'Well tell them that. Stick to your guns.'

'What guns? I'm tired, Jack. I'm achy. I'm confused. I don't think it has really sunk in yet, what's happened. I don't have much fight left in me right now. I just want to get it over and get out.'

At that moment the monitor on the table squawked. 'They are telling us time's up,' said Stephenson and pushed his chair back.

Hera stood up. 'Are you going to be in there?'

He shook his head. 'I can't. I'm booked to get down to Suva as soon as I leave here. Hope to find Elvira is still with us. But I'll come back as soon as I can.'

Hera nodded. 'Good. I'm glad. Give her my love.'

Stephenson held out his hand. 'Good luck, Hera. Watch out for Diamond, he's a dealer in dirt. Used to work on divorce cases. Now they use him as their hatchet man. And don't go waving your arms about when you're talking. It makes you look . . . comic.'

'Point taken.'

The door opened, revealing Kris. 'Dr Melhuish. This way, if you please.'

Tania was there too. She had a funny expression on her face and shrugged when she saw Hera.

'Can't see what the fuss is about. A few candid memos. Nothing like the ones I used to send you and which you obviously destroyed. And they want to query our science, whatever that means. We should be out in half an hour – and then we are going for a drink. Dr Kowalski's orders.'

They were led down a long corridor with opaque office doors on either side. At the end was a lift, which took them down a floor to one of the transverse wings. This lift opened into the anteroom of a small concert chamber.

People were milling about, and again there were reporters and cameras. Hera hurried past. 'No comment' was all she would say.

A balcony ran all the way across the concert chamber. Facing this was a small stage built on two levels. On the top stood a table with an ornate padded chair behind it. This was for the official who would be conducting the hearing. Below that were two smaller tables which faced one another. One was for the ORBE representatives and the other for the Audit Unit. Below that, at ground level, was a table for whoever was making the record. A woman already sat there, her hands folded.

Kris led Hera and Tania to one of the facing tables. It had two plain plastic chairs. Looking up they could see that the balcony was already quite full, with more people entering all the time.

'I thought this was just a meeting to answer some questions,' said Tania.

'It is,' answered Kris.

'So why all the people?'

'There is a lot of interest in this case.'

'So it's a *case* now, is it, and not an inquiry?' she snapped.

'Sorry. Slip of the tongue. I'll leave you now. If you need anything, I'll be near the door.'

Arranged on the table was a carafe of water, a single glass, some blank sheets of paper and a pencil. The table facing them was similarly equipped, except that the chair behind it had a high pointed back more suitable for a church.

'All very theatrical' was Hera's only comment.

Hera heard her name spoken and glanced up at the balcony. There she saw the sullen and angry faces of William and Proctor Newton glaring down at her. Lizzie Pears was sitting away to one side. She was concentrating on her nails, nibbling at them, her face blank. And what had she done to her hair? It was all spiky and seemed to have rags tied in it. Several leading members of the Settlers' Agricultural Association were also present, huddled together. Hera had the impression that they didn't want to look her in the eyes. She looked away. Hera felt strangely detached from proceedings, as if they were happening to someone else.

'Now listen,' said Tania. 'Don't let them rush you and don't let them fluster you. They might try to do both. And if you get stuck, give me a nod and I'll step in. I've stopped bigger inquiries than this when I was in California.'

Hera nodded.

Stefan Diamond, carrying a large black legal case, entered and took his place at the table opposite. He did not look at the two women. Everything about the man was heavy, Hera noticed. Heavy jaw, heavy brow, heavy stomach. She pitied his chair. Diamond

54

settled himself, undid the button of his jacket, scratched under the jacket while he looked round the assembly with a somewhat imperious gaze and then, finally, began to unpack the case. He set out his papers and folders carefully while gradually the auditorium fell silent.

Hera's attention was interrupted by the arrival of the Space Council member in charge of proceedings. He was a dapper little man with receding hair and bushy eyebrows. He seemed a size too small for the red legal gown he was wearing.

'All rise,' someone called. And everyone did.

The chairman sat down after nodding briefly to the assembly. There was a scuffling of feet and some coughing as people made themselves comfortable.

'We'll call this inquiry to order,' said the chairman. He then went on to give a brief outline of the reasons for the inquiry – that certain allegations had been lodged against the ORBE project management – and the protocols that would be followed. Questions would only be put by the representative of the Audit Unit, but there would be opportunities for public comment at the end of proceedings and for Dr Melhuish to make a final statement should she so choose. He then invited Mr Diamond to begin.

Diamond rose to his feet and in a deadpan voice outlined the details of the audit that had just been completed. Hera listened with her head on one side. How different, she thought, was Diamond's account of the process from her own perception, and yet factually he was correct and she could not fault him there. And somewhere between it all was the truth, she supposed. She found her attention wandering, looking at the mosaic pattern formed by the acoustic tiles on the wall.

'Now, Dr Melhuish, do you recall making the following statement? "We must not confuse culture with civilization. Hunter-gatherers were just as clever as we are and probably had a more coherent view of the universe, and their place within it, than we have. By and large they did not damage the landscape, taking only what they needed, leaving Nature to regenerate of her own accord. It was with the coming of agriculture that the damage started. The first farms led to enclosures, to selective breeding, to the damming of rivers, the moulding of hills and ultimately the desire to manipulate Nature rather than cohabit with her."'

Hera had to think hard. 'Yes, I think those were my words. We were on a panel. Me and some others. We were students at the Institut des Hautes Études. Over thirty years ago. You *have* been digging deep.'

'It would seem, then, that from an early age you were critical of farmers, indeed of agriculture in general.'

'That panel, if I remember rightly, was dealing with environmental issues, trying to get at why things had gone wrong on Earth. I was merely pointing out a significant but sometimes overlooked revolution that took place in the prehistory of Earth.'

'I repeat. "It was with the coming of agriculture that the damage started." Your words, Dr Melhuish. Moving on.' Diamond picked up a sheaf of notes. 'The following is an extract from the founding charter of the Observation, Regeneration and Botanic Expansion project on Paradise. "The ORBE project undertakes to make its scientific expertise available to help the settler agricultural sector in its efforts to create sustainable agriculture on Paradise." You signed this document when you accepted the position, Dr Melhuish. We note that in your application for a position with ORBE, you state that you can support "all aspects of the charter". In view of your later record, Dr Melhuish, it would seem that you were being circumspect with the truth, presumably in order to gain employment and, perhaps, to be near your mentor, Professor Shapiro.'

'Objection.' It was Tania. 'Mr Diamond's presumptions are misleading and irrelevant.'

'Sustained. Mr Diamond, please restrict yourself to the facts.'

This kind of exchange set the tone for the inquiry.

Little by little, by cutting and pasting together comments made by Hera, Diamond was able to create the picture of a tyrannical wasp-tongued woman who was intolerant of the problems faced by the descendants of the settlers and interested only in her own projects.

At first Hera tried to defend herself, pointing out the importance of context. But Diamond was not to be drawn; he simply ignored her and moved on. 'Here is Dr Melhuish writing to an ORBE project worker who answers to the name Pietr Z. It was written shortly after she had taken over the leadership of the ORBE project from her mentor and friend, Professor Shapiro. "No wonder they call them aggies,' she says. "Aggravating, agoraphobic, aggrieved and aggressive."'

'That was a joke,' said Hera wearily.

'Yes, but at whose expense? And who was laughing?' snapped back Diamond. 'Or were you merely trying to continue the tradition established by your predecessor, Shapiro?' Hera merely shook her head. There was hissing in the auditorium.

Tania leaned close. 'Why does he keep making these digs about old Shapiro?'

'No idea,' whispered Hera.

'Here's Dr Melhuish again,' continued Diamond, 'this time offering advice to a new appointee who has had an argument with one of the members of the SAA. The recipient of Dr Melhuish's good advice, Dr Tania Kowalski, is the lady who has accompanied her here to this inquiry. I will read this memo in full, for it reveals Dr Melhuish's hardening intransigence towards the agricultural sector.'

Memo to Tania Kowalski.

You ask why the aggies are so difficult. They are having a hard time, no question, but underlying that is the traditional xenophobia which seems to spring up so easily in secluded rural communities. This can be fuelled by jealousy, a sense of personal failure, a vision centred on the past, by insecurity and, of course, ignorance – all of which are true here. When reason fails, men turn to strange gods. When things continue to get worse, they look for an enemy to blame. We are it. We give them solidarity. If we were not here it would be the Space Council or they would start feuding among themselves and setting up little fiefdoms. But they never look within. Sad really, because the first settlers were men and women of vision, the pick of the bunch; but that spirit has now dwindled and we are left with these secretive and suspicious people who have so upset you. Take heart, brave lady. The other problem is that they see themselves as the true inheritors of Paradise and want something to hand on to their descendants. They resent us as interlopers. I once suggested that they should stop trying to farm but should just sit back and enjoy Paradise and watch the forest grow. From their reaction you would think

that I had suggested they ate their children. Also, like all ignorant people, they are frightened of our knowledge.'

It took five minutes for the chairman to restore order after the
reading of this letter. Hera sat silent, no longer staring at the wall
but at a place on the ground some metres in front of her. Even Tania
was silent.

A newspaper report published the next day described Hera as
sitting 'hunched like a woman drunk or immersed in a compelling
story, while the storm gathered about her'. Fatigue was taking its
toll. She was hearing her own words but remembering the occasions which gave rise to them. Hearing how easily Diamond's
flat delivery killed any lightness or wit. She realized too that Jack
Stephenson was right: she should have stayed on Paradise. 'The big
boys don't play fair and they play for keeps.' Who had said that?

'You have nothing to say, Dr Melhuish?'

Hera roused. 'You don't tell the full story. Why not tell them
about the time I stayed up all night and was midwife when the girl
up there, Elizabeth Pears, was born?'

Diamond cut in smoothly. 'No one doubts you have your fine
and gentle side, but this inquiry is concerned with the standard
of your leadership, your objectivity and the professional decisions
you made.' He paused and then added. 'However, in deference to
Dr Melhuish's demand that I tell the full story, I will now read the
full text of her letter to Senator Jack Stephenson concerning tourism.' There was an immediate murmuring in the crowd, for the
tourism issue had been, and in some quarters still was, a cause for
dissension.

From Dr Hera Melhuish to Senator John Stephenson.
Dear Jack
Re Tourism Proposal

Thanks for keeping me informed on progress. I have just had a
long and difficult meeting with the members of the SAA. The
tomato crop we had high hopes for after starting the seeds off
world, putting the plants under polythene and hand pollinat-
ing every flower, has failed. Dova Rokka, on whose farm we had
helped locate it, found out this morning. She brought some of the

tomatoes to show us. They had turned black. I cut one open and inside it was just mush and water. I've sent them for analysis of course, but I don't think analysis will help much. All I can think is that there is something in the air of Paradise that we can't feel but the plants can.

Rokka and the rest took this badly. I had not realized how much they had pinned their hopes on a few miserable tomatoes. I think Rokka is ready to call it a day. She has relatives on one of the lunar outlanders and is thinking of going there and starting again. However, she may not. Dai Tattersall has come up with a scheme, backed by the mad, bad Newton twins, for developing their farms as tourist resorts. Apparently there is money available to back this scheme – private investment assisted with some Central incentive solas – and he is all excited. He's gone so far as to draw up some sketches. Honeymoon cottages on the Bell Tree Islands, Scout camps and the like in the Organs. You get the picture? What worries me is that they have obviously been talking to someone at Central. They were very shifty when I pressed for details, and Proctor did his imitation of a mushroom and pulled his hat down over his eyes. He probably has cute ideas about establishing a little white church on a little green hillside under fleecy little clouds. Over my dead body!

Up on the balcony someone shouted something and the chairman immediately stopped proceedings and warned that if there were any more disruptions he would consider clearing the gallery. 'Continue, Mr Diamond.'

I know we have been through all this a hundred times, but they don't want to hear. What you are going to have to do, Jack, is get a protocol through the Space Council. Something very definitive. An absolute prohibition on any commercial development. Especially tourism. I know you see the dangers as clearly as I do, but this idea has got to be stopped now, stamped on hard, once and for all. So put your boots on. I'll keep you informed if I hear anything new.

And while you are shaping up the anti-tourism proposal, give a thought to this. As you know, I firmly believe that there is a place for experimental agriculture on Paradise, but having the two organizations – the SAA and the ORBE project – both concerned with the bio-development of Paradise really makes no sense. We pull in different directions all the time. It would make a lot more sense for the agricultural sector to be put under ORBE control. Then we could keep an eye on it, get rid of the commercial supply imperative which weighs like a rock, and treat agriculture as the experimental arm that it really is. The aggies would hate this, of course. They'd fight us like cats in a barrel. Already they talk about their ancestors as if they had been here for centuries – and I quite like that. I feel the same way about Angelique-over-Io. But while Io is thriving and expanding, Paradise is not – and the dream they have of handing on neat little pastures to their descendants just ain't going to happen, not until we get a handle on the crop failures. Sorry I am going on a bit. Let me know if there is anything I can do to help scotch the tourism plan and tell me what you think of my idea of making SAA part of ORBE.

Best wishes to Elvira when you see her.
Hera.

When he had finished reading the letter, Diamond looked across at Hera. His only comment was 'Well, Dr Melhuish, if ever you wonder about conspiracy theories regarding Paradise or people or where the climate of suspicion comes from, you need look no further than your own bathroom mirror.'

It was a cheap shot, and one which Tania immediately tried to rebuff, but her words were not heard so great was the outcry. Cheap or otherwise, it was effective. Insults were thrown from the balcony and Tania found herself in a fierce exchange with Dova Rokka. Order was not restored until a couple of members of the SAA had been removed from the gallery. Tania was also cautioned, and when she shouted at the chairman she too was ordered out of the hearing.

Hera was now alone. During all this Diamond had closed one of his folders and opened a second. He stood impassively while the chairman dealt with the disturbance. When all was quiet again Diamond continued in the same steady and unemotional voice: 'However, appalling though this record of manipulation and disparagement may be, there is another side to this issue which I would now like to examine.' He paused theatrically, as though pondering a difficult and perhaps distasteful matter. 'Dr Melhuish, how well did you know Professor Shapiro?'

The question was sudden and Hera hesitated. 'I don't think I understand.'

'Well, we know that he was your teacher, that he supervised your PhD, that you became colleagues. But was he more than that? A close friend, a confidant possibly, someone you were intimate with?'

'I don't see—'

'The reason I ask is that aspects of the science he preached, some of the heretical views he propounded, views which have been widely condemned by the wider scientific community, would appear to be exactly the ones which you have adopted . . . in the manner of a disciple, say, a willing and biddable pupil.'

Hera was up on her feet, her arm outstretched, when she paused. She saw the trap. Of course he was doing this. Winding her up with innuendo. Goading her. Getting her to make herself look ridiculous. She sat down again. She spoke very slowly and distinctly. 'That I admired Professor Shapiro is widely known. That I was honoured by his friendship is also true. Your use of the word intimate causes me some concern and I would ask you to explain exactly what you mean. Are you suggesting that Professor Shapiro, a man older than my father, and I were lovers? If so I shall ask you for the grounds for that assertion.'

Hera looked to the Space Council representative, who in turn looked at Stefan Diamond and said, 'Clarification please, Mr Diamond.'

Diamond pondered. 'I was merely suggesting that you were close friends, not alleging that you were lovers.'

'In which case,' cut in Hera, 'may I register my objection and ask that the misleading words be removed from the record.'

'Objection sustained. The word intimate is to be struck from the record. And Mr Diamond, may I ask you in future to refrain from using words that have implications that you can not substantiate. Please continue, Dr Melhuish.'

'Thank you. I would never seek to deny that Professor Shapiro and I did share intellectual interests. Anyone who can read can see that. As regards his science, when he died the world lost one of its finest scholars: creative, generous, better read than any man I have ever met, fair-minded and fiercely honest. Rare qualities, you might agree, Mr Diamond.'

'As rare as temperance in speech and good leadership, Dr Melhuish. Be that as it may.' He consulted his notes. 'Now, towards the end of his life, Professor Shapiro published a short work called *Genius Loci* for which you wrote the introduction. Correct?'

Hera nodded. And then before the chairman could instruct her said, 'Yes. That is true.'

'Could you tell us a bit about this book, please?'

Hera frowned. 'It covers rather a big subject.'

'Well, briefly then.'

'The essays, many of which are reworkings of earlier lectures, all centre on the ancient idea that there might be an indwelling spirit or energy which protects, shapes and informs things.'

'Things?'

'People possibly. Mountains. Groves. Buildings. Trees. Standing stones. Monuments. Temples. The idea comes from a time when all creation was thought to be animated by spirit forms.' Hera broke off. 'Could you tell me where this is leading? Perhaps then I could focus more accurately on whatever it is you are after.'

'Could a planet, for instance, be thought to have a *genius loci*?'

'Of course.'

'Paradise, for instance.'

'Certainly. That was the main thrust of the essays, as I am sure you are well aware. Shapiro was using the ancient concept in an attempt to articulate why Paradise seemed to have changed since the days of the first pioneers.'

'Become more hostile?'

'Let us just say changed. We do not yet know the dimensions of that change.'

'But it has become more hostile, hasn't it? Plants from Earth don't grow as well. Toxins have increased in native plants that we used to enjoy. And we have more than one case of unaccounted death among the settlers. Surely those changes can be seen as more hostile, at least to us human beings?'

'Yes. But I insist we do not know the dimensions of the change. There may be good things too.'

'Well, it is nice to speculate. This *genius loci* that Shapiro writes about, can you see it, smell it, feel it?'

'Some people claim to be able to.'

'Can *you* feel it, Dr Melhuish?'

There was a long pause. 'I feel that before I am prepared to answer any further questions I would like you to explain what you are trying to achieve. You are dealing with things which do not have a simple yes or no answer.'

'What I am trying to ascertain, Dr Melhuish, is whether or not, as a scientist, you have any personal experience of this mysterious essence. But perhaps we can approach this another way. What *scientific evidence*, and I stress that phrase, is there for the existence of this *genius loci*?'

'Well that, precisely, is the problem. That is what interested Shapiro. At the boundaries of science we reach the limits of our ability to prove. The *genius loci* does not respond to litmus tests or spectroscopic analysis. Even so, it would be good to keep an open mind. I mean, 200 years ago who but writers of fantastic science fiction would have dreamed of fractal points? Yet now we take these for granted.'

'So there is no conclusive scientific evidence?'

'Yes. Correct. There is no conclusive evidence.'

'But you feel there is some merit in the idea.'

'I have an open mind.'

'Surely a bit more than that? In the preface you write, "No one of sense can have visited the surface of this planet without being aware of mystery. To sit as evening comes and feel the pause between 'Breaths', to see the deep green glow of the world as darkness falls, is to draw close to its soul." Not exactly a scientific analysis, is it?'

'I was not trying to provide a scientific analysis but to evoke a feeling.'

'I spent over a week on Paradise, Dr Melhuish, as you well know, and I certainly felt nothing out of the ordinary.'

'That does not surprise me,' said Hera. This caused some laughter which was quickly stifled. 'Incidentally, the Breath is measurable. That is the accepted term we now use for the band of change which follows the setting sun and precedes the rising sun. We can detect the change when it occurs, but what the change is, in its essence, is not certain.'

'The breathing of the *genius* of the place, perhaps.'

'I try to avoid simple anthropomorphic parallels.'

'Then Shapiro was more radical than you. In the essay entitled "Dark Angel" he speaks about the history of the idea that a planet can react to the presence of humans. He cites works of fiction, *Solaris, Death World*, *The Burning Forest*, to name but three. Works of *fiction*, though.'

'New ideas often manifest themselves first in fiction.'

'But science, Dr Melhuish, if it is to have any validity, must deal in facts. In the essay "The Unseen Shadow" Shapiro seems to suggest that ghosts, miracles, flying saucers and things that go bump in the night might be manifestations of energy forms, your *genius loci* and the like.'

'The same has been claimed for the passage of fractal points across the face of the Earth.'

'Junk science, Dr Melhuish. We can track fractal points, or are you suggesting that you have evidence that the failure of agriculture on Paradise is the result of fractal passage?'

'No, I do not. It is an idea.'

'And in the essay "Shadow over Paradise", an essay which you single out for special praise, Shapiro goes so far as to suggest that it is our own darkness that is being reflected in Paradise. What does he mean by this? Unable to find a decent theory, unable to accept his own failure to protect the planet placed under his care, he turns in desperation to mysticism of a kind which once sent people to be burned at the stake. Our darkness! Does he think there is a devil in human beings, or that we carry some mental pestilence which can strike down alien life forms? Surely, Dr Melhuish, this is the stuff of dotage. The tragedy is made worse, however, by the fact that this deluded old man was able to put his dark imprint on a mind as fine and gifted as your own, and that you then perpetuated his heresy, thereby discrediting yourself and the able scientists who have had the misfortune to be associated with you.'

'Not at all. It is a well argued—'

'It is fantasy and dark metaphysics and you should be honest enough to admit it.'

'No. Let me sp—'

'Scaremongering, then.'

Hera was now up on her feet. 'No. Shapiro was—'

'You agree with him. You are an advocate of mystical science.

So tell me, Dr Melhuish, whose shadow is being reflected by the hostility of Paradise? The poor farmers who plant the seeds and whom you have treated so badly, or is it your darkness, Dr Melhuish?'

'Shapiro was merely setting out some ideas. Things for people to think about. Good God! When you stop people doing that, we really are in trouble. Next you'll be burning books, kicking down doors and starting a witch hunt.'

At that moment there was a commotion on the balcony above Hera. Proctor Newton was on his feet and pointing down at Hera. 'It's you,' he shouted. 'You are the witch. You are the black witch of Paradise.' And before anyone could stop him, he picked up the wooden chair on which he had been seated and threw it down at Hera.

The chair struck her on the shoulder. One of the legs hit her in the neck and tore her ear. She was knocked over by the weight of the chair and fell against the stage. The last thing she saw, the last thing she remembers, was faces staring down at her. Proctor Newton had grown huge bat ears and his nostrils were flared like those of a horse, and the hands that gripped the balcony rail were giant claws with bronze talons. She saw Stefan Diamond open his mouth and a vast blue and fork-tipped tongue came poking out, flapping and feeling towards her.

That is what she remembers.

What she does not remember was the shouting in the room and the people on the balcony grabbing Proctor Newton and dragging him back. Nor does she remember the young man, Kris, running forward and lifting her up. And the chairman shouting for calm. Nor does she remember struggling to her feet and being supported, cradling her arm and leaning back against the table. She does not even remember speaking. But this is what happened, no matter what fantasies her mind dreamed up.

She said – and she was looking up at Proctor Newton, pinned now between two other men – 'You must hate me very much. Very much. But you have said a wicked thing, and a wrong thing. I never wished you harm, but you would never listen – and now, and now we have all lost Paradise. I am not a witch. How could you think that? I would have given my life to save Paradise. I would have given my life to see just once the great Dendron striding on the plain. But so much has been lost, and we must find out why. We must ...'

And at that point she did faint.

What is one to make of this hearing? On the surface it seems unfair and hurried, but one suspects that a longer hearing would have ended with the same result. Having read all the papers and transcripts, I have to admit that the correspondence used in evidence at the hearing shows Dr Melhuish as a woman at the end of her patience – angry and undiplomatic. And one might also argue that Hera Melhuish showed bad judgement in leaving such a clear paper trail for the bloodhounds to follow. But, as Hera comments, 'It's with O'Leary now.'

In retrospect, the correspondence Diamond quoted at the hearing merely heated the atmosphere. The allegation which destroyed Hera was that she indulged in 'mystical science'. This touched deep and irrational fears in the community at large, and inspired anger and contempt among the scientific community in general, and especially among those ORBE scientists with whom she worked on Paradise.

However, as we shall see later, it is her willingness to face mystery that ultimately proved to be Dr Melhuish's greatest strength.

The ending of this part of her story can be told briefly and bitterly.

Hera was rushed to the hospital on Central, where she recovered consciousness. She made it known that she did not want any action to be taken against Proctor Newton. She received fifteen stitches to the cuts to her face, neck and ear. She was given the comforting information that had the chair leg struck her just a few centimetres higher then she could have lost teeth, possibly an eye, or worse. Both her right arm and her collarbone were broken and she had bruising to her ribs. These were treated in the normal way, and she was pronounced in no danger, but in need of bed rest. Her body would mend. Her mind ...?

While in hospital Hera received the formal recommendation of the inquiry. It stated, 'Dr Melhuish, while cleared of any implication of financial impropriety, has in her actions and leadership fallen below the standards expected of senior administrators. As a consequence we recommend she be suspended forthwith from her position as head of the ORBE project.' The letter had the stamp of the Space Council and was signed in the green ink of Timothy Isherwood.

Worse, though, was the damage done to Hera's reputation. The excellence of her early work notwithstanding, she was now branded as an advocate of weird science, mystical science, and hence a crank and a fraud. The 'case', for so it was described, was seized on in the popular press, and headlines such as PARADISE GURU ACCUSED OF BLACK ARTS and ORBE LEADER EXPOSED AND DUMPED glared at her. The hospital was besieged by reporters, and it was only with the help of the hospital administrator that she was able to escape. As soon as it was safe for her to move she fled as a fugitive to Io, the place where she grew up. Her arm was still strapped in a sling and the injuries to her face and neck were hidden under a hood.

The paparazzi were waiting for her at Angelique-above-Io and Hera refused to disembark but stayed on for the next stop, which happened to be Anchor Hold-over-Europa. A lucky *chance*.

Anchor Hold-over-Europa is a monastery dedicated to the memory of Julian of Norwich, and it was here that Hera found sanctuary. She was already known to Sister Hilda, who was in charge of the monastery, as Hera had been there more than once when she was younger.

However, those who took her in and gave her a room and simple food never suspected the depth of the damage done to Hera. Nor need we dwell on it. But she felt her life was ruined, and so, the night after her arrival, she waited until the small community on Anchor Hold was asleep and then, in a state of black despair, she took a knife and attempted to kill herself.

And she would have succeeded had it not been for Sister Hilda, who *by chance* found Hera collapsed on the floor and summoned one of the night sisters, a surgeon by profession, and together they saved her. This attempt at suicide was previously only ever known to a few of the sisters at the monastery.

I have italicized 'by chance' since Sister Hilda, by her own account, awoke from a dream in which she was warned that Hera was in danger, and it was this that sent her hurrying to Hera's room.

When chance events become persistent, they cease to be chance but part of a new order of knowledge. Such I believe to be the case here. As we shall see, as Paradise awakes, so the rational order whereby we regulate our lives becomes disturbed by chance events.

Coincidences mount up and heightened intuition becomes a cause for action.

We have reached a turning point in Hera's journey.

It is now time for us to know more about her.

5

Sister Hilda Speaks of Hera

While researching this book in the Julian Library on Anchor Hold-over-Europa I found the following handwritten reference among Sister Hilda's papers. It is a letter, written many years earlier, in support of Hera's application to join the ORBE project on Paradise.

Dear Professor Shapiro

When Dr Hera Melhuish came to me recently asking for a reference, I at first refused. I know nothing of her academic qualifications. But Hera was insistent, as she can be! She assured me that she did not want an academic reference but something more like a testament, a document that would speak about the other sides of her being.

While not a frequent visitor, Hera, as a young woman, visited us in her hour of need. She came to us, seeking to reconcile two sides of her being. On the one hand she was still the dreamy and innocent little girl who, perched atop a laboratory stool, watched her father as he pruned and grafted and 'chuntered' to his plants, 'mussing them with his blunt, soiled fingers', as Hera put it. It was there, listening to his storytelling, that she learned her plant lore and discovered her own intuitive understanding and deep love of Nature.

The other side of her being – one she identified most closely with her mother – is the high-achieving committed scientist, who can flare up in anger when she feels her beliefs are challenged. This anger, which so troubled Hera and frustrated her social life, is the dark side of her honesty. Her ardent desire to protect life forms is a simple reflection of her maternal instinct. The paradox (and I am not sure that Hera has finally come to terms with it) is that her anger derives from the same source as her innocence.

However, this does not excuse it. Hera does not have much patience for those she sees as fools or for those who, having achieved a position of power, fail to use it openly and in ways which she would consider wise. She makes her point of view known, bluntly and openly. She can be a ferocious critic and a thorn in the side of anyone in administrative authority whom she sees as stifling initiative.

That said, I have said the worst about her – and I dare to suggest that it is people such as Hera Melhuish who have, in times past, given us a wider vision of what is possible by daring to challenge orthodoxy. I am thinking of our patron, Dame Julian of Norwich, who put herself at risk by daring to call God 'Our Mother'.

Of course, Hera gained enemies. But the inner truth of Dr Melhuish, one which her critics fail to understand, is that, to her, to hold a flower is to draw close to heaven. When she sees the complex economy of nature – everything in its place, nothing wasted – she swoons. The underlying drive behind all her work is her desire to express her delight in things living. Those whom she battles and who see only a woman with piercing blue eyes, possessed of a ready wit indeed but more importantly of an absolutely dogged determination, they never suspect the tender, somewhat mystical creature that lives within.

May I wish you well in your deliberations.

Sister Hilda
Julian Retreat,
Anchor Hold-over-Europa

As we know, Hera gained the appointment, and some ten years later became head of the ORBE project on Paradise following the death of Professor Israel Shapiro, a position which she held until the planet was disestablished and the project closed down.

So there you have her – an anatomy of Dr Melhuish. All that I wish to add is that sometimes Hera Melhuish has been her own worst enemy, but not in terms of her anger as Sister Hilda suggests. Hera's passion, her quick manner of speech and her extravagant physical gestures (allied to her smallness of stature) made her an easy target for caricature – and there is always something slightly ridiculous about the excessively zealous, is there not? But, strange to relate, those who were most successful at mimicking her were invariably those who liked her and admired her the most. Those who wished merely to belittle and ridicule her revealed only their spite, for they failed to understand the inner truth – the water of the woman if I may so put it – so well conveyed by Sister Hilda in her final sentences.

It is with sadness that I record that Sister Hilda died just fifteen days before the publication of this volume. May she rest in peace.

We return to the living Hera, recovering on Anchor Hold.

6

Count Down to Vigil

To Hera, the period between her attempted suicide and her first night alone on Paradise seemed a 'long, dark, necessary journey'. During that time she had more or less given up direction of her own life. In retrospect, it seemed to her like a life being lived by someone else.

Be that as it may, to us that 'journey' is filled with paradox and mystery. I am aware that many things need to be explained in this chapter. I am also aware that many things cannot be explained. One of the differences I have discovered between writing fiction for children and this fact-based documentary writing is that fiction can be made consistent, reality can not.

For the first time we begin to see clearly that the life of this woman who has been pilloried for being a 'mystical scientist', is itself patrolled by mystery. Why and by whom remains unknown. And perhaps the questions are more important than the answers for the moment. We will begin with questions.

At what point did Hera's life begin to change and shape her for Paradise? Was it when she applied for a position with ORBE? Or when she decided to write the preface to Professor Shapiro's little book of wisdom? We could probably pick any one of several points of entry and all would lead us inevitably to the conclusion that there were forces beyond her control shaping her life. For the most part they retain the mask of the ordinary, by which I mean that they have acceptable causes and predictable effects. However, as we come closer to Hera's solitude on Paradise, strange events manifest and the normal rules of life begin to change. For a start, comedy begins to take over from tragedy.

*

It is two days after Hera's failed suicide.

Sedatives have had a disastrous effect and Hera has spent the days collapsed in her bed with a headache like 'the worst black hole of a hangover'. Hera has a massive thirst for cold water, but even the clink of ice cubes in the glass is like the detonation of cannon between her ears. Urination, necessary frequently, is achieved crouched over that ancient symbol of civilization, a chamber pot. Anchor Hold maintains interesting links with tradition so that the humble and human is never lost from sight. During the crouching, Hera, much to her embarrassment, is supported by one of the junior sisters, who sits vigil with her. Meanwhile, the room moves as though viewed from a swinging pendulum

On the morning of the third day, always auspicious, Sister Hilda hobbles into the room, her stick in one hand, a letter in the other. It is a genuine old-fashioned letter and it has been delivered by fractal transmission. It bears the impress of the Space Council and, although stamped confidential, has been opened.

'I opened it by mistake,' says Hilda with a twinkle in her eye. 'Sorry.'

Hera, for whom the world is now becoming more stable, acknowledges this with a small sober nod and removes the pages. She reads.

Memo to Dr Hera Melhuish
Anchor Hold-over-Europa

With regard to the ongoing Disestablishment of Paradise, I am authorized to offer you the position of interim director of the ORBE programme. Your duties will be to oversee the welfare of the departing staff, the termination and completion, as far as possible, of current experiments and the elimination of any dangerous experimental materials. You will be reinstated on full pay (plus holiday allowances) for the duration of the Disestablishment process. A speedy reply would be appreciated and should be addressed to T. Vollens, Office of the Secretary General.

The letter bore the official stamp of the secretary general.

T. Vollens was not a name that Hera recognized, but she did not consider that significant since staff changes were frequent in the Space Council. T. Vollens, whoever he or she might be, was clearly an administrative assistant.

After discussing the matter with Sister Hilda, Dr Melhuish replied from her bed. She accepted the appointment, subject to her body healing satisfactorily, and added just one personal and highly significant request. This was that she be allowed to stay on Paradise 'alone if needs be' during the period between the departure of the last shuttle and the final evacuation of the shuttle platform over Paradise. During a Disestablishment there was always a gap of several months between the two events. In explanation, Hera maintained that with the use of an SAS flyer she would be able to use this 'grace time', as she called it, to complete some personal projects. She added that she would not expect to be paid for this work.

As directed, she addressed the letter, 'For the attention of T. Vollens'.

It is important to understand that, since the ordeal of the hearing, Hera's sense of commitment to Paradise had strengthened. She wanted to find out what had gone wrong there. This, she now believed, could best be accomplished alone.

Before accepting the letter for transmission, Sister Hilda perched on Hera's bed and stared deeply into her eyes. Her gaze was of flint. 'You are not thinking of trying to kill yourself down there on Paradise, are you, Miss Melhuish?'

'No. I give my word. I'm a big girl now, Sister Hilda.'

And so the letter was sent.

Dr Melhuish had no real hopes that her wish to be alone on Paradise would be granted. It was, as she confessed to me, 'the last sad endeavour of a wounded woman'. So it was with a mixture of sadness and hope that, two days later, Hera found herself holding a letter of reply, again transmitted by fractal delivery, and again from T. Vollens.

This letter had not been opened, and Sister Hilda lingered at the door to find out the news. The envelope was large and it contained a sheaf of documents. Hera spread them out on her bed. The letter was quite different in tone from the previous one. It thanked her for her work, expressed the hope that she was feeling better and made clear Theodore Vollens' pleasure that Hera had accepted the position of interim director. Accompanying the letter was residency certification allowing her to stay down on Paradise during the grace period. Another document authorized the use of a Delta-class SAS flyer – these being the most modern type available. There was a booklet of supply and services request forms made out in her name. With these she could commandeer essential supplies from someone named Ernest de Lava, who was the newly appointed Disestablishment marshal. A copy of the documentation plus a covering note had been sent to Captain Abhuradin, who would be administering the Disestablishment from the space platform. All documents were authorized by Theodore Vollens, and all had the official stamp of the secretary general.

As you may imagine, Hera sat for a long time reading and rereading this material.

Following her instincts, Dr Melhuish did not reveal this letter or mention it to anyone except Sister Hilda. However, she did try to contact Mr Vollens at the Space Council only to be told that there was no one called Vollens working there.

So here was a mystery. At first Dr Melhuish suspected a hoax. A cruel one and an absurd one, but no more cruel or absurd than some of the things she had witnessed. But who would take the risk of perpetrating a hoax such as this? After much deliberation she contacted Captain Abhuradin via a fractal voice link and asked her very casually whether a new posting for her had come through. Inez Abhuradin, who sounded hassled, confirmed that she had indeed received an official letter informing her that Hera had been appointed interim director of ORBE with authorization for her to stay on the surface after the departure of the last shuttle.

'Is it genuine?' asked Hera.

'Well it has all the right signatures and a priority coding and the salary provisions are correct so, yes, it looks bona fide to me. Why do you ask?'

'I just wanted to check on the surface arrangements,' said Hera hurriedly.

'Yes, I thought that was a bit strange too. Are you sure you want to go through with this, Hera? It is a lot they are asking of you, especially in view of all that has happened. Solo on a planet, even with us up here, can be a very lonely place.'

'I'm sure I'll cope,' said Hera, and then she added, 'but for personal reasons I'm not letting people know.'

'Very sensible,' concluded Abhuradin. 'I think you must protect yourself.'

And there Hera let the matter rest. She speculated, though, about Abhuradin's words, 'It is a lot they are asking of you.' This made it sound as if the order had been presented to Abhuradin as an initiative from the Space Council and not a request from Hera. Mystery on mystery.

And there is more. While preparing this book I consulted the archives at the Space Council to obtain copies of the papers allowing Dr Melhuish to stay alone on Paradise. No such orders could be found, though the transcripts of the hearing and the letter of suspension were present in Hera's file. Hera's copies were lost on Paradise. Captain Abhuradin's copies had disappeared with most of the other files relating to Paradise when the barge containing them was *by chance* mislabelled and shunted into the garbage trajectory in the direction of Leo's Eye, the name of the sun that shines on Paradise.

So who was Theodore Vollens? Was there ever anyone called Theodore Vollens? Did Hera have a guardian angel in the Office of the Secretary General? Or did Timothy Isherwood feel remorse for something?

The mystery remains a mystery.

Ten days of rest was enough for Hera.

With her arm strapped up and her stitches out, she bade farewell to Sister Hilda and took passage for Paradise. But before departing she contacted Captain Abhuradin and arranged to disembark as discreetly as possible. This proved easier than she had feared since Alpha Platform-over-Paradise was frantic with hundreds of people coming and going. No one took notice of a small woman wearing the overalls and mask of a shuttle cleaner as she shuffled through the arrivals gate on Alpha.

The Disestablishment was in full swing. Cargo shuttles were in continuous twenty-four-hour service, as were the much smaller and faster personnel craft. Inez Abhuradin arranged for Hera to travel down to the surface with one of the demolition crews, and it was thus that Hera first met Mack. It was not auspicious.

'Been in the wars, lady?' he said, noticing her arm in a sling

'You could say that,' she replied and turned away.

And that was the limit of their conversation.

Mack shrugged. He was quickly coming to the conclusion that

most of the people on Paradise were touchy and odd.

Safely down on Paradise, Hera went straight to the ORBE HQ. The building was full of crates and cases and tired people who looked as if they had aged in the brief time that she had been off planet. No one had warned them that she was coming; not even Hemi the administrator had been told.

So when Hera walked into the ORBE HQ and said, 'Hello, everyone. I've been appointed interim director,' her announcement was greeted with a surprised silence. This was followed by muttered greetings and some enquiries about her health. Then people found urgent things to do elsewhere. The truth was that many felt betrayed by Hera and considered she had let them and the whole ORBE enterprise down. They did not want to be associated with mystical science or the ridicule and anger that had followed the inquiry. Hera took this hard.

Only Hemi made her welcome.

He sat her down in his office, which was in a state of chaos, and brought her coffee. He made her show him where the stitches had been and describe what had happened. Finally, he said, 'I would have made you more welcome. Got a cake or something. I've only just now heard from old Ahab about your appointment. That's why we weren't ready for you.'

'I didn't want it announced before I got here. I thought it would be better this way. And I certainly didn't want a cake.'

Hemi smiled. 'Yeah, well, you know what I mean. I'd been starting to wonder what to do with your things . . . hoping to hear from you . . . but now I suppose you'll see to everything.'

'I'm interim director, that's all. Appointed to take care of the close-down.'

Hemi nodded and shrugged but did not smile.

'You don't seem very pleased.'

'No, it's not that. It's just that this place . . . now . . . it's like a body without a heart. Everyone seems angry or else they're always linking up off planet. I've probably blown next year's budget with communications alone.'

'Well, is there anything for me to do?'

'There's forms to sign – performance certificates, equipment sign-off registers – but hey, Hera, it's nothing really. Nothing I can't cope with.'

'So what are you saying, Hemi?'

'I'm saying I think you should take a holiday. This place'll break your heart else. Go out to one of the islands. Swim a bit. Get some sun. I'll stay in contact. You can take your old SAS. I'll fix the books. Write it off.'

'You are very kind. I was told I was receiving a new one.'

Hemi looked surprised. 'First I've heard of it. But hey, what's new?' Then he looked at her almost shyly. 'And there's a bit more too, eh? You know when you appointed me administrator?' Hera nodded. 'Well I told you then I didn't know much about plants and science and things, but I knew how to organize. I hope you've no regrets about appointing me. Perhaps I could have protected you better, but—'

'I've no regrets at all. In fact, you were one of my best appointments.'

'See. I'm not sure what's going on round here now, but I hear things. And, well, what I want to say is, with me, with my people, we have no problems with the idea that trees have souls and spirits. One of our gods is Tane Mahuta, Great Lord of the Forest. And if that's what is upsetting them buggers up there,' he raised his eyes, 'then I'm with you, Hera.'

Hera was about to reply when Hemi stood up. Being well over six feet tall he towered over her. But he bent down towards her and before she could move, he pressed his nose against hers firmly and flatly. 'Kia kaha, kia māia ahakoa te huarahi ka whāia e koe.'

'What does that mean, Hemi?'

'Not easy to translate, Hera. But .... . "Be strong. Be confident. Despite the path you have chosen." That's about right, eh. Goodbye, Hera.'

In the next few weeks the people who had called Paradise home began to move off planet. And as the offices and houses were cleared, the men with the sledgehammers and crowbars moved in.

Hera, having followed Hemi's advice, set up her own living quarters at one of the research stations on a distant part of the planet. The place she chose was called Monkey Terrace Station. Originally this had been a supply depot for MINADEC workers, but it had then been taken over and refurbished by the ORBE project. The station was set back from a ledge of rock above a long stretch of water called Big Fella Lake. It stood amid a stand of ancient monkey trees – hence its name.

MINADEC workers had chosen names which reflected the way they saw things. Monkey trees had the unusual characteristic of sending pairs of fibrous roots down from their upper branches on the downwind side. Finding the soil, the roots dug deep and hardened. As the trees grew they gradually leaned and the roots took the weight. So it was true that, from a distance and with a bit of imagination, the trees could look like a giant ape hunched on the ground with both arms forward as though ready to run. These trees gave the station protection from the cold winds in the winter and pleasant aromatic shade when the summer sun was high. The view from the terrace looked straight across the lake to where tall dipper palms reached out over the water and rose and fell steadily. Beyond them were gentle hills of deep forest called the Scorpion Hills, and it was here that a large *Dendron peripatetica* had been observed by one of the first MINADEC survey teams. The Dendron was heaving its way down to the water and they watched it as it waded right through the lake – hence the name, Big Fella Lake. Far beyond the Scorpion Hills, and just visible on a clear day, were the white but smoky fumaroles of the Chimney. So, all in all, Monkey Terrace Station was quite an historic place, and normally it was very peaceful.

It was here that one morning Hera was wakened by the clatter of two craft coming in low over the lake and preparing to land. She pulled on a pair of overalls, quickly coiled and pinned her hair and slipped her feet into the soft meshlite survey boots that she wore for outdoors work. Not elegant, but so what? She didn't really want visitors, and her greatest fear was that someone would arrive to tell her that the order allowing her to stay had been revoked. By the time she ran outside, the two flyers had landed. One was a wide-bayed demolition transporter, and it had settled on the beach below the terrace and there created a small sandstorm. Men wearing the blue and green of demolition workers were already jumping down onto the beach and starting to unbolt their cutting wheels and portable generators. They were led by the tall solidly built man we have already met, Mack.

The other craft was a brand new Delta-class SAS flyer. It had come swooping in over the house in a display of virtuoso flying and had settled on the station landing pad. The pilot who stepped out was none other than Captain Abhuradin in person. That lady, elegant as ever, greeted Hera as she came out of her door. 'Well there you are, Dr Melhuish. Special delivery. One Delta-class SAS flyer that answers to the name of Alan. You must have friends in high places. This is one of the newest models. Arrived yesterday. So I thought I'd bring it out myself and see where you were and how you are and what you are doing. I thought you'd be pleased.'

'I am. No other news?'

'Nothing special. Except that I needed a break. Too many people in my life at present.'

Hera grinned. 'Not out here.' She turned. 'Except I see you have brought some friends.'

'They're nothing to do with me. I gave them directions yesterday. Caught up with them this morning and guided them through the Chimneys. I thought perhaps you had requisitioned them.'

'Not me.' Hera grinned at the suggestion. 'I leave all that to Hemi.'

'So how are you? Are you comfortable?'

Hera gestured around the small enclosure 'Well, what you see is what there is. Big Fella Lake, a jetty, a boat, greenhouses full of dead plants, a garden full of Tattersall weeds, a table under the monkey trees, a nice little shilo with all facilities and a view that is forever changing.'

Abhuradin whistled – a very masculine sound for one so feminine. 'Impressive.'

'And as for me, I'm fine.' Hera flexed her arm. 'No pain now, but still a bit mixed-up inside. Up here.' She tapped her head. 'You know. I'll be all right though. Why don't you go and have a look round inside while I see what these lads are up to? Make some coffee if you want. Everything's in the kitchen.'

Hera turned to face the men who had followed Mack up the steps from the beach and were now standing around waiting. She addressed them from a distance: 'Is this a social call, or are you boys here on business?'

'We're ... er ...' Mack removed his cap and rubbed his jaw, which had two days of stubble. 'We were sent out here to take this place apart. Lucky the captain was coming out this way or we'd never have found it. No one told us there was still someone living here.'

'Well, there is and she's staying. So there'll be no demolition out here.'

Mack looked at his men. 'OK . . . Well you probably haven't heard the news, living out here miles from anywhere, but this planet Paradise has been dis-es-tab-lish-ed. Now, you know what that means. Everyone is supposed to be off world in a couple of weeks' time. We don't want to rush you or anything like that, but . . .'

Suddenly Hera understood. This big ape of a man thought she must be one of the settlers, and from the way he was talking, he had already had some dealings with people who didn't want to go.

'I know all about the Disestablishment. I am – was – part of the ORBE project. But I have special permission to remain. I'm staying down here.'

Mack nodded slowly, weighing this up. 'You mean until everyone goes.'

'No, *after* everyone goes.'

'Uh huh.' There was a pause while he thought that over. 'That means you'll be, er . . .' There was a longer pause while he thought some more. 'You'll be staying down here on the planet, *all alone*, right?'

'Right. You've got it. Spot on. Give him a coconut, someone. And I'll be living *here*. So that's why I don't want you, or any of your men, tearing the place apart. Savvy?'

Mack nodded again. 'So what happens when the platform goes e-vac and we all bugger off back to Birmingham?'

'You what?' It was Hera's turn to stare.

'When we leave. Shut up shop.'

'I'll be coming off planet when the platform clos— Look, I don't want to stand here all day arguing the toss. If you don't believe me, you can ask Captain Abhuradin. But I'll tell you this – I'm staying, and if one of your men touches so much as a screw he'll have me to deal with.'

Mack lifted his hands as though to ward off a blow. 'OK. We hear you. That right, you fellas?' He turned to his men, all of whom were looking on with a variety of expressions on their faces. Then one of them could contain himself no longer. He turned away and exploded into laughter.

'Dickinson, get a hold of yourself.'

'Y-yes boss.' Then he broke down again, held his sides and

stamped on the ground. Hera started to laugh. It was Mack's face that was so funny. Next the other men broke ranks. Only Mack was left, looking from one to the other. 'Is there something I don't understand?' he said.

'I hate to interrupt a party . . .' It was Captain Abhuradin. She had freshened herself up and brushed her hair and now stood holding a tray with beakers and a full jug of fresh coffee. 'But would anyone like a coffee?'

They would. They did.

And it was while they were having coffee that Mack suddenly slapped his leg and pointed at Hera. 'I know who you are. You're that Captain Melhuish. You're that lady that had the chair thrown at her by that mad bugger with the funny hat. Remember him, lads? The one who set fire to his house before he'd removed the furniture. We had to belt him one to stop him trying to get back in.' They all nodded, still grinning. 'Well if we'd met you first, I'd have belted him twice. Pleased to meet you, Captain. I'm Mack and these are a few of my team.'

'Pleased to meet you,' said Hera. 'But I'm not Captain Melhuish. I am, if you have to use titles, Doctor Melhuish.'

'Yep, that's right. Doc Melhuish. Sorry. Hey, we met coming down on the shuttle. Briefly. If you remember.'

'I don't remember. And it is not *Duck* Melhuish,' said Hera, exaggerating Mack's pronunciation. 'It is *D*oc Melhuish. Open the vowel, man.'

'Yes, Doc. Whatever you say.'

Hera looked at Abhuradin and that lady coughed and looked into her coffee.

'You feeling OK now, Doc?' asked Mack.

'Yes, fine.'

'Well, seeing as we're not going to do any demolition . . . That is correct, Captain Abhuradin?' She nodded. 'Then is there anything we can do to help? We know how to build things as well as knock 'em down. So if there's anything needs fixing – doors, windows, roof laminates – just let us know.'

There *were* things needed doing. The Tattersall weed needed to be chopped back in the garden. Close to the shilo the irrigation system was blocked where plants had grown into it, and the dome-house laminate was torn. Hinges needed greasing, the twin doors to the auto-hangar needed to be rehung after a minor crash and the small boat Hera used on the lake was overdue for a good clean-up and service. This was the kind of maintenance which had to be undertaken all the time on Paradise. Left for a week, the vegetation moved in and took over.

'No worries, Doc. But then we'd better get back to base, eh Captain? It'll take us a good ten or twelve hours to get to New Syracuse at the speed we move, and then we have that museum to clear.'

'What museum?' asked Hera.

Mack consulted his notes. 'Sorry, I've left my glasses in the flyer.'

He held his notes up for the man called Dickinson to read, who glanced at it casually and said, 'It says, "The ORBE collection of bio-form memorabilia".'

'Yes,' said Hera. 'I know it. The Shapiro Collection. Quite valuable in its way.'

Mack took back his notes. 'It's to be crated up and shipped to Mars. That sound about right?'

'Yes. I shall want to have a hand in the packing of that.'

'No worries. We'll be starting there in three or four days. I can give you a call if you like?' Hera nodded. 'OK, lads, on your feet. We've got some maintenance to do.'

The men were up immediately, glad to be doing something. They thanked Abhuradin for the coffee, putting the mugs down carefully on the tray and grinning. They were obviously on their best behaviour and showing off a bit for the ladies. While one of them took the tray inside the shilo to wash the mugs, Mack divided the rest into teams and before long the small enclosure was filled with the sound of whistling, hammering and the occasional stifled curse.

The two women were left alone, and for a while they said nothing. Neither knew quite what to say. Relations between Hera and Captain Abhuradin had never been easy. And yet ... different as the two women were in almost every way, a grudging respect had grown between them. There was a lot to say. It was starting that was hard.

Down at the jetty one of the demolition workers broke into song. He had a passable tenor voice and the song was Italian and floated on the air. It eased the atmosphere between the two women. 'Nice men,' said Abhuradin finally. 'Quite different to the ones I have to deal with. Little men with long lists. That's why I decided to get away for a few hours and bring you the SAS.'

'I'm glad. I've . . .' Hera hesitated, trying to find the right words. 'Thank you for your letter. It helped. I'm sorry for the way I spoke before. I think I was out of my mind.'

Abhuradin smiled, but it was a tired look. 'Don't,' she said. 'I'm not going to bear any grudges. None of us wanted this. We were both outmanoeuvred.' The two women lapsed into silence again, but it was obvious that something was preying on Abhuradin's mind. Finally she said, 'There is something I need to ask you. It is a bit personal.'

'Ask what you like; I've not many secrets left.'

'How did you arrange to get permission to stay down here?'

'I didn't. I asked in a letter and it was agreed to. Some fellow called Vollens . . .'

'There is no one called Vollens at Central. I checked. Do you know that?'

'Yes.'

'I think this is all totally unofficial. The Disestablishment marshal doesn't know about you.'

'Are you going to tell him?'

'No. It's none of my business. I have the authorization. As far as I'm concerned you are here with the Space Council's blessing.'

'Thank you.'

'But you are going to have to make me one promise, Hera.'

'What promise?'

'OK, listen. When the evacuation is complete, you'll have about three months alone down here, give or take a few days, while we get rid of all the stuff tethered in space. I'll be staying until the end. And then, when everything is closed down, my final job is to open the platform to space before I leave. But before I do, I will send one last shuttle down to the surface. For you. I'll give you plenty of warning, but you have to promise me that you'll be there to meet it. Promise me that. Promise you'll be waiting there, at the old shuttle port, when the shuttle arrives, and that you will climb aboard and join the rest of us. Because if you are not aboard, and the fractal ship has to leave without you, then I will never forgive you, Hera. Never. Have I made myself clear?'

Hera seemed to hesitate. For a moment Abhuradin thought she

was going to break down, but then Hera rallied. She thought briefly of Dame Hilda, who had made a similar stipulation, and she said, 'OK. I promise. No games. No going bush. No silly things. I'll be there.'

Abhuradin let out a sigh of relief. 'OK.'

There was an embarrassed moment between them, until they shook hands like men that had brokered a deal. But then, feeling that to be inadequate, they leant forward and pressed their cheeks against one another, and were still for a moment. Only then did they smile properly.

'So,' said Hera. 'Enough about me. What about your plans, Inez?'

'Oh. I take each day as it comes. It's a madhouse up there. You wouldn't believe—'

'I meant about getting married,' said Hera quietly. 'Is it all still on track?'

Abhuradin coloured slightly, caught off guard. 'Oh, that. Yes. All is well. I hardly dare think about it . . . and no one else knows, Hera. So not a word. OK?' Hera nodded. 'It will be a new life for both of us. We try to talk for a few moments every other day. It keeps me going.'

'What's he like, your man? What does he do? Is he in the service too?'

'Hell no! He's an artist, a painter. Or at least, he wants to be. We met two years ago, in Peru. I was on leave and . . . well, we got talking, and I saw some of his paintings . . . I don't know how these things happen, Hera! We . . . Well, we fell in love. That's all. We were both surprised. But it is real, Hera.' Abhuradin smiled, and Hera could see her happiness. It was there in her face, in her eyes and in the way she held her body. She was a different, softer Abhuradin, quite unlike the strong-willed and somewhat glacial presence she presented when on duty. 'At present he makes a living designing wallpaper, would you believe? But soon. When all this nonsense is over . . . well, with my pension from the service we might just have enough money to buy a place . . . somewhere quiet and lovely, with room for a big studio at the back, and a garden with a swing, and I might retrain . . . as a teacher, perhaps. Or I might just open that little hotel with a café on the side and—'

'I am so sorry for that remark,' said Hera. 'Please, Inez, forgive me. It was unbelievably rude. I don't know what possessed me.'

'Nothing to forgive, Hera. But please, I don't want to talk about happiness any more. It makes it too hard. Dreaming. I just want to get through the present.'

Hera saw that Abhuradin was close to tears, and she reached out and squeezed her hand. 'It will happen. Inez. It will. I promise.'

Abhuradin nodded. She breathed deeply, taking control of herself. 'So. Onward and upward!' She dabbed at her eyes and looked at her face in a small pocket mirror. 'No damage done. Now, I want you to show me round this place, Hera. Tell me about all these plants you love so much. Show me how you'll live, and what you are going to do down here when you are "all alone."'

Any embarrassment was over. For the next hour Abhuradin was given a grand tour of Monkey Tree Station. Finally she sighed and stiffened her back. It was time to return.

Two of Mack's men winched Hera's old SAS flyer out of the hangar and Abhuradin climbed aboard. Before closing the door she turned. 'You promised, Hera.'

'I'll be there. Don't worry. And then we'll have some tales to tell.'

The door closed and minutes later Hera's old SAS grumbled into the air and turned to head across Big Fella Lake, its twin rotors rippling the surface of the water.

That afternoon something strange happened at Monkey Terrace Station.

Two men working in the garden heard a sound like a whip crack. It came from a giant Tattersall weed at the very end of the garden, one which had been allowed to grow to its full height. When the two men looked they were astonished to see that the tree's spiky limbs, normally held high, were slowly lowering. As they did so the flowers at their tips were closing and dropping.

'Hey, Mack. Look at this. Come here. Quick. Bloody tree's moving.'

Mack had been working on the cutter, and he came pounding up the steps from the jetty. Hera had heard the calls too and she came hurrying out of the shilo. Others stopped what they were doing and all gathered to watch.

The long ropey arms of the weed rested on the ground for a moment, and then they twitched and writhed like snakes and began to withdraw towards the main trunk. As they did so, the whip-cracking sound increased.

'What's happening, Doc?'

'Well, you lads are in for a treat. The Tattersall weed is going to put on a performance. It is going to shed its seeds. In about five minutes.'

'What's that cracking noise?'

'It's the sound of the fibres in the branches. They're contracting and compressing the sap. It's a kind of peristalsis. Wait here.' Hera ran over to one of the supply sheds and came back moments later with a bag containing loose meshlite masks with goggles. 'Here, put these on. Quick,' she said. 'Now watch. See how the branches are pulling back and winding round the trunk.'

'Like a coil spring.'

'Exactly, like a coil spring. One that also contains a fluid core at high pressure.' The cracking sound had now become higher in pitch, and it made the men wince. It was the sound of something approaching its breaking point. When it stopped, the tree was thin, like a tightly furled umbrella.

Suddenly, with a roar, the branches uncoiled, lashing out like the arms of an athlete throwing the discus. At their furthest extension there came another roar as seed ducts opened and thousands of small seeds, each with a long sharp blade-thorn, were flung into the air amid a fine spray of sap. The seeds shimmered like a cloud of bees, arcing high, and then fell to earth, clattering on the meshlite of the masks and catching in the men's clothing.

So great was the effort made by the Tattersall weed that the branches, having swung full circle, now swung back again, but there was no power in them. The branches were torn and broken. Some had detached from the tree completely and lay like long hairy snakes on the ground.

'That's it,' said Hera. 'That's its death knell. One fling and then they die. You can take your masks off. Show's over.'

Mack pulled the mask off his head. 'Well I'll . . .' He was lost for words. One of the seeds was lodged in the meshlite. He pulled it free and examined it. 'What a wicked little bugger. That could cut you open. See, it's even got a barb.'

Hera nodded. 'Yes, it looks like a barb, but that's just an accidental resemblance. That barb is a little duct, and the root grows out from there. The hook is to anchor the seed in the ground, but it also decays quickly and provides some nutrient to the seed. Paradise works quickly and efficiently. By tomorrow a lot of these will have rooted and I'll be going round the garden with a rake pulling them up. But I like to keep one or two Tattersalls close by, for the show when they seed, because the flowers are so beautiful and the perfume . . .' She breathed deeply. 'The early pioneers used to call them blue waltzers – you can see why – and it is a nice enough name . . . but these flowers had a bad reputation too.'

'Why's that then?' Mack was looking carefully at the dying tree.

'People used to say that if you dreamed of one of these it was an omen of death. And it's true: a lot of people had accidents near them. And there were creepy stories about them being able to move.'

'Move? You mean like walk?'

'More a crawl really. But hey, don't look so worried. I've been here a long time and I've never seen one shift. But the old stories persist.'

Mack looked at Hera closely. 'Hey, how do you know all this, Doc?'

'It's my job to know. You know how to pull down buildings. I know about the bio-forms on this planet.'

'Well if I were you, Doc, if you don't mind my saying, I'd keep my eyes open behind me with these Tatty whatsits on the loose. They could slice your head off if you was too close when one of them went off.'

'I'll bear that in mind,' said Hera. 'But you get to know what to look out for when you are working round them all the time.'

'And you want to be down here alone! Hell, Doc, you must be one very brave lady, or off your perch.'

'Bit of both, probably,' said Hera. 'Welcome to Paradise.'

The demolition men left in the evening with Mack guiding their lumbering demolition bus up into the sky. The cargo doors were open and some of the men sat with their legs dangling out, drinking beer and waving to Hera.

As they disappeared noisily across the lake Hera felt, for the first time, lonely. She had enjoyed their banter, their sly digs at her, their comic-book lust for the shapely Captain Abhuradin, and their general sense of fun. They, if no one else, were enjoying this Disestablishment. And they had certainly made a big difference to

Monkey Terrace. The place was cleaned, tidy and the doors didn't squeak.

Hera was misty for a moment, but then her practical mind asserted itself. She'd been lonely before and she'd be lonely again. She was here by choice. So get on with it.

During the week following Abhuradin's visit, Hera received a handful of farewell calls from some of the ORBE staff who were heading off planet. These were sad calls filled with hearty and well meant promises to meet up at some date in the future. Hera felt the planet emptying of all the people she had known and cared for, and she felt sad too, for many of the people she had thought of as friends neglected to call and just left.

Last to leave was Hemi. He'd accepted a job with the Space Council as part of the Office for Economic Planning. That made them both laugh. 'So I'll be able to keep my eye on you,' he said. 'Kia ora, Hera.'

And his was the last of the calls. But then . . .

Ten days after Hemi's departure Hera received a radio message from Mack saying sorry for the delay but they were about to start packing up the Shapiro Collection. If she wanted to be part of it she'd better get back to New Syracuse as soon as possible.

Hera was airborne in her new flyer within minutes.

She came in low over New Syracuse. Most of the prefabricated buildings were gone. All that remained were a few walls, still being unbolted and then hoisted onto giant carriers ready to be transported to the shuttle port. The little two-storeyed Shapiro Museum was still standing, though its doors and windows had been removed, giving it a vacant, bombed-out look.

Mack was already there. He was looking up, ear protectors on, and he waved briefly as the SAS circled overhead and landed. But he was not smiling.

'Not pleased to see me?' said Hera as she stepped out of the flyer.

'No, it's not that. Some bugger got in here before us. Hell of a mess up there. Sorry. Oh, and I brought you these.' He handed her a pair of heavy gloves. 'There's a lot of broken glass and widowmakers. Be careful where you tread. Follow me.'

And it was a mess. The entire building had been ransacked. Burn marks on one wall showed where someone had tried to light a fire. Upstairs entire shelves of books had been tipped over. Glass-fronted cases lay shattered. Drawers were pulled out and their contents strewn over the floor. Someone had sprayed red paint on the walls and there was a smell of urine.

'Hope you find what you wanted.'

'I can cope,' said Hera.

'OK. Well, I'll be back in the evening with a Demo Mule. We're way behind schedule. See ya.' Mack left her to it.

Somewhere among all this mess was a wooden box with a label attached saying SHAPIRO MEMORABILIA. This was all that interested Hera. Methodically she began to lift and clear the books and papers, working slowly from room to room.

When evening fell she had still not found the box. Inside the library, single lights blinked on and began to glow. She worked on, dragging aside filing cabinets that had been tipped over and shelves that had fallen. Some time later Hera heard a transport mule in the distance. She knew that Mack would need to start clearing the library soon. She didn't have very long.

She pushed a door, trying to open it wider, but something was trapped behind it. A coat. And there, under the coat, on its side but still intact, was the wooden box she was looking for. Hera lifted it carefully and carried it to a small table. The catch which secured the lid was still intact and closed, but the label had gone.

Carefully she opened the lid. Inside, wrapped in plastic, she found Shapiro's journals, field books, some handwritten speeches and a few letters. It was Hera who had packed them when Shapiro died. There also was his edition of Baudelaire and a small polished box which contained a few personal items: his dissection kit wrapped in a stained blue cloth, a tape measure, a pipe still with fragments of burned calypso in it and a couple of tri-vid tapes.

Hera repacked the box and was about to load it into her satchel when the lights failed. They just went out. No noise. No flicker. Just out. The darkness was total. It took her a moment or two to realize what had happened. With her hands up in front of her, Hera felt her way over to the wall. She had to climb over the boxes she had sorted and stacked. Finally, she found the light switch and flicked it on and off. Nothing.

So now what? She stood for a moment. She remembered she had left the radio control link to the SAS flyer in the shilo. Worse, she had disabled the voice link during the journey and forgotten to reinstate it. Here was a lesson. Alone on Paradise she could be in trouble if she did that, especially if she fell and hurt herself. OK. Nothing for it but to work her way outside and over to the flyer and find one of the beacons.

Feeling round the walls, Hera finally reached the stairs. To get there she had to tread on tri-vid cubes and books, something which she hated to do, for she could feel them shift on their spines under her feet like fish. She had just negotiated her way round a pile of boxes on the landing when she saw a Demo Mule approaching outside. Moments later, there was a beam of light. It raked across the building and flashed through one of the downstairs windows. She heard Mack's voice: 'Hey, Doc. You still in there?'

'Yes,' she called. 'Is it a general blackout? I forgot to bring my torch.'

Mack reached the front entrance and shone the light up the stairs, forcing Hera to shield her eyes from the glare. 'Sorry.' He shifted the light to the wall. 'This is happening all the time now. We rigged a cable up to the shuttle port, but it keeps shorting out. Bloody plants – worse than mice. Did you find what you were looking for?'

'Yes. Everything was intact.'

Mack shone his torch on the steps and started to come up. 'I've brought some candles. Amazing isn't it? Able to reach the stars, but we still need a candle in an emergency.'

'You need matches too, or are you going to rub a couple of sticks together?' said Hera, retreating into the room.

'Enough of the smarts from you, Captain Doc,' said Mack as he joined her. 'You're as bad as my lads.' A match flared, was touched to a wick and a moment later the wavering but strong light of a candle shone out. The candle was lodged in a hole drilled into a flat piece of wood. 'We come prepared.' Mack put the candle down on the table.

Slung round his shoulders was one of the tough canvas bags that the demolition men used when they were clearing sharp rubbish such as broken bottles. 'Now, the only thing is to be careful we don't set the whole bloody place alight. So what did you find, Doc?'

Hera pointed to the wooden box. 'Some of Shapiro's private notebooks and journals. That's all I wanted. Towards the end he stopped publishing as he was getting such a hostile reception, but he kept his notes. Now I want to use them. I've set myself a project for while I'm down here, Mack. I want to try and find out what has really gone wrong with Paradise. I think Shapiro knew.'

'So how do you plan to do that?'

It was on the tip of her tongue to say, 'You wouldn't understand,' but she bit back the words in time. Instead she said, 'I'm going to try to relate to this world in a more personal way. I don't know *how* exactly, but I think I can find a way. Shapiro had some ideas.'

Mack nodded. 'That's sort of what I do when I have to take down a difficult building. I talk to it. I use a pendulum. Tell it to show me the dangerous places. It works. The lads think I'm a bit daft. But hey, I'm still here and I haven't lost a man yet. Talking of which, I bet you haven't eaten today, have you?'

She hadn't and confessed as much. Mack shook his head in mock severity. 'I don't know how you're going to cope down here on your own. You haven't a clue how to look after yourself. Just as well you have a guardian angel.' He fished in his bag and produced a small bundle which, when he unwrapped it, contained sandwiches, a chunk of cheese and some apples. 'And don't ask what's in the sandwiches, cos if you're a vegetarian, you don't want to know. Just eat the bread. It's all I could find in the canteen.'

'I'm not a vegetarian. What gave you that idea?'

'Just thought you might be. You have that look about you.'

'What's that supposed to mean?'

'Nothing. Don't get your feathers in a twist.'

'We tend not to eat meat down here simply because . . . well, meat is in short supply,' she said, sounding more prim than she had intended. 'Once they brought in cows and goats, but they never thrived and the idea of livestock was abandoned. Except for chickens. The chickens did all right for a while.'

'Well tuck in then.'

'What about you?'

'I'll have an apple. Oh, and I brought this . . .' He produced a bottle of wine. 'Courtesy of that mad bugger – what's his name?'

'There are a lot of mad buggers, Mack.'

'The one who tried to kill you with a chair.'

'Proctor Newton. He didn't drink.'

'Well, when we pulled the Settlers' Club apart we found a cosy little cellar underground. There were racks where they kept their bottles – imported stuff, mark you, not local rubbish, and expensive too – and one of my lads spotted Newton's name on one of the racks. So we liberated everything. And before you ask . . .' He produced a corkscrew and a pottery mug and set them down. 'Shall I open it, or are you against drinking too?'

'What do you . . .' She saw she was again being teased. 'Do I always seem so . . . cut and dried about things? No, on second thoughts don't answer that. Open the bottle.'

Mack obliged and Hera settled and began to eat, realizing that she was very hungry indeed.

'Can I have a look at one of the notebooks?' asked Mack suddenly. And before she could say anything he displayed his hands to show they were clean.

'Yes, sure.' Hera opened the box and selected one of the field journals. It was the book that had accompanied Shapiro during a long journey up to the northern polar continent called Ball. Mack held the dog-eared and work-stained book as though it was made of porcelain. He turned the pages delicately. There were lots of drawings and he studied them closely in the light of the candle.

'What's that?'

'The miners called it a Crispin lily – but it's not a lily at all. A proper taxonomy is one of the things we were working on before all this.'

'Oh.'

'Native of the far north. Those petals are luminous at night. The miners used to sew them together to make slippers. Sometimes they used to put petals in their boots. They said it helped ease blisters. I know the petals look delicate, but they are as tough as pigskin.'

Mack nodded, and leafed on. 'What's this?'

'Fart in a trance.' She watched for his reaction.

'What? But it's pretty. Look at those little flowers.'

'Yes, but can you see the small bulb under the flowers? If you tread on one of those, they explode and the smell . . . Well, if you have ever smelled one you always watch where you are putting your feet in future.'

'Why do they smell so bad?'

'They don't really. Just to our noses. Plants don't have noses. The sap, because that is all it is, is a very good growing medium, except none of us could ever bear to use it without a mask.'

He turned more pages. 'What the hell is that?' He was looking at a drawing of a giant plant similar to an aloe vera. A man lay beneath it and a human skull hovered above.

'That's one of Shapiro's whimsies. Have you ever heard of the great Michelangelo – used to be called a reaper?'

'No.'

'I have never seen one, but the MINADEC men and a few of the first settlers did. They were frightened of them and so they burned them or bombed them. We think they might be extinct now. No one has seen one for over sixty years. You see, despite all the hype about how fertile this world is – and it is fertile, make no mistake – the ecosystem is fragile, and interlopers like us cause a lot of damage very quickly.'

'So what did it do, this Michelangelo, that was so bad?'

'We don't know exactly, but according to the old tales it was a plant that could steal your spirit. They said it could create images, hence its name. But whether they meant images in the mind or real images was never clear. People who encountered one of these plants just lay down. They didn't always die immediately. Sometimes they just lay there, but if they weren't found in time, they did die and shrivelled. People thought the plants must exude some kind of drug that took away people's will . . . and so they destroyed them.'

'And you are really going to stay down here on your own? What if you meet a Michelangelo?'

'Most unlikely. But I'd love to. That and a *Dendron Rex peripatetica* and a few others. That would be wonderful, but like I say, a lot of things have gone for ever. They're with O'Leary.'

Mack pointed at the drawing with his blunt finger. 'Do you all do drawings like this?' he asked.

Hera thought for a moment. 'I suppose we do. It's a bit like you said about candles. Cameras and tri-vid cubes can break, but it takes a lot to destroy a pencil and a notebook. You can learn how to sketch plants quickly and when you've had a bit of experience in the field you know what to look for. Don't look so surprised. Of course, some people draw better than others. Shapiro's sketches are beautiful. My drawings aren't so good.'

'He meant a lot to you, this Shapiro, eh?'

'He did. He was a great teacher. A great man. He taught me a lot of things. I have not met his like since.' Hera's manner, as she spoke, had undergone a slight change, a withdrawal. Mack sensed that his question had crossed some threshold, but he was not sure what. 'Well, I suppose I'd better get going,' said Hera, brisk again. 'Thank you for your help.' She stood up and Mack placed the book carefully in the wooden box and closed the lid. 'Thank you for being so thoughtful with the sandwiches, they were . . .'

'Herring and ham.'

'You finish the wine.'

'Can I give you a hand carrying anything?'

'No. I am capable. I have to begin to depend on myself.' She picked up the box with both hands.

'Well, let me at least carry the torch, unless you want to hold it in your teeth.'

She let Mack carry the torch.

The door of the SAS flyer slid open when she touched the lock plate, and all its lights came on. Mack stood well back and watched her climb aboard. His instincts told him that if he came too close she might again feel . . . not threatened, but exposed a bit. In the flyer Hera turned and waved. 'Thanks again, Mack,' she called. 'Will you give Captain Abhuradin a call and remind her to let me know the day the last shuttle will be departing? I want to be there to see it go.'

He nodded. 'Sure. Hey, do you want me to give you a call? I'll be on the last shuttle.'

'OK. Yes, that'd be good.'

The door began to close. Mack called, 'Oh, and one thing. Not that it matters, but I'm vegetarian.'

A week later, Hera was in a stony valley deep in the Chimney Mountains. She was sketching a pod of red Valentine poppies that had settled there after drifting high over her shilo. The tinkle of water on stone and the moaning of the wind through the high passes – sounds she had come to enjoy as much as any of her music – were suddenly lost as the alarm on the SAS ululated. It was Abhuradin. The schedule had changed. The last demolition shuttle would depart at midday. The evacuation part of the Disestablishment was complete. If Hera wanted to see the shuttle leave and bid it farewell, she would have to hurry.

She did.

Even as Hera packs her books and small tent into the SAS, Paradise is preparing to say farewell in its own way.

Already, as Hera guns the SAS through the mountain passes and sets course across the sea for New Syracuse, the sky is darkening.

A cold wind is stirring on the high plateau, lifting dust and grit.

PART TWO

Alone on Paradise

7

Elegie

Whether they be the broken temples of antiquity or the submerged follies of our recent ancestors, buildings, when no longer cared for, quickly fall into ruin, achieving thereby a melancholy beauty.

As on Earth, so on Paradise.

This shuttle port to which Hera is winging with such speed is typical. When first built it was the model of its kind. Carefully positioned among picturesque foothills, it was provided with its own shelter belt, its own power station and social amenities. The shilos and gardens which surrounded it were the best then available, and those who lived there were proud to call Paradise home.

Once upon a time, friendly house lights glowed amid the tall Verne palms. There was music and the flicker of tri-vid programmes on the curtained windows. When the breeze came from the coast, you could smell the baking of bread and the brewing of beer, for Paradise had its own brewery located on the road to New Syracuse. In the evening, when the bugle notes of the forest trees announced the setting of the sun, you could also hear the sharp cries of infants protesting at bedtime. Were you to have seen all this in its prime, you would have exclaimed, 'How like Earth!' And you would have been right.

That was, of course, the intention, for many who came here tried to create their own vision of what Earth had once been like in happier times. As we now know, that was one of our first and one of our greatest mistakes: for Paradise, despite appearances, was never anything like Earth; not like Heaven either, I suppose.

Now, abandoned, the shuttle port has become a windy place of grit and ghosts.

Just a few months earlier it was from this very port that the teams of demolition workers, summoned for the Disestablishment, spread across the surface of Paradise. Soon their green and blue uniforms were everywhere. They flew out to the distant communities, to the isolated homesteads, to the processing stations, to the mines (for there were still a few) and to the research stations. They stood by while angry and grieving people made their last farewells to the planet which had been home to them for three generations. Some settlers preferred to burn their houses, tossing a blazing rag through a broken window and then watching as the flames licked and leaped up the walls. It did not take long before the framing timbers fell with a crash and sparks billowed into the sky. Then gradually the flames got smaller, until finally all that was left was a smouldering ring of ashes, which, within days, would be overgrown and obliterated by the ever pressing vegetation of Paradise.

The green and blue demolition angels helped people pack. They shifted crates of personal possessions, and then, when the families had moved out, they began their real work – ripping down the public buildings, re-coiling the miles of irrigation tubing, disconnecting the pumps, scuttling and sinking barges that could no longer be serviced, greasing and vacuum-sealing any machinery that could be re-used, disassembling bridges, reclaiming buoys from the running tides and packing in hermetically closed crates the entire contents of the New Syracuse Library, the Distance Education Studios and the ORBE HQ. The temples, mosques and churches were picked apart and sent off world. So too the sheds, shops, restaurants, amateur theatre studio and the whorehouse on the waterfront. The Settlers' Club had its roof, walls and floors plucked away, revealing its secret wine cellar. The Settlers' Museum was pulled down and its contents, documenting the hundred and fifty years since Paradise was first occupied, were sold off to private collectors, dispersed to whichever universities expressed interest or burned.

Snapped up immediately was the quarter-size statue of a *Dendron peripatetica*, extinct now for over a generation. The tall sculpture was carefully cut into pieces, each piece numbered and crated and the whole assembly shipped out to end its days as the sole inhabitant of a crater on the dark side of the moon: bizarre but appropriate.

This demolition took only a few months, for Paradise, despite the aspirations of the first colonists, had never become more than an agricultural world. 'We only scratched the surface,' was the official assessment of the impact of Earth on the planet. Even so, those scratches went deep. The first fifty years during which Paradise was the exclusive territory of the Mineral and Natural Resource Development Company left their mark.

The planet's face was scarred by strip-mining for an aromatic gum which brought a fine price, and for a grey oily substance that burned dirty but hot and was used for local smelting. Some dams were built and rivers diverted in an attempt to make the deserts fertile. Many miles of forest were burned or defoliated to make room for the farms which were planned but never planted.

There were other effects too, invisible ones that could not be remedied, such as the extinction of plant species, the pollution of waterways and radioactive contamination from a misplaced power station. Records were few and no one knew where refuse was buried, or how many drums of unwanted and unnamed chemicals had been weighted and dropped into the deep blue trenches of the sea. Without records showing time and place, such things did not officially exist – and memories fade. Perhaps most grievous, however, was the unknown and unsuspected impact of the human mind on the invisible, passive and slowly awakening sentience of Paradise.

What the demolition workers could remove, they did. What they could not, they burned. And what they could not burn, they broke and left behind for time and the weather to dispose of. Official policy: nothing of use was to be left intact. Why? Well, no one was quite certain any longer. Originally, when the forces of Earth made their first moves into space, there were fears that an alien species might somehow be able to derive advantages from the refuse of earth. But in the time that Earth had been able to explore space beyond the solar system no evidence of a rival technological civilization had been found. Life? Yes. Diatoms in tepid pools, microbes in sulphur ponds, ferns. Just occasionally tantalizing evidence of civilizations long dead was detected under frozen seas or entombed in lava flows. But, of the hostile monstrosities that had peopled the popular imagination since Wells put pen to paper, there was no sign.

Nevertheless, the demolition workers were very careful, for strict legislation had been passed by the Space Council that any spillages must be cleaned up, and any damage they caused to the environment put right. It was curious legislation, the legal equivalent of slamming the stable door when the horse was already a galloping speck on the horizon. As the various conservation agencies kept pointing out, most damage to a planet was done during the first years of its exploitation, when the adventurers from Earth, the commercial companies which sponsored the exploration, were gaining a foothold. That was when the legislation was needed. But it was never enforced. The war between those who wished to protect and conserve and those who wanted to expand and exploit never ended, and the no-man's-land between them was littered with dead legislation.

Now this work of demolition and cleansing was complete. Plants were already crawling over the concrete, reclaiming every damp corner and niche. The army of men and women shipped in to do the pulling down, packing and handling had gradually shrunk from thousands to less than fifty. Those that remained were small professional teams, specialists in the last phase of Disestablishment – razing, burning and burying.

Today being the final scheduled work day, they had hoped to be finished by noon, off planet smartly, into the showers and then into the long boozy party which always followed the safe arrival of the historic last shuttle. And they might have done so too, except that one of the half-track Demo Mules out on a final scavenging run threw a track and the repairs caused a delay.

From Hera's point of view, the delay was fortunate, for she was late.

The day wore on.

The wind came.

The sun, which had shone so brightly in the morning, gradually dimmed to a pale disc, which finally disappeared in the deepening haze.

Steadily, the wind strengthened until it reached gale force. It became heavy and brown with sand and grit stripped from the high plateau. It howled and swirled round the remains of the lonely buildings. It shrieked in the broken gutters and tore at the roofs, lifting the few remaining corrugated panels and sending them wheeling across the compound like playing cards. It tore up the few straggly plants of Earth, all that remained of the kitchen gardens. It drove before it huge tumbling balls of Tattersall weed, that shallow-rooted ubiquitous plant of Paradise. It made sad music in the tall perimeter fence which surrounded the shuttle port with its rusting barbed wire and ceramic insulators.

Standing alone in the middle of all this, solid and squat on its launch pad, was Supply Shuttle P51, the last demolition craft. It was the only source of light amid the gloom – a single yellow beacon at its apex blinked on, off, on, off. The shuttle was awaiting the return of the disposal team stranded in New Syracuse when its Mule broke down. The damage had been repaired and the Mule was on its way back. As soon as it was safely stored inside P51, a small ceremony of flag lowering would be performed, and then the last shuttle would lift.

Meanwhile, the sand flowed round the squat shape like water round a rock. It teemed down its scarred and pitted sides. No human creature could live outside now. Only iron and stone and concrete could survive – and the omnipresent Tattersall weed.

But yet there was one human creature.

8

The Witness

Upwind of the shuttle port, and moving unevenly, a light appeared out of the gloom. Gradually a human figure could be seen beneath the light. It was helmeted and enclosed in a survival suit. Occasionally it stopped, crouching to avoid being knocked over by the fierce wind. Finally, the figure reached the perimeter fence which it gripped tight. It was at a place which overlooked the soon-to-be-abandoned port.

Secure now, with no danger that it could be sent cartwheeling by a sudden gust, the figure began to move along the fence working from handgrip to handgrip. It was heading towards a place where two lines of reinforced perimeter mesh met. Here an iron gate stood open, its frame twisted from a collision with a demolition truck. Just beyond the open gate stood the remains of a curved concrete wall, all that was left of a fuel depot. The wall deflected the wind and created a small haven. Cautiously the figure reached the twisted gate and was about to move through when suddenly it ducked. A massive ball of Tattersall weed came bounding out of the gloom behind, struck the perimeter fence so that it shook and sang, hung for a few moments and then tore loose and rolled on. It banged against the P51 shuttle, caught briefly against one of its stubby legs, and then barrelled away to be lost in the murk.

Cautiously, the figure stood up, looked into the wind to make sure that no further dangers were bearing down, and then crossed quickly to the safety of the concrete wall.

Dr Hera Melhuish pressed her back against the wall and breathed deeply. Much as she disliked concrete, on this occasion she was glad of its solidity. But even had the wall not been there, she would have coped. She would have found a place somewhere to hunker down out of the wind and flying debris, for she was not tall, could imitate the mouse if she had to, and was very determined.

Hera Melhuish took a few moments to catch her breath and then reached up and raised the visor on her helmet. She felt the cold air touch her cheek and, for the first time since leaving her SAS craft, heard the full roar of the storm. She sniffed the wind, noting the bruised lavender smell of the plateau. With it came a whiff of burning rubber and the sweet tang of the Tattersall weed.

Hera looked round at what remained of the rest of the shuttle station. She had not been here since collecting the Shapiro notebooks. The former administration block had been converted into an incinerator. A fire, presumably lit that morning, was consuming old tyres, machine oil and the plastic remains of restaurant trolleys and trays. It was sending out clouds of heavy black smoke, which billowed along the ground before being torn apart by the wind.

With her single light and her face no more than a glimmer in the darkness, Dr Melhuish waited patiently. This was a private mission, one she had promised herself: to witness the very moment when the powers of Earth finally withdrew. The very fierceness of the wind gave her a kind of satisfaction. There was even a hint of a smile on her face. But it was a grim smile.

After the shuttle had gone, she would be alone.

Hera stared at rough old Shuttle P51. It had been in service since the last modification of the platform. It squatted on six absurdly short legs which looked like a child had made them. For the rest, it was shaped like a blunt-nosed bullet. At its very apex, where the small beacon flashed, there was a dome of sullen grey-white crystal, and even as Hera watched, the crystal flared and then began to glow with a soft milky light. The beacon stopped blinking. Moments later the door of the cargo bay lurched, and then began to crank open, like a mouth. An access ramp rolled out noisily on small iron wheels and lowered into place. Lights came on inside. The shuttle was coming alive. The glowing crystal meant it was initiating a link with the space platform in orbit above, and that meant it was preparing to depart. Hera had arrived just in time.

Above the open cargo bay a line of quartz lights flickered into life and then grew steadily brighter as they warmed, bathing the concrete landing pad in a harsh white light. They revealed a single white-painted flagpole, above which flapped and snapped the blue and green insignia of the Space Council under whose aegis the planet had been established.

Dr Melhuish watched and waited. Time was now on her side.

The wind had moved round a few points and now whipped the fine sand into tight pirouettes, sending them into Hera's small enclosure. She felt it pepper her skin, slammed the visor on her helmet down and adjusted the air flow.

Suddenly there came a shriek of metal on metal and there were lights on the road.

Not far from where Hera stood, the main entrance gate jerked and then crashed to the ground as the last of the Mules – the one which had broken down – demolished it and came grinding home. The Mule had obviously been out scavenging a mile or so down the valley. Its flatbed was piled high with oddments of furniture. Hera could see a roll-top desk and a wooden bookcase. Perks of the job, she guessed, but damaged now by the rasp of the sand.

The vehicle clattered into the departure compound where the merchandise sheds had once stood. It slewed round on its half-tracks and steered directly towards the loading ramp. Slowing, it ground its way up the gentle incline. Hera saw sparks glitter briefly where the tracks slipped over the warn studs of the ramp. But then the squat vehicle revved its engine fiercely, pumped out dark smoke through twin nostrils in its rear, lurched forward and climbed steadily into the dark hold.

Once inside, the tail lights blinked on, red and white, and then flickered and died as the engine was switched off. Immediately cargo engineers ran forward with magnetic clamps and secured the vehicle. One man, tall and strongly built, came to the cargo door and stared out. He was wearing a half-helmet and kept his hand raised to stop the sand getting into his mouth. His gaze followed the perimeter fence until it came to the place were Hera was standing. Seeing her light, he removed his own helmet light and waved it above his head.

Dr Melhuish hesitated for a moment and then responded by flashing her light.

The man then cupped his hand to his mouth and called something. But the wind blew his voice away. He pointed to the earpieces of his helmet, held up three fingers and then opened and closed his hand like a duck's mouth.

Understanding the sign language, Dr Melhuish switched on her radio and tuned to Band 3. Immediately she could hear the crackling of static and the sound of the man breathing.

'Hearing you loud and clear,' said Hera. 'Thought you might have stayed up top and started the party already.'

She heard him laugh. 'Hi there, Doc. No, not me. I always like to be last off the job. First on, last off. That's the rule.'

'Very commendable. And was it you who knocked the perimeter gate down just now?'

'Yep. I couldn't see it for all the dust.'

'Huh! Well, I see you got yourself some nice junk.'

'That stuff? That's for one of the fellas up top. Says he collects courthouse furniture. Had us keep it back.' He laughed again. 'Hey, your mate Captain Abhuradin's on board. Came down for the send-off. You want to speak to her?'

'No. Not now. We've said our goodbyes. I'll just stay here and watch. But you can tell her I'm here, if you like.'

'OK. Will do. So what did you do to the weather, Doc? We were promised a fine day. And look at it. Damn near blew the Mule over.'

'It's unpredictable, Mack. Anyway, I prefer it like this. It suits me. Suits my temperament.'

'What? Stormy?'

'Yes, and full of grit.'

'I'll remember that.' Mack gestured round the deserted station. 'We've left you with a bit of a mess to clean up, Doc.'

'That's all right. I never travel without my broomstick.'

'I'd hoped we'd have got rid of all this crap but we've run out of time. I've had to leave one of our old Demo Buses down in the town. God knows when we'll get to pick it up. I asked for another day or so. I wanted to at least get the perimeter fence down, but they couldn't change the schedule.'

'Not to worry, Mack. Honestly. I like it like this. Surreal. It has a special kind of beauty all its own.'

'You've got a funny taste in art, Doc.'

'Who's talking about art? Anyway, what's new?'

'There's real logjam up top. About a hundred and fifty barges waiting to go fractal. Even if they can get them off two at a time, I reckon you'll have three or four months minimum down here.'

'Suits me.'

At that moment a siren sounded aboard the shuttle. 'Here we go. The brass is arriving.'

Hera, suddenly shy, switched out her light and pressed her body back into the shadows.

Moments later a small party came down out of the cargo bay. All were wearing survival suits which revealed their rank, but Hera did not need to see stripes or blue stars to distinguish the tall figure of Captain Abhuradin. Even wearing a survival suit and pummelled by the wind, she still managed to look elegant. Beside her was the short and earnest Disestablishment marshal sent by the Space Council whose name actually was Ernest de something-or-other – Hera had forgotten. There were several other officials and a couple of ratings, one of whom wore a diagonal red sash across his white survival suit. Mack and a few of the other demolition workers stood in the hold, looking out, their arms wrapped around themselves like patient gravediggers. Not being part of the military, they had no formal part in the ceremony, but a Disestablishment flag-lowering was always a sad occasion, being by its nature an admission of defeat, and many liked to show their respects.

The small party braved the wind and its members marched as well as they were able. They came to attention in front of the flagpole. As they did so, the anthem of Earth began to play from loudspeakers set up in the hold. Its sound reached Hera's ears fitfully through Mack's microphone, which he had forgotten to switch off. When the music started, Mack gestured to his men and they too came to a respectable semblance of attention, many of them having already served time in the military or as members of the Rapid Intervention Security Corps. Hera heard them singing the anthem in their own variety of sharps and flats. Mack's voice was loud and clear and surprisingly rich, and she realized that this little ceremony probably meant a lot to him. The end of a chapter. Another job done. Although he had smashed down the perimeter gate, she knew from working with him at the disassembling of the Shapiro Collection that he was the kind of man who would take pains to make sure that windows were not broken unnecessarily and that delicate things were packed properly. She admired that. And now, hearing him singing, she was moved – and more than a little saddened too, for she knew that she had become cynical about everything to do with the Earth.

At the end of the anthem, the rating who was wearing the sash advanced to the flagpole and lowered the flag. But the wind had made a meal of it and the once-bold banner which reached the ground was little more than a frayed rag. And as though that were not bad enough, a sudden gust caught the flag just as it was being handed over to Captain Abhuradin, and whipped it out of her glove. It sailed up high and away, tumbling like washing that has escaped from the line. Making the best of it, Captain Abhuradin saluted crisply and turned sharply.

The ceremony was over. Captain Abhuradin led the small party, now walking into the wind so their uniforms were plastered against them, across to the ramp and up into the cargo hold. As she passed Mack, Hera saw her issue some instructions and Mack gave his equivalent of a salute. She could see him speaking but could not catch the words, though she did hear her name. Captain Abhuradin paused, nodded and then came to the front of the cargo bay and, holding tightly to one of the side supports, looked out in the direction of Hera's refuge. She raised her hand briefly. Hera blinked her light in acknowledgement. That was all. The captain turned, staggered slightly against the wind and rejoined the small party, which was waiting for her in the depths of the cargo bay. As a group they moved away to the lift which would carry them up to the control deck.

Mack watched them and then turned back to Hera.

'Looks like we're off straight away. No messing about. I thought for a minute she was going to send us out to go looking for that bloody flag.' Mack pressed a switch at the side of the cargo bay and the heavy access ramp began to withdraw into the shuttle. 'Now listen, Doc.' Mack's voice had taken on a more urgent and serious tone. 'If you ever find yourself down in New Syracuse, I've left a few bottles of good stuff for you, courtesy of the Settlers' Club. I know you enjoy a glass of wine. They're in a case in the concrete bunker just near where the marina used to be. You won't miss them.' The ramp ground to a halt. Mack pressed another switch and the magnetic bolts slammed home, locking it in place. The tall cargo doors began to close. 'And hey, listen, Doc. You be careful out there. Keep your emergency beacon with you at all times. I'm serious. And if you get in any trouble, get stitched up by a Tattersall or anything, just hit the beacon switch and we'll be down to get you quicker than a horse snickers. Remember. Ciao.'

He waved once and the cargo doors hid him from view as they began to close.

'Goodbye, Mack,' Hera called, 'and thank you.' But whether he heard these last words or not she did not know.

Now things moved quickly. Hera heard a loud *clang* as the ramp wheels locked. Then came a muffled *thump* as the magnetic bolts closed inside the doors. Moments later plumes of dust were ejected from around the cargo door as the air was squeezed out from within, establishing a vacuum. A dribble of oil appeared round the rubber door-seals, and the wind-driven dust stuck to it. Overhead the bright working lights went out one by one. The compound was suddenly dark save for the crystal on top of the shuttle, which now burned with a stronger intensity. The shuttle was almost ready for departure. A lone siren above the perimeter gate began to wail – standard procedure before all departures – a mournful sound, made fitful by the wind.

In the old days, when the shuttle port was full of activity, the siren would have been a warning for all personnel to clear the compound. Faces would have been pressed to windows to watch, for the departure of a large shuttle such as a P class was always a spectacular event. The siren reached its crescendo and then began to whine down. From high in the sky a blade of intense light spiked down, appearing almost solid in the thick air and wheeling dust.

The beam was slightly out of alignment and struck the concrete floor of the compound, defining a sharp-edged oval of brilliance. The guidance engineer up on the platform adjusted the angle of the beam by fractions of a degree, and gradually the pool of light moved across until it touched the side of the shuttle, where it created strange patterns of light and shadow. It moved on, slipping up the rough metal, until it reached the crystal dome. Immediately the dome glowed more brilliantly as it absorbed and transformed the photon energy.

The crystal began to pulse, sending its own flashes of white light surging upward. Hera Melhuish adjusted the filter on her visor. The two beams flared for a moment as resonance was established between them, and then they fused into a single scintillating column. The colour changed from white to a steely silver and finally to a clear violet at which it held steady. There came a crackling sound and electricity danced around the legs of the shuttle. Slowly P51 lifted and accelerated steadily – the similarity to a giant spider dangling from a silver thread was uncanny – and then it retracted its legs.

Hera stared up into the streaming clouds following the shuttle into the murky heavens. Soon it was above the clouds, no more than a speck in the sky, visible only because of the steady violet beam of light blazing down from the space platform, with its glittering photon generators, some sixty-five kilometres above.

Already the Disestablishment party would be in full swing, with dance music playing and the lights turned down. There would be corks popping; men and women all spruced up and ready to dance, swapping yarns and laughing. In the canteen the tables would be set with red tablecloths. Gleaming cutlery would reflect the light of perfumed candles floating on water. Someone would have decorated the room with streamers and balloons as though it was Christmas, and there would be a big cake on which would be piped, in blue icing, 'Farewell Paradise'.

Beyond Hera's small sanctuary the wind howled.

Hera shivered, but not with cold. It was one of those involuntary movements of which our great-grandmothers would have said, 'Someone just walked over my grave.'

9

Lux in Tenebris

For a few seconds Hera stood there in the shelter of the wall, absorbing the fact that she was now the only human being left on Paradise. How small she felt. And how alone. Of course she'd known this would be the case once the shuttle departed, and she had tried to prepare herself mentally – but even so the reality was a shock and she felt a peculiar and quite unexpected stab of fear. For a few panicky moments she was tempted to open the radio link and call the shuttle back. But her hand did not move. She became a block of wood – as Hilda had taught her to be when faced with temptation. And when the temptation had passed, she was able to examine her frailty for what it was: a sudden reaction to fear, nothing more. And of course to call the shuttle back now would be to admit defeat absolutely, positively, irrevocably. *No way*, thought Hera, smiling grimly at her own fading panic. *No way!*

But what did she feel now that she was alone? Hera looked up and was still able to see the small worm of light turn as the shuttle climbed. She must feel something. After all, that small spark of light represented the last of her human companions. She would not see another human face for three months at least, assuming there were no accidents.

Loneliness was to be expected, and that Hera could cope with: she'd been lonely before. But there was something else, something deeper than loneliness. Something that made her quite calm. It was *relief*, she decided finally. Relief that the waiting was over. Relief that no fresh orders had come rescinding the one which allowed her to stay. Relief, also, that she didn't have to worry about meeting any of the settlers. Relief that she could move without being observed and just be herself, whether laughing or crying.

Relief that at last she could get on with the task she had set herself, in her mystical science way, and work alone with the planet.

For Dr Hera Melhuish was a singular woman, and like all such, when she devoted herself to an idea or a cause, she put it at the centre of her life.

Hera stood for a long time staring out into the deserted compound. There was no reason to stay – no sentiment or satisfaction to be gathered from lingering. She had hoped that the departure of the shuttle would somehow be conclusive, and that she would set out to accomplish her purpose like someone newborn, but it was not so.

She was the same Hera she had always been and she knew that no one and no thing would have taken the slightest interest if she had simply hunkered down in her concrete retreat for the night. No thing, that is, except the automatic landing and navigation pilot on her new flyer. This, noting the length of time since her departure, would send out a brief radio inquiry which would activate the radio system of her survival suit. But even the autopilot would not have given her an instruction. It, or Alan as she now tended to think of him, was there to take instructions.

Finally Hera, that woman of resolute will, took a deep breath and spoke aloud. She said, 'Pull yourself together, woman, and get going.' It worked. She looked out with a deeper sense of purpose.

The wind had definitely subsided. It was still strong, but it had lost that hard drive and was blustery rather than fierce. Hera closed her helmet, switched on the bright halogen beam of her helmet light and, bracing herself, moved out from behind the concrete wall. She discovered to her relief that she could make headway against the wind without too much trouble. Surprisingly too, she could see quite well – better than when she had arrived. Despite the onset of evening, the sky had lightened as the heavy dust and sand settled out of the air. High up above, the last rays of the sun were still just catching the clouds with a pink light.

Torn-off branches and stripped blue flower heads from Tattersall weeds clogged the perimeter fence. Some of the broken branches were swinging about in the fitful wind and the long prickles scratched on the concrete and made marks in the driven sand. For Hera to get through the gate she had to stoop low, and she both felt and heard the scratch of the thorns on her helmet and shoulder.

Once through, she moved well away from the perimeter edge. She began the trudge up the middle of the road, scuffing in the sand. Occasionally she walked backwards, looking back at the sad remains of the shuttle port. It was not merely that the buildings were gone or broken that made the former port a sad spectacle, but that what remained was a statement about something that had failed, an idea that had gone wrong, a potential that had never been realized. And how could that not be sad? She remembered a poem that her father had liked, about a face staring up from a desert. *Well,* she thought, *the ruins of a great civilization may speak volumes about time and tragedy. But this? All this was avoidable. This was our fault. My fault as much as any. I should have been stronger.*

Walking backwards has its perils, as does letting the mind drift in sad recrimination. Hera caught her heel on a piece of iron fencing that lay half buried in the sand. The next thing she knew she was down on her bottom in the dust. She accepted this as a warning and, as she picked herself up, offered thanks to whatever god protects drunks, children and small women walking backwards. But she knew that such gods only give one warning, and so she turned her back on the past and walked up the road towards the empty parking place where she had left her survey and survival flyer.

Hera was surprised at how quickly she reached it, and this merely served to remind her how difficult and dangerous had been the journey down from the flyer to the shuttle port. Touching the controls strapped to her forearm, she saw the lights on the SAS craft flash on and begin their steady blinking – guidance for a person lost in the dark . . . or a sandstorm. In her ears was a steady whine which changed pitch depending on whether she was facing the SAS or turned away. 'Cut the siren, Alan,' she ordered, 'and the beacons. I can see you.' Immediately the calm voice of the auto landing and navigation unit spoke in her ear. 'Welcome back, Hera. Are you receiving me loud—'

'Loud and clear. Yes, and I can see the effects of the sandstorm on you. You look as though you've been spring-cleaned with a wire brush. You're all polished on one side. Half your insignia has been scratched off.'

The autopilot made no answer. As she approached the SAS, its door opened smoothly. 'Are all your circuits functional? No damage?' she asked.

'All systems are functioning.'

That was a relief. She'd had a nagging worry that one of the tumbling Tattersall weeds might have wrapped itself round the SAS. The vehicles were tough and built for arduous conditions, but a Tattersall, tumbling like the one she had seen strike the fence, might have damaged an aerial or got tangled up with the rotor cover. At the very worst it might have toppled the flyer, and that would have been a problem.

But it hadn't happened. *I must stop doing that*, she thought. *I must stop worrying about things that might go wrong or could have gone wrong, but didn't. Be positive.* She climbed into the flyer and the door closed behind her and sealed. She removed the control panel from her arm and then her helmet and plugged them both into the battery charger built into the door. Later she would need to clean the helmet, as fine dust had clogged round the visor. Then, as she was undoing the insulated cuffs of her gloves, she heard soft music begin. Kossoff's 'Serenade to Alien Seas'. A nice touch this, she thought. A clever and sensitive piece of design, to incorporate an instruction into the autopilot's log of duties saying, 'Play sweet music when the pilot returns.' The effect was, as intended, soothing.

During the month since Captain Abhuradin had delivered the SAS to Hera, the autopilot had noted the pieces of music she liked and turned to most frequently. From these he had made a selection. Hera felt the charm of the familiar music reach out to her as she stripped out of the survival suit, unzipping it completely. 'Serenade' was part of a series of melodies each interpreting poems by the mystical twenty-first-century poet Yvegeny. It wasn't complex music or demanding in an intellectual sense, but it spoke to something inside her. All of the poems dealt with spiritual questions of one sort or another. Anyone who travelled into deep space or who contemplated the vastness of space or who found themselves alone amid alien fields, ended up asking the questions which have no ordinary answers. The poet had imagined himself to be a boy sitting in the sun by a bottle-green sea and sifting the sand through his fingers. As he sits by the shore he hears a voice. It is the sea talking to him and asking him about himself: where he has come from and what he has seen and what he hopes for as he grows up. One of the things that Hera liked about this composition was that the music did not pick up on any mood of sadness or romantic loneliness present in the translation – that would have been unbearably sentimental, in her view. No. The music rather challenged the thoughtful mood of the poems. It pulsed with strong rhythms. A male voice chorus provided the many voices of the sea. Accordions, harp, double bass and violin provided all the melody. But, weaving through all like a thread of silver was a clear solo alto voice. In this recording, a soprano with a voice like a bell took the boy's role. Hera had decided long ago that this was a voice to die for. And, indeed, if there were something called reincarnation, Hera wanted to come back as a petite soprano with a voice that could shatter glass. She hummed along with the melody in strict tempo and then nodded like a conductor for the solo voice to enter, distant and strange like the call of a sea bird. The first song was optimistic as the boy talked about setting out on his life, like an adventure story.

Hera hung her survival suit in the cleansing and detox closet, spreading the arms and legs wide. The boots too went into the closet, upside down on pegs. The door closed and sealed. Seconds later she heard the cleansing system switch on and begin its cycle. The suit would be chemically cleaned and dried. Equally important, it would be repaired with a liquid plastic which was absorbed by any torn fibres and then dried to close with the rest of the laminate.

Beside the detox closet was a normal shower unit. Built to accommodate the bulkiest of men, it was luxuriously large for Hera. 'Turn up the music, Alan. I'm going to take a shower.' Obediently the level increased. Moments later, had anyone been listening, the sound of the music was joined by the sound of water and then by the warbling contralto of Hera.

In the song cycle the sea was gradually turning from green to grey.

The shower did not last long, but was effective for all that. Hera gave herself the pleasure of a long slow dry under the heater fans. She emerged clean and dry but with her hair hidden beneath a shower cap. It was still pinned back in the tight no-nonsense bob she preferred – except when she slept.

Clad now in only the light cotton pyjamas that were all she

wore inside the SAS, a towel round her neck and with her feet bare, Hera ran up the spiral stairway that led to the control cabin. Apart from narrow structural panels which curved up to form the roof, the control room offered a 360-degree view. All the windows were dark.

Two small tri-vid screens occupied the space to the side of the main control consul. One of these had a wide cone of vision which could show what was happening to the sides and below the flyer. It possessed frequency filters that were permanently scanning and which, at optimum sensitivity, could have revealed any residual heat resulting from Hera's footsteps as she approached the SAS. The other screen operated only in the visual spectrum and was fitted with a powerful telescopic lens which could explore above or below.

Every effort had been taken to make the cabin comfortable and cheerful. Colours were bright, edges were rounded and surfaces were firm rather than hard. The control chair had been tailored to suit Hera's size. It could tilt back to provide a bed or, when configured as a chair, could swivel and glide over the floor. But it was always anchored by magnetic clamps, which would lock in the event of a sudden tilt or shock. Hera perched in the chair and studied her clean pink fingernails, noticing that one was very ridged. 'Now what does that mean?' she wondered out loud.

The music was just beginning the penultimate poem, and the boy, older now, having waded into the pale grey sea, was beating the palms of his hands flat onto the water and singing, 'If the Lord of Love on high . . .' Hera settled herself further into the pilot's seat and checked for any messages that might have come in while she was away. There were none. 'Quits his mansion in the sky . . .' She peered out into the darkness about the craft. No moon had risen yet. In a couple of hours or so the mottled silver and grey face of Tonic would rise to be followed some time later by the smaller golden Gin. But for the moment the darkness was total, as though the windows had been painted over, as though the small ship was stranded at the bottom of a well.

'If he comes, my soul to save,/ Will he find my lonely grave?' The music lingered while the voice soared, like a bird riding the wind up into the sunshine. It was a beautiful evocative moment, sad and brave, and Hera loved it. The voice faded, leaving only the wash and flow of the sea as the boy waded deeper. But then the water became dark and rough while storm winds grew.

'Stop the music, Alan.'

'There is one track remaining.'

'Later.'

The sound of the waves died away.

Hera stared into the darkness. Then she reached out and switched on the beacon light and bright landing lights. Revealed about the ship was the scattered rubbish left by the storm. Nothing moved. The wind had completely gone. At the edge of the parking lot she could just see the first fringe of Tattersall weeds, their flowers pale, leached of their colour by the light from her beacon. It was like looking at an old still photograph, or a stage set. The stillness was unreal. Something should be moving, a leaf drifting down, a whirl of dust . . . something.

What happened next needs explaining. Hera was not aware of it at the time, but Paradise was already beginning to work its way deeper into her mind. The consequence was uncertainty and a turmoil of the spirit. The following are Hera's own words of explanation as I recorded them in my studio.

Hera What then? I turned round and looked out through the windows behind me. But it was all the same landscape, the same still photograph – light fading to darkness, and it was the darkness that finally held my attention.

Olivia Were you afraid of the dark?

Hera Not afraid, no. I have dived, remember, in vast caves beneath the surface of Mars. Sometimes I slept in the water, cocooned in just my survival suit. I can cope with darkness – like it, even – but this darkness had a different quality about it. More . . . tangible, somehow. I thought of our ancestors, for whom a flickering fire at the cave mouth meant warmth and security. How well I understood that. And I thought about my beacon, pouring out the photons at the maximum speed an object could attain.

Olivia Were you aware of a change in yourself?

Hera I think so, but it was not like hypnotism. I seemed to see things more clearly . . . and symbolically too.

Olivia Go on.

Hera The beacon light . . . I imagined the edge of that light cutting into the darkness of space. Light pushing back the darkness. The known pushing against the unknown. The assertive yang against the passive yin. But no matter how hard yang pushed, no matter how much yin yielded, mystery would always remain, for the boundary between them could not be crossed. I began to cry then, because I think in my heart I knew that, despite everything I could do and offer, I would always be the outsider.

Olivia Hera. You don't have to—

Hera You see, I knew . . . I knew that this longing I felt towards Paradise, a longing which pre-dated my coming to the planet by many years, was profoundly irrational. And then when I found Paradise, well! Sometimes the yearning was so strong that I had to find a quiet place alone while the mood worked its way through me. I was so powerfully aware of the life current of the planet that it hurt . . . but it was a sweet pain too. And it made me act foolishly sometimes, like the time I stretched out on the ground in the forest, arms spread, face in the earth, and prayed to the planet, wanting it to loosen my stiffness, enter me in some way, fill me, temper me, chasten me, bring me some understanding and relief . . . Don't look like that, Olivia! I know what you are thinking. I know how resonant these words are of . . . and that is their truth. Ecstasy, like love, is finally indivisible. Like it or not. Have you not acted foolishly from pure emotion sometimes?

Olivia This is not my biography. I'll tell you when we are off the record. Did you ever talk about this to anyone?

Hera Shapiro. Once. But listen . . . I knew I was not mad. To be irrational sometimes is not to be mad. Is it? To be able to feel a divinity in a place is not mad. To be in love is not mad, is it? But, if it is a love unrequited? In verity, that is hell! To be aware of divinity is one thing. But to be ignored by that divinity is terrible. Though I might knock at the door, I might not be bid enter. *That* was what I feared above all, Olivia. In my darkest moments, I knew that I might just be wrong. Paradise might just be a world, unique indeed, but one that I had dressed with my own desires and vanity.

Olivia Yes. I can see the danger. And we do that, don't we? Dress things up. But doubt is often the companion to faith, so I am told. Go on with your story.

Hera Well. The other strange thing is that even while these thoughts spilled through me, I nevertheless had a sense that they were . . . I don't know the word.

Olivia Induced? Abstract?

Hera No. More like . . . liberated. Like when you face something terrible and it leaves its mark but fades. I knew that revelation does not come just because you want it. I mean, waiting for revelation is like waiting for someone else to do your dirty washing – you'll wait a long time. But then I thought of a phrase that my father often used, 'Fortune favours the prepared mind,' and I thought, *Do I have a prepared mind?* That stopped me in my tracks. It was as though I had been looking at a painting of someone I did not know, and then suddenly realized it was a mirror.

Hera felt suddenly weary. Words and questions! Words and questions! For a moment she put her head in her hands. Then she sat up and banged her fists down on the control desk. There was a time when she would not have had to ask that question about having a prepared mind. Or if she had asked it, the answer would have come back as a resounding YES. But now the simple symbolic truths that were her only understanding when she was a girl were crusted over with doubt and fear, anger and worry. What had happened to her in all these years?

She knew there was no going back. The innocence and simple sensuality of childhood is a consequence, in part, of ignorance. But she was a grown woman, in her fifties no less. Time to grow up. But how? How?

Back to Hera.

Hera Sitting there, feeling cornered and compromised, I suddenly felt a deep anger well up inside me. You see this was what was happening. I was not really in control. I was like ashes that glow when they are fanned.

Olivia Who was doing the fanning?

Hera Wait. I have never known a fit of anger like it. The first victim of my anger was myself. I was angry with what I was, with what I had let myself become. Angry too with being an angry, frantic woman. Angry for what I had lost. Angry I had squandered my gifts. Angry I had lost my innocence. Angry with Saturn because

... because! Angry with my mother – so energetic and distant. Angry with my father – so slow and patient. Angry with Shapiro – that smug, drugged, clever bastard. Angry with the god I didn't believe in. Oh, how I would love to slap him about the ears. Angry that I needed gods at all. Angry with darkness. Angry with Paradise because it held me trapped and took my love and left me hungry .... HOORAY!!!! I let out a great scream of rage. And that woke Alan up.

Olivia I can imagine.

Hera 'Hera,' he said, in that sweet rational voice, and I roared at him, 'And you keep out of it too! Bloody go to sleep or turn your-self off or something!'

Olivia And?

Hera Nothing. He didn't reply. But at least I felt better for the out-burst. I sat there in the silence. Nothing. No ideas. No thoughts. No will, my mind a block of wood. Then I reached forward and, with one sweep of my hand, I switched out all the exterior lights.

Blackness outside. Nothing to focus on. But something surprising. Something quite unexpected and quite wonderful. Hera found her-self staring at her own ghostly image reflected in the window. She could see herself seated upright, one arm extended, while about her was the small cabin, which glowed, lit by the softly illuminated desk and the cherry-red control lights. But there was more. She could see the reflection of the windows behind her, facing out to darkness, and framed within those windows was the reflection of her back ... and behind that, smaller and more faint and slightly raised – but there nevertheless – was again the reflected image of her face ... and so on, and so on. These images, each slightly out of phase, each getting smaller and dimmer with distance, curved up ... and up ... and on to infinity ...

She and they seemed to be waiting for something.

What a strange moment that was! Quite beautiful and unfore-seen. Hera knew that she was facing herself in a different way. She had been here before – in this quiet space where the mind, like the retreating sea, starts to yield up its monsters. Hera was not by nature a quitter. She was a woman who could learn. Having reached an impasse, it was necessary that she start to climb back. Slowly Hera felt her mind ease and her thoughts start to flow.

The billions of Heras looked on.

To herself she said, *I think a prepared mind must be a peaceful mind – always patient but always ready. I think it is one that is not troubled by paradox. It is like Yvegeny's bird that flies above the storm. I closed my eyes, summoning the music, and my mind rested on the image of the seabird that hung still in the sky, and then slid gracefully down the face of the wind until it almost touched the breaking waves before soaring up again into the sunlight. It seemed to make no effort but was in complete command. How I would like to be that bird! But I learned that a prepared mind is effortless too, and that is its strength.*

Aloud she said, 'Let me find that mind. Let my time on Paradise be a time of discovery and a time of pleasure. I might have got everything wrong in the past, but that is all right so long as I can walk away with contentment. I am so tired of being clever. I am so tired of being angry. Let me just *be* for a while, and if I can be of service here, then I count that a bonus, a rich reward. I might have to learn to freewheel for a bit. But that is what I want – to stop pedalling for a while – and I want to stop peddling too. Stop hawking my wares? Let me go about my business. Do what I can for Paradise. And if a call comes, let me be ready. And if it does not come, let me be ready for that too.'

Hera did not know the moment when her mind had slipped from speculation to prayer, but when the words stopped she was content just to sit, her mind feeling spacious and dark and curiously alive. She might have stayed in that state for some time, but something made her open her eyes. It came to her like a sigh from outside.

Immediately she was aware of movement. The blackness outside her windows was changing to a rich and mottled green. The night-time glow of the plants of Paradise was slowly returning, and the landscape was gaining depth. High on the hill she saw a group of candle palms, always among the brightest, pulsing gently as they shed the surplus energy of the day. Above the foothills of the plateau one or two stars were peeping out. At the edge of the parking lot the deep dark blue flowers of the Tattersalls were nodding in a light breeze, their petals picking up and reflecting back the small light from the sky. She could see the outline of their branches as if lit by moonlight, though no moon had yet risen. Closer to her, on the ground, the dead plants and leaves had begun to glow as their fibres softened and deliquesced, their juices flowing back into the soil of Paradise.

Then she became aware of a ripple of light moving slowly over the hills. It was so faint that she could only really see it if she looked to the side, but it was there and it was getting stronger. This was something she had never seen before, on Paradise or elsewhere.

Quickly she switched out all the cabin lights. The reflections vanished and the view outside became clearer.

She watched the line of light move down a distant hill like a cresting wave, getting brighter as it approached. She looked for the source of the light, having concluded there was some beam playing over the trees, but then she saw that it was the forest itself that suddenly glowed and faded, as though a current had briefly touched the roots as it swept by. She realized too that this energy field, or whatever it was, would pass by her or through her, and there was nothing she could do but wait and watch. But she was not passive, not a block of wood. She was conscious and alert.

As it came closer, she saw the trees jerk and rear and at the same moment they shone briefly. At the perimeter of the parking lot, one Tattersall weed flailed so vigorously that the branches broke, scattering flower heads and petals onto the concrete.

It was at that perimeter, where the concrete began, that the light was lost. There were no trees or bushes to reveal it. But still something advanced. A swirling of something like smoke, but heavy, like a gathering wave of dark water, flowing towards her.

Her head shaking in denial, Hera watched as the tide of darkness slowly advanced across the parking lot. It absorbed her light and sent back no reflection. It approached the SAS and Hera felt her spirit shrink inside her.

The darkness swirled up outside the windows and then flowed into the SAS as though the walls did not exist. It rose quickly through the floor, enclosing Hera's legs – which felt nothing – and then the control panel vanished and with it her hands. Her last conscious thought as the tide rode up over her was the wish that she was wearing something more substantial than light cotton pyjamas. Then she shivered violently and her throat was so dry that, though she wanted to call out, she could not.

The shivering was no more than a spasm and ended as soon as

the darkness had passed through her. Hera found herself in a blackness more total than anything she had ever experienced before. She put out her tongue but could not feel her lips. She lifted her hand but could not feel her face. Indeed, her hand seemed to pass through the place where her face should have been. She could feel no chair supporting her, nor solid deck plates beneath her feet. She was a point of consciousness, that was all, and the wonder of it was that she did not feel terror. She was denied the dimension of terror, but her mind . . . her mind seemed as clear as a polished mirror. She could think positively and was self-aware.

In that state Hera tried to open her mind to whatever presence had embraced her, dark or not. She was, in a way, eager. If we translate her desire into words, it comes out something like 'I am.' Or even 'I will.' Or at its most brazen 'I am willing.' But if this offer was heard or understood, nothing answered.

Instead she felt herself twisted, wrung out like washing in a strong woman's hands, but without pain. And then her mind was 'rifled'. That is the very word that Hera used when recalling this moment. Memories were lifted from her. There was no rhyme or reason that she could detect. Passive, she yielded up some of her most intimate memories.

The first memory was of an event that had occurred during a trip to old Europe. Her mother was attending a conference in the Alps and took little Hera with her for company and to show her some of the grand sights and old treasures before it was too late. They were at Chartres and already stonemasons were at work taking the cathedral down. Her mother was standing in the aisle and she pulled some wooden chairs aside, making a loud scratching sound on the stone floor. Flamboyant and theatrical as ever, she pointed at the dark slabs and said, 'See, that is where the pilgrims crawled on their hands and knees to gain forgiveness for their sins. Faith can make people do strange things, Hera.'

This memory was replaced by one of her father, stooping over his plants at Angelique-over-Io and cutting into the wood of a rose so that he could insert a small closed bud. His knife was very sharp. It could cut your finger without your knowing, as Hera had already discovered to her cost. He finished the graft and wrapped the joint with tape. 'Does it hurt the rose when you do that?' asked Hera. To which her dad replied, 'Not if you are careful and not if you are quick. Think of it this way: you are giving the roots something to do, something to look after – and they like that.'

The next memory was very brief. Hera standing on a table, a bit drunk, with a bottle in one hand and her rolled doctoral certificate in the other. She seems unsure which to drink from.

There were many other memories that were plucked out and discarded, but one of the strangest came last. Hera saw herself as an older woman. She is seated in a strange room. There is another woman with her who is just standing up, her tumbling red hair held in place by a plastic comb jammed in at an odd angle. Her face is merry but wears marks of suffering too.

That is all. In later years Hera always wondered who the other woman was. And now she knows. Me.

How long she was held in the blackness Hera does not know. At one point she wondered if she might be experiencing the celebrated life-flashing-before-the-eyes experience. If so, it seemed very relaxed.

And then there came one final spasm of shaking and she saw redness before her and felt a sudden startling pain in her hands. The darkness moved on. Solidity returned.

Hera opened her eyes. She was still in the cabin. She found herself leaning forward, her breasts pressed flat on the control panel, her elbows splayed and her hands clasped together so fiercely that her nails had pierced her skin. She immediately felt ridiculous, as though caught in an indecent posture.

She laughed at herself, released her tight hands with difficulty and then sat back firmly in her chair and breathed deeply. Her heart was pounding in her chest, but she was alive. She could still think clearly. No harm, as far as she could tell, had come to her. Somewhere she heard a fan start up. Everything was normal. . .

. . . except nothing was normal any more.

Hera sat very still.

The good news, she realized, was that there was now no doubt about there being a special consciousness on the planet: she had felt it, it had brushed her, she had sensed the might of its presence. At the same time, considered coolly, nothing very much had happened. A bit of fear, a bit of sensory deprivation. An enforced trip down memory lane. But there had been no revelation, no sudden leap in consciousness, no joining of mind and spirit with . . . with whatever it was. There had been no – she searched for the right word – no sense of divinity, no majesty.

Is that what I wanted? she wondered. *Is that it?* She smiled at that, recalling the phrase from an earlier time. *Well, perhaps I was lucky. Women usually die when gods reveal themselves. But that was not a god. No. No god worth his salt would come as darkness. That was a . . . that was . . .* She had no word for what she thought it was. *That was just a wake-up call,* she concluded. But from whom or what, she did not know. *Next time, I'll be ready.*

Hera was aware that her thoughts were somewhat frivolous, and she put that down to a reaction. *Better to be frivolous than morbid or mad.* But she was also aware that her mind had retained a certain clarity of thought, as though the brush with the alien had increased her sensitivity and quickened her consciousness.

She sat for a while with her knees pulled up and her arms wrapped around her, gazing out into the quiet night.

Outside the flyer a light breeze stirred the distant Tattersall weeds and there was no strange darkness lurking at the perimeter. It had gone. Passed on. But the sky was not dark. The silver disc of Tonic was already high in the sky – full moon tonight. It was brightening the tips of the trees and casting shadows. With the rising of the moon, the phosphorescence of the plants had faded. The stars were out too, with their mysterious zodiac patterns that as yet had no history. A golden glow was strengthening beyond the rim of the plateau. It was the light of Gin, just rising. She turned and looked out of the window behind her. In this silver and shadowy green world, she could see the road down to the former shuttle port and even the fence where the strands of Tattersall weed hung limply. She knew she could walk there with safety, but yet she felt no inclination to move. The stillness was sweet. She thought, *If I had my time over, I would do things differently – who wouldn't? But now I will enjoy being a quiet woman for a change. Enough of planning and head stuff. Now I am going to let things just happen to me for a change – sit back, treat my time down here as a holiday and see if that makes more sense. And if called, I will be ready and patient. And if not, I'll enjoy the swimming.*

She yawned suddenly and then sat up. She thought, *I am a very lucky woman. I have got what I wanted. I have this place to myself now, for a while*' Then she spoke aloud. 'I'm here,' she said, speaking distinctly. 'I'm here. Now.'

'I know you are, Hera.' The voice was a shock, and Hera felt the adrenalin rush in her arms and neck and her heartbeat leap. But it was the voice of Alan, the autopilot. 'Have you been sleeping, Hera? Are you all right?'

'Better, I think. God, you gave me a shock. Better than I was.'

'You were upset before.'

'Sorry.'

'Were you speaking to yourself, just now?'

'Yes, to myself. But no more questions, Alan. I've had enough questions for the moment. Now I want to sleep. Music, maestro, please.'

'Very well.' Softly, the music returned and Hera settled back in her chair. The great rhythmic ebb and flow of waves filled the small cabin. It was a long musical section, and when the words of the poem finally returned, the boy was far from the shore, and swimming.

With every stroke he is growing older. He has swum with mermaids and dolphins and a strange dark creature that lolls on the surface between feeds. He has drifted by coral and iceberg. The long-dead of the sea have visited him and told their yarns. Now, finally, he is an old man, and he knows the time is coming when he must dive. To celebrate this moment Yvegeny adapted lines from a mystical old Irish poet he regarded as his master. The soprano has been changed for a bass. He sings while the accordion plays, 'Winter and summer, and all the day long . . .'

Hera stood up and stretched. She had pins and needles in her legs. And her arm ached. There was blood on her fingers. 'My love was in singing, no matter the song.' Hera padded across the cabin to the central stairwell. She paused and had one last look round. Then she went down the steps and into the cabin she used as hers.

The music followed her, surging and falling: waves breaching a headland and dying noisily on a stony shore.

Hera crawled under the duvet. The bed was already slightly warm. Comfort for a chilled worker on a lonely mission. She snuggled down and drew her knees up. Outside, the poem was coming to its end: 'Now must I lie down where all ladders start/ In the rag and bone shop of my human heart.'

So saying, the old man dived under the waves and found he could breathe water.

But Hera did not hear those words.

Hera was already asleep.

Much later I asked Hera to explain what she now thought had actually happened to her during that first night. Here is her reply.

I did not know it at the time, but that was my first encounter with a Michelangelo-Reaper. And I was very lucky, because it was more concerned with establishing its domain than in being familiar with an entity such as myself, otherwise I might have been in trouble. I was lucky it came when it did, as it gave me assurance.

When it encountered me it paused because I was, after all, strange, and it examined me with the same casual interest that you or I might use when we find an interesting pebble. When it was satisfied, or because it had more urgent things to attend to, it put me back because, you see, it did not understand me.

Had I stayed another night it might have come back hunting. And that could have been bad news for me.

But that contact gave me a presence in the psychic world of Paradise, and at a deeper level than any other human has attained, except for those born on the planet like young Sasha Malik. By opening up my mind, it inadvertently ensured that my 'scent' was there.

This explains why later, when the Dendron was in need, it was able to contact me. So that also was a lucky accident.

There is a lot of 'lucky' in all of that.

The fact is, Hera was there. She was IN, and the pace of change on Paradise was hotting up.

10

The First Day

Foul becoming fair.

That was Hera when she woke up. The euphoria of the previous evening had faded and she was aware of violation. For a while she lay there, examining the feeling, turning it around in her head.

Memories, no matter how innocent, are private (she reasoned) and she did not know how much else of herself she might have revealed in those moments when she had hovered in the darkness with the alien presence wrapped round her. Memories, she reminded herself, are not like objective recordings but are shaped by our imagination and our emotions. In which case Hera knew she had probably revealed all – love and hate and the difficult bits in between. Moreover, her sense of violation was complicated by an awareness that she had hoped for contact and had actively sought it. Otherwise, what the hell was she doing down here, hanging about? Given what she already knew of Paradise, why should she be surprised that contact, when it came, took this mental form? Had she hoped that the alien mind, to whom telepathy might be as routine as breathing or sleep to us, would politely ask permission before barging in? If so, how would it do this? In any case the alien mind of Paradise, whatever it was, would be based on a wholly different set of sensory assumptions, and nothing of hers could have meaning to it beyond the fact that she was alive and different. No, if you play with fire, you get burned. If you play with aliens you will find your sense of dignity challenged, for better or worse.

By the time she had worked her way through this chain of reasoning she found that she was more than a bit critical of herself. 'I've got to toughen up. Not take everything so personally. And what is more,' she added, 'I'm fed up with everything having a sexual slant.

Why do I do that? Violated? Ha! It didn't mess me about. I took a chance. I could have had my mind scoured and left as empty as a seashell. But that did not happen. Instead I yielded up a few nice memories, and if they revealed the depth of me, well so be it. I have nothing to hide. I am what I am. And they can take it or leave it. Alan?'

'Yes, Hera?'

'Coffee!'

She threw back the duvet, and as she moved heard the SAS respond to her being awake – the whisper of filters in the bed-chamber, the shower system warming up, the priming of the coffee machine and the fluttering sound of a meteorological report being received. Significantly absent was the news bulletin normally broadcast from the shuttle platform over Paradise.

Some time later, showered and dressed, Hera was conscious that her mind felt very clear and focused. Polished was the word she used. So perhaps the alien visit had released something in her. She felt a quick energy too, and wanted to be up and doing. Though doing what she was not yet certain. Her intuition told her not just to wait passively for a further communication, but to be active.

Hera ran lightly up the spiral stairs and into the main cabin. It was a brilliant sunlit day and she had to shield her eyes from the light. Outside, a stiff breeze was stirring the flowers of the Tattersall weeds, making them nod in a curiously human way. The only evidence of the energy wave she had seen pass through them was broken branches and some trees which remained twisted gro-tesquely and were now losing their leaves.

Breakfast was brief, and Alan signed his own death warrant when he said, 'Good morning, Hera. I let you sleep beyond your normal pattern as you were so late going to bed and your schedule does not indicate any pressing duties.'

'Thank you, Alan. Most considerate.'

She replied evenly in a tone which would, had she been among her ORBE workers, have sent them running for cover. For some time Hera had wondered whether she should suppress the circuits which gave the computer its human voice and solicitude. She was aware of how easily she had begun to talk to the machine as though it was a human, and the last thing she needed was a surrogate male to distract her.

'Alan?'

'Yes, Hera?'

'What do I do to change your presentation index?'

There was a slight pause – how subtle it was, how clever the programmers! – and then Alan's voice replied evenly, 'A full range of possibilities can be found by speaking the moclay Alanstyle.'

Hera pronounced the word Alanstyle clearly. Immediately a checklist of the ways in which Alan could be modified flashed up in the tri-vid screen in front of her. Within minutes, Alan was reduced to a silent but alert slave – his voice restricted to essentials.

'Shall we depart, Alan?' Hera asked, and waited. Normally Alan would have replied, but this time there was nothing. Not even a hum in the air. 'Begin pre-flight procedures,' she instructed.

Immediately the SAS came alive.

Pre-flight procedures were fully automatic. The SAS, in a soft neutral voice, announced the different systems as they logged in and became fully operational. Hera felt much more comfortable. She heard the magnetic bolts take hold throughout the whole SAS, anchoring charts to tables, dishes in the cleanser, clothes in closets, drawers and doors. There was a soft whine of hydraulics as the rotor blades came out of their protective cover, straightened and stiffened.

Moments later the twin blades began to turn, slicing the sunlight. Hera slipped her hands into the pilot gloves and the machine became an extension of her body. A slight pressure with her index finger and the SAS begin to lift. Smooth and easy. She guided the ship in a tight spiral.

Looking down, she could see the remains of the shuttle port dropping away beneath her. At 500 metres she held steady and then began to cruise towards the sea, following the supply road.

The journey took little more than a minute. Hera guided the SAS down over Ben Haroun Park, where the whistle reeds would still be piping in the morning. She flew slowly over the remains of New Syracuse. It was not even a ghost town – only the roads and foundations of houses remained. Still intact, however, was the long curving sea wall constructed during the early, prosperous days of

MINADEC to shelter a fashionable marina and its complement of tall yachts and pleasure boats.

Hera followed the line of the sea wall and then flew low over the chessboard squares which were all that remained of the ORBE precinct. She looked at the burned dark space where her office and the Shapiro Museum had stood and felt no strong emotion.

Moments later, the SAS kicked up a small sandstorm as it landed next to a concrete bunker. Hera left the engine running and the rotor blades turning slowly while she jumped down and went looking for Mack's booty. As he had promised, there was a crate containing bottles of wine and a demolition sack into which he had stuffed a few luxuries – tinned salmon, perfume, preserved dates, a ripe round cheese, spare sunglasses, a book of poetry, candles, matches, a first-aid kit and anchovies – as well as a combination knife and corkscrew.

The goods safely stored, Hera took one last look around. How still the scene – like the stage of a desolate theatre! Then, satisfied, she climbed back inside the SAS and closed the door, which hissed as it sealed. Seconds later the flyer hammered into the air and set a steadily rising course straight out over the sea.

Hera had decided she would revisit some of the places that had been important to her when she first arrived on Paradise. Thus, half an hour later, she was far out above Dead Tree Sea and hovering. She had reached a place called Jericho Rise, where the seabed was close to the surface and gave an anchorage to many marine plants. Immediately below her was a large colony of yellow lip kelp, the individual plants moving slowly in the water like eels, sliding under and over one another, pushed by the wind and their own small water jets.

Hera brought the SAS down in the middle of the feeding kelp, settling it gently on the surface of the sea. She opened the cabin door and sat on the extended steps with her feet in the water. Soon the small mouths of the lip kelp found her. The peculiar feeling as they nuzzled and fastened to her toes brought back memories.

One day, shortly after she had joined the ORBE project, Hera had taken a cutter and, along with a few friends, sailed out from New Syracuse to the Jericho Rise.

There she had donned an aqualung and slipped into the warm clear water. Her last adventurous swimming had been on Mars, where the water in the underground lakes was thick with salts, and visibility by headlamp was usually little more than a metre. Sometimes she'd had to climb over ice, trailing her lifeline. But here . . .

Being a strong swimmer, she deliberately headed directly into the midst of the kelp and let the small hungry mouths pluck at her. Swimming steadily, she came to where several arms of kelp joined together. There she dived, pulling herself slowly down the plant, until she came to the main stem. The small mouths, being surface feeders, detached as she went deeper. She was about ten metres down when the water became suddenly turbulent, spinning her round, and she felt a powerful tugging on the stem she was holding. She gripped tight. Looking down, Hera could see where the stem curved away below her and how it was bending round in the water like a thick yellow snake. Faintly she saw a large dark shape gradually rising from the depths. Hera kept her nerve. *There are no sharks or octopuses on Paradise,* she reminded herself. And she told herself that repeatedly as the giant organism rose closer.

Hera had read about this plant. She knew she was seeing the giant bellows of the kelp, the organ which drew water in and expelled it with force. It would rise until close to the surface, where it would bask for a while in the warm water before sinking again to the bottom, where it would pump steadily for an hour or so before rising again . . . and so on and on, in a cycle that would only end when the plant became too large for its foot to hold it in place on the seabed during a storm. Then it would tear loose and drift until marooned on a shore. The small individual yellow tubes would then detach and swim away to become, unless consumed, giant kelps in their own right. Hera knew all this. Even so, she was not prepared for the huge dark ventricle, twice the size of her own body, which opened in front of her face. When the ventricle closed there came a great jet of water which pushed her away, detaching her goggles and breaking her grip from the slippery stem. She tumbled in the water, and then let herself slowly rise to the surface, where again the small nuzzling mouths greeted her hungrily. She let them hold her and roll her on the surface before retrieving her goggles and swimming back to the cutter.

Afterwards, she often wondered what the kelp must have felt as it filtered the cells from her human body. Exotic food indeed.

Alien food to the kelp. And she had never quite rid herself of the notion that the heart of the kelp had risen to find out where the strange taste was coming from. Later, when she returned to ORBE HQ, Shapiro had pointed out that she had taken a silly risk. 'What,' he asked, 'might be the consequences if the kelp has now taken a liking to human cell tissue? Can you not see the headlines? KILLER KELP STALKS THE SHORELINE.' He had given her his old-fashioned look. 'Don't be fooled by this place, Hera. It is not a kindergarten like Mars. Our interaction with Paradise is complex.'

She had answered by pointing out that every time anyone breathed out, something of their organic nature entered the biosphere. 'Not to mention the miners and loggers who piss and shit wherever they want.'

'I know,' said Shapiro. 'That's what worries me. Does Paradise learn as well as give? If so . . .' He had never finished his sentence, preferring, in his irritating way, to be enigmatic.

Now, after half an hour playing with the kelp, Hera finally detached the small lips. She closed the cabin door and gave instructions for the autopilot to take off gently while she got dried.

When she again entered the control room they were hovering at 300 metres, and the kelp beds below looked like many small yellow nebulae with hundreds of swirling arms.

She flew on. Beyond the kelp the sea became choppy and blue, sure signs that they were above deep water. Blue sea, blue sky, clear horizon – Hera was suddenly filled with a tremendous optimism and a surging love for where she was and what she was doing. It felt right, and any residue of discomfort over what had happened the previous night had vanished.

Hera adjusted course slightly and steadily increased her speed until she reached the limit of the gyro blades. To go faster, the SAS needed to change its mode of flight, which it did. For a few seconds they glided and then, with a surge that pressed her back into her seat, the SAS leaped forwards, climbing as the jet unit took over. The course she had chosen would take her directly over Dead Tree Spit, a famous landmark she had not seen for many years.

Hera loved speed. *Free*, she thought. *And abandoned too.* She stretched her arms above her head.

Some time later, the autopilot sounded a cheerful bell and Hera came awake to find that she was now cruising slowly and approaching the dark rocky shore of Anvil. This was a harsh coast of hidden reefs and surging waves. It took the brunt of any storms that struck from the north-west. Since there were few safe anchorages, many ships had foundered here during MINADEC times.

Hera took over the controls and steered along the coast until she came to an inlet. This gave access to one of the few places where a ship could anchor. But you had to know the complicated tides. As so often on Paradise, when both moons pulled together the passage was closed by massive waves, which came thundering through, driving all before them, only to waste their energy on the quieter water within. The place was a graveyard.

Looking ahead, Hera could just see the first faint outlines of the Staniforths. These were the highest mountains on Paradise and permanently covered in snow. The peaks, floating serenely above the clouds, always reminded her of the mountains on a Chinese silk fan that her mother had owned, which decorated the wall of their small apartment on Io.

Beyond the cliffs a bay opened and at its centre was an island. This was what Hera had come to see. Standing on the highest point of the island were the ruined remains of a giant Dendron, a mighty *Rex peripatetica*, famous and unique, the so-called 'walking tree' of Paradise, now extinct. Its tall twin branches and broken stump still faced the passage to the sea defiantly. Hera flew around it slowly and then brought the SAS down to land on the shingle shore.

As part of her introduction to Paradise, Hera had been sent on an orientation visit to Pietr Z's famous umbrella tree plantation at Redman Lake. This was located just a short distance inland from the bay.

One morning, just before dawn, Pietr Z had come tapping at her window to tell her he was going to hike over the Scorpion Pass and down to the sea. Would she like to join him?

This was an unexpected honour. Pietr Z's knowledge of this part of Paradise was unrivalled. But he was also a man who loved his solitude and who would on occasions (and much to the exasperation of his wife) disappear into the wild hills and not emerge for a week, regardless of who was coming to see him. So Hera had caught him on a good day.

It was mid-morning when they finally reached the top of Scorpion

Pass. For the last fifteen minutes they had been climbing through mist and the only way they knew that they had crossed the pass was when the path levelled and then began to slope downwards. They could neither see nor hear the sea, but they could smell it.

'Bad water here,' said Pietr. 'Very bloody dangerous. Great slab waves, lift from nowhere. Come swilling at you with the speed of a running horse. You heed my words, young Hera, if ever you have to sail here, don't trust it. And don't bloody swim!'

He led the way down the steep winding path to the shore, where tiny waves lapped the sand peacefully. Pietr grunted. Then, almost as though he had willed it, one of the waves reared up and came tumbling up the shore and washed round Hera's ankles. Pietr spat into the sea. 'Don't trust it,' he said.

Part-way up the hillside, and well above the high-water mark, was a boathouse with a long slipway that led down to the water. Pietr led the way up through the brevet, and Hera admired the wiry strength of the old man as he climbed with a springy step. When they reached the boathouse, the mist was lifting and the sky was clearer, but little could be seen of the bay.

Inside the shed was one of the all-purpose ORBE cutters. Pietr waved for Hera to climb into the front and put on a life jacket. Pietr meanwhile, stood at the stern and prepared to winch the boat down into the water. 'Why so high?' asked Hera.

Pietr winked at her. 'When the bastard waves come in, the whole shore goes underwater. That's why I built it like this, and that's why I come out here once a month to make sure it is OK. There's twenty people still breathing thanks to this little boat.' He banged its side with his fist. Pietr was obviously proud of the winch mechanism. He had both designed and made it himself. 'Watch this, Hera.' Pietr eased the winch and allowed the cutter to slip slowly down towards the sea and then stop. 'Now imagine this. Bastard sea running. Waves coming up at you like mad dogs. Wind in your face. You have to judge your moment to enter, or they'll have you. You'll be upended and down under before you can piss yourself. So you watch. And when a wave is just passing, you let her go. And get your bloody revs up! Now hold on.'

So saying he released the dog shackle and let the boat accelerate down the last few metres into the sea. He laughed when he saw Hera's expression as the boat hit the water, and the screws, already whirling, drove it forward. 'You understand, young Hera? You have to be self-reliant to live out here. If there's only me to launch the boat and there's a real bastard sea running, and some poor bugger is out there clinging to driftwood, well the only way to get out through the surf is to hit it running. Today it's calm. Tomorrow we might have two-metre waves to deal with. The day after that, who knows? Mad bloody planet!'

He guided the boat out into the fog. Pietr was steering by compass, but he slowed every so often and stood up to peer at the sea in front of the cutter. Once he swung hard to starboard and the boat bumped against a huge submerged trunk that ran along its side with a harsh scraping sound. 'Bloody things move, you see. Currents always changing.' Pietr swore for a few moments in whatever language it was that he called native. Moments later they were free and again in open water. 'That was part of an old Dendron,' he said. 'When they get waterlogged, they only show about 5 per cent above water. So if you hit one, you know about it. There are a lot of them round here – a regular graveyard. Lots of other rubbish too, but they are the worst.'

Hera peered into the greyness, looking for any telltale ripples or small waves suddenly appearing on the flat surface. 'What do you mean a graveyard? Do you mean like people used to say with elephants? That they went to a special place to die?'

'Naw. Perhaps some of them got a bit adventurous and tried to walk over to Hammer and then got into trouble when the water got deep. Dendron couldn't turn quick. They weren't bloody goats. And if they lost their footing or got swept away there's nothing they could do. Just here the current runs up pretty fierce. Yes. And if the wind is from the north-west, it blows them in here. Once anything gets washed in here there's no way out. It's a bloody trap. Has been for millions of years. They're here till they rot. Tell you, Hera m'girl, if you want to make your fortune, just excavate down here. There'll be wishbones by the ton.' Wishbone was the fanciful name given to the girdle of tough flexible fibre which gave the Dendron its shape and allowed it to walk.

The cutter entered deeper water and Pietr increased speed. The boat began to pitch in the swell coming from the deep ocean. Hera was aware of a change in the light – the mist was blowing away – and then, for the first time, Hera saw the island towering in front of them, and there, at its top, just emerging from the mist, a pair of giant curved horns rearing up to the clouds. Absurdly, she was reminded of the twin towers of Chartres cathedral, until, when the mist lifted completely, she saw the monument for what it was: an old dead Dendron, twin trunks and a broken body.

'There he is,' called Pietr, 'The old man of the sea. Still on guard.' He steered the boat through the shallows around the island. When they were close, Hera slipped over the side and, holding the painter, guided the boat until it ground up onto the shingle shore. They pulled it up high and Pietr tied it to an iron post concreted between a pair of rocks. Then he led the way up a rocky path, which had been marked with splotches of white paint. As they climbed, the massive remains of the Dendron seemed to peer at them over the crest of the hill. However, it was only when they got to the top and were climbing the last few metres that its true size became apparent. The two front legs joined to form a giant arch which at its apex was some ten metres high. Hera stood under this, looking up. She could see the gentle curve of the twin trunks soaring up to where they were broken.

Pietr, out of breath, sat on a flat rock and watched. 'You wouldn't have stood there if it was alive,' he called. Hera grinned. She'd seen pictures of a Dendron when she was a little girl on Io, seen it running with its strange three-legged gait, stamping its back foot deep into the ground and rocking forward while the tall trunks flexed and the Venus tears rang like bells. Dendron could move fast when they had to.

Hera squeezed out between one of the front legs and the place where the Dendron had slumped as it died. She touched its side and was surprised at how prickly it was. Pietr saw her pull her hand back. 'Dendron aren't like most of the plants here,' he said. 'When the fibres dry out, they don't rot; they get sharp and brittle and then they flake. They must have carried a lot of minerals, eh?'

Hera nodded and walked round the Dendron, looking up to where its twin trunks ended bluntly. 'How tall was it when it was alive?'

'More than a hundred metres from pad to flag, I guess.'

'Quite a big one.'

'Not bad, but there was one measuring a hundred and thirty

metres seen up in northern Chain. Can you imagine something like that heaving its roots up out of the ground and setting off to find a mate?'

Hera laughed. 'How did it die?'

'Shot. Like most of them were. For sport and profit. The old folks reckon it was the crew of one of the barges sailing out of New Syracuse. One of the crew must've seen Old Man Dendron climbing up the hill here. This barge had some kind of gun with exploding shells. So these boys did some target practice. The first shot hit the crest. Completely blew it off. The Dendron was trying to turn when the second round hit it. *Bang*. Right there between the twin trunks, and that blew its lights out.'

'Someone should have blown their lights out.'

'Yeah, well. In all the times the Dendron were hunted, not one of them ever tried to fight back. The people who shot at them were hoping they'd put up a fight – in the interests of sport, you see. They made the mistake of thinking Dendron were like us, like animals. They weren't. They didn't have minds – well, not the way we think of them. They couldn't think, and so they couldn't come up with clever ideas like defending themselves. They just sat and took whatever hit them. And they died.'

'And now they are extinct.'

'Yep. And now they are extinct. Poor dumb buggers.'

As he spoke the sun broke strongly through the clouds. The dull grey of the Dendron became patterned with blue and green as though it had feathers or scales. Pietr Z kicked about in the shingle and scrub behind the Dendron. Eventually he stooped and picked up a long black thorn with a thick wavy stem, like a kris. 'Here,' he said, handing it to Hera. 'A memento of your visit. Part of the Dendron's crest. Now imagine that coming at you with a thousand tons of Dendron behind it. How is that for lovemaking, eh?'

Standing there now, many years later, looking at these pitiful remains, Hera felt the tears well up inside her. She had cried then too, on the way back to shore after her first visit, imagining the great Dendron walking, bright red flags waving at the very tips of their branches and the sharp tinkling sound as the Venus tears hit together. 'I hope a comet blazed in the sky when the last Dendron died,' she said.

Pietr cut the engine to idle and let the boat glide past the remains of a giant stump. 'Now there's a fine poetic thought,' he said, obviously surprised. 'And it is still only the afternoon.'

'The end of a species deserves a clamour!' said Hera. 'When beggars die there are no comets seen. The heavens themselves blaze forth the death of princes. Of all the plants of Paradise, the Dendron were surely the greatest. That's all. I wonder who saw the last one die?'

'Sadly,' said Pietr thoughtfully, 'we'll never know.' He started the engine.

Such then were Hera's memories as she climbed back into the SAS. The remains of the Dendron were far more decayed now than when she had last visited. Much of its rear pad had fallen away, revealing a gaping hole. The twin trunks had begun to break up. Deep fissures had opened across the back. The next gale could topple the entire thing and send it crashing down onto the shingle shore, where it would slowly break up in the tides. And that would be that.

Hera sent the SAS spiralling up and let it fly slowly over the bay towards the mainland. The sea was still littered with hulks. Wherever she looked she could see other debris too, far more modern and garish – dozens of blue plastic demolition cases which had probably blown off the wharf at New Syracuse, broken sheets of striped plastic, scraps of burned timber, the bottom of an upturned barge with a hole in it, broken bottles, an umbrella without its fabric, broken oars and hundreds of lengths of the bright red fibre used to truss up cargo for space and which here had become tangled and knotted among the trunks and branches at the water's edge. That stuff would last for ever. Everything had a pale brown lustre, the patina with which Paradise covered the things of Earth. She wondered how many other inlets there were around Paradise choked with the flotsam and jetsam of Disestablishment. Millions, she guessed, for Paradise was a planet of islands and bays. It occurred to her that here was a job if she wanted one – a fine, sad, solitary job, token indeed, but rich with meaning: to compile a visual record of the state of the planet as left; a statement revealing the true face of Disestablishment.

Hera circled the bay and was pleased to see that at least Pietr Z's boathouse and slipway were still intact. It was probable that Pietr had never registered it as a building and so it had been overlooked by the demolition crews. A Tattersall weed had grown right up over the boathouse, sending its long ropy arms and flowers down the walls. Left to grow, it would end up crushing or tearing the building apart.

Hera lifted quickly to clear the trees at the margin of the bay and then flew over the low dunes and turned inland to follow a narrow ravine. Below her was the road that she and Pietr had walked so many years ago. It had been well maintained until the Disestablishment. Now it was overgrown in parts but still visible winding up and following the twists and turns of a creek.

Hera had decided to visit Pietr Z's umbrella tree plantation. She, like many in the ORBE team, had never accepted that Pietr was dead. The thought kept recurring – the hope really – that Pietr might have survived out in the wild forest. If anyone could, he could. But she was realistic too. ORBE had mounted a search for Pietr Z as soon as he had gone bush after the Disestablishment was announced, and not a trace of him had been found. He had often said that he would never leave Paradise and that if anyone tried to make him retire he would retire himself. Perhaps he had simply decided that the end had come.

The SAS flew over the Scorpion Pass and began to descend. The breeze which had blown in from the sea had dropped away. Only the wind from the rotor blades moved the treetops, which otherwise stood stiff and still.

The valley opened before her. At its end was Redman Lake, surrounded by hills and with the Staniforth Mountains as background. This was one of the pictures that the ORBE project had used to advertise its operation. The lake was already in shadow and the mountain tops were pink. Evening was falling quickly, as it did in these parts. Hera let the SAS drift slowly down the valley. No rush. She would spend the night here.

Redman Lake was small by Paradise standards. Collecting different kinds of water plant had been one of Pietr's hobbies, and the lake contained examples from most parts of Paradise. In the midst of these and far out in the middle of the water was a floating island built up over many years, and on this Pietr had built his small house. It was reached by a wooden walkway which zigzagged out from some shyris rushes at the side of the lake. But most often Pietr had used a small runabout which Hera could see still moored to the deck outside the house. She guessed that Hemi had deliberately removed the name and location of Redman Lake Station from the demolition manifest so that it would be left in peace as a monument to old Pietr.

At the margin of the lake Hera studied the tall swaying umbrella trees, with their glossy purple domes from which streams of heavy sap slopped and dripped. Many of the trees were just reaching their full height, and it was now that they were beginning to extend their mature domes. The older the tree, the bigger the dome – that was the rule. Beneath them, permanently drenched in the sap, she could see the little ones called spikes. They grew up drinking the sap.

Hera banked the SAS and flew slowly around the margin of the lake. How she wished to see Pietr come out of his house, hand raised to shade his eyes, wondering who had come to disturb his privacy. But nothing moved. The door remained shut. There was no drift of smoke from the chimney.

Hera landed on the SAS platform which floated on the surface amid the dark bladders of the talking jenny. Disturbed, the jenny began gulping and voiding. When Hera opened the door the air reeked, and the flatulent calling of the talking jenny was deafening as Hera made her way along the swaying walkway to the deserted house.

The door was not locked. Revealed inside was the old man's cabin. It had grown with his habits. Modern equipment stood on old packing cases. The calendar pinned on the wall was three years out of date, but had been updated by hand. One corner was filled by a big soft-looking double bed covered with a brightly coloured woollen bedspread made by Pietr's wife. Beside the bed stood a wooden bookcase, its shelves bowed with too many volumes. The floor was strewn with rushes which, when walked upon, gave off a perfume reminiscent of cinnamon. A sliding window stretched from floor to ceiling and looked out across Redman Lake towards the umbrella seedbeds with the mountains beyond them. Tonic was rising, creating a silver path across the water. Facing the window was one of Pietr's famous armchairs – famous because he would carve them to order and to the dimensions of the occupant. This one was carved from the pad of a long-departed Dendron. He had oiled and sanded the wood, making it smooth and silky to the touch. On the table beside the chair was an open book, an ashtray and a water pipe.

Pietr Z, like Professor Shapiro, enjoyed smoking the dried flowers of the calypso lily.

Old men and their pipes, thought Hera, and was suddenly overcome by a wave of sadness for old Pietr Z. Everything she saw, everything she looked at, reminded her of him, of his funny way of talking and his thick accent and his sensitive eyes, never merrier than when teasing her, but still a man who knew how to listen. She began to cry quietly. Pietr had been a good friend and had stood by her on many occasions. And now he was out there somewhere in an unmarked grave. He had given so much, and had loved this place with a single, unwavering and uncomplicated devotion. 'God bless you, Pietr, wherever you are,' she murmured. On impulse she picked up the book he had been reading – *Tales of Paradise* by Sasha Malik. She slipped a bookmark into the pages, closed the book and put it into her pocket. She wished there was more she could do, but she couldn't think of anything, and so she sat in the armchair for a few minutes while the grief worked its way through her.

Hera shivered. Evening was advancing and the temperature had dropped quickly. She glanced out through the window. Tonic had a ring of light around it and high wispy cloud had gathered in the hills. Rain tomorrow, she guessed.

As she said goodbye to the room, she heard a mutter of thunder in the hills. She closed the door to the cabin firmly. She knew that neither she nor Pietr would ever return. Everything was left for Paradise to dispose of.

Hera hurried down the causeway, anxious suddenly to be back inside the SAS.

Moments later, inside but with the raucous noise of the talking jenny still ringing in her ears, she looked out from the windows of the SAS. Pietr's house was rocking gently in the evening breeze. Inside the cabin the automatic lights had come on and shone out across the water.

11

The Call

Hera was up by dawn.

By the time the sun had risen above the Staniforths she was standing at the edge of the SAS landing platform, fully kitted out in a survival suit and with a machete slung across her back for good measure.

The rain that had come in the night had now passed, but the wind was still strong. Hera watched it send swirling cat's paws scampering up the meadow towards the umbrella tree plantation about a mile away. The wind was also carrying winged seeds. They arrived in clouds, lifted from the Kithaeron Hills and the High Staniforths. The seeds spun and fluttered on white and blue wings and were so dense that at times she could not see the further shore of the lake. They landed on the surface and floated, moving with the waves so that Pietr's little hut looked as though set in a freezing sea. They swirled round Hera, plastering her survival suit. They clung like coloured snow to the windows of the SAS.

Looking east across the water, Hera could just see the tall umbrella trees flexing, buffeted by the wind, bending and nodding like spectators at a carnival caught in a shower of rain. When the trees dipped, they revealed their gleaming grey domes and heavy sap running in slow white waves and falling like lather onto the plants beneath. Wherever she looked, she saw an active scene. Everything seemed alive, busy even. This was Paradise untroubled, as it had been for millennia. But the weather was worsening and Hera knew that if she wanted to inspect the umbrella tree plantation before the rain came or the wind worsened, she needed to start moving.

Hera's plan for the day was simple. First she would work her way to the plantation and see how the tree nursery was faring.

From there she would be able to see down to where the Tattersall weeds had encroached on the experimental seedbeds. However, getting to the plantation proved difficult. The pathways over the water meadow were defined by yellow plastic mesh which both floated and was held taut on posts. Originally established as a temporary measure, the plastic paths had become permanent despite Hera's offer of funds to establish a proper walkway. Although the surface shifted like the deck of a ship, walking *was* possible, as old Pietr Z often used to demonstrate. He would walk with a graceful gliding motion, almost as if he were cross-country skiing. Any ORBE apprentice working with Pietr had to master this art, and usually did, especially after falling two or three times into the talking jenny and the soft stinking ooze which was waiting on all sides.

Before her, the posts supporting the plastic mesh followed a wide arc, leading to the heart of the plantation. Occasionally the path divided, with a new arm curving away, heading to distant corners of the plantation.

In some places the talking jenny had sprouted right up through the mesh and was impossible to avoid. The name talking jenny was a euphemism. The plant possessed a soft brown cigar-sized fermentation bladder which floated on the surface. To feed, the bladder sucked in floating seeds with a gentle peristalsis. These it transformed into nutrients and gas. When it had finished digestion, it expelled the stinking residue as a spray with a raucous flatulent sound. During the previous night the talking jenny had fed well, filling millions of fermentation sacks with the fluttering seeds. Wherever Hera looked, there were small fountains of brown sputum staining the air. It was impossible to avoid being sprayed.

Almost an hour later, bemerded but unbowed, Hera stood close to one of the umbrella trees – a true giant. It was moving with the wind and she could hear the stress in its trunk, like a ship straining against a wharf. She waited until a column of the slimy, bubbly sap had fallen and then stepped smartly under the vast umbel. Here she was safe. The quality of the sound changed and the raw noise of the talking jenny became muted. At some time Pietr had carved a simple armchair into the roots facing down to the lake. Hera was glad of it. Survival suits were fine garments and had saved many lives but, like all such, they left something to be desired when it came to getting rid of sweat and body heat. Hera opened all the vents and lifted her arms, linking her hands over her head.

From here she could see the purple spikes and cups of the saplings which would, in the fullness of time, become tall umbrella trees in their own right. There were hundreds of them, all growing in the tree's drip line. When she looked across at the other mature trees, it was the same story. They all had their families gathered about them. Many of the offspring would not survive, simply because of competition, but those that did would be strong and vigorous and so the forest would advance and gradually take over the land. In the days before MINADEC, this entire valley had been a marsh filled with the majestic trees.

Occasionally, as she sat looking at the young plants, one of the spikes would slowly unfurl its leaves and then open like a clam. It would stay open until some of the rich nutrient from above had filled it, and then would close. The flow of sap never stopped, and so eventually, despite the wind favouring one direction, the waiting cups were all filled while others opened. The ubiquitous Tattersall weed was greatly in evidence, its blue flowers clustered round the smallest of the saplings.

As she sat, Hera became aware of a change in the air about her. The surface of the lake was blue again, reflecting the sky. The seeds that had covered it in the morning had all gone, sunk or eaten, and the wind too had faded away. The jenny were quiet and Hera opened her helmet and breathed deeply. It was a scene of perfect peace. Even the blue of the Tattersall weeds had a rightness about it, though they stood like an invading army, knee-deep in the experimental seedbeds.

Time to move! Cooler, Hera scrambled down over the roots to where a new section of the walkway began. This was called the Avenue and ran right through a stand of the tallest trees before heading back into the lake and entering the experimental park. *Walking with giants,* she thought as she glide-walked along. *I'm walking with giants!*

The last umbrella tree she visited was indeed one of the giants and its ribbed dome spread far out over the marsh. Looking across the lake, she could just see the SAS on its pad, shining in the sunlight. She touched the control panel on her arm and saw its beacon light flash once in acknowledgement. All was well.

Hera had just passed the tree's drip line when she heard what sounded like a trumpet call, high and clear. The sound startled her and she stopped. The single call was joined by other notes in quick succession until together they formed a dissonant chord. The overall pitch changed too, sometimes diving, at other times soaring up until the sound was lost to her . . . only to begin again with a low growl.

It was the 'pipes' of the High Staniforths – the wind blowing over the wide, open mouths of long-dead plants called tuyau which grew like giant vines in the mountains. The final chord held steady. It was not unlike the sound of an accordion as it is slowly squeezed to silence. That itself was a warning. The music had stopped because the pipes would now be clogged again with snow. Bad weather coming.

And in that moment, completely without warning, Hera felt something strike her from above. It might have been a sack of eels or a bucket of tripe. It completely covered her head and some of the material slopped over her face and down inside her collar. It flowed heavily over one arm and slipped to the ground. Surprised, she screamed, staggered forward, tripped and, in trying to recover her balance, fell off the narrow walkway and into the marsh.

It was her training on Mars that saved her. She relaxed as she fell. She gasped air before her head was engulfed. She did not struggle, for that might have entrapped her in the strong tangled roots of the jenny. She kept her eyes closed and her breath tight. Her helmet with its built-in camera fell away. Only when she felt her shoulder touch the soft ooze of the bottom did she gently push upwards. She let her buoyancy lift her slowly through the viscous liquid until her head bumped against the rough plastic underside of the walkway. Reaching out she was able to find the edge and steadily guide herself until her head was out from under the walkway. She could not stand but, with head bent back and lifting herself partially onto the edge of the walkway, she was just able to breathe. And that first breath was very heaven.

Everything was slippery. The stalks and bladders of the talking jenny gave no support, but began to void. The survival suit was heavy, and getting heavier, for the weight of the falling sap had torn open some of the seals and water was entering. When she tried to lift herself, her legs floated up under the walkway, pushed by the current flowing towards the lake.

Hera held tight, just breathing steadily. She was safe as long as she didn't panic. She surveyed her options. She could call up the SAS. But then what? She would still have to climb ... She could work her way hand over hand through the marsh, but the current was strong and with the heavy suit dragging ... Her third option was to abandon the survival suit and climb up onto the walkway. She could then make her way slowly back to the SAS. This was the option she chose.

With her chin clamped over the edge of the mesh, Hera removed the SAS command pad and pushed it safely onto the walkway. Then she simply pulled open the seals and unzipped the suit. A few wriggles and it was off her shoulders. Once her arms were out, she was able to push the suit down and away from her. The water felt suddenly cold but at least she could move freely. She limbered herself up from the ooze until the top half of her body was lying on the plastic. Two more kicks and she felt the legs of the suit slip off her feet. Freedom! With a final pull, she was kneeling on the walkway, her head pressed down on the SAS control pad to make sure it could not slip away. She was safe, and as though that were the cue, her senses came back. She could again smell the putrid air, for she had woken the dormant jenny with her struggles, and taste the foul water that had run into her nose and past her lips. But she was alive.

Hera stood up slowly, breathing deeply. She watched as the talking jenny gradually reoccupied the place where she had been. A minute after climbing out there was no sign of her presence or her struggle in the water. The survival suit and helmet with its precious camera, despite their buoyancy, never emerged. *How easily Paradise robs me of the things of Earth,* she thought. And then she laughed. What would Old Pietr have said if he could have seen her standing there in just her underwear?

Hera was tempted to go straight back to the SAS, but some grit in her nature, some determination to make up for lost time, made her move on down the pathway towards the seedbeds and the bobbing blue flowers of the Tattersall weeds. The air became a strange amalgam of umbrella tree slop, talking jenny eructation and the sweet perfume of the Tattersall weed.

Hera came to the place where the walkway divided and the regeneration seedbed began. Wind-driven pumps delivered frothy sap to a long line of small protected plants. Hera came to the first, and it was dying. The pumps were still working vigorously, delivering their measured quantity of sap, but the sap fell on open mouths slack and unable to close. It dribbled down and into the marsh. Plants that had their spike closed were turning black and beginning to buckle and droop. Hera walked along the line. She passed a thousand plants, and all were dying.

So much for a bold experiment! How pathetic they looked, these drooping plants! Why had they started to wilt now? The thought came to her that perhaps they had died because Pietr Z had died. There was no denying that sometimes clocks stopped, pets died and pictures fell when someone who loved them died.

She came to the last plant in the row. Its cup was open but the stem was broken and black so that it looked for all the world like a hanged man. The desolation of this plant summed up them all. Hera sank down and stared at it. *How sad! How bloody, bloody, sad!* It was an indictment of all that had gone wrong on Paradise.

How long she sat there she did not know, but her reverie was suddenly interrupted by a call from the SAS. 'Meteorological report. Storm system building in the Staniforths. High winds and rain from the north-west forecast. Present location insecure. Imperative move to a more protected landing.'

Hera roused herself and looked about her. The mechanical voice came at her again, and louder. 'Meteorological report. Storm—'

'I hear you,' she called. She looked at the mindless nodding pumps feeding the dead plants. 'I'm on my way back now. There's nothing I can do here.'

Hera stood up painfully, for she had begun to stiffen while seated on the mesh. The path she was on would soon intersect with the one she had taken that morning. She could see the SAS with its beacon flashing.

Signs of the coming storm were already all about her. A darkening of the sky. A shiftiness in the breeze. A deadness in the air. The talking jenny had begun to void in earnest, perhaps in anticipation of another seed feast.

149

Hera reached out and touched the dead umbrella sapling with her fingers. That small touch changed its balance and it collapsed forward across her arm, fell into the marsh and slowly sank. They would all fall in the coming storm. Paradise was cleansing itself.

Still bemused, Hera glide-walked her way down the path towards where a clump of Tattersall weeds stood tall amid the former seedbeds. As she approached, she saw one of the weeds jerk stiffly and then become still again. She was immediately on her guard, remembering the energy wave that had shaken the plants on her first night alone. She regretted the loss of the machete.

But as she approached, she noticed that the Tattersall weeds were growing in clusters. What's more, they were gathered round the places where the umbrella spikes had been planted, as though feeding. Despite the urgency of her situation, Hera's curiosity got the better of her. She approached warily. Gently she lifted one of the tangled arms of a Tattersall and was able to peer into the space within the plant. Her face was very close to one of the big blue flowers, but it was not its perfume that made her heart race.

Within the cluster of plants she had expected to see the pump working and a dead, black stump. But the pump was gone, broken by a Tattersall branch, and the flow of nutrient had stopped. In its place, growing vigorously, was an umbrella tree spike. It was already quite tall. Tough-looking roots had grown laterally out from the stem and had wrapped firmly round the lowest branches of the Tattersall for support. Higher up, the spike of the umbrella tree was partly open, like the mouth of a fledgling in the nest, and thousands of small fibrous roots had grown out from the mouth and pierced the upper branches of the Tattersall weeds. Where these entered the trees they had created running wounds. Even as Hera watched, one of the wounds bled sap which dribbled down and was hungrily absorbed into the root. Not only was the umbrella spike using the Tattersall weed for support, but it was feeding upon it. The invader was itself invaded.

Symbiosis is common in Nature, but where was the advantage to the Tattersall? To Hera's eyes it looked as if the weeds had deliberately set themselves up here in order to help the umbrella spikes. But (and it was a big but), if they had grown here deliberately then it suggested altruism, and that was distinctly rare in nature.

Hera could see that the Tattersall weeds were no longer vigorous.

She touched one of the thorns and it was soft, like the thorn on a young rose. The plants would undoubtedly die as the umbrella spike drank their sap. Then presumably new and bigger Tattersall weeds would take their place, to be devoured in turn. She looked down. They were already there, new Tattersall weeds, springing up.

How many Tattersall weeds would have to sacrifice themselves before the young umbrella tree began to create its own sap? Thousands. But that did not matter. There *were* hundreds of thousands in the nearby hills. The umbrella trees would survive. What she was witnessing here could be replicated wherever the star-shaped waterborne seeds of the umbrella tree could lodge and where there was a Tattersall on hand to serve as wet nurse.

Carefully Hera lowered the branch of the Tattersall weed and stepped back. The implications of what she had seen for the future of Paradise were enormous. Paradise was looking after its own.

'Priority warning.' The voice of the SAS was loud in her ear. 'Emergency rescue procedures will commence in one minute. Imperative return to base.' The storm was building with alarming speed. The Kithaeron Hills were already blotted from sight. The whole world was becoming abnormal.

'I'm on my way,' shouted Hera. 'Begin take-off procedures. Be ready to lift off as soon as I'm inside.'

She ran down the walkway. The Tattersall weeds gave her some protection, but when she came out into the open she could feel the full bluster of the wind. The talking jenny rose and fell in waves. The sky was a jumble of lowering clouds which seemed to move in two directions at once.

She came to the place where two paths joined. Brilliant flashes of lightning were followed moments later by a tearing crack of thunder, as though the sky was filled with stones banging together. In front of her she could see the SAS, its blades turning steadily, its beacon flashing. It was rocking on the platform, tilted by the wind. Then the first rain started, and it came like arrows. More lightning, almost above her now. Two flashes met horizontally, and at the point where they collided a brilliant violet star was created and slid slowly down the sky while the thunder roared and rolled.

The walkway was now heaving up and down in the waves and she was sure it would tear loose before long. She could no longer walk upright so she crawled, gripping the mesh with her fingers. *Only about fifty metres to go.* The wind veered round and came from behind, pushing her while the mesh heaved and strained. Then she was climbing, pulling herself up onto the pitching landing platform and running crab-like for the door, which stood open. She threw herself inside, shouting, 'Go, go, go.' The door slammed and the engine roared and Hera was pinned to the ground as the SAS lifted and banked and ran before the wind, its twin rotors hammering.

This was the worst journey Hera had ever experienced. She scrambled into the shower cubicle but could do nothing but hold on while the SAS dipped and dived and shuddered. She managed to slip her arms through the webbing of a safety harness and grip tight. Once the SAS dropped, like a stone down a well, but the autopilot, responding faster than any human, brought it round and into the wind, and its engines throbbed and the whole craft shook, but it began to gain height again.

This was what the SAS ships were built for, and why the automatic landing and navigation computers were so expensive. Every circuit would be involved as Alan calculated probabilities and stress factors – always mindful of the vulnerability of the small speck of life that stood, braced and frightened, in the shower cubicle. The engine beat its way through the storm, occasionally dipping, but always rising again and slowly gaining altitude.

Once they took a broadside hit, as though struck by a wave, something that came swirling out of the dark clouds, but that marked the beginning of the end of the storm for them. Thereafter the buffeting, while still considerable, gradually diminished. Hera was able to make her way up to the control room. She found they were very high. Higher than she had ever flown before in an SAS. Perhaps at the limit of what an SAS could accomplish. Looking down, she could see the storm racing below her, like a wide grey river containing within it curling black eddies. The SAS was flying across the tops of the clouds, following a diagonal path. 'Where are you making for, Alan?' she asked.

The reply took the form of a change in the navigation screen. The screen flickered erratically, but she could see they were heading down the rift valley and would seek shelter behind the St Louis Mountains. A place called Damien's Gully was highlighted. It was close to the site of one of the early homesteads where an emergency landing pad was located. Then the screen cut out.

'Are we badly damaged?'

There was a pause and the Alan's peaceful voice spoke. 'Small damage, so far.'

'How serious?'

'Nothing I can't fix. Nothing structural. Some circuits.'

'Will we make it?' There was no answer. 'Ignore that question.'

They flew on in silence. The buffeting now ceased altogether as they moved away from the storm and began to descend.

Music started, but it was scratchy and the tones were all wrong.

'Nice try, Alan, but stop it.' The music cut out. 'So tell me, Alan. What is the damage? What happened?'

There was a long pause. When Alan's voice came it was slow. 'Detailed report. Servo coupling links to FIX 387-8 slave monitor malfunction at—'

'Hey,' cut in Hera. 'I didn't mean that. Cancel it. Just give me the broad picture.'

There was another long pause and then Alan's voice, speaking normally, said, 'I think you would say we were lucky.'

'Lucky? I thought you autopilots didn't deal in luck, just probabilities.'

Long pause. 'Very well, *you* were lucky. If you had been a few minutes later, the 95 per cent probability is that I would have been blown off the landing pad and into the mire. There is a 99 per cent probability that I would have been rolled by the wind, and although I am strong, I cannot take off when I am on my side in water. Without me to shelter you, there is a 75 per cent probability that you would have been drowned. But that game is dead, because it did not happen. We were struck by lightning, several times, but our chances of survival improved with every foot of altitude we gained.'

'We dropped suddenly.'

'Inversion trap over the Kithaeron Hills. We fell to within fifty feet of the ground. But I found good air. And we climbed up and entered the storm again. That was when I lost the domestic circuits.'

'Did you send out a mayday?'

'Yes, when I thought we would crash.'

'So they will be sending a rescue team from the—'

'I cancelled the mayday when I knew we were safe.'

'Good.'

They lapsed into silence. Hera decided she could take a little more human warmth and adjusted the Alanstyle settings accordingly. When she asked, 'What is our ETA at Damien's Gully?' it took a while for Alan to reply, and the voice was still slow, but warmer.

'Well, if I keep constant speed, and there are no more problems, I should have us down in about half an hour. I'll need an hour of shutdown for repairs, and we could be back on our way by evening. That is unless you want to stay . . . .'

'I'll decide later.'

'Whatev—'

'Can I take a shower?'

'Yes, but the water will be cold. Sorry.'

'I'll cope.'

'And don't ask me to make a hot cup of tea.'

Hera had not realized how dirty she was until she saw the water on the floor of the shower. It was brown from the talking jenny. The mucus from the umbrella trees had dried like rubbery glue, and when she pulled it off, she found that her skin underneath was blotchy and puffed up. This was nothing new and there was a lotion in the first-aid cabinet that she could rub in.

The cold water flowed onto the back of her head, dividing her hair and coursing over her shoulders. What relief that brought! She had had two lucky escapes this day – several more if Alan was to be believed. And she had made one momentous discovery. Not bad for a second day. That deserved a celebration. She closed her eyes, turned and lifted her face to the water and let it pour over her eyes and nose.

That movement, while she did not open her mouth, reminded her of the dead umbrella plant she had seen. Remembering this brought her what she later came to call a 'moment of small enlightenment'. She explained this as follows.

It may have been simple reaction – relief at being safe – or the fact that I had witnessed something that I thought was close to a miracle, but the faces of those two plants, the dead one I had sat before in such sadness, and the magnificent live one that was growing with the Tattersall weed . . . well, both fused in my mind. For a moment I became, as it were, both of them. That, in turn, became my moment of small enlightenment, for suddenly I saw them as two alternatives. The polarity sparkled before me: one side spiralling up to infinity and light, the other coiling down to darkness and death. Darkness and light. Hope and despair. Yes or no. Knowledge or oblivion. There are so many ways of saying it. I saw then that it is all in the choosing and oh I wanted life and love and to be part of this great tumultuous change that was taking place on Paradise. It quite overpowered me.

And then it was gone, as a vision, but the memory lingered on.

Moments later Hera was working lotion into the angry red blotches on her skin and humming when she heard the change in pitch as the SAS dropped lower and then the bump as they landed. The voice of Alan came to her.

'Closing down . . . Suggest . . . food in freezer. Repairs now . . . No distractions.'

'Point taken. Will do. Let me know when you are finished.'

There was no reply. Alan had gone.

One by one she heard the fans stop and the gurgle as the water pumps lost pressure. The doors slid open and locked and then the lights blinked out.

Hera did not bother to get dressed, but just threw a wrap around her shoulders. Through the open door she could see the warm sunlight and smell the crushed brevet where the SAS had landed. To stretch on that bright blue and green carpet would do her good, she decided. She had a lot to think about. So, having collected what she needed from the dark kitchen, she stepped outside.

Again in her own words:

I was feeling giddy. Safety after danger does that, you know. And being naked outdoors was fun too – nice but naughty, and not something I did normally. I spread a tablecloth on the brevet and set out a glass and plate and some cold food and, of course, one of the bottles of wine that Mack had given me. I did everything with great deliberation. Everything, even the most trivial act, the pulling of a cork, the coldness of the bottle when it accidentally touched my thigh, everything seemed filled with significance. I was safe. I was alive. I was not a young woman – but I felt young.

They had landed in a clearing above the river. Looking down, Hera could see the meandering Damien Stream and the ruins of an old shilo. A watermill was still in place and turning, though whatever it had been built to drive was long gone.

Hera poured the wine and ate some fruit. She lay back in the sun and wondered for the first time for quite a long time – and somewhat to her amusement – what it would be like if she had a man on hand to share things with. But then, with that fond thought in mind, as she lay back, glass in hand, enjoying the fact of being alive, naked and longing, from nowhere it seemed . . . the planet spoke to her.

We are approaching an important moment in Hera's story – a moment which was the cause of heated discussion between us. Here are the very words that Hera spoke as I recorded them, sitting in the calm of my study.

Hera The planet spoke to me – it was unmistakable. Don't look so surprised, Olivia. It spoke . . . not just to my ears, not just to my mind, but to all of me in one divine voice and in one divine moment. It was my name that was said. Hera.

Olivia How did you know it was the planet speaking?

Hera I just did. It was unmistakable. If you had heard—

Olivia Ah yes, but I didn't.

Hera It was a two-way thing. You know that when someone speaks your name you have an involuntary reaction. Emotional. It could be pleasure or . . . whatever. When I heard the voice, I reacted with knowledge. It was not a strange voice. It was a voice I think I had heard before but never distinctly. I think it was always there but I had not been able to hear it before.

Olivia But now you were on the right wavelength?

Hera Yes. Something like that. I think intuition has something to do with it too. I remember when I was a student reading a paper about Paradise and I got this tingly feeling. So even then something was happening, but I didn't know what. We usually don't know, do we?

Olivia Like falling in love.

156

Hera I was like one of the girls who used to drop pebbles into a pool at full moon to see the face of the man they would marry. They knew they had fallen in love already; they just didn't know who with.

Olivia Women gamble on happiness too often.

Hera Olivia, stop it! So when I heard the voice it was like a voice I had known for a long time.

Olivia Was it a man's voice?

Hera Yes. No. Not really. But not a woman's voice either. But I know what you are driving at. It was deeply sexual. That's what you're wondering, isn't it? At least my response was. It warmed me as a woman. I just couldn't help myself. I was caught by surprise. The voice was like a shower of golden rain . . . so was my response, in a manner of speaking. (PAUSE) Why are you looking at me like that?

Olivia I am thinking your name should be Danäe not Hera.

Hera I thought of that too. God, they had the truth of things, who-ever first composed those old stories. You're thinking of the legend aren't you? Danäe, mother of Persus, who was locked in a tower by her father, yes? And Zeus came to her disguised as a shower of golden rain. Is that the story? Well take it as literal. But don't get too hung up on the sexual side of things, Olivia. Everything in our life can be seen as sexual . . . but it is what that leads us to that finally matters – at my age anyway. And in my case I felt my eyes were opening. The process which began when I was a girl and which accelerated during all the things that happened to me at the ORBE project at the Space Council, at Anchor Hold and in the night alone on Paradise . . . all, all simply came together. The planet speaking simply continued the process. Even now.

Olivia I hope it never lets you down.

Hera How can it let me down. It is in me now. No matter what. Even after everything that has happened. But there is something else you must know. And this was new. It's nothing to do with feeling good or complete or sexy. I was aware of pain too. Not in me. No. Not my pain. But pain in the voice. A discordant note. A stain . . . I don't know how to tell you.

Olivia Were you hearing the damage done to Paradise?

Hera Yes. Partly. But this was something more specific, like a cry in the night. I know now that this was the first stirring of the Dendron. It was aware of me.

Olivia We'll come to that later. One last question. Now, here, at this very moment, sitting here with me years later and with all that has happened to you, do you still believe that it was the voice of the planet that spoke to you, or was it something inside you trying to get out?

Hera It was both.

Olivia I was afraid you'd say that.

Hera In those few moments, sitting in a meadow on an alien world, I received the purest communication that I was capable of receiving at that time, and it spoke to me in the only language I could understand. The voice warmed me then, and it still does, even now. It was like the golden rain of Danäe, or a golden light inside me, or beautiful shimmering music. It, whatever *it* is, had enlarged me so that I could understand – and so I did . . . well partly. There was a reason I was there at that time. I understood as much as I could. And if I had understood more the knowledge would have destroyed me, like putting hot water into a cold glass. I would not be here now. I would be insane or with O'Leary, or a stiff and lacquered little corpse on Paradise.

Olivia But now? What can you hear now?

There was a long pause. I saw Hera drift away. My question had caught her off guard. I saw her eyes dart and flicker as though waking up in a bright light, and her lips purse, and then the black stains on her face became more pronounced. Hectic. Finally she mumbled something and moments later she sighed and her eyes closed. When she came back to herself, she was tired.

Hera You must not do that to me, Olivia. You must not put me at risk. You and your questions. You are worse than all the scientists in Christendom. What would you do if I died before the book was finished? (AT THIS POINT SHE SMILED AT ME WEARILY AND SEEMED TO LOOK THROUGH ME.) But Paradise is still there, and is changing, and they are all alive, so all is as well as can be expected.

I heeded the warning. I did not press her to explain further. And there we must leave our discussion. I am sure an entire library could be written about the complexities of communication with the alien, and the common ground which must be discovered before any communication can take place. I know that the demanding of proof can be a kind of blindness. But, having accepted the enigmas of the fractal, I wonder what could be stranger? Like many of you perhaps, I wish I could venture to Paradise and witness it for myself.

We return to Hera on Paradise. She is sitting in the meadow, naked and with a glass of unsipped wine in her hand. The echoes of the voice she has heard inside her are slowly fading.

Hera sat for a while, in that present moment – holding it, unwilling to let it go.

And the next thing she heard was music. Bach. Toccata and Fugue in D Minor no less. It came from the open door of the SAS. This was Alan's way of telling Hera that the repairs were done, the SAS was ready.

She smelled coffee too, and that was his way of saying that normal service had been resumed. Hera stood up and wrapped the tablecloth round her. Hera is not sure why she did this, but it definitively marked the return to her habitual self.

In truth she felt a bit let down – a bit, I suppose, empty, unfulfilled. She wanted more, but once again nothing tangible had been communicated except a sense of delight, as well as that fine thread of pain she mentions. Most positive was the realization that communication of a kind had taken place. It was a kinder communication too ... kinder than the abrupt seizure of her memories on that first night, and more personal. She was hungry for more. Being sensible, she knew she must be patient, for the timing was not in her hands. Being human, she was restless and full of longing ...

... for home.

An hour or so later the sturdy SAS barked into life. The two rotors began to carve the air and moments later the flyer lifted. Hera was at the controls and she set a direct course for her Monkey Terrace home.

She followed the rift valley and watched as little by little the Mother Nylo became bigger as more tributaries entered it. At the place where the Mother Nylo was joined by the Lazyboy stream, she turned west, and then she handed over the controls to Alan. Night had by now fallen. Hera fell asleep in her chair.

Twelve hours later, when she awoke, the SAS was cruising over the Chimney Mountains. By mid-afternoon she had reached Big Fella Lake and could see her small shilo at the end of the water. How peaceful it looked. How welcoming!

Some washing she had left out to dry when she went to bid farewell to the last shuttle was still flapping on the line. The large and straggly monkey tree was white with blossom and small Tattersall weeds were sprouting up in the clearing. How differently she felt about the weeds since seeing the umbrella tree plantation.

An hour after landing Hera was swimming in Big Fella Lake. She had had enough of travel for the time being. There was a lot she needed to think over and a lot to absorb. As she lay back and floated, her hair loose in the water and arms spread wide, she could, if she relaxed, just hear, or see, or feel, that shimmering music, that golden light, that warmth that was now part of her.

And always it was also there, woven through the experience – that fine thread of pain.

12

Tattersall Errant

Hera did not sleep well after returning to her shilo. And when she did sleep, her dreams were vivid and scary. She also found herself waking at strange hours. A great restlessness led her to wander about at all hours. 'All symptoms,' she said, 'of turbulence in the psychosphere of Paradise.' She did not feel that she was again being called or contacted as such; it was just that she was now aware of movements, sometimes quite violent, such as sudden squalls in the lake or strange lights in the sky.

Then one night ... Shortly after midnight she started awake, every sense alert. She had heard something move outside. The popping of seed pods did not occur at night and the only sounds that normally disturbed the night were the creaking of the nearby trees or the slap of waves on the shore. The sound she had heard was not like these. It was a scraping sound. And then, unmistakably, she felt as well as heard something bump against the wall of the shilo.

Pulse rising, Hera slipped out of bed and crept over to one of the windows. The two moons, riding almost together, were high above the clearing, and their light cast the shadow of the window frame starkly onto the plastic blinds. Not wanting to make a sound, Hera eased the blinds open and looked out into the clearing. No breeze was disturbing the tops of the monkey trees. She scrutinized the table, the greenhouse, the sheds, the hangar, holding her gaze on each until she was sure there was no movement. Then her eye fell on a Tattersall that had grown beside one of the sheds .... There was something happening there. As Hera watched, the plant trembled. The movement started small but gradually increased until the entire shrub was shaking. *It will shake itself to death*, she thought. And then the shaking ceased and the entire plant fell forward onto

161

the ground, its branches spread in an untidy tangle. She could see where the shallow ball of its roots had detached from the ground.

Again Hera was reminded what strange plants the Tattersalls were – beautiful, sweet but with a presence that made her uncomfortable. Always she was aware of that tainted reputation. And now this one had shaken itself to death. Why?

She heard again the scraping sound that had wakened her. Then there came a distinct but muffled thump against the opposite side of the shilo, the side closest to the forest. It was as though the wall had been hit with a mop. Quietly she crept across the room. Above her was a sloping skylight through which the moons were shining. As she watched, a shadow moved across the window. There was no mistaking its shape – it was a Tattersall flower, fully open. Hera ran to the kitchen where she kept a ladder. She set it up just under the skylight, which had been left propped slightly open due to the nights being warm. Hera climbed up stealthily and peered out through the narrow opening. As she did so, a limb of the Tattersall came over the roof like a thrown rope and the thorns scratched on the hard surface of the window. Hera almost fell off the ladder, but she steadied herself, slammed the window shut and slid the bolt. Lying across the window was the branch. She saw it begin to contract, and the long thorns struggle for purchase, but there was nothing now for them to hold on to. The branch slipped back and fell heavily outside and with it went the flower.

Shaken, but more surprised than frightened, Hera climbed down. She crossed to the front door and made sure that it was secure and then hurried to all the other windows and the small back door, making sure they were closed and locked. Shilos were strong, built for frontier conditions on strange worlds, and she had no fear that a Tattersall weed could rupture the walls or bring the roof down. Nor did she feel under attack. As she explained to me, 'Strange as it may seem, I rather accepted what was happening as just another manifestation of how quickly things were changing on Paradise. I thought of myself as a kind of beacon, a candle flame attracting strange things – experiences. Mark you, I was careful and on my guard. I was not afraid of being attacked, but more that an accident might happen. The Tattersalls were very clumsy!'

Satisfied that all was now secure, Hera returned to the ground-floor window. The Tattersall that had trembled and fallen was moving again. It had contracted and the roots had pulled well clear of their hole. Then part of it convulsed and one of the upper branches was thrown forward, towards the shilo. Other branches uncoiled and, when they had reached their maximum extent, twisted. The long thorns pressed into the brevet. Now began another slow contraction. Some of the thorns tore from the soil, but many held and slowly ('painfully slowly' said Hera) the root ball of the weed was dragged forward.

It was one of the most grotesque things I had ever seen. At ORBE we knew that Tattersall weeds sometimes behaved a bit like vines. That is in the nature of many invasive plants, and we knew that the thorns could give support when they got lodged in the foliage of some local tree, but we had never imagined that the thorns could be used as crampons or that the mechanism which allowed the seeds to be shed could be adapted to allow the plant to travel overland. I am still convinced that this was a new development, simply because the Tattersall weed I was observing was so inept at crawling. Even when the roots were able to add their little scamper, the energy expended for the advantage gained was ridiculous. Evolution is more efficient! But the Tattersall had tenacity, a simple kind of dedication and there was something comic about it, though I do not remember laughing.

Hera watched the Tattersall crawl slowly towards her shilo. Sometimes it moved more sideways than forward, but there was always a net gain. Behind it, the Tattersall left a path of torn earth. Then came the moment when it arrived directly outside her window. Hera had by now opened the blinds so that she could see clearly. She witnessed the way it compressed and then pushed its branches up against the wall of the shilo until it was leaning there like a drunk who, having lost his balance, does not know why he does not fall over. She saw the Tattersall gather two of its branches for one final fling. The branches coiled, tightened and then released. The tops of the branches snaked up and some of the hooked barbs caught on the gutter above the window. She saw the Tattersall contract and pull itself bodily upright. It was now standing against the wall. One of the blue flowers, its petals ragged, was pressed against the window.

163

The last action she observed was in the roots. The tree remained in the same spot but shook as its roots worked at the soil, digging themselves in like worms. This took a long time. Hera concluded that the Tattersall had simply run out of energy. However, it had saved its most unusual manoeuvre for last. There came a moment when all motion ceased, and then it suddenly bedded down.

It looked for all the world as though the roots and trunk had been tugged firmly from underground and then tied off. Immediately the whole tree stiffened up and became still. Then slowly it wilted. All the branches except those that were holding it drooped down and rested on the ground. Its flowers closed and fell, scattering their petals. I think it fell asleep!

The sky was beginning to turn grey. The crawl from the shed to the shilo had taken just over three hours.

Hera's next actions were very characteristic. Many of us would have decided to escape the house, but she got out her drawing book and made sketches of the way she had seen the Tattersall move. Then she made herself breakfast, and when that was finished and the sun was streaming in through the window and casting the shadow of the Tattersall across the room, she climbed the ladder again, opened the skylight and climbed out onto the roof.

Three Tattersalls had reached the house in the night and now lay draped across it. Others at the edge of the clearing had also moved. Two had managed to climb into one another and now lay in a tangled heap. Another had approached the monkey trees and, attempting to climb one, had become stranded, its roots dangling above the ground. That one was already dead. The leaves and flowers had fallen and its moisture was dripping from the ends of its flaccid branches.

Hera climbed back inside the shilo and locked the window behind her. She left the house by the back door and went round to the front, keeping well clear of the newly arrived Tattersalls. She was uncertain what to do. Her first thoughts were to get a scorch gun and trim the weeds back or dig them out. That certainly is what she would have done a few months earlier, but she was now not the same Hera. Of one thing she felt certain: the shilo had not been attacked. Plants tend to gravitate either by seed development or by root movement to those environments that are most congenial. So, the Tattersalls – in their own ungainly fashion – were finding the outside of the shilo convivial. Well, she should feel honoured. She would not be casual around them, but nor would she walk in fear. Nor did she see any reason to change a plan she had made to visit the Island of Thom. And if the Tattersalls had gathered round her front door when she got back, well, she would deal with that when the time came.

If in reasoning this way Hera appears to be somewhat foolhardy or naive, that is merely a measure of how far she had moved from the cautious attitudes of Earth and how much faith she placed in those few moments she had spent in communication with Paradise. She felt protected.

Hera touched the control panel strapped to her wrist. 'Alan. Prepare for take-off. Destination Island of Thom. Duration of time away five days. Departure time asap. Out.'

No sooner had she spoken when she heard the hangar doors begin to crank open. Moments later the compact form of the SAS emerged – fully charged, spruced and ready for action.

13

At the Heart of the Labyrinth

The land Hera was flying over had never been settled.

Rugged, wild and prone to earthquakes, it could not be farmed and even the early MINADEC prospectors had found little to interest them. It was a land of steep windswept hills and dark plunging valleys. At the bottom of these, dark lochs, shrouded in mist, showed hardly a ripple or even a reflection of the daylight.

The SAS crossed a ravine. A spring gushed from between two rocks and filled a small circular lake. This emptied over a worn stone ledge, from which the water fell sheer, disappearing into the misty depths. However, it was what Hera saw beyond this which astonished her. She sat up suddenly and shouted, 'Stop, Alan. Stop. Hold steady.'

The SAS banked in the air and the rotor blades changed pitch as the craft hovered. Below, where the ravine widened, Hera saw blue-flowered Tattersall weeds. Nothing really surprising about that, except that the plant had been absent for most of the journey so far. But now, suddenly, here they were in their thousands, and instead of being randomly spaced and growing wherever the seed fell, these had sprung up following a very precise pattern: a spiral. The lines of the spiral were not perfect – they followed the contours of the land – but the basic shape was unmistakable, it was like a frozen blue whirlpool, with the centre hidden under what was, in effect, a bouquet.

This could not be ignored. Quickly Hera checked the ORBE reference records stored in the memory bank of the SAS, hoping to discover whether there had ever been any project work done here. There had not. Out-plantings had been undertaken at the coast and in some of the valleys close to the shore, but little work had been done elsewhere. This land had been left alone. A footnote indicated that in the early days Mayday Newton had led a small expedition through here hunting for different varieties of the Paradise plum. It had been unsuccessful. And that was all.

Certainly, if anything like these rings had ever shown up on the satellite images which formerly tracked changes on the surface of the planet, ORBE workers would have come running. But the satellites had been among the first things closed down when the Disestablishment began. So, this formation was a relatively recent phenomenon, and one that would not have been observed had Hera not chanced to pass by. Hera wondered if the presence of the Tattersall weeds meant that a rescue operation was in progress. If so, for what?

Hera guided the SAS down slowly and held steady as soon as she detected the slightest turbulence from the rotor blades among the Tattersall flowers. She adjusted the magnification on the tri-vid screen to maximum. Immediately, the image of the flowers filled the screen and their blueness brightened the cabin. But Hera could not see through them. At maximum resolution she could see the individual thorns and stalks of the Tattersall weed. They came into and out of focus as they moved in the breeze. But nothing definite could be seen below them. Hera tried other filters – ultraviolet, infrared, sonic imaging – and they all told the same story. Certainly there was something at the centre. It was small, dark and warm; but that was all she could tell.

If Hera wanted to know more, she would have to go down and see for herself.

'Find a landing place, Alan. As close as you can to an entry point into that labyrinth.'

The SAS cruised slowly over the spiral. The weeds grew closely together with no obvious breaks. In speaking to Alan, Hera had used the word labyrinth in a casual way. She had not realized how accurate her description was. And, had she known, would she have behaved differently? Probably not. But she would have been more careful.

The best landing place Alan could find was a small rock-strewn plateau where the side of the ravine was less steep. It was just above the rows of Tattersall weeds. The small stream, after its hectic journey from the pool above, meandered nearby, and provided a natural opening through the plants.

Thoughtfully, Hera donned meshlite overalls and a helmet and visor. After witnessing the antics of the Tattersall weeds at the shilo, she did not know what to expect and so added a small scorch gun to her equipment. Then she climbed out of the SAS and slid down the bank to the stream.

Crossing the stream was easy and Hera soon found herself standing in a narrow avenue with tightly packed Tattersall weeds towering on either side. She reasoned that if she followed this natural path round for several circuits she would eventually reach the centre. She set off at an easy jog, heading down the slope. She splashed across the stream again at the lowest point, and then climbed up the hill on the other side. From the top she could see the SAS perched on the hillside.

With each circuit the path got smaller. Soon the giant weeds were packed so closely together that they seemed like a wall. The way became darker too, and it seemed as though she had entered a tunnel, for the plants now met overhead in a tangle and she could no longer see the sky. The air was still and heavy with the perfume of the Tattersalls. She jogged on while the path steadily narrowed until it finally stopped at a wall of weeds. The centre would be just beyond this.

Dropping to her knees, Hera was able to crawl under the lower branches. Emerging from under these, she found herself facing another wall of branches. But here there was nothing random. She was facing what, if she had been on Earth, would have been called a formal hedge. The tall Tattersall weeds were bent and tightly intertwined as though they had been plaited to make a basket. There were no gaps.

Hera comments:

I knew that whatever was being guarded by Tattersalls was on the other side, but there was no way through. I moved on round what was now quite a small circle. I was very aware of the noise that I was making. But I tried to be quiet, the way one does in a church or a museum. I remembered the time when I was a student and someone had an epileptic fit in the library. The noise of the chair being knocked over and the harsh gasping could be heard in all the rooms. Terrible. Then there was the time when my mother and I were on our travels and in a big gloomy building in Italy, and someone dropped a bottle of wine on some marble steps and it shattered and the echoes seemed to go on for hours. These memories came to me with great force.

Surely there must be a way through. And there was.

She came to a giant Tattersall weed, one with a trunk wider than her outstretched arms and branches that supported masses of flowers which tumbled right to the ground. A guardian tree if ever she had seen one. So densely packed were its flowers, they were like a wreath. But the lowest branch formed an arch about two feet above the ground, and so, down on hands and knees, like a humble pilgrim, Hera was able to crawl through to the other side, and so to the centre.

I found myself in a vast cistern. The walls formed by the Tattersall weeds rose sheer and unbroken, towering up until they grew inwards like an ancient beehive tomb. And the roof was a canopy of blue flowers speckled with sunlight.

I could feel a tremendous energy in the air – a bit like in a greenhouse – but an energy that was, as it were, latent or held in perfect balance. Have you noticed how a pan of water goes still just before it boils? Have you stood and watched the golden light of dawn spread through the sky as the sun rises – a sight which should be greeted with trumpets and cymbals, but there is only silence or the ring of a lonely cow bell? O Olivia, it took me a great effort to move out from under the tree and stand upright. My fear, if fear it was, was that my presence might just tip the balance and I would trigger the boiling, or be crushed by . . . what? A shower of gold?

In front of Hera, in the middle of the clearing, a small plant was growing. It stood alone in the bare soil. Though she had never seen one live, Hera knew what it was from early descriptions. She was seeing the thing called a Michelangelo, or a Reaper – a young one, one that would now in the fullness of time, become a giant.

Dark tapering leaves, no more than a metre tall, rose from the ground and then spread open like cupped hands. Growing up from its heart I saw many stems, and each ended in a cluster of small black berries. They moved slightly, bumping one another, and occasionally entwining their stalks like snakes. All of them had clustered on the side facing me. They were interested in me. And I saw a dark liquid began to drip down from the small beads, and I became aware of the smell of the plant – a sharp astringent odour, like bitter lemons. It made my lips feel dry.

Hera realized she could feel the 'aura' of the plant touching her. It made her scalp tickle and caused a slight feeling of nausea in her stomach. She crawled forward but stopped when she was a metre or so away. Kneeling up as tall as she could, Hera was able to peer down into the cup of the plant. She could see the start of its bulb – a red and black mottled ball which at this early stage of development was akin to the head of a mushroom just pushing up through the soil.

Hera wanted to touch it. It was a tender feeling. Later she thought of it as the woman in her responding to the infant before her. She knew too that the small plant wanted in some way to touch her as well, to feed from her. She felt her own will responding, and watched with a smile as her right hand begin to reach out, while her left hand took her weight on the ground.

At that same moment a shadow moved over her. Her legs and body were gripped from behind. She cried out as thorns pierced her meshlite suit, pricking into her skin. The giant Tattersall weed had moved. One of its branches from above had coiled round her in one convulsive move, lifting and turning her so that she found herself staring into a mass of its prickles. These, still contracting, scratched the hard plastic of her visor and were deflected past her ears and throat. Right in front of her eyes was the bud of a flower, and, as she stared, it began slowly to open. The bud casing tore and fell away and the blue petals unfurled. The flower angled round and stared into her.

Hera could neither move nor scarcely breathe for fear that the branches would tighten their grip, pushing the spines deep into her body – but how long could she stay like this? One leg still touched the ground and this gave her some balance, but soon that would ache and then the weight of her body would press her onto the thorns. In front of her she saw two more flowers open, and then more, until she seemed to be surrounded by a fierce blue gaze which never wavered. The perfume of the flowers was so intense that it made her want to cough, and that too was the last thing she wanted to do.

Hera could feel the sticky wetness of blood inside her overall. The pain in her legs and arms was becoming unbearable. She had to move. As slowly as she could she tried to straighten and then lower her arms. The plant did not resist but the blue flowers shifted, angling round. Finally she was standing more or less upright on the one leg that was free. Even so, she could not escape as the tree was coiled around and above her. One twist from the plant and she would be crushed. One darting blow and she would be impaled.

Trees have a different timescale to humans, and for all Hera knew the Tattersall weed which now held her might remain in this position for a long time, perhaps years. She would die from loss of blood within hours. She would hang there in the tree, in her meshlite suit, as the seasons passed and her blood would form little brown discs, like coins, scattered about her. She felt her mind weaken as the perfume of the brilliant flowers dulled the pain somewhat. She still hurt, but it did not seem to matter so much.

In this befuddled state a thought was struggling to be born in her. She seemed, for a moment, to hear a distant whispering voice. It came to her like a wind blowing over a desert. She turned her head slightly as though to hear better. And as she did so she recognized the voice. It was the one she had identified as the thread of pain.

It called her name: 'Hera.'

Once heard, it became stronger.

14

Mack the Dreamer

At the same moment as the impaled Hera heard her name being called, several other things happened on and about Paradise. Most immediately, Mack, who had been asleep on the shuttle platform high above the planet, woke with a start having himself called out her name.

He had been dreaming uneasily, for the Disestablishment was not going well. The problems were not of his making, but he and his team of demolition workers had become unofficial troubleshooters. That very day they had had to unpack and then repack some of the barges tethered in orbit round the platform, and that meant suiting up and going outside into the cold vacuum of space, and this Mack hated. His feelings were released in his dreams, which this time had seen him tumbling uncontrollably in space, his safety cord adrift, stars spinning round him and the certain knowledge that he would end his days a forgotten human satellite – one of many – turning round some cold world. But the fierce quality of this dream changed at the moment Hera was attacked. He saw her face in pain, called her name and woke up.

He sat up suddenly in the small cabin, aware of the echoes of his own voice. He was sharing with three of his team, and the other men were all sprawled on their beds in various positions of rest. Some had fallen asleep before they could get undressed, having completed a double shift just three hours earlier. They moved in their sleep and mumbled, but did not wake.

The memory of Hera's face was vividly before him. He sat in the semi-dark of the shuttle, breathing deeply, and felt the dream loosen its grip on him. He swung his legs out of bed and stood up on the warm plastic floor. He needed a drink, something cold and fresh – fresh lemon, crushed ice and a spike – then a bit of a walk round the platform to calm him down.

He was mixing his drink when Dickinson appeared at the door of the small galley.

'You OK, boss?'

'Yeah. Just a bad dream.'

'Just, I heard you shout out and—'

'Yeah. I'm fine. Going to go for a wander. You get some more sleep.'

Dickinson nodded, and then grinned. 'Hey, boss. Gutsy lady, eh?'

'Dickinson . . .'

'It's OK, I'm on my way. But you get some sleep too, eh?'

The shuttle platform never slept. When one team finished, another took its place, but still the work dragged on. A shortage of fractal transporters, botched packing of the barges, a food-poisoning scare in the kitchens, communications breakdowns in the fractal link, inexperienced administrative staff sent out by the Space Council for on-the-job training – all these were taking their toll. Everyone was tired.

Mack headed away from the bright glaring lights of the deep-space depot. He took a glide path down to the lower levels of the platform; past the steamy, noisy kitchens; past the bright, noisy repair shops; past the old cargo bays and the cool stores; and on down to the silence and emptiness of the big hangar from where the shuttles had once departed on their regular service to the planet. The hangar, of course, was deserted, though emergency lights were on and stared down bleakly. It was like the hold of a ship and the air smelled faintly of oil and disinfectant.

Standing alone in the vast chamber Mack felt some relief. He breathed in deeply and blew out lustily several times. It helped. Feeling more himself, he looked about. Everything was neatly stowed away, just as he had left it. The hangar was ready for use, ready for the last trip down to the surface, the one that would bring Hera back if . . . He did not finish that thought but walked on.

Here was stored old P56, the workhorse of the station. This veteran would probably be used for the last trip, he guessed. They would need its vast reserves of power to lift Hera's SAS and probably the demolition bus he had left at New Syracuse. Mac intended to be part of the crew for that journey and had presented a fanciful but official-looking inventory of all the important stuff they had been forced to leave behind. But if power on the shuttle platform was low, then Abhuradin would send one of the four small personnel shuttles. These neat sleek machines, little more than vacuum-proofed pods really, could reach the surface in little over twenty minutes. Each was parked in its own gantry from which it could be launched. They were all fully charged, he observed, but one had developed a minor malfunction in its auxiliary vacuum pump, so it would not be making the journey. He made a mental note to tell Maintenance.

Mack wandered on round the hangar, just checking, sipping his cold drink casually, making himself busy while he calmed down. Eventually he made his way to an alcove with curved window-walls, and made himself comfortable at the table. This place had been a small cafeteria when the shuttle was in regular service and it gave splendid views of the planet beneath and the stars above. From here you could watch the brilliant particle beam which powered the shuttles' ascent and descent.

He felt much calmer now. While walking idly he had been thinking hard. He had realized that the dream might have been fuelled by something that had happened that day while he and his boys had been floating in space. A door seal on one of the barges had malfunctioned. This itself was a consequence of an earlier failure to equalize the internal pressure of the barge with the near vacuum of space. The result was that as soon as Mack activated the lock to open, the door simply peeled back on its hinges. As it did so, objects such as a garbage bag, some spare rivets, transit cages and a broken box of pressure pens – things that had obviously just been tossed into the barge by whoever had closed it – came hurtling out. Luckily, most of Mack's team were on the under-side, but Mack himself had been outside the door and it was only because he saw it shift slightly before it broke that he had been able to jet away to safety. The rubbish went tumbling out into space. Had he been hit, the rubbish bag alone could have broken his safety lanyard.

Luckily the magnetic clamps which held the barge steady in space did not release when the barge bucked. Otherwise they would have had a real problem with a rogue barge tumbling about near the shuttle platform.

As far as Mack was concerned, it had been a near miss but he was still alive to talk about it. However, for the rest of the two shifts, he had found himself checking and then double-checking all connections and links. This slowed the work down and his men got jumpy, for few of them liked working outside.

Sitting now with his back to the solid wall and his arms spread and resting on the portal frames, Mack had the chance to reassess his dream. Perhaps, he reasoned, he had simply grafted his memory of the near accident onto his fears for Hera and had come up with a nightmare. It was a theory, though Mack was not entirely convinced. He tended to trust his dreams, especially those that came like commands, but they were never quite what they seemed and he was cautious.

He could imagine the expression on Hera's face if he raised the alarm based on a dream . . . and what she might say when awoken from her honest sleep on Paradise. No, on balance it was best to keep quiet for the time being, but he promised himself that he would find time during the next shift to ask Captain Curvaceous if she had received any news from Hera. He also knew that Hera could look after herself. She was serious and resourceful and not the type to panic. Tough too, and determined. He remembered her at Monkey Tree Terrace standing up to him, hands on hips, getting angry. He laughed at the memory and then at himself, at his balled fists and his worrying mind. *Truth is, you've got it bad this time, Mack m'boy . . . and you just might make a fool of yourself.* He rubbed his jaw, a bit embarrassed. This was the first time he had really acknowledged to himself that there was something about this clever woman called Hera that both challenged and attracted him. *Hell, I might just be making the whole thing up*, he thought, *just so I can go busting in like Fractal Man to the rescue.* Getting sterner, he spoke to himself: 'You're over fifty, Mack, and you're behaving like a kid of twenty, and she's so high class and intellectual that she probably won't even remember your name. Get a grip.' He felt a bit better after this dressing-down. More earthed.

Below him the planet turned. There was a lot of cloud and Mac could only identify a few features. This side of the planet and the shuttle platform were both moving into twilight. Leo's Eye still gleamed on the horizon. And the two moons? Mack could see they were more or less coming into alignment and he could imagine a great wave rushing round the planet, scouring and cleaning it. *Bet she's loving it down there*, he thought.

He heaved himself out of his chair and continued his patrol.

Mack was a man who always took an interest in his environment. He was the kind of man who could not help tapping a barometer as he walked past, tightening a screw if it needed it or checking if security doors were locked and keys in place. He was in all things watchful. And if this seems a bit fiddly and interfering, he was also a man who would walk the long way round a desk to avoid seeing letters that were not his and who was overly generous when it came to paying his way. So Mack, when strolling past the control cabin, could not help but notice that the red operations light was still on at the control desk for the shuttle. This meant that the shuttle had not been closed down completely but merely put on standby. Thus the circuits that fed the master beacon which generated the beam down to the surface were alive and warm just as they should be. Being the man he was, he could not help but try the door to the shuttle control room ... a door which he found locked ... but he also noted the type of lock and the door construction and the security wiring. All standard. He'd dismantled a hundred like that. He knew three ways of opening and disarming a door like that within five minutes.

He whistled to himself as he returned to his seat in the canteen.

'Hey, Mack. You down there?' It was Dickinson. He was at the top of the glideway holding a tray in one hand and a bottle and two glasses in the other.

'Yeah. I'm in what's left of the café.'

'You alone?'

'Yeah. Yeah. Yeah.'

Dickinson stepped onto the glideway and descended holding up the bottle like a trophy. 'Hope you don't mind, boss, but you didn't look your normal shitty self up there, so I thought maybes you needed a spot to eat and a drink.'

Mack didn't reply, but he nodded in the direction of the chair opposite him.

On the tray was a plate piled with whatever Dickinson had been able to filch from the kitchen and some fresh bread, still warm. Dickinson had struck up a relationship with one of the women who worked in the kitchen and everyone was happy.

He filled two glasses and pushed one over to Mack.

'So what do you reckon, Mack?'

'About what?'

'How long we'll be on this job. I think we all need a break. You included. A week off at Cleopatra's and we'll be new men. What do you say?'

Mack nodded. 'Could be.'

'I mean, we started on this job, when? Months ago, and don't get me wrong, I'm not complaining – it's better than a monastery – but a man needs a change now and then.'

'I thought you were well provided for in that department.'

'I am. I am. But it's the others I'm thinking of. Even Polka and Annette are getting a bit stroppy.'

'Very considerate of you. Well, OK. I'll have a word with Captain Abhuradin.'

'She can come too. She's got her eye on you. Now that would be a straddle you wouldn't forg—'

'Dickinson, will you just—'

'Sorry. Sorry. Here, have something to eat. Take your mind off it.'

The two men shared the wine and ate in silence. Finally Mack spoke.

'You used to work at a shuttle port, didn't you, Dickinson?'

'Yep. On-board mechanic when I was eighteen. Got my ticket as a controller when I was twenty-one. Made for life. But I fancied something more glamorous, so I became a demolition grunt instead. Why do you ask?'

'Did you ever work one of them?' Mack nodded in the direction of the shuttle.

Dickinson stood up and wandered over to the control room window and squinted through. 'Yep. These big crystal mothers were state of the art when I was training. I helped install one at the shuttle over at Gerard's Barn. You ever seen that place?' Mack shook his head. 'The shuttles are all shaped like hearts and they're done out with black leather and crimson velvet. They've got little golden cupids spraying perfume from their cocks. It's supposed to be erotic but it smells like a monkey's armpit. When a shuttle's docking they have this big knob-shaped lever that comes up and . . .' He stopped and looked at Mack, and then came and sat down. 'Listen, boss,' he said slowly, 'you wouldn't be thinking of doing what I'm thinking you're thinking of doing, would you?'

'You know your trouble, Dickinson?' said Mack, standing up and draining his glass. 'You think too much.'

15

Ordeal in the Labyrinth

People who have survived torture sometimes recall that, at the moment of greatest torment, they became distanced from their broken bodies. In this state they heard the voices of loved ones or sometimes saw luminous images of a deity. Such encounters enabled them to survive. At the summit of anguish our state of being may change and we become both the sufferer and the observer of our own suffering. Such I believe was Hera's case.

In her words:

Hera My first thought was, *This is not happening to me.* But the pain was real enough, and the sight of my blood. I remember being surprised. But my situation was changing quickly. I could feel the tightness of the branches and a terrible dark awareness grew that they were settling into me, that they would never move and I would be there for eternity.

Olivia Did you ever doubt?

Hera Doubt?

Olivia The wisdom of what you were doing, the wisdom of actually being there, down on Paradise?

Hera I was a bit too preoccupied for doubt, Olivia. Doubt is a luxury when you are pinned in a tree with spines growing through you.

Olivia Sorry. Go on.

Hera And still there was my name being sounded. It just went on and on – an echo that never faded. And the name seemed to flow in my blood. That doesn't make sense, does it? What I mean is that the name was in me like my blood, and I was so very aware of the blood. You see, being tilted the way I was, the blood from the cuts inside the meshlite flowed out through my collar and even into my mouth. I know I was very confused and I think I must have blacked out several times. One of the spines of the Tattersall was pressing into the place just under the patella in my knee. Another was in my thigh and a third in my back. Others were in my arms. I still have the scars.

Olivia You don't need—

Hera The pain of these, flower or no flower, perfume or no perfume, threatened to overwhelm me. They were like fire and ice. I had no idea how deep the cuts were. Severe pain induces vomiting. Did you know that, Olivia?

Olivia Yes.

Hera Well, It surprised me. My body took over and I must have convulsed uncontrollably. What a sight I must have made. Being twisted the way I was, the vomit fell to the ground – I saw it . . . I'm not boring you, am I?

Olivia No, I . . . Sorry, I'm a bit squeamish. Go on.

Hera Well, a kind of heat came back at me and immediately a growling. It was my name again, but spoken by a lion. I thought, *This is it*, and hoped it would be over soon. You see my convulsions had driven the spikes deeper. That was when I floated away. The pain was great, but I was elsewhere, on the other side of it. I think I had accepted death.

Olivia And yet you lived on. Your spirit was not broken?

Hera There was a moment of darkness, as though the sun had flickered, and I thought, *No more. Please. Let me pass on. Let me go.* And then, in front of my eyes, one of the lovely blue Tattersall flowers suddenly closed. Then opened again and closed again. Another higher up did likewise. Others followed. It was as though they were controlled by strings, snapping open and shut. And then they all closed and the tree started to shake.

Olivia Good God. And that hurt too?

Hera I was past caring. But I realized that the pressure on me had lessened. For one thing, I could feel that the weight on the one leg that touched the ground was heavier. That brought its own problems, but I pushed against the thin branch locked round my arm, and the branch eased off. The crucial thing is that it was not like a spring. It did not leap back, or worse, tighten even more. Well . . .

Olivia Go on.

Hera You are not going to like this at all, Olivia. I got this strong urge to push and to move. Suddenly I had an image of a Dendron, like the one that young Malik talks about. You know, when she sees it churning up the water at the bottom of the rapids.[2] I was urged to . . . It urged me to have the strength of the Dendron. That was the thought, and a surge of strength did come to me. And – mark this, because it is important – the same surge must have come to the Tattersall weed too, for almost immediately another of its branches pulled back. The spines – I saw them, red-tipped and wet – lifted from me slowly. I turned my body with them. I didn't want to be cut as they withdrew. How is that for clear thinking, Olivia? They came out cleanly, except for one, and the blood followed them.

Olivia Good God.

Hera And now we come to the silly part. I still only had one foot on the ground, because my other leg was still trapped. There I was escaping, but if the Tattersall weed moved any more, it would lift me up off the ground by one leg. But then that branch loosened its grip too. For a moment I tottered and thought I might fall towards the small plant in the centre. At that one same moment the giant Tattersall weed froze and all its flowers flashed open. If I had ever been close to sudden death, that was it. But I did keep my balance – don't ask me how, but when I was a girl I was a bit of an athlete, being small, you know – so that must have helped. It seemed like an eternity. Both of us still. And then I saw the flowers slowly close, one by one, and it let me drop.

When I looked up at the Tattersall weed, it had one branch raised higher than all the others, and I was reminded of a samurai warrior standing over me with his great sword raised. I kept very still. But then that branch . . . it too just wilted and dropped. Something had killed it.

Hera lay on the ground for some time. She was aware of many things. Of pain and of relief, certainly. Aware too that the presence that had given her the strength of the Dendron had also, perhaps inadvertently, given her knowledge. That would need long pondering.

[2] See Document 6.

She squirmed round and looked at the small plant, the young Michelangelo. It had closed up completely. It had lifted its leaves and wrapped them around its black and red heart so tightly that it now resembled a slim green vase of the kind that can only hold a single flower. 'What are you?' breathed Hera.

Hera had seen a truth about Paradise. The small creature at the centre of the clearing *was* a child. A powerful child. It had played with her and it might have killed her with the same wanton unconcern as a child plucks the legs off a daddy-long-legs or the wings off a cicada – without a trace of malice. Likewise, the clumsy Tattersall weed had thorns, not to attack but because they helped the branches to climb and grip. It was neither vengeful nor cruel.

Hera Paradise is very simple on one level – or it was at that time. The biggest danger I ever experienced down there was when I let myself think of the bio-forms in human terms or credited them with human emotions, and of course intellectually I knew that. But you know, Olivia, it is almost impossible not to. Our emotions are the greatest dynamo within us. Can you prevent love? Can you resist it? Is it not the greatest generative force of which we can conceive? And does not the great imaginative act of empathy begin within us too? (LONG PAUSE) At the same time, we do have to hold back sometimes in order to reach further. Poor Shapiro couldn't, and look what happened to him. Of course there is some overlap between us human beings and whatever the creatures are that live on Paradise – the very fact that we are all subject to time ensures that. But as Shapiro said on many occasions, 'We are children of the same universe, but it is a universe full of contradictions.' As long as you realize the bio-forms did not act with malice and had no concept of death in the way that we have, or any fear of death, you can start to understand the nature of Paradise – as it was. In fact, I did not know it then of course, but I was about to be useful to them.

Olivia Did they think of you as useful?

Hera You are so wonderfully pragmatic, Olivia. I think they saw me as just what is . . . what was there. To hand. Rice in a begging bowl. You know I sometimes think what we call wisdom is nothing more than the ability to foresee the consequences of our actions, and to hold back before they become our fate.

Olivia Can I quote you?

Hera I'd rather you didn't.

Olivia I have one question.

Hera I have a hundred, but go on.

Olivia Was the Tattersall weed that grabbed you protecting the small Michelangelo? Because, if so, that shows intention or motive in a way that we can understand.

Hera Mm. If I were a herbalist, and knowing what I know now, I think I would rename the Tattersall weed the mother-of-all-kindness flower or some such old-fashioned name because it seems to have always had an urge to protect. So, in grabbing me, you *might* say it was protecting the Michelangelo, or you *might* say that it was protecting me – and remember that the Tattersalls are very clumsy – for I reckon the naughty little Michelangelo had designs on me, don't you? But the truly important thing is that the voice of a Dendron – an extinct creature, as I then believed – crying out in pain, was heard by the only creature that could help it. Little me, Hera. Put that in your rationalist pipe and smoke it.

Olivia I will.

To return to Hera lying on the ground.

The adrenalin that flooded her system had a limited life. She needed to move before she stiffened and before too much blood was lost. The SAS could not reach her here, and so the first thing was to retrace her steps through the labyrinth. She crawled back under the giant weed, stood up and began to limp along the widening avenue between the Tattersalls. She has little memory of this journey beyond an impression that it got easier as she moved along. So we must imagine the small limping warrior battling on, her path becoming brighter with every dragging step.

Hera does remember clearly the moment when she finally waded across the stream, but she was not where she had entered; she was much further down the hillside at a place that was more like a meadow.

Hera was too far gone to ask questions and under no illusions. She was on borrowed time. She tapped the emergency code into her control pad and instantly the cool, unruffled voice of Alan spoke in her ear. 'Tracking your signal, Hera. ETA thirty seconds and counting.' Even as he spoke, Hera heard the engine roar and saw the SAS lift above the labyrinth far up the ravine. Having no human crew to consider, it bent in the air at a sharp angle and within a few seconds was hammering over her. What a wonderful sound! The wind from the rotor blades flattened the nearby Tattersalls and pressed Hera to the ground. The door opened in the side of the SAS and a small ladder snaked down and stiffened.

Hera dragged herself upright and sat on the bottom rung. There she undid the top of her meshlite overall and gingerly eased herself out of it. In some places the blood had dried and the meshlite was stuck to her. But she was able to loosen it and the fresh air on her skin felt good. Finally she undid the hip tags and pushed down. This was the hardest part, for to stand was painful, and yet if she sat down that hurt too. But she managed. She stepped out of the uniform.

A casual inspection told her that the cuts where the spines had entered were not as bad as they might have been. They looked like little mouths. No bones were broken. Though she had lost blood, that could soon be made up. She would heal. But her knee worried her. It had swollen and was very painful to touch. She feared that a tip of a spine might have broken off and be lodged inside.

Hera left the suit where it was, on the ground. I am glad to record that she had not lost her sense of humour. 'I must stop stripping off and leaving my clothes everywhere, or I'll have nothing left to wear when I leave Paradise,' she said as she gingerly stepped onto the ladder and held on. How prophetic!

'You are hurt, Hera?'

'A few scratches. And before you ask, the answer is no.'

'You don't want me to make a cup of tea?'

'That's not what you were . . . Oh, bugger it. Yes, make me a cup of tea. Just do it. Then head for home. I need to clean myself up.'

Back at Monkey Tree Terrace she made her way to the shilo, walking stiffly. She'd had some bright notion that she would shower and dress her wounds and then find clean clothes and . . . But as she lowered herself onto the bed, the room turned around her and she passed out.

She slipped to the floor and lay still.

With Hera's agreement, I wish to add a comment to this account. Hera has called me a rationalist, and I suppose that, in comparison

184

with her, I am. However, for once I am the one being somewhat mystical, albeit in a rather down-to-earth way, for I have thought long and hard about labyrinths, considering them a gateway between realities. We are close to a universal law.

The labyrinth Hera had followed on her way in to the Michelangelo undoubtedly defined the power outline associated with that small entity the Michelangelo-Reaper, just as iron filings define the power lines of a magnet. That it should take a spiral form should not surprise us, since that is one of the fundamental creative patterns of nature.

My contention is that the path she followed to escape was quite different from the path of entry. The escape path did not truly exist when she entered, or existed only potentially, that is in a veiled way, available only to the person of knowledge. Hera's experience in the labyrinth brought her that knowledge. What is more, I think a fundamental acceptance of her by that psychically lively world had taken place. The key moment was when she kneeled down and reached out in love to the small entity. That act triggered everything. Had it been anyone else – Shapiro, say, or me – a death would have occurred. Only those like the wild girls of Paradise such as Sasha, or perhaps a man like Pietr might have been safe.

My belief is that the new path was revealed by a will greater than that of the Michelangelo. We can call it the will of the Dendron, for it is assuredly that which saved her. Through her simple act of love, the Dendron came to know her. The trees parted, a way was found, and I am very sure they closed ranks again when she had passed. The mischievous little Michelangelo again took charge.

Having stepped in so far, I will go further. To me, there is no doubt that Hera should have died in that clearing. How could anyone survive that ordeal and walk out? It is my belief that there was a moment of choice in which one reality was replaced by another.

Labyrinths, as I said in my introduction, are pathways of knowledge. As such, they have only one right way of entering if you wish them to fulfil their purpose. Hera entered the labyrinth the right way, and faced the ordeal it offered, as well as her own fear. She triumphed. She thereby gained mastery. She was thus her own salvation. The intelligence of the heart, strong in faith and toughened by experience, can achieve what, on the surface, seems to be impossible. The mind is the cause; the effect is the miracle.

There can be no cheating with labyrinths. Had Hera spotted a narrow path which looked like a short cut, and had she taken it in order to enter, or had she cut and burned her way, she would have found the going hard. Perhaps, mysteriously, she would have found herself walking out again. But if she had battled to the centre, she would, as it were, have gone against nature, and no friendly Tattersall weed or long-dead Dendron (as she then believed) would have saved her.

She was no real risk to the child in the clearing, but it would have had her and consumed her in its way, and all that would now be left would be another small desiccated corpse lying on the surface of Paradise and a scrap of meshlite.

No book either!

16

Convergence

'C'mon, boss. You don't get overtime for lying in bed. Brought you some tea.' It was Dickinson. He was shaking Mack's shoulder. Mack growled something and rolled over. Then he came awake with a start. It seemed as if his head had just touched the pillow. But there had been no more dreams.

'You feeling any better?'

'No. But I'll cope.'

After breakfast Mack's demolition crew kitted up for outside. They completed their buddy check and one by one passed through the airlock and out into space. They emerged at the end of one arm of the shuttle platform, close to where certain barges that had already been filled but then rejected as unsafe for fractal were tethered. These barges had not been filled correctly and needed to be repacked and resealed before transit.

High above them a fractal freighter was angling down, its beautiful silver and black panels catching the sun. It had emerged during their sleep break, being already several days late. In a few hours it would lock on to a brilliant silver photon beam from the platform, and that would lead it into the docking web, where hundreds of transit barges were already waiting. However, by the time the photon beam came on, Mack's team would all be safe inside the shuttle port, for the raw energy of the beam did strange things to the space nearby.

Mack's team assembled outside the airlock, linked safety lanyards and then, using a permanent skim line, crossed as a group to an assembly point where four or five of the barges were tethered. There they separated, each person linking to one of the several skim lines that connected up all parts of the holding pen. Using simple magnetic induction and a small hand-held field generator, they could move up and down the lines with the skill of spiders. Already a charged mesh net was in place around a couple of the barges to make sure no cargo was accidentally spilled into space when they were opened. They were not taking any chances.

Mack was about to launch himself down a line when he heard a call on open frequency. 'Hold it, Mack. Don't engage. Your harness is loose.'

Annette Descartes, one of the two women in the demolition team, came skimming down the line. She tethered next to Mack and drifted round him. 'Hell, Mack. You're as undone as a whore at a barbecue. Who was your buddy?'

'Yeah, I was told,' said Mack. 'Thought I'd done it.' He felt the straps tighten and the magnetic clips lock.

'That's what comes of staying up half the night with that arsehole Dickinson!'

'I heard that,' said Dickinson, who was hanging clamped to the side of the barge. He had been first out and had set up the mesh. 'We were discussing the pros and cons of French philosophers.'

'Well, you should look after the old man better. There you go, Mack. Engage now.' She touched her helmet to his – the deep-space equivalent of a quick squeeze – and then gave him a push. Mack shot along the line. At the other end, the other woman in the team, Polka, was waiting just in case there was some malfunction.

The truth was that Mack's mind was not on the job at all. The unease he'd felt in the night was still with him. He'd tried to contact Captain Abhuradin to see if there was any message from Hera, but she was already on duty in the fractal control room and could not be disturbed. And now he had started to make mistakes. He knew that something was wrong with Hera, and the feeling would not go away.

'You OK, boss?'

'Yeah, fine. Just a bit dozy this morning, eh?' He did not see the members of the team hanging round the mesh make small hand signals to one another. Mack's reply had convinced no one. They would be watching him closely.

Mack was a man of hunches. Usually they came to him like sudden certainties and he would hear himself say things like,

'Everyone check your shackles – now,' or, 'We're going to back off from this one.' And, sure enough, moments later some problem would be revealed. The feeling he had now was less specific, just a deep unease. It was the uncertainty that was undoing him. Later that shift he welded shut a case that had just been opened for checking.

'Hell, boss. You're getting to be a liability.' It was Cole Barata, the man who had just spent twenty minutes cutting the case open.

'I am too,' said Mack. And he switched his welding torch off and went on open transmission. 'OK. Private talk. Barge 7. Everyone secure your work and then come on over.' One by one the members of the team assembled. Some came down, walking the mesh on magnetic soles; others came gliding in using the skim lines. When they joined they linked magnetically to whoever was nearest and then plugged in for private radio connection.

'Fire away, boss.'

'All on closed circuit? Transmitters off?'

A chorus of voices said, 'Yes,' all sounding very loud and without the space echo that sometimes made conversation on open frequency difficult.

'You've all noticed that I'm, er . . . not quite myself this shift?'

'Ye-es.'

'Well, those of you who have worked with me for a while will know that I sometimes act on instinct. Like I sometimes get a feeling that something is wrong and I stop work and get us out. Don't worry, there's nothing wrong with this job. This job is just a pain in the arse, and if we weren't getting paid double we wouldn't be out here cos we've got contracts waiting on Proxima Celeste and the Moon Dump and—'

'Get to the point, Mack.'

'Well, I've got a bad feeling now, but it's not to do with us. It's . . . er . . . it's to do with . . . er . . .'

'Not that pretty little professor woman who threw us out of her place on Paradise when that tree shed its seeds? What was her name now – Sheila Belich?'

'Hera Melhuish. Thank you, Dickinson. Yes, it is her. She's on her own down there. Don't ask me why. Some people are plain dumb when it comes to looking after themselves. But I keep getting this feeling that something really bad is happening down there. And I want to do something to help, but I don't know what.'

'Did Polka and me ever meet this woman?' This from Annette Descartes.

'No, you weren't on that trip. Just me and a few of the fellas.'

'I get the picture. And a few bottles of wine. And I bet you wish you'd had that Abwhoradin woman there too.'

'She was, actually.'

'This gets better. So what does this little professor woman have that Polka and I don't?'

'Can I answer that, Mack?'

'Quiet, Dickinson.'

'Yes, boss.'

'So ... er ... that's why I'm not quite myself,' finished Mack lamely. 'Sorry.'

There was a pause. No one was sure what to say. They were looking at a side of Mack they had hardly ever seen before. They had seen him thoughtful, but rarely shy. The idea that he might have fallen for a woman – especially a high-powered scientific one – surprised, pleased and amused them. But Mack was obviously unhappy. He was not love sick, he was worried sick, and his mind was not on his work. This needed sorting out, for all their sakes.

Finally, Polka lifted her hand to show she wanted to speak. This itself was unusual, as Polka was the quieter of the two women. 'So tell us, Mack. What would you like to do? You're no good up here while your mind's down there.' Several voices murmured assent. 'Do you want us to get Captain Headdown to give this Hera woman a call? Make sure she is OK and everything? Annette and I can arrange that, can't we, sweetheart?'

'Not a problem. She and me are like that!' replied Annette with a gesture.

'Excuse me. Can I offer a suggestion?'

'What is it, Dickinson?'

'Polka's idea's good. But it has one problem. You can't trust the radio cos clever people can lie, you know, and that lady is clever and determined and if she thought you were on your way down or were worried about her, then she'd lie through her teeth just to keep you out because she's proud, man. She's proud. I know it sounds a bit far-fetched, but here's what I think we should do. I suggest we break into the control room down below and steal a shuttle. Cole and Annette stand guard up here. No fucker gets past them, right? Everyone else acts as normal. I guide the shuttle down to the surface; you fire up the old Demo Bus we left down there – it'll still fly – and then you get your arse over to Monkey Tree whatsit and see what the fuck is going on. Then when she kicks you out, we do everything in reverse and no one is any the wiser. And the best time to do this is in about an hour when this freighter is docking and everyone is up top watching the fireworks. See, Mack. I only mention this because I know you'd never think of such a brilliant idea for yourself. But I've been in your team for, what, eight years now, and I would have been fried twice, crushed once and jetted out into deep space if it hadn't been for you and your hunches. If you think something is wrong down there, then I reckon there is. *Carpe diem*, Mack. Take the chance while it's on offer, because we can cope up here. Right, everyone?'

Everyone, despite their space helmets, was clearly astonished at what Dickinson had suggested, but they gave their support. They looked at Mack.

'Thank you, Dickinson. The thought had crossed my mind. But I don't want word about this to leak out. I mean it is a bit . . . it's not as if I was a young . . .'

'*Amor vincit omnia*, Mack,' said Dickinson. 'Do it.'

The rest of the team chimed in, agreeing. As Dickinson had said, they were all busting for a spell off planet, and if they couldn't take leave, well, a bit of quiet adventure, intrigue and thumbing your nose at authority would fit the bill. Finally Mack agreed.

Brilliant red lights began to blink on beacons stationed all round the shuttle port. Only fifteen minutes before the photon beam came on. Everyone working outside would have to move inside the platform or enter a security pod. Mack's team moved inside the platform.

As they were waiting to go through the airlock. Annette Descartes touched her helmet to that of Dickinson. 'Listen blue-eyes. What did that *Amor vincit omnia* stuff mean? Is it French?'

'No, a bit of Latin I picked up when I was cleaning windows in the convent. It means love conquers all – and if you meet me in the shuttle bay after we've got the old man down below, I'll give you a practical demo, OK?'

At some time during the journey home to Monkey Tree Terrace, Hera must have woken up sufficiently to crawl into bed before again passing out. She does not recall this. Nor does she recall the announcement from Alan that they had landed safely.

Some ten minutes after landing Alan began to play music which gradually got louder. He warmed the inside of the SAS and made sure there was boiling water available.

Finally Hera shifted and opened her eyes. She had trouble orientating herself for a moment. She felt sore all over. 'Turn the music off,' she said huskily.

The music faded. 'Hera. You are not well. I can detect blood.'

'So? I can cope. I don't need help. Women's business. Not yours.' Then she thought to herself, *Why the hell do I have to lie to a bloody machine?*

'You did not drink the tea I made.'

'Right. Sorry. I fell asleep. I'll drink it now.'

'I have disposed of it.'

'Then why— Aaah.' Hera had put her foot on the floor, and the pain in her knee made her wince. Despite that, she was determined. 'I am turning you down, Alan. You're starting to Hal me.'

'Sorry. I was—'

'Shut up. I'm in a shitty mood. All right? It happens! Now, when I have disembarked, put yourself away and check all your circuits and make sure you are fully charged. I may need you. Understood?'

'Understood.'

Among the medical supplies aboard the SAS was a pair of crutches. With these Hera was able to climb out of the flyer and make her way over to the shilo. Behind her the SAS closed its door, folded its rotor blades and trundled towards the maintenance hangar.

Inside the shilo Hera managed to strip off her pants and top, cutting them from her where they were stiff with dried blood. Examining herself with the help of a mirror, she saw that the wounds needed serious attention. She washed each cut with a damp antiseptic towel, pressed the skin gently to see if there was pus forming or any discharge, and then dressed the wound.

Her arms and legs were puffy and bruised, and the skin was yellow and tight – but there was nothing that wouldn't mend. The wound in her abdomen needed attention. She applied anaesthetic pads to reduce sensation, then she made sure the cut was clean and clipped the lips of the wound together. Primitive but effective. Finally, she covered the area with an adhesive pad of synthetic skin.

Her face . . . She did not remember being hit in the face, but her left eye was swollen and partly closed, though it did not hurt. At least she could see. The cheekbone below was puffy too, and bruised. The other side of her face was completely unharmed, giving her countenance a Quasimodo look. 'No beauty prizes this trip,' she murmured.

Worst, by far, was the knee. It was dark and swollen with internal bleeding. Clearly there was something still in there. An anaesthetic pad would kill the feeling in the surface of the skin, but to dig deeper she would need an injection. This was tricky, not least because to sit up and lean forward to reach the knee put stress on all her other wounds. But what were the alternatives? Contact the shuttle platform? *No.*

Hera made careful preparations. She placed a mirror so that she could see the front of her knee. She made sure all the instruments she would need were sterilized and laid out with a beaker of disinfectant to put them in when used. She chose to sit on the floor with her back to her bed, and she placed pillows and absorbent towels so that her knee would be lifted at as easy an angle as possible. Finally she prepared a hypodermic needle. It was a low dosage – she preferred to cope with pain rather than risk unconsciousness. Her idea was simple: to open the wound, reach in with tweezers, remove whatever was causing the problem, close the wound and reseal it with a synthetic skin pad. As long as the local anaesthetic held, she knew she could do it.

And she would have too, but she had miscalculated just how weak she was. She was unaware that the thorn from the Tattersall weed was still alive and reactive with her flesh. Nor did she understand that her mind was awash with the strangeness of Paradise. So . . .

She injected herself, and felt the needle go in. She pressed the plunger. Withdrew the needle. Felt a warm numbness spread, and then, just when she was reaching for the scalpel, the room spun once, her one good eye fluttered, and she slumped back, mouth open, her wrist knocking over the tumbler of antiseptic.

Strange dreams began.

It took Mack just two minutes to neutralize and disarm the lock to the shuttle control. Dickinson slipped into the control seat and began tapping out resonance coordinates. The automatic station, still active underground at New Syracuse, came alive and flashed a signal back. It would only take a few minutes for the ground plate to warm and then they would be in business.

Mack, meanwhile, keyed in the access code to the airlock in front of one of the shuttle pods. The small cubicle came to full pressure and seconds later the first door opened.

'OK. Here goes,' he said to Polka, who was standing by.

She handed him a demolition satchel containing concentrated food capsules, a small laser gun, a fixed-frequency radio transmitter, quartz light and universal batteries, a navigation map, medical supplies and a change of clothes. 'Now remember. Be in contact. When you want to come up, let us know. We'll be ready. Good luck.'

Mack slipped through, and the door closed and locked behind him. Seconds later the door to the fast transit shuttle opened and he was in. He placed the satchel and his tool belt in a locker and closed it. Then he eased his bulk onto one of the couches and lowered the cushioned body plates until they fitted snugly but not tightly over his torso. Behind him he heard the door slide closed and the magnetic locks seal. Fans came on and the lights dimmed. A soft female voice said, 'Welcome to the—' but Dickinson overrode it. He heard Dickinson's voice counting: 'Thirty, twenty-nine, twenty-eight . . . . Get yourself strapped in, Mack. Tight is better than slack. When she drops she drops. Keep your eyes and your mouth shut. Breathe through your nose and don't gulp or you might swallow your tongue. You're going to make the fastest descent on record. Don't worry, I'll bring you out smooth but you'll feel up to five Gs. You'll feel it but don't fight it. I'll pace it. You'll have ten minutes to get out at the other end. Do you read me?'

'Loud and clear. I'm all strapped in.'

'OK. Hold on tight. And it's five, four, three, good luck, one . . .'

The shuttle pod dropped from the station and began to accelerate. It was following a thin line of light which coiled and twisted but stayed coherent. Mack was pressed up against the restraining pads and his nose and mouth were both forced into the soft fabric. He managed to breathe by turning his head slightly.

After about three minutes he felt the acceleration stop and he could breathe more easily. He was now falling fast. He opened his eyes and could see a bright cherry glow spreading out as entered the outer atmosphere of Paradise. A few minutes later and he felt a slight checking of his speed and could imagine Dickinson bowed over his control desk, studying the tolerances, giving Mack as much speed as he dared and figuring when to start to slow him down.

Mack suddenly felt heavy and was pressed into his bunk. Deceleration. He sensed his face pulled out of shape and his hair drawn back from his scalp. He could not have lifted his arm to save his life. He thought his nose would break and his eyes be crushed – it had happened – and he could no longer tell up from down or left from right. Then suddenly things were easier.

A voice spoke: 'Three minutes and you're there, Mack. You OK? Have you blacked out?' The shuttle descent eased more.

'No, I'm fine. Just hard to talk ... when you're fighting ... for every breath. I'm fine now.'

'Slowing now. She's a lovely machine you're riding there, Mack. What's the weather like?'

'Can't see. I'm in cloud.'

'We'll soon have you under that. You've got half an hour more of daylight and then it'll be black, Mack. Black. No moons for hours. So make good use of the light.'

Moments later Mack was under the cloud. He was falling faster than the rain.

He could see the hills, dark and misty.

'Six hundred metres.' After a few seconds he felt the deceleration ease. 'And two hundred. Bang on line. Mouth shut. Breathe through your nose. One hundred. And ... sixty, forty, twenty-five, fifteen, easy, five ... .' There was a bump. 'You're there, boss. Careful when you get out. She might still be a bit hot and you'll stagger a bit too.'

Mack saw steam rising around the shuttle. He released all catches, fastened on his tool belt, slung the demolition satchel over his shoulders, put his helmet on and strapped it under his chin. 'Ready when you are, Dickinson.'

He heard the door locks slam back and then the hiss as pressures were equalized. 'Good luck, boss. That's from all of us. Now move.' The door hissed open.

Mack jumped down onto the concrete of the landing pad and ran out from under the shuttle and into the rain. He didn't stop running, either. He ran with that easy almost slow-motion lope of big men which does not look hurried but covers the ground quickly. One thing about his line of work, it kept him fit. He stamped over the gate he had flattened with the half-track, turned right and headed down the main road leading to New Syracuse. The road was already breaking up as green shoots from below pushed their way through the cracks. The gutters were clogged with rubbish and water spilled out over the road. Mack splashed through. The roadside was thick with Tattersall weed and long branches sprawled across the road. Mack jumped them and ran on.

Ten minutes later, starting to feel the strain but now in sight of New Syracuse, Mack glanced back and was in time to see the shuttle rising just before it entered the clouds.

The light was fading fast as he entered New Syracuse. Keeping to the road, he turned the corner where the courthouse had once stood. In front he could see the marina and the sea. There was the bunker where he had left the wine for Hera. Not far now.

He ran along the seafront, past the hole in the ground which marked the site of the former Settlers' Club, and there he came to a stop. Something lolling in the tide at the water's edge had caught his attention. Some shapes are unmistakable. Mack jumped down off the road and crunched through the shingle to the water's edge. Lying face down in the water, arms stretched above his head and with his hands half buried in the sand, was the naked body of a man. Mack gripped the cold hands and dragged the body up onto the shore. It was surprisingly light and Mack fell back on the shore, having pulled too hard. He fumbled for his torch and shone the beam down on the face. It was an old man with two days' growth of stubble on his chin. A wide gash was open in his chest and one arm lay at an angle that told that the bones were broken. On one shoulder there was a tattoo of a dragon, which curled around the name of a woman. Mack turned the hand over and there on the back was the letter M and a number. The same letter and number was present on the right leg. No doubt whatsoever. This was a MINADEC worker, and yet the company had stopped operations

196

on the planet over a hundred years earlier. Mack did not know what to make of it. If he'd had misgivings about Paradise before, they were now a certainty. He dragged the corpse further up the shore and there he had to leave it. Back up on the road, he turned inland and ran towards a metal fence which had once enclosed a repair shop for SAS flyers. It was here that he had parked the old Demo Bus.

It was still there, its blunt crab-like shape dark against a wall and half buried in sand and rubbish. That was OK. These Demo Buses, old and lumbering though they were, could lift concrete beams and land in fire if need be.

Mack climbed the fence, jumped down into the compound and ran over to the craft. He cleared a way through the tangled rubbish to the door. Before opening the door, however, he climbed onto the roof. Lengths of red plastic space tie had been wrapped around the rotor blades. Quickly he cut the tape away, throwing the pieces downwind, where they caught on the fence and fluttered. Satisfied, he climbed back down and tapped in the lock code.

The door opened without delay and he threw his satchel in and climbed after it. Inside in the cargo bay he removed the heavy tool belt and stripped out of his wet overalls. Feeling lighter in every way, Mack climbed up to the control room, settled himself in the pilot seat and inserted the key. The moment of truth was upon him.

He switched on.

Nothing. Not even a flicker on the dials. This was ridiculous. Even if he'd left the lights on there'd still be reserve power. What had he forgotten? Ah! The main breaker. That turned off when the door locks were engaged. Mack climbed back through until he reached the racks of batteries. The master switch was down. He reconnected it and heard the systems come alive.

Back in the control room the dials were dancing as the Demo Bus performed a self-check of all circuits. The most important reading for Mack was the power reserve, and that slowly increased until it settled at just under half charge. That should be enough to get him to Hera's retreat. If not, he would have to put down somewhere and wait for the batteries to recharge in the sun. At most he would lose a day. So why wait any longer?

Mack pressed the start button. There was no sudden roar of engines, but he heard the torque regulator hum and the pumps begin to cycle. It would take a while for everything to warm up, then the sparks would fly. Meanwhile, Mack tapped the destination coordinates into the memory bank, then he switched on the fixed-band radio.

Cole's voice came on line. 'Hey, boss. Reading you. OK?'

'Just about to take off. Did they find out?'

'No worries. Nobody knew a thing. Just for the record, we've signed you on for cabin rest. Overwork syndrome. Nurse Polka has taken responsibility. No visitors allowed. She reckons you'll be back on your feet in a few days as long as you behave and get lots of sleep. I've taken charge of the team. We'll be back on the job in an hour or so.'

'Might be a bit longer than a few days.'

'Well, we'll worry about that when we come to it. You do what you have to. OK?'

'OK. I'm on my way.' He touched the engine relay. The overhead rotors began to turn slowly and then faster as the engine came alive with a deep and hungry growl. 'See ya.'

'Ciao, man. Ciao.'

Mack increased the power; the rotors became a blur; the big machine stirred on its wheels and then lifted steadily. It rose above the remains of the buildings and into the full force of the wind and rain. Then it swung round as the autopilot took charge and set a steady course south-west, hammering into the darkness. The journey would take all night.

Hera remembers little. Her life was like a dream in which some parts were in colour and some parts in black and white. These were separated by periods of complete darkness.

Best were the parts in colour, because they were fantastic and unpredictable and full of strange adventures. She began as a white feather blown about in a green wilderness. Her first discovery was that she could do the most wonderful acrobatics, twisting and turning in the air, swooping down and then soaring up. But there were no landmarks, nothing to tell her where she was or how high or low – just a shifting mist. Then as she was letting herself spin end over end, faster and faster, she realized she could control what was happening. She stopped the spinning.

She was in her own body, standing ankle-deep in clear water. In front of her, a hundred metres away in deeper, bluer water, stood a Dendron. It was back on its stump, and with its two front legs extended so that she was reminded of a dog that wants to play. Some dog! It towered over her. She had never witnessed anything so powerful. It was aware of her too. She knew that. The Dendron lowered the twin branches of its horns until they were right in front of her. She could grasp the huge black and red spheres on their tough stalks. She thought she would climb in among them, but then, just as she was leaning forward, the dream turned red, as though someone had drawn a razor across it. In that one moment she felt such longing and such pain and she must have woken up because the world became black and white.

The lights were on in the shilo, and through the skylight she could see it was dark outside. That meant nothing. She was just a bundle of rags on a stick. Somehow she dragged herself up off the floor and through to the kitchen. Going to the toilet was agony, but it was accomplished. Going back to bed was achieved by crawling over the floor. Hera dragged a bucket with her. She levered herself up onto the bed. The knee looked ghastly, but she was so tired, so very tired, she would deal with it in the morning.

The red tide swept over her.

And so it went on. In her dreams she seemed to be a much younger Hera. Once she was more like young Estelle Richter from the *Scorpion* – dancing across the tops of the waves – and that felt good. Once she was deep in the ocean swimming with the giant kelp and passed through the ventricle of its heart and was hurled out into the sea in fragments.

But always she came back to the Dendron, and it was the dominant presence whether out at sea beyond sight of land or deep in a river or climbing a hill with great flowing strides. She came to dread those moments when it would stop and seem to be aware of her, for these were always quickly followed by a return to the black-and-white world.

And in this world she was aware of fever and of trying to take care of herself, but her hands would not behave and her arms were like dough. Hera explains:

There came a great darkness which filled all of space and I knew I was contracting to a fine point of light. Then that light too began

199

to fade ... slowly, slowly ... No pain, just darkness pressing against it.

But in the darkness awareness too. A door crashing open, a shaft of white sun, the smell of a Tattersall weed. A giant bear standing in the doorway and peering in. There was reason to fight.

So much to tell. So much to do. Surely, one last big effort ...

Heave up like the Dendron, crying, 'Help me! *Help me.*'

Mack woke up, disturbed by an irritating sound that would not let him rest. A panel on the control desk was flashing and a message moved across it. Mack touched the screen and the noise stopped. It was a warning message. The batteries were running down and would soon need to be recharged. Mack looked out of the window, noticed the first light of dawn in the sky and the fact he was flying over water. He could see away to his left, where waves were breaking against islands. That would be the Bell Tree Islands, which meant that he was already well past Blue Sands Bluff, which marked the eastern limit of Chain. Soon he would come in sight of the Chimney Mountains, and once over these he would be in sight of Big Fella Lake and almost there.

He thought of Hera, and felt a certainty that if he paused to recharge he would be too late, that the bad thing, whatever it was, would be complete.

He didn't hesitate. He flicked open a catch on the dashboard which revealed a red emergency button. He pressed this and held it down for three seconds. The navigation screen lit up. Methodically he began to eliminate all non-vital functions aboard the Demo Bus. He switched off the heating in the crew quarters and all non-essential lights. The fans which pushed warm air round the bus ceased their hum and all lights went out. The Demo Bus was now nothing more than a flying engine. Mack unbuckled and using his helmet light made his way back to the cargo bay. There were a few things he could jettison. He heaved open the cargo door and began pitching things out. Spare seats, bits of machinery, heavy-duty concrete cutters, welding cylinders – all these he threw out and watched as they vanished below. He even drained the water from the tanks and flushed the toilet. Soon there was nothing else to lose. It would have to do. When he scrambled back into the cockpit, the craft was already climbing into the Chimney Mountains – pink in the dawn light.

The entire mountain chain was composed of volcanoes. Most were extinct, but in some places wraiths of steam were rising amid the snow. Many of the high calderas had lakes in them, and these showed as discs of silver in the dawn light.

The Demo Bus did not try to climb over the mountains but took the lowest path, passing between steep slopes and swinging through canyons. It was a well known route, fractionally longer than the direct climb but more economical on energy. It was cold, and ice formed on the inside of the windows of the cabin. Mack crouched, knees up and with his hands tucked into his armpits.

On the dashboard were four red lights which indicated the status of the batteries. Three of these were glowing a steady red and the fourth flashed every ten seconds.

There was nothing Mack could do but sit and wait and watch and hope.

By the time he began the descent from the Chimneys, the fourth light was flashing every five seconds. But now he had only the length of the lake to run.

Mack sat stone-faced as the Demo Bus dropped to within a hundred feet of the surface. The machine droned on steadily. But they were losing power more quickly now. A third of the way across, the light was blinking every three seconds, then every two seconds. There was a sudden hesitation in the engine note, but it picked up and droned on. Mack roused himself, donned a life jacket and strapped himself in. If the worst came to the worst he would swim – except he couldn't swim.

Within sight of the terrace the light was blinking every second and then it stayed on. All lights were now red. Technically the Demo Bus was out of power. Mack was flying on whatever dregs of energy the machine could garner. And then the engine cycled, the ugly sound of a machine pushed to its limit, and the Demo Bus started to drop. Mack took over the controls. He guided the craft as well as he could towards the base of the cliffs. He could actually see Hera's shilo. Finally the engine cut completely. The controls went dead. The machine began turn over in the air, but before it could flip completely it touched the surface of the lake. It rolled once like a clumsy broken toy, but lurched upright. Mack scrambled out of the safety harness. Water was already seeping into the cargo bay. When that filled they would sink fast.

Mack prayed to the gods of demolition workers that the escape door would still open, and they must have heard, for when he applied his strength to the eject lever, the door cranked half open on bent hinges and he was able to squeeze through and jump.

In the lake now, bobbing in the water, he paddled away from the old craft and towards the shore. It was only a few hundred metres away. After a couple of minutes, he heard behind him a muffled explosion – the batteries, he guessed, exploding on contact with water – they were probably under the surface by now. Moments later a wave broke over him.

In the trough after the wave his feet touched bottom, and some minutes later, after some vigorous paddling, he could walk. When he was waist deep in the water he stripped off the life jacket and threw it away. Weeds tangled in his legs but he just strode through them. In his determination and energy, was there was a passing resemblance to a Dendron?

Leaving the water, he ran up the steps to the rock terrace.

No sign of Hera. She would surely have heard the explosion and come running. So . . .

Mack ran across the clearing to the shilo. A Tattersall weed, now in full flower, had grown across the doorway – a bad sign. The door, when he tried it, would not open, and so he put his shoulder to it and heaved. It crashed open.

One question was answered immediately.

Hera was there. He saw her. She lay still amid the ruin of the bed, propped up on bloodstained pillows, one pale hand flat on the sheet, a blank eye staring sightlessly from her damaged face.

There was no mistaking it. She was quite, quite dead.

Mack leaned against the door frame while the water ran unheeded from his clothes onto the floor. After the excitement of stealing the shuttle and the tension of the journey here, it was hard to comprehend the anticlimax. All for nothing. Too late was the same as never. He forced himself to look at the still body.

There is nothing quite like the stillness of a corpse – and he had seen many. One still expects to see an eye flicker or a finger move even in a coffin, to tell you that it is all a joke and has not really happened. But no. A dead body is unnerving, because everything is as it should be, except for the absence of that one indefinable and indispensable thing called life. Finally, it is the realization of the absoluteness of death which crushes us.

Mack moved slowly round the bed. He shifted the bucket carefully and looked down at the small frame of Hera. Then he placed her cool hand under the sheet, closed her one staring eye gently and drew the sheet up high over her face.

He would have liked to cry, but there was a dryness in him.

He stood, uncertain what to do next. Should he contact the shuttle platform and tell them what had happened – that would start all the official wheels turning – or should he do the right thing by Hera and wash her and tidy her, and comb her hair – lay her out and give her dignity? In the event he did neither. He went into the toilet area and stripped off his wet overalls and hung them in the shower.

His spare clothes had been lost when he abandoned the Demo Bus and so he wandered about looking for something to wear. Finally, he opened the door to the supply room attached to the shilo. There, hung up amid the heavy-weather gear and waders, he found an old pair of brown meshlite overalls. They were left over from the MINADEC days, but were clean and serviceable. They were just big enough for him, though still a bit short in the arms and tight on the legs. But they would do. He wasn't going to a dinner party.

He moved back into the shilo and reached a decision. Bugger the authorities! He would clean Hera up. He wasn't having some medic fussing about or someone making a tri-vid of her looking like that. Then he would tidy the place, make it decent, and then they could come and have their inquiries and inquests. He didn't really care. One of the first things was to get some air into the room. It stank of ... stale air.

Outside it was a fine morning, with a bright sun and a few white clouds drifting high. He went back inside to the kitchen. As Hera had done before him, Mack took the ladder, climbed up and opened the skylight. Immediately the scent of the Tattersall weed entered the shilo.

It was while he was fastening the catch to the skylight that Mack heard a sound in the room. It was like a sigh. Mack felt the hairs on the nape of his neck rise. Turning to look down at the bed where Hera lay, he saw the still form under the sheet slowly sit up. Such things happened, Mack knew: dead bodies belching and contracting and sometimes twitching. He had never seen it himself but he had heard. But this was such a definite movement, almost inhuman in its slowness, and one which required prodigious strength. It was as if the body was being lifted. Mack could not move; he just stared. Finally the corpse was sitting completely up with the sheet still draped over head and shoulders.

Mack was a brave man, but he climbed down slowly, never taking his eyes off the corpse. He approached the body. He had no idea what he would see as he reached forward and took hold of the sheet. Pulling it aside took all his courage.

It was still Hera. One eye remained closed, but her mouth hung open and he heard again a gentle sigh. A drop of saliva ran from her mouth, and that more than anything told him she was alive. How? By what miracle? He did not care, but he stroked the good side of her face gently with the back of his fingers and then said, 'It's all right, Hera. Relax now. I'm here and you're going to be all right.' Supporting her back he lowered her, though he had to push slightly before the stomach muscles yielded.

The transformation in Mack, while not as remarkable as that in Hera, was extraordinary in its own way. Gone was the hesitant man, out of his depth. Mack became purposeful. He knew exactly what to do. He checked breath and pulse. He made sure she was lying straight but with her head raised slightly. He placed her arms outside the sheets, so that if she had an instinct to scratch she could do no harm. He took the pail and flushed away the contents. He gathered up the surgical instruments, which were where Hera had left them, and set them in a pan to boil. He found soup in the kitchen and put it on to warm. He pulled out clean towels and sheets and pillow cases and a duvet with a cheerful cover and set them ready. The largest towel he could find he laid flat on the floor. He shifted the entire medicine cabinet into Hera's room and set it up where he could reach things easily. He placed a chair by the bed. Then he filled a large bowl with warm water and set it down on top of the bedside table. Finally, since there were no surgical gloves that would fit his huge mitts, he scrubbed his hands, trimmed his nails back, scrubbed some more and then dried them on a fresh towel. The soup was warm, but he turned it off. Hera was weak but not malnourished, and there were other tasks more urgent.

Carefully, he stripped back the sheet from her body, soaking the fabric where the blood had dried and stuck to her skin. He saw the wounds and it did not take him long to deduce what had caused them.

He worked on down, steadily easing back the stained sheet.

Finally he uncovered the knee. It was horrific. It no longer looked like a knee joint, but was blue with yellow patches and a gash on one side. It had swollen to the size of her thigh and smelled. Mack studied it like he might study a jammed pulley block. He had seen such wounds before. There was something inside, something locked within the tissue, and while that was there it could not heal. This, he decided was a separate problem.

He began to wash Hera. The face was healing. He checked as well as he could to see if her cheekbone was damaged. It did not seem to be, and the eye under the swelling was clearing. As he checked the face he became aware that she was smiling and her lips moved. Some hidden drama being worked out in there, he guessed. But she did not wake.

Many of the wounds had bled, but the dressings that Hera had applied had done their job and the flesh showed signs of healing. Hera's neat clips had held and there was no sign of infection apart from in the knee.

With the wounds treated and her body washed, Mack slipped his arms under her. She groaned briefly as he lifted her and laid her down on the towel on the floor. As quickly as he could he stripped the bed, rolling up the wet and soiled sheets. He turned the mattress over and remade the bed with the crisp clean sheets.

Hera was so light he could have lifted her with one hand. He placed her carefully on the clean sheets and covered her with the towel, leaving the wounded leg exposed. Then he placed a pillow under the knee and packed more towels around the joint.

What to do with the knee? His first inclination was to open the wound and let any poison out, but he was no surgeon and would have been cutting blind. He opted for the oldest treatment of all – a poultice. And he made one of those intuitive leaps, the kind of thing that either succeeds, and you are called a genius, or fails, and you are considered a fool or worse. He went outside into the sunshine. He found a Tattersall weed flower that had recently opened and he pulled off its thick blue aromatic petals. Perhaps he was thinking of the drunkard's cure, the hair of the dog that bit you.

He placed the fresh petals on the wound and covered them with a towel soaked in hot salted water. Five minutes later, when the poultice had cooled, he checked and there seemed to be no rejection. If anything, the skin looked slightly pinker. He applied the poultice again, and then again. Finally, convinced that there was no anti-reaction, he found a hot water bottle and used this to keep the petals warm. By experiment he found that a petal would only last for three poultices before it lost its colour, and so he went outside with the ladder and little by little stripped the Tattersall weed of all its petals.

With the knee treated, Mack reheated the soup. He was able to spoon some of it into her mouth and saw her swallow. While he did this, he noticed that Hera's one good eye was open, and that it stared up at him. When he moved round the room, the eye followed his movements. But there was no hint of recognition. She growled once, and he growled back. Anything to help.

Hera slipped back and forth between worlds – like the salmon that becomes a princess and then a salmon again.

While days passed in Mack's busy world, for Hera there was no sense of time.

Sometimes she saw the great brown bear shambling round her room. Sometimes she was aware of strong arms lifting her up, dragging her back from the lovely green meadows, of food being spooned into her mouth and of coughing. At other times her arms and legs were moved as though she was a limp manikin filled with damp sawdust. Sometimes the bear growled at her. And the knee ... the bear was always fussing with the stupid knee. And sometimes the bear hurt her and she screamed and hit out at it – but then she would slip away.

But the dreams were changing.

Hera Everything was becoming more intense. There is a lot I don't remember, but one occasion stands out clearly. Again I was on the shore. And again I was watching a Dendron swimming towards me. Only the tips of its twin trunks were visible, cutting through the water like blades, its pennants snapping back and forth, and I could hear the Venus tears sounding together like chimes.

It came rearing up, with the water streaming off it and great

206

waves lapping, heaving out of the sea towards me. It was urgent. But then, just when I thought it would crush me, it started shuffling. I stood absolutely still and it walked right over me. I was in the private space between its two high arching cathedral legs. The bulk of its body was over me!

Olivia Go on.

Hera Well, with an animal such as an elephant or a horse, I would have been aware of genitalia. But here there was just a great pulsing sac, the thing Sasha calls its codds. It is not a sexual organ of the kind we understand, but still I had the impression that the Dendron was exposing itself in some way. It was showing me its pain, which was also its need. And then, finally, I understood. It wanted to divide. That was its message. It wanted to divide. Its need *was* sexual on that level. It wanted to divide in the same way that you or I might want to have a baby. Does that make sense?

Olivia Yes. Were you starting to think of it as female? That would be scientific heresy, would it not?

Hera Indeed, but I was a bit beyond such niceties. And in any case I was dreaming. I responded as a woman. And I suppose if I am really honest, I *did* think of the Dendron at this moment as female, simply because it was the one that would become two from its own body. But that is not important. What *is* important is that this was the first time I began to understand that there might be a Dendron still alive on Paradise.

Olivia Can we just go back a bit? What did you mean when you said, 'I responded as a woman'?

Hera Resonance. I translated its yearning into terms which I, a human woman, could experience – and, yes, I responded physically, wildly. And I am not going to explain that, Olivia. Just use your imagination. Like the old poem says, Salt and honey. Fire and ice.

Hera woke up slowly. She was truly herself again and she was seeing in colour – the sun streaming in, her lying back, and her bare leg held firm . . . and . . .

The brown bear was sitting on her bed, its hunched back towards her, crouched over her knee, doing something. She struggled up onto her elbows, and for the first time she saw him clearly and knew who he was and what he was doing. 'What the hell . . .'

But let us not get ahead of ourselves.

Mack, the nurse, knew nothing of Hera's visionary adventures.

After a few days he could tell that the poultices were working and whatever was lodged in the knee was being brought to the surface. Hera seemed more at rest too, though she never seemed to regain proper consciousness.

Mack established a rhythm. Every morning, after he had fed Hera soup, he would tease open the wound on her knee so that the skin did not close and trap whatever was within. That done, he applied new poultices in the morning, at midday and in the evening.

One night, the very night which Hera has described, he was woken up by her groaning. When he switched on the light he saw that she had pushed off the light covers and was rolling her head back and forth on the pillow. She began to breathe in gasps, calling something, and she was running her hands up and down her body. Mack thought that she might be reliving the crisis when she was injured and was up from his bed on the floor in a moment.

He touched her lightly and Hera became calm but was still breathing deeply, and then suddenly she stretched out her legs and twisted her body violently as though some demon had seized her. She was crying out now as she twisted round on the bed. All Mack could think of to do was to hold her down by the arms, and when that did not work, he lay on her, not totally, not flat, but so that she could not injure herself.

And we must just imagine his astonishment when she kissed him fiercely in the sensitive place behind his ear.

Mack was not a fool – he could read what was happening and was shaken by it. When Hera was again resting quietly, half turned on her side, her hair spread out on the pillow, he noticed there were none of the flickering eye movements that had so characterized her earlier trance states. Nor was there any fever.

If someone had told Mack that in those wild moments Hera was not responding, as it were, to a man, but that like a weather vane, she was simply caught up and buffeted by the mighty sexual gale of the Dendron, well, he wouldn't have believed it. Would you? I wouldn't. But that was the truth.

The next morning, Mack went through his usual routine, opening the skylight, letting the sunlight in at the windows, putting water on for the poultice and for coffee. Hera was breathing easily and so he did not try to wake her. He drew back the sheet, folding it neatly over her thighs and tucking it between her legs for modesty's sake. He sat on the bed to inspect her knee, placing a pillow under it as he usually did. As he feared, the exertions in the night had had their effect. The wound had split open and bled a bit. It was a red gash, and something, like a black hair, was lodged inside. He looked more closely. Within the wound but pointing up were two small jagged points. Mack squeezed the wound slightly to see how tender it was, and Hera sighed. Quickly he selected tweezers from the medicine cabinet. He sterilized them and then, very calmly, he set to work.

Hera moved but he held her leg firm under his arm. He could not stop now. He felt her struggle up onto her elbows.

'What the hell are you doing here?' Then she must have reached down to the sheet and discovered that she was more or less naked from the waist down. She screamed and tried to wrench herself free, but Mack held her leg as in a vice. 'Let me go! Get your hands off me!' With her good leg she kicked him, jarring his elbow.

Mack exploded. 'Stupid woman. LIE STILL!'

She was so surprised, she did.

Moments later, Mack blew out his breath in a long sigh, released her and stood up.

Hera immediately pulled the sheet down.

Mack turned and looked at her. 'Well, I suppose I didn't expect gratitude,' he said and extended his hand. 'Here, these are yours.'

Onto the bed he dropped two thin pieces of what might have been dark seashell, but smeared with red blood. One was about an inch and a half long and curved like a blade. The other was a pointed hook with a nasty twist in it. He shrugged, for he had no more words, and went outside.

Hera tried to feel outraged, but that didn't work. She tried to feel indignant and that was better, but it begged too many questions. She looked at the two splinters of the Tattersall weed and, like Shapiro before her contemplating the seeds of a Paradise plum, realized that they were still alive. Thus it followed that inside her knee had taken place the most implacable battle of all: the instinctive and absolute rejection of the alien by her human tissues, and the desperate struggle of the alien to survive. Between them, they would have torn her apart – and nearly did. She knew that if the thorns had died inside her and deliquesced, her blood would have been fatally tainted. So perhaps, in a strange way, she had been lucky. It was all so complicated! And then there was the poor Dendron out there somewhere, aching. It too had taken up residence in her mind, demanding attention to its needs. Ah, how she would like to serve them all. And Mack . . .

She looked round the tidy room. She smelled the soup warming on the stove and the coffee that he had not yet drunk. She saw the clean towels laid out, the bedding freshly aired, the open windows. All the evidence of care.

So little made sense. She saw the sheet that covered her and realized it had been used more to conceal than reveal.

Hera worked her way to the edge of the bed and stood up on her good leg. When she put weight on her other leg it hurt, but not in that piercing way. She knew it would heal and she would run again. Her crutches were nowhere to be seen and so she hopped to the door. Mack was not in the clearing. 'Mack,' she called, and heard a shout from down near the lake.

Moments later Mack appeared at the top of the steps, puffing. 'You get back into bed, Hera,' he shouted. 'I haven't wasted days and nights looking after you so you can throw it all away.'

Hera didn't move. 'I wanted to say I was sorry.' It was not what she meant to say, but those were the words that came out.

'OK. Well, you've said it. Now get back into bed.'

'Hmgh! Men!' If Hera could have stamped, she might have. But instead she hopped back to the bed and flopped down.

Minutes later Mack arrived at the shilo. 'I suppose you'll be telling me next that you want some coffee?'

'If there's some going, or some soup. But I'm *so* sorry, I'm *far* too weak to get it for myself. Would you be so kind . . . please?'

'Hmgh!' It was Mack's turn to growl. But it was a funny sort of growl because he was smiling.

17

Things Fall Apart

During the rest of the day they started to get to know one another.

Mack explained how be came to be there.

'You mean you stole a shuttle, flew a half-powered Demo Bus halfway round this world, came here, crash-landed – and all on a hunch?'

'A pretty good hunch, eh?'

Hera did not reply. She was too surprised. What Mack had just told her, in such a simple way, was the most extraordinary thing anyone had ever revealed to her – and yet he seemed unaware of it. Men – by which she meant the men she knew – didn't just go taking risks and chancing everything on a hunch ... and now here was Mack, one of the least fey and otherworldly of all the men she could ever have imagined, and he had. So, what was going on? Why had he brought her back from the brink of death? Was he too obeying the will of Paradise? She sat and stared at him with her quick little intellect buzzing.

And that was the problem. Her questions so preoccupied her that she didn't really see him, not Mack the man, himself, the bear, the grunt, the lover, loyal to death. What she saw was a piece in a pattern. Her educated mind still hid too easily in abstractions, not yet being developed enough to be earthy.

She stared until Mack became uncomfortable. Finally she said, 'I want to tell you something. It is very important, and very exciting. It happened when I was in a dream world.'

Mack looked interested. 'Go on.'

Hera took a deep breath. 'I think there is a Dendron alive on Paradise.'

Mack did not move. From his expression it was impossible to tell what he was thinking or what revelation he had expected: certainly not anything to do with a Dendron, we can be sure.

'It is true,' she said, oblivious. 'When I was out for the count, I had these visions – no, adventures – and most of them involved a Dendron.'

'Really? And what happened?'

'Oh, it used to come to me, and it was so real. I believed I was there, with it, and it was in pain and needed help. Of course it could have been an ideal Dendron because I've never seen a live one.'

'What does an *ideal* Dendron look like?'

'Well, you've seen the pictures of them. I suppose it is a composite made up of all of them. All the best bits.'

'So it is something you made up in your mind?'

Hera was uncertain. 'Possibly. Hey, what is this? I start to tell you the most important thing on my mind and you seem to want to make me doubt it, or make me feel that you don't believe me or something.'

'No, it isn't that. It is just that I saw you when you were unconscious, many times, and I listened to your cries. To me you were often afraid, though you did smile occasionally. The last time I had to hold you down or you might have really hurt yourself.'

'Really?'

'Yes, really. You were out of control. Thrashing about. Getting in a . . . lather. I wondered what that was all about. If I had not seen you, if I'd just heard you, I'd have thought you were . . .' He stopped. 'Ahh, it makes no sense.'

'Go on. You'd have thought I was what?'

He looked straight at her. 'Making love.'

Hera's face coloured. 'Some things are hard to explain.'

'So what did it do to you?'

'Do? Nothing. It just stood there. Vulnerable, hurting, yearning . . .' There was a long pause. Finally Hera said, 'I don't know what words to use. I was overwhelmed.' She hesitated. 'Why are you looking at me like that? Do you think I would make something like that up? I don't know what happened. There was some brute force in the air and I responded.' She looked at him. 'Women respond to a lot of things and a powerful sensual feeling is one of them. Surely men are like that too.'

'Can't speak for other men,' said Mack, 'but for myself I respond to a woman who is real and flesh and blood and able to love with everything she's got and be a bit crazy too. And who doesn't have to imagine a monster tree to get her thrills.'

They sat looking at one another, appalled at how bad the situation had suddenly become between them. Finally Hera said, 'I don't think I've explained things very well. I wanted to tell you about something quite lovely, but you wouldn't let me. Not everything makes sense the first time you meet it, Mack. Look at you. You knew I was in need and you followed a hunch and came to me. Does that make sense? Weren't you carried away by a feeling? Why did you come to me? Why?' Immediately she asked that, she wished she had bitten the words back. In the moment of asking she suddenly knew the reason – call it a woman's hunch. The idea that he might have done this from love frightened her.

'It seemed a good idea at the time,' said Mack, standing up. He too was out of his depth. He had said more than he meant and revealed more than he wanted. He was angry and confused and felt a bit of a fool. 'Perhaps now you are back on your feet, it's time I got going.'

That night he moved out of the sick room to sleep in the SAS.

The next day they were polite to one another. The unfinished conversation was left unfinished. Hera walked to the terrace top and back to the shilo several times. Mack brought her sandwiches.

Mack began to make plans to leave. Having repaired the cutter, he cruised out to where part of the crashed Demo Bus stuck up out of the water and recovered a few possessions – the small radio for one thing.

It still worked. Sitting there in the boat, he contacted his team. He coped with their questions. Yes, he was OK. Yes, Hera had been in danger but now was fine. Yes, he would be back soon. Evidently the cover-up they had planned was working well and he had not been missed. Mack signed off before there could be too many questions.

Hera, meanwhile, was preoccupied. She had found she could manage her 'green' times better. She discovered that, if she let her mind rest open and summoned up the image of the Dendron's huge arch, she could immediately feel its living presence. But beyond that she was uncertain and worried. She felt something was about to break, something ominous, and she made the mistake of thinking that it was the Dendron. She knew there was something she needed to do, but what? What? Though the truth was staring her in the face, she was still not equipped to see it.

That evening they sailed a few miles round the lake, to a place where a flat rock jutted out into the still water. It was surrounded by a floating flower not unlike a lotus. These plants, sometimes known as shyris or occasionally shut up shop, rose to the surface with the first light of dawn. Then they opened, their leaves flat on the water. Finally, when the sun touched the buds, the flowers opened and fluttered like fans in a breeze. They stayed open for a few minutes only, and then shut up shop and dived again, only to reappear an hour or so later and repeat their performance.

Hera was lying back enjoying the last of the sun. 'Shall I cut my hair?' she asked suddenly.

Mack did not look up. 'Why do you want to cut your hair?'

'I'm asking you a question, not telling you.'

'It's nice the way it is.' They lapsed into silence. Finally, still without looking at her, Mack said, 'How long have you had your hair long?'

'Most of my life .'

'Well then—'

'But I've not *worn* it long, if you see what I mean.'

'Well, wear it long now and see how it feels. If you don't like it you can chop it off. But it's nice hair.' There was a pause.

Then Hera asked, shyly, 'Will you brush it for me?' Mack made to move and then stopped. 'No, you can brush it yourself,' he said. 'It'll be good exercise.'

Hera was so surprised by this reply, so uncharacteristic of Mack, that she sat up and looked at him. 'Are you all right, Mack? Are you still brooding on yesterday? Do you want us to sort things out? We got things the wrong way round.' She was surprised to see that his jaw was set in a way that made him look strained and angry. He looked straight at her.

'I think you can cope now, don't you? I'll be leaving tomorrow.'

'Leaving?'

'Yep. Tomorrow. I'll take your SAS back to New Syracuse, if that's all right. I'm sure Alan's clever enough to find his way back here.'

'But why? Surely not because of—'

'Like I say, you can cope now. And I think you've found what you wanted down here, and there's not much need of me now. Maybe you'll meet your Dendron and . . .' He reached down and picked up the radio.

'And what?'

'And I hope you're both very happy.'

'Mack!' He did not look up. 'Mack, please. You can't leave now.' He still did not look up. 'Mack. Please. Look at me.' He did look at her then, and for the first time she really saw the hurt on his face. 'Mack, you can't leave. Not now.'

'I can. I will.'

'But Mack, there's so much I want to tell you. When I've got things sorted out in my head, I thought we might work together. Might work like . . .' She was lost for words. 'Like a team.'

'Aye. Well I have a team, thank you, and they are waiting for me right now, up there. They put themselves on the line for me, so I could come down here. Come to help you. Well, I've done my bit, so now I'm off back. If you're getting fed up with this place you can contact Captain Whatserface up top and she'll come and get you. Me? I'll make my own way. Alone.' It was the longest speech he had made for a long time. And when he had finished, he stood up, extended the short aerial and switched the radio on. Distinctly they could hear it tracking and then locking onto its wavelength.

They heard Polka's voice respond, small and distant. 'Hello, Mack, is that you? Come in, please.'

All he had to do was open the transmission.

PART THREE

Saving the Dendron

18

A Team

They travelled back from the long flat rock in silence. Both were left with their thoughts.

Mack retired early to the SAS. Hera went for a walk in the woods.

I saw it then. Alone under the trees. I had let myself be so besotted by the Dendron. I had not seen what was there before me. I had taken Mack for granted. I don't think I had even thanked him properly for all that he did. And of course he never told me. Well how could he? That I had kissed him when I was swept away by the Dendron's ... whatever. What a fool! How could I have been so blind? And now I had lost him.

That really left me with only one choice.

In the morning Hera made sure she was up first. When Mack climbed out of the SAS he found a table spread in the clearing above the lake. Breakfast was waiting and coffee was fresh and steaming. Hera was sitting, her hair pinned back tightly and wearing a lightweight unisex meshlite overall. 'I thought we ought to talk before you went,' she said without turning, and poured him a coffee.

Mack sighed. He had half-expected this, and feared it. 'You're too clever for me,' he said finally. 'Too clever with words. I don't know what to do or what to think when you get talking. It's best I go. But I wish you well. I'm not angry now. It just ...' He shrugged. 'Take care of yourself, Hera. Don't go waltzing with no Tattersalls. OK?' He ignored the coffee, turned and walked towards the SAS.

'Mack,' called Hera, 'could you just do one thing before you go? There's a box I want down from the supply room. It's one of the blue vacuum cases. It's got some seed boxes and incubators I need. It's too high for me, and too heavy. Could you get it down before you go, and bring it out here?'

Mack stopped, looked at her, shrugged and then nodded. He headed into the shilo.

Minutes later when he came out with the box, which was indeed heavy, he found Hera sitting where he had left her. She still had her back to him and was gazing out across Big Fella Lake. The sun was making the surface steam and, round the shore, the lake was turning purple where the shut up shop were just opening.

'See you,' called Mack, and he headed for the SAS.

A few moments later she heard him speak to the machine asking the doors to open. Then she heard the sound of his fist hitting the side of the SAS. Five minutes drifted past, and she heard him approach and come round the table to face her.

'The door is locked. Alan's not answering.'

'I know. I've told him not to answer you. And I have hidden the override control where you will never find it. It's the only thing I could do to stop you. And now I want you to sit down and listen to me. There are things I need to explain. Things I didn't understand myself until last night. So, please sit down, and when I have finished, you will be free to go. I promise.' Mack paused and closed his eyes for a few seconds, as though strengthening his resolve or counting to ten to keep his temper in check. Then he eased himself into the chair facing her. He put his hands flat down on the table in front of him in the manner of a card player who does not want to be accused of cheating and looked directly at her.

'There is one other thing,' added Hera. 'I do not want you to interrupt. No questions, just listen. Agreed?'

Mack nodded, a short jerk of the head.

'I think last night . . . yesterday . . .' There was a long pause, and then Hera took a deep breath, and said quietly, 'I think I have grown up a bit, Mack. I'm experiencing things I've never known before so . . . so, please forgive me if I get things wrong. I'm feeling my way and trying just to let my heart speak – the way you do. Sometimes, you know, I'm too clever. I've always been clever. Clever at maths. Clever in debate. Top of the class. I think I learned to use being clever as a protection – I can see that now – but being too clever is the same as getting things wrong, isn't it? It is not allowing someone else to be right. So, now I'm down there, Mack, where all ladders start, in the foul— Sorry. I'm being clever again. Just listen and don't judge Hera too quickly. Now I want to start with a drawing.' Hera placed a piece of paper between them. On it she drew a circle and then within it another circle which just touched the inside of the outer one. 'This was something my dad used to do. When he had something he found difficult to explain, he used to do drawings – he often used circles. Just look at it while I'm talking.

'There are a lot of things I can't explain, a lot of things I do not know, but I have to start somewhere. And I am going to start with that wonderful, brilliant, courageous hunch of yours which brought you down here and which saved my life. No one does something like that without a strong reason, and the strong reason you did that is because you had fallen in love with me. No, no, no. Please don't get up. We have an agreement and if you do not like my choice of words I can't help that. I'm not playing games. The stakes are too high for me. I can't find a better word, and I have tried. And it is as difficult for me to say as it is for you to hear. You are the lucky one, believe it or not. Anyway, what was it that triggered that love into action? It was when I was hurt, wasn't it? That was the moment. And you knew it. And, because you are the man you are, you didn't just take a pill and go back to sleep or go out and get drunk or something. You acted out of the goodness—'

'I wouldn't call—'

'Shh. Please listen. Look at the diagram. This inner circle is your life.' Hera put a dot on it. 'Let us call this dot the moment when I was hurt.' She traced round the inner circle. 'Now all this is you stealing the shuttle, finding that body in the water, getting the old Demo Bus going, flying over here, crashing it, running up the path and finding me dead.' The pencil stopped at exactly the point where the inner circle touched the outer circle. 'Now we could continue round the small circle past this point. Let's say you clean the shilo, wash me, call the authorities and so on . . . but all that doesn't mean anything now, because that isn't what happened. At the moment you found me dead – as you thought – you jumped circles. It was because of your love for me. And the action which began way back here because of your love for me suddenly gained a new dimension. You are now on the outer circle.

'OK? Now, what was happening to me?' She drew two new circles, one inside the other and touching at one point as before. She

221

put a dot on the inner circle. 'Now here's me. Off I go, flying to the Isle of Thom, but I decide to investigate a strange phenomenon, something that drew me like fish to bait, and here I am in the labyrinth approaching the little Michelangelo, and bang! Catastrophe! A Tattersall weed grabs me, punctures me and I scream for help. I didn't scream for you, Mack, but you heard me. I screamed for whatever would hear me – anyone, anything – and the call was answered both by you and by some creature I believed extinct. A telepathic link had been forming for some time, and my cry for help formed a kind of bridge of some kind. I don't know quite how it happened, but that does not matter any more. All that matters is that it happened.'

She placed her finger on the circle. 'We are here now, approaching the place where the two circles meet. I get back to the shilo somehow, am overwhelmed by what has happened and drift into dream time. I am dying, there is no question of that. The light is fading, and then a bear arrives, kicks down my door and comes striding in full of love, faith and courage. At that moment I jump circles. I choose life. And now I am on the big circle too. Look at the two drawings, Mack. They are almost identical, no?' Hera slid the two pieces of paper together so that they were mirror images. 'Both involve a shift onto a new level. New meaning. It is a beautiful figure of symmetry. And it will express itself in other dimensions too. Because that is what this world does. Finds correspondence. And we are joined, Mack, you and I, whether you leave or depart.

'But for the moment let us stay with my adventure. What is happening to me at the moment you arrive? I am drifting, Mack. I may be on the point of death. But I am now linked to the planet in a way I had never imagined possible. And I am in contact with the most powerful psychic energy you or I can imagine. You asked me what I saw. We see what we can imagine, Mack. But the *truth* is something we know. The real Hera, the woman I keep hidden down here, in my dry heart, she knows the truth of the Dendron. She recognizes a kinship and shares its passion, and relishes it too, and wants it – because she has never really known it in her life.'

Hera stopped suddenly and turned away. 'I've got something in my eye,' she said. 'Please don't get up. I can manage.' Moments later she turned back. 'That moment, that moment of lovemaking . . . It wasn't physical lovemaking of the type we know about, even if it looked like it. We humans don't have many ways of expressing ecstasy, you know. We can't think like a Dendron, but we can be sure it was not intending me harm. It was just being what it is . . . . and more than being. It was crying in pain. And you are right, I might have been injured if you hadn't restrained me in the only way you could . . . so again you were the right man in the right place.

'That moment, we can think of it in many ways. Think of me as having no more will than a limpet on the side of a boat, Mack. I had to go where the boat went. That's not how I saw it, but it is true. To me, I felt suddenly free in a way that I can only dream of. Every part of me was carried up on that great surge, that wave, that energy that was simply the Dendron's joy in living. And the only way my body could give expression to that feeling was in the most intimate and primitive and precious act of love. That is all. Pain and ecstasy can be surprisingly close. Salt and honey. And I do not need to go there again. It was a threshold that I passed through, or over or . . . and it was you who made that possible, Mack, because it was you who saved me and it was you who was taking care of me.

'I have power, now, because of it, and knowledge. This Dendron, this creature which inspired young Estelle Richter, which inspires anyone with the wit to see it, which filled this world with its vitality, which was hunted to extinction for its wishbone, which had comic books for children written about it as well as some of the loveliest songs and meditations I have ever read. Well . . . there may be one such still alive. One. One only. *One* in the whole of the entire universe. *One*. Think of that. One. The last. The only. The never, ever, ever to be repeated. And you and I are here to help it. That is the circle we are both on. And we are there –' she pointed at the paper '– and we are here, in this clearing above this lake, because of what we are and what we can do.'

She paused. 'It was an act of love which started your journey to save me. But love is indivisible, Mack. Once you start to love in the simple generous and innocent way you did, well, it just spreads out. It is such clean energy. It resonates. When you saved me, you jumped circles onto a bigger circle. The new adventure is just beginning. Can you feel the resonance of your first act?' She paused. 'Forgive me, Mack, and don't be offended, but you know what resonance is?'

Mack stirred himself and looked up from the two drawings. 'It's what happens when you hit a piece of pipe in one room and a glass next door answers in sympathy.'

Hera smiled. 'Too right. And you hit the pipe so bloody hard that every glass on Paradise is ringing! Think of that when I give you the keys.'

There was a long pause, and Mack finally cleared his throat. But Hera spoke before he did.

'I haven't quite finished yet. I want to talk about you and me.'

There was an even longer pause before Hera finally gathered herself. She began hesitantly. 'I could not have done what you did in coming here. It's not only that I do not trust my own heart well enough – I mean my feelings, my desires and all that kind of thing – it's just that I am a bit of a coward, really, when it comes to loving. I am so abstract sometimes, so clever, and I hate myself for it. What I want to say is that you know more about love, about loving, about men and women in love, about being human in love – God, I'm making a balls-up of this – you know more about loving in your little finger than I do in the whole of my body. That is a terrible thing for a woman to admit, but it is true.'

There was another long pause while Hera fidgeted a bit and made several false starts. Finally she got going again. 'In view of what you said yesterday, and obviously the way I behaved when I was in the dream world, I feel I ought to tell you that I know little about the physical act of loving; it frightens me rather. I know so little about men that you'd think I'd spent my life in a convent. I think men frighten me, though I have no reason to feel that, as the men who have figured in my life so far, except for one, have been gentle and kind. I need to learn how— I'm sorry . . . I'm not saying all this very well. Perhaps what I mean is that I am frightened of loving, of how I might respond to . . . I mean, I don't lack passion, but I don't like to lose control. I know you can't have both. Please look at me when I'm talking otherwise it's like talking down a well.'

Yet another pause, but not so long this time. 'You see, Mack, I want to love, but I don't quite know how. There aren't any books about that, are there? I missed out, somehow, when I was young and all my friends were falling into love and out of love and getting messed up by boys, and messing boys up, and doing things on the sly and then being full of secrets afterwards – secrets I could not share in because I was such a dreamy girl. I was always lost in my dreams so I never got toughened, or tender. But yesterday ... when you said you were going to leave, it was as though you had put a dagger in my heart. It hurt so. And I didn't know what to say. I hurt, and hurting is easy – we do it all the time – but I didn't know how to say the good words, the words to make it right. I wanted to say something but the words stuck in me. But I can learn. If there is one thing Hera Melhuish can do it is learn. Please just give me that chance. Let us enjoy the big circle, Mack, the Dendron circle, because that is what it is, and let us see where it leads us. Let's be a team of two.' She stopped, frowned. And took a deep breath.

'Anyway,' she continued, 'I've said my piece. I'm sorry if I was rude or seemed ungrateful yesterday – I'm neither. Please think about everything I have said and make your decision.' She pushed the two drawings in front of him and then turned over a plate revealing the override control to the SAS on the table. 'There you are. You are free to go.'

She sat very still while Mack picked up the control and the two drawings. He said nothing. She studied the distant mountains, her face set and devoid of expression. She heard him walk away towards the SAS, the click as the lock opened, the welcoming voice of Alan as Mack climbed inside.

She waited like the block of wood she so easily became. A few moments later she heard the door to the SAS close and seal with finality.

And then, surprisingly, footsteps coming back. She sat unmoving, with her back to him, staring out over the lake. He came up behind her, close behind her, and stopped. Then she felt him pull the pins out of her tight hair. Released, the hair tumbled down over her shoulders. Mack said, 'Keep still, Hera, while I brush out your hair.'

Silence.

Hera sat very still with her eyes closed while Mack ran the brush through her hair. Then he paused and said, 'Can I ask you one question?'

'Anything.'

'If there's only one of these Dendron, why can't it just scatter seeds, like a Tattersall?'

Hera smiled. 'Because they don't do it that way,' she said. 'You need two Dendron to tango.'

'Oh.' Mack nodded to himself and went back to brushing.

They might have talked on, or they might not.

She might have asked him how it was that he had one of her hairbrushes.

They had no choice. Suddenly, outside the shilo, an alarm bell started to ring. It was a warning set up during the ORBE days to tell anyone who was working outside that a live message was coming in.

Abhuradin Worried

'I'll take the call,' said Hera. 'I think they've found out you're down here.' She ran her fingers through her hair, pushing it back. 'I think you ought to keep out of sight, Mack. Just in case.'

Hera moved inside the shilo and opened contact. The face of Captain Inez Abhuradin, looking uncharacteristically frazzled, appeared in front of her. 'Hera. Are you all right?'

'Yes. Fine. I had a brush with a spiky Tattersall weed, but apart from that I'm fine. You?'

'Good. Yes. No. Well, I don't want to frighten you, but I have reason to believe that the demolition worker who calls himself Mack may have come down to the surface and be trying to get to you. He stole a shuttle. You may remember him. He was the boss of that demolition team that came out to your shilo when I delivered the SAS. I'm sending a squad of specials down.'

'Mack?' said Hera. 'Of course I remember Mack. Actually, he's here now.'

'What!'

Hera called, 'Mack. It's Captain Abhuradin. It seems your visit here did not receive official approval.'

Mack came round the door and into the communications room. Captain Abhuradin saw him. 'What is going on here?' she demanded.

Before Mack could speak, Hera cut in. 'He saved my life, Inez. I would be dead now if Mack hadn't stolen the shuttle. I'm not joking. I contacted him, sort of, and he had the wit to answer.'

'Stealing a shuttle is a serious—'

'Yes, I know. But the rules in this game are changing. This is not the same world as you left a few weeks ago, Inez. It's changing so quickly. Please. If you are thinking of sending people down, don't. They will not be safe here. The planet is changing so fast. I'm safe. I think Mack is safe, but no one else would be. Believe me.'

'What do you mean, the planet is changing so fast? It looks the same.'

'You'd have to be down here to know. I can't explain. So much is happening. Please, please believe me, Inez.'

'Are you sure you're all right, Hera? That's what I want to know.'

'Perfectly.'

'Able to leave if you want to?'

'Completely.'

Mack intervened. 'Hey listen, Captain. I'm not a kidnapper or anything else you may be thinking. If Hera wants to go she is free to do so. I only came to help. But I want to make one thing clear: I was the only one involved, OK? None of my team had anything to do—'

'Well, that is strange. I have one here. Dickin-something . . .'

'Dickinson. Yeah, I know Dickinson.'

'He says it was all his idea. That he bet your team that he could get you down to the planet and back without us finding out.'

'Well he's lost his bet then, hasn't he?'

'That is not the point. You shouldn't be down there anyway. Hera, can I talk to you . . . alone? Tell him to go away for a minute.' Mack moved outside and closed the door. 'Hera, I don't know what's going on. You shouldn't be down there. He shouldn't be down there. And meanwhile I have a catastrophe like you wouldn't believe on my hands with this Disestablishment.'

'What's the problem?'

'The fractal gate is playing up. Everyone's frightened. Freighters coming here find themselves at Alpha Centauri or some such. And it's a lottery as to where the outgoing ones end up. Meanwhile, I have a tail of twenty barges waiting to depart; no one knows what's in them because they weren't marked properly, and then your Mack there steals a shuttle . . . I don't know what to think.'

'It's all breaking up, Inez. All part of the Disestablishment. And Paradise is playing its part. But listen, Inez. Don't worry. When the time comes to lift off I'll – or we'll – be there. And for the rest, the official stuff, just pull out a form, write Mack's name on it, call him a research assistant or something, stamp it official and stick it in the folder. I mean, who the hell is going to care what we did in a hundred years? Think of your painter man. Think of the life you want. Think of life beyond barges and the rest. I'll keep in better contact now. I promise. I promise. And I'll find time to tell you about things. Mack is a good man. We're working as a team now.'

'A team! Hera, do you know what you're—'

'Don't worry about me, Inez. Take care of yourself. We're both fighting on the same side. Remember?'

Captain Abhuradin nodded and then her expression changed. 'Hey, I was trying to warn you about danger, not looking for counselling.'

'Take help where you find it,' said Hera. 'Look after yourself. Don't send anyone down. Let things ride. I'll be in contact. I promise.'

'Do so.'

The line went dead. Inez's face contracted to a point of light – and vanished.

20

A Moment of Peace and Reflection

What are we to make of them? This pair, unparalleled?

She already over fifty and he just a year or so younger, so not young.

Those of us who are compelled to live in the conventional world can but stand and wonder as he outruns Romeo for foolishness and she, not as chaste as Desdemona, but with something of that lady's fierce honesty, makes plain her feelings.

I suspect that in their naive approach to love, they touch the heart of Paradise. However, neither Hera nor Mack were social beings. Their walls did not come down easily. They had to dismantle them brick by brick.

In deciding to speak about herself, Hera was matching honesty with honesty. Mack had come to her in an honest and uncluttered way. She was offering her own vulnerability to balance his. In so doing, she felt she had said enough for a lifetime. It was vastly more than she had ever said to a man. It was more than she had ever said about herself to any fellow human being, with the possible exception of Sister Hilda. She was surprised at herself, and pleased too, for the opening-up did wonders for her. A light had been turned on inside her, and it lit all parts of her being. She gained a deeper sense of herself. She could actually feel herself regaining her health and she took walks in the forest alone, pondering these things in her heart and exploring the knowledge inside her.

That knowledge! I have mentioned it several times but have never explained it. Nor can I explain it fully. The sculptor who moves round his block of marble or wood, cutting and chipping, thinking in three dimensions, following his instincts ... he has a million and one possibilities, and from these he makes one decision. His knowledge of exactly what to do – that was the kind of knowledge she received. It was also an awareness of her own mind – that great resonator (to use Hera's word) – alive, responsive, reaching beyond the confines of herself and engaging with Paradise.

For Mack, Hera's speech had rocked him and freed him. The gamble he had taken in coming down to Paradise had been right. Now, as he accepted he was there for the long haul, he found an outlet for his need to protect and nurture. It gave him an opportunity to put his great big male body at the service of his most tender and delicate sentiments – and I am not talking about making love. He was never happier than when he found something that needed to be mended, or straightened or bent. And he felt he had purpose too, something much deeper and more satisfying than 'the next job'. He liked the idea of riding the bigger circle, of being needed, of helping a poor dumb Dendron. And this perky and prickly, bright and beautiful, mysterious and sensual woman would, he knew, provide him with more than his fill of delight – should she be willing, and he live that long.

If you had been down there on the planet with them, you would not have noticed much difference in their behaviour. Mack slept in the SAS. Hera kept to the shilo. They contrived not to get in one another's way but to give each other space. When they met during the day they were polite and pleased – a bit like children who keep looking at the presents waiting to be opened at Christmas. They also explored tangible ways of showing their pleasure. Hera, who was adept with needle and thread, adapted some overalls to fit Mack's height and broad shoulders. What matter if the bottoms of the legs were of a different colour to the top? They fitted, and they gave Mack a change of clothes. For his part, Mack made Hera a set of hairpins from the thorns of a Tattersall. Mack had discovered that if he boiled the spines briefly, they hardened and did not lose their structure. He could then shape them with a file.

Mack also became hungry for knowledge. He had seen still pictures of a Dendron – there was a permanent exhibition up on the shuttle platform – but for the life of him he could not work out how it moved. He needed to see one, and he turned the shilo upside down looking for tri-vids, but all had been packed and removed before the Disestablishment. And so he sat on the stone terrace with his legs dangling over the edge, staring across the lake. He was trying to imagine what it had been like when the first Big Fella came crashing its way down to the lake and had wandered out into the water. Then he took a hybla leaf and stretched it on a frame and tried to draw one.

Hera, on her way to explore beyond the monkey trees, saw this and stopped. She approached quietly and then, seeing it was a Dendron he was sketching, she tiptoed back to the shilo and returned with Sasha Malik's little book, open at the story 'Shunting a Rex'.[3] She handed it to Mack, who had put his drawing down quickly. He held the book for a moment and then handed it back.

'Read it,' said Hera. 'This young woman knew the Dendron well. She rode on one.' Hera wondered what she had said that was wrong, for she saw Mack's face change.

'I can't read it,' he said finally. 'I can't read.'

'What do you mean you can't read? Every—' Hera stopped herself in time. 'Oh, Mack,' she finished. 'That's terrible. Oh, I am sorry.' Hera knew as well as anyone that there are always people who slip through the net, often very gifted people. 'But I saw you—'

'No, you didn't. Polka does the accounts and Dickinson does my reading for me. I can spell things out if I have time, but I can't read like nor—'

'Don't you dare say "normal people". I'm going to teach you to read.'

'Dickinson tried.'

'Dickinson isn't me!'

'True.'

'But now I'm going to read you Sasha's little story, and then you can do a drawing.'

This she did. She sat down beside Mack. She leaned partly against him. And she read the famous words, 'The shunt I want to tell you about happened when I was nine.' She imitated Redman shouting 'Now move, you fucker' and bright young Sasha saying 'It's curtains, bon-bon, unless you can climb a sunbeam.' And when she had finished, she shut the book with a snap and left it with him. Mack's eyes were shining, for he liked a good story as much as the

---

[3] See Document 6.

next man. Then out of the blue he said, 'I love you.' And Hera (God forgive her) pretended she hadn't heard, and so Mack pretended he hadn't said it, and life went back to normal.

That afternoon, walking in the forest, Hera found two graves, the bodies – shrunk and dry and peacefully exhumed – lying on the surface. She called Mack and together they burned the corpses.

The same force that was making the fractal gate unstable and causing Captain Abhuradin so much trouble was accelerating change on the planet. The increasing reappearance of corpses was just one manifestation. But it was not only bodies. Anything that had been buried was brought up: barrels, concrete foundations, old bottles, old kettles, bones, broken cans, scraps of paper . . . Everything. One must just imagine, if one follows the logic of all this, that every pound of turd, every pint of piss, every gobbet of phlegm and every dribble of blood found its resting place somewhere on the surface of Paradise; there not to rot but be embalmed. Unmoving. Unloved. Derelict and redundant.

A kind of resurrection was undoubtedly taking place. A movement that had begun years ago when a Paradise plum became toxic was now gathering momentum. A planet that had dozed, happy since its first oceans formed, was asserting itself, and cleaning itself. For humans this process had sinister implications.

Though Hera's body had healed, her mind was more troubled. As the smoke rose from the funeral pyre she said, 'I'm glad you're here. I'm glad you can share it with me. I get these funny ideas. This afternoon I thought, *I wonder if events are casting their shadow backwards in time? So we hear them before they happen.*'

'That's what hunches are,' said Mack. 'Shadows from the future.'

'Do you ever get frightened of your . . . hunches?'

He thought for a moment. 'Well, I used to accept them. Never thought they were strange until I grew up. But now, here on Paradise, I can't read the future so I'm taking things as they come. "And how can a man die better than facing fearful odds,/ For the ashes of his fathers, and the temples of his Gods".[4]

'Where did you learn that?'

---

[4] Thomas Babbington Macaulay, 'Horatius', verse 27.

'My granny. Always spouting poetry, she was. Couldn't shut her up.'

'You are amazing.'

At that time, while they were aware of external changes, they were more preoccupied by the changes happening inside them. They were like people learning a new language who gradually realize that the words are starting to make sense without having to translate them. But other forces were at work.

Some days after Hera's conversation with Captain Abhuradin, after Mack had talked to his team and told them he would not be coming back until Hera did, and after the good Captain A had simply granted a retrospective licence for Mack to remain on Paradise, giving him the honorary title of research assistant, the sky suddenly darkened over Hera and Mack, as though a giant bird had flown over the sun.

21

The Path of the Pendulum

At the moment when the sun seemed to flicker, Mack was working on the roof of the shilo, pegging back the Tattersall weed that had become rampant since having its flowers stripped. He straightened and looked up. There was nothing wrong with the sun and nothing flying either. It was Mack's optic nerve that had, for a moment, been pre-empted. He blinked, shook his head and then, as though a door had opened in the sky, found himself engulfed in a thunder of ringing. The sound knocked him down to the ground, where he knelt, head down, while a wave of nausea made him gasp.

Hera, deep in the bush behind the monkey trees, being more attuned to the changing ways of this planet and therefore more able to ride them, let the sound wash through her. Keeping her eyes closed, she concentrated and was able to distinguish the presence of the Dendron from the background roaring. The feeling it conveyed was vastly more of pain, panic almost, certainly a cry for help. But not directed to her especially. Broadcast to whoever could hear, anywhere.

The fractal gate high above hiccoughed at that moment, and a freighter vanished.

Hera had been preparing another funeral pyre. She had come upon two more graves, a man and a woman. They had lain beneath the soil for over a hundred years but had now been returned to the surface with considerable disturbance and lay, shrivelled and dry, on the dark soil. Their skin was tight and brown and shiny and the clothes they had been buried in were leached of colour and stiff as boards.

Hera left the bodies without striking the flame and ran back to the shilo.

'Did you feel that?'

'My stomach did. I fell off the roof. Is that the voice you talk about?'

'Yes. No. Similar. What you felt just now was a cry for help, Mack. We have to go. We can't ignore it. You can't stop a baby coming once it starts.'

'A baby?'

'No. Sorry, that's misleading, but the same idea. The Dendron needs to divide. Fission!'

Some minutes later it was Mack who applied a flame to the small pyre. The bodies burned quickly, like paper dolls, like old parchment, and the bones glowed white before collapsing into ash. Even the skulls burned, turning to roaring balls of fire which flared up and died. Mack watched thoughtfully and then shook his head and made his way back to the shilo.

Hera had already brought the SAS out of the hangar and was ticking things off verbally. 'Larder's fine. Water's fine. Power's at max. I've restocked the medi-kit. I see you've made yourself a nest in the control cabin. Very comfortable.'

'Only place I can stretch out.'

'There's a spare berth.'

'I'm OK where I am. Now I know something you won't have thought of.' He ran back to the shilo and emerged moments later carrying his tool belt. 'If you want to make a demolition man feel naked, take his tool belt off him.'

'Thanks, I'll remember that.'

The SAS came to power and Hera took them spiralling up into the sky.

High above the monkey trees, she looked down. The last of the smoke from the pyre was curling above the trees. The SAS flew in a circle. 'So which way?' asked Mack.

Hera looked at him blankly. Then she looked out of the windows as though for inspiration. 'I . . . I don't know.' She looked at him. 'Mack, this is silly.'

'Well try. Just relax and do whatever it is you do.'

Hera leaned back and closed her eyes. She thought of the Dendron arching above her. With the image came emotion but it was everywhere, and nowhere, and shapeless. She opened her eyes. 'I can't, Mack. I get no sense of direction.'

He looked at her a bit hesitantly and then said, 'Can I try?'

'A hunch? Why not?'

'Some people don't like this,' said Mack. 'Especially scientists. Can I have a couple of long hairs?' That surprised Hera, but she loosened her hair, combed her fingers through it and held up several hairs. 'Here, take your pick.' Mack took two and twisted them together and laid them on the control panel. He had a ring on his little finger – Hera had meant to ask him about that sometime – and he worked it off and tied it to one end of the hairs. 'Now don't ask any questions. I don't mind if you watch, but if you want to ask questions go down below and make a sandwich or something.

'I'll watch.'

'OK. But no questions.' He took the hairs between the finger and thumb of his right hand and let the ring dangle. Almost immediately, it started to swing, oscillating back and forth, towards him and away. His lips moved. He seemed to be talking to it and moments later the swing of the pendulum changed and it began to describe a circle, swinging clockwise. 'OK,' she heard Mack whisper. 'Thank you.' Hera thought of her father, who used to talk to his plants the same way. 'Now,' continued Mack, still concentrating, speaking each word carefully, 'show me the direction in which we must fly to find the Dendron that is hurting so much.' Immediately the pendulum slowed, its movements became random, and then it began to oscillate in a straight line but at a diagonal. Mack took a compass reading. West by north, say 283 degrees. 'Thank you.'

'Amazing,' whispered Hera. 'I don't believe it. How do you—'

'Sh . . .' But the pendulum movement had lost its authority. 'I hadn't finished. You had to open your big— Well, at least we now know in which direction to go. But please, Hera, the next time I ask you to be quiet, please shut up.'

'Sorry.'

'Just get flying, will you? Two eight three degrees west by north.'

'Is it far?'

'*That* was exactly what I was going to find out.'

'But how do you know that's right? It could have swung anywhere.'

Mack groaned. How often had be been through this? 'OK. Do you have a better idea?' Hera said nothing. 'Well, do you? This is my science, see. Old science. Your lot haven't caught up with it yet. Now fly before the bloody Dendron starts ringing its bells again.'

Hera adjusted the course and the SAS swung round and headed west by north. She took them up to 1000 metres and concentrated on getting a direct map alignment. 'This will take us over Paraffin Island and then on to Horse. And beyond Horse we'll be into the Largo Archipelago.'

The engine settled into a steady distant hum.

Hera switched on the view screen linked to the camera under the SAS. She entered instructions and drew simple Dendron shapes on the screen.

'What are you doing?'

'I'm setting up a pattern recognition programme. If it detects anything moving, or sees a repeated pattern or certain shapes, it will notify us and then we can decide whether to go down and investigate. It'll see things we don't. OK. That's it set and working.' She spun her chair round to face him. 'So how did you learn that trick?'

'Old fellow I used to work with. He could find where wires were broken under a floor or which rivets might spring loose or whether a weld was sound or not. He had fancy electronic diagnostic gear he could have used, but he was a little fellow, not much taller than you, and he hated carrying heavy stuff about, so he used a key tied to a bit of cord.'

'And it worked?'

'As well as the scientific equipment did, and more specific.'

'Why doesn't it like questions?'

Mack scratched his head. 'Well it's not so much the questions as the mind behind them. There are some minds that simply stop things happening.'

'And you think I'm one of them?'

'I didn't say that. But it's not a party trick.'

'No, Mack. I know.' And then she laughed. 'I was just thinking, if Galileo had studied Earth magic as well as maths and optics – well, there's no telling where we would be now. It would be a different world, Mack. Less prejudiced? Less afraid of the dark?'

238

Mack sighed. 'I wouldn't know. I'm not a very educated man.'

'Don't be sad, Mack. We're both going into the unknown.'

'There's a lot of life I've missed out on. The only thing I know about is work. I pull down buildings. That's what I'm good at. Like you're good at sewing overalls and such . . . But I've got this too.' He held up the pendulum. 'And I know what I know. And no fucker can take that away. Now why don't you have a go?' He handed her the ring dangling from the hair. 'Just play about with it. Don't be afraid and don't be clever. Just be interested and don't judge. Remember you talked about another Hera that hides inside you? Well, let her have a go. Ask it if we're travelling in the right direction to find your mate the Dendron. See what happens.'

Hera took the ring and weighed it in her hand. It was surprisingly heavy. Warm too, from where Mack had been holding it. 'It's a nice ring,' she said.

'One of a pair. My brother got the other. Given us by our granny. She said, "A man without a ring on his finger will always find trouble."'

'I see,' said Hera. 'So I'm trouble now, am I? Well, I'll give it a go.'

But before she could, the PR screen began clamouring for attention. It had found something and the SAS was now hovering, the tri-vid plate that showed the scene below focusing down.

There was a pattern on the ground. At first it looked like a spider's web made of strands of blue wool spread out over the trees and hills. But as they zoomed closer they could see that the blue colour came from the flowers of young Tattersall weeds, some in their first blooming.

Hera recognized the pattern – not quite a labyrinth but close. She was not surprised to see, at the centre of the web, a deep dark valley with a stream running through it. She took the SAS in a wide arc over the hills. They could see the web in its entirety, stretched out, blue strands over the green hills.

'Well if that's a spider's web, I wouldn't like to meet the thing that made it,' said Mack.

'It isn't a spider at the middle, Mack, it's a Michelangelo. When I was injured, the Michelangelo I saw was just a little one. The one down there must be huge and old. It must have kept itself well hidden, but now . . .'

'Did yours have a web like this?'

'Not really. Mine was more like a whirlpool, but it didn't look like a trap. If I had seen something like this, I might not have gone blundering in. Whatever is in there is no baby. It will be big and strong – dangerous too. Some were called Dark Angelos, or simply Reapers.'

'They're probably all dangerous. Anything that can make the bloody Tattersall weeds stand up straight deserves resp— Hey, look. Look there. In the middle . . . There's something moving.'

At the very centre of the web, at the dark hole, something was emerging. At first it was like the white snout of an animal, but then it rose on a thin stem until it was high above the forest trees. As they watched, it unfurled slowly. In shape it was like a feather, but so white as to be almost silver. And as it opened more, so it spread out flat and began to shine with an inner light, like the filament in a light bulb. Finally, they could hardly bear to look at it directly. Then, when it was like a mirror reflecting the sun, it became suddenly transparent – but still with a hint of violet. In size it now covered half the area of the web.

'Take us lower,' said Mack. 'Let me see that.'

'No,' said Hera. 'I don't trust it.'

'Oh, look at that . . . It's still opening and growing.'

Hera did not look but steered them away, rejoining their course. Mack didn't try to stop her, but he stood watching the vast pale shape as they flew away from it. Finally, when they were some distance away, he saw it begin to spin, like a whirlpool of light, gradually getting smaller, until all that was left was a silver ribbon, twirling at immense speed.

'What was all that about?' he asked.

'I have no idea.'

'How the hell could a stem as slim as that support something so huge?'

'Welcome to Paradise.'

'You're not impressed?'

'I'm thinking of the Dendron.'

'I think that was a good omen,' said Mack after a few moments. 'I mean, a white shape like a feather. That's what you thought you were when you were in dream time, wasn't it? And if we had been on the wrong track, something like that could have stopped us. Don't you think so?'

'Either that, or make us forget what we were here for.'

They flew on in silence and by nightfall had come to the sea.

'I think you need to teach me about the Dendron,' said Mack suddenly. 'Everything you know.'

'I don't want to disappoint you, Mack. There's a lot we don't know.'

'Could they swim?'

'I'm not sure. We know that often when they crossed the sea or a lake, they walked along the bed. Sometimes all that was seen was the tips of their twin trunks with the cherries and Venus tears bobbing about. But I feel sure they could swim too, although they weren't very buoyant. They were heavy, Mack, heavy. They carried a lot of fluid. They used to get toppled if they were far out at sea when the tides were strong.'

'So how did they find their way about?'

'No one knows how they navigated, if that's what you mean. That's one of the big questions we would have liked to answer.'

'What about those black ball things, the "cherries" that Sasha wrote about? Weren't they eyes?'

'Evidently not. Quite a number of species on Paradise have growths like that – well, similar. The plums for instance. Shapiro believed they were some kind of organ of sense. But not like eyes.'

'So if they couldn't see what did they do? They didn't just blunder about. How did they find one another?

'Sasha suggests telepathy.'

Mack nodded slowly. 'No wonder it knocked you silly.'

'Yes. But telepathy presumes a brain, Mack.'

'So? Perhaps it was all brain. What about the black balls? Perhaps it kept its brains in its balls, like Polka used to say about Dickinson.'

'That's as good an idea as any.' Hera smiled.

Mack sat looking at her for a while, thinking, his brow wrinkled. 'The point is . . .' he said finally, 'we don't know enough, do we? That's the problem.'

Hera nodded. 'That's the problem. It always has been. If only we'd had a live Dendron to work with. But the last recorded sight of a Dendron was long before the ORBE project got going. After the MINADEC onslaught, there must have been one or two left wandering about, but they were never recorded and probably killed.'

'But they divided, right. Fission. They split. One becomes two.'

'Right. Parthenogenesis, we call it. Virgin birth. There is always one that cuts and one that divides. The one that does the cutting is a kind of midwife.'

'I'm getting the picture. What was the one in Sasha's story?'

'Sasha called her "she", so I reckon the one that wrecked their camp was looking to divide. Looking for another Dendron to do the carving. But every Dendron fulfilled both functions. They did the chopping when needed, and then got the chop themselves when they wanted to divide.'

Mack shook his head. 'I thought some of the fellas in my team were a bit rough with their women, but these Dendron could teach them a thing or two.'

'I know you're joking, Mack, but beware of thinking of them as men and women. They would all split at some time and become two. And they would all do the cutting, perhaps many times as they hoofed round their planet. Their function depended entirely on what part of their sexual cycle they were in. Most of their life they were roving cutters, but then, when the time was right, they settled down to divide.'

Mack looked at her. 'And our Dendron. She wants to divide, right?'

'I'm sure *it* does.'

'Great. Can you do me some drawings?'

'I'll try.'

So for the next hour they stayed head to head, Hera making drawings and Mack asking questions. Hera explained what she knew of the anatomy of the Dendron. They discussed technical points in the story 'Shunting a Rex'. She watched as Mack tried to replicate a Dendron's movements using his thumb as the stump and the two index fingers as the front legs. It was surprisingly realistic. She saw his eyes smile when she explained about the coloured crest which rose and unfurled like a fan, and which could slice down whole trees with one sweep. Finally she told him the story 'One Friday Morning at Wishbone Bay'.[5] In this article Marie Newton, one of the early aggies, described an encounter she and

[5] See Document 7.

her daughters and son Tycho had with a pair of Dendron performing severance.

As Mack sat and listened, observing Hera's enthusiasm and imagining every cut and thrust, in his heart he wondered if she had any real understanding of what she was hoping to accomplish. How could they understand the ritual of the carving? How could they butcher a creature that size?

But Hera was sad too. 'No fossil records – Paradise doesn't do fossils. No live specimens. Just a few vid-cubes, a few wishbones in museums, a few stories and poems, and piles of carved earrings and knick-knacks. Ever since I've been here, the planet has been changing, but the change has been going on for years. The plum becoming toxic is just the most spectacular example. The early scientists wasted years trying to make this world conform to what we know from Earth and finally they packed it in. The planet functioned, but no one knew how. And then, when it was almost too late, ORBE started. You with your pendulum are probably closer to the Dendron than we ever were. You see, that's why the ORBE project, was so important, Mack. We who worked here, we were among the pick of our kind. We were "smart fuckers", as Sasha would say. But the one important thing about all of us was that we accepted that we didn't understand Paradise, and so we tried to find out starting from base zero. That's where Shapiro was so clever. He wanted the brightest and the most radical minds. And when he'd got them here, he relied on the enigma of Paradise to keep them hooked. No wonder we never got on with the aggies. We were everything the aggies were not. Look at us – pirates like old Pietr Z, hard-knuckle feminists like Tania, randy drug addicts like Shapiro . . .'

'Bantamweight prizefighters.'

'You're getting the picture. Agriculture was the last thing on our minds. We were ready to create a new science if need be, a new botany, a new biology, a new taxonomy, a new way of thinking. A new physics was already coming in with the advent of the fractal, and God alone knows where that will lead us. We used what we could of Earth when it helped – I mean, if something has roots and it grows in what looks like soil, and it likes water and sunshine, well, there is a lot you can do with it. And the exciting thing, Mack, was finding where Earth ended and Paradise began. And what happened? We were shot out of the water, Mack, like most of the

Dendron. And so if I get upset from time to time, that's why. And now there's only you and me left – travelling the circle.'

'The brawn and the brains.'

'I'm not that strong, Mack!'

Later, when the SAS announced they were in sight of the shallows of Paraffin Island, Hera ordered Alan to find a high place for a landing. 'If a Dendron stamps within a hundred miles of us,' she said, 'we want to know.'

Hera had gone beyond her strength and with a sleepy yawn retired to her cabin. Mack sat in the control room, wide awake, staring out through the windows. They had put down overlooking the seashore. In the pale golden light of Gin he could see the waves breaking.

A long time ago his granny had told him that his brother would be the rich one, but he, Mack, would have the adventures and one great adventure to cap them all. Well, she was right so far.

Glancing round the cabin, Mack saw that Hera had left the ring pendulum among the sketches of wishbones and tapering horns and strange dangling fruit.

Idly he picked it up and let it swing.

With the pendulum moving freely, he asked, 'Will we find the Dendron tomorrow?'

Immediately he received the answer: 'Yes.'

'And is the Dendron OK?'

The pendulum swung on a diagonal. The answer was inconclusive. Yes. No. Maybe.

Mack opened the chart of Paradise and moved his finger over it, tracing their course onward while all the time letting the pendulum swing in his other hand and asking for guidance as to where they would meet the Dendron. His finger had just crossed the Chingling desert, which filled the inner plateau of Horse, when the pendulum reacted. It was very specific.

'And will we be safe?' The pendulum again made the movement which told him that the outcome was inconclusive. Mack knew that words like safe were too vague for an instrument at precise as the pendulum, for they were not safe anywhere. He could have made the question more specific, but he chose to be content with what he already knew.

He had, however, one last question: 'Is helping the Dendron the big adventure my granny told me about?'

Though he always tried to keep his expectations neutral, it was with some surprise that he received the answer no.

2 2

Dendron!

They were flying high and fast.

Mack had marked on the map the exact place where he believed the Dendron to be. He had repeated the dowsing cast that morning and Hera had seen with her own eyes the authoritative way the pendulum changed.

Now the desert named Ching-ling was unfolding beneath them. The arid brown dunes were as clear and firmly sculpted as ripple marks on a beach. Every night the winds came up and the dunes shifted slightly, burying anything that could not escape. One river entered from the south and fanned out into the sand before disappearing underground. This had provided the last green they had seen. Occasionally they passed over sharp rocky mountains, which cast long, distinct shadows over the sand.

Far in the distance, but becoming clearer by the minute, were the tall mountains of north-west Horse. It was somewhere there that they would find the Dendron.

'Reaper below,' called out Hera, and switched the view screen to magnification.

They looked down on patterns in the sand, but these were not like the labyrinth or spider-web they had seen the previous day. These patterns swirled and coiled out across the desert sand as though drawn by a child. But still they had a focus – though it was not at the centre. A small ring of standing stones surrounded and hid the Michelangelo in their midst. As they watched the desert roll past beneath them, the pattern in the sand suddenly changed. New valleys and dips appeared, sand rose in spirals and a ripple of light spread out from the centre.

'Just letting us know it's aware of us,' said Mack.

Hours passed, and then, far in the distance, amid a maze of ravines and tumbled rock, they saw what seemed like a wavering line imprinted on the desert floor. At first they thought it might be the remains of a MINADEC water channel, but as they drew closer they could see it was not a single line but a series of small craters, each containing a small pocket of shadow. Hera took the SAS down to a hundred metres. Though she had never seen the spoor of a live Dendron, she knew what to look for. 'Look, Mack,' she said steadily. 'Look. Look. Look. There. We've found it. That's the mark of its stamp.'

To Mack it looked as if someone was planning to build a fence and had dug a series of post holes. They came wandering up from a deep ravine and entered the sandy desert between two massive pillars of rock. The fence maker must have been drunk, as the holes were not in a straight line, but wandered all over – even sometimes doubling back and crossing themselves. Between the holes were trail marks where something had been dragged and there were smaller impressions to either side.

But Mack's attention was on the ravine over which they were now drifting. It was sheer-sided, as though the roof of a subterranean cavern had fallen in at some distant time in the past. Smooth meandering pathways showed where water had flowed, perhaps quite recently, though now it was dry. Mack also saw the shadow of caves in the depths, and steep-sided overhangs. His guess was that there could be any number of interesting things hiding down there.

Away in a corner at the very bottom of the ravine was the merest hint of a spiral pattern, which ran along the floor and up one of the cliff faces. *Another of them*, he thought. *They're everywhere! Wherever there's action!*

Hera was busy guiding the SAS, following the tracks. They were not recent and she frequently lost them where the sand had drifted over them. But the general movement was in the direction of the foothills, and so a small time spent scouting in a circle was all that was needed to find the prints again.

The rounded dunes were giving way to stony terraces, which emerged like the backbone of a buried creature. Twice they came to places where the Dendron had obviously stopped for a while. Stamp marks formed a ragged circle, and the ground was scored and torn where the Dendron had scraped at it.

'I'll make a guess,' said Mack. 'I'll bet that's where it was broadcasting. I think it was looking for water. Look how it has torn up the ground and kicked those boulders aside. And there, look. What did I tell you?' Unmistakably, where the Dendron had stamped as hard as it could, crashing its stump into the desert floor, there was now a pool of clear water, visible only because it reflected the sky. 'I bet it sat there for a few days, thinking things over.'

Finally, as they were approaching the hills, the footprints vanished. The ground became flat rock, and not even a Dendron left a trace here.

They flew on slowly and came upon the first signs of vegetation – low plants which crept into the desert and had wide black leaves. Mack pointed out where several had been flattened and others torn out of the ground.

The stone plateau gave way to cliffs of shale and they could see where the Dendron had tried to climb and had slipped down, not once but several times. 'Why did it try to climb there?' wondered Mack. 'That's the hardest place of all. If it had come a mile east it could have easily got up that ridge, couldn't it?'

'Perhaps it wasn't bothered about finding the easy way.'

'Perhaps it was crazy! What's it weigh do you reckon? Hundreds of tons! Whatever it is, that's a hell of a lot of Dendron to go heaving about. Given the amount of climbing since its last stop, it would be getting pretty tired by now. That's when things make mistakes: animals, plants and machines. Once fatigue sets—'

He never got to finish. The sky suddenly darkened in a way which they recognized. Hera screamed and clutched her ears. At the same moment Mack felt as though he had been clubbed from behind. Both heard a roaring, as though sky and earth were about to be slammed together or torn apart. They braced themselves for the onslaught and then ... were left hanging. There was no sudden peal of bells or roar of thunder. Instead they felt what Mack later described as 'pins and needles in the head'. And that too gradually faded.

They looked at one another, both afraid, both like people who had felt an earthquake tremor and now awaited the main shock. But there was nothing. Just a hollowness which had its own kind of energy.

Finally, speaking softly, dryly and without emotion but very distinctly, Hera said, 'From all the evidence we have, it seems that we have just been spared . . . or protected.'

Mack could not speak. He was standing very still and with his eyes closed, but he nodded. Hera continued: 'I think we were shielded because we are here, and useful. Let's hope so.'

Then, tight-lipped, she took the SAS up higher. She could still feel the presence in her mind, but she was under no illusions. The Dendron, raw and untutored, had cried out as it would have cried out had a thousand other Dendron been in the region. It was a cry of pain and desire, innocent as a knife. But what, she asked herself, had intercepted that cry? What had absorbed it and made it palatable to their minds? If not the Dendron, then the only other creature she could think of that might be able to do such a thing was the Janus-faced, dark and formidable Michelangelo-Reaper.

She guided the SAS up and over the shale bank. The place where the Dendron had finally torn through the top of the shale was just beneath her. Now the vegetation became more dense, and some distance inland they came to a pool of grey water. The SAS hovered, and its rotors made the surface erupt into small frothy waves. A river emptied into this pool, but since no water flowed from it, they presumed the river continued underground. Facing them were three heavily wooded ravines which came down from the foothills in a broken zigzag pattern. Hera had expected to see the telltale web of a Michelangelo, but there was nothing except the camouflage jumble of bush and tree. The path of the Dendron, however, was unmistakable. It had marched straight through the lake and had entered the middle ravine, crushing everything in its path.

Hera guided the SAS up into the ravine, following the Dendron's track. Below, the stream tumbled white over rocks. After many twists the ravine gradually opened into a narrow valley and this led up to the first plateau. Looking back, Hera could see the desert behind her. It was shimmering in the sun, and the shadows were a dark blue. They had already risen some 500 metres.

In front was another lake, and here the water ran clear. A colony of talking jenny lay crushed and torn in the middle of the lake, a sure sign that the Dendron had passed through, and recently too. At the edge they saw a delicate lily, its flowers just opening.

It would have been a peaceful scene, except that facing them at the end of the lake was a huge Tattersall weed. Its blue flowers glowed and glared in the sunlight. Some long heavy hairy branches rested on the ground and in the water. Taller branches reached out to the sides as though barring the way. Even from this distance, Hera could see the thorns at their tips. They were in clusters, black and curved. In all her time on Paradise Hera had never seen a Tattersall weed like this. Things were changing, evolving quickly.

Mack stood at her elbow. 'Might have known we'd find one of those buggers hanging about.'

They could clearly see the stamp line where the Dendron had left the water. Hera guided the SAS along the margin of the lake and directly towards the Tattersall weed. The Dendron had stamped on past it, breaking and crushing some of the lower limbs. Mack nodded in approval.

As they approached the Tattersall weed, they saw it move. It began to wind up slowly, dragging its branches in so they tore the soil. 'Go high, Hera,' said Mack. 'There's something mad about it. Even for this mad place.'

They passed high over the tree. It did not lash out at them, which was what Mack had expected, but some of its giant flowers opened and closed quickly, and that was disturbing in its own way.

They entered a gently rounded valley which climbed on into the mountains, but not steeply, and here the vegetation was lush. The stream flowed quickly between dark banks, and where the Dendron had stamped were pools of clear water.

The valley widened, but a spur, jutting out from the side, hindered their view of its higher reaches. The top of the spur was crowned with a monkey tree which crouched as if ready to spring. Tattersall weeds grew beside the stream and up the slopes.

Hera guided them round the spur, following the river, and they entered a wide wooded canyon where the stream tumbled over rapids. There she brought them to a stop, hovering in the air.

They had found it. The Dendron. It stood just a few hundred metres in front of them, surrounded by the blue of Tattersall weeds. They both stared, for whatever they had imagined, nothing had prepared them for this.

Olivia So tell me, what was it like?

Hera Unbelievable. You can see as many pictures and tri-vids as you like, but nothing compares to the real beast, in the flesh. It was majestic. Beautiful. It filled up my mind like it filled up the space. It was standing side on to us, its front legs astride the stream, and its stump buried deep in the water. It stood as though on display. The classic pose, like the statue that used to stand at the shuttle port in New Syracuse, but that was only a quarter of the size of this one, or less. The only things that moved were its twin tapering trunks, which flexed back and forth slowly, as though feeling the air. To be honest, I hardly dared look at it. I felt crushed by it.

Olivia And Mack?

Hera I glanced across at him and he was standing with his mouth open. I think we were both used to the velvet green of Paradise . . . or of flowers like the shyris or the Tattersall. But here was a Dendron in all its gaudy pride. He had not expected the colours: the black of the stump, the blue of the back and the red of the twin horns. Or the music.

Olivia Music?

Hera With every move, even the slightest, the Venus tears rang.

Olivia And the crest?

Hera The crest was folded down. But as we watched it opened. I think it was to acknowledge us. Mack thought it might be a challenge. But I said, 'Nonsense!' It was honouring us. Have you ever seen a peacock open its tail?

Olivia No.

Hera Shame. It was sort of like that. But the quills were not feathers, they were serrated blades, hard as ivory and so sharp! The shadow of the crest fell right over us as it lifted. And that broke the spell. I took us up high, just to be on the safe side. But then, as we looked down, we saw the whole creature shake and shiver, and I thought, *It thinks we are leaving it in pain.* And so I took us back down and landed just up the hill from where it waited.

They climbed out of the SAS and stood looking at the Dendron. Slowly it closed its crest of blades and they heard a ruffling sound as it did so. Then it slowly moved its twin trunks, first to one side and then to the other, until the tips were just touching the ground. After which it straightened again.

'Why is it doing that?' asked Mack.

'It's saying hello, or welcome. I think it was a message, Mack.'

Mack pondered. 'You're sure it knows we are here?'

'It knows! And it's waiting for us. This is it, Mack. Payback time!'
'Payback for what?'
'Saving me.'

23

First Close Encounter

If the Dendron was aware of them it gave no further indication, except perhaps that its crest lifted partially and then locked. The codds were quiet except for the occasional small gulp. The heave up the slope must have taken its toll. It would need to rest, and with a Dendron a rest could mean a complete close-down before it was roused again by its need to divide.

Cautiously, they made their way down the slope and approached the Dendron. The sense of its living presence as they came under its shadow, combined with its stillness, was unnerving. They stopped while still some distance away and faced the great arch between its front legs.

Mack looked closely at the sweep of the Dendron's arch. He saw the way its curve might suggest the sensitive place in a human where the neck meets the back or, more crucially, the place where the thigh curves in and down. He looked at the soaring twin trunks and the codds – so suggestive and yet, if Hera was to be believed, nothing to do with sexual organs. Mack thought too of the story of Redman, and wondered how the hell that man had had the guts to get right up under a beast like this when it was charging. Ecstatic or not, symbol of sweet fulfilment though it might be, to Mack a Dendron at full stamp was the very stuff of nightmares.

But other things distracted him. At close quarters the stench of the Dendron was almost overpowering. He couldn't believe they always stank like this, otherwise there would have been more comment. What was it that young Sasha Malik had said – that they smelled like pineapples? Mack put his lips close to Hera's ear. 'If that's what pineapples smell like,' he whispered, 'then I never want to try one.'

'It's not what pineapples smell like,' answered Hera, also whispering. 'Sasha got that one wrong. She'd never tasted a pineapple. That'll be its sap. And it does smell strong, I agree. If you imagine that smell diluted then it would be OK, but I think something is wrong. It could be all part of its condition. We'll find out.'

Hera didn't want to say more. She wanted to dwell in the moment. Being close to the Dendron, the enigma of the creature increased. In the literature the 'sap' of a Dendron was described as a viscous green liquid. She imagined it now, pulsing through its body, passing through membranes, driven by that great bellows. Someone had once calculated that the pressures inside the Dendron were enormous, every movement being a transfer of fluid. No living creature could contain them, but here it was. She murmured, 'I wonder what it does to relieve the pressure? It'll have some venting mechanism, or cooling system. Steeping would help it but ... No wonder they don't like to get too far from water. That trip over the desert must have been hell for it. There'd be a build-up of impurities and that could account for the smell.'

Mack nodded but said nothing.

Then they heard a sound not unlike that of a talking jenny. Mack frowned. It came again, but much louder, and moments later the sides of the Dendron shivered and dark green sap began to ooze from its rough blue hide. It ran down its sides and dribbled into the stream. There was a sound like soapy hands meeting in a slap and the green sap stopped. 'What did I say?' said Hera. 'That must be it equalizing pressure.'

Mack shook his head and turned away, fanning his face with his hand. 'It's just air and water, Mack.'

'So is a fart.'

'Oh, pull yourself together. No Dendron has been seen on this planet in living memory. You're privileged to stand here. And if it wants to fart, it can fart.'

'I know. I know. It's just when I was growing up ...'

'Well, grow up some more. Seize the moment. Look with understanding eyes. I don't want to hear any more silly ideas or schoolboy humour. For all you know, the Dendron might think you stink, or worse. What you are looking at just did you the honour of farting in your precious presence. This Dendron is one of the most efficient engines you'll ever meet, and it's alive and you're going to have to help it. Soon. And with honour, and with care, and with love.' The sudden flash of temper subsided. 'Now. Just give me a few minutes. I just want to be on my own.'

Hera moved away. And she deliberately breathed deep. To her the smell was distinct and sharp, not of putrefaction and not like the talking jenny. It was a smell of life and dark mystery, a smell to get to know. Anyone who fouled that concept deserved what they got!

She shrugged off the anger. She didn't want it to spoil these first precious moments of encounter. Couldn't Mack feel the energy of the beast? What a strange man! So earthy and capable, and yet so easily distracted by something so childish. She looked at the swell of the Dendron's back and the great crest stark against the blue sky. What a beautiful thing it was, so perfectly balanced, so economical and clear in its lines. And practical!

Hera walked deeper into the shadow of the Dendron, then she made herself walk close. Its presence was wonderful and terrifying and she knew what Sasha had meant when she said she was thrilled by the energy of the creature. Hera could feel it too, as though inside her. She stood right beside one of the front legs and looked up, staring directly up the swaying, tapering trunks to the flags, which still hung limp. It made her dizzy, just looking. She touched the fibre of the leg with the tips of her fingers. It was hard, like frozen string, but prickly too where the tough strands had broken off. *They must be shedding their bark all the time*, she thought. *Bark. Hm. Can it feel me touching it, I wonder, like I can feel a fly on my hair?* She reached up and touched the place where the fibre started to turn blue, and that was softer. Still strong, but softer and more pliable. Almost like meshlite. It was able to stretch too.

She placed her palm flat and could feel a slight vibration in the beast. *There must be hundreds of small pumps working in there all the time, or the beast would slump. I wonder how she copes when the moons are full and pulling together. She'll feel them inside her. Oh yes, she'll feel them all right.* Hera looked down at where the trunk-sized feet of the Dendron were pressed into the soil. She knelt and disturbed the soil with her fingers. Just under the surface she could see tiny white roots which fanned out all round the foot and dived down. Perhaps that was what it was doing now. Growing down, bedding down. Those roots definitively answered one question: it was waiting to divide. Waiting for its prince to come with shining armour and a swift sharp sword.

The stream flowed between the twin legs. Steadying herself with a hand against the front of the leg, Hera stepped down into the quickly flowing water, which rose to her hips. She waded out to the middle of the stream and stood between the legs, looking up. It was a very deliberate move. The memory of her dream was vivid, but not overpowering. The inside of the arch was darker than she remembered – a mixture of blue and black. But then all Dendron differed, didn't they? 'But this?' she murmured. Within there, deep inside the dark arch, would be the living wishbone, oil-rich, tough as spring steel, smooth as ivory and 'smelling of primroses'.

Hera made herself walk right under the Dendron. What a private space she was in. She examined the twin codds – good name for them. She liked that name. They arched right into the body with great folds, like a concertina. They would have to be able to work independently, she realized, one blowing while the other sucked. And be able to reverse quickly too. That must be how they managed the twin trunks right up to the cherries and Venus tears. Sometimes, like when the beast was walking, they'd have to work together like one single bellows. What power! To be able to shift as massive a thing as that great black stump! And where was its consciousness? For it was inconceivable that something as organized as this could just be . . . just . . . *be*. Or had she got that all wrong, and just being was a higher wisdom?

At that moment the codds obligingly gave one gulp, and she could hear the strive and gurgle of fluids within the Dendron as they began the long surge through its body. Hera reached up and was just able to touch the bottom fold of the codds, but she immediately snatched her hand away in surprise, for the dark matted fibre was warm and moist. And why should it not be warm? Fluid moving under pressure gets warm. And what better place for a safety valve? She smelled her fingers, and it was just the rich ooze of the plant. *Must remember to tell Mack about this the next time we drink wine*, she thought mischievously. She washed the sticky juice from her fingers. Then she waded on further and touched the stool. It was like stone, hard and cold from the river. She walked round the stool and out into the daylight. One last look at the rounded rump of the beast – no anus of course – and the shimmering crest that could carve and crush. It had not moved. And she was done.

'OK, Mack,' she called, 'I've had my little tour. You can come out now. Sorry I got ratty. Let's decide what we're going to do. It's putting down roots. It will be dormant now for a little while, but then the anguish will start up again unless we're able to bring it some relief. Are you OK?'

While Hera was making her tour round the beast, Mack had moved up the stream, which meant he was also upwind of the Dendron. He'd been upset by Hera's sudden outburst, but he'd understood too. This was her moment. How would he feel if he'd been invited to take down something as beautiful as, say, the Parthenon, and someone had come along and pissed against a pillar? He'd do more than give them an earful.

He was not just being fanciful in thinking of the Dendron as a building. To him there was something monumental about it. Still as the Sphinx, but living too. And Hera was right: he had to get past stupid knee-jerk reactions if he was going to do anything to help. He'd been surprised, that was all. Surprised that such a human sound, as he thought, could come from a creature so inhuman. But already he was adapting to it, getting the relative proportions sorted out, working out how it moved, looking for danger points. If it reared now, he would be frightened, but he would watch it carefully too.

Mack watched Hera step into the stream and walk right under the creature and knew it would take a lot to get him to do that. He was too aware of the weight pressing down. But his thoughts were complicated by his unthinking assumption that the Dendron was male. It was the codds that worried him, for they were altogether too like a giant scrotum. No doubt Hera was remembering her dream. The irreverent thought came to him that if ever the happy day came when he and Hera made love, he hoped she did not expect him to perform like a Dendron . . . but he wouldn't mind trying.

Mack moved further away. He moved to the side, up the hill, and lay down on the ground. Out here, sitting with his arms round his knees, staring at the twin trunks, he could see the cherries and the discs of pale mineral fancifully called Venus tears. Their tinkle reached him faintly.

He studied the Dendron, trying to see it whole. He tried to

imagine the strong springy structure that gave it shape. This 'wishbone' thing that Hera talked about. He would have to study her drawings again if he was to make sense of it. Because it didn't make sense. There was more to it than just a few springy bits of bone. But if he could work out its logic – why, then it should be no more difficult than dismantling an old building with all its stresses and weaknesses. As long as it did not die on him, or shake him off or start to run. Best not to think of that. Now, if he had his team here ... Young Annette would already have shinned up one of the legs and be calling for ropes. Polka would have her eyes on the tears, thinking of earrings probably. And Dickinson ...? It was hard to know what Dickinson would do; he was a strange one. He'd probably climb up and sit on its rump and wish he could ride it.

At that moment the Dendron gulped and the codds heaved. Mack was reminded of the time he had seen a baby kick in its mother's stomach. His thinking turned over and he began to think of the Dendron's codds as a womb, of the beast as being female. Of course, he knew it did not have a womb, but he shifted from thinking of it as male and something that he had to *battle* against, to it being female and something which he needed to *help* through its own battle. Such a little shift, really, but he felt altogether easier in his mind.

Mack wished his team could see him now. They would be wondering what he was up to. Hell, what a show this would be. And then he thought of the tri-vid camera mounted on the SAS. That could send signals up to the platform. Why not? Let them share? They might even have some good ideas to help him.

It was at this moment that Hera called to him, and waved. He roused and went to join her. 'Satisfied?' he asked.

'Yes and no. I want to get started.'

It was hard to believe it was only just after midday, so much had already happened. They had eaten with a growing sense of urgency, and were now planning.

Mack had studied Hera's sketches, puzzling over them, trying to work out what was missing because there was a lot missing. He'd had her relate again and again what she could remember of Marie Newton's description of a severance and he sat with his head in his hands, trying to imagine the sequence and understand it. He quizzed her for details that just were not there. And she was getting tetchy having to say 'I don't know' or 'There's no evidence that ...' or 'If only.'

Why had the crest been chopped off first? He'd assumed that it was to do with disarming the Dendron, but there must be more to it. And why did the Dendron doing the cutting pay such a lot of attention to the big cut down to the codds, when it would have been simpler and safer and faster to cut away the main body closer to the front legs? So why ...?

'I don't know,' said Hera, for the hundredth time. 'You've got your blessed pendulum. Why don't you ask that?' She stood up and crossed to the window of the SAS and looked out at the Dendron, which had still not moved except that its crest had lifted slowly to full and now stood stiff and erect.

'I will when I need to.'

Hera was impatient to get started. She felt the seconds ticking away. She dreaded the moment when the Dendron would scream again – for that was how she now saw it – and she wanted Mack up there, on its back, axe in hand and chopping or whatever demolition men did, so that it would know that relief was at hand. *But Mack was so slow! So slow and plodding.*

Had she been able to read his mind, she would have seen that Mack was not being slow and he was certainly not plodding. As the problem of how to take down the Dendron became more real to him, so he was becoming professional and objective. He was actually coming to grips with the problem in a deep way, and this, to those who knew him, was manifesting as a change in his manner, a deliberateness. This she misunderstood. Mack was thinking about all sides of the problem, sounding out the logic, and not least among his worries was whether he could manage on his own. Hera's quickness of temper was irritating him, because it wasted energy and might lead to mistakes. His feelings for Hera were not involved in this. His love was a constant flame, but he seriously wondered if she was capable of helping, because she didn't seem to understand what was involved. She seemed to think he just had to wave a magic axe or something and it would all happen – well, there was no magic in demolition, just ruthless logic, some luck and the careful application of controlled and unremitting strength.

'Can we just get a move on, Mack? Make a start. Marie Newton says the first thing to be cut is the crest.'

'You know the real problem, Hera? We don't know where we are in the Dendron's cycle. If I went in there and started chopping away at the crest, we could trigger disaster. That Mayday woman didn't understand what she was seeing. There's more to it. And we have to work that out. What stage is our Dendron at right now, if we compare it with the story? Has our Dendron just come out of the sea? No, we know it is more settled. But by this stage did the Dendron in the story, the one she calls Mustard, know that help was there? Yes, it did. Does our Dendron know we are here and want to help it? We don't know. It might, it might not. So how do we trigger that understanding? It is all in the first approach. Marie Newton says, if you are remembering it correctly, that the crest on the one that was going to be carved—'

'Mustard.'

'Yes, Mustard, did not go down until Mustard had been touched by the other Dendron. That's what is important. Only when it knew the other Dendron was on hand and ready to do business did it give up its pressure. That's what we have to do first. Right now it's under full tension. I know about it putting down roots – you've already told me that a hundred times. I know it has farted and voided! But that was just a burp. Look at the bloody crest, woman. What's holding that up? Wishful thinking? No, it's pressure. The Dendron's confused. All it knows is that it needs to be split open. Right? So what we have to do is to relax it. Let it know that help is here. Then it'll relax, and then the crest'll come down. Then, and only then, can we start cutting. So how do we convince it to give up its pressure? How do we get to that?'

'You're the demolition expert.'

'Right. I am. So listen. From what you told me, something happened after the Dendron put its horns between the horns of Mustard. They touched cherries or something, and I think that is what our gal down there is waiting for. Are you with me?' Hera nodded. 'OK. Now there is one other thing, and I want to get it cleared up now so we don't have any misunderstanding later on. Who is in charge? Who's the boss up front?'

'Mack, I just want to get moving. I don't want to waste time having a stop-work meeting in a logging camp. You can be boss man if you like. I just want us to *do* something.'

'You don't understand.'

'I just—'

'Will you just listen, for God's sake? If this were a job on a demolition site, I wouldn't have someone like you near me. I'd kick you off the fucking team so fast your arse would reach the moon before you did. And the reason I'd do that is because I can't rely on you. You're too used to having your own way. You're a bully when it comes to decisions. And you'll do the wrong thing in a crisis. You'll think clever, or you'll argue the toss, or you'll get stirred up and shitty. You'll take more time being looked after than you're worth. You've never worked in the real world. I have, and I can take orders better than you. I'm talking about survival. If you're the boss and you say stop, even if I'm in the middle of a chop, I'll do my best to stop, because otherwise it might be my last. But we've got to know that we can trust one another. I'm not talking about master and slave; I'm talking about knowing where we stand. And I'm putting you in charge. I'll take my orders from you. Your call.'

'Mack I . . . This is silly.'

'I've given you a starting point.'

'Mack, why are you doing this? You're manipulating the situation.'

He turned away in anger and then turned back. 'Clever people! For an intelligent woman you're pretty bloody stupid sometimes. You'll argue about who carries the bucket while the house burns down. You're in charge. Make a decision.'

'I don't want to be in charge. I want us to work together.'

'Oh, we can work together. But when the ship is sinking, who says jump?'

'OK. OK. I understand, Mack. I don't want to be in charge. You know about all of this better than me. You are in charge. You're the b— Sorry. You're in charge. You give the orders. There.'

He looked at her and she could not read his expression. She did not know, but in those moments Mack was deciding whether to go ahead and try to do this job on their own, or whether to contact the platform, explain the situation and have Abhuradin send his team down. He'd have Hera locked up if need be, to stop her getting in the way. Hera did not know until later how close she came to losing that battle. But perhaps something guided her for she said, finally,

'Mack, I do understand. I've been on dives in the dark with just a line to communicate. And you are right. It's in the crisis when it counts, isn't it? I won't let you down. I'll jump when you say. And I'll try to shut up too.'

He grinned. 'Fat chance of that.' But there was no smile when he said, 'A deal?'

Hera nodded. 'A deal.'

'Well, if I'm an honorary research assistant, I'm going to make you an honorary demolition worker. Do this.' He spat in the palm of his hand, and held it out. She looked at him and saw he was serious. She spat in the palm of her hand, and they closed hands. 'See you on the other side,' said Mack.

'See you the other side, Mack.' They released. 'Other side of what?'

'What do you think?' And then she understood and was grateful to be trusted with someone's life.

'So what do we do now, boss?'

'I'm going to chop down one of those tall trees over there and trim it. I want you to take the SAS up and fly round the Dendron, but I want you to land every few metres or so with a thump. Pretend you're a Dendron, right. Get a good rhythm. Shake the earth a bit. Let it know in its roots that you are here and stamping round. But don't get too enthusiastic and break the bloody SAS cos we're going to need it to get out of here. Then we're going to drop the log down between its horns, rock it about in a friendly way and pull it out and see what happens. See if she gets the message.'

'What about the cherries?'

'I'm working on that.'

And so they did.

Hera woke Alan and explained what she wanted. 'Practice landings in a difficult terrain. Show me what you can do. Let me feel us shake the ground.' Minutes later the SAS lifted and flew round the Dendron, maintaining a radius of about a hundred metres, giving the earth good periodic *thumps* using its heavy-duty skids rather than the wheels.

The other rhythmic sound in the valley came from Mack. The tree was quickly felled and he soon was trimming it with the axe, giving his muscles a warning of things to come. He left a few small

262

branches sticking out about two thirds of the way up its trunk. For better or for worse, these would serve as the cherries. While chopping he had had a clever idea.

Mack was developing a theory about the Dendron, but he could not have explained it to Hera. He imagined the flow of fluids through the codds and round the giant body, and this suggested a generator. He guessed that the Dendron might carry a high electrical charge. Two Dendron touching might share their potential, and this could have all manner of effects from setting things on fire to raising consciousness. At the very least the Dendron in the river would know that something was happening. And if he triggered the release . . . well, then he could move on to stage two.

Satisfied with the trimming, Mack ran an extension cord he had found in the SAS tool cabinet up the length of the trunk and tied it in place near the small branches. Then he cut off the plug, bared the ends of the wires and nailed them into the branches. He was going to give the Dendron a different kind of shunt to the one described by young Sasha.

When he was ready he signalled to Hera and she brought the SAS over, bounced it once near him for good luck, and then landed so that its skids were astride the log. Mack attached the smaller top part of the log to the meshlite rope of the hoist. The SAS hammered into the air slowly, lifting the log, dragging it and its electric cables towards the Dendron, which all the time had never moved or given a sign of life, except for the occasional gulp.

Hera flew between the flags of the Dendron. The wind from the rotor blades made the limp flags flutter. Once past the twin horns she hovered and lowered, at the same time reeling in the meshlite rope. The front of the log lifted and she was able to drag it up between the twin trunks. She dragged it as far as she could past the cleft between the trunks, but without touching them, and then she lowered the tapered end of the tree until it was just resting in the cleft between the horns. On the intercom, she heard Mack's shout of relief when the log was in place.

'Nice flying. Now hold her steady. Keep the slack out of the cable, but not lifting. And if the Dendron moves. Cut loose and fly straight up. You're right in the path of the crest if it takes a swat at you. Understood?'

'Understood. You be careful too, Mack.'

Mack grunted and set off. He climbed up the sloping log using hands and feet. He too kept a wary eye out in case the Dendron decided to move, though his options were limited if it did. Hera, watching through the underside viewer, saw Mack as he clambered up and came level with the two soaring trunks. He was high above the ground. He stood up straight and climbed on with his arms spread like a tight-rope walker. He passed the cleft and came to the place where he had left the short branches sticking out to simulate the cherries. One of the bare copper leads had been twisted back on itself, and he knelt down and bent it back into shape. Then he shuffled on until he came to the end of the log. Carefully, he sat down, his legs astride the trunk, and undid the shackle, knocking the heavy bolt into the palm of his hand and guiding the cable free. Just as he began to stand up, the codds heaved and the Dendron shook itself briefly, like a horse after exercise. Mack threw himself flat, and as he did so he heard the SAS roar and lift, reeling in the cable as it went. There was a slight shift as the log settled, but that was all. The Dendron became still again. Cautiously Mack stood up. Everything was still in place. Perhaps the Dendron was telling him to get a move on.

His next job was to re-attach the cable to the thick end of the log so that it could be lifted and then rocked between the horns, thereby chafing the cleft and hopefully igniting the Dendron – so to speak. To re-attach the cable he had to walk back down the log. It was while he was doing this that he missed his footing, tripped and fell. He landed on the wide back of the Dendron. His uniform protected him from being scraped too badly, but his elbow was jarred. Otherwise he was all right. Thus Mack was the first man for a long time to actually sit on a Dendron, and to his great surprise he found that its back was quite soft, like the floor of a pine forest. Not so the flame-red cleft, however, which was hard and ungiving. He climbed up carefully and back onto the log.

'You having fun?' It was Hera's voice in his ear.

'Yeah. Bloody magic down here. Could you lower the shackle at the blunt end and then land.'

'On my way.'

Mack shaded his eyes and stared up as the SAS again flew slowly over the flags and then began to reel out the cable.

Moments later Mack jumped to the ground just as the heavy

shackle reached him. He passed the cable round the end of the log a couple of times and then bolted the shackle in place. He gave it a final wrench for good luck. They were ready for the big experiment.

The SAS landed. After one last look round, Mack gathered up the rest of the electric cable and ran over to the SAS, threw the cable aboard and swung up after it, leaving the door open.

'OK, Doc. Take her up about fifteen feet. Easy there. Take in the slack. Now back up a bit. Gently does it. There, the log's lifting. Dendron'll be feeling the full weight now. Back up until you reach the point of balance. Easy now. Almost there. Easy now. There. Hold there. Stabilize.'

'Holding.'

'Now what I want you to do, Doc, is make it rock, OK? A bit up and a bit down. Give your sister a thrill. OK? And if you see a sudden movement from her, hit the release, and get the hell out because she'll come for us like we were trying to steal her child. But if we're lucky and she likes it, we'll get the silver solas.'

'What are you doing, boss, while I'm giving my ... er, sister a thrill?'

'Attaching the electric shock leads to the generator. We want to wake her up, don't we? So when you're ready, Doc.'

Hera was amazed at how easily she took orders – it was quite nice to be spoken to in the language of the team.

She eased the SAS up and she eased the SAS down. She watched the log in the cleft as she rocked it. Up and down. Up and down. Up and down. Mack rejoined her in the cabin. 'All set below,' he said. 'How's she like it? Any change? Any reaction?'

'Nope. Just tell me, Mack, apart from the obvious, what makes you think the cleft there is a sensitive place? More sensitive than the codds, for instance?'

'Dendron divides there. That's the biggest junction in its body. That's where one becomes two. That's where it knows it's a Dendron, like you know you're a woman. Forget the codds. The codds are just a machine. Dispensable. Remember that Mayday woman's Dendron – it just ripped Mustard's codds out and threw them away. I reckon that with a Dendron the more tender you are at the beginning, the easier everything gets later. This is where it starts to give up its consciousness. Trust the Buddha! OK? Here we go. If she isn't primed with that she won't fire at all. Ease back now. Start to drag. Nice and slow. Keep it steady, steady. Keep it on line in the cleft. Don't twist the trunk or it'll come out of the groove. Great. Wait till the little branches reach the cleft then hold steady. Lovely. Lovely. Lovely. Oh, you sweetheart! Stop there. Now let's see what happens.'

Mack had brought a transformer with him into the control room. He edged it to 25 per cent and they saw a spark jump from one of the cable ends to the top of the left-hand cleft.

Hera was about to protest, but she bit down hard. She looked up at Mack, at the sweat on his brow and the intensity of his glare at the Dendron.

'Now take it,' he said and pushed the charge up to 50 per cent. 'Any movement?'

'No movement.'

'Take your revs up but hold position.'

Hera gunned the engine but changed the pitch of the rotors so that they absorbed the change. They shifted slightly in the air. 'Hold her steady!' Mack pushed the transformer up to 75 per cent. Lightning danced from the cables to both sides of the cleft and back. Sparks flew. But still there was no movement from the Dendron. 'Come on, you bugger, do something,' shouted Mack, and he pushed the transformer to maximum. Thin fingers of blue electricity fluttered up the twin trunks, and red fibres on the cleft smoked and caught fire. 'Give me full power. She's almost there, I know it. I know it.'

Hera took the engine to full and red warning lights flashed on the control panel. Alan began to speak but she overrode him with one sweep of her hand. Then suddenly the power cut. The burned-out cable fell away from the Dendron.

'Ease off,' shouted Mack. 'Hold steady but pull back to safety.'

Hera throttled back, and one by one the warning lights went out.

'OK. Back up. Pull the trunk out. Slack off the cable just before she falls.'

The trunk, burned and still smoking, pulled free from between the twin horns of the Dendron and fell down with one end in the river.

'You can land if you like, Doc,' said Mack. 'Let's look and see what damage we've done. But don't turn the motor off. Keep her running. We might have one hell of an angry Dendron wants to kick our arse.' They watched.

Then Hera pointed. The flags had moved independently for the first time. They had lifted and then fallen again. But then the crest twitched, as though hit by a sudden breeze. It closed suddenly and then immediately opened again. 'She's getting up steam,' said Hera. And no sooner were the words out of her mouth than the Dendron shook as a mighty energy was released and green sap began to pour from every orifice. It came from holes in the Dendron's side. A wave gulfed from the cleft and poured down between the twin trunks. Heavy green fluid poured like oil from the tip of the twin trunks, down and over the cherries and the Venus tears, and fell in heavy drops down into the stream.

'She's been holding that in a long time,' said Mack. 'No wonder she stinks. Maybe's now she'll smell of primroses.' The crest opened and closed again with a crisp slicing sound, and more juice flowed and this was a darker green.

'Clearing her tubes,' said Hera, and Mack nodded.

'Yeah, best thing,' he said. 'She'd have died in another day or so. Maybe had one more run in her. What do you reckon?'

Hera nodded. 'So now there's just one last thing.'

They watched as the crest opened one more time, and then slowly twisted to the side and lowered open and flat. The sharp tines dug deep into the soil beside the river, and all movement stopped.

Hera cut the engine. The rotors turned more slowly and then reversed briefly and came to a standstill. 'You did it, Mack. She knows we're here and we're going to help. You're a clever fucker, aren't you?'

Mack shrugged. 'Just an ordinary day at the office, Doc. Come on, let's go and get us a drink. She can rest now. She deserves it. What a relief! She had me worried there.'

The codds gulped quietly.

'Now I need to do some research.' He turned his granny's ring on his finger and slipped it into the palm of his hand. 'Mind if I have a bit more hair?'

Hera, who now wore her hair in a pony tail, took a few strands and pulled them out. 'Here,' she said. 'Keep a few for good luck.'

'I will. And now if you'll excuse me I want to work a bit on my own. I'll tell you all about it later. But I need to keep my mind uncluttered for a while. OK?'

'You're the boss. I'm going to spend a bit of time down by the river. I've a feeling that's the right place for me.'

Mack wandered round the Dendron but kept quite a distance from it, muttering to himself, occasionally taking notes and always with his little pendulum oscillating in his hand. Once or twice he stopped and kneeled down with his ear to the ground; sometimes he lay flat on the brevet with his arms and legs spread.

Hera, meanwhile, maintained a vigil of her own, sitting in the shadow of the crest where it dug into the soil and letting her mind ride with the easy consciousness of the Dendron. It knew they were here. In her memory Hera revisited some of her memories of the green time, and was content.

Just briefly she heard a ringing of bells as from a distance and felt a shadow pass over her, and the codds beat twice, strongly. 'Easy,' she murmured. 'Easy.' And she reached out and touched the hard crest, rather as one might encourage a shy but willing horse.

Then she heard Mack calling and roused herself. The sun was low. Mack had returned to the SAS and was preparing some food. His silence was heavy, like a man containing bad news. But Hera knew better than to ask.

That evening Mack remained quiet and thoughtful during the meal. Occasionally he grunted to himself, or said 'Hmm' as though listening to an internal dialogue. Hera sat quiet, biting back her impatience. But when she moved to clear the plates he stopped her. 'What's going on up here, Mack?' she asked, gently tapping him on the forehead. 'Can you share, or are you too worried and tired?'

'A bit of both. I'm trying to work out what we do tomorrow.' She noticed that Mack had arranged his fork and spoon and plate in a pattern, as though using them to think. And when he spoke, he addressed them. 'See, there's one big difference between me and the Dendron that did the chopping with that Mayday woman – what was her–'

'Marie Newton. Yes?'

'And that difference between us is time. The Dendron could work quickly. Proper equipment. Knew what it was doing. It took ... what? Little more than twenty minutes from first chop to final sever. But it's going to take me a couple of days, and that's if I have good wind and decent help.'

'Did I do all right today?'

268

'You did fine.' He stopped and looked up at her. 'Let me just tell you one thing, for next time you're working on a demo team. It's considered bad form to ask questions like that. Because you're part of a team. Now don't go looking upset. You weren't to know, and you'll learn. But if you do want to pay someone a compliment, or say something personal or friendly even, do it in a backhanded way so they don't feel embarrassed. Like when you said to me, was I enjoying myself when I nearly fell off the Dendron. That was spot on. I knew you were watching. I knew you were there. And I knew you'd be down in a flash if I was in trouble. OK?'

'That wasn't a compliment, Mack, I was—'

'You paid me the compliment of caring. Same difference. Anyway, that's not what I wanted to tell you.' His focus returned to the table. 'Now, taking two days over the job wouldn't matter, except I think there's a question of life and death involved. What I'm thinking is that with this fission business, there must come a moment when the old body dies and the new bodies take over. And if they don't overlap properly, you get three deaths, and it's – what was it that kid said – "Curtains, bon-bon" for all eternity. So where, I ask myself, does the old Dendron – the big gal we've got sleeping down there – where does she keep her life? Put that another way: at what point does the old Dendron have to die so that the new kids can live? My worry is that if I rip out its codds tomorrow before I'm ready to split the other two off, they'll all die. So we have to try and keep them all alive until the last cut of all. So how do we do that? Logistics really.'

'Well, where do you think she keeps her life? In the cherries and tears?'

'No, it's not in the cherries, or the tears. My guess is they are wanting to become independent. They're part of the new life. They don't want to be worried by the old girl any more.'

'Gotcha,' said Hera. ' They'll be going through a pretty complex adaptation of their own right at this very second.' She thought for a moment, and then tapped the table with her finger. 'I've had an idea. You remember I mentioned the front two legs have already rooted?'

'Yep.'

'Well, they'll be getting all sorts of information from the roots, won't they? About being a new young Dendron – how you ring your bells and shake your cherries and contact the nearest Tattersall weed, and—'

Mack sat up straight. 'There's a thought. They'll be trying out their voices while the old part of them is still alive but dormant. But if the old part wakes up before the job is done – can you imagine! If it broadcast that pain! Hell, they'd need the protection of all the Michelangelos in the region and then some. Us too.'

'Is that what you felt today?' asked Hera.

'Of course. There's been a Michelangelo hovering about for a while now.'

This was news to Hera, for she had felt nothing except for the one flicker and she'd thought that came from the Dendron. 'How do you know it's a Michelangelo?'

'Just do. For one thing, it makes it impossible to dowse. Its patterns are just too powerful. I can't get past them. It's friendly, for want of a better word. At least at present. And it's taking a keen interest in things here'

'Oh.' Hera wondered what else Mack might have picked up. The man opposite her was suddenly stranger to her, more unknown, but not a stranger. He was still Mack. 'So, going back,' she continued, 'if its life is not in the cherries, what about the wishbone? That's what people shot at when they went hunting.'

'Yeah. That was its weak point. That stopped it being able to move. If you shot it in the wishbone you'd cripple it, but not kill it. You could strip it of its wishbone, and still it wouldn't die. Dendron take a long time to die, I'm thinking. Years, probably. They have to be killed properly. Quickly. Efficiently. Like that galloping Dendron killed Mustard in that Mayday woman's story.'

'And if they aren't killed properly?'

Mack looked at her. 'My guess is that if a Dendron isn't killed properly, it will war with itself. It will want to sever, like our gal down there, but it can't move. All it can do is cry for help while with every passing day the need to sever and die gets stronger.'

'Like being in perpetual labour, with no hope of a birth.' Hera shuddered.

'You can imagine them screaming their pain, can't you? We heard it. Just a bit of it.'

'Getting louder as the years slip past. Because it could take years, couldn't it?'

270

'One voice becoming three as the young ones get stronger.'

'And still no one comes. God, that's terrible. God, imagine it. All that screaming. One day I'll show you Dead Tree Spit, Mack. There's a Dendron that took a long time to die. You can still see it.'

'Aye, we'll visit it. When this is over, one way or another.'

Hera sat very still. Then she said, 'Mack, I want you to promise me something. If we can't make it separate, we mustn't let three lives linger. It's all, or nothing.'

Mack nodded. 'So that's our problem, Hera. Where does it keep its life? I need to know so that I can kill the old one quick when the young ones are becoming independent. Or I kill them all. That's why I'm quiet. I'm thinking. Can't do too many things at the same time, you know.' He stood up. 'I'm going to sleep outside tonight. Look at the stars and see what they have to say. Tomorrow'll be a big day, one way or another. Tomorrow we'll start to disestablish the Dendron. Who's on dishes?'

'Alan.'

Mack grinned and left her to it. But he was back in a moment. 'One thing, Hera. I had a thought. We'll be shifting the SAS right up close to the Dendron tomorrow and there's a mobile tri-vid mounted on it. I'd like to open a link up to my team on the platform. They'll be interested to see what we're doing, but more important they might have some thoughts that'll help.'

Hera stopped, and then she beamed. 'That's a brilliant idea, Mack. Why didn't I think of it? I think my brain's going to sleep like the Dendron. And they can record it too, so that if anything happens to us down here, there's a copy.' She paused and added, 'You know, there's one thing I don't understand, Mack.'

'Just one? And what's that?'

'I'm thinking about what we were talking about. With all the pain the Dendron must have been broadcasting, I can't understand why the Michelangelos didn't come like a swoop of avenging angels and simply wipe everyone out. They could have treated the human invaders like a pestilence, and got rid of them.'

'And how could they do that if they didn't know how to hate?' Hera had no answer. 'I think the Michelangelos had no more understanding about what was happening than the Dendron. If you want to know the truth, I think they were stunned, and so they backed off, sharpish. You've got a bit of a down on them because of what happened to you. But I think they're the jokers in the pack.'

'Well, I hope you're right. And if we end up with three deaths, well, there'll be two more little bodies on Paradise beside them. This place is not getting friendlier. I just hope we don't fail.'

'Fail? "But screw your courage to the sticking-place,/ And we'll not fail." '

'It's unlucky to quote *Macbeth*, you know?'

'Who's that? I was quoting my granny.'

'Hm! Get out and do your thinking. I'll call the platform now.'

24

A Closer Ecounter

Hera did not sleep well that night.

Though she had tried many times, she had failed to make contact with the platform above. She had always known in the back of her mind that the shuttle platform was up there, a last line of retreat, available if needed, though she was determined not to use it. Now it could not be contacted at all, and that made her feel very isolated. Her unease was compounded by a growing feeling that her presence on Paradise had become more marginal. She was still important, still had a part to play, but events seemed to be moving on past her.

She lay still and thought of Mack. Perhaps he was asleep by now, or still out there by the Dendron, trying to work out the quickest way to save the two young trees. Or perhaps he had reached his conclusion and was now lying back and staring at the stars, gathering his strength for the morrow, or snoring like an ox. Hera could not hide from the fact that Mack now seemed in some ways more at home here on Paradise than she. The Michelangelos which frightened her didn't seem to bother him. And what was more, he seemed better able to grasp the realities of their situation, and that of the Dendron, than she. That intuition of his carried him deep, to the very heart of things. Was she jealous? I think she was, a bit.

Finally, at four o'clock, she slipped from her bed and went up to the control cabin and instructed Alan to try again to contact the shuttle platform. One last try! She heard the tracking signal, the calibration, and then the call sign. Several minutes passed, and then – just as she was about to close down – the call signal was answered. Alan locked on immediately, a link was made and Hera found herself looking at the tired face of a young tri-vid operator.

Hera identified herself and asked to be put through to Captain Abhuradin as quickly as possible. The operator hesitated. Obviously Hera's name meant nothing to her and she was under strict orders. 'Captain Abhuradin will be resting. Shall I log the call for delayed transmission?'

'Check the coordinates I'm calling from first, sunshine, and then put me through.'

Hera saw the operator's surprise, quickly followed by the long-suffering look the young reserve for those seniors who insist on causing trouble. Hera was pleased to see that look change to one of near disbelief when the coordinate check was complete. 'It says here you are calling from the surface of Paradise. That's not—'

'So tell me about it. Now put me through.' Hera saw her nod and then establish the cross links. 'Sorry for the delay, Captain Melhuish, but all the communications have been crazy of late. Strange things have been happening. You are through now.'

Inez Abhuradin's face appeared, but Hera hardly recognized her. The face was puffy with tiredness and her fine features were partly hidden behind a large dressing. 'Hera, I've had half an hour's sleep in the past forty-eight, so this had better be good, even from you.'

'Inez. What's happened?'

She groaned. Not in pain, but at the prospect of explanation. 'Of course, you don't know, do you? Just a minute.' Abhuradin moved out of view and moments later, when she reappeared, she had a glass of water with some pills bubbling in it. 'I'll make more sense when I've had this.' She downed the contents in one swallow and blew out like a swimmer that has just finished a race. 'I've had everything, Hera. We lost a freighter a few days ago coming out of fractal. It just vanished. Blink, like that. We sent a trace in and it vanished too. We tried to contact the Space Council, and nothing was getting through. And then it was discovered that the fractal point had vanished. Gone. It took a few hours for things to sink in, and then I had a riot. People thought we would be trapped here for life and panicked. People thought we were going to run out of food, so the kitchens were attacked. I had to declare martial law and there were running battles. Up and down the corridors. Can you believe that?'

'What happened to your face?'

'I stopped a bottle. It's nothing. Cheekbone not broken, thank God. But don't make me laugh, all right?'

'Are you OK now?'

'Yes, order restored. But then yesterday, just when we'd got the situation under control, all the communications gear went dead. Power failed. Lights out. Even the solar panels were on the blink. We switched over to emergency and I started to evacuate whole wings. I really thought we were coming apart, Hera. We have forty-eight hours of oxygen in reserve, that's all. I tried to get a message down to you. There was nothing I could do. And then suddenly everything came back on. Like nothing had happened. And the fractal point was back too, and the freighter just coming out of it. We tried to contact it, but no response. It was drifting. You know that old story about the *Marie Celeste*? That's what I thought of. So I sent one of the tugs out and we brought the freighter in by remote. We docked it today and – you are not going to believe this. When we opened it up, all the people on board were children – eight-, nine-, ten-year-olds. It was the crew and the passengers. They'd been regressed, somehow. I've got a couple of fractal engineers here now and they are going crazy trying to fathom it. So then I had a platform full of crying children. Everyone is very frightened up here, Hera. But at least we are functioning again.'

While Abhuradin had been talking Hera had been remembering Shapiro's prophecy linking changes on Paradise and the fractal.[6] She was also remembering the stunning effect of the last howl of the Dendron. They had been protected, but the shuttle station had not. 'I think I can guess what happened to you, Inez, and it's connected to what has been going on down here.' Inez frowned. 'I'm not going to be able to explain, and there are time anomalies that don't make sense, but there is a link between the way Paradise functions and the way the fractal works. We've discovered a lot, Inez, and we've been through a storm of our own, but ours was psychic. We were protected because . . . because. Hell, this is so strange. We were protected because we were on the track of a live Dendron.'

'You were what?'

Hera spoke slowly. 'We were . . . No, I'll give you the update. We've found a live Dendron. Now don't go asking me more

[6] See Document 11.

questions because we are both too tired, and for the moment don't tell anyone. It is probably the last, and . . . But listen, this is what is important for you. For some reason, the Dendron are able to generate an incredible psychic energy, which links to the Michelangelos, and . . . when it gets out of balance, it can twist space and time and you and me and . . . That is what happened. But I think you'll find it will be quiet now, because we've found the Dendron, and today, tomorrow, whenever it is, we are going to try to divide it.' Hera paused. 'Why are you looking at me like that, Inez?'

'I haven't understood a word you've said. But you have found a live Dendron?'

'Yes.'

'Are you all right, Hera?'

'Yes and no.'

'You haven't been . . . taken over?'

For the first time Hera was able to laugh as she understood what Captain Abhuradin was thinking. 'Hell no. Nothing like that. There's a lot to tell, and no time to tell it. When we're up with you again, we can sit down and I'll try to explain . . . if I can. But the longer I'm down here the less I understand. But it all sort of makes sense too. Even children coming through the fractal – a kind of renewal. But we have to accept that we're not in control.'

' "We"? Do you mean you and that Mack fellow? How is it working out with him? Is he behaving?'

'I think he understands this place better than I do. But look, time's short. Just take my word for it. I think you'll find that the fractal will have settled down now. But I would move people off the platform as fast as you can. Forget the cargo – junk it, fire it into the sun – because if we fail down here, then there could be trouble up there. Not could be, would be, will be. I'm serious. Please, please, trust me on this, Inez. I know it doesn't make sense, but you've seen what can happen when the fractal goes just a little bit crazy. Next time it will be worse.'

Abhuradin nodded.

'Now, something else I need to tell you. I want you to keep this link open. I want to feed it to our tri-vid. That means you can see what we are doing. Originally Mack just wanted to make a link so that his team could see what he was doing and help us with the Dendron. But now you've told me about your problems, I think it will be good for you to see too. And make a recording, because there is a real chance that if things go wrong, we'll never make it out. I don't want to seem dramatic – OK? But again I'll just have to ask you to take my word for it. What is more, you may even be able to help us. OK?'

Abhuradin nodded. 'I hear you, Hera. I don't understand, but I hear you. What's this Dendron you've found? Like the ones in the pictures?'

'Exactly like them. It *is* one. A live one. Different colours. But so beautiful it makes me want to weep. And I've found out that it is a creature of unbelievable energy – sometimes we feel it as sexual energy.'

'Hera! Hera, what the hell are you talking about?'

Hera again realized the gulf of understanding. 'Forget it. It's misleading. Forget I even said that.'

'I'll try.'

'Listen. Are any of my people still up there?'

'One or two. There's someone called Valis Umaga. Looking after some of your ORBE samples, I think. We've had to repack—'

'Right. Tell Valis under any circumstances not to try to send any stuff from Paradise through the fractal. Tell him straight from me.'

'OK.' Abhuradin was writing. 'OK. Got that. And there's a tough-looking mama called Tania Kowalski. Do you know her?'

'Yeah. Biochemist. Great woman.'

'If you say so.' Abhuradin, it seemed, had a different opinion.

'Get Tania on line when we link tri-vid. She knows a lot about the Dendron. Did a special programme on them. She'll understand. She can explain better than I can what we're doing.'

'OK. Anything else?'

'Just take care of yourself, Inez. I hardly recognized you. How's your painter man?'

Captain Abhuradin smiled for the first time, and winced. 'He's here now. Asleep over there. Hell, Hera. Life's short and this job looked like it was going to drag on so . . . a few weeks ago I arranged for him to transfer. Best thing I ever did.'

'Good. I'm glad. And you did right. We've a lot to talk about. Last thing. Mack is outside—'

'Are you and he—'

'No. Nothing like that. But he's asleep, I hope, and doesn't know I'm talking to you, but I know he'd want to get a message to his team. He treats them like family. Just tell them ... tell them he's having a great time. Tell them that the water's warm, he's learning to swim and he wishes they were here. Tell them that. They'll understand.'

'Will do.'

'I'm linking to tri-vid now. I'll leave everything running. Don't worry. Go back to bed. We've a few hours of sleep yet. We'll talk again.'

The transmission closed, but the line stayed live.

'Alan?'

'Yes, Hera?'

'Net this link to the shuttle platform. Priority Alpha, and join it in with the local tri-vid. Got that?'

'Mobile link or static?'

'Can you give me both, or cut between them?'

'Intercut.'

'Do that. Keep it live no matter what. But if there is a break, try to re-establish. Got all that?'

'Yes. Do you want inter-edit delay facility?'

'No, Alan. This is *cinéma vérité*. We send it out raw. Out now.'

Hera yawned. Now she knew she would sleep. Outside, looking through the control room windows, she could see the great bulk of the Dendron. Tonic had risen and in its silver light the Dendron was like a boulder. There was no sign of Mack.

As Hera snuggled under her covers, she thought how interconnected everything was. Inez Abhuradin, the woman who never mixed business with pleasure, now had her man with her. How could Hera ever explain that this decision was partly because there was a Dendron still alive on Paradise and Dendron did strange things to women when they wanted to divide, or join or ... didn't they? *Did they do the same for men?* she wondered. Mack seemed colder, somehow ... No, not colder, more distant ... but that might be the Michelangelo ... the Reaper ... Now if the Dendron are odd ... Reapers are really ... .really ...

Hera was woken when she felt the SAS move. Mack was up, had started the flyer and was moving it closer to the Dendron. By the time she climbed out, still tugging on her meshlite, he had it parked and the tool compartment was open. He was pulling out tools and setting them out. Chainsaw with battery. Solar generator. Pressure pump. Pneumatic nibbler. Scrub cutter. Three axes. Pick. Mattock. Rake. Sledgehammer. Wedges. Long saws, hand saws, solar saws, spades. Everything was out and lined up for inspection.

When Hera came round the SAS, Mack was busy putting a final keen edge onto an axe.

'It's going to be long day, Hera. Glad you had a good sleep.'

She nodded and yawned. 'I got through last night. Finally. They've had troubles on the platform. Amazing stuff. But I have the tri-vid link working. It'll be on now. Live.' If Hera had hoped for a warm response to her news, she was disappointed. Mack merely grunted and went on sharpening the axe. 'So,' she continued, 'if you want to talk to any of your team, I'm sure they'll be pleased to hear from you.'

He nodded. And then he put the axe down. 'Listen, Hera. You're going to have to deal with all that. If I need to talk, to get help or something, I will. But apart from that I don't want to talk to anyone. That clear?' She nodded, disturbed somewhat by his manner, by his quiet and his intensity. 'Today is the make-or-break day, Hera. Once we start there's no stopping. By the end of today, we'll know whether we can save her –' he nodded casually at the dark blue side of the Dendron '– or not.'

Hera absorbed this. He'd said as much last night. 'Is she . . . still all right?'

'As far as I can tell. Her codds are warm so she's thinking about us. She's drinking. Had a bit of a pee about dawn. The cherries haven't started to drop so the two lads up front are still fine. So, all in all, we're in there with a chance.' He smiled at her for the first time.

'Have you eaten anything, Mack?' she asked. 'Had a coffee or breakfast?'

He shook his head. 'My stomach was in knots this morning.'

'I'll get something ready while you finish sorting the tools.'

She was on her way before he could argue.

It was strange setting out a table near the vast shape of the Dendron. Hera noticed that the smell had changed. It had lost the sour taint that Mack had found so unappealing. It was the same kind of smell but sweeter. Not primroses or pineapples. Itself.

Once, as she was bringing things out, the Dendron's codds gave a great heave and Hera nearly dropped the two bowls she was carrying. Mack, up on its back, using a paint spray to mark the places where he would cut, paused and was ready to jump. But the beast didn't move.

Then, as Hera finished pouring the coffee, a call sign rang out from the SAS, and she jumped up to answer it.

Perched on her chair in the control room, Hera could see the trivid picture of Mack working on the back of the Dendron. It was clear and sharp, and this was the image that was being transmitted up to the shuttle. On the line she heard a man's voice: 'Hi there, Captain Melhuish. Dickinson here. Just thought we'd call to see how the old man's treating you. We've got your camp on visual. If you could open the lens a bit wider, we would be able to see the tips of the Dendron's horns – if that's what you call them. Looks nice down there. Nice stream. Miss Annette Descartes wants to know, and I quote her verbatim, "What the fuck is that thing the old man's climbing about on?" Is that a Dendron?'

Hera laughed. 'Yes. Believe it or not, we have to try and help it divide. I can't really talk now. And I know that Mack doesn't want to be disturbed so . . .'

'Say no more. We know what he's like. When he's thinking he can't talk. And when he talks, he sure as hell isn't thinking, half the time. Just tell him the reserves are all on the bench. He'll know what I mean.' A woman's voice cut in. 'Tell him that Polka and Netty send him a biiiiiiig kiss.' Dickinson came back on line. 'You got that all right? That was Polka. She's the polite one.'

'Yes . . . er, I'll give him the message.'

'Now, there's someone here wants to talk to you. Over to Miss Kowalski.' There was a thump and a scraping sound, and she heard Dickinson's voice off mike saying, 'You're standing on the cable, Miss Kowalski. You can sit up here with me.' Then Tania was there, very loud and breathless.

'Hera. Hera. Tania here. Is that for real? I can't believe it. Shit a brick, Hera! I mean . . . after all these years. Is it OK? Is it alive? Hera? Hera?'

'I'm here, Tania. Just let me get a word in.'

'Yeah, yeah. When I heard the news I tried to get that cow Haveagin to let me come down. But she won't. She—'

'Yes, and you mustn't, Tania. You mustn't. It's too dangerous now. Forget everything you ever knew about Paradise. Everything. I mean it. If anyone comes down here just now we could be in trouble. What we have is a brand new situation. Nothing like we've ever seen before. We have Reapers back, and you know what that means. Even the Tattersall weeds are getting mobile. The planet's rejecting everything of Earth. Bodies coming back to the surface. But it's good too. I'll explain as much as I can, later. I'll come back on line as soon as I've given Mack his breakfast.'

'What the f—'

Hera cut the volume. Tania's reaction was predictable. But Hera now saw what Mack had meant. She was dizzy with other people already. And the questions that could not be answered. She got Mack to come down and eat. Which he did, finally. Still absentminded. Still thinking. 'Can I talk to you?' she asked when he had been sitting for a minute.

'Sure.'

'Did you figure out the problem?'

'Which problem? There's a lot of them.'

'The er . . . what did you call it last night? The place where it keeps its life?'

'Oh that. I think so. At least as well as I can. It's a gamble, Hera, but where's the safest place on a Dendron?'

'Up with the cherries and tears.'

'Nope. Those are its hands and eyes. Why do you hide your brain in your skull?'

'For protec— You don't mean the stump, do you? But that's just a . . .' Her voice trailed away.

'Just a what? Why is its stool standing in the water now? What do the codds connect to? Why did that Dendron the Mayday woman talked about, why did it attack part of the stump so hard and rip parts of it apart? Now I have no idea what a Dendron's brain is like, nothing like our brains that's for sure, but that's where it keeps it, in that dip in the stool. And that's what we have to keep alive and happy, if we can. Until the second-to-last cut. You'll be helping with that too. I'm not going to do things the way the other Dendron did. It had time and strength on its side. We have neither. So I hope

281

you're feeling fit, Doc, cos I'm going to need a lot of help today.'

Hera nodded. She read the change in their relationship. She was Doc again. 'You'll get it, boss. Can I have a few minutes to finish a call?'

'Take your time. I'm laying out the cutting plan. I'll be half an hour or so. And then we start.' He stood up. 'Oh, er . . . was there anything in from Dickinson or Cole and the team?'

'Yes, Dickinson was there. He said to tell you that the reserves were all on the bench.' Mack nodded. 'And some people called Polka and Netty said to give you a kiss.'

Mack grinned. 'That all?'

'That's all.'

'It's enough.' He finished his coffee and reached his arms above his head and stretched.

While Mack finished planning the cuts, Hera returned to her conversation with Tania. She explained as well as she could their new understanding of how the Dendron functioned and what they were trying to do.

Tania started with lots of questions, but these gradually ceased as the story unfolded and became stranger. And when Hera paused for breath, Tania said, 'Hera, if it was anyone else but you telling me this, I wouldn't believe a word of it. But because it's you, Hera, and because it all makes a weird kind of sense, I believe half of it. OK. I'll ride the tri-vid at this end – put a commentary on it when I can. But . . . O Hera, I wish I was down there with you. This is everything we ever dreamed of, and more. Now, one thing. Give me a bit of a wider angle if you can and tilt up a bit – I'm missing the flags. And, if you get time, try to zoom in if there's something really interesting, like when you get right inside the Dendron.'

Dickinson came on line again. 'Couldn't help hearing what you ladies were saying. All sounds pretty normal to me. But hey, Prof. If you want, you can tell your AP to connect us through to your control line. I can link with it up here. Then we can do the camera work by remote, if that'll help. Then you don't have to worry about it. I've ridden camera when I was working security for the Vatican and I can get that focus tighter than a chicken's—'

'Thank you, Dickinson,' said Hera. 'Just hold a minute, will you? Let me check.' She switched through to the autopilot. 'Alan, can you connect a tri-vid control line up to the shuttle?'

'Yes, Hera. If they can provide a triception boost and negative interface.'

'Hey, Prof.' It was Dickinson again. 'Got that. Leave it to me, eh? If your AP wants to talk techno-babble, so can I. We'll sort it out. OK? And if big-bum Titania here will just give me a bit of room . . .' In the distance Mack could be heard calling. 'Mack wants you, Prof. Leave it to us. Alan and me'll have a chat. Good luck.'

Mack was waiting on top of the Dendron when Hera climbed the ladder. He had brought some of the tools up. 'You're going to be gofer. OK? You *go for* this or you *go for* that. OK?'

'Right. With you.'

'The first thing I'm going to do is try to disable the crest thing, so that even if she wakes up she won't be able to take a swipe at us. To get to the fulcrum, we're going to have to cut a trench down her back and round the heel of the crest. I don't know what we're going to find, but it is a complicated joint, so it should be easy to disable it. Here's a mattock and a spade. Go for it, Doc. Follow the blue lines I've marked out. Now dig.'

So they started. Each one working from a different side of the Dendron, they cut a trench along its back. The deep red of the Dendron's back was soft, as Mack had found when he fell on it. It cut easily with a spade, but removing the cut was hard as all the fibres went downwards and they did not tear easily. Below the tufted red fibre, the inner body was green. Hera began by trying to be very neat. But the Dendron's flesh would not yield to that approach and so she soon found herself using the mattock and tearing the matted fibres out in clumps. Everything in her screamed out against this brutal treatment of matter, but she could see no alternative. The heavy green flesh slipped and slithered down the side of the Dendron and fell noisily into the stream. There it floated away.

One problem emerged quickly. The sap of the creature came welling up, filling the trench, and they soon found themselves knee deep in slippery mucus. Mack lost his footing when he swung his mattock and slipped over, narrowly missing one of the sharp tines of the crest. He sat in the hole he had dug like a man in a green bath. 'OK. Change of plan. Get me the chainsaw, Doc. We'll talk to it with that for a while. Cut some drainage channels for all this pea soup.' Hera buried the head of her mattock in the side of the Dendron and

283

climbed down the ladder. Mack threw a rope down to her. 'Here, tie it to this.' He watched her closely. 'What's that knot you're using called?'

'A bowline. We use it on the boats all the time. It can't slip and—'

'I know what it is. Up she comes.' He pulled the chainsaw to the top of the Dendron. Hera climbed back up the ladder. 'Now, Doc, have you ever used a chainsaw?'

'Yes.'

'Right. I want you to cut a couple of trenches here at the end of the Dendron so all this slop can drain away. Get your feet secure first. And watch out cos these things start with a hiss and a roar. No grace clutch or anything.'

Hera cut and the saw ran through the flesh of the Dendron easily. She cut a V and was able to use the flat of the saw to send the cut flesh sliding away. The green water began to gully down the side of the Dendron.

'Good. Now there is only one problem. We need to cut lower and round the underside if we're going to drain this lot away. Any suggestions?'

Hera didn't bother to answer. She tied the rope round her waist and handed the end to Mack. 'If you'd be so kind as to hold this, boss, I'll lean over the side and cut a beautiful deep drain.'

'Hook your toes in the lip of the trench then.'

Holding the saw away from her, Hera leaned out from the side of the Dendron. Mack took her weight until she was almost inverted, and then she began to cut. It was surprisingly easy. The blue fibre fell away from the blade and the only problem was the green liquid from above, which found its way inside the leg of her overalls, ran down the underside of her body, came out at her neck and used her chin as a spout. Some inevitably ran into her mouth, nose and eyes.

It was at about this time that the tri-vid camera on the top of the SAS suddenly moved jerkily and panned round. It then retracted and advanced its lens. After a pause it turned smoothly to follow them. Hera, despite the dribbling juice, was cutting steadily, making a deep trench in the side.

'Stop,' shouted Mack. 'Don't move till the saw's stopped. Your hair's come loose.' Hera held the saw away from her and felt the harness of her overall begin to lift. Then a hand seized her by the back of her meshlite and hoisted her upright.

'I ought to cut it off,' said Hera.

'Like hell. Just needs tucking in and tying down tighter. You should see young Polka's hair. Red as this Dendron. Lot bushier than yours. She tapes it down. So do Jason and Akira. If I had hair like this, I'd have it long.' All the time while he was talking Mack was tucking Hera's hair back and then anchoring it. 'With all this sticky shit in it, it'll probably set before long anyway, and then you won't have a problemo. OK. There you are. Over the side again, McGinity.'

Ten minutes later, Hera was upright again and easing her back. Mack was whistling. He undid the rope round her waist from behind. And as he did so, she heard him whisper, 'Don't look now, but they've got that camera working on remote. It'll just be Dickinson arsing about.' Out loud he said, 'You did bloody well there, Doc – for a beginner. Go and get yourself cleaned up a bit. I can take over now.'

Hera found her legs were shaking as she climbed down the ladder. But one thing, one thing above all pleased her. Mack was cheerful! She realized that as soon as he was working, the worry lifted. He was into the job. She had no doubt he was thinking as hard as ever, but it was not sullen work, but lively work, full of . . . She looked for the word. Wit. Fun. Sport. All fitted. She was aware of the camera following her as she reached the bottom. She gave it a thumbs up and headed into the SAS for a change of overalls. She heard the saw start up on the top of the Dendron, followed by the steady *swish* and *slop* of the liquid pouring down the trenches she had cut and tumbling into the stream.

By the time Hera emerged, hair taped back, face clean and wearing fresh overalls, the trench was complete and Mack had cleared a crater around the heel of the crest. The crest had not moved. 'Bring your drawing book up,' called Mack. 'You'll want to get a sketch of this for your grandchildren.'

'You serious?'

'Sure. I'll be doing the next bit.'

Hera fetched her sketchbook and clambered up onto the high point of the Dendron's back. From there she could see deep into the Dendron. Revealed was a wide flat ball-and-socket joint where the crest could swivel. Thick straps of creamy wishbone joined the crest to the joint and then disappeared down into the Dendron.

'These here,' said Mack, tapping the exposed straps of fibre, 'control the crest. I reckon there's one for each of the blades – that's about 240. That explains what that Mayday woman meant when she said it "chops and cuts". I remember you saying that. It's a good description. Makes maximum use of the effort. It means that the blades can be made to move either together like an axe blade or separately like a saw. They come down in a chop, and when that stops, they rip. Very bloody ingenious.' He rested the blade of the saw on one of the wide straps of creamy fibre. 'These attach directly to the stool. They've got to, as it is the only solid thing in the vicinity. These straps of wishbone are what give the whole crest its stability – whether it's resting up or going into battle. I reckon that hump there where you're perched is one of the main anchor points in the Dendron's body. It takes the shock of the chop and distributes it through the rest of its body, and the weight of the stool gives the chop its drive. Perfect. If I had one of these in the team I could get rid of Dickinson. Now, the Dendron you told me about chopped straight into all this stuff – rip, shit and bust. That right?'

Hera nodded.

'Well, we're not going to do that because of the danger of damaging the Dendron before we can liberate the two trunks up front. We don't want to create bad feedback. Could ruin everything. You remember?' Hera nodded again. 'So what I'm now going to do is cut through the main straps, then sever the crest.' He picked up a small blade and plugged it into the power pack on his belt. 'This little brute can cut through steel,' he said, brandishing the saw. 'Let's see what it makes of the wishbone.'

Hera realized that what she had just heard was one of Mack's briefings. He probably did this before every job. She began sketching quickly, trying to capture the poise of the joint and the way it attached to the crest, and the neatly plaited fibres. She would have loved, just once, to see it open now, and watch the wishbone straps tighten and feel the pulse of its huge strength as it took the strain right underneath where she was sitting. She could imagine the great heave and flow – and the heat too. There would be a lot of heat generated. That would be an obvious reason for steeping, simply to keep cool. A body like this with a thatch on top could overheat quickly. She thought back to the desert. The Dendron's achievement in trekking across the desert was ever more impressive.

Mack was ready. He raised the blade. 'Let's see if this'll talk to it.' He studied the joint. 'I'm going to cut this big strap first. You keep back on the hump there, Doc. There might be a recoil.' He got down on his knees in the ooze, worked his body under the tines of the crest and braced himself.

'Mack, there's no danger the crest can come down and pin you, is there?'

'No. I wouldn't be lying here if it could. If anything, it might rise a bit as the tension comes off here. You be on the lookout.' He braced himself again and held the saw blade just above the pale strap of wishbone. He clenched his teeth with the effort and the saw began to spin. His first cut was shallow, a mere etching of the surface, and he looked to see if there was any change. He saw some of the cut fibres, like fine hairs, open and peel back under tension. 'It's definitely going to lift. You keep well back.' He made a second shallow cut, following the guide of the first, and saw more fibres peel back. 'You'll feel the strap under you contracting. It's lifting the crest a fraction.' He made another cut, a deeper one this time, and saw the wishbone begin to stretch and open. Dark green fluid with the consistency of engine oil seeped from the cut wishbone. He saw the fibres sever, and heard them snap like the breaking of violin strings. The tension on them had been greater than he imagined. For a moment he wondered whether the Dendron might, in some way, be trying to help. That was logical, wasn't it? It wanted to split. Logically, if he was doing what it wanted, then he could in some strange way be giving it pleasure, and it would cooperate – or was he just being daft?

The last fibres parted suddenly with a snap, the cut ends contracting and twisting like burned plastic. The crest lurched and lifted. It was for a moment eccentric, seeking a new point of balance. In lifting, one of the black tines slid over Mack's shoulder. He felt it catch and snag in the saw harness. It began to lift him. Mack was not a light man, but his weight meant nothing in this contest, and he felt himself dragged to his knees, and then hoisted higher until he hung suspended with his feet several inches above the soft mushy surface. He could not reach round to release himself because he could not get purchase. He was bent over, like a schoolboy of the past, awaiting the cane.

Hera felt the change in tension through the thick pelt of the

Dendron. The hump on which she was sitting lifted slightly and there was movement under her feet like a wave passing. Then everything settled down. But what was Mack trying to do?

She stood up and made her way down the trench they had cut. Finally she could see where Mack was hooked on the crest, harness stretched tight between his legs. Hera worked her way round the ball-and-socket pivot point. She could see that Mack's face was red with the effort – and perhaps more than the effort. 'Are we comfortable, sir?'

'Just unhook me, and none of the wisecracks, OK? And careful you don't jiggle the thing. I don't want to join the altos.'

'No, sir.' However, releasing him was not that easy, for Mack was a heavy man. Eventually she had to cut through the harness and he dropped down onto his toes and then his knees in the ooze.

He stood up and adjusted himself with obvious relief. 'All right, you've had your little laugh. Now come and look at the other side. I'm going to cut that strap too. What surprises me is that even this wishbone fibre has fluid in it. Everything is managed by fluid – tension and release, tension and release. I'm starting to get the hang of how this Dendron mo— Stop bloody laughing, will you? I'm serious.'

The next cut went smoothly. The dark green 'oil' bubbled out and Hera collected a sample. The strap, when severed, rolled up like a wood shaving. The crest dropped back down sharply and tipped to one side. It could no longer be lifted by man or Dendron.

'That's that finished,' said Mack. 'Now. Look at this wishbone stuff. It's got amazing tensile strength. You couldn't pull it apart in a month of Sundays. You have to cut it. Was an analysis ever done on what it is?'

'MINADEC did a whole lot of analyses. Tania knows the details. The problem is, once a Dendron is dead the original wishbone becomes brittle pretty quickly. They used to grind it up and drink it.'

'You pulling my leg?'

'No. There used to be a big trade. Men found the need of it, apparently. Helped their virility. You might've have needed some too, if I hadn't cut you down in time.'

'You're never going to let me forget that, are you?'

'I'll think about it. But Dickinson probably got it recorded anyway.'

Mack groaned.

During their lunch break Hera checked with Tania Kowalski and Dickinson to see how the recording was going.

'Fine. Fine,' said Tania.

Hera detected evasion. 'So what's the problem, Tania?' She looked closely. 'Are you wearing make-up?' She glanced across at Dickinson. 'And you've got a brushed-up casual look about you, Mr Dickinson. You're very cosy, the pair of you. What's going on?'

'I think you need to have a quick talk to the captain,' said Tania hurriedly. 'Things are a bit more advanced than the last time we talked. She was here just a minute ago. Hey, did you see where the captain went, Dickhead?'

'No, I didn't, Titania,' replied Dickinson.

'You two er . . . getting on all right?' asked Hera.

'Yeah, great,' said Tania, 'as soon as we got a few basics sorted. That right, Dickhead?'

'Well to be honest,' said Dickinson judiciously, 'she didn't go down too well at first. But with a bit more practice and a mouth as big as that, she should impr—'

'*Dickinson!*' It was both women speaking.

Captain Abhuradin was located. Hera was relieved to find her transformed. A crisp clean uniform. Hair brushed and shaped. Even the bandage on her face was stylish and her poise was back. But she was a worried woman. 'Hera, I don't know how you are going to take this, but there was nothing I could do. Sorry.'

'About what? Why is everyone talking in riddles?'

'So they didn't tell you?'

'Tell me what?'

The captain took a deep breath. 'Word got out about the Dendron. A news team came through the fractal about half an hour after I had spoken to you last night. I didn't know they were here. They'd come to interview some of the children, but then they—'

'Get to the point, Inez.'

'Well they heard from somewhere – probably that cheeky little communications clerk from Central – that you were down there – you know what gossip is like on the platform – and they heard that a Dendron had been found – people remember the Dendron, you know . . .'

'Yes, and . . .'

'Somehow they found out you were doing a live broadcast. And one of them contacted the chief press secretary at the Space Council and he spoke to Tim Isherwood and got permission for the Time and Space Network to take live coverage. Official.'

'So what's this mean?'

'It means that what you are doing down there is now being broadcast to any station that wants to take it.'

'*What? WHAT!*'

'Apparently there has been a high pick-up rate. So . . .'

'This is wrong, Inez. We're not running a circus.'

'I know. I know. I wanted to get a message to you. If it's any consolation, your two people here, Dr Titania Kowalski and Professor Kenneth de Kingson, are doing a brilliant job. People can't take their eyes off the programme, Hera. She's explaining the biology and history and he seems to be able to explain everything else. They're brilliant together – and so entertaining. The banter . . . They must be good friends, yes?'

'They rub along. Look, are you telling me that everything we're doing down here is being broadcast via the fractal to whoever in the explored zones cares to tune in?'

'Not the audio line. But everything else is seen in tri-vid. Kowalski and de Kingson interpret the action for the viewer. It is very documentary. Very science-based. Kowalski's good, isn't she? I see what you mean about her.'

'It's a bloody outrage. When I get my hands on them . . .'

'No, Hera, they're doing a good job. Very professional. None of this is their fault. Media rules, Hera. You know that.'

'It's still a bloody outrage.'

'Well, there's something else you ought to know. Evidently the level of support for what you are doing is breaking all viewing records. The dial-in channels are overloaded with callers. That time when you went over the side with the chainsaw. Well, my heart was in my mouth. I never realized how big the Dendron are! You're a brave lady, Hera. What's more, people want to know why ORBE was closed down when there was such an important endangered species on the planet. It's all media hype, I know, Hera, but at least it's on the right side. You are not going to be on Timothy Isherwood's Christmas card list.'

'Just as well.'

'Hera, I'm sorry about this. But I can't talk now. There's a lot to tell you. Later. When you are back up here. I have to go. I'm being interviewed on the arrival of the children in a few minutes. I'm nervous as hell. Good luck. I'm handing you back to Kowalski and Kingson.'

The line, as they used to say, went dead. And then came alive again.

Hera found herself looking at Tania and Dickinson.

Dickinson spoke first. 'Before you say anything, Miss Melhuish, just be glad that we're here. When the story broke that we were in live contact with you, Time and Space wanted to take the lot over – get their own techies in and some blue-eyed ponce who does popular science programmes. We stopped that. Well Titania did, actually. Very impressive demolition job. Are all you ORBE women like this? No, don't answer that. I don't want to know.'

Tania cut in: 'As soon as we realized what was happening, Dickinson installed a ten-minute delay so nothing gets out without our knowledge.'

'So what is happening now, at this moment?'

Dickinson consulted a side monitor. 'Just now they're running background documentaries. *Early Days on Paradise.*'

'They've contacted Rita Honeyball and Moritz to talk about the plum. But the moment you start again, we'll be covering,' said Tania.

'And, what is more, people find us entertaining and informative. Is that not right, Dr Kowalski?'

Tania did not look at him but spoke directly to Hera. 'I know Dickinson behaves like a prat, Hera. But as prats go he's not bad and, give him his due, he knows the electronics. And just for the record, he came up with these fancy names while I was laying into their news director. By the time they'd wiped him up off the floor, people were calling me Dr Titania and him Professor Kenneth, for fuck's sake! Anyway, Hera, we can pull the programme if you say so, or you can just turn it off at your end. It's as simple as that. Of course, we would lose the data – and I'm measuring everything.'

'Unfair. Tania, you—'

Dickinson interrupted: 'I want to add something, Doc. It is over to you as to whether you tell Mack. But listen up. As long as he thinks it's just me arsing about, he'll be happy. But I tell you this: if he discovers the tri-vid is going out to the great unwashed, he'll tear the bloody cables out of the wall and I suggest you start running right now cos he won't be taking prisoners. Your call, Miss Melhuish. And I don't envy you one little bit.'

'OK,' said Hera. 'Just give me a minute.' She began to tick things off on her fingers. 'There's a ten-minute delay so you can edit. There is no live audio signal going out. You are the only two doing the interpreting. Am I right so far?' They both nodded. 'How do you know they're not picking up our tri-vid signal when it arrives up there?'

'Oh, I'm sure they are. And recording it,' said Dickinson. 'And trying to sort it out, and scratching their heads. But it won't do them any good. Your lad Alan and I agreed some encryption protocols before we made the link. Your broadcast is secure. If anyone tries to hack in, well . . . if they're lucky, they'll get garbage. If they are unlucky, it's wall-to-wall Mahler.' He tapped the side of his nose with his finger. 'Trust Professor de Kingson. They'll have the tapes of what *we* broadcast, of course. But that's all. Naturally, Mack won't be too pleased when he sees himself getting hung up by the balls on prime time. And then this morning, when he fell down in the green soup, I fell off my stool laughing. I always told him he'd missed his vocation and should have gone on stage.'

'*Dickinson!* Can we get back to the subject? Are you sure the Network can't break the code?'

'Does the Pope wear woollen bed—'

'Answer the bloody question!'

'Yes. Yes. Yes. Yes. Yes. I'm sure.'

'OK. One other thing,' said Hera. 'It just occurs to me that Time and Space may be trying to pull strings with the Space Council to get the shuttle platform opened so they can get down here. Now, that mustn't happen. You've got to stop them. Not just for our sake, but for everyone's sake. Broadcast the warning so that if they try anything they can be held to account. Don't ask me to explain why, because it would take too long. But just as you helped Mack get down here to save me, so trust me on this now. Don't let anyone come down here. Scare them shitless, if need be. Mack and I may be safe, simply because of what we are doing

– but there are other forces at work too. So over to you.'

'I think we can do that,' said Tania. 'Don't you, Professor?'

Dickinson nodded. 'And in any case, I can always fuck up the shuttle. I've still got the keys.'

'Don't worry, Hera,' said Tania. 'Leave it to us. Get back to work now. Save that beautiful big beast for us.'

'Yeah,' said Dickinson. 'And look after the Dendron too. But it's still your call, Doc. Remember.'

In the afternoon Hera and Mack worked on, extending the trench right down the length of the back of the Dendron. They had struck up a good rhythm, working together. Mack cut with the chainsaw and ripped with the mattock while Hera worked with a bucket, scooping and clearing the slush over the sides. Working as fast as they could all day, they had managed to clear about as much of the surface material as the Dendron in Marie Newton's diary had cleared in one cut with its crest.

But now Mack began to cut more carefully. If he was right, then the main organ of sense – the 'brain' of the Dendron – would be found somewhere under the crest's pivotal joint. Its exact location was not known, and the situation was complicated by the fact that they must now be getting close to the top of the great twin pumps, the codds.

Mack was six feet six inches tall. Now, when he stood in the hole they had excavated, his head was well below the back of the Dendron. Both he and Hera needed a ladder to get in and out. Both were soaked with the heavy juice, which had got inside the mesh-lite overalls and made them sticky and uncomfortable. The heat was not helping. The clouds that had filled the sky in the morning had cleared and the sun now shone down from a clear blue sky.

Finally Mack said, 'To hell with this for a game of spacemen. I'm stripping down. You make yourself comfortable too. If you're worried about the recording we can always turn the bugger off.'

Without more ado he unzipped his overalls, stepped out of them and threw them down to the ground. He was wearing red and green shorts underneath. He had long since abandoned his boots, trusting his bare feet. Hera decided to do likewise and soon stood in just a top and loose shorts. Her face, neck, arms and legs were plastered with the green ooze. She appraised Mack. A strong body with broad shoulders. Hairy chest, but not too much. Powerful arms – but pale. Not having seen many male bodies close to, she did not want to seem to ogle. At the same time, not to look would seem prudish, childish even. 'You could do with some time lazing in the sun, my lad.'

'I could too,' he replied, looking at her. 'But there's this woman, you see. As soon as I lie down with a book in the sun, she wants me to go chasing all over the country hunting Dendron.' Mack stretched, and then scratched his chest and back. 'By God, it feels better without that meshlite stuff on. I know it's safe and strong and all that, but it's the wrong gear for this kind of job. Can I ask you how you are coping, having been injured so recently?'

'I'm fine. I feel better for the exercise. One thing, though. This green stuff. It reminds me of the jelly from an aloe vera plant. Have you ever heard of it?'

'Vaguely.'

'Well, it's very good for the skin. And I've just peeled some of this off and my skin feels clean and soft. That's all I was trying to say.'

'Well I'm glad to know that. We'll keep some in a jam jar to take home.' Mack jumped down into the hole and was immediately knee deep in warm ooze. 'I want you to come down here and bring your bucket. We might have a problem. Here, jump down.' He lifted his arms to help her. But his hands being covered with the juice and her top being loose, his hands slipped when he tried to hold her, and although Hera was not heavy, she fell down against him. Complicating matters was the fact that his hands caught in the loose shirt and it rode up and under her arms, exposing her breasts. In that state he put her down on her feet.

'Sorry about that,' said Mack. 'My grip slipped.' Hera didn't reply but pulled her damp shirt down. 'Didn't know you weren't wearing a bra.'

'Some of us don't have to. Now let's get on. What's the problem?'

It was one of those moments.

Each was suddenly deeply aware of the other physically. This had been happening for some time. How can it not when a man and a woman live close together and are attracted? But neither had quite acknowledged the attraction. In fact they had carefully avoided it – and that, of course, made matters worse, or better. For Mack the sudden sight of her breasts, nipples raised and nicely rounded, simply took his breath away. He could still feel them pressed against him and it made his throat dry for a moment and he felt very clumsy and breathless. For Hera it was more confusing. The shock of feeling her shirt ride up and not be able to stop it clashed with her sudden sense of the man's arms and strong body being very, very close. The clash tied a great knot in her and she found herself breathless, embarrassed, pleased, a bit dizzy and warm – but above all she was aware that she wanted – no, more than wanted, needed – that big knot untied.

Habit took over, and she hid her feelings under a brisk exterior, but later she would examine those feelings. Mack, a bit less protected by habit, had no choice but to let his pounding heart subside.

For the time being, Hera was down the hole they had cut.

Mack said, 'This is the problem. We're close to the codds and I don't want to damage them. We might be near whatever it uses for a brain, and I don't want to damage that either, yet. So first of all, feel about with your feet. Can you feel any difference on the bottom here?'

Hera moved round the hole, sliding her feet through the mush, feeling with her feet like a child at the seaside ankle deep in the sand. Mack retreated up the ladder.

'It feels a bit warmer here,' she said. 'This would be over the codds, wouldn't it? And I think I can feel ridges. If I work my toes . . .' She did this, concentrating visibly.

As that moment the Dendron gave a heave. The codds went through their great gulping and, moments later, green water was released on the back of the Dendron, flowed down the trench and cascaded into the hole. Within seconds the level was rising. Hera was in no danger, but what had most surprised her was that she had felt the movements like a great rolling wave under her feet. She had felt the ridges on the top of the codds open and close like a concertina. She felt a sudden warmth too, and when she stepped back there was a tingling in the liquid, like little pinpricks or as though something had scampered lightly over her feet. The bottom of the trench was a lot softer here. It was very different. She might have felt the start of the brain.

Mack had climbed out of the hole, and he now reached down and offered her a hand and helped her up the ladder.

'No doubt about it,' she said. 'You're right over the codds. I could feel them contract. And over there ... That was hard to describe. There was something different down there.'

'OK. I know what you mean. I felt it too. Just wanted to be sure I wasn't imagining.'

The green water reached the top of the hole and began to flood over. It ran away and out through the channels Hera had cut in the morning. They felt the Dendron shake and the remains of the straps which Mack had cut twisted and curled, unfurling like tongues. Those straps which were still intact contracted and the ball joint moved, stirring the crest. But without the two main support straps attached, the movement could go nowhere, though the black-spiked tines turned and flexed and cut the air like scissors.

'Is it trying to lift its crest? Why?'

'I think it's saying, "Get a move on!"'

Hera turned, and then cried out and pointed. One of the two front trees, one of the horns, had begun to droop. Its flags had no life and hung listlessly. Three of the cherries detached and fell to the ground, landing beyond the Dendron with a heavy thud.

Beneath them they could hear the codds labouring like old bellows, and for the moment there was nothing they could do but hang on. They knelt down while the Dendron shook, and they held on to whatever they could, including one another.

It seemed to last for a long time, but then gradually the shaking subsided. The front horn had straightened, but several more cherries had fallen.

Mack stood up. 'That's a warning. The two up front are in bad shape. They could be dying. The Dendron gave them what it could, but it's failing fast too. Remember in the Mayday woman's story, the Dendron that was doing the cutting at one point put its own horns up against the other and rubbed. I'm sure it was giving comfort or energy of some sort. We are going to try a big gamble, Hera. Have you got a good head for heights?'

'No, terrible.'

'Then now's the time to learn. It's payback time. Look at me. I'm going to rig it somehow so I can get you up there. I want you up there – don't worry, I'll make it safe – but I want you to get through to the two front trees. I think that's what the cherries are for. Use your body, use your mind. Touch them with your hands, let them feel your life. Remember anything you can about the Dendron, anything that you saw in the dream time. Everything. All of the good memories – it playing in the sea, it coming up and over you. And the way you felt. The waves. The redness. The way it swept you along. The sex. Yeah, *that*. Remember *that* especially. Everything, all the details and as much as you can. You said that knowledge came to you, yes? From the Reaper! From the planet! From the Dendron! It doesn't matter where from. Now give it back – from your heart, your womb, your mind, your . . . everywhere. Give it back to them a hundred times more. Let them know we're here because I think they have forgotten, and I think they are very, very frightened. Pour your love and life into them like they were your own children. Go and get changed quickly. Put on warm things. It'll get cooler when the sun goes down. You might be up there a long time. And start remembering, now.'

Hera heard his words and knew what he meant, as well as those things that could not be said. Mack was right, 'Payback time'. And wasn't this really what she wanted? She hurried down the ladder and into the SAS.

Mack came down after her. From the back of the SAS he brought ropes, a light chain ladder and a large multi-spanner. He sat in the back of the SAS and fastened his boots, lacing them tight. Then he attached a pair of the light crampons demolition men use when working on wet timber or in icy conditions. Lastly, with a long auxiliary strap, he wrapped his tool belt tight round his waist. Two big breaths and a flexing of the hands and he was ready. He climbed back up onto the Dendron and dragged the extension ladder up after him.

At the base of the strongest of the twin trees he rammed the ladder down hard so that the feet bedded into the turf of the Dendron. Then he pulled the ladder up to maximum. Its top was still far short of the first branch of the cherries, but at least at that height the trunk was smaller and he could get his arms round it to climb. He now draped one of the long ropes round his shoulders so that it couldn't drop but would cushion his head against the tree. He attached the folded coils of the chain ladder to the back of his belt. It hung down like a tail. He made one last check to see that he had everything he might need: spare cords, knife, ring head cleats, hammer, eye pulleys and the wrench – he touched each piece as he said its name. Satisfied, he set off up the ladder, fast and agile – the balanced climb of a man who knows ladders and their tricks well.

Behind him, on the roof of the SAS, the small tri-vid camera turned and tracked him. It was good that Mack did not know that all the members of his team were now packed into the small tri-vid studio watching, or that, beyond the fractal limit, millions of others observed as he climbed high above the Dendron. Professor Kenneth de Kingson described every precaution and every danger in glowing prose.

At the top of the ladder Mack wrapped his arms round the trunk and, using the crampons for purchase, began to climb. Push, lift, grip. Push, lift, grip. It was painfully slow progress, but it was progress nevertheless and eventually he was able to reach with one hand and take hold of the lowest of the cherry branches. With one big effort he heaved himself up. His arms were aching, and he sat for a minute in the fork of the tree to recover. *Not getting any younger,* he thought. *This might be my last big adventure, whatever granny says.*

Sitting astride the branch and with his back to the trunk, Mack lashed the chain ladder to the branch and then let its length go snaking down. It banged against the top of the extension ladder, which it overlapped slightly. To test it, he took a firm grip on the tree and stepped gingerly onto the top rung. It didn't give. Feeling more confident he jogged up and down lightly. All was well.

Lighter now, and with good footholds and places to grip, he climbed quickly from cherry branch to cherry branch. There were only three levels of branches, but at each level were four or five separate limbs sticking out. The Venus tears tinkled against one another as he climbed past.

Perched on the last of the cherry branches, Mack loosened his webbing belt, passed the strap round the tree and buckled it again. Then he leaned back, stiff-legged, and let his weight hold him safe against the tree. He could now use his hands. He uncoiled the rope from his shoulders, located an end and tied a large loop. He then leaned out from the tree and cast the loop so that it fell entirely over the crook on the opposite tree where one of the cherry branches sprouted out. The distance between the two trees was not great.

Dickinson, watching closely from the shuttle studio, guessed what Mack was about to attempt. 'Ladies and gentlemen in the studio, and you viewers at home. What Mack is attempting is one of the hardest manoeuvres we ever have to perform when we are working alone at the top of a high building – often in a high wind and with freezing temperatures. We call it hangman, for obvious reasons. You can see how Mack has attached himself, like a man on a telegraph pole. Now he has tied a noose to one end of his rope. What he is attempting to do is establish a rope bridge between the two trunks. We emphasize that none of you viewing this at home must ever try to do this manoeuvre alone. One slip is all it takes. There, he's reaching out now ... ready to throw ... and steady, steady, steady ... and there it goes ... And he's got it the first time!'

The team jammed in the small studio, as well as a few of the off-duty shuttle workers and some of the bemused children, burst into spontaneous applause and cheering.

'You can hear the reaction of the people up here on the shuttle platform over Paradise. Mack will now draw the noose tight. There it goes. He's pulling the rope to make sure it's tight ... And it is. The treetops are linked, ladies and gentlemen. A double bridge will now be made between the two trunks, one rope above the other. I'll explain its purpose later. For the moment I am now going to hand over to my colleague Dr Kowalski. She has news of the state of the Dendron. Titania ...'

Tania's voice took over. 'Thank you, Professor. The former head of the recently abolished ORBE project, Dr Hera Melhuish, is now ready below ...'

Tania had just been talking to Hera and knew what she was going to be doing.

Mack, oblivious to all this, tied off the rope ends to the tree. He had his two-rope bridge in place. Now all that remained was to test it. He climbed back up to the top rope, selected one of the pulleys with a steel dog clip and gripped it in his teeth. Then he took hold of the upper bridge rope and swung out between the trees. As he did so, his shoulders bumped the clustered cherries, one of which detached and fell.

Between the two trees he hung by one arm while he anchored the dog clip over the bridge rope. And then he swung back. That manoeuvre took its toll. His arms felt as though they had come out of their sockets. Big men are not meant to swing in trees.

'Mack. Mack, what are you doing?' It was Hera of course, standing on the riverbank beside the Dendron. 'You've got the ladder. I can't get back up.'

'I'm making it safe for you up here. I'll be down in a minute.' His last task was to fit the rope through the pulley. He realized that if he had been thinking properly, he could have threaded it before attaching the pulley. *Next time I'll know better,* he thought and swung out again.

To Hera, watching from below, it looked terrifying. *What if he falls? What will I do then?*

But Mack didn't fall. He got the rope through the pulley and, gripping it in his teeth, swung back to the tree. There he tied a bowline loop round his chest and under his arms. 'Coming down,' he called and swung out between the trees. Elbows clenched against his body, he began to lower himself down, paying out the rope as he went. He stepped off at the bottom. 'I'm not showing off,' he called down to Hera. 'I just wanted to show you that it's safe. OK? Now, you're going to need a seat of some kind.'

He removed the extension ladder and set it up against the side of the Dendron as before and climbed down. While Hera climbed up the ladder, she could hear Mack inside the SAS. He was thumping about, and then she heard a tearing sound. Minutes later he emerged holding one of the moulded foam seats from the mess area. The advantage of this was that not only was it comfortable, but it had moulded holes in it and these he could use to tie it securely. He carried the chair in one hand while he climbed back up onto the back of the Dendron. Quickly he tied the rope to the chair so that it hung free. Then he lifted Hera up and sat her in the chair. 'That comfortable?'

'Fine. I think.' She gripped the arms of the chair. 'But what if I . . .'

'OK. I'm tying you in so there's no way you can fall out.' Mack passed the rest of the rope round her waist and then round her legs and through the holes under the chair. He pulled it tight and then hoisted her until she was swinging a couple of metres above the Dendron. 'OK. Try and fall out of that.'

Hera twisted a couple of times. 'OK. I believe you.'

'Hold tight. I'm going to hoist you up a bit.' He pulled on the long pulley and Hera's chair rose. She sat quite stiff and the chair spun on the rope. 'I could fix that,' he said, 'but when you get up there, all you have to do is hold one of the cherries or one of the bridge ropes and you'll be able to stop it spinning yourself. Do you feel OK?' Hera nodded.

She didn't feel OK. She was terrified, but she wasn't going to say so.

'It'll feel pretty strange at first, but you'll soon get used to it. In fact, you might start to like it once you're up there. Anyway, it's the best I could do given the time and I guarantee you're safe. So. Good luck, Hera. Remember what I said. I'll be down here if you need me. Here goes.' He pulled on the rope and Hera rose. She spun one way and then the other. Several more pulls and she was level with the bottom of the chain ladder. She was now not spinning so much. The first of the cherries was not far away. A few more pulls and she could almost touch them. One more pull and she was in the midst of them and she could reach out and grasp them. The chair jerked a couple of times as Mack tied it off. And there she was. She could not touch all the cherries, for some were on the far side of the trunks, but she could reach a lot of them and she also found that she could almost stand up in the chair. She forgot about being high off the ground. She concentrated on the black and red balls that clustered about her and the pale discs of Venus tears that she could make ring just by brushing them with her fingers. She tried to concentrate on her memories of the Dendron, but those memories would not settle. She caught herself remembering the way her shirt had rolled up and the surprised look on Mack's face when he saw her bare breasts and how nice it had been to brush against his body and the crinkly tickle of his hair.

'You started all this, you know,' she said to the Dendron. 'Oh, but I want you to get well and to grow big and strong, like Mack down there, and then go wandering all over your lovely planet and crush Tattersall weeds under your feet and stamp where you want and send your thoughts out into space. They aren't thoughts, are they? They are your sense of being. Of life and energy and . . . love. No wonder we all respond to you. We wish we could all be as wild and carefree and lusty as you.' She reached out. 'That's what you've got waiting for you – a lifetime of sea and moonlight and sunlight and of rivers and tumbling streams, and then, at day's end, you will want to surrender and give all of it back to the sky and the sea and the shore and the earth and be ripped apart in one last, long, carefree rending. You see how well I know you? I know your tides,

301

both your coming in and your flowing out. You are what we all want to be, in our deepest, deepest, deepest core – and we are that – but we forget sometimes. I'm going to do something silly.' She loosened the upper part of her coat. She had, as Mack had advised, dressed warmly. But she drew her clothes aside and, with her arms spread, embraced the warm cherries of the tree, touching them to her breasts and holding them in her arms and yes … yes … she held one of the lower cherries against her womb.

What the poor, sick, close-to-dying twin Dendron thought of this we will never know. Perhaps they paled like the poor husband of Israel Shapiro's sister when faced with another demand to deliver.[7] But I think not. Perhaps for a brief few moments she did manage to speak their language – or enough of it for them to understand – and they knew they were loved and not alone crying out in their solitude. For Hera sang to them too, as she suckled them. And touched them and rocked them and kissed them. The music was from Kossoff. The inspiration from Yeats. And the sound was of the sea.

> Winter and summer, and all the day long,
> My love was in singing, no matter the song
> But the best songs of all, are those from the heart,
> The secret dark place where love's ladders start.

Mack worked all the rest of the afternoon, digging and cutting close to the hump between the two trunks. When he finished, he had worked his way down to the great wishbone which linked together the whole of the front of the Dendron. He had observed a thin purple line which knitted across the wishbone: it was a natural line of cleavage. It was here he would tomorrow sever the two young trees.

But for the moment Mack had worked himself to standstill. He needed to rest, and he thought the Dendron might like a rest too.

As the sun set, Mack stood at the foot of the ladder and called to Hera, 'Can I get you anything? A drink? Something to eat? Would you like to come down for a while?'

'I'm very comfortable,' called Hera, her voice dreamy. 'This was a good idea of yours, Mack. I'm very warm and comfortable. I'll stay

[7] See Document 5.

for a while longer. Don't worry about me. We're very comfortable.'

Mack pondered this. She sounded a bit drunk. That might not be a bad thing. He called again: 'Well, just as you like. I'll be sleeping outside again, so if you change your mind I'll be here to let you down. OK?'

There was no answer.

Mack got himself some supper and then made his bed outside.

He lay back as the moon rose and could see the little chair dangling between the horns of the Dendron. How lonely the tree seemed. And the small human figure, now its only defence, hunched against the darkness. *A brave lady.* Mack realized that he had offered up the woman he loved to satisfy the needs of this world. He wondered what she would be like when she came down. *Would she be different? Would she have changed? Would she even know him? Would she care?*

At some point when the moon was high he woke up. He walked over the silver grass and climbed up onto the Dendron. 'Hera,' he called softly. 'Hera. It's me, Mack.'

A few moments later a voice answered: 'Where are you, Mack? I'm so cold and empty. Take me down, please. Make me warm.'

He lowered the chair and lifted her out. She *was* cold. Her clothes were all undone. He'd told her to wrap up warm. He covered her as well as he could and carried her down the ladder and up the hill to the place where he had set up his bed. There he laid her under the covers, and then he crawled in beside her and put his arms round her and felt her turn like a little animal as she snuggled close, accepting his warmth.

All this was of course recorded – but not transmitted.

2 5

Sirius

It was about an hour before dawn that Hera woke up. She was immediately aware of Mack's arm around her, warm and protective, of the gentle regular grumble of his breathing and of the pressure of his thigh. She felt no inclination to move, but she turned her head slightly so that she could see the stars. Neither Gin nor Tonic now being present, the stars shone out boldly. One was prominent for its brightness, and this she knew was Sirius, the same Sirius that we can see from our solar system, the Sirius that was studied by the ancient Egyptians in the time before the pharaohs and which they associated with their great goddess Isis.

Of course the constellations were different, there being no jewelled belt for Orion or pointers from the Plough, but it gave her a feeling of security to know that at least that one, important, brilliant star was visible to her at this moment, and that it was, in the poetic way of such things, looking down on her too.

She turned gently, not wanting to disturb the sleeping man, but her hands, following a will of their own, sought out his warmth. Then it was the work of a moment for her to slip out of the clothes and covers that he had used to keep her warm but which now seemed too hot. She pushed them right out of the bed. She turned in his arms, raising herself on one elbow so that she could just see his face in the starlight, and her hand stroked his cheek, and his neck, and his heavy arm with its strong muscles, so unlike her own. He stirred then – who would not? – and, stretching, his hand slipped naturally up to her breasts and thence to her hair and back to her breasts. His eyes opened at the moment she kissed him.

Thus, in the next several minutes, was accomplished something which they both had thought about, both had feared, both had made too complicated, and which, when it happened, was natural, easy and normal, and full of surprise, strangeness, delight and fire. At its peak, Hera twisted beneath him and buried her head in his neck and kissed him as she had once before and cried out fiercely and whispered, so softly that he might almost have imagined it, 'I love you . . . Mack.'

Mack, that man of iron if ever there was one, in that moment turned to water.

Down the slope, where the SAS stood beside the sleeping Dendron, the all-seeing tri-vid camera was still recording, but it was pointed up at the stars, and at Sirius, which it studied to the exclusion of all else.

26

Third and Final Encounter

It was Mack's turn to lie awake.

The turmoil he was feeling made him happy, and had that been his only problem he would either have slept like a lion or simply lain awake anticipating the next time he could turn his drowsy lady. But he had heard something in the outside world, a sound that did not fit, even though this was Paradise and the unexpected was becoming the norm. The sound was grinding and rough, like something heavy being dragged, and it came from the hills which surrounded them. At first he had suspected a storm might be approaching, and so was alert for the stirring of trees and the sound of rain sweeping down the valley, but yet the sky remained clear, the stars bright and there was no hint of lightning. Everything was wonderful, except . . .

He must have dozed, because the next time he started awake the sky was brightening with dawn and the stars overhead were fading. Moving very carefully, he lifted Hera's hand from his chest and slipped out from under it. He replaced it carefully under the covers and drew them up. The wet grass outside the bed was cold on his legs and buttocks. Much as he was tempted to crawl back in, duty was a stern taskmaster in one such as Mack. Hera muttered something in her sleep, turned and snuggled down into the warm place where he had lain.

He relaxed. The covers were wet with dew and dew also sparkled on her tousled hair. Mack hoped she would sleep on, and, let it be said, he wished this more for his sake than hers. He wanted to dwell for a while in the memory of the lovemaking. He wanted to savour the tumult he now felt inside himself. No matter how much you love someone, such things are best done alone.

Naked, he walked down to the stream to a place where the water ran deep. He sat with his feet in the water while the air lightened about him. Though he shivered for a moment, he did not want to get dressed. It was a pristine moment. Never to be repeated. He reasoned that now, if ever, a man should be naked! What a romantic!

Everything was very still. The grumbling in the hills had ceased. Away to his right towered the bulk of the Dendron, its colours and scarred, damaged back beginning to emerge from the dark of night. He was able to count the cherries, and none had fallen in the night. A good sign. While he could not pretend that the twin trunks had changed in a dramatic way, they were at least holding their own. By evening he hoped to see two trunks growing gracefully apart, and a dead stump. Then, job done, there would be time for Mack and his lady to explore themselves: 'Merry as thieves, eating stolen honey', another line from his granny's store. Sitting there by the stream, he heard the first flute-like calls as plants released the night air and drew in the morning. The patient Dendron gulped several times. A short time later a dribble of liquid bubbled from its sides, but it lacked urgency. The Dendron was dying.

Time to start. Mack would think about breakfast when Hera woke up. On impulse, he plunged forward into the cold buffeting stream and came up blowing hard. The cold shocked the romance out of him, and he climbed out of the stream quickly and jogged to the SAS for towels and clothes.

The camera moved, following him as he passed. Dickinson was on duty, unshaven and red of eye. He was missing nothing, and having talked about the stars he was now describing dawn on Paradise to an audience who, whether it was day or night where they were, kept watch with him. In the night he had heard the Dendron labouring. He had also heard the high sharp ringing of its Venus tears, and as he told the millions listening, 'How could that not be a hopeful sound?'

Dry now, and wearing fresh shorts and a T-shirt, Mack climbed up onto the Dendron. First he inspected a deep channel he had carved while Hera dangled above. The cut was close to the critical place in the creature's anatomy. Following the logic of the separation, cutting here had already brought some relief to the Dendron. He had dug down until he could actually see the top of the wide plaited straps of fibre which held the Dendron together. When he cut through these, the main body should fall away, leaving the two trees still attached to one another but free to grow on their own. He had also cut up from below and had reached the place where the giant arteries carrying the green sap from the codds to the twin horns and the two front legs divided. He could see where the pliant wishbone thickened before joining the great arch formed by the creature's legs. It was here he would make the day's first big cut, severing the young from the old.

During the night the black joint line he had noticed the previous evening had begun to open. It was under pressure, the two young front trees already trying to pull away. And when they did, the old body would then need to be killed, and quickly too, before its pain could infect the two young trees.

Mack, having now some experience of working with the wishbone fibre, considered that he would not have too much trouble cutting at this place as the wound would be opening and so the blade should not bind.

Satisfied that all was well, Mack turned and moved down the back of the Dendron. Under his feet its fibres were soft but without resilience – a sodden mattress. He reached the deep trench which he and Hera had cut first of all. Here, the ubiquitous wishbone was exposed. It took the form of small segmented pipes which wove together like basket cane. When the creature was running, Mack could imagine how these pipes slipped over one another, stretching and compressing, sending fluid coursing through the entire beast.

As a man with more than a passing interest in engineering, Mack intended, when the separation was complete, to cut one of the pipes open to see what kinds of valves were involved.

The trench was draining well, but the deep hole they had cut above the codds was half full of green slush. The previous night, just before the light failed, Mack had bored into the side of the Dendron and fitted a drainage pipe. He supposed it must have blocked. Using a stick he poked about in the hole, feeling for the opening to the tube. In so doing he stirred up some pale fibres, small tubes like pieces of straw or small segments of bamboo. He did not remember seeing these before. Finding the opening to the tube, he plunged the stick deep into it. Moments later he heard a slopping sound on the outside of the Dendron and the level started to drop.

Reaching down into the hole Mack scooped up some of the fibres. They were all of different lengths and diameters. Some were as thick as his finger and some no thicker than hairs. But all had one feature in common – the ends of the tubes were covered by a membrane. Spreading out from this he saw small yellow lips. He remembered Hera mentioning something like this once. The tubes moved in his hand, not like worms but like individual mouths, and he could see the ends opening and closing.

After a few moments exposure to the air, all movement stopped and the tubes became limp. The first stage of their liquefaction had already begun. He threw them over the side of the Dendron.

Most of the liquid had now drained away and Mack could see the bottom of the hole. This was the place where Hera had stood. He could see the ridges which signified the top of the codds. On cue the Dendron gulped once and the ridges opened and closed like a concertina, stretching the fibre between them. One touch of the chainsaw, and the fabric would fold and tear. He would also attack it from beneath – and while it would be messy, he had every confidence that he could rip his way right through to the 'brain' of the Dendron and put it out of its misery. The 'brain'? That was another enigma.

In the bottom of the hole, below the outflow tube, more of the small tubes had appeared. When their tiny mouths closed they ejected drips of dark green liquid. What were these, then? Some kind of parasite? Some kind of fluke? But why just here? Why not in other parts? Why had he not seen them before? He'd seen enough of the inside of a Dendron and of its fluid, and anything flopping about in there would have been obvious.

Sap flowed into the hole and the level began to rise. Blocked again, and by these little tubes. The pool was in turmoil, with tubes bobbing up, gulping and diving. He saw some of the tubes join up to make a chain, which pulsed as a unit for a few moments and then broke up again. So they could organize themselves. Smaller ones could slide into bigger. Chains of different lengths could be made.

It occurred to Mack that what he was seeing had a sense of purpose. These were not parasites. These creatures – if that was what they were – had an important function in the life of the Dendron. They seemed to be emerging from the sides at the bottom of the hole. That meant they could be coming from very deep, from the space behind the codds, from the stump itself, even. He climbed down into the hole, being careful not to put his full weight on the codds' membrane. He plunged his hand in among the small fibres. Immediately they attached themselves to him and he felt small pin-pricks where their mouths nibbled. There might even have been tiny electric shocks. He could not be sure. He held his hand there for a few moments and then lifted it slowly, dragging up the small tubular creatures that had attached themselves to him. He tried to shake them off, but they were persistent and finally he had to pull them off and throw them into the stream. In the place where they had been attached were small round sucker marks, and the larger ones had actually managed to prick him open and draw blood. He examined one of the tiny mouths, and crushed it under his fin-gers. It felt gritty. Silica, perhaps, the same as the Venus tears. *Now why ...?*

That part of Mack which enabled him to look at a building and work out how it was put together, his 'demolition imagination' as Hera called it, took over. He imagined the great bellows of the codds opening and closing, creating a siphon, sucking water in from the sea or a river or a lake, and then driving it up through this chamber of tubes, of flukes, of suckers, whatever ... Imagined bil-lions of them, many billions maybe, some so small they could only contain a molecule of water, others big enough to draw blood with their teeth. All of these, individually or forming chains, would take the water in and pass it on. Then others would suck that water in and eject it. The water would in effect pass through a tremendous network of pipes, being energized at each transition. If each tube was in some way unique, like having its own charge or nutrient, then every molecule of water would have its own experience – call it knowledge – which it could perhaps transmit. This surely was significant. Is that not what a brain is? Millions of little connections being made and broken. Perhaps, too, the fibres in the Dendron, drenched as they were at all times, contributed their own energy. Mack had no idea what all this activity might mean on the local level. But on the big level, the macro-level let us say, it became a Dendron, alive and conscious in every fibre. A great siphoning ball of psychic energy. Mad with energy and lust. He thought of the pictures Hera had drawn; he thought of Sasha's intuition regarding the Dendron's sensibility; he remembered Hera's description of her dream time in which she had drifted with the Dendron. Perhaps that was the Dendron waking up, starting to move and becoming aware of its needs – and it had captured her, for it would broadcast indiscriminately and she was the only prepared mind, ready to receive.

It made sense! He had to tell Hera. He had to wake her up. Quickly he bent down, scooped up two of the flukes and climbed out of the hole. 'Hera. Hera.'

'Good morning, Mack.' She was there, at the table by the SAS. Preparing breakfast. He had been so busy that he hadn't seen her and she had kept quiet because she wanted to surprise him.

'You've got to see this. I've got an idea about the Dendron ... about its brain.' And without waiting he climbed down the ladder and hurried over to the table. He put the two small creatures down on a plate on the table, where they twisted lethargically. 'What you are looking at is part of the brain of the Dendron. I'm sure of it. There are billions like these.'

'Mack. Mack. I don't want to depress your enthusiasm, but have you noticed we've got company?' She nodded behind him.

Mack turned, and the sight that met his eyes stopped him in his tracks. The hills were now covered with Tattersall weeds, their blue faces staring down like spectators at a games. They had come in the night. Mack now knew what had wakened and troubled him. It was the sound of thousands of Tattersall weeds crawling close and then setting down their roots and bedding in. He pointed to the far hillside, where the Tattersalls had formed up in rows, creating a pattern like a whirlpool which stretched over the hills. 'I see there's a Reaper advertising his presence too.'

Hera took his hand, slipping her palm into his. 'I saw the Tattersalls when I got up. I know you don't like them, but on balance I think it's a good sign they are here. They always seem to gather where something needs healing.'

'Well, I'm glad there's Reaper on hand to keep them in order. So. What now?'

'We eat. You tell me what you've discovered. We make a plan. Then we make an end of it, and quickly too. We don't have long. I'm so happy, but I feel so heavy too, Mack. I can feel the Dendron dying slowly within me. Last night, up there –' she nodded to the

311

two trunks '– it was a two-way exchange. You were right. The Dendron is at war with itself, Mack. It wants to divide, but it doesn't want to die either. It has never had a life. Never made a carving. And now it's grieving. That is what has brought the Tattersalls near.'

Breakfast was an urgent affair. Mack explained quickly how he thought the Dendron functioned: 'We use nerves to carry messages to our brains, well perhaps the Dendron uses its fluid to send messages throughout its body. It doesn't feel physical pain like we do – other pain, psychic pain, perhaps. So the fluid has something like memory. It says, "I want to move," and seconds later the legs move. It's not such a daft idea, because it is also the fluid that makes the legs move. Anyway, here's what I plan. First up, I'm going to take down the ropes we used last night. Then I'll build a platform across the stream under the codds so I can get in to cut. Then, when we're ready, I'll cut the front joint. The main body will collapse and I'll carve the codds up.'

'And what do I do?'

'You'll be up on the Dendron with the high-pressure hose. I want you to flush away everything I cut, all of these flukes. We have to get rid of all of them, into the stream. We do it as quickly as we can, because the time between when I sever the two trees from the old one, and when the old one dies and stops transmitting its pain or sadness or whatever, is critical. Its pain could become their guilt – or kill them, even.'

While Mack stripped out the rigging and built a platform and set up the high pressure pump, Hera took the opportunity to talk to Tania.

Following a request from Dickinson, she unhitched the camera and gave them a tour of the Dendron, explaining in detail what they planned.

'And what about last night?' asked Tania.

'Last night?' said Hera in astonishment. 'You know about last night?'

'We could see you.'

'What!!!'

'Yes, up there in the funny chair that Mack rigged up.'

'Oh, that . . .' Hera recovered quickly. 'Let's just say I was trying to bring comfort to the twin creatures.'

'It seems to have worked.'

Dickinson coughed. 'Well you certainly brought comfort to one creature,' he said. This remark was swiftly followed by an interesting sound effect: a loud *thump* followed by the sound of Dickinson falling off his chair.

Mack was ready. Stripped to the waist, chainsaw in hand, he stood in the channel he had cut between the two horns. Hera was at the other end of the Dendron, braced against the remains of the ball-and-socket joint where the crest had stood. She held the hose in both hands. The compressor at the pump was throbbing and would go to full power as soon as the trigger was engaged.

After pleadings from Dickinson and Tania, Mack had repositioned the camera high on one of the trunks to give a better view of all that was happening on top of the Dendron.

'One last thing,' called Mack. 'And I'm talking to Doc now, not Hera. Remember the golden rule?'

'What golden ru—'

'If I say jump, you?'

'Jump.'

'Over the side.'

'Over the side. Gotcha. Good luck, Mack.'

'OK. Here goes.'

The saw whined and Mack began to ease the blade back and forth, cutting deep into the wishbone. Fragments of white fibre sprayed into the air, and Hera kept the wound clear of debris with a steady stream of water. The air should have smelled of carnage, but it smelled of flowers instead.

As Mack cut deeper, he could see the wishbone curl as the pressure built. The cut was opening gradually of its own accord as the front legs of the Dendron strained forward. Mack had severed the first layer of fibre and was beginning to cut through the pipes. As he did so, a jet of liquid held under enormous pressure spurted up and knocked him back. Hera shouted something and pointed. One of the tall horns was wavering and beginning to wilt. Mack stopped the saw and crouched down and watched. The amount to which the trunk tilted was critical – too far and it might tear, and that could be very serious because now, with the pipe cut, there was no way of replenishing the fluids. He had explained this danger to

Hera but had also pointed out that the Dendron must have a solution of their own. In the Mayday woman's story the Dendron which had done the cutting had been far more ruthless than he was now, and there had been no problem.

As they watched, the drooping stopped, and the trunk hung steady and swayed. Mack's guess was that somewhere within the front of the creature a valve had closed and the precious fluid was retained. He started the saw again, cutting steadily while the fluid poured over him.

He severed the second pipe and watched the other trunk slump, but not as much as the first. Mack nodded in satisfaction.

Now the cut became more difficult. Mack was deep inside the front of the Dendron. Sufficient of the dark fluid had drained away, helped by Hera's directed flow of clear water, and he could see the place where he was cutting. He crouched down and, holding the saw vertically, began to ease the blade back and forth. He could hear it biting deep and steam rose – a tribute to the toughness of the wishbone fibre. But it was yielding. He changed sides and, after a few seconds of cutting, heard a snap and the part of the body on which he was standing lurched. One of the main fibres had broken before it had been cut. That was a warning. The stresses within the cut must now be immense. He again applied the blade. This time he both heard and felt the joint begin to break open of its own accord. He stepped back onto the main body of the Dendron and watched as, slowly, the section with the two front legs began to tear away. The separation was slow, but it was now being done by the Dendron.

There came a moment when the movement stopped, and Mack could feel the pressures beneath his feet build ... and then the Dendron broke with a tearing sound that ended with a loud *snap* and both parts of the Dendron lurched. Mack was almost shaken loose, but the twin trunks were now straightening and pulling away from the old parent. He could see the stream beneath him. As the separation widened, the full face of the cut he had made became visible. It was a wall of woven wishbone with a honeycomb of pipes at its centre.

According to his calculations, the main body he was standing on should now slump down to the stream. But it didn't. Instead it started to straighten and lift. Mack was not sure what was happening. The lifting might just be a temporary easing, and he waited and watched. But it didn't stop.

Mack slung the saw over his shoulder and began to climb, wedging his feet into the pipe holes and heaving himself up on whatever he could grasp. Hera, meanwhile, had no idea what was happening and kept spraying the trench until she saw Mack's arm and head appear. The body of the Dendron continued to lift.

Mack shouted, 'Hera. Cut the water. Get down off the Dendron.'

'What's wrong, Mack?'

'Jump! Now!'

Hera threw the hosepipe down the side of the Dendron, and as she did so, she saw the escape ladder slip sideways, pushed by the rising body of the Dendron.

'Jump for the stream!'

This time she did not hesitate. She jumped straight down, entering the water with a splash. She felt her feet touch the bottom and pushed up strongly, breaking the surface close to the bank and away from the sharp tines of the crest. Three strong strokes and she was at the side and able to pull herself up and out of the water in a second.

Mack, meanwhile, had climbed out and lowered the chainsaw to the ground. He too was preparing to jump. But the Dendron lurched, and he lost his balance and fell into the trench that they had cut along the back of the Dendron on the first day. At this angle it was like a slide, and though he grabbed for the edge and did manage to catch some fibres, they tore loose and he continued to slip. He tried desperately to wedge his body across the trench, but it was too steep and with a cry he fell into the hole above the codds. Since the moment of severance this had filled with the white wriggling flukes, and there was nothing for him to hold on to. Mack might still have been able to clamber out, but the Dendron was gulping wildly and beginning to droop again. Then, as Mack was reaching desperately for something to cling to, the membrane above the codds gave way. To Hera it looked as though he had been pulled from below. His upper body and head and arms vanished down into the dark hole of the codds, and she heard him scream.

Hera ran onto the platform Mack had built that morning under the Dendron. She could tell where he was struggling inside the great bellows. But she knew this was the strongest part of the

315

codds, used to rough treatment, and there was no way he could tear it.

The electric chainsaw had landed nearby. Hera ran over, grabbed it and climbed back onto the platform. She reached as high as she could and made a long raking cut. Part of the sagging codds fell open and water and flukes came tumbling out. Mack was still moving and this told her where he was. He was trying to make it to the gash. She moved along the platform and slashed again, trying this time to cut through the pleats of the codds. Mack's boot appeared and she could see where the other foot was kicking. But then the Dendron gulped one more time and the boot vanished. She had no choice but to cut blind. She made the cut as shallow as she could and heard a muffled scream. She moved to the side and cut again. This time Mack's arm appeared. She seized it and pulled, putting all her strength into it. Once the elbow was out Mack was able to grip the side himself and pull. Hera moved as far away as possible. She started the saw again, hoisted it as high as she could, and plunged it deep, raking it from side to side. She must have cut something important, for the codds began to tear apart of their own accord and with their last strong gulp Mack was ejected.

He slithered down onto the platform. His entire body was covered with the wriggling white flukes. He twisted and turned as he tried to claw them from his face, but his arms and hands were covered and they were in his mouth too. Hera grabbed him by one boot and pulled, and pulled again, dragging him slowly across the slippery platform and onto the bank. There he writhed, trying to pull flukes off his skin.

The compressor was still chugging and Hera, quick thinking as ever, chased the hosepipe, which had fallen into the stream, found the nozzle, pointed it at Mack and pressed the trigger. At this range the water must have seemed like being punched, but it worked, and the jet prised the flukes free from Mack's skin and sent them tumbling into the stream. She hosed his hands, arms and neck and he was able to pull the flukes from his face. She hosed his legs, and when he staggered to his feet, she hosed his back. They were in his shorts too, and he pulled them off and picked the flukes off one by one while she hosed his buttocks.

His body was bloody. It was as though someone had pressed bottle tops into his skin until they drew blood. On his thigh was a more serious cut where the chainsaw had grazed him. But the cuts didn't bother him. Mack had reached a point of frenzy. He picked up the chainsaw and went back onto the platform, ignoring the flukes still writhing about. He hacked his way into the Dendron. There was no finesse. He raked what remained of the codds with the saw, and then tore the pieces away by hand, throwing the bits into the stream.

Next, he heaved himself up inside the cavern of the Dendron and cut at a membrane which he now knew contained the deeper parts of its brain. He was rewarded with a cascade of the flukes, larger ones this time, and darker coloured, which tumbled over his shoulders. Hera was behind him and hosed away any that attached. He climbed on, right into the beast. He cut the sides and he cut the top; he cut down and he cut across, and all the time the small wriggling creatures came tumbling out.

Finally Hera heard the chainsaw rasp against the hardness of the stump. The saw stopped and Hera heard Mack call, his voice echoing, 'Hera! Do you want to see?'

Hera stopped the hose. Mack's arm came reaching down out of the Dendron and hoisted her up. 'It's all right now: I've got rid of most of them. It was a nest. Just here, and that's all that's left now.' He pointed at a large white open-mouthed worm which grew out of the dip in the middle of the stool. It groped around blindly like an arm without fingers. Hera recognized one of the roots of Paradise. This was larger than most she had seen. When the Dendron tore free to go walkabout, the root went with it. 'Do you want to finish it, or shall I?'

For an answer Hera took the saw and placed its tip at the place where the wavering root rose from the stool. One brief burst and the whirling blade severed the root, which fell to the platform, twisted as it rolled and fell into the river. 'Sic transit gloria mundi,' she murmured. 'Now, what about the little ones?'

'I've not finished yet,' said Mac. 'Last job.'

He climbed out from under the newly dead Dendron, which was slowly collapsing, went straight to the tool chest and selected the heavy axe he had sharpened on the first day. Then he collected the ladder, which had fallen to one side, and set it up so that he could climb up to the twin trunks, which were still joined, forming an arch over the stream.

Hera followed. She picked up his shorts. Thought for a second and then threw them away into the stream. *Why distract a man with something as trivial as clothes?*

'I'm going to finish this bloody job now!' said Mack as he propped the ladder up against the arch. 'I'm so steamed up I reckon I could tear these two apart with my bare hands.'

With that he climbed the ladder, the axe poised over his shoulder. He positioned himself between the trunks and began to chop. Splinters of wishbone flew, and within five minutes he had cut a trench round the fine dark line which marked the place where the two trunks were joined. It was a growth line, slightly jagged, as though joined by a master carpenter. He touched it lightly with the sharp blade and saw the fibre peel back. The trunks were straining apart.

All he now needed to do was cut a V straight down and the Dendron would do the rest. Mack made two clean cuts. Satisfied that his line was good, he started again. He struck a rhythm. Chips of wishbone flew again.

Hera watched. It was the first time she had ever seen a man such as Mack taking full pride in his strength. He was totally absorbed. Naked too. Primitive and casual with his beauty. She saw the way he lifted the axe so that he didn't waste energy, and the way he let the weight of the axe do most of the work but guided it just at the moment of impact so it stayed true. Periodically he turned and attacked the other side of the arch so that the two sides did not get out of balance. She was intrigued by the different patterns of muscles that stood out during the course of a single swing of the axe – it was the artist in her – and she found herself thinking of some of the statues she had seen of athletes – wrestlers, discus throwers and the like, and of the ancient Celtic warriors who ran naked into battle, confident of rebirth. Surely Mack was descended from them.

Some ten minutes later, Mack paused. 'Getting near now. Get that wine open?'

'It's already breathing,' she called.

'So am I, and thirsty.' He started again. After some four cuts, he stopped. 'Come round the front and watch. This is it. This is what we call the butcher's cut. The axe will find its own way out.' He positioned himself carefully, legs spread, shoulders relaxed, and raised the axe. He brought it down fiercely, not cutting sideways but straight. There was a cracking sound and Mack hopped onto one side of the arch and held on to the trunk. The cracking grew stronger until, with a *bang*, the entire joint tore apart. Slowly and gracefully, the two sides of the arch that had been joined for so long straightened and found a new balance. As they did so, the trees shook and the Venus tears rang out.

Hera clapped her hands. And although she and Mack couldn't have heard them, all the people at the space platform Alpha-over-Paradise, riding high above the planet, cheered too, for the scene was being projected in the dining room. And further afield, far, far, far away, in the crowded main debating chamber of the Space Council, representatives who a short time ago had voted to terminate the ORBE project now put on a brave face as the people about them went wild with jubilation. Was Theo Vollens somewhere there? I feel certain he was: if not in person, then sipping champagne in spirit.

Estimates vary as to how many other people were watching from the inhabited worlds that day. I know I was – in this very studio where I am now sitting writing – along with many, many millions of others, at a conservative estimate.

And there was Dr Tania Kowalski, keeping her excitement in check, saying, 'Of course, it is early days yet and the severance is just complete. But all seems to have gone well. Both the new Dendron-to-be seem stable, the trunks have a balanced curve and they are well bedded.' And then she added, 'The Space Council is to be complimented for its foresight and wisdom in allowing Dr Hera Melhuish and her research assistant to complete this important project. We hope to speak to representatives of the Space Council shortly,'

Mack and Hera knew none of this. Mack climbed down and Hera met him with a glass of wine. But before he could have that she kissed him and that was the first kiss they had enjoyed in and of and for itself. Simple pleasure.

It was much later. Evening sunshine still filled the small valley, but clouds were gathering in the hills, and Alan was predicting rain.

During the afternoon Mack had taken the SAS up and dragged the remains of the Dendron's body across the clearing to where the trees started. On the way he had crushed a few Tattersall weeds, in true Dendron fashion. Now the Dendron's remains could liquefy in peace. Hera had hosed down the stool to get rid of any soft matter. The stump, where the Dendron's 'brain' had been hidden, now contained a small pool of clear water. The stream was running clean too. Mack had steeped himself for an hour in its cool water and his cuts were dressed. And Hera and Mack were now sitting at their table and feeling proud of themselves.

Hera, after a long struggle with her conscience, was about to confess to Mack that the scenes shot by the camera had had a wider audience than just Dickinson and Tania. In fact Dickinson and Tania and the whole demolition team were standing by to talk to Mack in case he was upset. The space-wide broadcast was over, though the camera was still turned on and recording. Dickinson was hoping to be able to set up a reverse link so that Hera and Mack would be able to see the people on the shuttle.

Hera had just filled Mack's glass and uttered the time-honoured phrase 'There's something I want to tell you' when they heard a scrabbling sound. It came from a stand of Tattersall weeds which they had flown over when they first saw the Dendron. Mack stood up guessing it might be a weed on the move.

There was more noise, and then a thick hairy limb, bigger than anything they could have expected, came probing out from the trees. It had thorns like claws and the thorns dug into the ground. Another limb followed it and it too dug in. Both contracted, scratching the earth, and the uprooted body of a giant Tattersall weed dragged into view. It was the one they had seen at the mouth of the valley three days earlier. The similarity to a giant spider was undeniable.

They saw the tree draw itself together. When it released, more branches were thrown forward, three or four this time, all in a powerful but uncontrolled way, like puppet arms. Any other plants in their path were simply knocked down. They dug in and dragged, and even before this movement was complete, more of the limbs of the plant were coming at them, creeping forward and plunging their thorns into the ground. Ungainly and uncoordinated though this movement was, it nevertheless had urgency. Two more casts and it would be upon them.

On the top of the SAS the camera swivelled and focused.

Moments later, one of the limbs flung forward and crashed down in front of it.

Mack grabbed Hera and together they ran to higher ground, to the place where they had slept. When they turned, they saw one of the heavy arms strike the SAS, buckling its roof and the rotor blades and cracking the windows of the control cabin. The tri-vid camera was sent spinning over the ground and ended up in the stream. Then the body of the tree, with its giant ball of root matter, was dragged right over the SAS flyer, which rolled, crushing its rotor blades and solar panels, to end up on its back, its tail in the stream and its siren howling mournfully.

The giant Tattersall weed moved on for two more casts. Then it righted itself and settled some twenty metres from the two new trees. It prepared to set down its root.

They saw the squirming white root emerge and enter the earth. The ball of side roots settled over it. On either side the long heavy branches rested on the ground, steadying it. 'Like an old man squatting on a pot' was Mack's description. Finally, its bright blue flowers came out and they could smell its fragrance.

PART FOUR

Paradise Menacing

27

Love – a Transcript

We are at another turning point, and our story becomes, for a while, internal.

Unlike the Dendron, where one became two, with Hera and Mack two are becoming one.

But, as with Romeo and Juliet, we see that the best laid plans can be overturned. The Michelangelo-Reaper, which we have only encountered once so far, will shortly move from the shadows and become important.

Hera and Mack looked down from their small exposed campsite. They watched the Tattersall weed as it settled near the twin trees. It trembled once as its roots dug deep, and then it became still. Mack picked up a stone and, with the unerring eye of a demolition worker, threw it high and hard so that it bounced off the branches of the Tattersall and then tore one of its flowers.

'What's that in aid of?' asked Hera. 'Are you trying to provoke it?'

'Just wanted to see if it had any more kick in it. It's done enough damage already.'

'I don't think that old man's going anywhere fast. That climb completely knocked the stuffing out of it. I think that Tattersall weed's settling down for a long, long rest. They're not really equipped to go charging about.'

'Well, I don't trust them.'

At that moment there was a rumble of thunder. Looking across the valley they could see that rain was already falling. They also noticed that more Tattersall weeds were on the move, dragging themselves down to where the twin trunks swayed in the gathering breeze. Already there was quite a congregation of Tattersalls, and Hera, remembering what she had seen at the umbrella tree plantation, was under no doubt that they would be offering the trees whatever help they needed, whether sap or physical support.

Olivia   You must have been terrified.

Hera   I think we were more shocked than terrified. But with the rain coming we had to move quickly. We crept down the hill to the SAS. If we met a Tattersall on the move, we simply dodged round it, but they were not bothered with us.

Olivia   Was there anything left to salvage? I thought the SAS was crushed.

Hera   It was. The craft was completely ruined. The fluid drive mechanism had fractured and the roof had been torn open when the rotor blades were ripped off. The cabin was half in the stream, but we could still climb aboard. All the electric circuits were dead, except for the siren, which had its own small battery and which Mack silenced with a fist.

We salvaged what we could: backpacks, clothes, a tent, food. The distinction between needs and wants became critical. But we were more fortunate than many. The SAS was a survival craft, remember, and the problem was not what we needed, but what we could carry. Mack found the small fixed-band radio, which seemed none the worse for being soaked, but its batteries were almost flat. I located a solar charger and a small stove. We carried everything back to our camp.

The first thing we did was erect the tent. The clouds were coming down from the hills and then the rain arrived. We simply threw everything into the tent. Then we sat in the tent, huddled together, and watched as the light fell and the mist gathered about us.

And that was frightening, because we could hear sounds down by the river. Scraping sounds. The Tattersall weeds were on the move, but we couldn't see them. Fear focuses one's mind wonderfully. I reasoned that our tent was set well back and close to where the dense trees began, and no Tattersall weed would make its way through them. And I reasoned too that the Tattersall weeds were not actually aggressive. Blundering, yes. But as long as they did not blunder our way, we were probably safe.

But there was something else. When I looked into myself, I realized that I was not actually afraid of anything. It was not because Mack was there. It was because I was so proud of what we had done for the Dendron, and I was so pleased with myself, because I knew that I had, for the first time in my life, fallen in love. Fear just did not exist. I felt warm all over. Nothing in all my reading had ever prepared me for what I was feeling. It was so wonderful. And it was so interesting, I mean what it was doing to me – mentally and physically. I couldn't say anything about it to Mack: I just had to sit there. I didn't dare touch him. I think I was a bit afraid of what I might do.

After about an hour the rain eased and then it stopped completely. Some time later I saw the first stars above the hills. Then more stars came out as the clouds moved away. And the natural green glow came from the plants. The world became tranquil for me.

Not so Mack. He was not tranquil. He felt the need to work out a plan. I was more content with the *now* of things, and that was a big change in me. But he still needed to organize in order to feel secure. And he wanted to protect me too, I knew that.

And we had had a plan, a very beautiful plan, before the Tattersall weed destroyed our means of escape. Our plan centred on our caring for the Dendron – the two of them – for a short time until we knew they were secure, and then caring for ourselves. I say it was beautiful, because our plan gave us space and time and a purpose while we got to know one another properly and began to make all those adjustments you have to make when you fall in love.

Afterwards? I suppose we would have decided to quit Paradise and face the world. We knew we couldn't stay. Paradise was becoming too unpredictable and there was no place for us there, not really. We were not a new Adam and Eve. If anything, we were more like the old Adam and Eve and on our way out. I felt my work was done. My life had clicked round and a new circle was beginning. I think I was hoping for new challenges – and I knew that loving someone was the biggest challenge I might ever have to face. And Mack? Well, he had made his feelings pretty clear, and so both our futures were suddenly wide open and full of completely new and exciting possibilities. You have been married, haven't you Olivia?

Olivia   Three times.

Hera   Then you know what I mean.

Olivia   Divorced three times too. But don't let that stop you. Go on with the story.

Hera   Well, *we* thought the possibilities were exciting. And then this Tattersall weed had come blundering in like a drunk at a party and had destroyed our plans just as certainly as it had broken the SAS. We were no longer in charge of what we did. We could not escape. The SAS was kaput. We were again trapped by circumstance. That is what I think Mack found hardest.

I watched his reactions. He became very practical – well, he always was practical – but very much the man in charge, sorting things out, trying to find order in chaos. This is what he proposed. First, charge up the radio to make sure it was working. Then get a message up to the platform and arrange a rescue. I was not sure about that. I still felt that any action by Abhuradin and her forces might trigger some kind of avalanche, but not because the planet was vengeful, you understand. Paradise doesn't work like that. But because it had evolved in response to what we had done there and was now poised to reject the alien. Cut the string and the weight falls. Pollute the streams and the fish die. Damage a planet and it returns the compliment with interest. It is the way. Totally comprehensible, simple and absolute. And it does not need malice or anger.

I felt that we were more or less safe, barring accidents. But the arrival of a rescue party, armed with laser cannon, their minds hardened by the will to save 'those of their species', or some such. Well, that thought might be all it would take to trigger the antiresponse. Paradise, remember, was a psychically reactive place. We were safe as long as we did not provoke change.

Olivia   What do you mean, 'We were safe as long as we did not provoke change'?

Hera   I was thinking of the Reapers, the Michelangelos. To me, at that time, those were the most dangerous of all the creatures on Paradise – well they still are, really, because, you see, they are totally unguessable. They seemed both kind and terrifying. With them, I felt none of the warm vital energy I experienced with the

Dendron. I only had to think of a Dendron and I became happy, because of their wild carefree energy. And yes, that energy was sexual, simply because most of our good energy is sexual in some way. Well, isn't it?

Olivia No comment.

Hera But the Michelangelo-Reaper ... I never knew what to call it. It was like being told a joke that you don't get, or having a dream that you feel is important but that just doesn't make sense, and besides ... look at the power they had. Read Sasha.[8] Look what they did to me. There was no doubt in my mind at that time but that they ate humans in some way. Now, of course, after what happened to Mack, I see things differently, but at that time ... I was a bit concerned too because I could see that they didn't frighten Mack in the same way they frightened me, and I didn't understand that.

Anyway, I let Mack go on with his planning and prepared a simple meal. We were neither of us really hungry but I had saved the wine. That was important. It is amazing how a little luxury like a bottle of wine does you good when you are in a tricky situation.

So, then, when we had eaten, I made sure he was comfortable, and I said, 'Mack, I have two things I want to explain.'

He settled back and said something like 'Fire away, Doc.'

I was feeling guilty, you see, because I had not yet told him about the broadcast and I wanted there to be no secrets between us. 'The first is that when you were freeing the Dendron, it was not just Dickinson and Tania who were viewing, it was being broadcast to anyone.'

He looked at me. 'What do you mean, "anyone"?'

'Anyone!' I said. 'It was live on the Time and Space Network. A fractal transmission that could be picked up by anyone. At the Space Council, or out on Churchill, or down on Earth, or the Angelique torus, Gerard's Barn even.'

He nodded, and I didn't know what he was thinking. And then he said, 'Well, I hope they enjoyed it. I should have guessed. He's got a bloody cheek that Dickinson. But no harm's done, is there?'

[8] Hera is referring to Sasha Malik, 'If You Go Down to the Woods Today ...' here published as Document 8. She may also be thinking of the strange lines that Malik wrote at the end of her short love story 'Getting Your Man' (Document 2).

'No. No harm's done.'

And then he said to me, 'I'm glad you didn't tell me before. I think it would have stopped me working. Thanks for keeping quiet. Now what was the other thing?'

And I had been expecting an outburst! People are very surprising sometimes.

'The other thing,' I said, 'concerns us.' His face fell and I saw I had used the wrong words, loaded words, and now he feared the worst. Quickly I said, 'Don't worry. It's nothing bad. I just want to put an idea to you.' And then I told him my fears of what might happen if people came to rescue us, and I added, 'But that's not my only reason, Mack. I'd like to spend some time with you alone. Just the two of us. And I don't want to stay here in this valley. Now the Tattersall weeds have arrived they can take over. They'll know what to do better than us. They couldn't have done what we did to help the Dendron. That was our task, our big circle, and now it's done, and a new circle is beginning. And it's you and me, Mack, and I don't know where it's going. So I suggest we walk out of here. I suggest we make our own way over the planet. I'll teach you to read and you can tell me your stories. It can be done, Mack. And yes, we'll stay in contact with the platform, and if things get too hostile or if we get into real trouble, we'll call them up and take our chance. Perhaps something small and humble could come and find us. But it might not be necessary, Mack. We both have something of us lodged in this planet. We know the situation, and if we try, we can "bugger off back to Birmingham" on our own. What do you say, Mack?'

Olivia And what did he say?

Hera I can't remember. I think he was a bit puzzled. You see, he was expecting to be rejected. And then when he finally got the idea he said something like, 'You mean you want to trek with me over Paradise?' And I said, 'Yes. That's what I'm talking about.' And he looked pleased and then doubtful and then happy and then he said, 'It'll be hard, you know.' And I think it was at that point that I hit him.

Olivia And then?

Hera And then we made love. Out there on the grass. It was very different. Abandoned but quite premeditated too, full of talking and sudden kisses. Passionate but not blindly so, and very, very

330

exciting. I was very surprised at myself, and I think Mack was too
. . . I say, Olivia, you're not going to put this in the book, are you?

Olivia   Of course not.

28

The Courtesy of MINADEC

They were up before dawn.

They watched the sunlight creep down the side of the valley, making the ground steam. High above, the clouds scudded across the sky, sending shadows across the valley.

The tent was down. The solar charger was propped at an angle where it would catch the maximum daylight, and the fixed-band radio was attached. Hera returned briefly to the SAS. She was in search of music. Flamenco, no less! For Hera intended this journey to be memorable. She also rescued Pietr Z's edition of *Tales of Paradise* and Professor Shapiro's notebook. These were the only documents to accompany Hera when she left Paradise.

During the night the area around the twin trees had changed. Many more Tattersall weeds were now gathered close, some with their flowers pressed flat up against what had once been the Dendron's front legs. They heard the Venus tears ring, and the flags, while not yet flying, looked definitely more lively.

Over a breakfast of soup, rehydrated cherries, left-over rice and muesli they discussed their route. There was not much choice. Either back to the desert or up and over the Gilgamesh Heights and down to the Sea of Ben Ben. They chose the latter.

Thereafter their plan was of necessity less precise. The idea was to keep to the coast until they came to the foot of the Staniforth Mountains. They would then follow a well established trail – Hera knew it well – up to a pass in the range and so make their way down to Redman Lake and thence to the boathouse where Pietr Z's boat would be waiting.

By the time the sun arrived in the clearing, the two packs were standing ready.

The small radio having partially recharged, Mack chanced a call. They heard the call sign and then a sleepy voice said, 'Receiving. Who's calling?'

'Annette. Is that you?'

'Yeah, Descartes here. Who the— Hey, Mack, is that you? Where the Calcutta you calling from, man? We've got a team lined up to come and—'

'Yeah, yeah. Now listen.'

'Trouble is there's some fuck-up with the system. We thought you and the little lady were . . . Is she still OK?'

'Yeah. Hera's fine. The SAS was wrecked but we got out of the way.'

'Shee-it, that was some mother of a spider, or what the marysuck was that thing, Mack?'

'A Tattersall weed. Not very dangerous. Now listen, Annette.'

'Good to hear your voice, man! We all thought it'd walked right over you. So, like I said, we've organized a team to come down there. Some real raw-knuckles drafted in to help with the barges. I mean fingers-down-the-throat ass-kickers who don't take prisoners. Nastee men! I love 'em all, or I'm trying to. We thought we'd just be picking up bits but now we know you're *in corpore sano*. Well . . .'

'You've been seeing too much of Dickinson.'

'Oh, Mack. Dickinson! Shit, Mack, you'd have been so proud. He got that smarmy little fat-mouth from the Space Council, Tim Wishyawould or something, for an interview on prime time. And Dickinson, he started out all smooth and sicko-fuckin-phantic like and then he just let loose. He verbalized that bastard so fucking hard his lights went out on zero and you'll be buying him diapers till Christmas. Seems this Timothy shite was responsible for giving your little lady the hard back-shaft, and so Dickinson decided to lobo him off at the knees. Demolition time. Then that big dyke Titania got in on the act and stamped on what was left. All on prime time. All on the record.'

'Descartes. Will you just hush a minute and listen.'

'Yeah, boss, what?'

'Don't send anyone down here. It's too dangerous.'

'Hang on, boss. Polka's woken up; she wants a word.'

'Hi, Mack. Polka here. We'd given you up. We'd given you up for—'

'Polka. For fuck's sake. Will one of you two women listen?'

'I'm listening, Mack.'

'Descartes says you're trying to send a team down to rescue us. Don't!'

'Don't?'

'Don't!'

'So why's that, Mack? I mean we saw something like a bloody big spider come after you and—'

'It wasn't a spider. It wasn't after us. We're safe. But if you send a bunch of specials down here, it might just tip the scales against us. This place is dangerous. It's psychic.'

'Psychic. Like voodoo.'

'Yeah, something like that. Or a hand grenade with a loose pin.'

'Wow.'

'So. We're gonna walk out.'

'Uh uh? Walk out?'

'Yes.'

'OK, boss. You're the boss. I'll tell them.'

'We've got the radio. We'll keep in contact. And if we need you to come, I'll tell you. Hey. This battery's getting flat. I'll need to recharge.'

'You do that. How's your lady? We thought she was pretty good, the way she hosed you down when you were covered with those lice things. Tell her she can come and join the team whenever she wants. We need a bit more feminine pluck.'

'Hera's fine. Thank you, Polka.'

'OK, Mack. I'll give them the word. No rescue until you call. I'm starting to lose you, boss.'

'And tell them . . . tell them . . . tell them it is appreciated. OK?'

'They know that, boss, but I'll tell them all the same. OK. Enjoy the cherries.'

The radio went dead. Mack looked at Hera and nodded and grinned. 'Well, I got through. Just.'

'I gathered. How did she know we'd been eating cherries?'

'Well . . . she didn't. She meant something else.'

'And what does it mean to "lobo someone off at the knees"?'

'That? Well it seems like Dickinson found an opportunity to have a go at your mate Isherwood. My guess is he lured him into an interview about Paradise, softened him up with a couple of patsy questions and then put the boot in. He can do that, can Dickinson. Very quick-witted when he wants to be, and educated too. He said to me once, "If you want to attack someone, and you want to make it stick – do it in public." So that's what he did. From what Descartes said, that was a *big* public link-up. I don't think Mr Isherwood will cause you any more problems.'

'And why do you call Annette, Descartes?'

'It's her name. Would you believe she is the direct descendant of some French philosopher?'

'OK,' said Hera. 'Then why is the other called Polka?'

'Because her name's Dorothy, of course.' Mack was getting impatient. 'Come on, Hera. Time we were on the road.'

They set out heading up the stream, taking them directly past the giant Tattersall weed that had wrecked the SAS. Mack paused in front of it, staring up at the tree, and Hera thought he was going to speak to it. Instead he walked to the nearest of the big blue flowers and tore one of the petals off. He folded it carefully and neatly and stuffed it in his shirt. He saw Hera looking at him. 'I like the smell,' he said. 'Let's go.'

There were of course no paths, but they were able to make their way easily up the riverbank, where the plants were well spaced out. It was a steady climb, and they made good time. Soon they were high enough to be able to look back and see the clearing and the twin trunks. It all looked very peaceful. Then the river led them round a hill and the scene was lost.

This turning marked the real beginning of their final journey.

Sometimes they talked, but more often they walked in silence, lost in their own thoughts.

By the time they stopped for lunch they were high in the Gilgamesh Heights and the stream which they had followed was now small and tumbled over rocks noisily. It was Mack who called the halt and eased his pack off his shoulders. He was still a bit sore from where the flukes had attached themselves when he killed the old Dendron, and the rubbing of his pack was making matters worse. 'Here's hoping,' he said and tore two large strips from the Tattersall petal. These he tucked under his shirt and over his shoulders. 'Thought I'd put that ugly bugger to some use.' He patted the leaves through his shirt, and nodded. 'Might just do some good. Do you want some?'

Hera put a couple of small strips inside her boots where she thought she could feel the start of blisters.

Lunch was simple, and although Hera made several attempts to start a conversation, Mack was lost in his thoughts, but it wasn't a moody brooding silence. Finally he said, 'One thing I don't understand. There was one Dendron. Now there are two, or there will be when they grow up. But what happens then? Say one of them gets to maturity first, goes walkabout, decides it wants to split, comes back, finds the other, gets it to do the honours. And then there are three: one old one and two kids. Now the old one goes walkabout and wants to split, but there are only the little ones. So what does it do? It wanders about, aching like the one we've just split, broadcasting its pain to all and sundry. But we're not here to give it a hand. We're long gone. Maybe we're off planet, maybe we're dead, because we don't know how long it takes for a Dendron to grow from being a little tree, like the ones we left down there, to the full monster. I mean that is some growing. So what does it do? It dies, that's what. You come back to the same problem. Two is not sufficient for the Dendron to prosper. I reckon you need a minimum of four active ones for them to start to prosper without outside intervention. What do you reckon?'

Hera thought for a while. 'Well,' she said finally, 'I can't fault your maths. But one thing I do know about this place is that it seems to be able to speed up its evolution pretty dramatically. Look at the Tattersall weeds. When the *Scorpion* arrived they were just jolly blue flowers with a sweet smell and people slept with them under their pillows. Now look at them. And that has happened in what? Less than 200 years. I've studied lots of examples of how bio-forms adapt in response to danger, but I have never seen anything so quick. It argues consciousness of some kind, and not the random hit and miss of our evolution.'

'You mean, you think the Dendron will evolve so they don't need to split; they can just peacefully fold apart like a choirboy opening his prayer book?'

Hera looked at him and shook her head. 'I don't know where you get your similes from. Your granny?'

'What's a simile?'

336

'I'll tell you later. No. I don't think the Dendron will ever just fold apart like a . . . choirboy opening his prayer book. I can't imagine that. What a loss that would be! All that lovely passion and frenzy gone. Paradise wouldn't be Paradise without it. It'd be like . . . it'd be like a morgue at midnight.'

'Dark?'

'Silent! That's a simile. Use your brain.'

'Well, morgues aren't noisy at the best of times, so what's midnight got to do with it?'

'I was trying to give an example of a simile, but it didn't work, so forget it.'

'Morgues are—'

'Will you shut up about morgues? I'm trying to explain about the Dendron. Or do you want me to push you into that stream?'

'Sorry.'

'Where were we? No, I think something else will happen. Something new and quite unexpected. It may even be happening now. Or maybe the Dendron can adjust its life cycle, slow down its metabolism and so endure the long wait until its children catch up with it. I don't know. But we bought them time, and that is the main thing. I'm sure the Dendron will not die out. That doesn't fit the pattern, does it? Too many good things have happened – don't you feel it? – like you and me.'

Mack nodded. 'Sounds good to me.'

'So get your pack on, big man. I'd like to see if we can get to that pass up there before we make camp. I'd like to see the sea from there in the morning.'

And she did.

It took them seven days to descend the other side and reach Moonshine Bay, and by then they were experts at pitching their tent and striking camp, and they had not fallen out. They had used their time well, making camp sooner rather than later, giving themselves time. We must imagine them in the evening sitting together round their small stove with mugs of tea, or lying together in their tent, heads touching and talking fondly, sharing confidences. By now they were eating what they could forage and Hera's deep knowledge of the plants of Paradise was put to the test. Though there were plums in abundance, they avoided them and contented themselves with simpler foods. Even so, Hera always

337

used the ancient skin test, which was as reliable on Paradise as on Earth.

Here is a transcript of what she told me about the more intimate side of their journey:

Hera Mack was interested in everything. Always asking me questions I couldn't answer. Like, we saw quite a number of old Dendron stools in the river – all broken down and flaking – and he'd want to know how old they were, and I couldn't tell him. I used to get mad at that.

On the second day we had just come down from the pass. Everything was very lush on this side of the mountains and I spotted a thunderball plant not far ahead that was all swollen and waiting to explode – in fact it could have gone off just with us walking past.

So when we got close to it I said, 'Mack, stop a minute. Do you want to see some magic?' He was of course immediately suspicious, but he said OK. Now it was a very clear and fine day, you understand, and we could see right down to the Sea of Ben Ben, with all its islands. So I said, 'Mack, I bet I can conjure thunder out of this clear sky, but you have to turn your back and shut your eyes.' He said fine and turned away. He was very suspicious. So then I covered my ears and kicked the plant. It went off like a cannon. Loudest I'd ever heard. A hell of a bang, and Mack jumped out of his skin and the fine blue seeds came out in a cloud and covered him.

I thought it was funny. He wasn't too impressed, mark you, because some of them got down his shirt and he had to wash them off in the stream. I played lots of tricks on him and saw him relax. Another time I found some of the Valentine poppies and they were just inflating, so when we stopped for lunch I read him the story of Valentine O'Dwyer and Francesca Pescatti and he liked that.[9] We both got one of the big red pods and wrote messages on hybla leaves and tied them on and sent them off up into the sky. They caught the wind and went straight up the hillside and maybe back over the pass. Of course, we didn't tell one another what we'd said. That's the tradition.

[9] See Document 12.

Olivia And what did *you* say?

Hera That would be telling.

Olivia So what kinds of things did you talk about?

Hera Ourselves, mainly. You've got to remember, Olivia, it was all new to me, so I was a bit like a girl with her first love, and I was on my best behaviour, but also I couldn't help myself. I've never been able to hide my feelings, and I so wanted him to know me and love me and for us not to have secrets. So when my walls finally came down, they came down completely, and there wasn't a brick left standing. He was the same. A bit more reserved than me, but then he'd been hurt in love more than me, and so what seemed a game to me was a bit more threatening to him. But he did open up and talk to me, finally. And I to him.

Olivia Can you tell me?

Hera Well ... I suppose so. I've nothing really to hide. It's just a bit embarrassing, that's all. Things told in the intimacy of a tent can sound a bit silly in the cold light of day.

Olivia I know. But you might have to trust the reader a bit. All writers have to, and we get disappointed when our best efforts at irony and wit are misconstrued as mistakes. Even so, we take the risk. Not once, but repeatedly. I think you'll find that most readers will meet you halfway. For what it's worth, I think that anyone who has fallen in love will know what you are talking about, and you will remind them of what it was like.

Hera Mack wanted to know what other men I had made love to. I don't think it bothered him, but he wanted to know. Men are a bit territorial about things like that, aren't they?

Olivia Some are. Personally I quite like it. But that's just me. Go on.

Hera So I told him. I mean, it was a pretty pathetic record for a woman in her fifties. But I explained that my work had more or less been my life, and the idea of settling down with one person and having children never figured in my world, well not in a deep way, an active way. He wanted to know about my first experience of lovemaking and I told him I could hardly remember. That's the truth. I was a student at the School of Applied Science, Biology and Genetics on Luna. I was in my second year and we'd all been to an eclipse party, and I'd had a bit too much to drink and got silly and noisy, the way I do. Well, there was this young man I'd been dancing with ... I think he had red hair and I suppose I thought he looked a bit dashing . . . and we ended up on this sofa. I'm not sure how we got there but there was no one else about. And he was kissing me and I suppose I was kissing him. And I knew what he wanted and I thought, *Well, why not?* I mean, it has to happen sometime, so why not now? And I *was* curious.

But it was so embarrassing. He couldn't get his trousers undone and I ended up with my skirt up round my neck, sort of waiting. Then he ended up on top of me of me and I got a bit scared then. I'd sort of assumed that he would know what he was doing, that men – boys that is – knew all about it. And certainly he'd given me that impression. But now I think it was his first time too. And you know what they say – too many new things together is a recipe for disaster. Well he couldn't . . . he couldn't find his way, and I tried to help, and somehow I got his elbow in my stomach and I think he got my knee in his . . . codds. But we got started eventually and he gave this great big heave and that really hurt me, and that was it. He'd finished, and when I moved he asked me to be still. Said it hurt if I moved. And I lay there and I remember thinking, *Is that it? Is that what it is all about? I'd rather be doing algebra.*

Then he got up. And he was shaking a bit. And he was suddenly worried in case someone caught us. And I thought, *Well, it's a fine time to start worrying about that.* But he wanted to get going. I think he wanted to tell his friends. We were both embarrassed, and a kiss would have been terrible. I think we shook hands finally.

And then he said, 'I'll go out first and then you wait five minutes.'

And that really hurt me. I pushed him back and I went out of the room and slammed the door and locked it and went back to my study. And I sat up and I did do some maths. And then I cried a bit because I was ready to make love – I was of age, as Sasha would say – but it seemed so confined and a bit demeaning really. I went back to my books and tried to pretend it had never happened. And what *had* happened? Nothing really. But I made sure I wasn't pregnant.

Several times after that he came round to my door and wanted me to go out with him. I think he felt genuinely sorry and embarrassed, so I set him a puzzle. It's an old one and if you're not used to puzzles it can trick you a bit. I said, 'I'll give you six hours to solve this, and if you can solve it in that time I'll go out with you.'

But he couldn't, and I didn't. After that I got a reputation for being intellectual and arrogant and a bit of a man hater, and then my father died ... but I got first-class honours. And if I was in love with anything, I was in love with my subject.

Olivia You set him a maths puzzle?

Hera Yes.

Olivia What was it? Can you tell me it?

Hera It's very well known. I give you twelve identical balls, and I tell you that one is either lighter or heavier than the rest. I also give you a perfect balance. Now, you are allowed three weighings, that's all. And at the end you must be able to tell me which ball is the odd one and whether it is lighter or heavier. There is no trickery. Just logic. There are lots of puzzles like it, and if you can do one, then the rest are easy. But he couldn't. He was no more good at logic or maths than he was at loving.

Olivia Did you tell Mack this puzzle?

Hera Of course. Well, he asked me.

Olivia And did he try to do it?

Hera Yes.

Olivia And?

Hera He solved it. As I said, it's just logic, and Mack was very logical.

Olivia You're either a very brave woman, Hera, or a fool – and you're not a fool. What would you have done if Mack hadn't been able to do the puzzle?

Hera Done? Nothing. Well. No, that's not true. I would have made love to him and then shown him how to do the puzzle. It's not important. It was a silly thing and the only reason I gave it to the spotty student was because I wanted to show him up, humiliate him intellectually – and I did.

Olivia What would you have done if your spotty student had solved the puzzle?

Hera I would have gone out with him once, as I agreed. I would not have made love to him but I would have set him another puzzle. And Olivia, think on. I know lots of puzzles, including some that have no solution.

Olivia That's not fair.

Hera Nor is love.

Olivia I think you probably frightened men.

Hera I know I did. And some of them hated me for it. Especially after I became head of the ORBE project. But I was still curious. About sex, I mean. I knew a lot about the riotous goings-on among Martian bio-forms – but not much about humans. And my only other sexual encounter didn't add greatly to my store of knowledge.

Olivia Another frightened male?

Hera I was Shapiro's mistress on and off for fifteen years. One of them, anyway. And more off than on, if you see what I mean. Don't look shocked, Olivia. I thought you would have guessed.

Olivia Then you were lying at that hearing when that lawyer ... What was his name? Nasty, big pug jaw, always needed a shave ...

Hera Stefan Diamond.

Olivia Yes, him.

Hera Of course I was lying. They weren't interested in the truth; they were just digging for dirt, and I wasn't about to give them any. No one knew that we had been to bed together, of that I was certain, but if I had confessed they would have twisted that into all manner of nasty shapes, all of them damaging to ORBE, and I wasn't about to let that happen. Anyway, Shapiro was almost impotent. I think the idea pleased him more than the act.

Olivia He was considerably older than you.

Hera He was thirty-eight when I was born. Over sixty when I became his lover. Does that seem strange? It shouldn't. Age is not a barrier. Oh, I love the idea of young Sasha taking her man or young Estelle Richter making love on the shore when the *Scorpion* first landed. They somehow got things right. But me? All I can say is that Shapiro was the first man I had ever met who I could freely acknowledge was my intellectual superior. And I am sorry if that sounds egotistical, but it is the truth. And in those days the intellect came to matter to me a great deal because science is a very competitive world. Have you ever been intellectually infatuated with someone, Olivia?

Olivia Yes. It didn't last beyond the second Martini.

Hera Then you know what it feels like. It is the most wonderful submission, and can be the cruellest. I was his PhD student. Top in my class. Out to win the world. And suddenly there I was with this mild-mannered man who didn't seem able to shave himself properly but who seemed to have read everything, spoke two or three languages and who could cut through arguments with the ease of a hot knife through butter. He just knew so much and could select from such a range of sources ... And there was something a bit decadent about him too. It only came out when he had been drinking – hints of a dark inner life – and that was attractive as well. I was just in awe, and awe is a dangerous emotion, it makes you very passive.

Olivia I wouldn't know.

Hera So I was surprised when, after one of our PhD meetings at his home, we had a meal – he was a good cook – and a bottle of wine or two, and then he asked would I like to hear some music that his sister had just sent him from Earth? I said yes. It was a new opera by Kossof and Besser called *Chrysalis*. Do you know it?

Olivia Yes. Where the god Pan is born again of Earth?

Hera That's it. And we listened to it and it has that incredible end to Act One when Pan steps up to the mirror, looks in on our world and then breaks the mirror and steps through. Well, we were sitting close. I had my shoes off and I was sitting with my legs drawn up on the sofa. Very modest, but I was being a bit provocative too, I think. And I was loving the music but wondering what I could say about it when he just took my glass out of my hand and kissed me. I was so astonished. Little me. I felt as if Pan had kissed me. And then it was all so easy. I kissed him and slowly he undressed me and said I was the most exciting woman he had ever met and that some of my research work had stimulated him to go back and resume work he had abandoned on the effect of photo-dynamic resonance on cellular infarction in some of the subterranean aqua bio-forms that had been found on one of the deep lakes under Mars.

Olivia Any girl could be excused for going down after words like that.

Hera I'm serious! Those are sexy words, Olivia. And I think it was true because later he published a very well received paper on cellular resonance and my research was given full credit. What I need to tell you also is that, having almost undressed me, and having me willing and waiting, passive to his Pan, he fell asleep. Which didn't do much for my confidence. But I was hooked. And we did become lovers. Eventually.

We were more intimate than we were sexual, if you see what I

343

mean. Ideas were the aphrodisiac. Sometimes it was enough if I just held his hand or put it to my breast or kissed him, for he was a very sick man in the last five years. He was an addict to the plum. He had a pet one that he used to milk. He was a melancholic too, and knew a lot of Baudelaire by heart, and I was never comfortable with that side of him.[10] I also think he never acknowledged a certain homosexual inclination which, had he done so, might have made him happier. Who knows? But even to the end he could sparkle like no other, and ideas and theories still poured from him, and he remains the most original scholar I have ever met – or will meet. And he loved me. I know that. And cared for me. And shared some things which I will not talk about, for they belong with Shapiro in the grave.

Olivia Fair enough.

Hera Mack found this hard to accept. I told him. We all have dark patches in our lives which we cannot share. And finally he accepted that, because there were parts of his life too that he could not explain. I said to him, 'If you had met me in those days, you would not have wanted me, and I would not have known you. Now is our best time. Let's use it well.'

Olivia Do you believe that?

Hera Oh yes. Some are lucky and fall in love when they are young and retain an innocence that guides them. But for most of us I think we have to mature in life before we can cope with the demands of love. It took me a long time to shed my skin, Olivia. And when I did . . . there was Mack.

Olivia You were very lucky.

Hera I don't think luck has anything to do with it. Anyway, one night I said to Mack, 'Do you know what the most sexy part of a man's body is?' He looked at me as if I was joking and then said, 'His shoulders and his bottom.' Not bad guesses, eh? But I said, 'No, his brain and his mind.' He got upset then, because he thought I was putting him down. But I said to him, 'Mack, you are the most brainful, mindful man I have ever known. Who else could have taken a twist of my hair and a ring from his granny and found the Dendron? Not Shapiro or any other man I have

---

[10] For further information on Professor Shapiro and his addiction to the Paradise plum, see Document 5.

ever known. Who else would have so trusted his inner knowledge that he would shift down to a planet in order to save a woman he hardly knew, but believed he loved. Not Shapiro, for he didn't possess that insight or that courage. And who else but you could have worked out how to separate the Dendron? I would have destroyed it. Shapiro would have destroyed it. But you worked it out with raw intelligence and insight. And you had the strength to trust your understanding. You are the nonpareil, my love, and your Hera loves you like a flame that heats a pot. That's a simile.'

And do you know what he did, Olivia, this big dumb lovely man of mine? He had me sit back between his legs with my back to him, and his legs were tucked up under mine so that his heels were touching my bottom, and I was sort of floating upon him, my arms on his thighs. And then he let down my hair and he started to comb it out with just his fingers, and that is the most sensuous and intimate thing, I think, that anyone has ever done to me. I was water to his cup, and I felt his tears on my neck.

So have I answered your questions, Olivia?

What is the matter, Olivia? Why are you crying?

A surprise was waiting for Mack and Hera as they made their way down the shingle banks beside the river and turned right and so up into Moonshine Bay. Standing back from the shore was a cabin. It was a bit old-fashioned-looking but otherwise seemed in good condition. The windows had not been broken and the blinds were all down. Mack tapped at the door, perhaps thinking that someone might have been at home, or perhaps he was just warning the ghosts. In either case there was no answer and so he punched out a window, released a catch and climbed in. With the blinds up and the doors open, he could see he was in a luxury cabin, a retreat for the executives of MINADEC, a place to bring friends and girlfriends for a quiet weekend of R & F beside a clear blue sea and with a view of islands. The cabin was dry and clean and more or less as the last occupants had left it a hundred years earlier.

When MINADEC ruled Paradise, there was a small settlement at Moonshine Bay. It did not figure on any of the maps, hence, when MINADEC withdrew, the cabins were left intact. The ORBE project knew of them and had had some plans to use them for an outstation, but these plans remained on the drawing board. A few of the cabins had survived the seasons. They were, as Hera once described them to me, 'like a display in a museum panorama', and one wonders if there was more than chance involved in their survival.

The remains of a concrete landing pad – now rendered useless as it had lifted and twisted – could be seen in the foothills; the supports for a jetty, looking like so many broken teeth, could be seen stretching out from the shore.

Though other and more luxurious cabins might have been habitable, Hera and Mack liked the cabin they had first found because it was right on the shore. Ten seconds from bed to bathing.

They made themselves at home. There were big soft double beds – one each if they wanted – and showers which still functioned, after a bit of coaching, despite not being used for a long time. Everything needed airing so they simply carried the mattresses, cushions and quilts outside and left them in the sun.

It was Hera who found the wine. Some bottles were ruined, but enough were not. And she found some clothes that were the height of fashion during the MINADEC days. For Mack she selected a dinner suit with wide shoulders, flexible waist straps and a vivid red plastic carnation sewn in. For her, she chose an evening dress with low cleavage and lots of feathers in strange places and perfume from La Boutique de Paris. They moved the table out onto the beach and ate their simple meals while the sun set over the sea. And when it was dark, they lit candles.

'This is decadent,' said Hera, opening another bottle of wine, her eyes sparking. 'Do you want a cigar? I found some in a vacuum chest. Should still be OK? I'll get you one.'

'Later,' said Mack. 'For the moment, would you like to see some magic? If so, turn your back and close your eyes.'

'I love surprises,' said Hera. She poured herself a glass and turned her back. She heard a scratching sound.

'OK. Turn round now.' Hera did, quickly, and was in time to see a rocket fizz into the air. 'This is for the Dendron,' said Mack, and the rocket exploded into a sparkling crown of gold and red. 'And this one is for Shapiro.' The second rocket described a spiral as it shot upwards before bursting into blue sparks which fell like rain. 'And this is for us.' Two rockets shot high into the air. There they exploded and crackled in silver and red balls of sparks. They hung there for a moment before dropping and dispersing in the breeze.

It was a golden time. But nagging in the back of their minds was the awareness that it was borrowed time. The problems of the platform, far overhead, were a constant worry, despite frequent radio contact. Mack in particular felt that he should be 'up there' helping his team – though Polka, who had become the main contact, insisted they were coping and that the situation was 'not so bad' since the Dendron had been divided. Hera found herself torn between her enjoyment of the present moment and her knowledge of how far they had still to journey. She felt a strange kind of guilt in being happy.

When they went for walks beside the sea, they always carried matches because occasionally they found bodies, dried and shrunken, cast high on the strand during a storm. These they burned and watched thoughtfully as the smoke rose and the bones burned bright as phosphorus. They found old boxes and crates, and if they picked them up, none of the sand of Paradise clung to them. Mack shook his head. 'It wants nothing to do with us, does it?'

Lots of Dendron stools stood in from the beach and in the rivers. Some had decayed right down to ground level. Others still stood tall, and Mack hoisted Hera up so that she could stand on one of them and look down the margin. 'They go on and on and on', she said. 'Thousands of them.' They also found where the young trees had been cut down, sometimes with an axe, sometimes with a chainsaw. 'Your maths works in reverse too, Mack. Too much of this kind of thing and numbers soon reduce. But can you imagine the mighty carvings that took place here? And look at the size of some of these stools. These were real giants. We were lucky. Ours was small by comparison.' She lifted up one of the tines from a crest and it was taller than her. 'Imagine this in full swing. Now that's the stuff of romance.'

Hera found books in the house: novels and some technical works, as well as books for children, among which was a spelling book. Mack began receiving lessons every day, and it was a sight that touched her heart to see the big man sitting on a towel on the beach and picking his way through the words, repeating them to himself and then drawing them in the sand. His favourite text was one of Sasha's shorter tales, 'Getting Your Man'.[11]

[11] See Document 2.

Mack being Mack, he spent time exploring. So while Hera read and drew and prepared interesting meals, Mack checked out some of the houses. One had lost its roof and the wind and rain had done the rest, but most were in amazing condition. All had an unreal cleanliness, a lacquered patina, for, like the crates and the corpses, they were insulated from Paradise. He also searched through all the sheds, and in one he found something which he kept hidden from Hera. It was a boat, an old-style cutter, with a solar panel, a small fluid-core engine and a mast lying flat with meshlite sails furled round it. It was standing on a set of solid rubber wheels. He cut back the plants impeding the double doors of the shed and prised them open. Minutes later, with the help of a lever at the back and grease on the axles, he had moved the cutter out into the sunshine. Mack was no connoisseur of boats, but to his eyes it looked very comfortable, with bunks down below and a galley and lifebelts. He knew Hera liked boats and so this would be his present to her.

Each day he found an excuse to go off and each day he worked on the boat, checking the engine and the solar panels and the batteries. These were flat, but to his joy, since they were dry cells of the type developed for use in space, they soon began to pick up and hold a charge.

And then one day while Hera was busy trying to prepare something complicated and spicy from what remained of their rations, he trundled the boat down to the sea and manoeuvred it into the water. It floated. No leaks. He started up the engine. It took a while for the fluid core to warm before any moving parts could function. But he watched the temperature guide, and he watched the shore too, hoping against hope that Hera would not come out before he had it running.

The needles passed from the black to the green. He heard the engine turn and the torque plate take up the strain. Gently he eased the engine to forward. It coughed once – he had no idea what caused that – and then it engaged and the boat surged away from the shore. About a mile out, having heard no worrying torque squeals, he took it to full power and had the shock of his life. The boat sat back and then lifted and planed. The speed was frightening to one not used to such things, but he took it in a wide arc and headed back to shore. He had located the horn and now he sounded it. Three times. Moments later he saw Hera come running out onto the beach, wearing a bikini she'd found in one of the cupboards. He saw her hold up her hand to shade her eyes, for the sun was behind him, and then she ran back and seemed to be calling. He could not hear, but he guessed she was calling for him. She ran back onto the beach. This time he was close, and he cut the power and drifted in to the shore.

'Dr Melhuish, I presume.' He jumped down onto the shingle, took the painter in his hand and gave it to Hera. 'Here you are, sweetheart. It's all yours.'

Hera was breathless with astonishment. 'But it's . . . it's beautiful. Where did you find it?'

'Bought it from a friend in Birmingham. Do you like it?'

'Mack it's . . . O, Mack. What's it called?'

A name had been painted on the front and on the stern in Mack's new, careful handwriting: *The Courtesy of MINADEC*.

29

Round the Head of the Horse

The Courtesy of MINADEC made their lives even more interesting. They could now sail out to the islands, not using the engine when the wind was fresh but scudding over the clear water and tacking home. Hera was in her element with the dashing spray and the buffeting, but Mack was content to sit and steer and sometimes he was sick. He was never at ease on the water, and though he learned to swim, it was more of a wallow and he was nothing like the graceful minnow that darted beside him.

But both were aware that time was passing. The situation on the shuttle platform had again worsened. They had to field questions about where they were exactly. Had they been attacked again? Were they coping? They were very vague in their answers, but when the contacts were over they felt guilty because those who cared for them were having a hard time on the shuttle platform. The backlog of barges was being cleared slowly, but they were hampered by the media interest the broadcast on the Dendron had generated. To make matters worse, there were occasional inexplicable breakdowns leading to blackouts. Sometimes the fractal gate would close down completely. This happened most noticeably if something native to Paradise was being shipped out, so strict checks were made, and anything, whether it was a piece of carved wishbone or a painting on stretched-and-dyed hybla or a Venus tear, was removed. A whole cargo bay was now filling with the artefacts.

As Dickinson explained to Mack, 'The feeling here is that the whole place is breaking up, so the sooner you get yourself and your missus up here the better. There's talk in the team of coming down to get you. I know what you said about that, but we might just have to withdraw from the shuttle if things get worse. Captain

350

Eiderdown looks like she's ready to quit. I'm not being too subtle for you am I, Mack?'

Descartes was more direct. 'I'm frightened of that place down there, Mack. It's creepy. And Polka and me are having the shittiest dreams of our lives, not to mention pains at the end of the month. So the sooner you and your sweetheart get your big arses up here the better, and the sooner we shift out. Otherwise we're leaving you, Mack. We love you dearly and we always will, but Polka and I can't stand it.'

Captain Abhuradin was putting a brave face on things and confided to Hera that the only thing that kept her going was that she was pretty sure she was pregnant. She now only wanted to get the job done so she could concentrate on that. She wanted Hera to say how long she thought it would be before they reached the old shuttle port, as she had to think of scheduling. She wanted to know where they were and Hera had to be very vague. So, while Hera and Mack were happy in themselves, that happiness began to feel selfish. But there were other things too. Tattersall weeds, hitherto conspicuous by their absence, began to appear on the high hills. They saw three of them scatter seeds in one morning. The invasion had started.

On the morning after the final call to the shuttle platform, without it ever really being discussed, they found themselves packing up and loading things into the boat. A keen wind was coming off the sea and rain clouds were building against the mountains when they closed up their house. Mack had mended the window he had broken, and he had found the key to the door. So they locked it and hung the key where it could not be missed – a symbolic gesture. They knew that they were the last people who would ever warm the beds and clean the dishes and do their washing in the old house. Every step was now a kind of retreat and everything became symbolic.

Their plan was to sail west, round the shores of Horse, stopping if they found somewhere that took their interest, but as soon as they left they began to race. Mack was the most ill at ease. He could not explain why, even to himself. He sat in the cabin with a bucket and a towel as the boat dipped and rolled in the heavy swell. And when his head was up he watched the coast slip by. Occasionally they saw the swirling patterns of the Michelangelo-Reaper, not just marked by Tattersall weeds, but shaping the entire contours of the hillsides with tall trees.

On the morning of the second day they were sailing past cliffs. Hera kept them well out to sea, but the swell from the ocean was great, and at times when they were in the troughs they couldn't see the land, though they were only a mile offshore. Riding the crests, they saw the waves hit the rocks at the base of the cliffs and the foam climb high.

Hera was looking for something. They rounded a headland and came into calmer water, and there she spotted an opening in the rocks with a narrow passage of water between. 'You in the market for a bit more magic, Mr Mack?' she said. 'If so, shut your eyes while I steer us through here. In fact keep them shut anyway, cos you're not going to like this bit.'

He did so, and a moment later he felt the boat lifted on a surge and heard the waves echo all about them as they passed through the channel. Then, after a few seconds, Hera cut the engine and let them drift. 'Open sesame. This is called Valentine Bay. Can you guess why?'

The inlet was about a mile across and formed almost a complete circle between the shore and the rocks. On the landward side, gentle hills sloped up to the mountains. Several small streams entered the bay, tumbling white down rocky valleys. But that was not what held Mack's attention. All the shores, and the sides of all the river valleys, were covered with the bobbing red spheres of Valentine poppies. There were millions of them, stretching as far as the eye could see. They rippled like waves in the wind and occasionally a single balloon would break its stem and lift into the sky trailing its seed pod.

'Can you imagine that once a lot of the bays on Paradise were like this? The *Scorpion* logbook mentions bays filled with red flowers – we think it was these. This is the bay Sasha Malik mentions where Valentine and Francesca landed on their bed of osiers. The flowers took them here, you see. And, historically, a young couple lived here in MINADEC times. They'd run away from one of the camps and set up their own homestead just in that valley there. It happened a lot in those days – people just heading off into the wild, a bit like us, really. Well, when the ORBE project started there was not a single Valentine poppy here. Not one. They had all been harvested and sent off planet to make lampshades or something. So this was one of our first projects and one of the most successful. What do you think?'

Mack was nodding. 'It's beautiful. You can imagine lying down, can't you, on the ground, with all those red globes bobbing above you. It would be impossible to be sad in a place like this.' And then he added, 'I wonder where their minder is?'

'Minder?'

'Mm. Their Michelangelo. Isn't that right, that all gatherings of plants like this have their own minder?'

'That's a strange thing to say.'

'Is it?'

'I don't know what you mean. How do you know about this?'

Mack looked at her and there was something confused about his look. 'Sorry. I thought you must have told me. But it is right, isn't it?' For a moment Hera had the uncanniest feeling that he was not talking to her. Then he looked back at the bobbing flowers and she saw him smile again his normal gap-toothed smile.

'No. I never mentioned a minder before,' she said. 'I've always thought of the Michelangelo as being a more selfish and solitary plant. From the stories . . . from the little evidence—'[12]

'Oh no,' interrupted Mack, 'I don't think they're selfish. They like to play, that's all, and they play a bit rough sometimes. They don't understand us, you see. That's my impression, anyway, from all the patterns we've seen.'

'Would you . . . like to go ashore?' Hera asked slowly. She was looking at him closely. There was something different, a bit strange . . . something in his manner. She'd seen this before, she realized. Several times. An abstractedness. Then he turned and smiled and put his arm around her. 'Thanks for bringing me here. It's lovely. And that story Sasha wrote is special to me. You planned it all along, didn't you?'

'No, I just suddenly remembered as we came down the coast. But I knew you'd like it. The next time I get to speak to Tania I must get her to contact Rita Honeyball. This was part of her parish. She

---

[12] Evidence of conflicting attitudes to the Michelangelo-Reaper can be found in Documents 2, 8, 9 and 10.

used to give us Valentine poppies when we had a birthday, just when they were about to swell, and tie messages to them. She'll be pleased to know how lovely it is.'

They stood gazing for a few more minutes. Mack seemed to be looking for something and then, satisfied, he nodded. 'Time to go, Hera,' he said. 'You'll have plenty of time to walk down memory lane when you're back on the shuttle off planet.'

And that remark, too, bothered Hera. She brought the engine alive and took *The Courtesy of MINADEC* on a circuit of the bay, and then headed out through the narrow channel and into the open sea.

They were about half a mile down the coast when Mack looked back and pointed excitedly. 'Look. Hera, look. There's a message for you.' Rising up into the air above the hills was a cloud of Valentine poppies. There were millions of them, and as they caught the wind they flowed with it like a red carpet and passed high over Hera and Mack. And still they came. Hera cut the power and they turned in the swell and watched in silence as the balloons flew before the breeze and spread out.

'So what was the message, Mack?'

'Just saying hello, I think.'

She knew he was lying.

In the afternoon the wind slackened and for a time the sun came out. But it was a silver disc at best, and Hera watched as the high cloud gathered about it. Gradually the sky became heavy and leaden. They felt the temperature drop. When Mack asked what she thought the weather would be, she told him that the indications were inconclusive. 'Somewhere between bad and dreadful.'

That evening they reached the place where the southern tip of the big island called Lennon approached the coast of Horse, creating a channel between them. This, at its nearest approach, became the notorious Royal Straits where our story began.

Apart from the weather, Hera had been observing the tides and the moons. Without an almanac it was difficult for her to be certain, but she was pretty sure that sometime soon they would reach one of the periodic tides for which this channel was famous. She did not want to be bobbing about in mid-channel when the great waves came flooding through. The choice was simple – either to make a dash now while the tides were big but not too dangerous, or find a nice safe anchorage for fourteen days.

She explained this to Mack.

'It's too long, Hera.'

'Blame Paradise.'

'I say we make a run for it.'

'OK. I think so too. We'll rest the night here and make a start at first light. I don't want to navigate through here in the dark. Reefs.'

That night they lay together quietly, listening to the boat creak and the waves slap. Hera tried to sound casual. 'You seem quiet, Mack. Is something worrying you? Is the swell making you feel sick? Tell me.' She stroked his brow where worry lines had formed. 'Are you a bit frightened? I know you don't like the sea. Or have I done something wrong?'

'It's not the sea. And it's not you either. It's just ...' His voice trailed away.

'Tell me. You can tell me anything. I love you so much.'

'It's just ... it's just this place. It's got a hold on me. I don't want it to.' There was a long pause and then he began again. 'I've never been happier in my life. I never believed I could be so happy. Since I met you my life has opened up and got some daylight in it. God knows it needed it. For the first time since I don't know when, I began to look forward to the future. And now this.' He sighed. 'You do know. Don't you?'

'I know you love me. For the rest you'll have to tell me. I'm afraid I've become wonderfully ordinary since we saved the Dendron.'

'Why did it have to happen here? Meeting you. Why not somewhere else? Somewhere normal.'

'Like Birmingham?'

He laughed. 'Yeah, like Birmingham.'

'So what's normal, Mack?'

'I mean the kind of place where people can just rub along, get on with their lives, squabble a bit, make love a lot and grow old easily.'

'Perhaps it could only happen here.'

'I don't want to believe that. I want it to happen in the world I know, not here. I don't want magic; I want a wife. I want a place in the sun with people I know. I want to build memories. I want to be

355

"young and easy under the apple boughs". Like my granny used to say.'

'Are you afraid that when we leave here, we'll come apart? Is that it? That the love won't last?'

'I hadn't thought of our love not lasting. I hadn't got that far. Oh, I'd thought you might get bored with me. I mean I'm not— *Ow!*'

She had nipped him, hard. 'And I'll do that again, and really hard, and in a place where it really hurts, if you start that talk again.'

He sat up. 'That really hurt.'

'Good. Now you were saying that you'd never thought about our love not lasting. Go on.'

'That's grounds for divorce, for a start.'

'Shut up. Or I'll do it again. Now get on with your story.'

He lay back. 'Well what I meant was that I knew, deep inside me, that no matter what happened – apart from nipping – I'd still love you. I just couldn't help it. That's the way I am. But I'm afraid I'll never leave here. And I feel that this place is driving us both now. I can't explain it any better. Like the other day, after we'd talked to the people up top, I felt this great urgency to run. To get moving before it was too late. It was as though someone had said, "OK, Mack, you've had your holiday, now get back to it." Do you know what I mean?'

She did know what he meant, about the compulsion to move. She'd felt it too. The golden time had ended. 'That was because we both felt guilty,' she said. 'Here we were enjoying Paradise the way it ought to be enjoyed, and they were sweating it up top.' But it was his other words that had chilled her. She said, 'Why do you feel you'll never leave here?'

There was a long pause during which Hera did her best to keep perfectly still. Finally Mack said, 'Will you stroke my face, like you did that time before?' Hera propped herself up, adjusted his arm so that she was not leaning on it too heavily, and rested against his chest. She began to stroke from the centre of his forehead, moving out to the sides.

'I'm going to tell you a little story,' he began. 'When I was a kid, just three or four, I used to have dreams, terrible dreams that frightened me, and my granny used to stroke my forehead like that, and it always calmed me down. You've got the same gift she had. And then I'd find a way to tell her the dreams and she'd listen and sometimes she'd explain what she thought they meant. And sometimes she didn't, and that worried me. Anyway, I often used to dream there was something trying to smother me, not like with a pillow on the face or anything, but something within, something that grew up inside me. And it stopped my eyes so that I saw differently, and my mouth so I tasted strange tastes, and I used to hear this sound like a great rushing black wind. I suppose something happened to my nose too but I can't remember that. Probably just as well. And then this thing, whatever it was, crept out of me through my eyes and ears and out of the place just where your fingers are now, right in the middle of my forehead. And that was when I used to wake up. And I knew that if I hadn't woken up, I wouldn't have woken up or I would have woken up different. And the funny thing is, sometimes I wanted to let that thing come out, but I was very, very afraid. And I still am.' He paused and said quietly, 'You can stop rubbing now. I'm OK.'

Hera stopped, kissed him very lightly, and then snuggled down with her arm across his chest. 'So how does this affect you now?'

'Several things have happened. A lifetime ago you asked me whether I thought the future could cast shadows. Well that shook me, because that was something I'd realized when I was a boy, and I had passed them off as hunches. I could feel things before they happened. I could, but my brother couldn't. And I know that because I'd ask him. It wasn't knowing the future, like picking winners, but personal things, and even though they might be bad, I couldn't always prevent them, but I could feel them coming. As I grew up the dreams became less frequent and so did the hunches. But when they did come, they were irresistible, like a command. Like when you're taking down a dangerous building and your mate says, "Stop!" you stop. You don't think about it because thinking about it takes too long. You stop, or you jump or you hold steady or whatever. That was what it was like when I was coming down to save you. It was like someone had said, "Run!" and boy did I run. You think I had a choice? I didn't have a choice. It was you I was responding to, your pain, your need. You talked to me once about resonance. You don't need to talk to me about resonance. My bells and cherries were ringing for you from the first time I saw you all bandaged and full of fight on the shuttle down to Paradise.

357

'Anyway, I've wandered off what I wanted to say. Today I had a bad turn. Bad in one way, not in another. It was when we visited the Valentines in that round bay. When I looked at them, I had this vision of such beauty that it hurt. It did. It hurt me here in the throat. Not like when you pinch me but another type of hurt. And it was just like the dreams – it was something taking me over. I could feel it rise in me and start to smother me. And I asked you about their minder and suddenly realized you didn't know what I meant. And then when I looked, really looked, I could see it, the Michelangelo, right there amid the great dancing globes, and it was so merry. There were patterns there, but they kept changing, and that's why you couldn't see them. Great rippling waves of colour. Like a red sheet in the breeze. It was chasing the wind, you see, and then bucking the wind. And it was glad we saw it. It wanted me to go ashore. "That siren voice was sweet." It spoke with your voice, Hera, and I almost said yes when it asked me, but I made myself say no, and you sailed us out.'

They lay still. Hera did not know what to say because a chasm had opened before her. She had seen nothing that he had seen – patterns or merriment. There was suddenly so much she did not understand.

Mack suddenly pulled her close with the arm that was under her, half lifting her on top of him as if she were a blanket.'Another thing when I was a boy, my granny used to do the tarot cards. I used to ask her to tell our fortunes, but she never would. Said she couldn't do it because we were too close. But one day she'd been fiddling with this deck of cards – I think she'd made them herself – and out of the blue she said, "Your brother'll be the rich one, but you'll have the adventures, and the big one'll be your last." Well, she was right about my brother. Got more money than he knows what to do with. And me? I've had lots of adventures – I've done nothing but talk about them for the past week. And I hoped, hope, that meeting you would be my last and greatest adventure. But what do you think she meant, "and the big one'll be your last"? If I asked you, out of the blue, what you thought the last, biggest adventure in life was, what would you say?'

'I'd say . . . I'd say it was death.'

'That's what I think too. But there are different types of death, Hera. You could die being spiked by a mad bloody Tattersall

358

or chopped in half by a Dendron like that poor bugger Redman or . . .'[13]

'Or?'

'Or you could be taken by a Reaper.'

'And is that what you are afraid of?'

'Yes.'

'Can't you block it out?'

'I can. A bit. But like I say, part of me doesn't want to, and that's what frightens me most. I could slip away. Oh hold me. I know you can't fight off death. But we might fight off the agent of death.'

'Was that the message you saw in the flowers, Mack? The real message, when all those balloons were released at once? Was it a message of death, Mack?'

He took a deep breath. 'Hold me, Hera. Hold me. Hold me. Hold me as tight as you can. Crush me into you.' And he held her tight too, his arms as strong as any Tattersall weed, so that she could hardly breathe. 'What it said was – it was a choir of voices singing, every flower had its part – and what it said was, "All of these, and more, are yours. Such is my love for you." And it was your voice, Hera, because yours is the only voice of love I know, but it wasn't you speaking. So you have to get me off this planet. You must not let me out of your sight. Can you do that? Is your love strong enough?'

'It is. If you want me. It is.'

That night they never let go of each other, as though afraid that some beast might come clambering up out of the dark water to take them.

But it was a different kind of beast came. A few hours before dawn Hera felt *The Courtesy of MINADEC* turn on her anchor and the waves slap hard against her. The wind was picking up. It came from the east, and that was good for it would push them through the Royal Straits, but *The Courtesy* was a toy boat really, good for cruising in calm seas. Hera had no idea how it would fare in a real storm.

Before dawn she was up on deck, dressed in heavy-weather gear and life jacket, disentangling the anchor chain, which had managed to get caught up with a rope that had blown overboard in

---

[13] See Document 6.

the night. The sky was grey and already the wind was lifting the tops off the small waves and sending them scudding across the sea. Water which had been clear yesterday was now milky grey with bubbles and the small boat danced and skittered on the surface in the way that light craft do in a broadside wind. The sooner Hera could begin to make headway the better. Finally, frustrated by the tangle, she cut the offending rope and threw the tail end over the side. She set the winch to slow and the chain began to clink aboard and run noisily down into its hold in the bows. As the anchor chain tightened, so *The Courtesy of MINADEC* was pulled round until the anchor lifted from the seabed, at which point the boat leaped. Hera set the speed to slow, and when the anchor finally came on board, she went to neutral, took one last look round, and then engaged forward and upped the revs. *The Courtesy* surged ahead.

Out in the main channel the weather was fierce. The grey clouds streamed overhead, strained by the wind. Hera did not like the wind coming from behind, as the cutter had a low stern and could be swamped if a chasing wave broke over them. Hera would have to have eyes in the back of her head. But she was not really complaining. She had lain awake most of the night and was now glad to have something practical to do, to take her mind off the problems. She had left Mack sleeping. In repose there was something king-like about him, she had decided, his strong face and solid body, but the similarity came from the carved images she had seen on a sarcophagus. On balance she preferred the real man.

Lying awake, glad that he slept but weary herself, she had realized that a man such as Mack was very vulnerable. The very intuitions that were his strength opened him to danger, for they were psychic channels. For a brief time she had been open, after the voice of Paradise had called her name – how long ago that seemed – and look what had happened to her! Mack had a lifetime of openness and so might be easy meat for a predator Reaper. For that was how she saw the situation. She would be a woman going into battle to save her man. How dare that Michelangelo – she could think of other names – how dare it send *billets-doux*, valentines no less, and offers of love to her man? In some ways it was comic, she could see that. Comic and absurd. But she wished that at this minute they were both on the way up to the shuttle platform to rejoin the quick-witted Dickinson, the up-front Annette and the people she had come to love and trust such as Inez Abhuradin and Tania Kowalski. She had done her bit for Paradise and so had Mack; could they not now have their peace? Apparently not. So they must take it.

The Courtesy of MINADEC bucked as she entered the main channel. The water was lumpy and broken, and Hera could not cut through it without taking on waves and side hits. She adjusted speed in an attempt to match the speed of the waves which now chased the small boat.

It was an hour or so later that Mack stumbled up on deck. He looked a bit green and dishevelled, but alive.

'Put your life jacket on, Mack. Even if you lie down, keep it on.'

He nodded and stumbled back down into the cabin and the door slammed behind him. A wave took them from the stern and ran the length of the boat. The cutter was not well designed, Hera noted. The water did not drain away quickly, and in these conditions that was important. Must remember to tell Mack to keep the cabin door shut at all times. One wave in there and we'll be in trouble.

Mack came on deck again, bulkier now, and he had seen the danger and closed the door firmly. Conversation was difficult, but by shouting close to her ear he could make himself understood. 'Let me know if you want me to take a turn.'

She nodded gave him the thumbs up, and went back to trying to read the sea.

Hera had been in plenty of storms during her time on Paradise. It was here she had learned to sail, crewing on yachts out of New Syracuse or taking one of the ORBE cutters out on expeditions. She didn't frighten easily, and being light and small but strong, she could scamper safely about a pitching boat where a bigger man would stumble.

With every wave that hit them she was learning the tricks of *The Courtesy of MINADEC*. It was not the boat for these conditions, that was certain, but it was gutsy and pugnacious, she decided, and she liked that. It took the troughs and lifted easily and didn't dive too deep.

To Hera, every wave was an individual and to be treated as such, with constant adjustments of speed and line. She could detect patterns and sometime predict, but there were rogue waves too. These seemed to come from nowhere and were suddenly on you. One such took her broadside before she could react and the boat shuddered. And lifted. That was where *The Courtesy* was vulnerable. Like most boats, side on she could be rolled.

They survived that broadside, and they survived others. Slowly, as the morning drew on, they made headway, and while the weather did not ease, at least it did not get worse.

If there was a physical problem for Hera it was in her arms and back. The continual battle with the steering wheel was a strain which became an ache and finally she called Mack to the helm. Although he was not a natural sailor, he had an instinctive grasp of engines and how to coax the best out of them. Before she went down into the cabin, she watched to see how he was coping. He had observed her closely, learning how she reacted, seeing what she reacted to. Hera saw that he rode with the boat, spread-legged, and reacted quickly when the waves built up, leaning in to the wheel and not away from it. She gave him a thumbs up and went below.

She made tea for them both, holding the small kettle still. And when she had delivered him his cup, half-full, she stretched out below. Even while fully occupied steering the boat, she had been thinking about their conversation in the night, wondering what to do. It had brought their relationship into sharper focus for her, and made it more real too: less romantic, more pragmatic, and that felt good. When he had said 'I don't want magic; I want a wife' she felt her cup overflow. Was this the same Hera who had always seemed so job-driven that she had no time or interest in romance? Ha! No, this was Hera, the woman, awake and enlivened, and part of her own great tradition. They were a team, she and Mack, she knew it. Anyone seeing them now would think they had crewed together for years. She loved the way he trusted her. When she was boss, he jumped. He asked good questions too that showed he was thinking. He was protective, but not in a way that weakened her. She would fight for him, by God she would. And she would not let up until he said, 'Stay.' Like Sasha before her, she was there for the long haul – a wave hit them broadside and her tea spilled – as long as they survived the storm.

By late afternoon they had shared the work of the day and, apart from a few mishaps, all was well. They were tired but, most important, they were in sight of Royal Straits, and that cheered them. This three-mile channel – named after the Royal Seafood

Company, which specialized in gourmet seaweeds and had used to trawl these waters – had a bad reputation. The problem was that the straits were shallow, and so the twin-moon waves which surged round the planet here experienced drag and so could, in the right conditions, turn into mighty breaking tidal waves. Small boats could be turned end over end. The danger for a big ship such as a trawler was that it could survive the comber, but might then be dumped and dragged on the rocky bottom in the following trough and hence lose its propeller or keel. It was then vulnerable to being turned broadside on to the sea and the next comer could roll it. It had happened plenty of times, and the shore was dotted with wrecks. The question facing Hera and Mack was, simply, should they make a run for it now despite the gathering evening, or should they turn into Preacher's Cove and ride the night out?

Three miles. Not far with a wind pushing you and the prospect of safety at the end of it, for there were many good anchorages off the western coast of Horse and Hera knew this part of the coast well. It was here that she had been working to re-establish the pancake wrack when she first heard the news of the Disestablishment.

'Let's get it behind us,' she said. 'Then we can relax.'

'Whatever you say, boss.'

'OK. But if we are caught by a wave, I'll be taking us as straight as I can, and I want to know that you are tied on to the boat. Because it can get very steep and if you do get swept overboard ... well, I'd never find you. And you would be swept off, because a wave is stronger than your grip.'

'Understood.'

She upped the revs and set out. She had sailed the channel several times in fair weather and foul. Now she was trying to remember the tricky parts. On a fine day it was beautiful and the rocks on the bottom gave the water incredible colours and patterns. But today there was so much broken water that she could not have told a wave breaking on a rock from a simple clash of currents or spray drift. She knew the channel was safe as long as she kept just left of centre. The dangerous rocks were mainly to the side. But one of the things that made steering difficult was that the straits were full of cross-currents, and these would push the small boat sideways. She decided to go as fast as possible.

The tactic worked.

And they almost made it.

They had just reached the place where the pancake wrack was seeded and were in sight of the end when a giant wave started to build behind them. It was like the back of a whale rearing up out of the water – it just grew and they found themselves being lifted up its face. They stared down, and a hole in the sea seemed to open before them. The engine laboured as Hera fought to keep them straight. She was counting too. If the wave began to break now they were finished: nothing could survive that weight of water. But if it held its shape and they reached the crest . . . Five, six . . . It became dark. The light was cut off by the rearing wave. It was so close they could have touched it. Nine, ten . . . And then, just when they thought they must surely fall, the air lightened. They had crested the wave. They were through, and *The Courtesy of MINADEC* came level again. The hump of the wave passed under them with a hiss.

They dropped down its back, but a new wave was already gathering behind. It was not as big as the one they had just survived, but it was already breaking. Hera had no choice but to steer as straight a course as she could. 'Hang on tight, Mack!' she shouted as the wave surged over them, forcing them down. They went under. The boat shuddered with the weight of water. Hera had no idea whether they were upside down or right way up or how deep they were. But then, sluggishly, the prow broke the surface and the cutter rode up.

She was low in the water but the windows were not broken and the pumps were working. Seawater poured off the boat on all sides. Hera glanced behind. No monster wave was gathering and she sensed that they had changed direction slightly. The wind was no longer coming from the rear. It had lessened slightly. She could hear the engine labouring, but she kept the throttle pressed for full power. She knew they must be almost past the place where the shallows gave way before the deep trench. Soon the hills would give them cover. 'Go, you beauty. Go, you beauty. Fight it,' she shouted. With every second that passed her hope grew. She had no time to check for damage. All her attention was on the sea in front, and the nearby cliff which marched steadily past them.

They must be past by now.

They must be in deeper water.

She chanced another look behind and there, rearing up against the murky dark sky, was the next giant wave, but it was marching away to their left. All they would feel was its swell. She let out a great cry of triumph and slapped the boat with the palm of her hand. 'You beauty, you fighter! We're through, Mack. We've beaten the straits. Mack. Mack!'

Only now did she have time to take stock. She turned and there was no sign of Mack. Just a tangle of ropes in the stern. But then the ropes moved and an arm poked out. He had taken the full force of the wave and it had slammed him under the aft seats, where he now lay, wet, winded and wedged. But alive. And struggling to get out. 'We're through, Mack,' she shouted and pointed to the white-crested wave that was now accelerating away from them like an express train.

She eased back on the engine, lashed the wheel so they would hold their course and scrambled back to help him out. His nose was bleeding and his knuckles were grazed. But they were both alive and they crouched on the heaving deck and punched one another and laughed.

Hera climbed back to the wheel and began to look around for damage. The first thing she noticed was that the solar panel which kept their torque batteries charged had gone. All that was left were the bolt holes. That meant they were running on whatever charge was left in the battery. The gauge which told them how much power they had in reserve was broken and the needle stood at zero. Amazingly, the mast was still intact along with the tightly furled sails. The anchor cover had gone, ripped away. They were trailing ropes. But otherwise, superficially at least, they had come through well. They were still riding a bit low in the water, but that wasn't surprising.

'Mack. Will you go and check the cabin? Look in the battery chamber. See if any water's got in. Check for damage.'

Mack nodded and climbed below.

Hera studied the sea. They were well past Calypso Headland, which marked the northern tip of Horse in this latitude. The light was failing. The wind was still strong, but they were in open water and the waves had settled to a more predictable pattern. She had a decision facing her. Should she turn and head south and run for the safe coves of Horse, or should she head on for the distant shores of Anvil. They could go slowly overnight. There were no rocks, shoals or islands to worry about. They could take turn and turn about on watch, and perhaps the wind would die down a bit. If luck was really with them they could even set sail north-north-west for Hammer and New Syracuse. They would be there in a matter of days, and with luck would never see another Michelangelo.

Mack climbed back out on deck. 'What's the verdict?'

'Well the cabin looks as if Descartes had one of her binge parties: two of the batteries have broken loose and smashed. I think we have a small leak somewhere up front but I couldn't find it. Otherwise OK.'

'Sure it's a small leak?'

'Yeah. The anchor hold door's come off. There might be a crack round there. I can find it and fix it as soon as I clear a way through the mess.'

Hera considered for a few moments. She looked at the dark sea streaming past and made her decision. 'OK. Here's the plan. We're going to sail on. Ride our luck while we have it. This wind's in our favour. We might be in sight of Anvil by tomorrow.'

It was a good plan and they made good mileage, taking turn and turn about, until shortly after four o'clock when the engine began to fade. Once the power had begun to fail it dropped quickly. There was no time to get oil lamps.

Within minutes they found themselves sitting in the middle of a pitch-black heaving sea while a brisk wind beat them about the ears.

30

Haven

There is no blackness quite like the blackness of the sea at night.

It is an immense blackness which seems to smother you. Hold your hand in front of your face and you will see not a glimmer. Bring it closer and you will touch your nose and will still not see anything. You live and move by what you can feel and by your memory. If you have a torch it can be worse, for it merely emphasizes the blackness and the sea, which you can see rising and falling as it sweeps past you like so much black ink. The beam, when you shine it in the air, shows for a while in the mist and spray and then fades away in the immense cavern that now surrounds you.

Such was the situation of Hera and Mack.

With the failure of the batteries, all lights in the cabin failed. The merry red and green lights marking port and starboard, as well as the instrumentation, such as it was, dimmed and disappeared. However, the darkness was not Hera's main worry. The loss of power had revealed a serious design fault in *The Courtesy of MINADEC*. The steering was power-assisted and when the batteries failed the wheel lost its ease and became a thing of lead. Without power, unable to steer, they were at the mercy of the wind. And the wind would, simply by the physics of such things, turn them, and then the waves would come at them broadside on.

'Mack?'

'Yes?' He was standing right beside her.

'There's a torch in the wheelhouse cupboard, down to the right of the wheel. Could you fetch it?'

Hera felt Mack move round behind her. She sensed him reaching up to grip the cabin roof and then edging his way over to the cupboard.. She heard the click of the cupboard door. And moments later the flashlight beam cut into the dark.

'Now what?' said Mack.

'I want you to take the wheel. Keep us pointed so the wind comes from directly behind if you can.'

'Where are you going?'

'Getting a rope. I'm going to rig a sail up front. That'll give the wind something to bite on and keep us moving. Then we'll worry about the steering. Don't waste the batteries now. I know where I'm going.'

Being tidy at sea was one lesson Hera had learned when crewing a yacht. So, during her time away from steering, she had coiled and stashed all the spare ropes.

She felt her way round the ship, never moving without something to grip. The ropes were hidden under the rear seats and she was able to feel them, get a sense of their length and weight. She selected a medium-length cord about the girth of her index finger.

'Flash the light once, Mack, to give me my bearing.'

She saw the light, but just as she was about to release her grip, the wind tipped the cutter, and a wave came swilling on board and foamed round her legs before running away down the boat. Mack flashed the light again.

Holding the rope under one arm, Hera made it back to him in no more than four steps. 'Hold me by my life jacket while I tie on.' She felt his grip steady her against the rolling. Quickly she tied the rope around her waist. 'OK, here's what we are going to do. I'm going to tie myself on here to the wheelhouse so that if anything happens, like I get washed overboard, you can pull me back. And if that does happen, pull gently cos I might have a foot trapped or the rope up round my neck or anything. Now, I'm going up front and I'm going to release the jib sail. What I want you to do is this. Shine the torch to your right. Can you see that binding wheel with the rope coming out of it? That rope goes out to the jib. When you feel me pull once on my safety line, I want you to slowly release the line, that's anti-clockwise.' Another wave hit them hard. They heard it and felt the small boat buck and tilt, and then the spray came right over them and would have knocked Hera over if Mack had not been holding her. 'That's because we're broadside on. Makes life tricky. Keep releasing until you feel me tug twice and then stop and lock off. OK. One other thing: if I do go over the side, lock off the rope before you try to save me. Got it?'

'Yeah. Good luck, Hera.'

'Right. See you on the other side, eh?'

Mack grunted, remembering the lesson he had given her when they were saving the Dendron. 'Don't you want the torch?' he asked.

'Need both hands, Mack. You know me.'

Steadying herself for a moment, Hera pulled herself up beside the cabin and onto the narrow deck. She had plenty of things to hold on to and the only problem was that the deck was leaning anywhere from thirty to forty-five degrees, and so just keeping her feet on the wet deck was a challenge. She felt her way along the boat to the small jib boom. Here she tied herself on to one of the anchor guides and then braced herself and felt out along the jib. One by one she untied the jib lashings and felt the sail come free and loosen. Now. She gave one tug on the safety cord. Under her hand she felt the jib line move. Almost immediately she heard the jib start to flap as the sail unfurled. It was a sound like castanets. This changed as more sail was revealed, and she heard the sail bang as it took full wind. She hoped that Mack had a tight grip and would not let it out too quickly. The next thing she heard was the strain on the ropes as they took the full weight of the wind. She sensed the boat heeling round and steadying and starting to run before the wind. The wind was now steering the ship, and that meant they would buck about a bit. But they wouldn't wallow.

She tried to guess how much sail was up. Not too much. She didn't want to put a great strain on the boat, just enough to keep them pointed. Two sharp tugs, and the rope stopped moving. She could feel the movement in the cord as it was locked off. OK. Back now.

The journey back was a lot easier. That's the way of things.

'You're a bloody marvel, you are,' said Mack when she again stood by him, holding his arm for support.

'I thought you weren't supposed to give compliments.'

'I'm gonna revise the rulebook. I couldn't see where you were, but I felt the moment the sail took the wind. What a difference! What next?'

'Next we need to sort out a rudder we can control, otherwise the jib might slap about too much and begin to tear the sail or rip the rings out.'

'There was something like a rudder in the battery store. A big blade with two pins pointing down.'

'Sounds about right. Funny place to keep a rudder though. Look out for the tiller too – that's the handle that slots on the top.'

'Gotcha. Let me go and get it.' Mack made his way down into the cabin and slammed the door. Hera realized she was shaking. It was not fear, but her muscles acknowledging the strain. She braced herself against the wheel and stretched, trying to release the tension. Against her back she could feel the wheel shudder as the surging water struck the rudder below. It must be stuck fast, otherwise the wheel would turn. Whatever position it had been in when the batteries failed was probably the position it still held. She hoped it was straight. Certainly the boat had not been jiving about as much as she expected, and so it might be still doing its job. The trouble would come when they had to steer to get to land. But that was a problem they'd deal with when they came to it.

Mack was on his way back. He bumped his head, cursed whoever invented small boats and lugged something heavy up on deck. Hera shone the torch. Old-fashioned, varnished and never been used by the look of it, it was, undeniably, a rudder. The tiller was lashed to it. 'I'll tell you. It's bloody heavy.'

'All the better. Can you manage to hook it over the back?'

'I suppose so.'

'Well, let me get a rope on it first.'

And it was as well she did, as getting the rudder hooked onto the rings as the boat surged took all Mack's grunt and they lost it twice when it was knocked out of his hands by waves – but the third time it slotted. The tiller was soon bolted into place. And they sat in the bows while Hera tried to keep them steady.

They sat there for the rest of the night, only about an hour or so, and gradually felt the wind slacken. As dawn broke, grey and wet, they saw looming ahead of them the high headland which marked the eastern tip of Anvil. The sight of land, even though far away, rallied their spirits, and Mack departed to make a cup of something warm. *Thank God*, thought Hera, *they didn't install an electric stove as well.*

*

By mid-morning they were close, and the mountains of Anvil, the Staniforth range, dominated the skyline. Hera, who had stayed at the tiller for most of the time, was aware that *The Courtesy of MINADEC* was becoming sluggish in the water. She was starting to wallow, and there was no doubt that however small the leak had been originally, it was now serious. The constant strain of the jib sail had probably opened a seam in the old boat. Also, Hera had put up more sail to compensate for the boat's heaviness and the drop in the wind. All of that would be putting more strain on it.

Meanwhile, Mack had been investigating. The water was trapped between the walls and under the floor plate. They could hear it slop back and forth. When it eventually rose above the companion walls it would start to enter the cabin, and that would signal the end. They could not pump it out. The pump was linked to the electrical system and with that not working there was nothing they could do. *Madness!* thought Hera. *The Courtesy of MINADEC*, gutsy as she was, demonstrated what happens when you put too much faith in a single system.

The immediate problem facing Hera was where to put in to shore. The coast was almost unrelieved – cliffs and reefs, and where she could see shingle bays they were protected by lines of sharp grey rocks.

Hera had sent Mack down below to pack their equipment. The understanding was that if she found a place to put in, she would do so. It was up to him to be ready. Ideally she would beach the craft, but if that were not possible, they would have to swim and tow their things behind them. Fortunately the water was not cold, as seawater went, and they could certainly make it to shore, but the prospect of putting damp clothes onto an already wet body was not enticing, to say the least. So Hera balanced the remaining buoyancy of the boat against its ability to keep moving forward.

They rounded a point of rocks and for the first time a pale sun shone out and made everything silvery. There was a bay. The heavy swell from the storm made tight little waves against the shore, and these turned on themselves when they reached the shingle, almost like wheels. Hera read this as evidence of an undertow. It was nothing like the vicious rip tides she had seen, but it would make wading ashore difficult. What was more, she could tell by the way the water swirled and rippled at the entrance to the bay that there were rocks just below the surface. She hoped that the swell might lift them over. Hera called to Mack: 'On deck, sailor. I want you up front looking for rocks.'

Mack came up, dumped their backpacks and other bags on the deck and scrambled to the front of the boat. They got over the first reef with a bit of scraping. They got past another rock which had just its snout showing above the water and which rasped along their side. Then the water was flat and Hera steered for shore.

Mack was ready. As soon as the keel hit the shingle he threw their belongings high up the beach and jumped off. Hera followed. The boat was already slipping back, and Hera sank up to her ankles in the soft shingle. She threw her weight forward; Mack caught her arm and pulled her up the beach. With the next swell, *The Courtesy of MINADEC* lifted back off the shingle and slipped heavily out into the small bay. She turned when the wind caught the sails and drifted slowly towards the rocks. One more swell saw her lifted onto the reef. As the wave spilled away, with it went any remaining buoyancy. The weight of the boat dragged her down. She tore open along one of the laminated seams. Prow hooked on the rocks, she settled lower. With the next wave, the end came. She filled with water. Bubbles boiled to the surface. Cushions and papers floated away from her. She lifted briefly and then the stern went down and *The Courtesy* slowly slid under the waves. The tip of her mast, and part of the sagging jib sail, canted over at a steep angle, was all that remained visible. The cutter was grounded and would break up with the pounding of the waves. The next two-moon tide would see what remained lifted and smashed on the rocks.

The two people huddled on the beach paid *The Courtesy of MINADEC* the respect of watching her dying movements before gathering their things and heading inland and out of the wind.

Hera led; Mack followed. And then he turned and stared out to sea, his hair and beard blown back by the wind. Perhaps he had heard something. Certainly, in those few moments, he saw a pattern move across the surface of the sea. Briefly the waves moved in unison, stirred from beneath, as they lifted and broke on the shore.

31

Concerning Mack

Had Dickinson, or Annette Descartes, or any other member of Mack's team, seen him at that moment as he faced the sea and saw that swirling pattern suddenly shape the waves, they would have been surprised at the look of fear in his eyes. They knew him well, their quiet leader. They knew him as a man who rode with situations when he could, and confronted them only when he could not. They knew him as a man who had faced danger many times, liked it even, but they would never have seen that hunted look. They knew him too as a private man, one who rarely spoke about himself. He carried his history within. An interesting man. Unpredictable but dependable. Complicated too. It is time to learn more about him.

When I first asked Hera about Mack, she threw her hands in the air – one of her characteristic gestures – expressing impossibility. The following is extracted from several interviews I held with Hera.

Hera   Hopeless. Getting Mack to talk about himself when he didn't want to was like pulling teeth. He'd tell stories – and he had a lot of them, funny and tragic – usually against himself, but something got in the way when I asked him even simple questions about himself, about his own feelings. He would deflect enquiries with a joke. At the same time, when the pressure was on him – like when he was afraid of being captured by a Michelangelo – his feelings just poured from him, and I was glad.

I suppose I could have asked more, but I felt we were living on borrowed time – and we were. I made him promise once that when we escaped he would let me 'debrief' him properly. And he agreed on condition that he could do the same with me. Do you see the problem in getting a straight answer?

Nevertheless, some facts did emerge.

Mack was the elder of twin brothers. They were not identical twins – in fact it is hard to think of twins being more dissimilar. Mack's birth name was Arnold, a name with which he did not identify. His brother was called Jason, and that seems quite appropriate. The family name was Lorimer. 'Mack' was a nickname he was given when he was in prison. It was slang. Evidently anyone who was big and tough and used a knife was called Mack. The name stuck, long after he had left prison.

Both parents died when he was a boy. His father, Sergeant Tikka Lorimer, was Australian and a member of the UN Land Reclamation Force assigned to Bangladesh. Mack had a picture of him, and there was no mistaking father and son. Barrel-chested, same big frame, same gap in the front teeth, same curly hair – Mack was the image of his father.

The monsoon rains were late in Bangladesh that year. Then, when they did come, they just didn't let up. The result was a disastrous flood which took out some of the new dykes the UN had been building and buried crops in silt. Tikka Lorimer was helping families fleeing along a dyke top. He stayed too long and was swept away when the dyke collapsed. His body was never found, and all Mack retained was his picture and a letter.

Mack's mother was called Diana and she was quite a beauty, very striking with long dark hair. She was twenty-one when the twins were born. After Tikka died she received a pension and moved from Sydney to Perth to be closer to her mother. A few years later she was diagnosed with poly-cystic kidney disease syndrome and she died of renal failure after only a few months' illness.

A personal memory that Mack did reveal to Hera concerns the time he was taken to see his mother in hospital, shortly before she died. It seems he did not recognize her and cried and struggled when she reached out to hold him. A wasting and darkening of the skin, as well as hair loss, is one of the terminal symptoms of Larson's syndrome. In Hera's view, that experience marked him for life and perhaps explained his fascination with her hair. After the death of his mother, Mack and his brother were brought up by their maternal grandmother, herself a widow and a fortune-teller with a great love of poetry.

Mack's school career was not distinguished. He gave the impression of being a dreamer and was irresponsible. He was often late for school, failed to complete homework and frequently cited for truancy. By contrast his brother was a high achiever, outstanding in both sports and academic work.

Olivia I'm interested in why Mack never learned to read. I would have thought that a woman like his granny, who seems to have enjoyed literature, would have made certain that he did.

Hera Yes, well. You don't know Mack. My impression is – though I emphasize he never said this – that he deliberately decided not to learn to read. I believe he also actively fostered the impression that he was a bit simple.

It was protection. He knew he was different from the other boys. He was experiencing horrific dreams of being possessed and of sometimes being outside his body, and so to protect himself he played dumb. He was the one allowed to sit at the back of the class and doodle while the rest got on with their lessons. But he was quite good at maths. He must have been a difficult boy to understand. On the one hand he was indolent and dreamy, but yet he had enthusiasms and gifts. Also, he had this habit of disappearing.

Olivia Disappearing?

Hera Yes. He'd go walkabout. Wouldn't tell anyone and just go. He once let slip to his grandmother that he had gone off with a friend – and she knew that wasn't true – and that she was never to worry about him because his friend would take care of him. It was a spirit friend, you see.

There was his size too. He grew very quickly – he was already six feet tall when he was fourteen, and he had some kind of breakdown. He didn't remember much about it, or at least that was what he said. I think it was puberty more than anything else. I think he was going through a bigger change than most. Anyway, when he came out of hospital he became interested in bodybuilding – a lot of boys do, and he just bulked up naturally.

As soon as he could, he dropped out of school. He told his grandmother one time he was going on a 'long walkabout'. That was when she gave him the ring. It had been her mother's before her and her mother's mother's, and so on. She reckoned Jason would do all right, but Arnold was the one who needed protection.

And off he went. Into the desert.

I suppose it was a kind of pilgrimage or a retreat. He moved around, getting odd jobs, experimenting with his life. He lived with a woman in a caravan for a while and she gave him his first sexual experiences. She was an alcoholic and used to steal from him to buy cheap sherry. He didn't mind. He reckoned he was getting the best of the bargain. But the thing that struck him was that when she was drunk she was a different person, in fact several different people, and she would move from being comic and fun, to being broody and resentful, to angry and sarcastic, to crying, to comatose – all in the space of two hours. And he would put her to bed. The next morning she would wake up and not remember any of it.

One day when he was out doing a job, chopping wood or some such, he had one of his hunches. It was so sudden that he almost chopped his foot off. It was one of his rare visual premonitions, and in it he saw himself lying dead outside the caravan with a wound in his throat. So when he finished work, instead of going straight back to the caravan like he usually did, he went to a bar. Apparently the time after work was when they had sex. They'd got things worked out quite well. He'd leave in the morning before she had woken up. She'd wake up sometime, slop about, do some shopping, get the place tidy, and start to feel randy about four o'clock. By the time he got back after five she was ready to tear the pants off him. Have you ever behaved like that, Olivia?

Olivia   Get on with the story.

Hera   Well he stayed at the bar until it was late and then he walked to the caravan park. There were police all over and an ambulance, and he saw the woman being carried from the caravan on a stretcher. There was a man dead.

The caravan was sealed but his possessions were in there, so he did his dumb act and spoke to one of the police officers and got the full story. The man was the woman's husband and he'd heard about Mack, so he'd come to the caravan park with a gun, intending to shoot him. When Mack didn't come home, he broke into the caravan, found his wife half naked and already into her first bottle. They had an argument. He shot her and then himself.

He must have been a bad shot as he only wounded her, but he managed to blow his own head off. 'So you were bloody lucky, mate; you stayed in the bar.' That was the policeman's verdict.

Olivia What happened to Mack?

Hera Nothing. He was the intended victim, but otherwise he wasn't really involved. The police kept his things and he was supposed to be able to pick them up after the enquiries were over. But he didn't bother. He went walkabout again.

Olivia How old was Mack at this time?

Hera Sixteen. We then lose three years of his life. I think he was in the desert. Just drifting. There was always work for a 'big fella' – as he put it. And not too many questions asked, because anyone who went bush had their reasons. They were sorting themselves out and the desert was a wonderful place to be alone. Life on the margin, Olivia, an interesting place.

Olivia So when next do we catch up with him?

Hera Nineteen, going on twenty, high summer, northern Queensland, into drugs. 'A good time and a bad time' was how he described it. He was picked up for robbery, and the comic thing was that the drugs he and his partner had found had actually been stolen.

So he found himself in prison for seven years, and that saved him. That was when he got the name Mack, and it stuck. He went through a lot of hard times. He was very angry but he wasn't stuck in his anger – it was something that was passing through him.

You asked about him not reading. Well, in prison he had ample opportunity to learn to read, but he didn't. By now he had the idea that if he learned to read it would stop his inner life.

Olivia His intuition?

Hera Yes, something like that. What do you think of that? Has that idea got any merit?

Olivia Well, I've always thought of reading as stimulating the imagination –

Hera Perhaps Mack didn't need stimulating.

Olivia – and of helping you find the inner you, apart from the pleasure it brings. Access to ideas, new experiences, new thoughts. Look at young Sasha, finding her way.

Hera That's writing. And that's *if* you want to communicate. Mack didn't want to communicate. He had nothing to say. He was living too intensely. When I was a girl, I was a bit like Sasha – well, in some ways, in my interest and my curiosity. I sometimes think now that I would have been happier if someone had sat me down and said, 'You don't have to do anything, Hera, you don't have to explain or make judgements; just sit and look at this painting, and let the painting look at you.'

Olivia Inner knowledge, waiting to be born.

Hera Higher knowledge, possibly. You see, what's interesting about Mack is that he could do numbers, and I think that is a more important skill than reading. It gave him access to the abstract, but in a purer form than words. Words are so loaded, Olivia, and most of all when written. It's so hard to strip them to their essentials, that's what writers and poets—

Olivia Let's get back to Mack. He's in prison and . . .? What did he find hardest?

Hera The hardest was not having access to a woman – women. Hell, he was only twenty and he was fizzing. But being close to so much anger and hatred was very hard too. He could feel it like a burn. And so he kept to himself, and if anyone caused him trouble, he did his dumb act. And if they persisted he waited for his moment and hit them hard. Hit so he broke something. Hit so they had to be sent to hospital.

He had it all worked out. He trained in the gym – a lot. He kept himself very fit and he met men there who taught him about fighting. After a while he was respected, and they knew he wasn't so dumb.

Olivia OK. So what turned him round?

Hera Two things. The first was he learned a trade. Halfway through his time he was moved to a more open prison, an occupational prison. He became a mechanic. He could scribble his name if he needed to. Most of the manuals in the workshop had little drawings and so he could follow them. And the teachers . . . well, some of them were former inmates, and they said things like 'If you're a mechanic you get your hands dirty, and if you get your hands dirty you can't turn pages in a manual because you get the book dirty, and if you get the book dirty you can't read it anyway – so learn it in your head, Mack.'

Suddenly the days started to whizz past. He learned how to maintain the big magnetic torque trucks. He worked on scaffolding, and that led to platform construction, and that led to elementary space technology. He was a welder and a fitter. He took every diploma he could – and he could do the maths.

I mean . . . Let me put it this way, Olivia: if he had needed to read and write, he could have, I suppose, but he got through without it, and I'm not sure what that says about the system or our culture. There were always people on hand to help. Not being able to read became normal to him. Even with his demolition team Polka did the invoices and Dickinson handled any paperwork – and Dickinson, make no mistake, was very sharp. It was not until Mack met me and wanted to share more in my world that he decided to make an effort, and wasn't he lucky?

Olivia You mentioned two things that helped him.

Hera Yes, the other is a bit strange. One day one of the warders came round looking for volunteers to attend an experimental counselling session. Now all of them were used to this kind of thing, being guinea pigs for social experiments or prison reform studies or criminologists doing their PhDs and the like. And they used to sign up because sometimes it meant you got to go out on a visit and see women. So they were taken into the lecture room and sat down in rows.

After about five minutes the door opens and in comes this Buddhist monk all in his robes and with his head shaved. In fact he looked like one of them. This little monk sat down on the floor in front of them and just looked at them. He didn't say anything for a long time. He just looked.

Several of the prisoners just got up and walked out. They thought he was playing mind-fuck games and they knew all about that. Finally he said, 'Well, now we know one another a bit. I am here so we can help one another.' And that was all. He went back to sitting and looking at them. At last one of the prisoners said, 'Do we get to go on a trip?' He was being clever. And the monk says to him, 'Where do you want to go?' and he was being clever too, because the way he said it made it seem like a special question.

After half an hour the session ended. The monk got up, thanked them for their attention, said he would see them next week, bowed to them with his hands together in front, said a short prayer and went out. They all looked at one another, shrugged and went back to playing ping-pong or whatever they did in their spare time.

The next week there were only four volunteers, and the same thing happened. And the week after that there were only two volunteers, Mack and another fellow who was also very much a loner.

Finally Mack said, 'Is this what we do? Just sit and look at one another?' And the monk said, 'That's quite an achievement. But is there something else you'd like to do?' And Mack said. 'Yes. I'd like you to talk to us. Like, tell me how you are able just to sit there and look at us and not do anything.' And the little monk looked away, thought for a moment as if he was weighing up the question, and then he looked back and said, 'I think it is because I'm not worried about anything.' The other prisoner said, 'Aren't you worried about us? Most of the religious people who come here are worried about us.' And the little monk said, 'No, I'm not worried about you. You'll find your own way, now or later.' 'So what do we do now?' asked Mack. 'What do you want to do?' said the little monk. And so it went on.

Mack was fascinated. He noticed that if they asked a question such as 'How do you manage to sit like that? Don't you get pins and needles in your bum?' the little monk would answer them. But if they asked him a question which wanted him to initiate something, he would always turn the question back on them. He would never take the lead. And these questions went round and round and round. For Mack, it was the first time anyone had asked him what he wanted, and it was so difficult to come up with an answer – but that didn't mean there wasn't an answer. But he started to ask himself the question and eventually, eventually, eventually he started to get some answers.

He said to himself, *What do I want to do when I get out of here?* and there were lots of answers – find a woman, have a beer, get a job. But the biggest answer of all was, *Be of some use.* When he found that answer it really surprised him. And that very day word arrived that the UN was looking for drivers to take food into Sichuan. It was dangerous work, but there were people starving, and he signed up because he was a good driver and knew all about big trucks.

At the last session, before he left, he told the monk what he had decided and started to thank him. The monk stopped him and said, 'You did all the work. Good luck.'

So, no conversion. No sudden light of understanding. But a calmer mind, and I think finally that was Mack's greatest strength.

380

He drove relief trucks for six years, wherever he was needed. He was shot twice and came down with various fevers. But he survived.

He had lots of adventures. Lots of hunches. Lots of lovers. Lots of heartache. Lots of risks. After that he went into space. He helped build the Hercules space station in the shadow of Mercury and the stories he can tell you about that would make your hair curl.

He travelled out through the fractal to Proxima Talleyrand and worked on the shuttle platform there, and then, when the Outlander Dome colony was disestablished on Regit, he went into the demolition trade and that became his speciality. The people he worked with on that first job became the nucleus of his team. And they had been together ever since. So, when the Space Council decided to disestablish Paradise, Mack and his team signed up. And the rest, my dear Olivia, is history. One thing you learn about Mack – and it takes a while to realize it – is that he will never do something he doesn't want to do. Interesting, eh? The things he does are the things he wants to do. He could be a bastard. But he's the most unselfish man I've ever known. He cuts his own cloth – and still does, probably. And that is why he is still out there on Paradise, and why I am here.

Forgive me, Olivia. I don't want to talk about it any more.

So, we return to the story of Hera and Mack as they stumble about in their wet clothes, making camp inland from the small bay where *The Courtesy of MINADEC* sank. Tomorrow they will climb into the Staniforth Mountains.

32

The Watcher on the Heights of Staniforth

Soaked and cold from their boat journey, they made a fire under some trees inland from the shore and declared the rest of the day a day of rest. Hera put the tent up while Mack prepared a simple meal. Then she climbed into the tent before the food was served, intending just to change her clothes. But she fell asleep, on her face, where she lay. All Mack did, for fear of waking her, was to remove her boots and tip the water out. Later she stirred herself, pushed her damp clothes off and burrowed into him. He, flat on his back, didn't even notice.

Morning found them stiff and hungry but more optimistic. Their plan was getting simpler.

Hera knew pretty well where they had put ashore. Mack, in a rare oversight, had forgotten to pack the charts, but it didn't matter. She knew that if they climbed from the bay they would reach the foothills of the Staniforth Mountains. They would then have to follow one of the valleys until they approached the snowline, where they would be able to see the Organs. Once there, they could cross over a high valley which divided the peaks and then drop down on the other side to the Kithaeron Hills, below which was Redman Lake and old Pietr Z's umbrella tree plantation. It would seem, almost, like home. From there they would have half a day's walk to the coast where old Pietr Z had his lifeboat. Hera was certain it would still be there, remembering her first day alone on the planet when she flew over it. Then they would sail across Dead Tree Bay, just as Hera and Pietr Z had done many years earlier. They would round Dead Tree Spit and head directly for the shores of Hammer. The journey should take them no more than a day or two, depending on the weather. She knew that coast well and was confident she could navigate their way to New Syracuse. Then they would contact the shuttle. It would come down, they'd step aboard and within the hour they would be at the shuttle platform over Paradise and enjoying warm showers, drinks with friends, a telling of adventures, soft beds followed by a quick skedaddle through the fractal and . . . They neither knew nor cared what came next.

It sounded a long way, but Hera knew it was not. Her ORBE people would do a trek like that and not really think much of it. The only thing they had to do was avoid the Michelangelos, and she already had some plans for that.

By mid-morning of the next day they had made good progress. They followed a stream inland and then struck an old MINADEC bulldozer track, which led directly up towards the Staniforth Mountains. They could see the peaks, towering white and menacing in the distance, when the clouds lifted. The track was heavily overgrown, but only with dimple and hyssop flag and trefil wanderer, and these they could push through easily. The path led them back and forth around the hills but always upwards. By late afternoon they could see the Organs clearly and the first scatterings of snow which surrounded them.

The Organs were just that, big pipes. They were the mineral exoskeletons of plants called tuyau – so named by the French mineralogist who discovered them. These plants – which when living resembled thick, probing, green worms – had grown up from the valleys below. They burrowed underground. They split rock. They sent out side shoots which started new plants, and these in turn burrowed over and under, and sometimes through their parents. Those tuyau which had grown right up to the high plateau, snaking through the valleys and thrusting across ravines, died when they encountered the permafrost.

From studies of the growth patterns, such a journey might have taken a tuyau 5000 years, and in the case of the larger plants considerably longer. At the top they clustered like hundreds of broken mouths. It was the wind playing over these pipes which gave them their popular name. When the wind blew from a certain direction, they sounded alto, diapason, swell to choir, basso profundo and treble. It was mighty music, strange and spectral – and no two tunes were ever the same.

383

Mack and Hera climbed until evening. They reached a small shelf which had once been a turning place for the half-track grubbers, and here they pitched camp. Mack stood for a while shading his eyes and peering up towards the Organs. The setting sun caught them obliquely, making them look like gun barrels. Then he looked closer, squinting. 'Hera,' he called. 'Come here, sweetheart. Look. Up there. Doesn't that look like a man looking down at us? There. Near the big open pipe. Just in front. It looks as though he's sitting on something and has his hand raised.'

Hera looked, her eyes no better than Mack's in the fading light. And yes, she saw it now. It did look like a man. And yes, his hand was raised as though in greeting. But when she waved in reply, he did not move. 'Probably just a trick of the light,' she said. 'The frost can make strange shapes of the rocks.'

He was still there in the morning. In the clear light the shape was unmistakable. It was a man.

With the rising sun behind, his face was in shadow, but he seemed to be leaning forward as though to get a better look at them. He was still waving, and his other arm was back behind him, resting as though pointing. It was a strange, open posture – a sculpted pose, full of expression and energy.

Mack tried to guess what the white figure might be. Perhaps it was a statue, erected during the MINADEC days to honour some commercial baron – though why it should be placed in this remote place he could not explain. Alternatively, its very remoteness suggested a joke, perhaps played on a boss by disgruntled employees, like the grotesque drawings Mack had sometimes found on the wooden rafters of old buildings. Mack was sure that when he and Hera reached the figure they would find some crude and perhaps obscene effigy, and a scratched note referring to things long forgotten and people long since dead. Hera pointed out that, even at this distance, there was a fineness of composition and proportion, no hint of mockery, and Mack had to agree. His final suggestion was that what they were seeing were the frozen remains of some lonely wanderer who had got lost. Hera nodded at this, but she had her own ideas as to who it might be, and these, for the moment, she preferred to keep to herself. Neither could explain the pearly whiteness of the figure. It was not snow or frost, as the snow had melted and the frost had vanished with the coming of the sun. But the figure drew them to it, as much by its mystery as its friendly open welcome.

The path they followed wound back and forth, and for long periods it was out of sight, but then the next time they saw the figure it was nearer – and it was definitely a carved chair or a throne of some kind it was sitting on. Finally, they scrambled up a slope and came out onto the bleak platform where the figure sat. They had reached the place where the Organs began. Here, and on the neighbouring hills, were the grey and white pipes of the tuyau, jutting up out of the ground and pointing to the sky or twisting like serpents across the valleys. They moaned to themselves in the light breeze.

The view was magnificent. They could see right down to the sea, where the swell, still marching in from the storm in the east, formed great arcs in the water. Close to the shore the waves became foam-backed as they reared and broke. They could not see the bay where they had made landfall. That was hidden behind a hillside. Looking inland they saw the Staniforths magnificent against the blue sky. They were among the highest mountains on Paradise.

The figure on its throne was seated very close to the edge of the stone platform. In front of it the cliff fell away steeply. Mack approached cautiously from behind until he was close enough to reach out and touch its back. It was smaller than Mack had expected, but there was now no doubt that it was a man and he had once been alive. Even the tangle of his beard was preserved. But everything, his body and even his clothes, had been turned to a creamy white as though made from wishbone. He was wearing an open shirt and shorts. The scuff marks on his hiking boots and the laces, double knotted, and even the fibres of the laces, could be seen. The hairs on his arms, the knees – knobbly with age – the wrinkles at the neck, the thick splayed fingers of a man who worked with his hands, everything was perfectly preserved. At his feet was a small backpack, the top undone and the strap lying across his boot. Inside was a cut-down pipe and some leaves which could only be from the calypso. All were white. And the face?

Mack edged round in front of the figure and looked at the face. The man was smiling – a fierce kind of smile, but a smile none the less. One hand was raised, open-palmed – you could see the lines in the palm, and if you knew about such things you could have read his fortune. The other arm rested behind on the back of the throne, and seemed to be pointing to one of the large pipes. 'Go that way,' he seemed to be saying.

Hera had hung back. She had recognized the figure. It was, of course, her old friend Pietr Z. So this was where he had run to after escaping from the umbrella tree plantation. She might have guessed. He had often talked about the music of the Organs, and he knew more paths and ways to get here than anyone. She looked round the stone platform. It was one of his lookouts, no doubt of that. She could see where he had cleared the ledge, piling up little cairns of stones, each of them serving as a memorial to someone. She saw where he had chiselled and carved the chair from slabs of tuyau and bedded them into the rock platform.

Pietr Z often used to disappear on his 'sabbaticals', as he called them, for two or three days at a time and always alone. This was one of the places he would come to. Well, he had found a fine place to die. And he had no doubt planned it for some time. But it was very strange too. How had he managed to die with his hand up like that? And what kept it in position now? How come his body had not slumped? It was as though he had been frozen instantly.

She edged round to the front and reached forward and touched him, stroking his grizzled cheek. He was as hard as rock but with a hint of warmth from the morning sun. His body seemed to have fused with the slabs of tuyau that made up his seat. This was, Hera guessed, a more advanced form of the 'lacquering' that had so interested Shapiro.[14] Here, if Shapiro was right, the mind-matter of Paradise had done more than interfuse with human cells; it had taken them over completely, transforming them molecule by molecule into the material of Paradise itself. It would never weather. It would always retain this sharp and detailed clarity, for it was, in a way, alive, and would remain so as long as Paradise remained alive. 'Was this your reward, old man?' she murmured. 'Was this what you wanted?' She guessed that the answer to both questions was yes.

'So you knew him?' said Mack.

'One of the originals. In every way. Pietr Z. He came up here to escape. I'll tell you about him later.'

Mack sensed that Hera wanted a few minutes alone. He wandered

[14] See Document 11.

off to explore. The gaping mouths of the tuyau especially interested him.

Hera sat for a while with her back against the old man's knees, staring out. She looked in the direction he was looking. It was exactly the direction from which they had come. If you partly closed your eyes, you could believe you were floating. She found herself wondering if any of the red Valentine balloons had come drifting by this way. That would have been a sight!

'Well, old Pietr Z,' she said finally. 'I took your *Tales of Paradise*. Thought you wouldn't be reading it for a while. And you'll be glad to know that the last time I was at the plantation everything was doing well. And the bloody Tattersall weeds – remember how we used to curse them and chop them back? Well, they have proved to be a friend.' It was 'friend' which triggered her tears. Not heavy, and not causing sniffing. Just emotion coming out through the eyes. Tears for memory, and tears of gladness too, that she had had the good fortune to find him and say her last farewell. She suspected, though, that there might be more to this than just good fortune. In many ways her path seemed shaped. 'Did you hope I would find you, old friend? I think you did.'

Hera stood up and wished she had something to leave, some little token to mark her presence, and then she remembered how Pietr Z had always wanted her to wear her hair down. Men of his generation always liked women with long hair. Well, now she *was* wearing it long, and had got used to the pony tail bobbing at her back. She pulled a few strands loose, ran her tongue along them, twisted them, and tied them round the thumb of his upraised hand. 'There you are, Pietr Z. That's for you. You'll be glad to know I'm finding long hair very useful these days.' And as she released the hair, it turned white and stiffened and stopped blowing in the wind. When she touched it, it was hard and sharp, and although she did not try, she knew it would not break or bend, no matter how hard she twisted.

It was done, and it was good. With a last affectionate pat on his back, Hera turned away and set out to find Mack. As she did so, the wind blew across the stone ledge and several of the pipes moaned, their pitch rising and falling. It was a thrilling sound. An eerie sound. The true voice of the wind, but a gale was needed to get them really singing.

The weather, she noticed, was changing. The bright dawn was giving way to mist. Already the tops of the High Staniforths were lost in dark clouds, and she heard the rumble of distant thunder. This was the mountains, as ruthless as the sea. Here you kept one eye on the sky and the other on where you were treading. And when the mist came down, you stopped.

Mack was standing at the back of the platform of rock, hands on hips, staring down. Hera joined him and then stepped back hurriedly. At his feet was a precipice. 'Come back from the edge, Mack. I know you've got a head for heights, but a sudden gust and you'll be over.'

He stepped back and joined her. 'It's the same the other side,' he said. 'Steeper, if anything. These tuyau, or whatever you call them, seem to have burrowed up through the rock. Now how the hell did they do that? They must have come creeping up the valley, then up behind the hill over there, right through it maybe, and come out here. Bloody incredible. Anyway, do you want the bad news or the really bad news?'

'Give me the worst.'

'Well, the bad bad news is that if we want to get to the valley down there, we'll have to retrace our steps right back to where we started this morning and then drop down to follow that stream. I should have been thinking this morning when we set out. But then again we did want to see the old man, didn't we?'

'We did. So what's the bad news?'

Mack pointed down into the valley below them. 'Look there. The troops are gathering. Are they taking over the whole bloody planet or just the bits where we are?'

Hera had seen them too, the Tattersall weeds. They were standing in the valley just where she and Mack would have to descend. They would have to pass right through them. And they did look like troops, massed. Beyond them, in the far distance, right at the bottom of the valley, they could see where the small river, swollen by many tributaries, tumbled over rapids and emptied into a lake. 'There you are, Mack,' she said, pointing it out to him, 'Redman Lake. Remember Sasha's story?[15] And those are the rapids the Dendron came down, and the river there, that's the old Mother Nylo.'

---

[15] Hera is referring to 'Shunting a Rex'. See Document 6.

Mack nodded, but he was not paying close attention. 'The question I'm pondering is whether the old fellow came up that long way or took a short cut. Come and see what I've found.'

He led her across to the large and broken mouth of one of the tuyau. It was to this that the statue of Pietr Z seemed to be pointing. 'There, look at that.' Chiselled into the wall inside was Pietr's name and an arrow pointing down the dark passage within the pipe. Below the arrow were other words. Mack pointed at them. 'I can't figure these out.'

'Nor can I,' said Hera. 'That's his own language. None of us understood it. But, knowing him, it'll be something basic like, "This way to the best umbrella tree plantation on Paradise."'

Mack scratched his head. 'Why would he write directions in a language no one could understand?'

'He was like that. The message was for himself, his own mark, something personal. The arrow was for everyone else. It's clear enough.'

Mack was still bothered. 'You said he was escaping.'

'He was. He was afraid the authorities would send him off Paradise because he belted one of the inspectors during the Disestablishment. He came to a place that he thought of as his own, a place he knew well and where he would be safe. And make no mistake, Mack. He came up here to die. He'd got it all ready. And the message on the wall there is to help anyone who found him. Like us.'

In all of this Hera was correct – except, crucially, in her guess about the meaning of Pietr Z's hieroglyphics.

'So you reckon he climbed up and down here regularly?' Mack pointed down inside the dark tuyau.

'I'm sure of it. For years. This was his private path. And I reckon that if he used it, so can we. Why do you look so worried?'

'Look at it, Hera.' They both stared down into the pipe, which curved steeply away into the darkness. 'It's like a pathway to the underworld.'

'Well, it isn't. It is the internal cavity of a long dead plant and a short cut used by a kind old man whom I wish you could have met.'

'You're not afraid?'

'Of course I'm afraid. But if old Pietr points this way, that's good enough for me, and besides . . .'

'What?'

'Think about it. Mack. I've nearly been hung, drawn and quartered by a Tattersall weed; I've had a sexual experience with a Dendron – not to mention another big beast; I've dangled above a black sea at midnight on a boat that was nearly capsizing . . . This –' she nodded at the dark tunnel '– is nothing. All I want to do now is get you up and off this planet as quickly as I can. Then I'll start wearing white frocks for you and smell of lily of the valley and be a demure lady afraid of the dark, but till then bring on the demons. I'm Hera, remember, and my vengeance is legendary. Don't look so worried. You asked me to look after you and I am. Deal?'

'Deal! But I don't understand you sometimes.'

'Nor do I. But even so. Look over there.' In the valley below them the mist had settled, and rain had started to fall. The mist was already drifting past them. 'Are you telling me you want to go scrambling down through the wet and the Tattersalls? Or do you prefer a nice quiet stroll through a long-dead tuyau?' Above them the tuyau pipes called and answered across the misty valley, the sound stronger than before. 'Wait till these boys get going. They'll make Mahler sound like a Sunday school choir. Come on, Mack. The worst may be over.'

'Do you mind if I consult the pendulum?'

'I'd be delighted if you consult your pendulum. And if it says we don't go? We don't go. Meanwhile I'm going to bring the packs in out of the rain.'

While she did this, Mack fished out his ring with the twist of Hera's hair. By the time Hera had brought both packs up he was smiling. 'This is the best and safest route to the valley,' he said.

'Happy now?'

'Happier.'

'Then let's go.'

We may wonder what Mack had seen when he looked down that dark pathway into the earth. Was it another frightful memory from his dreams of childhood? Or some deep and almost inaccessible racial memory of the path to sacred knowledge? That path often traverses death and terror. Or was it simply that he associated the hole with the trap of the funnel web spider from his native Australia, or perhaps the dark place at the heart of a Michelangelo-Reaper?

Or was it none of these? My guess is that his instincts as a demolition man were jangling like a tocsin bell. The basements of a dying building are dangerous – you don't just go barging in. But since his intuition gave him no clear assistance, he turned to his pendulum, which never lied and always answered the question asked. And did it lie on this occasion? Perhaps he did not ask the correct question.

33

Down the Tuyau

They walked in single file. Hera went in front with the torch. This suited Mack, as he could see over her head. Above him there was ample clearance.

About a hundred metres down into the tunnel, at the place where it started to curve and they lost the daylight, they came across Pietr's campsite. His billy, his small stove, a sleeping roll, a spare backpack with clothes and a miner's helmet with a light, all were there. They took what they could use. As she was leading, Hera wore the helmet. Most important to her was the discovery of Pietr's wishbone walking stick. Pietr had carved the handle himself and he was rarely seen without it, even when doing routine work round the plantation. He had laid it flat on the ground, set apart from his other possessions. It was like an arrow pointing the way. Hera claimed it as her own.

They trudged on, getting deeper.

Rarely was their pathway straight. There were always bends in front, and surprises such as places where the tuyau wall had broken and branches poked in from the outside. At such places they had daylight and damp fresh air and, if they wanted, they could have climbed right out and made camp. But they went on, and as they got deeper such places became less and less frequent.

They found that walking in the tunnel took on its own reality. The outside world vanished. Their world contracted to what they could see with their small bobbing lights. There were just the walls, segmented by the slow growth of the plant, and the soft damp floor. The only sound, apart from the occasional tuyau moan, was the regular *pad-pad-pad* of their feet. They lost all sense of time and played games guessing how long had passed since they had entered. And they always guessed too short.

Talking as they walked was not easy and each remained in the private world of their mind. Having Pietr's stick gave Hera confidence and steadied her. For Mack's sake, she tried to look and sound braver than she felt, and when they stopped to talk she made jokes and teased him. But behind all this she was alert for any sign of a change in Mack. She had noted that he had become more passive since the visit to the bay of the Valentines. In part she knew that this was because he had tried to be a good crew member on *The Courtesy of MINADEC* – not the boss – but there was something else. He was, she knew, listening for a call and at the same time frightened of hearing it. He was like someone who is recovering from an illness and fears to feel the return of the symptoms. In trusting her, he had to some extent given up his mastery of events. So it was up to her.

Hera tried to keep her mind focused and practical, but it wandered to daydreams too. When she had mentioned wearing a white dress and smelling of perfume she was not joking. That was part of the new world waiting for her, a different world – not better, not worse than the one she knew, but a world she wanted to explore with him. She thought about how lonely she had been all these years. She had never realized. She wondered if Mack would ask her to marry him, formally, properly, in the old-fashioned way men used to. He more or less had, hadn't he? But then, when she became lost in such happy thoughts, she would stumble, or the light in her helmet would flicker, and she would be instantly on her guard. Daydreams could wait.

Mack, meanwhile, was trying to keep a grip on his fear. It was the dark, and it was being underground – but most of all, it was the growing feeling that there was something he had not understood. In those few moments in the Valentine bay, when the red globes danced in the breeze, he had heard a sweet siren call promising immortality, a new life, and it was still resonating in him. But for the life of him he did not know what it meant. It did not feel like death. But would he ever be free of it? Would he have a choice? Was he now condemned to wander with that tip of knowledge broken off inside him? And what of this woman who walked so confidently in front of him? She offered a new world too, a world in which he could let himself be vulnerable, because she was on guard. Sometimes he just wanted to pull down the shutters and curl up at her feet. Perhaps it would all be better when they were off this world, out of it, away. They would sit and talk, heads touching. And he would give her his granny's ring. When his mind settled on this, it became calm.

Several times as they were walking they felt wind sweep past them. Sometimes it came from in front. But most often it was from behind, and then it did strange things to their ears, making them feel dizzy. At such times they would hear a deep resonating growl which grew and grew until they could feel the air vibrate and they had no choice but to stop and crouch down with their hands over their ears. Sometimes the sound was like hammering. This made Hera sick, and she drank water and spat it out to clean her mouth. And then they would say things like, 'Lucky we weren't higher up or that would have been a real blast.' Or, 'Imagine what it must be like on old Pietr's seat now.'

Hera found that as long as she didn't let herself think about the weight of soil and rock above them, she could cope quite well. She told herself that the tuyau did not dig unnecessarily and hence most of the time they would be above ground, even if they could not see it. She studied the segments, each of which marked a year's growth, and wondered if old Pietr had ever counted them. Sometimes the segments were packed together. Not much climbing then, or perhaps all its energy was going into offshoots. At other times the segments were extended, up to ten metres between ridges. That was awesome growth. And did it just grow like a cucumber or did it wriggle? She would have to come back one day and ... No, she wouldn't.

Quite often they could see where Pietr Z had walked. The imprints of his boots and stick were distinct in the soft floor. The sight of the footprints was comforting, and Hera matched them, counting the paces for as long as she could. She was doing this, watching his footprints instead of looking ahead, when she almost fell down a hole. The tunnel suddenly dropped vertically, and when she looked down all she could see was a spiral and the reflection of her light in the water at the bottom. The tuyau must have been burrowing through rock here, as the growth was small from year to year and the walls were very segmented. *Steps*, thought Hera.

Pietr Z had hammered a cleat into the floor and sealed it with resin. A rope was attached to the cleat, and this vanished over the lip and down into the dark.

'Do you want me to go first?' asked Mack.

'No. If I go down and get stuck, you can pull me up. If you go and get stuck, you're stuck.'

'You're the boss.'

'And don't you forget it, sunshine.'

She took a grip and slithered backwards over the edge. This was the hardest thing Hera had done so far. She managed to dig her toes into the segments of the sides, but she hated the damp walls and the feeling of being totally enclosed, and she had no idea how deep the water might be at the bottom. But her training on Mars came to her aid again. *Concentrate on procedure.* She had an escape route. A man she trusted had come this way before. She had a rope and a big strong man on the other end of it. Mars had been worse. She would cope.

At the bottom her feet touched the water and she lodged her toes in one of the folds in the wall. She turned and, reaching out, could feel where the wall of the tunnel started to angle and become the roof of the new passage. She took another step down ... and she froze as she felt something brush against her ankle and move away. Her cry was involuntary.

'What's wrong? Drop your specs?'

'Ha! Ha! Very funny. I'm going into the water here and I got a surprise.'

She lowered herself one more segment and felt for the bottom with her toe. Still nothing. And so she went down one more. She was now well past her knees in the cold water, and again something brushed her leg. It felt like an eel. Twisting her body round, she could look down and see, in the light from her helmet lamp, where the tunnel curved and became level. The water did not extend far up it, so she must be in some kind of sump, and there was no telling how deep it might be. It could be very deep. It occurred to her that this might be the place where the plant rooted, the way all the plants did in Paradise. She thought about the Dendron and the Tattersall. Was that what she had touched? She tried one more step and the water came up to her waist, and this time she trod on the root – or whatever it was – but it didn't wriggle and she was on the

395

bottom. Cautiously she released the rope and began to wade. She came to a hidden step and almost fell forward. Now she was able to climb up onto the tunnel floor. The bottom was thick with sediment and the water became like thin mud, but she got through it by taking small steps. She was going up and, apart from the squishiness under her feet, she was all right. Moments later she was on dry floor again.

'Can you hear me, Mack?

'Yes.'

'I'm in the tunnel. On dry ground. The tunnel comes off that chimney. I'll shine my light so you can see. No problems. Except there's a hidden step, which was exciting. Could you just lift the rope for a minute and let me see its end?' The rope began to rise slowly. Where it had been immersed in the water it was twisted and muddy. There was more rope than hole, so that was what she had felt, and that was what she had trodden on. She shook her head at herself. 'You're getting too old for this kind of lark, m'gal,' she murmured, and then called out loud, 'OK, Mack. Start lowering the packs. No problems.'

She made two trips, wading back and forth through the water, and soon the packs were on the dry bed of the tunnel. Mack was descending. She saw his boots, and when they were about to enter the water she called, 'Hey, Mack. I think there's an eel or something in the water there. Gave me a bit of a bite. Just try and tread on it, would you?'

'You what?'

'Yeah. An eel. It's not too big. Might get up your trouser leg though.'

She saw him descend, and waited for the moment when he trod on the rope. And she heard him swear and then laugh.

'You'll pay for that.'

They moved on.

Steadily down.

The little adventure with the rope had been good for both of them. The tunnel had christened them, as it were, given them a fright, and now it was less threatening.

They came to a place where the tunnel opened up and became wide and high. To the sides were smaller tunnels. These were where the tuyau had sent out offshoots. Pietr Z had drawn little maps on the floor at these entrances, indicating where they led to. But Mack had no inclination to explore. He was looking at a blanket on the floor and the stub of a candle in a niche on the wall.

'The old bugger used to sleep here on the way through.'

'Well, he was older than you. A bit fitter probably, but he needed his rest.'

'But can you imagine that? I mean. Sleeping in here? Could you do that?'

'In the subterranean caves on Mars we had to sleep in the water sometimes.'

'Yes, but you had the right equipment.'

'Too right we did. The temperature was just above freezing.'

'But look at this, will you? A blanket and a candle. A bit bloody primitive.'

'He was a primitive man.'

'Even so!'

'I'm getting worried about you, sunshine. You'll be wanting milk on your muesli next.'

'Knock it off, Hera. And enough of that sunshine business! All I'm saying is that I admire someone who could sleep down here. I couldn't.'

'And he was alone too.'

'Yeah, that's true. He had some advantages.'

And so they went on.

If their humour seems a bit forced I invite you to put yourself in their situation. Forget the creepy VR games you play in which you are looking for Tutankhamen's bedroom or some such. Smell instead the damp air that Hera and Mack breathed. See the darkness in front and the darkness behind. Here you can't press SAVE and take time out. There is no sudden EXIT. Here any joke is welcome. Here any mistake is fatal.

Well? Say something funny.

As they got deeper they experienced the phenomenon of hearing the echo of their own feet. It always sounded as though something was following them. And it always stopped seconds after they did. More than once Hera turned round, and then Mack would stop and turn round and shine his torch up the passage. And they would laugh to one another, being careful not to shine their lights in the other person's eyes. At such times they would check to see that they were both all right and not getting too tired or hungry or thirsty or in need of a pee. And they would share out nibbly things such as the hard blue seeds of the thunder bush which Hera had gathered that morning before they set out, after letting Mack explode it. These had the flavour of aniseed and could be chewed for hours before they became bitter. And there were monkey nuts, which Mack had climbed for and thrown down for Hera to catch in her hat. Such little treats made the time pass more quickly.

And so they went on.

Down and down and down.

Hera's helmet light failed. They replaced the batteries, but the replacements didn't work. They must have been flat and Pietr had not disposed of them. Hera reached out for Mack's torch but it slipped in the transfer and dropped, and the bulb broke. So then they were down to their last torch and got ready to use candles. They made jokes about being old-fashioned.

Gradually the floor levelled. They both felt it.

Now they started to come to boggy patches where water had seeped in from the outside. They had to wade through mud, but undeniably they were coming to the end. It was twelve hours since they had started. By the time they emerged it would be night.

And the last part was the hardest. Isn't it ever so? They had to cut and fight their way out. Thick bushes filled the last hundred metres of the tuyau and had grown across the opening. These had to be cut through. Sometimes they were up to their waists in soft ooze, advancing only by inches as the heavy wet branches gave way. Much of this work fell to Mack and he was glad of it. He would cut a path through and then come back and carry Hera like a frog on his back.

Finally they felt their way up a bank, the air fresh and sweet, and at the top they were on dry land. The night was dark. No stars or moons shone through the heavy clouds. Their last torch showed only the trees around them.

Hera had a vague memory of something that Pietr Z had once muttered when they were out walking, something about a tuyau mouth just off the path. Perhaps this was the one he meant? In which case ... She pushed forward through the trees and shone her torch. There it was, overgrown now, but no mistaking it. 'Hey,

Mack,' she called. 'We must be close to where the three ways meet. One to the sea. One to the plantation and one to Redman Lake. We've come a long way. We're halfway home. It was worth it.'

Mack came stumbling through the trees, dragging the packs.

'Tomorrow,' declared Hera. 'We'll sort it all out tomorrow. Let's make camp here.'

They cleared a small area and pitched their tent. A candle wedged inside one of Hera's boots made it seem like a home from home.

While Mack went for a pee, Hera spread out the sleeping bags and a few things to eat.

Standing outside, they stripped off their muddy clothes, hung them over branches and crawled into the tent just as they were and snuggled into their sleeping bags.

'Welcome home. Have we done well, or have we done well?' asked Hera.

He leaned across and gave her a kiss. 'I've said it before and I'll say it again. You're a bloody marvel. Thank you, Hera.'

'Aye, but could we have done better?'

'What do you mean?'

'Well, we could have brought a corkscrew to open this.' From her backpack Hera produced a small bottle of wine. 'Courtesy of *The Courtesy of MINADEC*. I thought we deserved at least one treat.'

'Give it here.' Mack had it open in a moment, and they lay back, crunching seeds and drinking from the bottle.

When it was half finished, Hera leaned back. 'Do you want the bad news or the good news, Mack?'

'Give us the bad news.'

'A man's work is never done.'

'So what's the good news?'

'It's the same. And now you're going to set a new record for the longest kiss in history. It starts at my knees and it doesn't finish until you reach my ears, and I'm sorry about the mud, but you'll just have to get to like it.'

'I'm partial to a bit of mud.'

'Well there you are then. And then it's my turn. But don't blow the candle out.'

In the soft light of a candle, a tent can seem as large as a cathedral.

PART FIVE

Michelangelo-Reaper

34

Reaper – Mack

It was in the still dark dead of night that Mack woke Hera up, dragging her back from a dream of horses. She lit the candle and his face looked terrible. He was staring at her. 'Hold me, Hera. Hold me tight.' It was the voice of a man drowning. And she threw her arms around him and pulled him down onto her and said 'It's all right, Mack. It was just a dream, whatever it was. I'm here.' And she tried to rock him. 'Put your arms around me. I'm here.'

He wanted to make love and, while Hera would have preferred to lie still and comfort him, she was not going to risk seeming to reject him, so she welcomed it. It was frantic. He threw himself at her as if trying to use passion to blind himself, or her, to his nightmare. Looking back, Hera was able to say that it was the kind of love a man might make when he is going to abandon a woman. A last frantic gift of guilt. But of course she did not know that then, and she bound him to her, her arms around his back and holding him inside her, binding him with passion and hoping that he would feel her love and draw strength from that. And when he came, he sobbed and shuddered, and that was when she held him tightest, trying with her body and her love to say that for which there are no words, or ever could be. And she would not let him go when he wanted to withdraw. She whispered things that only lovers say and he stayed in her.

The medicine worked. He became still. She could feel his heart beating and there was sweat on his brow. He became still and soft and rested and finally dozed. That was when his weight became uncomfortable, but she was able to slip out from under him without him waking. She wiped his brow, and she wiped herself. And she looked at him and thought how noble he looked in repose. She thought of poor Shapiro. He had never looked noble; he had looked exhausted and dry and bony. But Mack? And she saw the slightest of smiles. One kiss, and then the candle was blown out and a last wry thought: *I'll be sore in the morning.* She draped his arm over her and went in search of sheep, not horses.

In the morning, when she stretched and squirmed round on her back, the tent was light and the roof was patterned with the shadow of branches. Mack was not there. Her first thought was that he was out having a pee or perhaps, if she was lucky, he might come tapping at the tent with a cup of something warm and a joke about women who couldn't take it. She groaned. She was too tired to start thinking up smart replies. But then with a rush she came to herself. She remembered the night and sat up. The bed was cool beside her. He had been gone some time. 'Mack?' No answer. '*Mack!*'

There came something like a spatter of stones thrown hard against the tent wall, and she saw their little shadows run down the tent to the ground. The shock of that got her moving.

'*Mack.*'

She stood up too quickly, and almost fell over when she caught her feet in the sleeping bags. Seconds later, down on her knees at the tent door, she was pulling at the Velcro ties, but the flap wouldn't open. Something was holding it from outside. She gave it one almighty heave; the fabric opened and she found herself facing the dark green spiky leaves of a Tattersall weed and a small blue flower just about to open. Naked as she was, she squirmed round the branch and climbed out into the small clearing she and Mack had stamped out the previous night. Tattersalls ringed the space. Perhaps they had been there last night. She neither knew nor cared. They were here now.

Mack's clothes were gone. She hopped in a circle as she tried to get her legs into her pants. She pulled on a top, still wet and a bit muddy, and then her meshlite overall with the zip up the front. Her hair got caught in the zip. She unzipped, pulled it free, re-zipped and then tied her hair back with a band. Boot was horrible and wet on her bare foot. And where was the other? In the tent with the candle. She pushed the branch out of the way and retrieved the boot. Forget socks. And all the time, even while she fastened her boots, she had an eye on the Tattersall weeds. There was one drooping that must have just scattered its seeds. Was that to wake her up? It was a thought. Hell, how could one know what the Tattersall weeds were about? Helpful one minute, threatening the next. And she was listening, all the time listening. Hoping to hear a step through the trees, a breaking of branches, a whistle, anything to say Mack was near or coming back from a morning stroll.

More organized now, she picked up her small backpack, which contained, among other things, their medical supplies and her own few treasures. Then she grabbed Pietr Z's stick and used it to push aside the Tattersalls. She barged through the branches that barred her way, jumped down to the path and looked around. No sign of him.

They had camped at a place where the small path turned quite sharply as it descended from the Scorpion Pass, which led to the sea. Only a hundred metres further down the path she could see the junction where the three paths met and where one of Pietr Z's silly signs was still in place. She ran down to the junction, and came to a place where the forest opened up. There, between the path that led up to Redman Lake and the path that led down to the plantation, a hill rose sharply, with a concave depression at its centre. Between its two arms, all the trees seemed blighted and bent out of shape. Some had withered, some had lost leaves. All had been leached of their colour and bent to conform to a pattern. She gasped when she saw it. It was the worst thing she could have seen: a whirlpool, a spiral, a vast curve of energy which travelled up the concave sides of the valley, over the top and so came back down inside itself. It was like a seashell: the unmistakable evidence of a Michelangelo-Reaper.

The only one way in was a dark arch that opened immediately opposite her. But follow that path and she would eventually come to the centre, the place where all the turning stopped. Hera remembered. She knew what she would find living there. Sitting in state, with its leaves raised like folded hands, would be a Reaper, but not like the little one that had played with her. This one would be big, really big if the size of its energy pattern was anything to judge by, and old too, presumably.

It had kept itself well hidden all these years, like a sleeping trap awaiting its time. There would be a stream nearby too – and yes, when she looked, there it was, meandering out from under the trees no more than a hundred metres from her, and then wandering beside the path that led down to the umbrella tree plantation. It had not been there before and was presumably the creation of the Reaper.

Had Pietr Z known the Reaper was here all the time and kept quiet? Of course he had.

Hera could see the marks on the dewy brevet where Mack had walked. The path led straight to the Reaper's door. Before entering that passage, Mack had removed his overalls, the ones which Hera had sewn for him, and had hung them on a branch. A sign for her?

A movement caught her eye. Something in the valley was changing. At the dark centre of the Reaper's hold a mistiness was gathering, and the air wavered and distorted like the air above a chimney where a fire burns but without smoke. She watched, her hand to her mouth, as up through the dark hole there grew a spiralling shape. It was at first like the tip of a black feather, with every plume distinct and perfectly traced as in an etching. As it rose it turned, and as it turned so its shape expanded. The feather pulled apart and re-formed slowly into a sphere, and that became something that Hera recognized as an eye. It was ill formed and clumsy but, as she watched, it became more precise. An eye with lid and lashes . . . Not a quick eye, but a surprised eye, or a wondering eye. Even as it turned she saw something of Mack there. But it was gone as the eye pulled apart and re-formed and became a hand – square-palmed with stubby fingers, firm and hard. It turned before her, slowly getting larger.

At this moment something shook Hera. It was as though a warm wind had blown right through her and she felt a sound inside herself like the breaking of a musical string. She sank down onto the soft green brevet and watched, all fear suspended. The world beyond the Reaper lost colour. Everything became monochrome except the changing shape in the air, and this gained colour and life and concentration as though warming. Hera was now – whether she liked it or not – within the sphere of the Reaper. She was no longer just seeing with her eyes, but with her imagination too. She was participating. No longer passive. She watched the hand open and close. The fingers flexed in the air and made strange complex shapes. The possibilities of the hand were being explored. For a moment it was a pianist's hand poised above the keys, and then a working man's hand. She recognized this. A hand for all seasons that could caress and wipe and become a hard fist when the need arose. She knew that hand too, and had held it many times. Even the little chip on his thumbnail was there, where he had damaged it on the boat.

The shapes were getting larger and swifter, growing with confidence, folding and unfolding through one another. They were high in the sky, turning and tumbling and changing with the speed of thought – no sooner done but thrown away. Many were abstract. Shapes and stains. But most were body parts, detached, but not in a bloody way. Reduced to form and line and texture. An ear became a toe became a nostril became the bulging biceps of a man with an axe. Everything was being explored, just as Hera would explore something exotic and strange that dropped from the sky, holding it up to the light and then shaking it to see if it rattled. Or . . . thinking differently, thinking of the Reaper through its other name . . . as a sculptor might explore the balance and form of a naked woman kneeling – changing the angle of the head, adding, taking away – before finally shaping his clay into a Madonna.

She was waiting for it, wondering, but despite herself she was shocked and pleased when the giant phallus, filling the sky above the valley, unfolded. What an odd thing it was, looked at this way, from a strange and unconventional angle. Ungainly and accidental-looking. An add-on. A single rose on a stripped tree. *And what would the Michelangelo make of that?* she wondered. Could it understand the organ's many functions beyond plumbing? Its slow erection and the blinding light that accompanied the movement suggested that Mack, in whatever form he now existed, was revealing all. But then again . . . Irrelevant thoughts teased her. *Where,* she wondered, *would he find a woman to tame that?*

Irresistibly, following the evolution, the phallus transformed to become his face. A surprised face, as well it might be. But what a composition! The hair, the eyes, the curl of the hair above the ear . . . The abstract and the real, holding together. The face was caught at a moment in time. Hera remembered the expression on Mack's face when she had confronted him at Monkey Tree Terrace and Dickinson had stamped on the ground laughing. So there was history too. Their history. Mack's history. A puzzled young boy. A grave-faced older woman. The Reaper was into his mind now, peeling him open. What more could be shown? Faces, faces, faces in all attitudes and emotions. She didn't want to watch. This was too private. We all deserve our darkness. This was becoming painful and dangerous. Hypnotic. Compelling. Hera began to lose her sense of who she was as the images twisted and coiled in the sky above. She wanted to look away – some intimacies should only endure the moment of their creation – but she could not look away.

But then, as though the artist had suddenly wiped his canvas clear, all images vanished save one. The last adjusted slowly, and Hera saw her own face staring down at her, with hair tumbling all over. She saw herself as Mack had seen her. Laughing as she teased. Crying briefly and then open-mouthed in ecstasy at the moment of climax. The Michelangelo, faithful recordist, humble archivist, saw the truth of them both.

The image grew until it filled the sky. It stretched across the horizon, killing the sunlight.

There came a moment of total stillness ... and then the face began to break up. The centre could not hold. And yet one more image managed to assert itself, just briefly. Hera could not make sense of it. She had to lie on her back to look up at it. It was like a tree, but with three trunks which grew into a complex knot, and at its top she could just see the tip of a gleaming silver blade-like flower. The tree held its shape for a few seconds and then began to waver in the air, and to revolve like something on a potter's wheel. And the faster it turned, the more quickly it contracted, centrifugal energy in reverse, vanishing like a column of water down into the dark chamber of the Reaper. Until ... finally there was nothing.

In the sudden vacuum Hera shivered and curled up on the damp green of the brevet. Then the warm breeze passed through her again. It was the Reaper withdrawing, its energy spent – and she lay for a few moments still. Then she sat up. Colour returned to her world. The blue of the Tattersall weeds. The patterned deep green of the brevet. The sky. The clouds. How unreal and empty everything looked after the tumbling brilliant images. But she was back in the real world, the world she knew. What she had seen was now only present in her memory, though undoubtedly alive in the world of Paradise.

Hera scrambled to her feet, picked up her backpack and, without hesitation, ran towards the dark entrance to the Reaper. She was remembering the story that the Reaper, after it had devoured its victim, returns the corpse and hangs it on a tree or some such.[16] She did not know the truth of the tale, but she wanted to know. Moments later she was under the trees. As she ran along the incurving path she found more of Mack's clothing. His vest. His boots. And finally his shorts. She could imagine. She had felt the grip of a Reaper on her mind. It would have forced him, stumbling, caught between the need to walk and the need to pull his clothes off. Plants could not understand clothes.

She ran on, round the path, which gradually became tighter and smaller. But it was well formed too. Welcoming even, with dappled shadow.

She ran on . . .

And on . . .

Until finally she stumbled through an arch of tortured trees. She had reached the centre.

There she saw the Reaper, and it was magnificent! Its great serrated leaves were raised. They were folded together like hands at prayer, and of a green so deep you could lose yourself in it. The edges of the leaves were rimmed with spikes which shone like silver. High above, on a thin stem, dangled the ubiquitous cherries of Paradise. These, as Hera knew well, were the sense organs that the Michelangelo shared with the Dendron and with other plants too. These cherries were very black and lustrous, and about each of them moved tendrils as restless as green snakes.

She was aware of the Reaper's presence, of its energy, of its consciousness as it allowed her to come close, allowing her in. Vaguely she realized that it was honouring her – a very human thought – though what this might mean to the Michelangelo-Reaper she could not guess.

She stopped in front of it. She saw the leaves move. She saw them start to open, to peel back, slow and languid; and as they did, the perfume of the creature came to her.

We talk of primroses and pineapples, of the foul combustion of a bloated cow and roses in the evening – it was all of this and more.

The leaves folded down, one by one, and lay prostrate on the

---

[16] Sasha Malik in 'If You Go Down to the Woods Today . . .' (Document 8) gives a humorous account of this kind of event.

ground. The last two opened – what was that image Mack had used once – 'like a choirboy opening his prayer book'? Well, it was not quite that, but there was something ceremonial and solemn about it. Behind the leaves stood Mack, his pose relaxed and statue-like. The great *David* she had seen in Rome stood thus, casual in his beauty. He was like an athlete after a race, not bent over and puffing, but using no more energy than is needed to stand. The muscles were firm but relaxed. She had seen Mack stand like that once: the moment after he had delivered the butcher's cut that severed the Dendron.

High above him hung a cluster of the dark fruit. It had become agitated with the prostration of the last leaf, and a rain now fell from each cherry, the drips making dark splashes on Mack's skin. Then the fruit lowered and Hera saw the care with which they touched him. His neck, his lips, his thighs, his feet – all places she had kissed at some time. And she saw the green tendrils wrap around his legs and arms and waist and then gently lift him.

He was carried up, held for a moment, and then brought towards her, the whole plant inclining. Finally, he was laid down before her like an offering.

The cherries withdrew high and drooped and the tendrils hung limp.

Hera saw Mack sigh, as though just waking up. And that small movement rolled through her like thunder. She knelt. And she was aware, more fiercely than ever before, of the pure lovely yeast-meal scent coming up from the dying man.

Hera closed her eyes and her heart turned to water.

3 5

Reaper – Hera

Edited transcript of interview

Hera O Olivia, if you could have seen him. He looked so handsome, lying there before me, younger in some ways but damaged too. He looked bruised, but those were the marks of Paradise on him – they were bruises of a different kind. He was aware of me, I could tell from his eyes. They were bright and clear and his gaze never left me. He could hardly speak. I could see the light fading in him. But there was an urgency about him too, and I came to realize that his coming back to me was an act of will. He was in some way keeping himself alive for me, when all he now wanted was to slip away. He lived elsewhere now, in the air and in the trees and in the roots of Paradise. Finally, I knelt down beside him and took his hand and leaned my head over his to catch his whispers – and sometimes we touched foreheads, just as we had so often in the past.

He had heard a call. It had come at dawn, and like me he had found it irresistible. He had simply followed it – docile, and yet filled with the habits which dressed him and made him close up the tent properly and even kiss me before parting. I discovered too that the Reaper that had summoned Mack had put the Tattersall weeds in place and made me sleep longer than I would have otherwise. There was nothing he or I could have done.

He whispered, 'Did you see me?'

I nodded. 'I saw you, Mack. Above the valley, in the sky.'

I saw his eyes soften. That was as near as he could now manage to a smile. 'Was I good?'

'You were very good.'

411

I saw him nod to himself, a small movement. He whispered, 'Wish Dickinson and the rest had seen me. They'd have laughed. Give them my love, Hera. I'll be thinking of them.'

He tried to move and I thought he might be in sudden pain. I tried to lift his head, but he didn't want that. 'Did it hurt you, love?' I asked.

'No pain. Just . . .' I saw him for a moment drift away, remembering ' . . . just the other. It's like my right hand now.'

I didn't understand that remark, but I could see the effort he was making, so I didn't push him. Now I know what he meant. He had taken over the Reaper as much as it had taken over him. It was biddable, and he, Mack, the true spirit of the man, not the sad being I was farewelling, was in charge. I was aware too of a depth of intimacy which I could not comprehend. It was more than my skylarking with the Dendron. Reapers take more and give more. Two had become one. He had entered its green darkness as surely as it had entered his mind and body, and there was something in me that was shocked by that, and if I am truly honest with myself, a bit jealous.

I saw him breathe deeply, and something of the old Mack was there in his eyes – like the times when he would spit on his hands before picking up the axe, or stretch in the morning so that I heard his bones creak or grumble before picking up his backpack. There was something he needed to say or do. I leaned very close, my head over his, and realized he would be seeing me at this moment as he had when being taken by the Reaper. That made me so happy. He whispered, 'Listen to me, Hera. You are in danger here and must get off Paradise as soon as possible. I am going to help you. But you must do something very brave. You—'

'What dang—'

'Sh. You can't know until you know. To be free from Paradise you must know more of Paradise. When you get back to Earth you must know more too. There will be many questions. You must be given knowledge. I jumped circles. Now, so must you . . . but not as far as me. Don't be afraid. I want you to stand and let the Reaper come close. Let it touch your skin. Don't be afraid. It will not harm you any more than I would harm you, and I will be waiting for you. It will be easier then, I promise. Take nothing with you. This . . . is too hard, too much in the head . . .' His voice just trailed away and I thought I was going to lose him, but he rallied. 'Let the Reaper come close. Do it, Hera. *Jump!*'

I was not clear what I was being asked to do. It was one of those moments when, if you think too much, you waver. The first time I slipped down into the dark cold waters on Mars I felt like that before I dived. All I could do was trust the words of my dying lover. I stood before him. And I felt shy as I undressed, for I guessed that was what he meant. But what was he handing me over to? Can you understand my fear, Olivia? What did he want? I felt terrible.

But, naked, I knelt down again. That seemed right. What else could I have done?

Olivia You could have said no. You could have run away.

Hera No, I couldn't. And where could I run to? There are times when you can't run, when you just have to trust. He saw my fear and struggled to his knees and he held my hands. His head was down, like a poppy before it opens, like one awaiting execution. And I thought, *This will kill him or me*. Then I felt sudden touches of rain on my skin. I looked at my arms and the marks were black. I twisted to look up and saw that the cherries were active, and their juice was touching me and staining me. And I knew I would carry those marks for the rest of my life. The tendrils too were reaching down. I struggled then and tried to stand and tried to pull away, but he held me and I felt the moment when the first of the cherries nuzzled my ear. I closed my eyes. Somewhere a scream was born inside me but . . . suddenly they were all around me like wasps, and still he held me . . .

No, Olivia, I'm all right. I'm all right. It is just that, as I tell it, so I see it and feel it. No, Olivia, I don't need a tissue, thank you.

Time. I have no recollection of time. But then I heard Mack's voice, and he said, 'Do you want to see some magic? You can open your eyes now.'

I did, and there he was, large as life, grinning from ear to ear. He looked perhaps a bit younger, and I thought, *That's allowed*. And I felt younger too, and I thought, *That's more like it*. I felt like I did that first morning after Sirius . . . and I was so full of energy and love that I tingled. He was wearing the clothes he had on when I first met him out at Monkey Tree Terrace, and me . . . I was wearing a white dress! I had never worn a white dress in my life.

413

I said, 'Why am I wearing this dress?' and he said, 'I was going to ask you the same thing.'

Think what that means, Olivia. And it took some getting used to. But oh, it felt so right.

Well . . . I glanced around. There was no Reaper. We weren't in the small clearing any more. We were outside in the sunshine and it can't have been too long after dawn either, as there was still dew on the brevet. My feet were bare.

He said, 'I thought you might like to see our children.'

I said, 'Really? We've got children now, have we? Well, I'd love to have had them first.'

He pointed behind me. I turned, and then I recognized where we were. It was the valley where we had divided the Dendron. And of course I understood what he meant. The valley was so different now. For one thing, there were thousands of Tattersall weeds and they were clustered round the two trees. The ground was torn with clawing. The twin trunks stood tall and looked magnificent. They had straightened and there was no sagginess about the bark. Even colour was coming back to them. One was deep blue like the parent Dendron, and the other was more purple. The flags were flying, the cherries were glossy and I could hear the tinkle of the Venus tears. But most impressive was that from the top of each tree there streamed a narrow beam of sparkling light and it went straight up into the sky.

'What is that light?' I asked.

He was amused by the question. 'That? You'll see a lot of that. On Earth too. Everywhere. It's the purest energy of all. It's the same energy that is in you when you sparkle. It's what drew me to you in the first place. There's probably a name for it on Earth, but I don't know it cos I'm just an ignorant demolition worker. It is what makes things happen. It's the "force that through the green fuse drives the flower", as Granny used to say when she was peeling onions. It's what holds things together, everything, body and mind.'

'Is it what makes your pendulum swing, Mr Galileo?' I made the question innocent.

He looked at me – and it was pure Mack. 'Yes. That too. That and more.'

'Like thought, you mean?'

'That and more. Hope and trust are good words too. And giving that which is best in you for the sheer fun of it. Love is not a bad word, if you want just one.'

'And where is it going, just up to the sky and then . . .?'

'Ah ha. I'll show you soon. It's a two-way flow of energy. Those flows are joined to a fractal point – and from there, who knows? That factors into untold dimensions.'

That phrase stopped me.

For a moment I had a sudden vision of such immensity, of the deep union of opposites. Of lines of energy that mesh the universes, giving and receiving. Interfused. Then I looked back at the two trees. 'Are they aware of us?' I asked. 'The Dendron was.'

Mack screwed up his face in thought. 'That's a tough one. Yes and no. They're sleeping, and will for many years. But in the way of this place. Everyone knows everyone else's business. You'll soon understand. Shall we go and visit the children?'

He took my hand and immediately we were standing on the two trees, him on one, me on the other, and we were each standing on the collar of the arch where they used to be joined. The holes that had been there were completely closed. 'Mack,' I said, and he pretended not to hear and to be polishing his nails or something. 'Mack, next time can we take it more slowly? I want to enjoy the ride.'

I stood with my back to the trunk and then I pressed my ear to it. I heard it gurgle. I tell you, Olivia, I've never had children, but that must be what it's like the first time the baby you're carrying kicks. Is it, Olivia?'

Olivia Well, I've had four children, but I've never heard a tree gurgle. But yes, I think it probably is.

Hera I called across, 'Are we here, Mack? Are we really here?'

And he said, 'Where the hell do you think we are
– Birmingham?'

'No. I mean, I'm not dreaming all this, am I?'

'You are here. Most of you. All the important bits. But there's also a little bit of you back there at the centre with the little bit of me too, and we are very safe and cuddled up together because there is one of the ugliest and meanest and toughest and most talented and brilliant of the Michelangelos looking after us.'

'Meaning?'

'*Me.*'

That took some thinking about

'Come on,' he said. 'Holiday's over. Now you've got to earn your keep.' Suddenly he was standing beside me. 'Let's go and spend a couple of minutes with that old fellow.' He nodded towards the big old Tattersall weed that had destroyed the SAS and which now sat peacefully in the morning sunlight and did not seem to have stirred since we had left. 'You want to float over. Is that right?'

I nodded.

'OK. But don't say I didn't warn you.'

And we did, Olivia, we did float, except I noticed that I didn't have a body, not until we landed among the Tattersall's giant branches. Then I was me again. My head was my head. My hands were my hands. And my feet were cheeky in the green brevet.

'I bet you didn't have breakfast this morning, did you?'

I shook my head.

'You see, as soon as I turn my back you stop looking after yourself. Have some of this.' He turned to one of the big blue petals. He called, 'Hey, Granddad, do you mind if my lady has a bit of this?' There was no reply. He turned back to me. 'He's not talking to me since I ripped the other one when we set out. Temperamental Tattersalls! He has no recollection of smashing up the SAS, by the way.'

'You're joking, aren't you?'

'Yes.' He tore a piece off the flower. 'Here, have some of this and let's sit down and think.'

We sat down between two of the branches, our backs to the tree. Mack would never have done that before. We were looking down at the baby Dendron and the river and the young Tattersall weeds. From behind us, in the depths of the forest and up on the hills, we could hear the fluting of plants which were still coming to terms with the daylight.

'Peaceful, eh? Pretty much like it was before the *Scorpion* came, wouldn't you say?' I was aware of a subtle change in his manner. 'Well, it isn't. I'm going to show you the problems of Paradise and you can carry the message back to Earth, Hera.

'People probably won't believe you, so you'll just have to find a way to convince them. But two things before we go. We're going to enter by the root of this old fellow and travel down. As we get

deeper you are going to feel very confused, because we'll be meeting up with the roots of other inhabitants until we come to the
place where there is only the one root and that covers the whole
of the interior of Paradise. That place is the most confusing of
all, because every plant on Paradise, every blade of brevet, every
fart-in-a-trance jenny, every umbrella tree, every plum, hybla and
monkey nut is linked at the deepest level of all. So there are no different "plants", as you called them, on Paradise. There is only one
consciousness, and it has many manifestations.

'There was a time when it basked quietly, this world which you
call Paradise, content with miles of ocean and the tug of the moons
and the winds and the tides. It was as unruffled as a deep pool in a
running stream. And the great charge and discharge between, say,
the Reaper that you know and the sky above was so effortless that
there were no stress lines to see. But there is a sickness now. It is in
the root, and you are going to feel it. If you are prepared to. I can
take you down, but I can't take you there like a tourist to a place of
execution or show you a picture or simply describe it because . . .
because that is not how things are here. You feel it, and then you
know the truth. You will, for a time, be part of the darkness. Is that
all right, Hera? Don't be afraid. That is one of the dangers. I won't
let you go too far, because I want you in a fit state.'

'For what?'

'For when I take you to the moons.' That reply I was not
expecting.

'You said one of the dangers. What are the others?'

'Ah yes. When we get down there and the going gets bad, don't
be surprised if there is a change in me. But try to stay very close.'

It was not so much his words but the tone that bothered me.
'What sort of change?'

'More me. More as I am . . . now.'

'How do you know all this, Mack? You've only been here an
hour or so.' He laughed when I said that. And he replied, 'Think,
Hera. Call me Mackelangelo, why don't you. Or Mack the Reaper,
if you prefer. I've been here a very long time. Since "Before the
Romans came to Rye or out to Severn strode".'

Of course I had forgotten. He was so like the man I knew. But
yet he wasn't the man I knew. Now he was as much a plant of
Paradise as a man of Earth. I had to keep reminding myself of that.

It was so like the old times, Olivia. And all the fun that was in him! I thought of all the fun we might have had together. It was a sad thought, really, but I couldn't feel sad. Sadness just wasn't an emotion that was available.

Olivia   And then he took you underground?

Hera   And then he took me underground. Except it wasn't like underground, like under the soil, at all. I was apprehensive though. I still remembered Mack's comment about the Tattersall weed being like an old man having a pee in a bucket or something like that when it put its root down, and that had sort of conditioned my attitude. I didn't like the idea of grubbing about in an old man's urinal. Don't look like that, Olivia!

But of course it wasn't like that. First of all, Mack talked to the tree somehow, and then he said we had its permission. I think that was all done for my benefit. The Reaper and the Tattersall weed would have a much more direct way of dealing with things. All I know is that moments later all the blue flowers on the Tattersall weed opened, and the one near me was very large – or I was smaller or something. Mack stepped up to one of the flowers and it closed round him. So I did the same. The next thing I knew I was like a small ball of light and I was travelling very fast. Whether it was down or up I had no idea. Then another ball of light joined me and fused with me and it was Mack. We travelled together. At first it was like . . . Have you ever swum in a strong river, and felt the current buffet you and throw you about, and when you try to swim against it, your arms are like blades because they just slip through the water, and you end up going backwards, so you just go with it, and let it take you where it will?

And then it changed. It was like . . . Have you taken a bath when you are very tired and you get the water just right and you lie down and just relax? Well, it was like that. But when I relaxed I saw moments from my life, happy moments by and large. I have a theory that since I can not experience what a plant feels, my mind, or whatever part deals with such things, goes hunting for analogies. So a talking jenny full of seeds 'burps' in contentment and that reminds me of one of Shapiro's famous post-graduation suppers where we were all full of wine and food. Or the wind blows through one of the beautiful girl-in-a-trance trees and I remember the fear and excitement of going up to the top of the Eiffel Tower with my mother and the wind in my hair. That kind of thing.

But later on, when Mack and I got right down, really deep, in the place Mack talks about where there is nothing but the energy of the root, I could not take any of it in. I was just there, and all about me was delicious fire and blazing energy. Ah yes, Olivia. I have used that language before, haven't I? I didn't have any precise analogy for that, just the lovely feeling of being stirred. I was experiencing a planet just getting on with its life. 'An ordinary day at the office', as Mack would say. But then things began to change. We reached a place where Mack became more remote. I could still recognize him, but he was edged with energy, like an aura, I suppose, and it pulsed very slowly. 'Be careful now,' he said.

Suddenly everything changed. I was on a road, and there were people throwing stones at me. I was running away hoping to hide in a stand of Crispin lily, but I only had one shoe on and my feet were cut. A stone hit my arm and I started to bleed. The people were catching me. Suddenly others were in front of me. I knew they were going to kill me. The people came very close. They formed a ring around me and one pushed me down to the ground. They were chanting, 'Whore. Whore.' There were men and women and children who pelted me with stones from close quarters. A child, a little boy, he couldn't have been more than three, ran up and threw his handful of pebbles in my face and then scampered back to his mummy and daddy for praise. And then, when I cried out for mercy, Mack stepped in and they became still, frozen like they were in an old tri-vid that had jammed. I could see the hatred in the faces, the raised arms, the spit in the air, the lust in cruelty, delight in injury and righteous indignation. One by one they softened like candles by a fire, but they turned into water, dark water, like tincture of nettle, and that water drained into the earth quickly, as it does on Paradise. I felt my terror and pain, and my anger too. How I wanted to kill them all. What emotions! So fierce! They took me over. But I too dissolved and drained away into the soil of Paradise. And finally I was me again. I remembered there had been a stoning, in the early days, over some infidelity or accusation of witchcraft. It was a community in Northern Chain. It had been hushed up . . . but it had happened.

The world turned about me. I was in a new place. I was young and very excited and I was holding my boyfriend's arm as he climbed down out of my window. It was dawn, and I was in my bedroom leaning out. My thick dark hair tumbled down. He'd stayed longer than he should. We'd both slept in. We were getting too confident. The danger was my dad might wake up, and then there would be trouble. My boyfriend jumped down into the garden and turned to wave, but my father reared up from behind a hybla and aimed his rifle and shot the boy at point-blank range right in the face. There, in front of me. I saw his head explode, like a melon. The blood reached to my face. Christ Lord love us, I had bits of his skull in my hair. If the shot had not woken the neighbours then my screams surely would. Again Mack was there and the scene froze. The angry father dissolved, the boy dissolved and I did too. We ran like blood in the gutter. And I was Hera again.

This story was one I knew. This was Sasha's story, wasn't it, about Valentine and Francesca?[17] Sasha made it a song of love, but I knew the truth. The real Francesca ran away from home that morning, and they found her next day hanging in the ravine at the bottom of the garden. Two months after the shooting Mr O'Dwyer, the father of the young man, poured kerosene under the Pescatti house and burned it down, killing them all. That was how the love story ended in the real world.

But we had not finished. Next I was a young woman up a ladder and I was picking Paradise plums in an orchard. My basket was half full. I paused to wipe my brow because I was sweating and my shirt was damp and clung to me, and I was suddenly aware of a man in the shadows. He had come from behind and was looking up under the tree, looking up where I was.'

'No, Mack. This I don't need. This I don't want. Stop it.'

Instantly he was there. 'Shall we get away from this place?'

I nodded and leaned against him and closed my eyes. 'I have seen enough to understand. Take me somewhere clean.'

I was not aware of motion, but I was aware of leaving that place. It was like a fly must feel as it pulls free of the spider's web.

Then suddenly there was water around me. Warm and slightly salty. I had swum in it often. We were out in a bay, Mack on his back doing his imitation of a whale. Me? I stopped in the water. I didn't want to swim. I wanted to make for shore and look for my towel and dry myself and put on my clean white dress and try to get the horrible images from my mind.

The water was shallow and the bottom sandy as we waded ashore. Mack shook the sand out of my towel and threw it to me. All the while he had not said a word, and I was glad of that because silence was safer for the moment. But I was aware he was watching me, and probably in the way of this world he already knew what I was thinking, but that did not occur to me then.

When I was dry I put on my dress and sat on the beach looking out to sea. I began, 'Let me see if I have got this straight. Correct me if I go wrong, Mack. The root of Paradise – let me call it that – at its deepest level, is the consciousness of Paradise. Is that right?' He nodded. 'And what has happened on Paradise, I mean the things that have happened – the conscious acts of cruelty, the deliberate violence, the hatred, rape and so on – they have carried a kind of dark energy. And that energy has flowed into the consciousness of the planet somehow. And now it is everywhere. Everything has now been stained by the hatred and anger that I have just felt. And it is us – I mean everyone who has come here since the *Scorpion* landed – who have introduced this pollution. That is what is meant, isn't it, by the people turning to liquid and draining away and into the soil?' He nodded. 'And that is the problem?'

'That and more.' He looked at me steadily.

'Go on. I'm not quite with you yet. I'm still . . .' I looked for words. 'I'm still down there.' I shivered.

'It is more than a stain, Hera. The very essence of what you call the root is that it is alive in a special way. It is more like your brain, really. It is dynamic; it can learn; it can change. But it is not a thing, like a root or a brain. If it were to die there would be nothing. It is not like wishbone, resilient and strong and able to spring back. If it dies it is gone. It would not leave a cavity, just an absence. And Paradise would be finished for ever. Just like the Dendron we managed to save would have been finished for ever. Remember your words: "One. One only. *One* in the whole of the entire universe. *One*. Think of that. One. The last. The only. The never, ever, ever to be repeated." A child of our universe – and we pulled it back from the brink, Hera. You and I. And for that you are honoured by being here now.'

He stopped and looked round. 'All of this, everything you see about you now, is a manifestation of that great energetic, creative force that we find at the heart of Paradise. It is not just here on happy little Paradise, it is everywhere; and everywhere it manifests differently. Earth has its own special and totally unique representatives, as does Paradise, as do all the countless worlds where consciousness has taken form. But here it is under threat, and the threat is now within for exactly the reasons you give. Paradise is a very reactive place. Look how the Dendron sought you out, and look how you reacted. Talk about providence in the fall of a sparrow! Here you only have to think of it falling and you have an impact. And that is of course what kept this world innocent and safe for so many eons. A world in which a Dendron could happily trample on a hybla and never know of killing, or malice, could now learn to kill intentionally.'

Mack saw the expression on my face. 'That may never happen,' he said quickly. 'Our little ones are safe. Your love is in them. And as long as I am here, it will not happen!' Then he shook his head sadly. 'But you see the danger. A world which never knew of violence, because here every end was always a beginning and the essence poured back into the soil, has learned the idea of killing. It learned it in the shells which felled the Dendron, the saws which toppled the trees, and the devices which were used to explode the Reapers, as well as in the hatred and blood which were in the air and on the land. Why do you think the first plums became toxic? Because they were fighting back? No. There was no way that could have happened. It was an accident; it was contamination from the root and it was felt in the plum first simply because, of all the forms on Paradise, the celebrated plum was the most sensitive and the most concentrated. The contamination took the form of poison because anger or hatred must always do harm to realize themselves. And some poor bugger ate the plum and got sick. And the Newton kid died. And then we, we Michelangelos, became Reapers, we Tattersalls gained claws and learned how to kill. But slowly. We are still pretty backward, otherwise I don't think you or I would have made it as far as Moonshine Bay.'

'Mack,' I said. 'This is me, Hera. I am not a stranger to you. You are sounding angry.'

'Ah yes. There is some of the poison in me, and that is because I spend time down there, there where the darkness gathers. The fisherman smells of fish. Sorry. I'm not angry in myself or worried for myself. Anyway, that same Paradise which welcomed the merry crew of the *Scorpion* because it did not know what danger was, has learned terror at the hands of the alien. Fear and hatred and anger – they don't *make* anything – they haven't the wit – but they contaminate. And that is now manifesting on Paradise. And that is why you are in danger and why you must leave. Remember that madman who tried to kill you with a chair . . .'

'Proctor Newton.'

'Yes, him. Or those people who hung a silly Tattersall weed outside your door to terrorize you. That was the instinctive reaction of rottenness to that which it knew was its enemy – something that could love. Well, that rottenness is here, now, and there is no hiding place for you. You are a double target. You are both alien and good.'

I had never heard Mack speak at such length or use language such as this. If I had not known before, I now was convinced that it was the Michelangelo that was speaking.

'Will Paradise close down?' I asked finally.

'Completely. We will play to our strengths. We will lick our wounds and we will learn to play again. And perhaps, in a million years or so, we will have Dendron again, running all over plants that are happy to be trodden down as the price for hearing its bells. You can see why I wanted you to come here. I know the touching of the cherries made you scream but hey, a small price for so much knowledge. There is so much to say, so much to show.'

'It's a lot to take in,' I said.

'It's all very simple,' he said. 'You know most of it already. You just needed a nudge. That's all you've ever needed.'

'Speak for yourself.' I looked at the beach and the trees, and then I lay back on the sand. At that moment I felt I could stay there for ever. Just lying still. 'Come close, Mack.'

He lay down beside me.

'I know I must leave soon, but there are so many things I want to ask.'

'We have a little time yet before I—'

'Sh. Tell me about the Tattersall weeds. I don't understand them at all.'

'Ha! The Tattersall weeds. Put your head on my arm and your arm across my waist—'

'Ma-ack.'

'And I'll tell you a story. Now hush. Once upon a time there was a big tall Tattersall weed that had never shed its seeds.'

'Not like you.'

'No, not like me. I'm a Mackelangelo and we do things differently. Now do you want this story or not? OK. Pipe down. Now the thing about Tattersall weeds is that they are always curious, always wanting to poke their flowers into everything. They are very sensitive to smell too. And this Tattersall weed thought himself really lucky because he had grown up in a place where there was a lot of talking jenny and fart-in-a-trance close by, which wafted every time there was heavy rain, and there was a sugar lily above, which dropped its nectar down on him whenever he wanted. Well, the sugar lily grew faster than he did. The result was that whenever he wanted some nectar, he would call out to the sugar lily and it would tip its prow in response, but the nectar would miss the waiting blue flower and hit the sleeping jenny instead . . . and talking jennys are indifferent to sugar lily ooze. Now, as I say, Tattersall weeds are all very curious, and this one found that if he flopped his frond over the lap of the sugar lily he could get a leg up, as it were, and hence have more chance of getting the nectar. He got quite good at this, and the sugar lily didn't seem to mind, but then one day, he gave an extra heave – the sugar lily had grown a bit taller, you understand – and *pop*, his root came right out of the ground. *I'm in trouble*, he thought. *Any minute now I'm going to turn to water. If only I can connect up*. And he tried to. He tried to flop back down onto his root. But he missed – perhaps the sugar lily had moved a bit – and he landed on top of the primed-and-ready-to-squirt orifice of the talking jenny. The jenny was not impressed, but squirted anyway, which gave the Tattersall weed such a shock that it jumped again and dragged the jenny, root and all, right out of the mud. At this the jenny decided that enough was enough – it was going to take retirement and turned to liquid on the spot. As luck would have it – and we all need a bit of luck in such things – the root of the Tattersall weed struck the root of the jenny and thought to itself, *Well, it's not my root, but it's a pretty good root. So why not?* And it linked up.

'And thus the Tattersall weed learned how to flop about and join up. It was never very elegant, but it could now satisfy its curiosity. And it discovered that it didn't need a jenny, or any other plant, because if it just lowered its root, the root would burrow in and link up with any neighbouring root. It told all the other Tattersall weeds and they started to clamber about, but only at night when the sun was out of the way, or they ran the risk of drying their roots. Time passed and all was well.

'But then the *Scorpion* arrived. And shortly after that, a lot of other new and strange and interesting beings came wandering about, like little Dendron, and there were new smells too, and so the Tattersall weeds became more active and started to hang round the houses and the rubbish dumps and the chemical latrines where the smells were very strange. But by now some of the damage we've talked about had already been done, and the lovely deep consciousness was stained, and so when a Tattersall weed put down its root, it could never be sure whether it would find a clean root or something tainted that would, in the way of such things, infect it. And when it got a tainted bit of root it started to lash out and it discovered it could kill. Not just chickens, either. It wanted to move more and so, instead of flopping and scraping with its branches, it grew tiny spines like it had on its seeds and found that with these it could grip the soil or other plants and drag itself along. Primitive, but it worked. And the consciousness of the planet put this to good use, and the Tattersall weeds became the great nurses of Paradise. But to this day, when you meet a Tattersall weed, you can never tell whether it has a rogue root or a healthy one. But you soon find out. Anyway, that is how the Tattersall weed learned to walk.'

'Thank you. And where did the Tattersall weed learn to help other plants?'

'It had always done that, with its perfume. So when it learned to move it just followed its instinct.'

'And are there a lot of rogue Tattersall weeds?'

'Not too many. More than there were. Enough. And increasing. Especially where there used to be towns and houses. But so are the good ones too. And now . . . listen.'

425

I heard a noise in the air. It came from beyond the headland, and moments later a flyer like an old fashioned SAS came over the headland and prepared to land. It set down on the shore about a hundred metres from us. On its side were stencilled the words SCORPION SURVEYOR.

'You always said you wished you could have seen the illustrious Estelle Richter. Here she is.'

The door opened and a woman jumped down. She was wearing a bulky meshlite suit and still had her mask on. I saw her open her mask and breathe. And then she lifted her mask off completely and threw it down on the sand. I saw her call to the others.

One by one, they came out. This was the crew of the *Scorpion*, Olivia, and they spread out and they called to one another and played a game on the sand. And then Estelle came along the beach towards me and Mack. She was holding hands with this tall lanky long-haired lad who was trying to grow his first moustache. They couldn't see us. Estelle came right up to me and . . .

Olivia And?

Hera And I'm sorry to disappoint you, Olivia, but we have all been too much influenced by that picture called *First Landing*, in which Estelle looks like Botticelli's Aphrodite. Estelle did not look like that. She looked better. She was a sturdy ginger-headed girl with freckles and blonde eyebrows. And when she laughed, her whole face lit up. The story is true about her bathing. It was a dare from her boyfriend, and she stripped off and plunged into the sea in her bra and pants. And she splashed water at him until he came in. They took their clothes off in the sea. Then they wandered away into the woods, where I trust and pray they made love because that is what Paradise is good at.

Olivia I prefer your version to the original. And what happened to you?

Hera Mack and I left them playing. We floated up for a while, and in the distance, far out to sea, I saw a Dendron which was making its way towards the shore in great holloping strides, coming to see what all the fun was about.

Mack took us up slowly. He asked if I was all right. It was strange being so high and without a suit or the walls of a shuttle – but then I didn't have a body either. But if you don't have a body, well . . . you don't worry about falling or breathing, do you? Soon we were reaching the edge of the atmosphere and entering the true velvet blackness of space.

We moved above the green, white and blue face of Paradise. He was taking me towards Tonic, and when we were close, I mean, ten or fifteen miles above its surface, he asked me to look about. I saw the stars. I saw my love star, Sirius, and all the colours of space. And Mack seemed sort of mischievous, and so I knew he was up to something.

Mack said, 'You see how things are?' spreading his arms and pointing round.

And I said yes, though really I had no idea what he was talking about.

Then he said, 'Now close your eyes. I'm going to count to three, and then open your eyes and tell me what you see.' This was just like the games we used to play. He counted one, two, three . . . and when I opened my eyes, I saw the space about us was beginning to change. New bright lights were appearing, but the stars were getting fainter.

'What are those points of light?' I asked.

'Fractal points,' he replied. 'At least that's what you call them. To me they are points of natural energy. "Therein all time's completed treasure is." Watch.'

I saw light spring up from the surface of Paradise until it was an incandescent ball radiating energy into space. The darkness backed away. All the bright fractal points joined up in a vast three-dimensional web, above and below and to the sides, and the energy that was flowing in that web was greater than anything I could conceive of. It was all about us. It was in the spaces between stars. It was more solid and stable than crystal or diamond and brighter than both. And still it grew. Connections made connections. Yet it was never confusing, and I knew where I was and who I was, and that if I had wanted to, I could have moved to any point in space or time. I could, Olivia. I could have gone back to my moment under the light of Sirius, to the death of my father, to Earth in the time before dinosaurs.

I said to Mack, 'What am I seeing? Is this the universe as it really is?'

And do you know what he said? I give his words to you as simply as they came to me. He said, 'All you are seeing now is the impress of our love. To see the universe as it really is, you have to see every atom and its history, every molecule and its history, and so on round and round the spiral until . . . and still you are not there, because there are dimensions beyond dimensions where finally dimensions disappear. Only then are you at the bottom of the ladder. But hey, I didn't bring you up here for metaphysics, sweetheart, but so you could see what you have done. Not bad for a little lady, eh?'

'I couldn't have done it alone, Mack.'

'Nah. That's true. The workhorse carries the load. But you did the steering. And does it matter, finally? How can you tell the dancer from the dance?'

God, I wanted to kiss him then. But it is hard to kiss when you don't have hands to hold with or lips with which to kiss.

Mack said, 'You have one last wish, Hera.'

'Need you ask, Mr Mack?'

We went back to the tent. The tent as big as a cathedral. At some point in the night I asked, 'Can a Mackelangelo reach as far as Earth?' I needed to know. He said, 'To Earth, yes, and beyond a million, million Earths. Love and thought do not obey the inverse square law of matter.'

I know you find scientific language unromantic, Olivia. But those were the words of love I wanted to hear. I now knew I would never lose him. Nor he me. Now and for as long as it matters, which can be an eternity for me. And at last I could go. Happy, free – as full as I need ever be of salt and honey.

And in the morning, he said, 'You like paradoxes, don't you, Hera? Well, here is one. I can reach Earth but I can no longer walk with you over Paradise, not even back to New Syracuse. That is beyond my parish. I will do what I can to help, but you will walk alone. As you walk, I want you to remember these things only: that you have all the knowledge you need to get home, and that you have more friends than you know. So, when the going gets rough, remember the Dendron. Got that?'

'Yes, Mack.'

'God speed, Hera.'

I was again at the clearing.

To my dear dying love, now so still under the watching cherries, no more than a few minutes had passed since I had left. But his breathing was almost still and only his eyes had light. I was kneeling beside him and words came into my mind: *We bring them into the world and we see them out again.* A woman's lot, Olivia, to see them into life and out of life, though it leaves us grieving.

He was looking at me and there was an intensity there. He was trying to say something but could no longer form words. I was holding his hands, and it seemed that the tension was in his right hand. I turned it and looked at it, and there was his ring, his granny's ring, still with my hair attached.

I took the ring and I held it before his eyes, and I waited until I saw him focus. Then I placed my finger, my index finger because it was a bit big for the others, in the opening of the ring. And slowly I slipped the ring on my finger. And then I closed my hand into a fist. The first was for love, the second was for strength. And he saw. And he knew. And I heard the rattle in his throat and I put my ear close to his lips. I heard his last whisper: ' "Till . . . the river jumps over the mountain . . . and the salmon swim in the street".' I watched his eyes. They were soft and warm, and then they slowly set as his spirit withdrew.

I moved quickly then. I do not know whether he was conscious or not, but I got the scissors from my first-aid kit and I cut my hair off. I cut it as close to the scalp as I could. And I laid it on him. On his brow. On his chest. Round his arms like a warrior. On his stomach. On his manhood. Round his thighs. Over his knees and down round his ankles. Thus I laid him out with my hair as his shroud. I was just in time. I saw the last light die.

And then, as I expected, I saw him dissolve. The body slowly turned to water. Not all at once, but gradually, and the parts in contact with the soil changed first. The buttocks and legs and back of his head became glassy, and then jellied and finally drained away. He sank lower into the brevet. I began to see the leaves through his chest and neck and through my hair. Then his cock, entwined with my hair, vanished into the soil. His smiling peaceful face remained for a moment, glimmering, and then it too slowly evaporated. And my hair went with him.

And that was it. It was an ending.

I was now alone.

And we who live on, must move on.

36

Disestablishment

Hera stood up.

She was aware of urgency now. She found her clothes and began to dress, but then an instinct told her that was not wise. Meshlite overalls were a clear sign of the alien. She would be better dressed in Crispin or even hybla. But boots. She would need boots. She would be walking over stones. And she would need the small pack too, with the radio and first-aid kit. The pack also contained two of her most valued possessions – Pietr Z's copy of *Tales of Paradise* and the Shapiro notebooks. She would not leave them behind. She slung the pack over her shoulder and picked up Pietr's wishbone stick, and set out. She remembered seeing a large Crispin at the entrance to the Michelangelo's labyrinth and she set out round the long curving path. Soon she was running. She imagined Mack running beside her and knew that as long as she was in the labyrinth nothing could touch her. The danger would be outside.

She reached the entry portal and it took her less than a minute to pull down one of the large Crispin leaves. It had the texture of fine chamois leather but, unlike the leather, it turned away rainwater and did not absorb it. She tore out the stalk to make a space for her neck and draped it round her shoulders. She punched holes for her arms and drew it close about her. Then she ran out onto the open brevet.

While she had been inside, some Tattersall weeds had dragged themselves onto the path and the way up to Redman Lake and down to the umbrella tree plantation was closed. *So they're moving closer*, she thought. *Friend or foe?* It was impossible to tell. Then one of the Tattersall weeds stirred and threw two of its branches forward, dragging itself crabwise.

Hera sprinted ahead of it onto the path before it could cut her off. The path to the sea seemed open, no Tattersalls waiting, and so she ran as quickly as she could up the gentle incline. The weed could not match her for speed and she had soon left it far behind. She stopped for a few moments to catch her breath and then moved on.

Several times, as she trudged along, she had the impression that someone was walking with her. They were not by her side, but behind her, where Mack had been when they were coming down through the tuyau tunnel. And that, she realized, was a kind of message for her. She was not alone, but she was not dependent either, and she would make it under her own steam. Once she was prompted to look up in the sky, and there was an oval cloud above the hill. It did not take much imagination to turn it into a face.

Soon she was at the crest of the pass, and from there she could look down to where the sea moved with an oily heaviness in the bay. In the misty distance she could see the gaunt cliffs of Dead Tree Spit. She could not see the remains of the old Dendron.

Hera jogged down the hill. The sun was now high and no cooling breeze came from the sea. Without her hair to protect her, sweat started at her neck and ran down her back. How wise she had been to make a Crispin cape. Meshlite overalls would have been chafing her by now.

Before reaching the bay the path became a zigzag, following the meanderings of the stream. This stream ended when it met a sandbank and formed a small clear lake. This had once been a children's swimming pool, in the days when families came to picnic by the sea. Beyond the dune was the bay, and Pietr Z's small boathouse on the hill.

On impulse, Hera removed her cape, boots and backpack and waded in, sinking up to her neck in the cool water. Stage one complete. For some reason she felt safer now that she was near the sea. She examined the blue-black smudges on her body and wondered how she would explain them: the marks of the alien.

Moments later, refreshed and dressed again in Crispin leaf, Hera made her way over the hot sand. The dune towered above her, and the fact that she could not see over it made her cautious. Also, she had heard a sound of dragging, and that alerted her. Hera climbed the side of the sandbank slowly and peered over. The first thing she

431

saw was a cluster of Tattersall weeds. They were standing on the shore, not far from the slipway below the boathouse. Their flowers were all open – a sure sign they were alert. Innocent-looking indeed, but there was a warning inside her.

Hera remembered the bay well. It was the place to which the tides carried all the flotsam and jetsam from the Dead Tree Sea and the waters round the Largo Archipelago. It was a natural slow whirlpool which trapped and never released. And there was a lot of rubbish now, bobbing in the swell and cast up on the shore. No doubt the last two-moon tide would have carried much of it, clearing the sea and casting the rubbish up on the strand. Looking closer, Hera realized with a shock that she was seeing bodies. Human bodies. Tangled heaps of them. Varnished, lacquered, embalmed, enamelled – use what word you like – they were there in their thousands. All who had died at sea in this region had found their last resting place, mixed with the rubbish cast from ships. What a mess and what a tangle. Pools of oil. Rusting canisters standing amid their voided contents. Broken crockery. Wire. Excrement. Children's toys. Plastic mesh. Books. What a place of death and ruin, but the air smelled sweet, no stench of decay.

Hera climbed over the top of the dune and began to make her way towards the boathouse. She knew she could outrun the Tattersalls easily if they showed any interest in her. She passed between the piles of bodies with their frightful faces. The answer came to her then, why the Tattersall weeds were here: they were learning about death.

When she was about halfway to the shed, she saw one of the larger of the Tattersall weeds suddenly hoist its root and take two heaving leaps towards her. At the same moment another Tattersall, one that she had not seen, heaved itself down onto the shore. It was now between her and the boathouse. Hera stopped. She saw both weeds gather to make another stride. Clearly their ability to move had improved. *Were they trying to imitate human behaviour?* This was no time to speculate. There was no doubt in Hera's mind: she was under attack.

While aware that she could still outrun them easily, it suddenly occurred to her that of course a Tattersall weed could not move in water, for their claws could find no purchase there. She changed direction and ran straight down to the sea. There she stepped as carefully as she could over and around the floating bodies clustered at the edge. Perhaps it was the effect of the seawater, but the bodies that lolled in the small waves looked like statues moulded from chocolate.

Behind her she could hear the *thump* and *scrape* as one of the weeds tried to follow her.

Hera closed the watertight seals on her backpack, thrust her hand through the thong on her stick, plunged into the sea and dived. The cape billowed and floated and she was able to swim under it, pulling strongly with her arms. When she broke the surface she swam on until she was about fifty metres from shore. There she trod water and watched as the Tattersall weed, in a kind of frenzy, beat the water to lather as it cast its branches forward, raking and tearing the corpses but making no headway itself.

Hera swam round to the slipway with the cape draped around her and dragged herself up. She crawled up the slipway until she was on dry wood. There she sat for a moment and checked that the seals on the backpack had not leaked. It was fine.

She felt something strike the frame of the slipway. Peering over the edge she could see other Tattersalls on the move. One had cast a branch up onto one of the supporting crosspieces and was preparing to climb. Another was close and a third was starting to coil, intent on casting its seeds. Hera climbed as quickly as she could, but carefully, for the slipway treads were uneven and narrow.

It was only when she was almost at the boathouse that she looked up and there saw another Tattersall weed waiting. This was the one she had seen before, when she flew over this part of Paradise at the start of her vigil. It had now grown right over the shed. One of its branches had poked in a window and a big blue flower looked out from inside.

Now why did that look funny? Why did that make her want to laugh? She had no idea. She climbed to the little landing in front of the shed and raised her stick. Nothing, nothing was going to stop her. And if this Tattersall proved to be a rogue . . .

She was amazed to see its flowers closing one by one. What this signified she did not know. *Could it smell her determination? Was it closing down in the face of her aggression? Was that a welcome?* As the flowers closed they filled the air with their fragrance. The smell, so astonishing and sweet, reminded her of the poultices that Mack had made a lifetime ago to heal her wounds. And she remembered Mack's statement that not all Tattersall weeds were afflicted in their roots. It might even be protecting the boathouse. Perhaps something of the spirit of old Pietr Z had rubbed off onto the Tattersall. Who could know any more?

She was in front of the doors now. She slammed the bolt back and the twin doors folded open, swinging outwards. Hera glanced back down at the Tattersall weeds on the beach and was in time to see the one that had been coiling release its seeds. Its branches flung wide as they uncoiled. But since it was standing close to the uprights of the slipway, these effectively chopped each branch off at the elbow and the seeds went everywhere. She felt the structure shake but that was all. More worrying was that the other two weeds, almost in the manner of Mack's little story, had managed to heave themselves up onto the lower supports of the slipway. One had its upper branches already over the edge of the slipway. However, its lower branches were entangled with the other Tattersall weed, which was attempting to climb up on the other side of the slipway. In effect, each was trying to climb up on the other, and neither was gaining.

Meanwhile, at the water's edge, the Tattersall that had attacked her first was in trouble of a rather gruesome kind. In its efforts to reach Hera it had managed to get its thorns stuck in some of the corpses in the water, and had lost traction. It was now thrashing about, turning on the spot and gradually drifting out to sea. *They were all so intense, these Tattersall weeds. So serious*, and again she found herself wanting to laugh. But . . .

She threw her backpack and stick into the boat and climbed in after them. There she stripped out the battery leads linked to the solar charger on the roof and connected them to the torque engine. Everything came alive. *Great*. She looked round and could see nothing else to be done. Typical Pietr, everything neat and in its place, and even a chair carved from wishbone for the helmsman. He had modified all the controls so that he could lower it himself, controlling the speed of descent while seated. Hera did not have time for refinements or to learn the ropes. All she now wanted was to get the cutter into the water as quickly as possible.

She pulled the boat's knife from its holder and simply cut the rope that held the craft in place. It lurched forward; she fell back. In this she was lucky, for otherwise she would have banged her head on the top of the door frame as the boat rolled out. It tilted at the top of the ramp and then began to run down the skids, gathering speed. It hit the first weed just as it was heaving itself up, and sent it tumbling down over the side of the slipway. There it landed on the now branch-less Tattersall that had cast its seeds. The cutter struck the second Tattersall weed, and the effect this time was more like a knife, as the running bar sliced through its branches. It too fell, but its root ball caught in the frame of the slipway, and it ended up hanging upside down, waving its branches aimlessly.

Hera, meanwhile, was crouched in the bottom of the boat and holding on to the carved seat, her legs wrapped round its supports. The boat hit the water at speed and sent up a great plume of spray. The water slowed the cutter quickly and its backwash slopped over the side and struck Hera just as she was standing up. She sat down again in the water. 'Enough,' she shouted, having noticed another oval cloud, innocent in the sky.

In no more than a minute the engine had warmed and Hera was steering slowly across the still water of Dead Tree Bay, watchful for anything submerged. Carefully she picked her way out through the hulks of long-dead Dendron, and then, when she was in deeper water, she pushed the cutter to maximum and locked the tiller.

Hera removed the small radio from the backpack. She extended its aerial and spread the small solar panels in the sun. She switched it on and, with relief, heard the familiar tracking sound and the crackle as it made contact.

'Hi. Dickinson here. You receiving me, Mack?'

'Not Mack. It's Hera. Your signal is very weak. Can you boost?'

'Hera! Hold it there.' She heard him call off mike. Then he was back. 'Sorry. I'm on emergency now. We're in the shit up to our haircut. Is Mack—'

'Mack met with an accident. I have to tell you he's dead. I buried him myself this morning. I'm on my way home alone. Things are bad down here. I'll give you all the details when I see you. Is Inez . . . is Captain Abhuradin there?'

'Yeah. Eiderdown's just coming. Tania's getting her. Well, that's bad news to go with everything else. There's going to be a big empty space at our table now.'

'Mine too.'

Abhuradin's voice cut in on remote. 'Inez here. Can you hear me, Hera? Are you all right?

'Yes, I'm fine. I'm just rounding the point at Dead Tree Bay. I'm in one of the lifeboat cutters. I'm on a direct course for New Syracuse.'

'Got you. We've been trying to contact you for a day and half. All hell has broken loose up here. We have orders to evacuate. I'm getting the women and children out now. We're breaking up, Hera. Do you have an ETA for New Syracuse shuttle port?'

'I'll have to call you when I'm closer. Say twelve hours, give or take a bit.'

'Fast as you can, Hera. I've no leeway. Is Mack OK?'

'Dead, Inez.'

There was a moment's pause. 'I'm losing you, Hera. Did you say dead? Was it an accident?'

'Well, I didn't shoot him.'

'No. Of course. You tell me about it when we get you off planet and we're all out of here. Out now.'

Night was falling. Hera sat at the tiller and rode the swell. The good humour that she had felt at the antics of the Tattersall weeds had deserted her. Now she felt tired and cold and just wanted to get across the sea as quickly as she could. She pulled the Crispin cloak about her.

Later she would go hunting for blankets in the first-aid locker, but for the moment memories were starting to crowd in and she couldn't keep them out. She turned the gold ring on her finger. Once she felt the cutter move as though someone big had just sat down, and she turned in surprise but, of course, there was no one. She heard her voice say, 'I'm missing you, Mack. God I wish you were here.'

With night the sea began to glow. She was entering the place where the seabed rose at the Jericho Rise. It was here that the yellow lip kelp fed, and when they were on the surface they emitted a pale green glow. Soon the wake of the cutter could be seen for miles, stretching out behind her.

Hera suddenly felt anxious that there might be something floating ahead, and she cut her speed just in time. One of the great bellows of the kelp had just broken surface and now lay heaving. She steered round the giant orifice and it blew at her wetly as she passed. *Perhaps I've caught Mack's hunches*, she thought, and again nudged to full speed.

By dawn Hera was running due west along the coast. And how different it was now! In some of the river valleys she could see the red of the Valentines, but most of the hills were covered with the blue of the Tattersall weeds. Evidence of Reapers was everywhere, and the hills were criss-crossed with the power lines of their labyrinths. In one place three Reapers seemed to be locked in some kind of competition, and even as she watched she saw ripples of energy roll over the hills. She imagined the glittering battle that would be taking place, if only she had eyes to see. She hoped that it was a rogue Michelangelo being subdued. If not it might be bad for her, as she was now close to New Syracuse. Even the sea was agitated, and the surface was broken into small choppy waves. She went further out to sea to avoid any possibility of being caught. Sometimes she saw patterns in the sky, flickering shapes of light and shadow, but they were meaningless to her. *God, what a mess!*

At long last she came in sight of the concrete blocks of the sea wall of New Syracuse, and there she contacted the shuttle platform. It was a long time before anyone answered, and then it was Polka.

'Hey, where in God's bollocks are you, lady? Don't you know the bus leaves in three hours?'

'I'm turning in to New Syracuse now. Tell Abhuradin I'll be at the shuttle port in just a bit over an hour from now. OK, Polka?'

'Will do. We'll get you out, lady. But be there, eh?'

The communication went dead.

New Syracuse was unrecognisable.

The concrete foundations of buildings had been torn open and toppled. Plants of all kinds sprang from any crack or cranny they could find.

Hybla, trifile wanderer and hyssop flag filled every space. Towering above all were giant Tattersall weeds. These trees, which now seemed more claw than tree, dominated everything and crowded right down to the water. They had, it seemed, torn anything down that could be torn down. There was nothing comic about these creatures. Everything about them was menacing.

437

How logical that these monsters should make their appearance at the very place where the greatest concentrations of humans had lived. The root would indeed be black near here.

Soon Hera was steering through rubbish and bodies, bringing the boat in to the shore. She was very aware of the subtle way the Tattersall weeds were adjusting their branches so that as many of their flowers as possible could follow her. Then, just as she was approaching the shore, several of the giants lunged towards her, their branches striking the water and sending up waves. Hera threw the tiller over and the cutter turned and headed out into the middle of the old marina. She cut the motor and stared at the solid wall of trees. There was no way through. As far as she could tell they had occupied the whole of the New Syracuse area, and probably right down the coast too. If she put ashore they would surely rip her to pieces.

She felt the raw hostility of the Tattersall weeds in their implacable blue stare. How stupid this was. She had come so far. There had to be a way. In a sudden rage she picked up old Pietr's stick of Dendron wishbone and brandished it. The smooth fibre was strong in her hands. At that moment she remembered Mack's words, uttered so clearly. Remembered too the magnificent towering Dendron that had come to her over the sea in her dream time and the moment when Mack had delivered the butcher's cut and the two young trees sprang apart. Those memories turned something on inside her, some deep energy. What had Mack said about this planet being so reactive? Well, where was the Dendron now that she needed it?

'Help me,' shouted Hera, and she waved the wishbone stick. 'Help me . . . *now.*'

And that was all it took.

For a moment her vision went to black and white. Familiar territory for Hera. She braced herself and was ready for the moment when the Tattersall weeds shook, their roots gripped by the presence of the Dendron. She heard the ringing of the Venus tears and smelled the green presence of the Dendron. Then, as though from a distance, but distinctly, she heard her name called: 'Hera.' And then stronger: 'Hera.'

She knew the voice, knew the caller. The Dendron that she and

Mack had saved, the Dendron which now lived on in the two trees and which contained in itself the entire history of Paradise, was answering her need. It was resonance, of course. A simple response to a cry for help cast in the dark.

Hera didn't even know she had done it. But in that moment something of the bright spirit of the Dendron found its way to her mind, and she turned and faced the trembling Tattersall trees without fear.

Everything became clear and shining. She stood up in the cutter and directed the small boat towards the shore. As she approached, the Tattersall weeds directly in front of her were pushed back. The boat crunched into the shingle, and it was a sound like thunder. She stepped out and raised Old Pietr Z's wishbone stick. In front of her a pathway opened, not by the magic of her wand, but in response to the exuberant spirit of the Dendron, which was in her and moved ahead of her, pushing all resistance aside. She felt the boisterous get-out-of-the-way-I'm-coming-through delight of the Dendron. A delight in strength. The brilliance of its being cracked in the hills round New Syracuse and the stamp of its stool shook the roots of the Tattersalls.

The Tattersall weeds bent out of shape. *Perhaps a Michelangelo was giving a hand too*, she thought. Some branches twisted and broke. Some weeds simply tottered and fell away, rooted out and cast aside. All of them were stripped of their flowers. Hera was unstoppable as she stepped into the lane that had opened between the trees, which fell away before her.

Hera headed for the shuttle port, following as well as she could the path of the former highway. As she walked along, the thought came to her that the Dendron was the purest manifestation of the planet's wild energy. It was anarchic and free – like her, now. She could feel the Dendron's mighty spirit surge in her. And if a Tattersall weed was slow to move, then it was *slam* as Hera hammered the earth with her stick and the Tattersall jumped.

She knew she was safe while the spirit of the Dendron was with her. But she also knew that behind her the Tattersall weeds had closed ranks, clustering close, and those that still had flowers blinked open their blue eyes.

Once, between the high branches, she saw a curling worm of

light in the dark sky. It was the shuttle descending. Not far now.

She walked on. At some point she took her boots off and threw them away. Later she tossed the radio aside and the small first-aid box. All she retained of Paradise were her stick, her cloak of Crispin and her small bag of treasures.

The shuttle landed. It was the old P64. All the small rapid-transit machines had buckled under the massive fluctuations of energy that had shaken the platform. It alone still burned with a constant flame. Captain Abhuradin, in full battle gear, ordered the shuttle to open its bays. The locks slammed open. The seals hissed and dribbled. The cargo doors opened a fraction, jerked, and then slid open steadily. The gangway pushed out and lowered its tip to the ground. Within the cargo bay and in other parts of the P64 a few men, all volunteers, stood at readiness.

The doors were open. They heard the creak and click of cooling metal. There was no Hera waiting.

Abhuradin consulted her watch. The time frame was very exact. She had just ten minutes. Then she would order emergency ascent, and the P64 would close and lift whether Hera was there or not.

No one moved. Everyone watched. All they could see beyond the small compound was the dense forest of Tattersalls. Some had been crushed under the P64 when it landed. All the weeds had their blue flowers straining to fully open, and their perfume was heady in the morning air. But then they heard something. It was like the rush of wind that comes before a storm.

'Five minutes, Captain, and counting.'

Abhuradin nodded but did not reply. She stared into the ruined shuttle port and along the broken lines of rusty wire that marked the perimeter. She was remembering.

A sudden silence. And then a ripple of movement passed through some of the Tattersall weeds near the perimeter. Their top branches waved as though they had been shaken. Trees toppled and fell. As they watched, space opened up under the weeds. The calm voice of the captain was heard throughout the ship: 'No one is to move or fire until I give the order.'

'Three minutes, Captain, and counting.'

Silence. Stillness. A holding of breath.

And then a small figure, looking lost and waif-like, with tufts for hair and wearing nothing but a torn Crispin cape, walked out from under the trees. She stepped carefully over the flattened perimeter gate and approached the waiting gangway. Abhuradin, her heart pounding and with a sudden dryness in her throat, advanced to meet her, but Hera stopped her with a gesture.

Hera stepped up onto the lip of the gangway, turned and stared at the millions of Tattersall weeds that thronged the hills and valleys. She raised the hand wearing the ring and clenched it like a fist. Then she opened it like a star and closed it again. Some of the Tattersall weeds answered her gesture with a blink of their flowers, but the majority stared back blankly.

Hera removed her cape and threw it down to the ground. Then she raised Old Pietr Z's wishbone stick as high as she could and threw it into the midst of the Tattersall weeds. Some of those present thought they heard a faint tinkle of bells when the stick landed. All of them felt the shock wave that moved away and flowed up the hills, gathering speed.

Freed from their restraint, the Tattersall weeds close to the P64 shook and some began to twist, as though preparing to cast their large clawed limbs forward. Flowers which had closed when Hera emerged from the forest now blazed open.

Hera turned and, with a sad wistful smile, entered the shuttle.

The cargo doors began to close. Abhuradin's voice was crisp. 'You men avert your gaze. Someone get the woman a blanket.' Then, more gently, 'Hera, you're all bruised. What did he do to you?'

'Just love bites,' said Hera. 'Well, I promised I'd be here. And here I am. Sort of.'

The cargo doors met, cutting off the view of Paradise. Immediately the old P64 lifted, climbing up its strong thread of light. As it did so, the Tattersall weeds moved in, joining ranks, filling the place where the shuttle had stood and scratching its squat legs with their thorns. Others spun violently, scattering their seeds. From all the hills and from the nearby plateau millions of blue flowers stared up as the shuttle dwindled until it was finally lost in the clouds.

Thus was completed the Disestablishment of Paradise.

DOCUMENTS

'Concerning the Fractal Moment', from the Daybooks
of Mayday and Marie Newton

The daybooks kept by Mayday and Marie Newton are the most valuable documents we have concerning the early days of agricultural exploration on Paradise. The Newton family were among the first pioneer farmers. They, along with the Tattersall family, came to Paradise aboard the first domestic fractal carrier. It had a cheerful name: *Figaro*.

Mayday Newton had a degree in mathematics and took a special interest in all scientific developments. The following extract is from the daybook which he began to keep while he was a passenger on the *Figaro*. This was his first passage through the fractal, and the scientific and philosophical implications of it fascinated him. Fractal studies became his hobby and he authored some studies on this topic in *News of Paradise*, published by Tom and Wendy Tattersall.

All such articles ceased when the two families fell out over treatment of a Michelangelo-Reaper.

•

Over dinner I had a good conversation with one of the navigation officers. He has the wonderful name Lorenzo de Lucia. I asked him about fractal technology.

According to Lorenzo, a fractal point is a point of symmetry in space, one where energies match and achieve a kind of balance. There are a lot of these points, evidently. What the first experimenters discovered was that they could send messages via these points and that the transmission was instantaneous between points. No speed-of-light delay. It avoided the Einstein limit. The next thing they did was to send out messages blindly via a fractal point, but equipped with a special programme that sent them back when they struck another fractal point anywhere. The returned messages were then analysed to see where they had been. Thus it became possible for fractal addresses to be mapped. Charts were prepared. Patterns emerged. Things were getting organized.

In the early days, when this technology was being developed, quite a number of live researchers were lost. Corrigan and Ortez are two names. They vanished into . . . well, that's anyone's guess. They volunteered, and vanished. The fractal point opens to an infinite number of dimensions, so the omniscient one is the only person who might have a clue where they are . . . and he or she 'ain't saying nuttin'.

Lorenzo asked me if I knew anything about maths and I said, 'A little.' And then he asked me if I knew anything about quantum mechanics and I said, 'Not a lot.' And he said, 'Good,' because, in his experience, people who knew a bit were harder to talk to than those who just had to take things on faith.

Here is a summary of what he said.

These fractal points of symmetry form a vast three-dimensional web in our space–time, and all the stars and planets and moons float within this web. In fact the physical stars and planets and moons, and all the rest, can pass through these points, and do so all the time. The fractal points may indeed account for ghosts or any number of strange phenomena on Earth – flying saucers and the like – because they carry enormous poly-dimensional energy. The easiest way to visualize this gigantic web is to think of a geodesic dome while remembering that there are fractal points within as well as without the dome. The fractal points can be imagined as being those points where the hexagons meet. Of course, there aren't any hexagons in space. It is just a way of getting a handle on the concept.

Now, I'm going to write the next bit down exactly so I can think about it later. He said, 'Just as the quantum universe can be seen as a labyrinth of passages, occupying overlapping dimensions, well, as below, so above. The fractal points are the entry doors into different dimensions, except you must not think of them as doors, because there is no point of transition. You are either in or you are not. We choose the moment of being "in", and that is the fractal moment when we are also "out" but elsewhere.'

Evidently the actual moment of transgression requires no time in our conscious dimension, though of course if you slipped dimensions you could be in trouble, like poor Corrigan and Ortez.

So, essentially, our journey to Paradise consists of: a) journeying through normal space–time to the fractal point, b) preparing to pass through, c) ¿WHAM?, d) recovering from the passage, and then e) journeying on through normal space–time to our destination. Simple as A?C. It has a lovely symmetry, with a great big question mark at its centre.

I asked him about the fractal points at the quantum level. Apparently the most up-to-date theory is that these also are interchange points 'where different energy-field realities meet and interact'. Lorenzo gave me one example. He said that dowsers, when they are looking for water, say, are interacting with the thing they are looking for via fractal points at the quantum level. It's a different way of getting at the truth. So there we are – a mixture of science and folklore. A bit like us, really: quite sophisticated on a technical level, but with a yearning to plant with our hands and eat what we grow. They call us pioneers, and I am proud of that.

I have enough to think about for some time, and if I can get up a head of steam, I might have a crack at the maths of fractal travel and try to see what is involved.

Sweet dreams are made of this.

'Getting Your Man', from *Tales of Paradise*
by Sasha Malik

'Big as your fist, healthy as garlic and sweet as nectar.'
Marketing slogan for the Paradise plum

The Paradise plum was a noted aphrodisiac. Indeed, there was a time when gourmets fought in restaurants for the last plum in the kitchen; when debts were paid in plums; when ageing potentates with young wives, despite the promise of their name, relied on the plum for virility. Sometimes the plums were preached *against* as a symbol of hedonism. Sometimes they were preached *for* as a promise of the heavenly delights awaiting us. Now we can only look back at a craze that went sour. More than sour – at a fruit that became poison. But they are still remembered for what they were, part of the brief golden age of Paradise.

The plum was a fruit like no other. It was not sweet, it was not sour, but like a good wine changed flavour as it was consumed. The effects of the plum could be detected on a person's skin within minutes of their eating one – a certain silkiness, I am told. Its fame as 'the bedroom food' was universal and attested: it provoked both performance and desire.

So what happened?

For the first account we turn to Sasha Malik, who tells a good tale. Sasha was one of the 'wild women' of Paradise – of which there have been many. These were women who forsook life in the camps or towns, preferring to live under the trees, surviving on what they could find in the deep, untrodden bush.

Sasha was the daughter of a lumberjack, 'Stammer' Malik. He, with his wife Donna, had shipped out to Paradise shortly after its opening-up to help take down stands of umbrella trees. A few months after giving birth to Sasha, Donna Malik ran off with a 'Gypsy-eyed miner from Chain' and so the child was brought up by her father. He treated her as part of his logging team, which means that he treated her well. 'I had one father, ten big brothers and twenty uncles,' Sasha boasted.

At the age of fifteen Sasha ran away with a carpenter called 'Big' Anton, a man twice her age.

Sasha and Big Anton lived happily for three years in North Chain, until Anton was killed when a log fell from a cart and rolled on him. It was grief at his loss that drove Sasha to live wild under the trees. Later, after many adventures which included riding a Dendron across Blue Sand Straits, Sasha returned to her father's camp, and it was there that she wrote the collection of stories that we know as *Tales of Paradise*.

Sasha and her father died just over a hundred years ago. The timber barge in which they were travelling rolled in a storm while crossing the troubled water we know as Dead Tree Sea. She was just twenty-one.

Getting Your Man

People blamed Big Anton for taking me off. They said he was too old for me and should have known better. But it was me that seduced him, and carefully too, and I am proud of that.

It was during the log push, and Father and the team were down the Old Nylo clearing the blockage where a rockfall had stopped the river and the logs were piling up. Big Anton pulled the short straw and was left in charge of the camp – and me. I was the one who drew the straws, and I cheated.

I'd loved him since I was little. Don't ask me how or why because I just don't know. I simply fell in love with him, and knew he was the one for me come hell or high water. But I knew too, the way smart kids do, that I couldn't have him until I was big enough in every way, like I didn't want another father and I didn't want an old man either or more big brothers. So timing was important. I also knew he loved me, though he didn't know that and would have been ashamed if he'd thought it. A good man.

449

I decided that the time was right when I was fifteen and very, very hungry. I was fifteen just before the log push. So when the team was gone and we'd waved them goodbye in the morning, I knew it was my time.

I'd already made Anton a love potion taught me by one of the girls in New Syracuse. You take the seeds of the plum when they are dry and then crush them. Some people throw the seeds away, but they are the best part and you can use them in lots of charms, but you never use them like pepper. You let them steep for a day or two in spring water gathered when both moons are in the sky. Wait until the water is starting to turn a deep blue. Then give it a stir with your finger and pour it off the seeds. Put it aside. It'll keep a few days out of the sun but don't put it in a fridge because that kills it. See, it is a living drink. Now, when your time is right, you need to add two more ingredients. Have a wee in a bowl, dip your finger in the wee and then stir the juice with that finger. Lastly, prick your thumb and add a few drops of your blood and stir it in well. Then choose your moment when your man is there and not about to go out chopping and there are no other women or people about – and serve it fresh.

Big Anton was not a man who worked if he didn't have to. He'd sit by a lake with a book, or yarn the day away, or whittle a toy for a man with kids. So that was where he was, snoozing after lunch – I'd made him a good one. Unsuspecting. Feet up on a stone. Boots off. Belt loosed. Hands behind his head. Muscles like rope. Handsome as a god at dawn. An untamed and uncivilized man. Mine. I loved him so much I was worried he would read my mind or smell my ache, and I would lose him. I knew he would be frightened of me when I came at him. He would run away if he could. He would swim over Redman Lake quick as a fish, and scrabble down Old Mother Nylo until he caught up with the men. I knew him, knew his mind. I was older than him in so many ways.

While he was sleeping I had a good wash. Brushed my hair like that pretty girl Baigneuse. I was so very nervous. It makes me laugh now, and cry too, for I knew what I was doing – I was growing up. I rubbed the skin of a plum on my breasts and between my legs and across the back of my neck. That was another trick the girls taught me. They reckoned the smell made the men come more quickly so that they could get done with more of them when the rush was on. That wasn't what I was thinking. I was just taking precautions because I didn't want a broken heart and oh, I wanted my lover, and though I feel pretty, I don't think I am really. I've got something else but I don't know a word for it. The girls had other tricks too, for slowing the men down, and I thought, *Time for that when we have nights together*. See I knew I was in for the long walkabout, and no fucker would stop me.

I squatted to wee, but I couldn't. I was all tight and moist. I jumped up and down and almost panicked. Finally I squeezed out a few drops and that had to do. Then I put on a loose blue dress I'd made from strips of hybla and dyed with juice from a waltzer.[18] Last of all I pricked my thumb and I said a little prayer as I squeezed the drips of blood into the drink and stirred it with my wet finger for luck.

'I'm bringing you cordial,' I said, nudging him with my toe. 'I want to know what you think of it.'

He snuffled, a bit like a horse, and farted and I thought, *Great. That's something else I'll have to get used to.* But he squinted up at me with his big daft smile.

'Like the way you've done your hair,' he said. ' Pretty dress too. Look a real lady, Sasi.' Then he reached up for the glass. Christ love me, if I'd been a step further forward his hand would have gone straight up under my dress. I almost dropped the drink.

He sipped it. Pulled a face. 'What's in it?'

'A bit of this and a bit of that. Don't you like it?'

He sipped again. 'I can smell a bit of plum. That right?'

'Might be. Drink it up.'

He took a bigger drink. And then he drained the glass. I think he did that just to please me. He handed me the glass and lay back.

I didn't know what to do next. What to expect. So I waited. 'Well?' I said finally.

'Well, what?'

'Did you like it?'

'Yes, it was all right. A bit more plum'd make it better.'

'Doesn't it . . . make you feel anything?'

[18] Waltzer or blue waltzer was the original name of the plant which later became known as the Tattersall weed.

451

He looked up at me. 'You're a funny one, Sasi. What's it supposed to make me feel?'

I shrugged. This was not going according to plan. 'Happy,' I said. 'Yep. OK. Gotcha. It makes me feel very happy.' And he stretched his body slowly, all five foot three inches of him like a great cat, a panther. 'Now I think I'll go for a swim.'

'No, don't do that,' I said, and I kneeled down beside him.

See, I know what the men do sometimes when they go for a swim. They swim round to the rapids where the Rex[19] came down, and sit in the foam and bring themselves off with their hands when they want relief. They all do it. Father too. I've seen them. I knew that if Big Anton went that way I would lose him. I didn't know what to do, but something inside me did. The next thing I knew I was out of my dress and my hands were all over him and I was kissing and kissing and kissing so that he couldn't speak. Was a woman ever bolder? And he was so big and hard in my hand and I thought, *All this is mine.* And I was flowing all over him like honey.

He said once, 'If Stammer—'

But I stopped him. 'Leave my father to me,' I said sternly, and straightway kissed him a hundred times so he would forget. 'Now, Big Anton,' I said, working my way under him like a tree dolly and him a fallen log, 'do your duty by your woman. I'm yours now, for good 'n' all, and I'm here as long as you want me, and there's no going back, so there.'

And there wasn't. Though I never did find out whether it was my love potion or me that did the trick . . . but we never needed it again.

When my love was dead, and I had set him to sleep, I rubbed his body with the skin of a plum and squeezed the juice between his lips. I ate the fruit myself, but it was not as sweet as the smell of his hair or the taste of his lips in the morning.

Beautiful in his stillness, like a man asleep beside a lake, boots off, belt undone, arms back, a god in his slumber, dreaming of whatever gods sleeping dream – perhaps of me.

I took him to a private place. There I have a Reaper friend who will treat him well. It is one who knows me and has felt me and has shown me myself.

[19] *Rex* was the early name for the *Dendron peripatetica*.

My Reaper friend, it took him in. There I left him, staying only long enough to see my golden dead love's silver flowers rise and know he is safe in Paradise.

End

Extract from the official report into illicit trade in
Paradise products: Paradise plum and Dendron

The date at which organized smuggling on a planet-wide scale
began is not known. It was, however, in full operation during the
last decade of the MINADEC administration and investigations
are continuing. The main centre for the processing was the island
of Scarlatti in the Largo Archipelago.

When investigating officers arrived on Scarlatti they found
presses and a bottling plant capable of handling several thousand
litres of juice at one pressing. The residue, the skins and seeds of
the plant, were deposited in a pit which was in the process of
being covered over when the officers arrived. In this operation
the plums were not picked individually, as this would have taken
too long and required too many people. Instead the entire tree
was cut off at its base and then loaded into one of the ore trans-
ports which had an open licence to move from location to location. In this way, entire regions of Horse, Northern Chain and
the western seaboard of Hammer were denuded of the Paradise
plum. The plums were picked while in transit and the wood from
the trees was disposed of at sea.

The fate of the Dendron is perhaps more spectacular. The
Dendron was hunted from the platforms of prospecting planes
which had been modified to carry cannon. Two such planes were
found on the ground at Scarlatti. MINADEC records revealed
that they had been declared lost at sea some years earlier.

No accurate estimate can be placed on the number of Dendron
killed and cut up for their wishbones, but the number must be at
least in the hundreds of thousands and possibly in the millions.
One index of the damage to numbers as a result of this culling

is the decline in the number of sightings of the Rex during the last decade of the MINADEC occupation. To date the number has continued to decline, and we face the prospect that the viable population of the Rex has collapsed.

This document is taken from an official report concerning smuggling. While MINADEC was withdrawing from Paradise a fractal barge called *Hoy Linden*, having taken on cargo and surplus mining equipment at the shuttle platform over Paradise, aborted its mission when just twenty minutes out from fractal. A leak in one of the containers in the cargo hold had been discovered. The manifest indicated that the crate contained used uniforms, but the material which leaked out was juice from the Paradise plum. The crate was opened and inside were jars of the juice. Some of these had not been made secure and several had broken at some point in transit. Discovery of this led to other crates being opened. Some were found to contain the cut wishbones of several hundred Dendron. Other crates contained juice as well as bales of dried calypso petals. Juice may seem a strange commodity for smugglers, but as already indicated, in those early days the belief was widespread that both the juice of the Paradise plum and the ground-up wishbone of the Dendron had aphrodisiac and generative powers. Calypso petals brought sweet dreams to even the most chronic insomniac.

There was a ready market for all of these. Two hundred millilitres of juice could be worth up to 200 solas. Dendron fibre, with its fine blue and green flecks and its perfume reminiscent of primrose, was worth even more, as it could be cut up to make little charms and jewellery as well as being ground into powder to be added to wines and cordials. The calypso petal was sold by the pouch. One pouch being a hundred grams. Combine all these with a bit of vodka and you had a tincture of renowned potency. Even sold separately, the ingredients were worth a fortune.

This report was never made public and, as far as I can ascertain, the only people ever brought to justice were those caught actually on the island of Scarlatti as well as a small party of hunters and their girls who, having enjoyed a weekend of sex, drinking and hunting, crashed their SAS on landing and were caught red-handed with the wishbones of twenty-seven Dendron in the hold. The report was certainly not known to the agricultural pioneers such as the

Newtons or the Tattersalls, who while they could see the physical damage done to native flora, had no true knowledge of its extent.

Further evidence relating to this case was destroyed during the mysterious fire on the MINADEC torus, the year before the first agricultural pioneers arrived. However, it is inconceivable that the managers and senior officers of MINADEC could have been ignorant of what was happening. That fire was, as one of the prosecuting offices declared at the time, 'convenient for the guilty'.

The report from which I have quoted only came to light as part of a routine research request submitted to SC Archives when I was preparing this book for print. I have taken steps to ensure that it will be published in full as part of a public archives project.

DOCUMENT 4

'Agricultural Developments and a Recipe', from the
Daybooks of Mayday and Marie Newton

The Newton diaries are invaluable, providing the only consistent
record of day-to-day life on Paradise from the point of view of the
agricultural pioneers. Reflected in these pages are the excitement
and the optimism as the small family settles in and begins to create
a new life. In many ways the Newtons were fortunate. The land
they occupied was virgin meadow and had not been cleared with
the herbicides used in Northern Chain and the Largo Islands. The
crop they chose to grow was native – the Paradise plum – and there
was a plentiful stock of young plants in the woods nearby. Their
house had one of the best views on Paradise, looking out over the
Blue Sand Straits and across to the high grey cliffs of Anvil. This
was of course a migration route for the great, and already nearly
extinct, Dendron. The following description was written three
years after their arrival on Paradise.

The final daybook entry was made by Marie Newton, on the
morning of the day on which Mayday was fatally injured.

It was one of the Mayday and Marie's grandchildren, Proctor
Newton, who hurled the chair which injured Hera at the ORBE
hearing.

•

Third anniversary. Marie is down at the bay. We saw a Dendron
swamped in a storm a week ago. There was nothing we could do
but watch as it was toppled by the big breaking waves. And now it
has been washed up at the bay, all flags and cherries gone.

Marie wants to do a book with pictures about the life of the

Dendron – or Rexes, as some people still call them. I told her to watch her step. It is not too long since someone came upon what they thought was a stranded Dendron and climbed up on it, and it got up and walked out to sea!

I've been down the line having a look at the crop. Very pleased. All the plum trees I put in a year ago are doing well. A good crop, I would say. The plums are maturing, black, blue and the deep red. In fact I somehow seem to have planted a few different varieties, as I see we have some green-veined plums and some that are bright like cherries. But they will all taste good, I'm sure. The first crop I sent sold out the morning it went on auction, so after we've paid the taxes and the land loan and the insurance and the equipment levy, we might, if we're lucky, have a bit left over, and that would be nice. First time in our lives.

Been talking with John and Gerda Pears – they've got twins Peter and Benjy, arrived last month – about supply lines. They are doing quite nicely, thank you, 'turning seaweed into solas' as Gerda put it. John thinks we ought to all get together and start a trust fund so we can purchase either a controlling share in the Paradise platform or the nearest fractal – or both! He reckons Paradise is about to take off commercially, and the last thing we want is some middleman from Mars controlling our supply line. He also talked about tourism, so he is thinking far ahead. I'm not sure about that, though. As soon as you get too commercial you lose sight of the mountains and the music.

I want to talk about the trees. Life is easy so I get time to experiment and think. One thing I don't understand about them is why they have such a bloody long root. The first time I dug one up I tried to dig the whole thing out, but the root just went on and on, getting deeper and deeper, till finally I had to give up and chop it off. This must be one of the characteristics of the flora on Paradise. Most of the plants I have dug up have a long root. Take the blue waltzer (or the Tattersall weed, as we are now starting to call it). It has a long single root too, but that root has a little knot in it so that it breaks as soon as you put pressure on it, like the elbow on a tomato. Not so the plum or the stink wort or the yellow trancers – they've got a root like a main drain. Why do they need a deep root like that if all their sustenance comes from surface roots? I mentioned this to

Deacon Syng, and he thought it might be an evolutionary remnant from the time when there was a shortage of water and the plants had to dig deep. He may be right, but I have seen no evidence of drought or desert in this part of Paradise.

I realized something the other day when I was scorching back some Tattersalls in the meadow bottoms. We are the true pioneers. It came as a shock. And do you know how I know we are the pioneers? Because there are no manuals. We experiment. See what works and apply that. For instance, I tried making compost, but you can't on Paradise. But you can make wonderful plant tea, which is just as good.

I am probably the world expert on growing the Paradise plum. I know that Tewfic and Sullia have a few plants up and coming. Now that secondary workers are starting to arrive, things are easier, They intend to plant out a hundred acres or so as soon as they have finished clearing their land. Tania and Sean, who have a massive holding touching two continents in mid-Chain, are also gearing up to plant the plum. God knows why they don't have any local ones, but I will supply them with rootstock. I think you could say that we, as a planet, are up and running. I love being self-sufficient and I have never seen Marie so happy. I am trying to make a solar hair dryer.

Gunter and Hirondelle are starting to worry me. I don't think they're going to last. Everything they plant seems to fall over. I went over in the cutter to see them last week and Hirondelle had taken to her bed in depression. She says living here is like living in a graveyard! I think she's a few fingers short of a fist. She is very fey, full of omens, and has designed a tarot card sequence for Paradise. She wanted to cast our future but I told her we were not interested. That kind of thing puts the willies up Marie. Me, I think it's just ignorant mumbo-jumbo. I suggested that Hirondelle have a smoke of the calypso lily and gave her a pouch. Marie was upset with me as she thinks it's addictive, but I think of it as a medicine. I like a pipe-full of an evening. It stimulates the mind.

Been talking to Tattersall and I think we need to start agitating for a research institute here. I am not sure who was responsible for the initial planning, but I suspect they thought this place was like Earth because it looks similar and because we can breathe the air and drink the water. But as the days go by I recognize ever more deeply how totally unlike the Earth it is. Not worse or better. But different, and we need to know how things function here. A bit of scientific nous would not go amiss, and less of Hirondelle's spooky nonsense. The last thing we want are freaks on Paradise. Gunter is as bad. He has this idea that you should pee on plants – so he does that, methodically, and I told him that might be why he can't even grow a decent Tattersall weed! But he just snorted.

Just got word. Literally just now came in: 'To Bola and Peta Silvio, a girl called Isadora'. I'm so happy for them. No complications. All the right bits and pieces and all in the right place. We are invited over for a party in a couple of weeks' time. Must think about an appropriate gift.

Marie has become really interested in publicizing Paradise. She's started an action group called WAM – Women Against MINADEC. It was after she heard about those drums of chemicals they found up on Palestrina. A lot has not been explored yet on this world. And there's a lot we don't know. The group is already having an impact. They went to the Bell Tree Islands and found the grave of the first child born on Paradise. It gave Marie and the rest of the party a real fright. They came to the falls, which were as pretty as anything you can imagine, and the little grave was off to one side. It was in what had once been a clearing, and there was still a signpost up saying Babycry Falls, but the whole place was now completely overgrown, as you might expect.

Marie has also started a cooking club. When we can, we all share recipes, and Marie wants to publish a little book of them to accompany the produce we send off planet. Those of us who are into native food production think it is a good idea, and there is a distributor on Mars who is interested. Marie experiments with the Paradise plum almost every day, so I am the envy of all the fellas! Here is one of her recipes. I provide the titles. I name this one

Isadora's Plum Delight – recipe by Marie Newton

Take some ripe plums (a plum the size of a duck egg or a fist is usually enough for one person) and lightly wash them, being careful not to bruise the skin. Set them aside on a dry towel and let them dry in the sun or air. Don't rub them, as the skin detaches very easily after washing.

When dry, slice with a very sharp knife and hold the plum together as you withdraw the blade. Hold it for a few seconds, then allow the cut plum to open naturally. You will find that the flesh of the fruit holds firm and that there is a ring of small black seeds surrounding a central yellow pith.

Using a small sharp spoon, scoop out the yellow pith and reserve in an egg cup or small bowl. Then remove the seeds with the spoon, and discard. If some of the seeds have been bruised, they may leak a blue liquid. This is not harmful but has a flavour close to fennel, which is to be avoided in this recipe. A dab with a twist of absorbent kitchen paper is usually all that is needed to soak up the blue liquid.

Mash the pith with a fork and add a herb of your choice. Hybla berries provide a nice contrast to the flavour of the plum. Spoon the mashed pith back into the cavity from which it came. Heat an oven to 200°C and place the plum halves in the centre. Watch as they froth up and change colour. When the liquid pith has firmed and the skin of the plum is reddish brown, they are cooked. It never takes more than five minutes.

Serve immediately with fresh warm bread. Each part of the plum has its own flavour. This can be an appetizer or a dessert – or a complete lunch. It tastes especially good with one of the range of Tattersall teas.

Enjoy.

DOCUMENT 5

'Plum Crazy', from the private notebook of
Professor Israel Shapiro

According to the date, and Hera's testimony, the following entry
was probably written only a few weeks before Shapiro died. This
would explain the sombre and apocalyptic tone. It shows the effects
of addiction to the juice of the plum.

•

To dinner with my sister and her husband in Cambridge. Tonight
we heard the Cantata Romana sung by the full choir of King's
College. Proceeds to go to the relief fund for Rome. Afterwards we
walked through the lovely grounds of Clare while a frost made the
air dry and pure.

They will have to move before the year is out, I fear. Their lovely
stone house is sinking! Oswald showed me the cracks in the cellar
and muttered grimly about the lack of endowments.

Fortuna came home while we were sampling the fruit of the
cellar. She was wearing a peacock-blue outfit and had been out fund-
raising. She said to me, conspiratorially taking my arm, 'I have a
special treat for dessert,' and my heart sank. How hard it is when
people mean well but do the very thing that hurts.

So at dinner there it was. As I feared. After the wine and before
the liqueur. Ushered in with trumpets.

This 'plum', as they call her, what am I to make of her? She sits on
my plate like a giant damson, inviting my fork and knife, her perfume rising like a vintage port – but I would rather plunge the fork
into my arm than eat this innocent creature, which contains more
knowledge than I do. Yet I do not.

Being one for whom politeness is like spelling, a cornerstone of civilization, I reason: my host, Oswald, will have mortgaged his pension to pay for these – retained in the caves of Mars, close to freezing, say 34.5 degrees of the old Fahrenheit, varying by less than point five of a degree, week in, week out. I should feel honoured. And they mean it as a treat for me, for they know I have had a hard time of late.

Fortuna and I both once had a cache of plums, an inheritance from our spendthrift father. Fortuna gobbled hers with her paramours. I, being the sober conventional one, ate some of mine, sold the rest to get research funds, and I doubt if Papa would ever forgive me for that or would ever understand. A few I kept back. Three remain. One is for H, whom I love. One is for me when I am dying – not to eat or drink, I have my own supply of liquor for that, but to keep by my ear like a shell, and I will whisper to it as I fade. The last is for Fortuna when I am gone, and I hope she guzzles it with the same generous gusto she has guzzled her life.

For I am an addict and both love and hate my vice. A kind of hypocrisy here. 'Nous alimentons nos aimables remords. Comme les mendiants nourrissent leur vermine.' This Baudelaire mood confirms my worst fears. I am moving on, away, off, losing the thread somewhere. The hunter may come home from the hills, but this ship will find no haven. I need a sip to 'shuffle the deck', as we say.

That's better. We were in Cambridge. Eating. Yes.

Fortuna is deft. Her twin-tined fork vertical in her hand and the sharp knife between the prongs, she slices like a conjurer and, lo and behold, the slit fruit splays as the fork withdraws.

She says, 'The seeds are bitter. Such a waste to discard. I am told they are good for lovemaking.' Oswald pales, poor sod! 'But better in the compost,' she adds kindly.

I think to myself, *The small dark distillation of matter we call seeds are its wisdom. They are its salt. Hold them on your tongue for as long as you can, until the blue honey fills your mouth and turns bitter. Then swallow swiftly.*

But I don't say this. Fortuna would try it. She would go out in a blaze of glory, knowing her. You have to build up slowly to achieve my stamina. I would have a bad conscience, and besides, I wish to die first. So, I obey convention and put the seeds to one side. They are not dead yet, I observe. That fine blue secretion tells me they are still viable, not as seeds but as centres of sense. Fortuna has been coy in her cooking, perhaps believing that a plum done rare becomes a rarer plum. They are not dead, that is what I want to say, for if they were, they would not bleed their blue knowledge. They would congeal like vile jelly.

But revulsion and addiction are at war. On the tip of my knife I lift a pale morsel. I apply it to a sliver of toast, and, like the addict I am, like all lovers, delight at the rush: salt and honey, guilt and pleasure.

Despite my knowledge I am no better than the rest, my nose in the trough, gobbling.

But a few days later I am back in my laboratory on Paradise. Tonight I will not sleep but I will dream. Before me is Prunella, the entity that has been my companion for fifteen years. Her roots pass through my floor and down, through the caverns of Paradise. With instruments I have traced that pale cable through sixty feet and it gets thicker and stronger the more it descends. It 'raps' with all the other roots of Paradise.

There is a prunella fruit – a 'plum' – which hangs before me, over my desk. It is large (say the size of one of H's breasts). There is a cut in this fruit I have kept open since first I had it brought here as a straggly vine. All I need to do is insert my scalpel and move it slightly. Moments later I am rewarded with a few drips of blue nectar, which I catch in a spoon and drink. Nine times a day – as often as I cast offending Adam out.

Does this operation hurt the vine? I think not. In fact I am sure not, as I would be aware if it did and it would by now have contrived some means to stop me. Perhaps poison me, and the truth is I have sipped enough juice to kill a regiment. No, it does not hurt any more than I hurt when I produce acid in my stomach or semen in my balls.

There is a parallel here, of course, and we will come to that. But for the moment I am still an ace of spades short of drunk, and want to lay some falsehoods while I can. How dangerous is popular wisdom! Estelle it was who first called this a plum, and anyone can see why. But if we called it the Paradise testicle, or the Paradise ovum, or the Paradise cerebellum or thyroid, people might not

464

be so keen to eat it. If we likened it to a fleshy chakra – a node of energy made solid, a halo that rings like silver crystal when you tap it with a fingernail – we would be closer, though still far from the truth. These beautiful red pendulous shapes, sometimes perceptibly warm to the touch on a cool morning, are of course its main organ of sense and feeling – but again language is betraying me, for what they sense or what they feel is beyond me, though maybe bright H will untie the mystery.

How I wish I could have been on the *Scorpion*! Would that there were more like Sasha or lovely, daft Estelle Richter, whose naked body splashing in the sea was the first knowledge this world had that there was a world beyond Paradise. Is there wisdom in innocence? I think there is, but there is a cult now of drab men and women for whom the world, and even life itself, is a kind of commodity. These critics, having eaten, now study their excrement to see what they consumed. On this they base certain conclusions. Their ignorance is uncompromising. Let us rather stand before the unknown in very humble, quiet observance and wait while it reveals itself.

Sadly, we have tended to export the fears of Earth to space. My dying hope is that the exportation will not be accepted, and just as the corpses of Earth are slowly delivered back to the surface of this world, there to lie and dry and never fester, so the madness of Earth will be exhumed before it can take root.

I am sorry for lovely H and the rest. It is not their fault – but it is our fault, the whole damn lot of us. Once I was a scientist, and a good one, but I never quite believed in science. In my prime I could see alpha and omega as glorious echoes of one another. Great resonating gongs beneath a sea whose waves brought rapture. But now I am a happy mystic, happy to be cryptic and in love with my Prunella, which I tease with my knife and which teases me with her knowledge. He who knows will understand what I say. He who does not know will not be enlightened.

I do not mean to be difficult, but if you men of the future wish to understand, you must make as a big an effort as I have, and pay as big a price as I have, and taste failure as I have. The sad truth is, everything you need to know is there before you, and always has been, on the lovely Earth we once called home. It is all in the asking.

It is all in the seeking. Perhaps if I had read more poetry I would have known this sooner.

Now I drink my blue nectar and lie down in the soil and seek the peace of God which passeth all understanding. Good night. Oh my sweet love . . .

'Shunting a Rex', from *Tales of Paradise* by Sasha Malik

To begin let us recall that, as a girl, Sasha Malik ran wild on the hills of Kithaeron while her father chopped trees. She danced, swam, dreamed and invented games as the mood took her. She was a clever girl with a quick eye, and soon it was Sasha who kept a tally of the logs sent down the Mother Nylo – both their length and their volume. And it was Sasha who kept the receipt books. By the age of twelve she was more or less running the household, and that included brewing batches of beer, cooking meals, mending wounds and cutting hair and beards – all for a price.

Never receiving any formal education, she nevertheless learned to read and write. Logging camps were the only social life that the young Sasha Malik knew, and her language and attitudes reflect this. She had access to tri-vids of course, but the texts she preferred were the magazines and books brought in by the woodsmen and miners. Lonely men may have their own kind of literature, but it would be a mistake to think that just because they had chosen a rough life they were unlettered or ill educated. Far from it. Men who seek solitude have questions to ponder, and it is to the classics of their language they often turn.

Sasha read widely and indiscriminately and acquired her own small library, which included Homer's *Iliad*, *Everybody's Home Medical Encyclopaedia, Volume 2*, *Salome* by Oscar Wilde, the *Contemporary Poetry Mars Collection*, *Romeo and Juliet* by Shakespeare, *Teach Yourself to Draw Animals*, *Wuthering Heights* by Emily Brontë and *Elementary Mathematics*, as well as a selection of brightly illustrated erotic works. Traces of all of these can be found in her writing. A photograph of Sasha at the age of twelve shows a serious-looking girl with an oval face and large eyes. She is holding a book to her chest. However, it was the eyes which were most often commented on, both for their green colour and because they seemed to belong to an older person.

We must imagine young Sasha in those days, sitting beside a campfire at night, cross-legged in cut-down dungarees, a blanket around her shoulders, lighting her father's pipe of calypso from an ember and handing it to him, unobtrusive but alert, unregarded but all ears, listening, wide-eyed and missing nothing while the men tell stories and boast. At some point she wrote down their yarns, their songs and their scary superstitious stories. She also wrote about the things she had seen and done. She did not have exercise books, and so she wrote on whatever she could find: the backs of old invoices, the linings of tea packets, which she found she could open and press, and in an unlined notebook given to her as payment by a freshly shaved MINADEC inspector. Many years later, these pages were discovered and published under the title *Tales of Paradise*.

As already revealed in the autobiographical story 'Getting Your Man', Sasha ran away with Big Anton at the age of fifteen, and it was after his death some three years later that she became a 'bush lady', living alone and surviving on what she could forage or what she was given if she happened to be close to a camp. Her reputation as a healer spread and stories grew up about her. It was considered lucky if you saw her. There are several accounts of her being met on paths, dressed in clothes she had made from Crispin, and of her handing over hybla letters to be delivered to her father on Anvil. None of these letters survive.

Sasha travelled the full length of Chain and out to the Blue Sands Bluff – the very place where Mayday and Marie Newton were later to establish their homestead. According to legend, Sasha crossed the Blue Sands Straits to Anvil riding on the back of a Dendron.

Eventually, after a year of wandering on Anvil, she showed up one night at her father's camp. She just walked in and sat down at the fireside and spoke the oft-quoted line, since known as Sasha's Hello.

'Any food in that pot?'

Sasha went back to a life of healing and cooking, like when she was a girl, but she also made it known that she intended to go off planet and write about her adventures in the wilder reaches of

Paradise. While she would rarely talk about those times, she clearly had something she wanted to set down and something that troubled her. Sadly, this was not to be, and we can only speculate on the stories that might have been, and the insights they would have brought to Paradise.

The following is Sasha's account of 'shunting' a Dendron – a Rex, as she called them. Although the incident occurred when she was nine, she probably did not write this account until she was nineteen or older. The ape nuts she refers to are the buds from monkey trees. Hollop is a word of Sasha's own coining to describe the characteristic motion of a Dendron when agitated.

Shunting a Rex

The shunt I want to tell you about happened when I was nine. Father and me were at the log-drop jetty when we heard shouting. It was Redman and Wynston, out in the log lake and paddling their little boat as fast as they could. They beached and came running into the camp, shouting that a Rex was on its way down the rapids. It had got a steam up. Redman reckoned it must have come hiking over from Horse and had worked its way up the gullies on the other side of the Staniforth Mountains. He was excited. Redman enjoyed a fight like he enjoyed danger, and that was why he was a tops cutter. But Wynston, he was new, fresh in from Moon college, only been with us a month, still earning his blisters and he had never seen a Rex before. His eyes were so big that the whites were like a ring-round-the-moon cake, and I thought they would pop out of his big face, and he just kept saying 'Stamp me blacker than the ace of spades, you see that mother?' till finally father told him to shut it.

'How long before he hits us?' That was Father.

'Ten minutes. Fifteen at outside. He's coming fast. Straight down the rapids. Big fucker.' That was Redman.

'You on for scout?'

'Anyone else offering?'

They banged fists like lumber men do, and Redman set off to get some Molotovs. We could hear the Rex by now.

This was not the first time we had been attacked. It had happened once before, and so the men knew what to do, and so did I. I didn't wait for father's eye but just ran back to our shilo and started gathering up whatever I could of our possessions and piling them into cone baskets. Clothes, razors and scissors, the solar stove that Father brought from Mars, my dolls, some of Mum's bits and pieces that I knew Father treasured. Everything went into the baskets. Big Anton came and helped me. He carried the baskets while I scrambled up the rock bluff above the camp and ran round to the diving ledge over the dark green pool of the Nylo. When I threw the rope down, Big Anton tied the baskets on and I pulled them up.

The diving ledge was the safest place. Father and I had discussed it, in case there was an attack in the night and we got separated. It was high above the log lake, and no Rex could get up there – like a man can't climb a sand dune while holding a sack of stones on his shoulders. And there was a cave up there, and at the back of the cave was water. The diving ledge was also the best vantage point from which to see what happened, and that was what pleased me.

Other men brought baskets of their things and I pulled them up and stacked them neatly. We could hear the Rex getting closer, and everyone spent as much time looking over their shoulders as they did hefting the baskets. When its flags appeared over the trees, the men stopped bothering with the baskets and got to their fight positions.

Now there you see is a funny thing. A Rex on the move always makes a shagger of a noise with trees pushed over and the stamp of the stool crushing everything. But yet they always seem to catch you by surprise. Forests are strange places for noises. One minute it can be quiet and all you can hear is the pop of the seed pods or the rattle of leaves. Then suddenly the trees shake and fall, the earth shakes and rumbles, explosions like when a rock splits in the fire batter your ears – and suddenly a Rex appears round the corner of the stream, heaving along and nothing can stop him, and his shadow is over you before you can stand, and it's curtains bon-bon unless you can climb a sunbeam.

And what was Father doing while I was protecting the home and our wealth? He was preparing a firewall round the big equipment – the diggers, the saw crane, the tractors and scuffers. In those days we used to build a wall made of a plant we called poor man's coffee. We wove it with lawyer-and-hang cord, which will tighten but never release. The perimeter wall was kept clear every couple of days by sending the tractor round it. Two of the men – Terry and Sanch – were detailed to maintain the wall so that if need arose, like now, they could run fuel into holes cut in the PMC and set it alight. Fire is the only weapon against a Rex when you are in the forest. That is the only thing they respect. Some places have a cannon that can shoot incendiary shells, but there have been a lot of accidents. If you fire a cannon in the forest, you'd better be sure not to hit a tree nearby.

Some people don't believe this, but when you are in the deep forest, well it is like being in a deep green fog. I have been places where, if you reach out a hand, you won't be able to see it when you spread your fingers. Mother speaks whereof she knows! There's men have put down their rifle and taken a leak and not been able to find it when they turned round. They've blamed their cobbers, thinking they were joking them, and sometimes fights have broken out. And yet there it was all the time, under the leaves, waiting till next time someone stood on it and maybe shot a foot off.

The other thing Father was doing was kitting up Redman with Molotovs – Redman liked being front scout. He reckoned that the only reason he'd been born was to fight, and that was all that he was any good for anyway. To be a front scout you had to have guts and smarts, and give Redman his due, he never faltered. He would go down towards the Rex shouting and swearing at it – although I don't think the Rex could hear, still less understand – and he would stand in its path with a couple of Molotovs held above his head. When it got very close to him he would throw the Molotovs under the Rex and try to burn its codds – not that it had a cock and balls of course, this is just what we called the big thing it had there. If it worked, it was a way of slowing the Rex down. Course, if you tripped or fell over because the ground was shaking so much, or a tree hit you, or you dropped the Molotovs before you could chuck them, well it was your own codds got scotched, and your goose too. Your best hope then was that the Rex would step on you and put you out of your misery with a couple of hundred tons of stamp.

Father was also distributing arrows and bows. I kid you not, an arrow can get through leaves and branches that baffle a laser. But he had a laser torch too, and only he or big Anton ever handled it since the time that One-Eye dropped it and burned half the camp down, including all the washing on the line.

So, I know that most of you will never have seen a Rex on the rampage. Many of you will have seen that famous tri-vid of the Rex crossing the Taff Straits with its flags waving in the wind, or that still picture of the Rex stopping to steep at Big Fella Lake in South Chain. Well, what I will do is tell you what I saw and what I know and you can use your imaginations, because as Jim Bury used to say, there's no way a picture can show you. 'You've got to be there.'

But first I want to tell you a bit about the Rex.

When a big Rex rips out its roots and goes walkabout, well, the earth shakes. I don't know how heavy they are, but they carry a lot of water and when that stool comes down it usually sinks a good metre or so into the soil with its stamp, and that shock makes everything tremble. Me, I love it. It used to make me shiver and go tingle just thinking about it. But I have heard my teeth chatter so loud when a Rex was near that you'd think they would bust at the gum. Your Rex don't like raw rock, but they don't mind a riverbed, and that is where they cause landslides if the banks are unstable. If they are walking through the forest they just barge their way through, and where they have passed, you could drive two tractors side by side without touching. Except your tractors would probably get stuck in the stool holes. I kid you not. If it doesn't happen on Mars, it happens on Paradise!

One laddo, a soft kid from Luna way, tried to make a tri-vid of a Rex approaching. Soft fucker climbed into a tree to get a good angle. Starts filming and making his spiel about how magnificent the Dendron carburundum is when the tree he's perched in starts shaking. Shook his camera to bits, it did. Five hundred solas that camera cost, and all he had left was the handle in his hand and a dribbly bit of mike cable strung round his neck. And meanwhile this Rex is getting closer and finally it pushes his tree over as if it was a shyris reed by the river. No one knows how the laddo escaped. Like Father said, he must've dug so bloody fast his mother was a mole, either that or he was God's stablemate. Up he popped when the Rex had passed and he started running. They reckon he ran straight across Anvil, jumped the Ditch, straight across Hammer, straight up the shuttle spout and he didn't stop running till he was back in bed in Birmingham.

But to return. You can smell a Rex, especially when it's running and its pores are open and steam is rising from it. I've never eaten a pineapple, but those that have tell me it smells like that. It also has what I call a green smell, the smell of water with sun on it and bubbles rising. Not a smell of decay, but a sweetish smell. It is the smell of Paradise that everyone notices when they first arrive. That is the smell of a Rex. Quite different from your blue waltzer or your ape nuts or the baby-needs-changing stink of the umbrellas. A special smell, and it gets stronger as the Rex gets close.

We could smell this one and it hadn't even reached the foot of the rapids.

So there I am on my ledge. The first thing I see are the tips of the Rex's twin horns, high above the trees, and with all its flags flying. They were flexing back and forth like a stiff whip as it walked, and the cherries and tears were banging together, sounding like rattles and bells. It paused when it reached the bottom of the rapids. And then lurched and moved on.

I watched as it came round the bend in the river and began to heave its way towards us. I saw the horns bend forward as though to reach out for us, like those things an insect has. But this was an appearance only. The Rex was making life easy for itself as it waded through the water.

It paused in midstream, and the current churned and eddied about its legs and splashed its stool and its codds too. Its size was wonderful. It towered above us and above the logs that bobbed in the water. It was like a giant cockerel, red-crested and black and green and gold. But it was nothing like a cockerel either. It was a proud horse rearing up, with flanks that shivered, or a pack-shouldered bull bellowing at the moon, and the movement of its horns would have scratched the black sky. But it was nothing like a horse or a bull either. It was raw life, like I see in my dreams, free and dangerous. But I was not afraid. I would have swum to it. I would have clambered up its rough wet sides until I could perch between those horns, sitting on the hump, knees spread and gripping with my thighs. I would have looked up through the spread of its horns to the black cherries and red flags and cried with joy. And would it have noticed me? You betcha! Like your elephant knows the ant on its back and the sequoia the dove in its branches.

Then, as I watched, this Rex started to unfurl its crest. Oh, so slowly, like Salome lifting a veil when she was getting serious.

Let me tell you, when you see a Rex walking it usually has its

473

crest hidden. If you look at the pictures of a Rex you will see a ridge along its back. Well, that is the crest when it is folded away. The crest is a branch really, similar to those you find on a fern, and it unfolds slowly like a baby's hand opening. On one side it has a range of silver thorns. I call them thorns but they are more like sword blades as they are very sharp and slightly curved and can be up to two feet long. As the crest rises the thorns unfurl too and become like teeth, like the tines of a newly sharpened saw. It is a fierce weapon, but it is not a weapon in the way we understand, and its unfurling had nothing to do with us.

By this rising, I knew that the Rex had sex on her mind. She was looking for a mate to carve her, for calve she must, perhaps had already sensed one in the hinterland of Anvil that was answering her cry for service. And this call had brought her on her journey, perhaps from distant Horse, and we were just in her way. Our Rex was dangerous simply because she didn't even know we were here. Or even if she did know, we were not of her being and of no concern.

From my perch I could see how the men had fanned out, facing the bank. Redman had climbed round the rocky shore and now stood holding up his Molotovs and shouting out a challenge like Achilles at the walls of Troy. When he saw the crest rise, he gave out a whoop. He knows sex when he sees it. Up on camp level were Father and the rest, all armed, all waiting to see whether the Rex would keep on up the river and pass us by, or whether she would turn in towards our small camp. Stanch was holding a burning torch ready to light up the firewall if the Rex went that way. Big Anton was over near the cabins and Father had given him the laser.

The Rex began to move. The tall horns twitched as though sensing, smelling the wind. And then she stopped in mid-pace, seeming uncertain. Perhaps she smelled fire. The crest closed and opened again with a ringing sound and sent a shimmer across the log lake. No one moved. Men waited to see what she would do. The Rex then turned completely round on her stool in the middle of the lake, her two front legs stamping like pistons, and again stopped. They don't breathe or anything, Rexes, not like a horse or a bull or a cockerel, they just stop. They set down the two front legs and settle back on the stool. Nothing moves except maybe the flags, which flap in the breeze and the cherries, which rattle and ring. Here's a problem for the human. Your Rex might settle down for an hour, for a day, for a week, for a year. No one knows. I don't think the Rex knows, because a Rex doesn't think about things the way we do.

So Father waits, watchful. And then the men get a bit fidgety, like they are looking at a bomb or something. Redman wades into the stream until he's just a few metres from the Rex. He's moving like a cat now. Millennia ago men moved like that when stalking a mammoth or walrus. Without taking his eyes off the Rex, he shouts to Father, 'You want me to rouse it? Throw a Molotov between its horns? Give it a wake-up call?'

Father thinks for a moment. Then he says, 'You fellas be ready. Light your arrows now. If it rears and turns this way fire for the base of the horns. Don't wait for orders.' The men did as told, but they didn't want to take their eyes off the Rex in case it moved. 'OK, Redman. Try your arm.'

I see Redman light the fuse on a Molotov, and then he brings his arm over like an overhead chop with an axe, and the Molotov sails high and smoky and passes right between the horns and falls into the river on the other side.

Wynston laughs, and I think to myself he will lose teeth for that at day's end. Redman heard.

'Just getting the range,' Redman shouts, cheeky fucker, but brave man, eh? Then he lights the second Molotov, takes aim and throws. This one smashes right at the base of the horns, right on the little hump they have between the horns where I'd sit. The fire runs down its front legs and into the river, and up one of the horns. I can see some of the tufts of fibres on the horns start to burn. Redman throws another Molotov, not bothering to light it, and scores another hit. Now the fire runs down the Rex's back and under it to where the codds are and round the base of the crest, which twitches. Flame also begins to lick up the other horn. Another Molotov, but this misses. And another, Redman's last, and this is really clever. He has thrown it high so when it hits the left horn it shatters and the fuel scatters down in a curtain which ignites with a whoosh.

'Burn baby, burn,' shouts Redman, wading backwards. 'Now move, you fucker.'

But the Rex doesn't move. It just stands there and burns. It doesn't know it is being attacked. If it knows it is burning it doesn't seem to mind. It has no idea it might die because it has no idea about death

... And then the flame reaches one of the cherries. I see it happen. A curl of blue flame licks a black cherry and ...

Then it moves. No preparation. No hunkering down to leap like a cat or drawing back a fist like a man. The front legs come up and reach forward like a horse charging. At the same time the stool stretches and throws its weight forward. In one bound it's at the bank, and I see Redman dive back into the river, his only escape, but whether he makes it I don't know. There is no red in the water.

The two front legs grab and claw the shingle and the stool stamps down, and as it does the two front legs clamp again. The men fire their arrows. Many miss because they are wanting to run. Some men simply stand in shock until their hands are burned, then they fire and run. The arrows that land catch and burn with a black chemical smoke. The Rex bounds again, turning back into the stream, and it stops and shivers for a moment. With one strong move it flexes its tall horns to one side and strikes the river with a sound like a whip slapping. The spray puts out some of the flames. I see Redman swimming away, strong. But the Rex flexes to the other side, again flailing the water just where he dives. And when it rears again the water is red. I see Redman's body without a head or an arm, and a little black hole for a neck.

The Rex turns again, and now it does run for the shore. The front pair of legs thrust and seize, the stool pushes and leaps. In three bounds it is there. I see Father fire an arrow which sticks in the crest. Other arrows fly, and again the Rex is burning. Terry and Stanch set the bamboo wall alight and the clearing fills with smoke and cracking fire. The Rex smashes through the flimsy wall, dragging it away and trailing fire behind her.

She hollops round the clearing and I see Big Anton standing firm and the laser starting to carve great black stripes across the flanks of the Rex. The lines smoulder and then burst into flame. I smell something like turpentine but cannot take my eyes away to see if something has spilled. I see Anton aim high and the laser beam sets fire to some of the Rex's flags, but it also starts a fire in the trees beyond.

I see the Rex sit back on her stool and her front legs claw the air as though she would reach up to touch her blazing flags. Surely this is pain, or can I step inside the cool mind of the Rex to whom nothing matters but to mate and move on? She reaches suddenly, her front legs stretching out and she crushes the small laser that has tormented her. I know I scream with fear for Anton, but I see him roll clear and then dart between her legs and round behind the stool, which is three times his height.

The Rex is turning away from the cabins, and Big Anton takes his chance and runs for cover into the trees at the edge of the clearing. The Rex is looking for water. I know that, I can sense it, and so she turns back to the river and moves towards where I am, perched above the swimming hole.

More burning arrows descend, but they do not distract her. She hollops into the water, sending up a wave, and the spray reaches as far as my hideaway. The swimming hole is deep, maybe thirty feet, once the site of a waterfall which perhaps came through my cave. She advances and I see the moment when she slips, or the ground gives way and she sinks lower until her legs and stool are completely under the water.

The burned flags and cherries are level with my eyes. I can reach and touch them, but I don't. I am too frightened, and the smell of the tree is making me gasp and my eyes water. But I look, and I see the red juice run from the cherries and small grains which might be seeds pour out and onto the cave floor. Is it dying before me? Am I seeing death? What a scowl!

There is shouting now and I can see beyond the great horns. What I see does not at first make sense. My father, driving the mobile crane with the big cutter we use to cut the tops off the umbrella trees. He has come to the edge of the riverbank, as close as he dare. And now I see the blade engage and start to spin. The bright teeth become a continuous diamond rim. The crane arm lifts and reaches.

The saw blade, horizontal, slices into the tall trunk that I have called a horn, for that is all it is, not bone or ivory, and immediately my cave is filled with soft, mushy, chewed fragments of fibre. They stick to everything and are in my hair and my ears and eyes.

As the limb falls away, I can see the mouth of a tube, another open throat. But this one fills with a dark green liquid which brims up like a pot boiling, and begins to slop over the sides. It comes in gulps.

The saw blade cannot reach the other trunk and so my father simply turns his attention to the crest, which still stands high. He attempts to cut it at its base, but the blade just clogs and the engine races and slips. We have had this problem before on Paradise.

But perhaps the Rex has had enough of play, and so, with sides burned, one horn gone, a great gash under her crest, her flags and cherries burned and her body bristling with spent black arrows, the great one rallies and heaves round in the water and with one strong hollop is beyond the range of the saw. There are no more arrows or flaming torches. All are spent. The men stand and watch as the Rex, spouting juice from her severed horn, moves out into the stream. Despite her injuries she moves steadily away. The mud is stirred from the bottom where the stool digs deep, but otherwise the water is clearing fast, except where the cut trees are tied at the head of the stream. That is where the remains of Achilles lie grounded, in the place where the jetty touches the shore. He is body-spent, all anger gone, a log in the water beside the ones he had worked so hard to cut.

And Wynston.

Ah, dirty fucker . . .

He's knee deep in the stream, washing the shit from his legs with his hands.

And a man still lies dead in the water!

End

'One Friday Morning at Wishbone Bay', from the
Daybooks of Mayday and Marie Newton

This report, published in *News on Paradise*, is taken from Marie
Newton's diary entry. When explaining the details to Mack, Hera
was quoting from memory and, as we shall see, her recall was
pretty accurate.

The Isaac Newton referred to in the first line was the second son
of Marie and Mayday Newton. At the age of eleven he died on his
parents' farm of poisoning, having eaten a Paradise plum. He was
thus one of the first victims of the toxicity that was starting to manifest in the plums, an irony worthy of Greek tragedy.

It was harvest time and everyone was working in the orchard.
His cries were heard by the farm workers, but when they reached
him he was already curling up in the tight seizure that later became
associated with plum poisoning. He never regained consciousness,
and Marie Newton never recovered from his loss.

Although extensive tests were carried out, none of the other
plums in the Newton orchard was found to be toxic and so the
poisoning of young Isaac was regarded as an isolated case. The
fact that harvesting and export continued for some years after this
speaks volumes regarding the demand for the fruit. However other
deaths were reported off world, and within a few years the trade
ceased completely, when the plum was declared toxic. It is significant that the toxicity appeared in all parts of Paradise and not just
in the Newton orchards.

The story 'One Friday Morning at Wishbone Bay' was celebrated
in its time. Marie Newton had gained quite a following for her
recipes using native foods of Paradise, and because of the stand
she had taken as first president of WAM. She also gained quite

a reputation for her paintings of life at Blue Sands Orchard and for her keen observation of life about her. Marie would no doubt be pleased to know that the story she dashed off as a diary entry and sent to Wendy Tattersall to supplement the pages of *News on Paradise* would, many years later, prove significant when it came to saving the last of the Dendron. That is an epitaph she richly deserves.

•

Busy. Try not to let the memory of little Isaac dominate but it is hard.

Mayday is off to New Syracuse to get the SAS serviced at the station there. I know we are lucky in many ways, but oh how I wish that the grieving would soften. I always thought myself so strong. But busy, busy. Despite the problems in some quarters with the PP, we are still getting more orders than we can fill. Mayday insists that we stay at the quality end of the market even if we have to pick the plums early.

Each plum takes a year to get from being the size of an elderberry to full, plump and edible. Mayday would like a quicker turnaround so he wants to plant more acres. He is a real businessman these days. I am not so sure. We have had reports back of some of the plums tasting bitter, and that never was the case! I don't want to rewrite my recipe books to say, 'Add more sugar!'

I had just got back from seeing Mayday off when Berry (she's the noisy one) came running in (about half past eleven) saying there was a Dendron coming in at Wishbone Bay. This was important. She had never seen a live one. They have become infrequent visitors these days. I used to tell the children stories when they were little about seeing the Dendron wading across to Anvil at Blue Sands Bluff, and of course they have seen the pictures I paint.

I dropped everything, called for Cherry (she's the studious one), who was as usual reading in Mayday's little library, and off we went in the Sputtor,[20] up over the ridge to Wishbone Bay. We picked up Tycho, who was returning from the back field after hearing Berry's shouting.

[20] The solar powered utility tractor used on all farms.

Ten minutes later we were at the top of the bluff looking right out over Wishbone Bay. It is wide and sandy and very safe for swimming, as it does not get deep quickly. There was the Dendron, about a mile from shore. It seemed to be steeping, but it was shaking its tall horns and we could just see the flags flapping, and once it did that sideways slam-slam in which it hits the water with the tips of its horns first on one side and then on the other. It was a still day and we could hear the *slap* on the water.

Suddenly Tycho pointed over to the hills. 'Hey, Mother, another's coming.' And it was. Moving as fast as I have ever seen one move. It was tearing through the wild forest to the west of us, smashing down trees, and its crest was up and swaying and slicing back and forth as it ran. 'There's going to be a fight,' said Tycho, getting excited. It veered round, and for one heart-stopping moment I thought it was going to come over the crest towards us, but instead it headed down from the highland, through the spinney and into the flat marshy area above Wishbone Creek. It stopped there. It was only about a quarter of a mile from us, but we were safe as the bluff is sheer. I doubt it could climb up, but if it tried, I could have had us out of there in seconds.

We could see steam rising from it, and it did a funny little dance. Next it threw its weight forward onto its two front legs, lowered its horns until the tips touched the ground and then, taking all its weight on the front two legs, lifted its stool and stamped it down as hard as it could. We could hear the *thump*, like someone chopping a tree, and we saw the marshy mud slop about. It did this twenty or thirty times, moving round in a circle between each stamp. 'What's it doing?' asked Berry. 'Stamping out the battleground,' said Tycho. 'No, it's not,' I told him. 'What you are going to see may look like a battle, but before long, if we are lucky, we might have two young Dendron trees growing.'

'One each for me and Berry,' said Cherry. 'Tycho can have the stool.'

I'd only heard about this, of course. I'd never actually seen a carving, though there are many stools round Wishbone Bay so it must have been a popular trysting spot. One year we'd had a worker with us, a saw doctor and engineer who'd come to Paradise in the MINADEC days and who went bush when they withdrew. He stayed with us shortly after Tycho was born, to help with the orchard, and he told us some of the things he had seen, including the birth rites of the Dendron.

Anyway. As soon as the Dendron that was steeping in the sea heard the other one thumping the ground, it reared up in the water and started to come inshore. As it waded up out of the water we could see its colours. I had never seen such a brightly coloured one. The horns were of tawny gold and gleamed where they were wet. The stool was of course black – they all are – but the body was a deep yellowish-red and the crest, when it unfurled, was a brilliant crimson. What a sight! And again I had forgotten to bring the tri-vid! It came up onshore, stopped, and then headed for Wishbone Creek, where Mayday keeps the cutter. It went right on past the little boathouse and on up the stream.

Two great heaves, reaching up with the front legs and pushing with the stool, and it was onto the plateau. The other Dendron moved out of the muddy area that it had pounded and started to prowl around the perimeter. I say prowl because that is what it looked like. It had its horns lowered in the front and was tapping them on the ground. It crept forward with small steps, stopped, dragged its stool up and stamped it down. It was just like a dance. Its crest, meanwhile, was stiff and erect – you get the picture – and the tips of the blades gleamed like butchers' knives.

We have a pair of those blades that Mayday found a bit further up Wishbone Creek and we keep them like crossed swords on the wall. They are very sharp, and the edge is serrated like a bread knife. They are quite light, and very brittle now.

The Dendron that was doing the prowling began to move each of the blades in its crest separately. It was as if each one had a mind of its own. Sometimes they rippled like the side of a stingray when it is swimming and sometimes they crossed like scissors. If you put your hands together but with the fingers straight and interlocked, and then move your fingers, still keeping them stiff, you get the general idea. It was obviously getting ready to cut and was trying out its weapons.

The one that had come in from the sea – Mustard, the girls had christened it – moved right into the middle of the swamp. Its crest was very erect. It too had its horns lowered and had them in the mud. It seemed to be looking for something. Then it reared up and did that slam-slam to either side they are so fond of. I don't know how it is they don't lose their cherries – they must be welded on – but they don't. Obviously they know what they are doing. Well. The effect of this slam-slam was significant. It made a trench in the mud but, more important, it must have dislodged some blockage higher up as I saw the water start to run more freely. It was still muddy of course, but it was soon clearer and flowing quickly. Then Mustard positioned itself so that its two front legs were on either side of the stream, and the stool – well, it stamped it down once really hard right in the middle of the stream and the water splashed up and the stool sank deep. The crest was very stiff and, after shaking a bit, didn't move.

The other Dendron, the one that had come overland – it didn't have much colour, just a dun browny grey, nothing like Mustard, though its cherries and flags were bright – now stopped its prowling and came into the circle and then it lowered one of its horns down between Mustard's horns until it rested on the cleft there. It rocked for a while, and I could understand that. It was a tender movement. But then it started to walk slowly backwards, and just at the moment when its cherries were being dragged between Mustard's horns, Mustard started to shake. Then the brown and grey one withdrew quickly, back to beyond the edge of the circle where there was a muddy pool, and there it stopped and steeped.

Great shivers ran through Mustard, and green water came from its back and from its hump and from its cleft. Water poured down its tawny sides and stained the stream. It looked horrible, the green dribbling down over the yellow, like one of my watercolour paintings when I get caught in a shower. The girls thought it was having a pee and they are young enough to giggle. Young Mr Tycho looked a bit disgusted, and since I could not think of any better explanation I kept quiet, though I am not convinced it was having a pee. Something else was happening. Like Mayday says, when we get some specialists out here, we'll find out all these things.

I could see the way the shivers started down at the stool and travelled right up through its body to the tops of the flags, and the flags flapped but they were wilting. When the shaking stopped they drooped and became heavy, and I think some water dribbled from them too. Then Mustard opened and closed her crest twice, and Berry and Cherry, bless them, waved back to her. We watched as, very slowly, the crest sank down. It didn't close onto its back the way they do when they are walking at sea, it lowered down right behind it and slightly turned so the sharp blade tips cut into the bank of the stream. My brave son saw this as submission. 'Yah, it's yitten,' he said. (I have no idea where he has learned that language.) 'It's not going to fight.'

Mustard waited, crest awry, still as a statue.

The other Dendron waited too, stiff and still at the edge of the circle, stool deep.

We all waited. Almost an hour. The girls started to get restless and Cherry wanted to go back and get her book. Tycho wanted to walk down and get closer, but I absolutely forbade that. I don't want to lose two sons.

There was no warning. Suddenly the Dendron steeping at the edge of the circle hoisted its stump, turned round and advanced slowly on our lovely Mustard. It came towards it, as it were, stool first, and its crest was hard and poised, like an axe over a block. It came up beside Mustard and I was interested to note that it was slightly smaller than Mustard. Smaller or not, we saw the saw blade strike, an oblique movement, and at the moment of impact the blades jerked so that it cut as well as sliced. In that one movement it severed Mustard's bladed crest, which fell to one side in the water.

The little girls cried out and held on to me, their arms round my legs, but I told them that what they were seeing was all completely natural and that Mustard hadn't been hurt. But they were a bit too young to understand.

Mustard started to shiver again and green water poured from the wound. I think the cut had also severed a connection inside her where Dendron have that great pump. She seemed to be gulping with shock. Then the smaller Dendron backed off, lowered one of its horns, put the tip under the edge of the fallen crest and, in one quick movement, flipped the whole crest right out of the swamp and down onto the beach. It landed among some rocks and dropped down into the water.

When the crest hit the water, the attacking Dendron seemed to fall into some kind of frenzy. It waved its own mighty crest back and forth, flexing the blades and scattering the inner parts of Mustard which had stuck to the tines. Then it stamped round Mustard again while her torn body shook and gulped. Finally it moved in. It was walking backwards again, crest to the fore, if you can imagine that.

It was working its way backwards until the sharp blades of its crest lay flat across Mustard's back. The blades swept along horizontally and began to shave great slabs of fibre from Mustard's body. The flesh revealed under the mustard-yellow thatch was a patchy green with strands of white. Horrible. Then, with one swift movement, it cut downwards, close to the stool, and we saw great plumes of liquid and dense matted fibre fly in the air as it hit the codds. It cut faster, and chopped down hard several times, digging the tines as deep as it could and working the blade back and forth with a rocking motion. Soon the blade was buried deep inside the still quivering Dendron. And when it was as deep as it could reach, the smaller one pulled away with a great heave of its body, using the weight and strength of its own stump to add pressure. It tore half the side of the Dendron out. We could just see the open wound where the codds had been. It was black inside and seemed to have small tubes clustered there. We saw it cut three or four more times until finally, with a heave, Mustard's stump separated from the main body. A white mush filled the river, like the contents of a stomach pouring out, and drained away. Mustard swayed but the smaller Dendron steadied her with its horns, running them right along the torn length of her body in long smooth strokes. Then it moved round to the front and slid its horns up the horns of Mustard and for several minutes the cherries of the two creatures touched and rang together. There was a sensuality about that, to my human eyes. I may be quite wrong, but that was what I thought. Like Mayday used to put his arms around me after little Isaac died.

Next I saw Mustard shake and curve the upper part of her body, as though testing to see if she could stand alone. She could, but we could see that without the stool to support it, the weight of the rest of her body was heavy on her and threatening to tip her back. The smaller Dendron moved round behind her and ran the blades of its crest under her. It was both supporting her and feeling for the place where the front legs joined the main body. It cut slightly, feeling with its blade almost to make sure that it had the right place. We saw Mustard heave slightly, as though to ease the entry of the sharp crest. And when it was in place the small Dendron began to rock back and forth, cutting upwards, feeling its way. We could see why – one wrong cut and it might slice one of the trunks and that could indeed be fatal. As it rocked and cut, so Mustard rocked too,

485

riding the blade until, with one final pull, we saw the tines of the crest appear up between the hump and the twin trunks and, with a tearing sound, the main body of Mustard fell away and collapsed into the churned mud of the stream.

More liquid came pouring out of the wound. But not as much as we might have expected. The butcher Dendron now moved round to the front. It placed its crest in the cleft between the two trunks and folded it down so that it became a single cutting blade, almost like a samurai sword. The two girls hid their faces at this. They did not want to see what they thought might be the *coup de grâce*. But I made them watch. This might be their only chance, and they would never forget and they could tell their grandchildren. I showed them how carefully the blade had been placed in the cleft. How carefully it was being raised. I showed them how carefully the Dendron was lifting itself up to gain the greatest cutting power. And then it struck down. One powerful, surgical downward cut. It was like a lightning strike. And then, when the power had gone out of the strike, it pulled away and the crest blade cut through the remaining tough fibre of what I knew was the wishbone. The severance was complete. And we cheered as the Dendron which we had called Mustard slowly straightened and split and became two trees, sisters or brothers – call them what you will – standing on either side of the stream.

The Dendron that had done the cutting staggered back. We had hardly given a thought to the energy it was expending. It stood for a while in the muddy green water, steeping. Last of all it lifted what was left of the middle body of Mustard and tipped it down onto the beach. I think that was as much as it could do, and then it made its way slowly down the stream and out onto the shore. Its crest was still raised and we could see that it had lost a number of tines, but it lowered slowly as the Dendron walked out to sea. Then, when the water was almost up to its hump, it stopped, and it did not move for a month.

Next day I took the girls down to the beach to look at what remained of Mustard's crest in the rocks at low tide. We gathered some tines to show Mayday when he got back. Then we visited our two new family members. We could see small white roots around the bases, and we knew that by now both trunks would be bedded deep. Scars had closed over where the wishbone had been cut. The

486

twin trees were straighter too. The stool was . . . the stump. The top had already poured away, and there was a big cavity in it, but the rest was unchanged, pitted, hard as iron, more hoof than tree.

Down on the beach the main body had already started to liquefy, but other parts – the remains of the wishbone – were hardening. I promised I'd cut them pieces off the bone for them to wear as pendants and keep for luck. But most important to all of us was that at the top of the two trees, though some of the cherries and Venus tears had fallen, the flags were flying high.

•

NOTE: This article was written some six years before Mayday Newton was killed while scorching back some Tattersall weeds round Wishbone Creek. It was regarded as a freak accident at the time, as Mayday was an experienced farmer. The exact circumstances of his death were never discovered. Suffice to say that this accident reinforced the doubtful reputation of Tattersall weeds.

Two days after Mayday's cremation, Marie made arrangements to leave Paradise, taking her daughters Berry and Cherry with her. Her son Tycho, who later married Isadora Silvio, chose to stay and manage the farm. They would continue the battle to grow crops derived from Earth-raised seed until the Disestablishment.

DOCUMENT 8

'If You Go Down to the Woods Today ...', from
Tales of Paradise by Sasha Malik

Records regarding the enigmatic creature called the Michelangelo-Reaper are sparse. No one knows when the two names were first utilized. They were certainly in common use during MINADEC times, and were frequently interchangeable. In general, Michelangelo seems to have been the more threatening name, Reaper being used more ironically. The Michelangelo who dallied with Hera was a child and so we must excuse its behaviour, for it had no understanding of its power. We do the same for Cupid with his little darts, do we not? Those readers who perused Document 2, 'Getting Your Man', will have noted Sasha's enigmatic note concerning the disposal of the dead Anton.

So what more is there?

Again we turn to Sasha. Her short story 'If You Go Down to the Woods Today ...' is a strange little tale that might have been composed as a bedtime story and must have come to her after many mouths had shaped it. I am sure it began as a fireside story and she added her own special gloss. It reflects the fear and wonder which this enigmatic creature inspired.

Note that a GB Pass was a free pass to any of the brothels, shows, gymnasia, clinics, etc. available on Gerard's Barn. They were sometimes given in lieu of bonus certificates to MINADEC workers. 'Grubber' was the nickname for a contract miner who would dig anywhere for wages and a percentage of the find. It is doubtful that Sasha would have known what a kipper is. The identity of Jemima, if indeed there ever was such a person, will probably never be known.

If You Go Down to the Woods Today ...

Long time ago, before I was born, there were two gum miners called Norris and Morris. They became mates because their names sounded the same, and they always worked together. They were what Father calls a double act, meaning that what one began to say, the other would finish, and they were always cracking jokes. They could keep their cross-talk up all day and it used to amuse the men in the camps to hear them. They'd begin in the morning as they were loading up their mechanical digger.

Norris Good morning, Mr Morris.
Morris Good morning to you, Mr Norris.
Norris I think we should go and –
Morris – dig for gold today.
Norris Gold? No, Mr Morris, something better than gold. Gum.
Morris Gum? Chewing gum!
Norris Gum to sell to the MINADEC man.
Morris Who took a crap in an old tin can.
Norris Used a banknote to wipe his arse.
Morris Then folded it neat like a GB pass.
Norris Put it in his wallet, put the wallet away.
Both And that why he's rich and we dig clay.
Morris I get your drift, Mr Norris, and I'm shifting upwind.

And so they went on. Making it all up. It doesn't look so funny when you write it down, but when they got going they could stop the whole camp and I hear that men fell down laughing.

The way they worked it in those days, the MINADEC surveyors would come in first and prospect by flying over the valleys and gullies. They had lots of ways of measuring things, and if they thought there was a chance of minerals or gum or anything under the soil, they'd whistle up a digger team of twenty or so grubbers and in they'd go like robbers' dogs.

Well, this was a gum dig where Morris and Norris were working. A big one. The camp was in the middle of a couple of thousand hectares of the tall silver-barked trees they used to call girl in a trance. Good name that, because in the spring the long trailing leaves turn blonde as straw. When the wind blows they swish and bob like hair. Not like my hair. I'm black as Tess O'Leary, but the leaves are beautiful and clear-looking.

Beautiful or not, in they'd go and cut down the trees as near to the ground as they could and drag the lumber away. They cut it short like that as the stump was a good solid foundation for the digger. And then they would dig until they'd turned up all the roots round the tree. It was the roots they wanted as the gum was inside them, little hard yellow veins of it, and they would cut the roots off as they went. Then they'd move on to the next girl in a trance and make her shake her head. They'd bulldoze a track as they went, so that they could send the roots back to the factory on Kossof Island.

Well, this was a good dig where Norris and Morris were working, and they were happy as they were finding lots of gum and making big money.

So, one morning, off went Morris and Norris in their old steam-driven half-track with the big auger sticking out the back like a tail and the root snips riding high. They were working at the bottom end of the stand of trancers and come midday they wanted a rest. There was a dark valley nearby with a little stream coming out of it. So Morris says to Norris, 'Where there's a stream there's –'

And Norris says, '– a place to swim.'

And Morris says, 'And a cup of tea with whisky'.

So in they went, up the valley, following the stream. And they came to a lovely deep pool with the sunlight falling on it and the water so clear you could see the sunshine on the bottom and the shadows of bubbles turning with the flow over the smooth round stones. Without a word, Morris dived in and Norris followed. And when they bobbed up, mouths open as if they'd been drinking like fish, Morris pointed and said, 'What's that, Norris?'

And Norris looked and said nothing. For the first time in his life he didn't have a word to say.

They were both looking at the cauldron bulb of a Reaper – but they didn't know that. They had never seen one. It had big blue knotty veins standing out round the bulb so you could tell it was an old one, and the background was a misty green.

Morris Looks like a Chinese vase.

Norris Bit big for a Chinese vase, unless we've shrunk. And what are those big black globes up in the air above it? Lot of them.

Morris Those are its eyes.

Norris If those are its ayes, I don't want to see its noes. I'd be voted out before I was in.

Morris You don't get a nose on a Chinese vase.

Norris Or eyes. Let's call them its *plums* then.

Morris Mmmm. You know what I'm thinking, Mr Norris?

Norris You're thinking you might shin up that tall stalk there, grab a plum for yourself, one for your mate, and then slide back down using your balls as a brake.

Morris And what will you be doing while I am intermasterbusti-macating myself?

Norris I'm going back to the half-track to get us some smokes.

And this Norris did. But when he got back there was no sign of Morris. But the air was filled with this perfume like almonds and lemon. And the plant had changed too. It had closed up so you couldn't see its cauldron. 'Mr Morris,' he called, but there was no reply. He got frightened then, because he saw the big clusters of balls moving above and descending. When he stepped back, he fell right into the pool.

He was in the water thrashing about when he bumped into some-thing and, thinking it might be a piece of wood, he hung on. But it had clothes on and a little screwed-up face like a puppet and hands like little paws. No mistaking who it was. Mr Morris.

Mr Norris let out a great big scream and swam downstream as fast as he could. He swam over the rocks and through the pools until he got to where they had left the half-track and he revved it up and shot back to camp.

He rang the fire bell, and the men came roaring and running back from where they had been working – all except Lucky Dip, who had chopped a toe off the previous day when an axe went through his boot, and he hobbled up on crutches.

Norris gabbled out his story. No one understood what he was talking about, but they all broke out their weapons and set off back to the ravine – all, that is, except Lucky.

Not one of them came back.

And that is the end of the story.

Finally, in the evening, Lucky raised the alarm. Next day some of the MINADEC 'specials' arrived – the big ugly ones they send in if there's been a slugging between camps. They found the ravine. They found the stream. They followed it up until they came to the pool. They found the Reaper too. It had changed. It was all open and on show like a fairground, all colours and with growths like big blue rubber hands coming up out of its cauldron. And the black cherries were bobbing about on the end of their stalks like bees on a string.

The specials also found the men. They were hung up in the trees like kippers, all dry and shrunken, with eyes like buttons and their muscles turned to white strands of Crispin. They had little black marks on them like someone had spattered them with black paint. The specials cut them down and retreated. One or two of them had started to feel funny with the collywobbles and wanted to lie down on the spot, saying they were tired. Dumb fuckers! They probably would have too, if the others hadn't kicked them down the stream.

They called up an incendiary grenade launcher, the type they use when they want to start a forest fire. Long silver body with a big black warhead. And they fired it up the gully and right into the Reaper. They say the bang could be heard up on Tonic, where it rattled the glasses on the MINADEC bar. And the smell came like a shock wave. I've never smelled a cow's stomach when it has lain dead in the field for a week, but I'm told this smell was worse. I've heard of latrines in the badlands of Byzantium that could stun an ox at forty paces and fell a man like a flying brick. But this I'm told was worse.

So you make your own idea up, Jemima. They said the smell stuck to you like tar and no amount of washing could get rid of it, and that I can believe, because what a Reaper does isn't *on* you, it is *in* you once you have breathed its perfume. And it will come out through your pores until your last kiss – I mean the kiss of death.

So that is why you don't go down in the woods, Jemima, leastways not without your Auntie Sasha. Sasha knows how to talk to Reapers so they smell sweet as honeysuckle and won't hurt a moonbeam like you.

End

•

COMMENT: Events such as this spread as stories. No one knows how many men and women were actually killed by Michelangelo-Reapers, but disappearances were common, and if someone went wandering off into the trees and did not come back, then they would say, 'The Reaper's for him.'

I think men rather like to have an enemy waiting out there in the dark when they're gathered round campfires, and the Reaper fitted the bill for the MINADEC workforce. It's a shame Reapers couldn't uproot and wander like Dendron! Then the MINADEC specials would have had a real nightmare to deal with, but the end would, I think, have been the same.

A mysterious thing about the Reaper was that it could disappear quickly. Once spotted, even a big Reaper would often vanish overnight. When this happened, it would leave nothing behind it except the large clearing where it had lived. This was usually a wide boggy depression in the ground, where it had sat and, in the middle of this, a knobbly root-end like a big black carrot. Obviously that was all that was left of its main root. There were no side roots and no parasitic roots trailing in the trees. It might take a hundred years to grow, but it was gone in a night. No one ever saw this happen, or if they did, left no record. This too added to the mystique of the Michelangelo-Reaper.

Official MINADEC policy was to destroy Michelangelo-Reapers whenever found. They were declared a noxious bio-form, which meant that a bounty was paid for each one destroyed. When a survey team encountered a Reaper it would deploy what was called a STET (specific target extreme temperature) bomb. These generated terrific heat for a brief period but had only a small explosive charge. They were quite heavy and had a sharp point at the front. STET bombs were regarded as environmentally friendly weapons, as they did not damage the nearby flora. A STET bomb could be dropped from about fifty feet above a

Reaper and so was extremely accurate. It cut through the upper part of the bulb, which Sasha calls its cauldron, and then, when inside the Reaper, it was detonated by a radio signal.

The Reaper put on quite a show, evidently, for despite its fleshy appearance it burned easily. A common belief was that this was caused by combustible gases contained in the cauldron. In effect, the small bomb triggered a private and devastating explosion.

'Child Spared Grim Fate' by Wendy Tattersall,
News on Paradise 27

•

Not all manifestations of the Michelangelo-Reaper were fatal. Here
is a brief account published by Tom and Wendy Tattersall in their
irregular round-up of events called *News on Paradise*.

•

We have all done it at some point: looked away while the children
are playing or become absorbed in a book. Or perhaps we thought,
Tom's there or *Sulia's on guard*, and closed our eyes for five minutes
too long.

So it was when we visited Sulia and Tewfic Rokka's beautiful
homestead, to help celebrate the birthday of their youngest daughter Krisima. It was a good time too, for a reunion with others from
the first ship, the good ship *Figaro*. Among those gathered were
Gerda and John Pears and their children Petra and Benji, and the
'Plum' Newtons and their offshoot Tycho (and another offshoot
to be, unless Marie has put on a lot of weight). Also present were
Eugenie and Estragon Lermontov, who came with their three boys
Sergei, Fyodor and Vsevolod. The Lermentovs were wearing the
same clothes as the day they stepped off the *Figaro* (some of us are
not so lucky). Lastly, we were pleased to see Tania and Sean Lysaght
and their daughter Cathleen, who is shooting up like a rocket. It
was a two-day party, and on the second day we went up the coast
in the cutter to Mad Miner Falls. (For the origin of this name see
News on Paradise No. 11.)

It was an ordinary day on Paradise. You know the kind of thing.
Bright sunshine. A light breeze offshore. The wind scented. A clear

sea. Dipper palms rising and falling on the headland. First vintage plum wine, and plenty of it.

Some time in the previous week a Dendron had come past and had left a big stamp in the sand which the children could hide in and which Mayday kept falling into, pretending he had had too much of his own vintage.

After lunch, Tom who-can-never-sit-down-for-longer-than-five-minutes Tattersall suggested we climb the falls to see if we could see the Dendron, as it would have wandered out to sea somewhere nearby and might be steeping. This we did, each of us carrying a child on our shoulders and taking another by the hand.

At the top there was no Dendron to be seen. The party split up. The 'adventurers' set off to explore, while the 'squatters' settled down in the shade to entertain the little ones more interested in playing with the kite seeds blowing down from the hills. The split-up was where the problem began. I was a squatter, and I thought Cathleen Lysaght had gone on with her mummy and daddy. But Tania and Sean thought she had stayed with me.

She was missing for three hours, and none of us knew.

It was only when the adventurers returned that Tania asked me where Cathleen was and I replied with the fatal words that no parent ever wants to hear: 'But I thought she was with you.'

There was no panic. Thank God for the basic RISC training. Within minutes we were organized into search parties. Tania and I elected to stay with the rest of the children, and we gathered them close, I can tell you. We all had our PSRs, so we could keep in contact with the parties who spread out. Some went down into the valleys; others headed for higher ground, where there was a small stand of trancers. We thought she might have gone up there as she has lovely long strawberry-blonde hair and there are none of those trees near the Lysaghts' patch. But no luck.

It was just after I had put the PSR back down after contacting the other teams when I heard Tania cry out. She was pointing. Not up the headland but across the dark ravines, where the forest bush was thick. And when I turned and looked, I saw it too. Rising above the dark green bush was something like a golden bugle but which drooped as it ascended, as though it was heavy. And then others joined it, each on its own stalk. Behind them I saw a spike rise high, and then another and another, and all of them opened into the most beautiful jade-green and pepper-red and cornflower-blue flowers resembling starbursts, like the lovely agapanthus I used to have in my back border.

Tania's cry was a cry of horror and I understood, for we both recognized the terrible signals of the Michelangelo. (They call it that to try to stop people worrying, but we knew, and the people who were here before us knew too, and we all called it the Reaper.) I was on the phone in an instant to Tom, who had headed in that direction, and his reply when he came in was a whisper. I've given the transcript of this, but I can remember every word.

Tom T   We can smell it from here. We're moving on. We can't see anything yet. It's a real jungle in here. Mayday is holding back so that if anything happens to me, like I get drowsy, he can come through and take over. (PAUSE) Sean? You on line?

Sean Lysaght had led a party exploring the cliff tops beyond the headland.

Sean   Receiving.
Tom T   I found Cathleen's sun hat just now. Suggest you and Tewfic pull back from where you are and join us. Wendy knows the direction.
Sean   On our way.

It was an open line, so everyone heard this. They would all be turning back by now. The next moments were terrible. Tom had his radio on and we could hear him pushing through the bush and swearing under his breath. He, of course, like the rest of us, had never seen a live Michelangelo, so he did not know exactly what to expect. For a few moments there wasn't a sound. Then very softly and quietly we heard this:

Tom T   I can see Cathleen. She is on her knees and she seems to be playing, drawing in the sand. I can't see her clearly because she is surrounded by ... I don't know what you call them ... They're not like plums; they're more like elderberries, black and shiny and all different sizes ... She seems all right and is talking ... I can't hear what she's saying. She's talking to ... I can see where the black berries come from. There are stems high above in the top of the canopy and they hang down from there. The threads are so fine I can only see them when the light catches them. Hell, I can see the flowers too, through the canopy. High, high above us. They're opening and closing slowly. (PAUSE) I'm not sure what to . . . I'm going to advance slowly. See if she'll come to me. I don't want to trigger anything . . . (CALLS) Cathleen. Cathleen. (WHISPERS) She's heard me. She's standing up and . . . (CALLS) It's me, Tom. Are you OK? (WHISPERS) She's waving. The black berries have lifted from round her. (CALLS) Time to go home now, Cathleen.

Cathleen (SEEMINGLY FROM FAR AWAY) I want to stay here. I'm playing a drawing game. Come and look.

Tom T I can't. We have to go now. All the others are waiting for you. Your mother wants to see you. She sent me specially.

Cathleen Bother. All right. I've lost my sun hat.

Tom T It's OK. I found it. You'd dropped it. Come on now. (WHISPERS) She's turning round. The plant there, the Reaper thing, its leaves are all up like an aloe vera so I can't see the bulb it's supposed to have. I'm sweating like a horse. The smell is getting to me too. It's not unpleasant. Cathy's lifting her arms and one of the berries has come right down and bumped her forehead. She's laughing and now she's given it a kiss . . . I wonder what she's seeing? She's not at all afraid . . . and now she's coming towards me . . . She's just turning back to wave. The Reaper hasn't moved. Now she's on her way again . . . She's here. (LOUD) Hello, Cathy.

Cathleen Hello, Tom. Thanks for coming for me. Well, wave to her. You always wave at least once when you leave someone's house. Goodbye.

Tom T We're on our way out. We're on our way out. God, my legs. Bloody legs are shaking.

And that was it.

As they left the forest we saw the giant flowers and trumpets droop and retreat and finally disappear below the level of the canopy.

Cathleen, of course, never knew what all the fuss was about.

Back at the Rokka farmstead she seemed none the worse for her ordeal. When we asked what she had been doing, she put her head on one side and her tongue between her teeth – the perfect image of the perplexed five-year-old – and then she said, 'There aren't any words for it.' And she's probably right. When she was tucked up in bed she said, 'We were sort of drawing in the sand. I'd draw something and then she'd draw something, and then I'd change what she'd drawn and she'd change what I'd drawn. And sometimes we drew things together.'

But we never found out any more.

End

•

COMMENT: A pretty story, but it's not quite complete. That same night the colonists had a meeting about what they should do. The Rokkas were very clear that they didn't want a Reaper anywhere near their homestead – in fact they wanted to destroy it. The Newtons and the Pears sided with them. The Lermontovs sympathized, but pointed out that the Reaper was not exactly on their doorstep and that the plants were not wanderers like the Dendron, and so on balance they thought it should be left alone. The Tattersalls were adamant that the Reaper should not be touched but left to get on with its own life. The Lysaghts had had such a scare that they had gone to bed and little Cathy was sleeping in their room.

At the height of the argument Mayday Newton suggested that perhaps Tom Tattersall had sniffed too much of the scent of the Reaper and his judgement was unbalanced. Tom T took offence and pointed out that he was actually the only one (apart from Cathy) who had actually been close to the Reaper, and was therefore aware of its presence, and that presence was not hostile.

They did not take a vote, but next morning at dawn Mayday Newton, Tewfic Rokka, John Pears and Estragon Lermontov took the cutter up the coast. Estragon had agreed to steer and take charge of the boat.

Shortly after dawn the Michelangelo was set on fire using homemade petrol bombs ignited by a domestic fire lighter. Its burning took just twenty minutes and they were able to return home in time for breakfast.

It may not be significant, but this is the last recorded sighting of a fully active mature Michelangelo.

'The Pity of It' by Wendy Tattersall, *News on Paradise 28*

In this brief article Wendy Tattersall reveals her feelings of outrage in response to the killing of the Michelangelo. This article marked a distinct split within the ranks of the original agricultural colonists – aggies, as they were known. The killing she is referring to is printed as Document 9, 'Child Spared Grim Fate', also written by Wendy Tattersall.

•

Two months ago something terrible happened on Paradise of which we must all be ashamed. A creature of this world, an inhabitant of much longer standing than any of us and which bears two contrasting names of our giving, the Reaper and the Michelangelo, was burned to death for no reason at all.

It had done nothing except give vent to its feeling for beauty with a display unparalleled in my experience, and it had given an afternoon of pleasure, a 'drawing lesson' let us say, to a little girl.

Now I, as much as any of you, know the reputation of the Reaper. We have all been fed the garbled stories told by drunken men in the MINADEC days, detailing how the Reaper would 'suck out your juices and spit out your corpse'. We have also heard the fantasies of men and women who lived in a deprived relationship with nature on this world of ours, and talked about a creature that made tapestries of your spirit.

But how many of us have looked with open and un-shuttered eyes upon the Michelangelo? Why do we have this knee-jerk reaction as soon as we encounter something we do not understand? Must we have a 'devil' on Paradise?

If so, it is a devil of our own making, and one that we have carried here in our own minds.

I call on you all now, let us redefine Paradise in our own terms. Let us look with kind eyes. Let us celebrate beauty as a manifestation of goodness. Let us disregard the folklore of old Earth, with its goblins and witches which lurk in the forests, and move on. As a wise man said once, long ago and with different intent, we have nothing to lose but our chains – and those chains are of our own forging.

I await your comments.

'Buster', by Professor Israel Shapiro

Hera Melhuish believes the main part of the following essay was composed sometime after Israel Shapiro's work had been attacked for its 'mystical' content. If so, its tone is far from defensive. It is a refreshing article, lacking the mordant voice of some of Professor Shapiro's other essays. In this we see glimpses of the humour of the man. He would perhaps be amused that the most recent research on the fractal tends to corroborate his intuitive understanding.

Buster

Among the many stunts attempted during the MINADEC days, one of the most spectacularly unsuccessful was the introduction of guard dogs on Paradise. The dogs usually died within three weeks of arrival. The vets could find nothing wrong with them, but the dogs were unimpressed by this and remained obstinately dead.

Most were burned on Scarlatti. Some who had been special pets were given decent burial and a few even had small tombstones erected above them. One such was called Buster, and I have him with me now.

In his prime he would have been all snarl and slaver, but now he is nicely enamelled. This creature, which was once a great biter of felons, is now as harmless as a hearthrug. He couldn't hurt a flea, even if he could find one.

I have had him for ten years, ever since he was lifted, rump first, from the potting mix. He is therefore considerably older than me. Originally he was placed in a metre-long coffin, paws crooked and tail brushed, but since they had made his coffin from woven hybla stalks it would have deliquesced within weeks, as is so often the case on this planet.

And that is the first point I want to make. That which is of Paradise deliquesces when it dies; that which is of Earth does not. As regards Paradise, this rule holds with a few notable exceptions: the Dendron body fibres harden to something like flaky quartz, the tuyau turn to a kind of organic stone, and a few others achieve a certain carvable permanence. Not so the bio-forms of Earth. They do not rot or turn to rock. The natural agents of decay so familiar to us on Earth, and evidently durable enough to travel with us, yea through the fractal, do not function down here. If you die up on the shuttle platform you rot, if you die on the surface of Paradise you are coated with brown enamel. The logical experiment of killing something at each moment of descent and observing exactly when the enamelling begins has not so far been conducted, though Dr Melhuish and I did achieve something similar with a dead dog, as I will explain.

It would seem that the change from mortification to mummification occurs at exactly the moment we experience the planet directly. There is a slight philosophical conundrum here linked to the word experience. I suspect that personal attributes are involved in the experiencing of Paradise. To some humans the Paradise experience may even be sensed while on Earth. To others, Paradise may be experienced as they emerge from the fractal platform Alpha-over-Paradise. But for most bio-forms of Earth the experience is most fully realized as they slip below the very Earth-determined environment of the shuttle platform and enter the green and milky-blue atmosphere of Paradise itself.

The rule would seem to be this. While you are alive on Paradise your normal functions continue within you, but they are contained within an invisible membrane. If you sneeze, any viruses die within inches of your nose. If you scratch, then the fine particles from your skin are contained and neutralized and wrapped by this fine patina which we have described as lacquer or enamel. I experimented on myself once. I combed my hair – this was some years ago – and immediately studied the particles under the microscope. They were enamelled.

It is as if everything organic of Earth is entrapped within this fine semi-permeable membrane, which filters and then neutralizes it. Nothing physical of a non-Paradise bio-form actually enters the life cycle of Paradise. And, at the moment of death, Paradise rushes in and takes you over completely. The semi-permeable becomes impermeable.

I can hear you say, 'What is the moment of death?' We have argued about that for years and have reached no final conclusion. Paradise, however, cuts through the problem. It knows when you are dead and takes action. It may be the moment, described in some philosophies, when the fine silver thread breaks and the spirit leaps free. It may be the moment when your brainwaves cease. If you are on Earth or in an Earth-simulated environment, such as the shuttle platform, then of course your body immediately begins a million and one dynamic processes, all the consequence of your death, and you decay, and so we bury you or burn you or fire you into the sun.

But not on Paradise. It is the stuff of horror stories to contemplate that you might yet have consciousness when Paradise decides you are dead. You live on in an eternal moment of whatever suffering you were experiencing as the planet closes about you. But I doubt that. That would not be consistent with everything I know and have experienced about Paradise. I would stake my life on the fact that Paradise knows exactly to the nano of a nanosecond when you are dead, and in a way which we, confused by categories and processes, do not. The Thanatos point may indeed be a moment bounded on one side by the grey-moving-to-black of decay and on the other by the grey-moving-to-green of life, but as a point of transition, of interface, the Thanatos point exists.

Here, on Paradise, we used to bury bodies, and for many years they remained intact, down there among the roots. There are no histories indicating that Paradise rejected the human in the early days. The first was, I think, a child, but that was during the agricultural pioneer stage and things were already going wrong. But now, some generations on, those same bodies 'rise again and push us from our stools'. We find we are not destroyed beneath the soil, as would be the case on Earth, but have undergone something akin to a sea change. Shakespeare would no doubt see it more clearly, but to the common eye the bodies that are found sleeping on the surface have shrunk as they dried and seem coated with lacquer. They become lighter too. They burn like chaff. They leave little ash. Even the bones ignite like phosphorus. We have not been here long enough to know these mummies' ultimate fate, but the healthy soil will not contain them and exhumes them by some natural working of its own. We should place sentinels on the graveyards of Paradise to watch the dead rise. (My God. If I had written those words a few centuries ago, I would have been talking about the Last Judgement. Let us keep Paradise clear of such thoughts.)

The secret to all of these changes lies in the interface between our bodies and Paradise. Buster and I have together studied this for some years.

My first experiment was of fourteenth-century simplicity. When I brought him home, dry and easy enough to carry, I cut a section across one of his claws with my scalpel. I suppose I expected to see a fine profile of the lacquer – a bit like the rind on a horse chestnut – and perhaps, if I were really lucky, I might even see it spread to cover the newly exposed part. No such luck. The fault is in the metaphor, for we are not dealing with lacquer or enamel or rind or any kindred process, but something vastly more subtle.

Where I had made the diagonal cut, the exposed surface was in no way different from the skin or the eyeball or the individual hair of Buster's coat. Either the change had come as I cut, or it had been there all the time. I am still not absolutely sure of the answer to this, although I have spent quite a time chopping bits off him, dipping them in different substances, boiling, freezing, etc. When I cut him open – a bit like cutting through stiff cardboard – I found his organs intact, right down to the contents of his stomach and bowels, and all in a perfect state of preservation. A cast, fired and glazed, could not have been more true. It was obvious that this cut-and-see approach was not getting anywhere.

My second major experiment was much more upmarket. I took Buster on a journey to the bio-security lab at I-HEDBET. I carried him in a sealed box containing the air of Paradise, travelled as quickly as I could and had prepared my way well. I had booked lab time and had made known the experiment I was conducting. Many research students and former colleagues wanted to assist.

The facilities of the bio-security lab at I-HEDBET are the best one can find anywhere. There I transferred Buster and his precious atmosphere to the vacuum of a hermetically sealed manipulation closet. I was hoping to exclude all non-Paradise contamination.

Within the HMC, I was able to amputate those parts of the dog which interested me. I took slices of hairs and tissue so thin they were just a few molecules thick. Whenever I cut I encountered the membrane. What I needed was to see into the interstices of the membrane, for this surely was the threshold which Paradise used to insulate itself from the things of Earth. Here I had a stroke of sudden good fortune.

Among our equipment we had an electron scanner. Despite its accuracy we found we could not calculate the nanometric wavelength of the membrane, since it was operating at a frequency smaller than the scanner could achieve. However, one of the research students had come up with a technique called resonance phasing. This uses a harmonic of the original image, and when we managed to tune to this, we were able to gain a visual image. We were in effect seeing the unseeable, looking beyond photons, and what we saw was a gleaming silver surface so bright and energetic it had to be damped down. As I made a section through one of Buster's hairs, we saw something that had the brilliance of molten glass (though no heat) flow from just in front of my blade. Remember, we are talking of quantum states, and the energy of Paradise (for such it was) was predictive, coming into existence just before it was needed.

My belief, and the belief of those who were with me, was that what we were witnessing in that blazing brilliance was a threshold. Any door or a gate has a threshold, and we were all reminded of the scintillation which occurs just before entering the fractal. We were seeing, as well as we could, the deep energy of Paradise. And what words can we use to describe that? If this threshold protected Paradise then it was the will of Paradise or the intention of Paradise we were seeing. It is only a small step to say we were seeing the thought of Paradise, but what that thought was, we had no way of knowing.

Even as we watched, our faces white in the reflected light and our eyes gleaming, we saw the brilliant image fade. Silver became grey and grey gradually became grainy and died away. For me that was a moment of awe-full truth. I knew, though how I knew I cannot say, that what we were seeing was the reality of Earth reasserting itself as the vitality of Paradise withdrew. We saw the old and familiar onset of decay.

Later, when I wrote about this, we got into a rare old row. To me, we had gone as far as the instruments would allow and reached the point at which imagination must take over if we wanted to go further. And that seemed to me quite appropriate. If what we were witnessing was the threshold of thought, then how better to approach it than with the imagination?

I was shaken. I had seen that brilliant threshold that could hold time at bay. It was then, and remains now, as awesome as it is terrifying. If you wish to talk of a gleaming sword that protects Paradise, then you need look no further.

With the experiment concluded I put the remaining bits of Buster in deep freeze. I went to visit my sister in Cambridge. Thinking too hard can get you drunk, and I am lucky to have Fortuna to fall back on, for she can always lift a hangover. Ideas are more intoxicating than wine, and she let me talk and explore contradictions, and sometimes, you know, she says just the right word and suddenly you can see things more clearly. When you live too long in your head, the reality you find there becomes too real, falsely real, and that is when you need the challenge of masterpieces to ground you. She played me Mozart and Haydn and stole my Baudelaire. We went to one of the twentieth-century revivals Fortuna is so keen on – Shostakovich's *Lady Macbeth of Mtsensk* – performed by a company from Peru. It was not to my taste, but that does not matter. It had a vitality true to that great and troubled century.

Feeling more myself, I returned to I-HEDBET. I had by then worked out my theory on how Paradise protected itself with a thin skin of thought. I now needed to observe more closely my theory in action.

My final experiment was decidedly prehistoric. I took Buster out of cold storage, stitched him together and left him decently covered with a sheet and lying on a trolley in the corridor outside the main bio-form lecture room. A hundred students tramp by every day. I left a note on Buster saying dead dog – do not look under this sheet, thereby ensuring that 99 students a day looked at him and breathed on him. After some days, my patience was rewarded: Buster began to smell. Two more days in an incubation box in the bio-security lab and he was ripe. Without the protection of Paradise, he had spontaneously begun to rot. In this state I shipped him back to Paradise with me, hoping he would pass through the fractal without his decay being arrested. He did.

Meanwhile I had Dr Melhuish come up to the platform. I made

her look at Buster and undertake microbial and DNA tests. With these complete, we travelled down to the surface in a private shuttle. At my request we journeyed as slowly as possible. We monitored the dog closely and within minutes of leaving the shuttle platform we noticed a change. Buster was becoming enamelled again. It spread over him and through him. I imagine the effect was instantaneous, but it took a few moments for it to manifest. Our instruments stopped recording and the smell stopped too. This proved one thing: that it was not the air of Paradise – for we were breathing shuttle air or platform air – but the presence of Paradise that caused the sea change.

We had the shuttle stopped and then taken up again, but could detect no change. Buster remained enamelled, which meant simply that the insulation of Paradise took a longer time to wear off than to be imposed. Finally we dropped down to the surface.

During this short journey we developed the most terrible sore throats. We also experienced stomach cramps which grew in intensity the lower we descended. We tottered from the shuttle, me clutching the dead dog and Hera making a beeline for the ladies. We both suffered from what I afterwards called Buster's revenge, until our systems were purged of all dead dog matter. In addition I had an itchy scalp and itchy skin, which did not really clear until I swam in the sea. We drank copious quantities of water. The symptoms did not last long, fortunately. Paradise deals swiftly with death.

But I had proved my theory. Paradise enclosed us. Prohibited decay. It was not something in the soil. And now we also knew why the early dog handlers complained of sickness after they had taken the dead guard dogs for disposal. And why, when others had brought in sheep and cattle, there were complaints from the shearers and slaughterers. Their sickness was caused by the particles of the dying creature that they had inadvertently consumed, which had then been lacquered by Paradise inside them.

People used to say that this was because there were no animals native to Paradise, only plants. This is the great popular misconception. The truth is that there are no animals on Paradise and there are NO PLANTS either. There are only the Paradise bio-forms, unique and singular, and they have a culture of total exclusion and the ability to impose it on elements from outside Paradise.

•

POSTSCRIPTUM (not for publication): Do I mean 'total'? Absolutes are dangerous. I think there is a *will* in the planet which can lift the veil of exclusion, but I have no idea how. I am teased by those lines of young Sasha when she says, in her love story, 'to see my golden dead love's silver flowers rise'.

I have seen that silver. I saw it in a lab at I-HEDBET, and I saw it shine on the sober, surprised faces of my fellow scientists. I see it still in my mind's eye. And I am bold enough to make a prophecy. As Paradise wakes up, as the bodies start to bob to the surface more frequently, as the toxins grow in leaf and fruit, as the rejection gathers strength – for all these are manifestations of the *will*, by which I mean the *thought* of Paradise – so you will find that the fractal connection will break down. They are kindred processes, and hence they work in sympathy. It is one of the deep laws of nature.

Let us return to Miss Malik. I think that witch-woman, the more-than-a-woman, the woman that any man would die loving (I am talking of Sasha, of knowledge) knew how to cross that threshold and she did that for her man Big Anton. His body will never be found, and nor will Sasha's. That I promise. At their death they simply dissolved like a leaf of the tough hybla that settles on the ground. They dissolved. Skin, juices, bones and all flowed into the soil of Paradise – to be reborn in some way of its own devising. For them the gate into Paradise was open.

As for me, well, I am pretty pickled inside, and I know I am hooked on Paradise, but I will not deliquesce. So, when my time comes, my wishes are very clear. To get me off Paradise before the last breath. I do not want that sudden insulation, that lacquered shroud. And burn Buster too, as a hero. But . . .

> Get me back to Earth, please.
> Cremate me when you can.
> And I who once knew Paradise,
> Will die a happy man.

End

'How the Valentine Lily Got Its Name', from
Tales of Paradise by Sasha Malik

The following is the story which Hera was referring to when she
mentions the tale of Valentine O'Dwyer and Francesca Pescatti.

Most references in the story are obvious, but it is worth remembering that there never was a child called Jemima. She was the fic-
tional younger sister or niece that Sasha imagined. Conventional
wisdom holds that this was wish-fulfilment, a product of Sasha's
loneliness. But I hold there is more. I think Jemima reflects Sasha's
desire to communicate and pass on her knowledge of Paradise. In
my reading, Jemima is the child which Sasha would never have.

How the Valentine Lily Got Its Name

Once upon a time, a long time ago, before I was born, there lived
in the small town of New Syracuse, on the planet called Paradise,
two families named the O'Dwyers and the Pescattis, and though
their gardens shared a common river that flowed between them at
the bottom of their gardens, they hated one another like fire hates
water. If Mrs Pescatti put the washing out, Mrs O'Dwyer lit a bon-
fire and the smoke always dirtied the washing because she burned
sooty things and fanned the smoke with her apron. If Mr O'Dwyer
was sitting down to watch a tri-vid of a distant conflagration, for
such was his passion, Mr Pescatti would start his lawn mower with
the faulty coil and mow the patch of brevet he called a lawn until
there was no plant left, and he would not stop even though the sun
went down until Mr O'Dwyer had come to his door in a rage and
shouted across the ravine which separated them.

Now the O'Dwyers had a son called Valentine, a tall handsome dark-haired lad much fancied by the girls of the town, who would hang out their washing in the rain just to catch a glance of him. But he had no eyes for them. He looked for and sighed for and stiff-ached for Francesca Pescatti, the only daughter of Mr and Mrs Pescatti. And she, Francesca, beautiful as dawn, with skin like the white Crispin lily which grows in the cold plains of Ball, and hair that was golden and curly like maid o' the lake, and full-breasted too, like her mother (but firm and tight, not slack and slouched, so that her mother had to keep adding darts and pleats to keep her decent) she moist-ached for Valentine.

Valentine and Francesca grew up like poppies in a coil of barbed wire. When they were little – I mean younger than me, about your age, Jemima – Francesca would put on a white dress, for she loved wearing white, and then she would slip through the loose fence board near the garden shed, hidden behind the family blue waltzer, which is, as you know, the protector of the good, and run down to join Valentine. He had come crawling through the hole he had cut in the Machiavelli nettle, which is, as you know, the protector of freedom, which he had lined with tin sheet so he didn't get stung. They would meet at the little bridge which crossed the stream which separated their houses and play quietly. They floated boats of hybla under the bridge and pretended to cook meals on a campfire. They didn't play mothers and fathers as that didn't seem much fun. But when the jenny bobbed up to feed, Francesca would put her finger to her lips and whisper she had to go home, and they would arrange the next time they were to meet. Once Valentine kissed her quickly, and she said she would tell, but the only person she told was the big blue waltzer, and he wasn't telling anyone. But her mother would catch her when she got home and say why was she wearing a white dress to play near the dirty back shed. And Mrs Pescatti would have to wash it, and no sooner was it pegged on the line when out would come Mrs O'Dwyer with her matches, like a smelly one after monkey nuts.

But they grew up, Francesca and Valentine, and the day came when she could no longer get through the fence and he had trouble with his tunnel. And besides, boat races and pretend cooking had lost their tang, so what were they to do? They didn't know it, Jemima, but they had fallen in love, like you will one day, and love is like a Rex with her fanny up – she always finds her mate.

Now there was in the town of New Syracuse a woman who had a shop where you could buy everything from pens and pins to prayer books and potions. So Francesca would hide her mother's prayer book and Valentine would hide his father's pencil – and they would be sent down to Mrs Lorentz's shop for replacements. And she looked on them fondly, for she remembered what it was like to be young and let them sit in her back parlour, face to face, knee to knee, holding hands and hurting for something they could not name. See, they had never been told what bodies are for, and they could not read very well so they couldn't go to the library and get a book about bodies. And they didn't have a nice big Auntie Sasha to tell them. Course, they knew that if they touched themselves in certain ways it was very nice and made them feel alive and drowsy at the same time. So they sat there aching and then they got to peck-kissing, and then they got to touching and then Mrs Lorentz threw them out because she had to shut up shop.

One day when Valentine was sixteen and Francesca was just fifteen, he said to her, 'Meet me at your blue waltzer tonight after the streets lights are out.'

'I can't,' she said. 'I'll be in bed.'

'Well, get out of bed when you hear your dad snore. Come down the stairs and don't slam the door.'

She told herself she wouldn't, but when the street lights of New Syracuse went out she was out of bed in a flash. There was no sound in the house but the snoring of her dad as she tiptoed down the stairs and outside into the sweet night air.

Yes they had stairs in their house, not like ours, and I don't know why they had street lights, Jemima. Perhaps so that people could read on their way home from the library. Now hush and listen, because this is interesting.

She tiptoed down to the bottom of the garden and went behind the blue waltzer, which was a big tree by now, and Mr Pescatti was thinking of cutting it down so he could see when Mr O'Dwyer was watching a tri-vid. Francesca looked and looked, but there was no one there. Then she heard a sound like *mee mee* – the sound a swing rope makes when first you swing on it – and she climbed up on the old fence and peeped over and there she saw something very strange. Four of the big red fly-by-night balloons were coming towards her, and dangling under them was Valentine, pulling for his life along a cord and getting closer. You see, earlier that day he had come over and attached a line to the fence to guide him. And he had practised for some time to see how many fly-by-nights he would need to float in the air and he found that four would carry him easily.

He climbed down at the fence. Tied his balloons to a piece of wire he'd fashioned earlier. Climbed through the fence because he'd already put one of the palings on a hinge so he could get in and out quickly. They were in one another's arms in a minute like that drawing I showed you by Mr Sergel where the lovers are eating one another! And then the two of them were in the shed. And she was only in her nightie. And then she wasn't.

What happened that night I do not know. Well, not exactly. And even if I did, I wouldn't tell you, Jemima. Not yet anyway. But soon there came the dawn. Night's candles were all burned out and sunrise turned the misty mountain tops to gold.

She ran to her bedroom and stood at her casement and waved as he pulled himself over the dark ravine. The balloons he rode on were red as the blood that she found on her nightie and washed out herself with pride, her mother never knowing.

That day she offered to clean out the shed and her father approved. She made improvements. Sharp things were hidden. A couple of cushions from the summer house made a big difference. A couple of plums picked at dawn set in a bowl. Clean water in a jug. A candle down low. Her father approved. 'I can come here when your mother is in one of her moodies,' he said. 'And get some calypso in, girl, and it'll be shining.'

Valentine came the next night, and the next and the next, until soon his garden was running out of the big red fly-by-night poppies and he had to steal from the neighbours. But their love grew with every touch and sigh, and soon they became bolder. He came to her earlier and left later. They felt like gods in their fortune.

And then one night, Mr Pescatti coming home late, smelling of beer and perfume, heard strange sounds in the shed while he was smoking his last pipe of calypso in the garden and relieving himself into the honeysuckle. He knew those sounds, heard his daughter sigh, saw the balloons, heard her love cry, went into the house and got down his gun, preparing to shoot the O'Dwyer son.

But he was cunning too, as well as mean. He sat up all night in the garden, and when the dawn, in russet mantle clad, touched the misty mountain tops, he saw the young man kiss his fair Francesca, long and lingering, one hand on her breast and the other above holding the balloon tether. Then Valentine swung away and pulled himself along his line.

Mr Pescatti hid until the girl was in her room and the boy was waving kisses from above the dark ravine, and then he shot him. Not him. He shot the balloons. One. Two. Three. Four. And the boy fell down into the stream and lay still among the rushes.

Francesca looked down from her window and she heard her father laugh and saw his bald head below, pale as a graveyard mushroom. She took the big Bible, the one she was given when she was eleven after her first bleeding, the one with the wooden covers and the big crucifix, and she threw it down from the window as hard as she could and she sconed him.

Then she ran into the garden, down to the fence, out through the hinged paling and down the path into the ravine. Behind her was confusion. The neighbours came running. Men in pyjamas. Women in nighties. They found the man stunned, the Bible, the gun and Mrs Pescatti crying that her daughter had gone from her bed and run away. No one knew what to think but they looked to one another in the knowing way that grown-up people do when they don't want to say what they think but want you to know that they are thinking it. They did not think, however, to go looking behind the wise old waltzer or down in the muddy ravine.

Francesca had found her Valentine. He was not dead but wounded. She plucked down osiers and wove a willow platform and placed him on it. She sang cantons, whatever they are, to the wanton air, whatever that is. And then she gathered nine fly-by-night balloons from a secret place she knew. Four for the head. Four for the feet and one for luck. She tethered them, and she lay down beside her Valentine. They folded together like hands at prayer, and she cast off.

They floated up from the dark valley and into the bright morning sunlight. The neighbours looked in astonishment and pointed. People came out onto their balconies and saw the bright red balloons of the fly-by-night as they lifted high above the town. Dogs barked and children rubbed their eyes and stared up from their windows in wonder. And all the lovers of the town rang their bells lustily, laughed aloud and fell upon one another.

The willow bed went higher. It drifted out over the sea like a small cloud, and then over the horizon like a lone bird, and was gone. Francesca and Valentine went to their own place, you see, a bay not far from here. And when they got there, they put down, built a house and lived happily ever after. And she had lots of babies and he wrote her lots of poems and made her laugh.

And as for the families, the O'Dwyers and the Pescattis, they took their fences down and became friends. They even built a bridge between their gardens. They had learned their lesson, you see. They had both lost children, and that is a terrible thing for a parent. They left the wise old blue waltzer alone and the pull-line in place and the hinged paling so that they never would forget the time Francesca saved her Valentine.

And that is why the fly-by-night is now called the Valentine lily, why the dashing silver stream that runs through New Syracuse is called the Valentine River and why every year, on the anniversary of that day, lovers of all ages write messages on hybla leaves to the one they love, tie them to Valentine poppies and send them up into the sky.

And you can do that too, Jemima, when you get a bit older.

Sleep now.

End

For a solution to the 12-ball problem on page 341, please visit www.phillipmann.co.nz, where you will also find more information relating to Paradise.